ALL GODS FALL

SEASON ONE: STORMS

CITY OF REVELS

CRADLE OF THE WORLD

BLACK HYPOGEA

TOWER OF SAMADEL

BOBOROS VALE

KEVIN WEIR

Zainab!
Enjoy the adventure!

This is a work of fiction. Names, characters, place, and incidents are the products of the author's imagination or are used fictitiously and are not to be construed as real. Any resemblance to actual events, locales, organizations, or persons, living or dead, is entirely coincidental.

Cover Art: Elizabeth Pieró
Map Design: Dewi Hargreaves

Paperback ISBN: 978-1-7773274-1-5

To staring silently into the middle distance and inevitible typos.

FREELANDS SEA
Nature's Grave
FORT ROCKHILL
MARJYAL, CITY OF REVELS
BROKEN ISLAND FORT
BLACK HYPOGEA
CASTLE ADATHIN
TEETH OF THE SEA
SEBANNA'S REST
DOTHRIN
SEBANNA'S ARCHIVE
BLASTED LAND MINES
BARROWFIELD
The Salt Flats
DANCER'S INLET
TOWER OF SAMADEL
SORROW SEA
BRUMAL BAY
GALIANOS
ISLES OF ELYSIUM
BANSHEE COAST
BANSHEE SEA
N
THE FORMER LANDS OF
ADATHIN

ALL GODS FALL: SEASON ONE

PART ONE

CITY OF REVELS

People like to believe history is written in stone, with undeniable truths about what occurred when. In reality, the past is a series of mysteries being debated and rewritten at every opportunity. Sometimes it's to hide painful revelations, to honor the dead, or simply because as time went on we forgot. The truth becomes more flexible the further back you go, and it's the survivors who decide what history is.

Or at least that's what I've read. I disagree. There are bad storytellers spinning the wrong yarn, but that does not change the truth.

I've travelled far to hear the tales we pass down from parent to child, but I always knew my journey would bring me back here. To a lonely castle in a forsaken land. Adathin. It's almost poetic.

See, I don't trouble myself with how rock was formed or the will of gods. I wonder how we got here. There are threads that bind all these incorrect retellings together. Primordials. Divines. First Gods. Land, Sky, Sea, Dark, and Fire. Cradle of the World. Chalice of Light. If I can take these seemingly disconnected threads, I can stitch together a tapestry of where we came from. And perhaps see what's going to happen.

But that's the end of the journey. I shouldn't get ahead of myself. If there's one thing I've learned from my work it's that once you start walking, there's no telling where you'll go.

—From the journal of Jovin Gutterwake

Chapter One

The Trail's End

Far in the distance — beyond the southern tree line — lightning flashed, promising a coming storm. Gaul needed to finish up in town and get moving before the rain caught him. He stepped out of the way of a carriage carrying men and women northward. He kept a wary eye on the massive horse, egged on by a grim-faced man.

Mud kicked up from the wooden wheels and coated Gaul's boots. It dried with a gust of chilling wind and joined the stains already on his pant legs. Adjusting the blade on his hip and the small shield hanging off the sheath, Gaul walked south down the main street. All the while, dark clouds rolled in.

Landus wasn't much more than that one street. Buildings had been cleared. The front doors left wide open to the elements. People had taken the essentials, leaving behind much of their furniture and decorations. Landus felt hauntingly similar to every other small-town Gaul had been through in the recent month. The further south he got, the emptier the world became.

The door to the alehouse rested against the wall next to its empty hinges. The sign above read *The Trail's End.* In the corner furthest from the entrance was a slumped over form with long hair, snoring in fluttering waves — the only figure among the many tables and chairs. Half of those chairs laid against the walls or rested upside down on the tables. There weren't enough people in town to use them. It wasn't simply people moving away. It was an exodus. Gaul rapped his knuckle against a nicked tabletop and waited.

An older man with a bushy brown beard entered from the back room. His expression turned from surprise to confusion. "You looking for work?" he asked.

"No," Gaul said.

"Good," the barkeep said, wiping his hands on his apron. "Most people are leaving town rather than hiring."

"What happened?" Gaul asked. He walked through the bar, each step returning with a loud creak.

The barkeep grunted. "An Imperium priest came through recently. Spouted off about some doom and gloom coming from the south. Got people scared."

"A priest?" Gaul tapped his palm on his striking shield. "White robes? Followed by six soldiers bearing golden eagle symbols?"

"Lightwalkers, yeah." The barkeep cocked his eyebrow. "These friends of yours?"

"Something like that. Did they buy anything?"

"You're asking a lot of questions, stranger." He leaned on the bar, staring Gaul down. "I have a lot of drinks no one's drinking. And a lot of food going bad in my coldbox."

Gaul chuckled. "I don't have any money. What about barter?"

"What've you got? Sword, shield, armor?"

Gaul pulled his jacket tighter over his leather cuirass. "I may need these where I'm going. How about my gloves?"

"Some ratty work gloves? What am I going to do with those?"

"These aren't 'ratty work gloves.'" He pulled one off and flapped it in front of the barkeep. "It's thick leather. Could catch a blade if you were feeling up to it. Look, I just want to ask a few questions."

The barkeep shrugged and turned toward the kitchen.

Gaul threw the glove on the bar and dug through his bag. "I have some food, salves, tinderbox. I have a couple sunstones. Just strike one against your—"

"I know what a sunstone is."

"Fine. I suppose I would be willing to part with my knife if it will get me some answers." He drew the hunting knife from next to his sword and placed it on the counter.

The barkeep pushed the knife back. "That's all you have?" he asked, leaning in. "What are you? A soldier?"

Gaul returned the knife to its sheath. "Something like that."

"Sorry, soldier," the barkeep said, running his hands over his large beard, flecks of grey showing his age. "I can fill three carts with the hunting knives I have, but a sword, shield, or some armor? That's actually worth something."

"Divine's name!" Someone cursed from the kitchen. A small woman with white hair poked her head into the room. "Stop being an ass to the man, Lucen. He's clearly travelled a long way, and not to be strung around the room by you."

Lucen grumbled something unintelligible and rolled his head side to side. "Of course, dear," he called.

The woman smiled at Gaul before disappearing into the kitchen. Gaul leaned against the bar, looking expectantly at Lucen.

Lucen ducked behind the bar. Something rattled and he reappeared with a tray full of cups. He set them down with a clink. "You clean, I'll talk," he said.

"Excuse me?"

Lucen directed him to grab the wash bucket from the back room. Washing for information. It could have been worse. Gaul threw his gear near the bar and followed Lucen's directions through the kitchen. The white-haired woman chuckled as he entered, only to turn it into a cough and return to cooking potatoes.

Ignoring the woman, Gaul brought the wash bucket back into the front and started cleaning the alehouse's cups.

"This priest," Gaul started, sliding a clean cup to Lucen. "He paid with trinkets, rather than coin, yes?"

Lucen placed the cup on the shelf before returning to his stool. "I would hardly call them trinkets. Paid with jewelry mostly."

"What kind of jewelry?"

"All in all for the few days of drink and food? Two rings and a necklace."

"What kind of necklace?"

"Gold."

"Just gold?"

"As far as I can tell."

Gaul grew quiet. The sounds of water splashing intermixed with the soft snoring of the figure still passed out at the corner table. "Did they buy anything else in town? Where did they stay?"

"They camped outside town. Landus doesn't have an inn. We don't have much of anything. People don't pass through." He tensed his jaw. "Normally. Look, kid, it sounds like you're looking for something. Just tell me what it is, and I'll tell you if we've got it."

"A chain necklace. One with gold and steel links."

Lucen sat back and considered. "Naw. Can't imagine anyone in town taking something like that. I felt bad for the guy, that was the only reason I took the stuff he offered. Sold them to some of the folks leaving town, figuring they can pawn them when they get up to Celtmeri."

Gaul had stopped listening. *The Priest still has it*, he thought. A chain with both gold and steel links was rare enough people would notice it, but too ugly to barter with. He was so close to the Priest. The mere thought of him made the fire rise in Gaul's gut.

"Pay attention!" Lucen leapt from the stool.

Gaul blinked. He looked at his hands. In one was a glass cup half full of water. The other, the broken lip of that glass cup wrapped in a wash rag. The fire inside dissipated as Lucen snatched both pieces.

"We don't have much of these glass ones." He looked over the broken shard. With a sigh, he placed it on a shelf below the bar. Gaul reached for the next glass. It disappeared in a splash as Lucen snatched it away. "Just wash the metal ones."

Gaul grabbed a metal mug — giving a sideways glare at Lucen — and started washing again. He didn't mean to break the glass. It didn't matter. Lucen watched him like a hawk. A scowling hawk. Gaul hid his annoyance. He didn't want to get kicked out of another town.

"When did the priest leave?" Gaul asked, handing the mug to Lucen. "Did he say where he was going?"

"About two days ago." He placed the cup on the bar, not looking away from Gaul. He hadn't even returned to his stool. "I didn't hear him mention where he was going. Hold on." He turned toward the figure in the corner. "Marta!"

The figure whipped their head back, revealing a woman staring in bewilderment. A long streak of drool ran across her bronze cheek that she wiped away with her sleeve. She attempted to stand, but her hand slipped off the table and she fell back into her chair.

"Her?" Gaul stopped washing. The drunkard put both hands on her table and, like a calf learning to walk, rose to her wobbling feet. "She seems to be a little… out of it."

"Don't worry about her. For Marta, booze affects the body, not the brain. She's still sharp as a tack."

A resounding crunch followed Marta stumbling over a chair and crashing into a table.

"A tack could be generous, though."

Gaul wiped his hands dry on his pants and offered it. Marta either didn't want it or didn't notice. She pulled a nearby chair closer and dragged herself into an ungraceful sit.

"Marta." Lucen snapped his fingers in front of her face. Marta's eyes focused on Lucen's. He patted her on the cheek. "Back with us. You drank with the priest and his guards, right?"

"I drank with the guards. The priest was a priest. He talked a lot, but never drank." Marta pushed her long hair back. A vicious scar ran out from the corner of her mouth. Did the drink slur her speech? Or the wound?

"Did you hear where they were going?" Gaul stepped closer. A tug on his collar put him back at the wash bucket. Lucen pointed at the water. The dishes weren't done. Gaul picked up a mug that looked like someone ate soup out of it, but kept all of his attention on the woman.

"The guards were very friendly," Marta said, flipping a limp hand toward Gaul. "They paid for drinks like they were water. One of the men made fun of my smile, but the rest put him in his place. Which was good, or I would have given him one of his own." Her laugh shredded the somber air. It wasn't that funny.

"Marta," Lucen said. "Did they say where they're going?"

She nodded. "They're going through Nature's Grave."

Lucen let out a low whistle and turned about. Gaul looked between him and the drunkard, swaying her head. He abandoned the soup mug — he had been rubbing the same spot for the past minute anyway. "What's Nature's Grave?" he asked.

Lucen stopped at the far end of the bar, staring out the window at the clouds forming above the trees. "It's a forest to the south."

"It's the end of the world," Marta added, curling her legs up to her chest. "And the beginning. Beyond it is the Kingdom of Adathin."

The tension in the room grew until it formed on his skin like a freezing breeze. Legends weren't uncommon on the road — sometimes whispered at a campfire and sometimes shouted in a loud tavern — but something was different about this one. Lucen still stared southward, an indecipherable look on his face.

"Someone's going to have to fill me in here," Gaul said.

"You're Ulkradian, right?" Lucen finally stepped away from the window.

Gaul cocked an eyebrow. "Why would you say that?" Sure, he was a few shades paler than the average person in the south, but that shouldn't make him stick out.

"Now I've never seen an Ulkradian with short hair, but your shield." He motioned to the wood and metal teardrop near the stool. "I fought in the Mirral Conflict for the Imperials. Saw some Ulkradians after they joined in. I noticed the reinforcement on the punching edge. I've seen many shields exactly like that, all on the arm of Ulkradian soldiers. I took a guess."

Gaul set his jaw. While he had been trying to get information out of the barkeep, the barkeep had been inspecting and inferring information about Gaul. It was impressive, despite the annoyance of being analyzed.

"Fine. I'm a foreigner. What does that have to do with anything?"

"I assume that means you know about the Cradle of the World?"

The barkeep spoke of faraway kingdoms and creation myths. If he was messing with Gaul, he played it straight. It had been years since Gaul thought about the stories of the Cradle. The land where gods rose and claimed the world from monstrous creatures. An allegory at best. An excuse at worst.

"The King of Adathin," Marta said. She closed her eyes and kept her knees against her chest. "He believed his kingdom was built upon the Cradle. He spent his fortunes and worked his subjects to death to find proof for his beliefs. When his subjects had been worked to their breaking point, they rebelled against the king. They hung him from the tallest tower in his castle and vanished."

"Or at least that's how the legend goes." Lucen ran his hand over his beard. "All you need to know is people who enter Nature's Grave don't come back. Or don't come back the same."

His gaze flicked to Marta, rolling her head around her neck. Her lips moved with silent words. Gaul squatted next to her chair.

"Thanks for the help," he said.

Marta's eyes eased open. She shrank away. "Please don't touch me."

Gaul retreated. Marta skittered back to the corner, her sobering giving her a level of balance. She swept her hands over her hair, putting it into an unkempt bun, then — deciding it wasn't worth the effort — let it fall loose again.

What a curious town this has turned out to be, Gaul thought. He snatched his jacket and bag from the stool.

"You're going to go to Nature's Grave?" Lucen leaned against a nearby table.

"Can't let a few trees scare me off." He grabbed his gear and moved toward the exit. "Sorry I couldn't finish those dishes."

"Could I ask you a question?" Lucen pushed off the table, keeping pace.

"I don't have any dishes for you to wash."

Lucen held up three copper marks. Gaul stopped. Having actual wealth could be useful if he ran into a situation like this again.

"What's the question?"

"Why's an Ulkradian soldier chasing an Imperial priest through the Free Lands? Is it about all that stuff he's preaching? The end of the world?"

"I don't know anything about the end of the world. He just took something precious of mine." Gaul backed toward the exit. "You can have that for free."

Lucen grabbed Gaul's arm and pushed the coins into his hand. "I'll pay for that one."

Gaul squeezed the coins. What happened to the ornery barkeep? What about Nature's Grave made him so generous? A heavy pit grew in Gaul's stomach. He pushed it away. Lucen's fear of the forest was contagious. But it was nothing.

"What's your name?" Lucen asked, putting his hands in his pockets.

"Gaul."

"Gaul, the soldier from Ulkradia. I think you were right about the sword and shield; you may need those where you're going."

Gaul couldn't think of a reply. These people spoke of the forest as if it was a death sentence. So, he nodded and put the marks into his bag.

"Hold on!" The little white-haired woman rushed from the kitchen, clutching a small pouch. "Consider it your dinner."

Inside were pieces of dried meat and two apples. The woman beamed and Lucen had the same indecipherable look he did when staring out the window. Somewhere between intrigue and concern.

"Thanks. It's very kind of you." Gaul put the pouch into his bag, now getting rather full. He left through the open doorframe.

The carriages had faded into the northern horizon. It was the same in every town all the way up to Ulkradia. Whatever the Priest said reached listening ears. Townsfolk fleeing north. Fleeing from what? The end of the world?

A few drops of rain splashed in a nearby puddle. Gaul flipped up his hood. Other people may be afraid of Nature's Grave, but he couldn't be. The Priest was closer than ever before. He wasn't one to get wrapped up in local legends. No reason to start now.

He hung his shield off his sheath and carried on south down the main street. The dark clouds had overcome Landus. Gaul puffed hot breath in his hands and stomped through a puddle. A few seconds later, there was a second splash. Marta followed him, standing in the middle of the road and staring.

"Hello?" Gaul called.

Marta smoothed back her wet hair, swaying side to side.

Gaul turned. "I'm going to go now. Okay?"

"No. Wait. Uh…" She mumbled something.

"What did you say?"

"…With you."

"I'm not dealing with this."

"I want to go with you!"

Gaul sighed. "No. You need to go sleep it off in a barn."

Marta shook her head. "I need to. I have a place to be." Her knees gave out and she fell into the puddle.

Gaul looked from Marta, to the Trail's End. No one came out to find her. The rain intensified and still Marta laid in the mud with her lower half submerged.

"You've got to be kidding me," Gaul muttered.

He scooped her onto his shoulder. She snored against his chest as he walked her off the street. He placed her on a bench where the awning would keep the rain away. Someone had forgotten a blanket near the entrance to the abandoned home. It didn't look like they would come back for it. Marta stirred as he wrapped it around her.

"He's waiting for me," she murmured in her sleep.

Peculiar woman, Gaul thought.

The rain turned into fingernail-sized droplets that pounded like tiny hammers. Landus' metal awnings rattled and the struts creaked with the whooshing wind, a cacophonous symphony and still Marta stayed fast asleep. Gaul lingered in the rain, watching her breath puff out from beneath the blanket tucked near her chin. Someone had to come for her soon, he thought, and he didn't have the time to wait. The Priest was close. He oriented on the forest line overtaking the horizon and the storm clouds that hung above. Ignoring the urge to turn back, he headed to Nature's Grave.

As far as I can tell, Nature's Grave didn't exist during Adathin's time. There are no writings of a forest of its nature anywhere in the castle library. Sure, forests aren't an exciting subject to write on other than the fact they exist, and it is still a number of days ride north of the castle, but I have to imagine it would come up. It's not a normal forest.

It stretches from one coast to the other, effectively cutting off the isthmus that connects Adathin to the rest of the world. It's not particularly thick when it comes to forests, but the winding paths and a heavy canopy disguising the sun can create an atmosphere meant to play tricks on the mind. Anyone who wanders into the Grave unprepared is guaranteed to never come out.

—From the journal of Jovin Gutterwake

Chapter Two
Nature's Grave

Rain fell in thick blankets that turned the distant forest into a blue-white haze. Only the crowded branches and leaves of the massive trees gave Gaul any solace from the downpour. The Anima of Storms unleashed her full fury. Gaul darted from cover to cover. The raindrops beat heavy on his leather hood while he moved — if it wasn't for his coat he would have been drenched to the bone.

The next few hours of travel were marked by damp roots and slick dirt. The bright side to the weather was the slim chance the priest would be moving too, it was Gaul's opportunity to close the distance. He went as far as the dying sunlight would take him. But, as night fell, the rain refused to let up and each step became more treacherous.

He moved away from the path, making sure he remembered how to return to it come daybreak. Not far into the brush was a thick tree whose trunk was misted with water. A pleasant enough place to sleep through the storm. He hung his bag off one branch while claiming a stronger one he could strap himself to.

Thunder crackled through the night, preventing Gaul from getting a restful sleep. When day broke, there didn't seem to be any change in the weather. Perhaps rain was the eternal state for Nature's Grave, a sobering thought considering there didn't appear to be an end to the forest.

He leapt off the branch he had tied himself to. His feet flew out from beneath him, sending him splashing into the flooded dirt. Muddy water seeped along his back as he laid in the puddle, taking deep breaths to control his anger. He eased to his feet, feeling the liquid pour out of his cuirass. A fire grew in his stomach. He resisted the urge to punch the tree, instead he took a moment and quelled the flames.

I'm better than this, he thought. *No need to get angry.*

He grabbed his bag off the branch and swung his jacket back on. His soaked shirt squished under the outerwear. He growled, shifting about in his armour. Breathe in. Breathe out. There was no use getting worked up about it.

The cool, dirt-smelling air was smooth in his lungs, filling him with energy for the next day. He fastened his coat up to his chin to protect against the chill in the air. The cold countryside of Ulkradia still came to him in the quiet moments, distance and time did not steal the memory of home. Though it did become fuzzier. Hopefully he'd find the Priest soon. First things first, Nature's Grave still surrounded him.

With the benefit of the small amount of sun that could make it through the clouds and trees, Gaul found the path he had been taking easily, still within sight of his sleeping spot. Strange, in the dark it felt much further away. He continued, dashing from tree to tree once again.

Hours passed before Gaul spotted an object in the path. He rushed to it, feet sliding along the slick ground in his haste. Mud gripped the wheels up to the axel and a large golden eagle emblem emblazoned the side. The Priest's cart.

One axle was snapped in half, both sides driven into the ground. A large log tied up with rope pinned the corpse of a draft horse to the bloody earth. The rope disappeared into the canopy above. Kill the horse and one could scavenge the cart clean. Simple, yet terribly effective.

The ground around the cart was a swamp of overlapping footprints and water both bloody and muddy. Here someone tripped. There someone ran. Whatever happened at the cart was lost in the mess of a panicked moment. There was a scramble, and there was death. Gaul crouched next to two deep grooves that went from the chaos down the path forward. A second cart. From there a dozen — no, two dozen — people took off into the woods.

If the Priest was captured, following the path would be the best way to find him. But if he had fled, the footprints into the forest would lead the way. Which one to take?

Gaul paced the ambush site. The Priest had a dozen Lightwalkers with him. Holy warriors of an unbreakable oath. If the Priest was captured, they would never run. So, Gaul picked the trail into the forest.

He was close to his quarry, but with the Imperium cart in such a state, how would he find the Priest? If the Priest died in these woods, or was taken to where Gaul couldn't follow, everything he had done was for naught.

For over two months, Gaul chased the Priest. From town to town it was goodwill — and a bit of thievery — that kept him alive. But the Priest was always ahead of him, taking a lackadaisical route through Eastern Ulkradia and south across Griffon's Gulf. Each Pantheon Church loaded his coffers for the trip across the Free Lands, where the Divine's weren't worshipped. None of the Order could tell Gaul where the Priest was headed. The Pontiff's Seal stemmed all questions. But dockmen, innkeepers, and bartenders all said the same thing.

South. Where the end of the world begins.

His words, apparently.

A splash of white caught Gaul's eye. Crushed under many footfalls was a once white cloak, now stained brown. Gaul lifted it out of the mud and gave it a snap. It had gold trim, as well as a gold eagle embroidered across the shoulders. A Lightwalker mantle.

The forest breathed around him. No telling what was out of sight, hiding among the raindrops and fog. Tucking the cloak under his arm and resting his hand on his sword hilt, Gaul continued forward.

Time froze in the horrid stillness of the forest. The sound of wind and raindrops were all that saved him from absolute silence. No birds chirped, no critters scurried. Save the trees, Nature's Grave was dead.

The forest brightened as the trees thinned into a muddy field.

Gaul's jaw dropped.

At least two dozen corpses littered the small clearing. The mud had already begun dragging them to forgotten graves. Most had nothing more than rags. Pathetic things wrapped in light capes to protect them from the elements — when they were alive, of course. Gaul only wished it was the first time he had seen something so terrible.

A couple bodies had on arming doublets meant to be worn under plate armour. The plate armour worn by Lightwalkers. But it was long gone. The victors had taken the time to strip the dead, but left the bodies of their allies behind to rot in the mud. A materialistic sense of priority. Scavengers, no doubt.

Gaul walked the corpse yard, taking care to not step on any half-visible body. The ambushers fought with clubs and rusted blades. Spears were nothing more than sticks sharpened to a point. Weapons remained discarded where they fell, or stuck into trees and mud like steel and wood tombstones. The amount of waste in one place — both in life and otherwise — made Gaul stop. The rain pounded on his hood, as if to push him to the earth as well.

"I'm sorry," he said. But the dead didn't care.

A ring of foes surrounded the fallen Lightwalkers. Gaul inspected the corpses, crouching at their sides. One had taken a crude arrow to the throat; the other had a deep red stain on her side around a hole in her doublet. They hadn't begun to rot. But the colour had left them and they were a couple days dead. While Gaul slept in the tree, they were already gone.

But they weren't the Priest. Hope remained. Gaul went from body to body, checking for that youthful face he had seen once in passing — but was burnt into his mind.

Across the field, a sword stuck out of the stomach of a body burned black. Gaul's heart fell to his feet. He grabbed what he hoped was clothing and pulled. Cooked flesh tore from bone. Another arming doublet. Gaul let out a breath of relief. The Priest yet lived.

Who were these mysterious, rag-wearing ambushers? They chased down the Priest and his armoured soldiers rather than taking the treasure in the cart. They even took the time to have a madman's version of a campfire. Was it an intimidation tactic? And where were the other Lightwalkers? Where was the priest?

Gaul rubbed his eyes. The journey had taken a sharp downward turn. There were too many questions. What was a Pantheon Priest doing this far south? Where was he going? Gaul assumed a trip to proselytize the Free Lands to the Divine Pantheon faith, but it appeared more like a pilgrimage.

A new sound reached Gaul's ears. Hidden amongst the raindrops striking the trees the water hit something more metallic. Gaul shut his eyes and focused. The sound was constant, mixed with the occasional clink and scrape.

Gaul spun toward the arrival. A Lightwalker, clad in their signature heavy armour, lumbered into the clearing. His helmet covered his face and in either hand he dragged a great sword, carving two lines into the forest beyond. Dents and scratches tarnished his armour, and his cloak was missing.

"Hello…" Gaul held out the bloodied cloak. "I think this is yours. What happened here?"

The soldier made no motion. His breathing rang heavy and hollow. The thin visor on his helmet was devoid of life. Every muscle in Gaul's body tensed. Adrenaline hit his heart like a cannonball. Death stood before him.

The soldier hefted both great swords over his head and covered the distance between them in a blink. Gaul tossed the cloak away, drew his falchion, and snatched the sword from the burnt corpse. Blade struck blade.

The great swords hit like a horse's kick. Gaul slammed one knee into the earth and wrenched his back, barely keeping the hefty blades at bay. A steady pulse grew in his spine. The soldier growled and swung again. Gaul flipped the rusted sword around in his offhand and embedded it into the mud. His shoulder popped as a groove carved into the earth.

Creaking groans came from the soldier's mask, along with hot, putrid breath. Gaul's arms shook. Another joint popped. He put his foot against the soldier's shin and pushed. The soldier held firm as Gaul slid away. A great sword parted the mud where he once was.

Gaul scrambled to his feet, the slick ground trying to take them out from under him again. The soldier stayed hunched and stretched out like a feral beast sniffing the air. As he turned his head, he revealed a gap in the armour's neck. One quick blow could end it.

The soldier tightened his grip on his swords — then exploded into motion. Handfuls of mud came with him. Gaul stepped into the armoured projectile. The soldier reared back, showing his neck.

There. Gaul thrust in.

The soldier slammed both hilts on the rusted blade, snapping it like a twig before it found its mark. Gaul looked at the shattered weapon and groaned. It was a good attempt.

Discarding the sword, Gaul grabbed the closest spear and went in again. The soldier turned and swung. The spear went wide. The breeze from the mighty weapon crested Gaul's nose. His spine screamed at him to not do that again.

The soldier swung in wild motions, accepting the momentum given to him by his great swords. He knocked one spear away and Gaul picked up another. There had to be an opening. Somewhere in that bladed maelstrom was a weakness. Gaul's lungs burned with exertion, but the soldier never slowed. Was there even a human inside that steel cage?

The next spear thrust slipped between the armour at the soldier's shoulder. There was resistance and a squish, but the soldier leaned into the hit, snapping the spear. Gaul danced aside and whipped the shaft against the soldier's helm. Like the clapper on a bell, it rang. The soldier groaned and held his arms to his head.

Gaul abandoned the broken spear and spun on his heel. Running from a fight meant surviving a fight at least. The soldier let out a heart-rattling battle cry.

Something big ripped through the air. Gaul dropped. One great sword sailed over his head. He rolled, snatching an arrow sticking out of the ground and pushing both feet off a dead body. He hurtled at the soldiers. The arrowhead slipped into the slit on his helm, penetrating with a grotesque squish.

The soldier froze. Gaul gave him space. The rain was all that dared to move. It pounded like a heartbeat as black, viscous liquid seeped from the visor. The soldier let out an inhuman cry, sending shivers up and down Gaul's spine.

The good news was he could be hurt, the bad news was it only seemed to make him angry. Gaul chose a direction that didn't have a furious freak of nature and sprinted away, sheathing his sword.

Run or kill. Every chance at surviving the beast trickled away. There had to be a better place to fight. A place where the soldier couldn't swing like a wild man. Gaul slid his shield onto his arm.

Arrows stuck out of the trees as he re-entered the woods. He snatched one and held it in his teeth. They were small. They could slip between the cracks in the soldier's armour. He grabbed a few more. Four arrows and no bow. It didn't matter what the soldier was made of, it had some body that could be destroyed. Hopefully.

Gaul burst through a thicket of bushes, and the world ended. He stumbled, sending dirt tumbling into a great ravine. Before him, a wall of grey fog. Below, oblivion. The rain slowed as if to taunt him.

The earth trembled at the soldier's approach. He walked through the brush like it was water. Branches and thin trees snapped to make way. The great sword's hilt creaked within his furious, inhuman grip. An arrow still jutted from his visor. Gaul braced himself to stand against the storm.

The sword came first. Gaul caught it on the flat with his shield and pushed it into the dirt. For a moment the soldier was off balance. Gaul pounced. He drove an arrow into the soldier's throat. Blood — or a dark imitation of it — spurted from the wound. The soldier swung back, snapping the arrow out of his neck.

Fury met fury. Gaul pushed the soldier's arm across his chest and unloaded blow after blow into his helm. Metal rang like thunderclaps. The soldier groaned and shoved Gaul back, swaying like a tree in the wind. His helmet bent inward at the nose and something cracked inside its dark interior. It almost seemed like Gaul was winning.

The soldier took his blade in both hands and charged. Too slow. Easy for Gaul to step aside. The sword dug into the earth and Gaul stomped it deeper. It had to go. He plucked another arrow from his mouth and plunged it into the soldier's elbow.

With a bestial roar, the soldier wrenched away, sending mud and grass skyward. But his sword remained. He swung a decapitating blow. Gaul stepped past the sword, into the arm, shield raised. The shield struck the arrow. The elbow popped, followed by a sickening crack as the sword left the soldier's grip. It skittered across the ravine's edge and plunged into the foggy depth below.

That wasn't enough. The soldier needed to hurt. Gaul's breath quickened. Fire burned in his gut. He took the last arrow and stabbed it into the visor. Black blood, hot against Gaul's skin, poured from the wound. Still Gaul pushed until he heard the arrowhead strike the back of the helm and the soldier staggered.

Only the soldier didn't fall. His arm hung dead at his side and vile liquid gushed from the gaps in his helmet, but his feet stayed planted. Held up by willpower or rage, there was no way to know. He grabbed the arrow shafts and pulled. Centimetre by centimetre they slid out of his skull.

"Just die!" Gaul shouted, swinging in with his shield.

With a snap, the soldier's arm went back into place. He caught Gaul's shield by the edge. Wheezing and groaning, he pulled him close. A sickening sweet smell wafted from the helmet. Was he already rotting?

The soldier swung for Gaul's head, pushing him back to keep his face on his skull. The ravine's edge made promises to give way. But like a cornered animal, Gaul only felt fury. He could let the fire in his gut consume him. He could be that monster.

The ground shifted. Gaul grabbed the soldier's collar to steady himself, then cracked him in the face. The soldier took the hit like it was an insect. He took Gaul by the shirt and threw him to the ground. The breath blew out of Gaul's lungs.

Then the soldier started punching.

Steel rain replaced water. Gaul got his shield over his body, but still his bones cracked under the onslaught. Blood filled his mouth. He crawled on his elbows, only for the soldier to drive his foot across his jaw. He rolled through the mud, landing face down. Gritty water filled his mouth. His skin went cold.

This is what dying feels like, he thought.

The soldier approached. His once gleaming armour covered with dark stains. He was going to be Gaul's end? Some freak in the woods. A story cut short.

The soldier fell to his knees at Gaul's side. Metallic wheezing came from his armour. He lifted both fists into the air and dropped the guillotine.

Gaul spun. Mud flew in all directions. He drove his shield into the soldier's descending chin. He grabbed his chest plate and in the next instant was on top of him. The foggy expanse of the ravine wasn't far.

The world became a crimson tunnel. Gaul unbridled his rage upon his enemy. Blood poured from his own mouth, intermixing with the soldier's. His chest burned as he collapsed the helmet flat. Each blow stoked the flames in his stomach. It was good. It was right. He screamed a breathless cry.

Then he stopped. The soldier still twitched, though his helmet could not contain a head. Red faded from his vision and he was left with a horrifying clarity.

How would she feel? Gaul thought, as the pain filled his body once again. *How would she feel if she saw you like this?*

The world shifted. Gaul's stomach flew into his throat as the ravine's edge disappeared into a landslide. A twisting root caught onto his shield. The soldier vanished into the fog, followed by the sickening crack of metal impacting earth.

The root shifted, dropping Gaul a few centimetres. His entire body screamed. His vision darkened. Thoughts became harder to fit together. There was nothing left in him to stoke the flames. Even if he wanted to.

He held onto his last good image, a beautiful woman with long raven hair. She reached for him. A gold and steel necklace hung around her neck.

"I didn't die a monster, Anori," he whispered. The last of his breath.

The root gave way. The clouded sky retreated. He slid along the side of the ravine, bouncing off rocky outcroppings and crashing to the ground below. His breath came out in wheezy huffs, stinging his lungs.

Shadows moved in his peripherals, joined by distant murmurs. As the darkness enveloped him, rain was all he could feel.

I've enjoyed searching the castle. It's filled with such rich history I could never have imagined before. I found a lab in an auxiliary building. They had been experimenting with lithoflux. Forms of crystals I have never seen before! These people were so advanced! However, what is missing is any indication of an uprising. The castle looks abandoned, not ransacked. The paintings are still hung and the dining room still has a number of silver candelabrums. It seems to me; any revolting subjects would take anything of worth when they left.

Searching the castle has also allowed me to find some books that were removed from the library for one reason or another. One such book describes Marjyal as a prosperous city of entertainment and luxury. The darling of the king's youngest daughter, she built it after giving up her hunt for the Cradle of the World. There does seem to be some conflicting information here, though. I found a document that implies the youngest daughter somehow poisoned her land and created a miasma that drove her people away. Perhaps Marjyal was another city she built? After the poisoning destroyed her original home?

The Marjyal I saw described in the books is nothing like the city I remember growing up in. They claim it was some kind of bastion for weary travellers, rather than the self-destructing pit of thrill-seekers and pleasure-hunters it is. Propaganda, perhaps? If it was ever like the city described in these books, all I can say is that city is long gone. All that's left is the City of Revels.

—From the journal of Jovin Gutterwake

Chapter Three
Marjyal, City of Revels

The sun burned Gaul's eyes as much as the pain burned his body. Half-conscious, he tried to sit up — only to feel a pressure on his chest pushing him back down.

He laid on a straw bed littered with many bumps. He strained his eyes to focus on something. All he could make out were bare stone walls and a figure placing something on his chest. Was he dead? Elysium was a disappointing place. He didn't deserve paradise.

Sleep overcame him.

The next time he awoke, the world was in much sharper focus. He was indeed in a stone room, bare, save the entrance across from the thatch bed he laid on. Above him was an opening to the sky, crosshatched with iron bars. A black cloth covered half of it, keeping the sun off. A man dressed in a ragged grey shirt and pants sat with his back to him. A twisting pattern of intersecting scars spread down his bald head and disappeared into his tunic.

"H—." Gaul's words caught in his dry throat, turning into a cough.

The man turned at the sound. He had dark grey eyes and a white goatee, with skin tanned to the point of looking like leather. "Good," he said. "You're awake." He tapped on his chest. "You can take that off."

Gaul cocked his head. *Take that off?* he thought. He touched his chest, expecting bare skin. Instead a white fabric with a black rune stretched from his clavicle to mid-torso and shoulder to shoulder. He gripped one edge and peeled it off. It pulled against his skin and hair until it tore free.

The man sitting on the stool took the fabric. "Your lung was collapsed." It disintegrated in his hand. "Most ribs were broken. Your back was... let's just say it was bad. You've been asleep for four days."

Gaul stood from the bed, stretching his spine out with a satisfying pop. His body felt refreshed, as though he spent the day before lounging in the hammock outside his home. But everything he owned was gone. The clothes he had on were torn cloth pants.

"Thank you." He cracked his neck. "I'm Gaul."

"Tora," the man said and offered a small cup of water. "Drink."

The water was warm, and tasted earthen, but it refreshed nonetheless. "Where am I?"

"Marjyal. Some recruiters found you in Nature's Grave." He eased himself onto the stool. He stretched out his left leg, wincing. "It's amazing you're alive, must have been quite the adventure to put you in the state you were in."

"I'm still figuring it out myself." Gaul rolled the empty clay cup between his hands. He lost the Priest's trail, if he was still alive at all. Three of his knights dead in the clearing — four, if that monster he fought finally rested. The Priest still had over half a dozen soldiers. If he was brought to this place, Marjyal, by the same people who saved Gaul, are they the same ones who attacked him? "Do you know if a priest and some soldiers came through here?"

Tora stopped rubbing his leg. He sighed and flopped his head back, squinting against the sun beaming down. "A few people were brought in barely a day before you. One had long, white robes. Well, they used to be white. Could've been a priest I suppose." He paused, narrowing his eyes. "He had a golden eagle on his chest."

Gaul placed the cup onto the bedside table. Finally, the Priest was closer than ever. "Thank you again, but I need to see that priest. Can you tell me where he is?"

"It's not that easy." Tora limped toward the exit. "Come with me, I'll explain."

A pit grew in Gaul's stomach. He followed Tora, glancing at the bars that sat between him and the blazing sun high above. They went into a tight hallway lined with entryways.

"This is the Marjyal Pits," Tora explained. They passed by many more rooms like the one Gaul awoke in. Everyone had iron bars for roofs, some bare, while others had tarps to shade them. A few had people in various states of injury, with one of the runic bandages somewhere on their body. "The people who brought you here are recruiters from the Guild of Boars. They scour the land, including Nature's Grave, for people with potential."

A groan came from a passing room. A young man was unconscious on a thatch bed. Another older man with the same interlocking scars Tora had wrapped a runic bandage over the young man's eyes. Blood was wet across the walls and a table of tools sat by the bedside.

"Potential for what?" Gaul asked, tearing himself away from the grizzly sight.

Tora pounded on the door at the end of the hall. "Tora Lautrec with patient." He turned to Gaul and spoke quieter. "Entertainment. To die in the Pits."

Gaul's skin went cold. A piece of the door at eye level slid aside. A man with a dead glare peered through. He scowled when he saw Gaul.

"He survived," he said.

"Yes, he did," Tora said, holding himself with a fragile confidence. "He's very strong."

"He's very lucky." He slammed the viewer shut and half a second later the door clicked and creaked open. Light flooded in. "And he just lost me a bet."

Beyond sat a massive courtyard. Within it were over three dozen people. Some sparred with wooden weapons. Others drank from the fountain tucked away in a far corner, hiding from the sun. A few sat against the wall, holding their heads, nearly comatose. A pair of soldiers watched over the commons from above.

The guard slammed the door behind them. He kept his eyes fixed on Gaul. "Keep walking, Untested," he growled.

Once they were far enough away, Gaul leaned into Tora. "What bet did I make him lose?"

"He probably bet that you'd die," Tora said.

"Oh. Glad to disappoint."

They paced the commons. Few people paid them any mind. Occasionally someone would nod at Tora, but there was no life in it. A grim energy followed them wherever they went.

Gaul kept his eyes on the walls. There were plenty of good cracks that could work as handholds, but the wooden spikes barbed with metal discouraged any climbers. Above that, a pair of soldiers waited with crossbows and whips. And above them, the spires of a city.

"Looking for an escape?" Tora asked in a whisper. He chuckled. "Everyone does. No one succeeds. The guards are more than willing to put a bolt through your leg and back under my care. Even if you do get out, Marjyal's a maze. The Sorrow Sea on one side and a wall on the other."

Gaul caught Tora by the arm. "There has to be a way out."

"There is." He brushed Gaul's hand aside. "Prove yourself and you can take the Champion's Walk to the Hall of the Appraised." He pointed to a gate set against the furthest wall. A gilded road glittered beyond. "Then, in time, you earn your freedom."

"This is lunacy."

"The more you win, the more the Praetors will put you in easy fights. Keep you alive for the audience." He stepped around Gaul. "Or you can give up, and perish quickly. That's the choice all these Untested had to make."

Gaul gritted his teeth. To take unwilling people and force them to fight, what kind of city would not only allow it, but endorse it? He followed Tora to a bench in a shady corner. "What about the Priest?"

Tora eased himself down. How could an old man like him survive this place? "What was that?"

"The Priest," Gaul repeated. "Where did he go?"

"Oh. I'm sorry but he was taken into the arena a couple hours ago. I imagine they'll be done soon."

"And then he'll be back?"

"If he survives." Sorrow crossed Tora's face "Where are you from, Gaul?"

"Ulkradia."

"Where's that?"

"North. Far north."

Tora lit up, if only for a moment. "Another one from outside Adathin."

"Adathin?" Gaul sat next to him. "So we are through Nature's Grave?"

"Unfortunately so. I'm from Yutha. A town of no repute in the Free Lands." He leaned his head against the wall. "A beautiful place though. Right in the prairies. I was hired as a doctor for a caravan heading east. We accidently dipped into Nature's Grave, got lost, and were taken by the Boars. They attack with slave soldiers in mass. It is…" He squeezed his fist. "Terrifying."

"A healer? Is that why you're still alive with that leg?"

"Yes. If it wasn't for my knowledge, I would probably be thrown to a torture show. Or some other such depravity."

Gaul conjured up words of sympathy, but they didn't seem right. He sat with Tora in silence. Strangers in a strange land.

The sparring fighters took regular breaks, drinking from the fountain before getting back into it. Others barely moved from their spots curled up against the wall. A loud bell rang and everyone stopped.

"What's that?" Gaul asked.

"The fight is over." Tora pushed himself to his feet. "But it sounds like someone's taking the Champion's Walk."

The Untested crowded around the gate to the golden road. There was no mechanism to move the bars. It was nothing more than a viewing hole. A stage to motivate the Untested to fight. Gaul pushed his way through the crowd with Tora at his heel.

Down the road, two guards pulled open an iron door with gold inlays. Figures emerged to the cheers of the Untested. A man in light leather armour appeared, blood trickling down his arm, but beaming in the applause all the same.

Behind him, using a guard as a crutch, was a man with delicate features. His hair the colour of a field of wheat, now stained red and black by blood. He wore the same light leather as the other fighters, but Gaul couldn't mistake his face, even though he only saw it once. The Priest. He was dazed, holding his left side. Blood flowed onto the gold below. His skin was nearly grey.

"Is that your Priest?" Tora asked, shoving through the crowd.

"Yes." Gaul took a heavy breath. "How do I see him?"

"He's going to the Hall of the Appraised. You'll have to go through the arena to meet him. Though you may not have that much time. That is a nasty wound."

The Priest stumbled. The guard had to catch him to keep him on his feet. "I must have been worse than that," Gaul said. "You brought me back."

"I'm a stupid old man who believes in the duty of a doctor. But here they use leech-bindings." He turned his head so Gaul could see his back. The scars that once crossed his scalp were gone. "I'm sure you saw them. They indicated that my life was bound to yours. Dark fluxweaving, if one could even call it that. You got some of my vitality, but if you had died, I would have as well."

"Even the healing is ruthless."

"Yes, well, for the doctors in the Hall of the Appraised it may not be worth the risk. Unless a Praetor demands your priest be saved, they'll let him bleed out."

The Priest disappeared through the doors. The crowd dispersed, returning to their previous activities. Gaul was so close. Too close to fail.

"You'll have to survive the Pits to get to him," Tora said.

"That's hardly a problem." The fire grew in Gaul's gut. "Surviving's what I do best."

Tora didn't stay in the commons for long. He wished Gaul well before returning to the infirmary. The other fighters were willing to spar, but none wished to talk. It's harder to kill someone you've gotten to know as a person.

Gaul moved from partner to partner. He made sure to never fight with any real skill, so not to give away his moves to a potential opponent. The smarter fighters were doing the same, he could be sure of that, but it was better than sitting in the shade waiting for the day to end.

The sun was about to touch the city spires beyond the commons' walls when the guards called for the fighters to return to their rooms. They led them out from the commons down a flight of stairs into a torch lit hallway of barred cells. Fighters who didn't enter of their own accord got shoved in. A guard grabbed Gaul by his shoulder and tossed him into a cell halfway down.

A simple straw pile was the only possible bed he could see, and a stained bucket his only toilet. He couldn't even spread his arms in the tiny cell and could barely lay down, only fitting if he curled up like a child. A foot-long blood smear decorated the wall to his left and a small square window was across from the door the guard slammed shut and locked.

Gaul approached the window. It was smaller than his shoulder width and the ground was at eye level, before plunging off a cliffside into the city below. Marjyal stretched onward into the dying sunlight, a chaotic sea of building tops crashing into each other. Tora was right, even if Gaul escaped it seemed easy to become lost in the urban maze.

He dropped onto the pile of straw. It was better than the stone floor, but not by much. The straw poked and scratched his bare skin. He trampled the bed into something somewhat comfortable and laid back.

All he had to do was prove his worth in the arena to finally catch up to the Priest. Then he could worry about escaping that abyss.

"Gaul."

The whisper came so faint; Gaul wasn't sure he heard it.

"Gaul." It came again.

He stood from his bed and moved to the window. The voice got louder, moving along the prison's wall.

"Who's there?" Gaul whispered, pulling himself closer to the bars.

A figure came into view. They wore a long cloak with a hood and mask. They flipped the hood down and knelt next to the window, rustling up their short, ragged hair. Gaul narrowed his eyes. How did this person know his name?

"There you are," she said and pulled down the scarf. A vicious scar ran from the corner of her mouth. A familiar scar.

"Marta?"

Gaul was long gone by the time Marta sobered up, still sitting on the blacksmith's bench. There was an armed soldier heading into Nature's Grave, with seemingly no fear of the land. Someone like that could easily help her get to her brother. She would have to convince him to journey deeper into Adathin with her. The Priest had refused, told her the lands south of Nature's Grave were not for sightseeing. She wouldn't give Gaul the option.

Lucen gave a half-hearted attempt to stop her, but he must have been relieved to see her go. She kept him busy with her time spent at the bar, but she heard him whisper. She heard everyone whisper when they thought she was too out of it to care. About her and her brother. How they came out of Nature's Grave years earlier.

Screw them, she thought, as she stole Lucen's knives and headed south.

She followed the main path at a fast pace. Gaul had a day at least on her, but she understood the woods better than him. He was guaranteed to get lost, and she could take that opportunity to close the distance. She reached into her bag and felt the exodus stone within. It put a chill across her skin. Too cold even for the already cold weather. She pictured Gaul in her mind, hazy as it may be.

The sun reached its apex when the sound of steel on steel reached Marta's ears. She sprinted toward the commotion in time to see Gaul and some knight disappear into a ravine. She lunged for the edge.

Gaul hung a short distance below, his shield caught in a twisting root. Blood stained his face and his eyes moved unfocused. He looked up, but stared straight through Marta. He mumbled something under his breath. Nature's Grave had taken its toll on the soldier.

Marta laid on her stomach. Her fingers brushed his shield. So close. A stone flew from the fog and struck the wall. The root tore from the dirt. The ravine's lip crumbled and Marta scrambled to not be taken with it.

"No!" she cried.

Gaul plummeted like a broken bird. He bounced off the cliff face and crashed into the earth far below.

Figures appeared from the mist in the valley. One spun a sling over his head. Marta pressed herself to the mud, peering over the edge. The one leading the pack had a boar's head as a crown. Marjyal had arrived.

"Shit," Marta whispered. "Shit, shit, shit."

The leader motioned to the numerous slaves to check the bodies. They swarmed Gaul, inspecting and prodding him.

"The sorry bastard's alive," one of them said, and the rest heaved the body into a cart.

Next, they moved to the knight Gaul had been fighting. They pulled at his armour and flipped him over.

"Put him in the cart," the leader shouted. "We'll have to cut that stuff off him."

With great effort they hauled the knight to the cart, tossing him next to Gaul's motionless body. The slaves pulled the cart into motion, bumping over the soggy grass and carrying Gaul off to the Marjyal Pits.

Marta shut her eyes. Gaul was alive, if barely. But he was going to Marjyal. The thought of going back there put ice in Marta's veins. She could return to Landus. Back to the Trail's End to drink herself numb. Her brother said he would return after all.

No. She squeezed mud in her hands until the water drained away. Fear wouldn't hold her back anymore. But she couldn't go alone. She still needed someone like Gaul — and it left a sour taste in her mouth to consider leaving him to the Marjyalians.

Marta crawled away from the ravine and dug through her bag until she found the exodus stone. A grey sliver of rock piercing a chunk of petrified wood. Not only was it cold, it was lighter than its materials would indicate. She squeezed it and thought of the towering spires and labyrinthine streets of Marjyal. All she would have to do was walk.

The landscape was solid trees and brush. The rain slowed until it disappeared, but moisture remaining on the high grass and ferns soaked Marta's boots. She had faith in her stone. As long as she kept walking she would be out of Nature's Grave.

It took another hour until the trees broke into a golden grassland, flat enough she could already see the spires of Marjyal on the horizon. It would take her until nightfall. That'll make it easier to sneak through the walls. Her legs shook as she took her first steps toward the city.

The last hours of sunlight did wonders to dry Marta. She was already less miserable by the time the sun went down. The recruiters surely had more than one exodus stone. Their lead would be substantial. There was time, though. As long as Gaul held on, one of the doctors in the Pits would save him. They had to, didn't they?

Even when the moon and starlight put Marjyal into nothing but a silhouette, Marta could see it clear as day. It wasn't easy to forget. Stone and wood buildings fell over each other into maddening architecture, the hundreds of spires jutted into the sky, and of course the Marjyal Pits sat upon a hill for all to see.

How long had it been since she left the City of Revels? She was a child. Her brother, years her elder, snuck out with her hidden in a cart. He would be furious, but she was doing this for him. To see him again. At least she wasn't going in blind.

The ten-metre masonry wall that surrounded Marjyal's eastern side had seen better days. She followed the exterior until she discovered some rubble crushing the grass. Not far beyond was a crack wide enough to squeeze through. She flipped up her hood and wrapped her scarf around her face as a mask. Visions of being a ten-year-old girl flashed through her head. Throwing knives at strawmen — and the occasional real one. Last chance to turn back.

Pieces of stone fell as she pulled herself into the crack. She braced herself on either side of the crumbling brick and concrete and eased forward, making sure each step was firm and quiet before moving on. Fortunately, Marjyal was more interested in keeping people in, rather than out.

She was halfway to the other side when the crack brightened. She froze. A city guard holding a torch strode in front of the crack. They faced toward the interior wall, putting their back to her. If he turned, she wouldn't have many good choices. Scramble back into the field? Lunge at them? Her hands felt slick on the walls.

Don't slip, she thought. *Don't slip.*

The guard sighed and continued their patrol. Marta finally exhaled, but not too loud. She waited until the guard's footsteps faded into hushed stomps, then exited the crack in the wall. If the guards found her they would assume she was leaving the city without permission, which put her fate in the hands of that guard.

The interior wall waited across a decaying garden heavy with shadows from dying braziers. A small window glowed in the distance, it might as well of been across the world. Moving torchlights littered the garden, and a few on the walls high above. She kept low to the earth and sprinted toward the window, making sure to give the braziers a wide berth.

She crouched below the windowsill, made sure the hallway inside was clear, and vaulted in. Her leg clipped a table, sending it and its contents crashing to the ground.

"What's that?" someone shouted.

Marta rolled with the momentum, back onto her feet and out the opposite window. She landed with a hopping stop on the city streets and yanked down her disguise. Keeping her eyes forward, she put her hands in her pockets and ducked into the closest alley. No one shouted at her to stop — she was another Marjyalian strolling through the restless city.

Lanterns on building walls and light escaping from nearby windows illuminated claustrophobic cobblestone streets. The city wasn't close to settling down for the night. People stumbled out and into buildings at random, hooting and hollering. Periodic screams echoed through the night, some of joy, some of pain. She was back in the City of Revels.

She felt sick just walking through the streets. Fifteen years had done nothing to fade the memory of crooked buildings and nonstop celebrations of nothing.

Marta's recollection was stopped by a nearby shout and laugh. She exited into a square filled with people, all facing a raised platform. A cheer rose from the crowd as some figures in charred white robes hoisted a thick pole with a naked man chained to it. The metal links cut into the poor man's skin, leaving red welts where they rubbed against his arms and chest. They crossed over each other like a marionette tied up in its strings.

One of the burnt cloak group lifted a white-hot piece of metal to the sky, joining the numerous torches already up there. He placed the iron against the chained man's stomach, awakening him into screams. The crowd cheered again. Marta gritted her teeth and continued out the other side of the square. There were no laws to stop such an action. Venerate Mar, Anima of Revels. That was all that mattered.

The side streets were choked with debris. The builders had added hazardous extensions to their buildings — held up by stilts — and jury-rigged stairs up to the rooftops. Marta shoved a drunk woman aside and climbed for a better view.

The Marjyal Pits eclipsed the sky on the southern-most hill. A massive amphitheater with a few auxiliary buildings attached and lit up like a beacon. She kept the arena in sight and made her way across the rooftops and makeshift bridges.

Atop the buildings it was much faster to get to the Pits, with the occasional need to hop across an alley. The buildings stopped at the bottom of the hill and Marta found a crumbling tenement to slide down before ascending the rocky slope. A few guards meandered the grounds. None paid attention to Marta as she walked around to the infirmary.

The infirmary was built into the earth, only the barred roofs that looked into the medical rooms visible. Over a dozen holes laid out in two columns, and Marta checked them all.

Doctors fawned over patients, working to exhaustion to keep them alive — knowing the death of the patient would kill them as well thanks to the leech-bindings. A guard stood over one such room, dropping small stones onto the patient and laughing when the doctor screamed at him.

At the far end was a room with a bald doctor. Gaul laid on a straw bed. The doctor poured something down his throat, but he wasn't moving. A leech binding laid on his chest. Marta allowed herself a moment of relief, before tapping a knife on the iron cage. The doctor looked up. His eyes widened.

"How is he?" Marta asked.

The doctor placed himself close to Gaul. "Excuse me?"

"How is your patient?" She squatted on the cage.

"He's injured. Very injured." The doctor looked at Gaul, then back up to Marta. "I can fix him, though. What's it to you?"

"I bet on him. How long until he's awake?"

"I'd give him a few days. If he doesn't wake up by then…" The doctor turned his back on Marta, grabbing the cup that had the concoction and placing it outside the room. He limped with every step. "I suppose then there will be two corpses in this room."

"A few days, you say?" She stood and started to leave, then stopped. "I'll be stopping by occasionally. Let's keep this visit between us."

"Sure. Doesn't really matter to me."

It would be days until Gaul woke up — if he woke up. That was a lot of time to spend in the City of Revels. But after that, she would see her brother. With that in her mind, she could survive anything.

She needed a quiet corner to hide in and plan. Those were rare to find in Marjyal.

**

"Marta?"

The last time he'd seen the woman she was passed out on a Landus bench. He blinked, expecting the hallucination to fade, but there she was. Proud smirk and new haircut.

"I almost didn't recognize you," he said.

"Oh, well, some weirdo in the market traded me some chicken for a bunch of my hair. Figured why not?" She scanned Gaul up and down. "You look well. Did someone steal your clothes?"

Gaul snorted and crossed his arms. "What are you doing here?"

"I'm here to get you out." She grabbed the bars and pulled herself closer. "For a price."

Gaul narrowed his eyes.

"If I help you escape," she continued. "You're going to help me get to the Cradle of the World."

Gaul started to say something, then stopped and turned to pace the cell. He pinched the bridge of his nose. "The Cradle of the World? Even if it is real—"

"It is real. My brother went there. He's been researching the King of Adathin's search for the Cradle and went on ahead without me. I got a little… held up and wasn't able to follow." She squeezed the bar. "So, let me get you out and you can watch my back as we head south."

"Wait." He rested his elbows on the windowsill. "Can you get me into the Hall of the Appraised?"

"Are you serious? That place is sealed tight, and I'm not exactly going to be breaking you out in a subtle way. I get you out, we run."

"Could you break me out of the Hall?"

"Are you—?" She shook her head. "You understand you have to go through the arena to get to the Hall, right? You can't guarantee you'll win; you can't even guarantee you'll get a fair fight!"

"That's not for you to worry about. Just focus on getting me out of the Hall of the Appraised." He flopped onto the pile of straw. It hurt more than he expected, but he refused to show any pain on his face. Instead, he laid on his back and stared at the ceiling. "Now walk away. I need to be rested for tomorrow."

Marta made a few grunts and groans then disappeared from the bars. Gaul craned his head back and stared at the window she had vacated. He was lucky enough to find the Priest, and lucky enough to have an escape plan. But luck had a habit of running out at the worst possible moment. Tomorrow, he needed all he could get.

I found a sparring arena at the back of the castle. It wasn't large, but there were seats for spectators, so I imagine it drew a crowd. In the outbuilding next to it were racks of wooden weapons. The people didn't fight to the death. They fought to display skill and glory. I wonder what they would think of the City of Revels *not far to the north and their Festival of Vultures. A Festival where death is the draw. I still think back and wonder what those terrible shows have to do with venerating Mar.*

I wanted to keep searching through the castle, but I've been having this weird feeling that I'm not alone. The only place I feel safe is locked in the grand library. Either I'm going mad from the isolation, or there are truly sounds echoing through the halls.

—From the journal of Jovin Gutterwake

Chapter Four

Festival of Vultures

In Marjyal's north, along the lip of where the city crumbled into the Sorrow Sea, six mansions sat on the highest point. Palaces, at least by Marjyal standards. Each had their own space, built with strong gates and high walls — as if the people inside didn't want to entertain the fact the masses sat on their doorsteps. These mansions made home to the rulers of Marjyal, as much as the city had rule. The six Praetors.

One mansion sat apart from the others. It was higher and further back. In the mornings one could see a shadow standing at the back window. Melifacto, Praetor of Owls, looked over the tumultuous landscape below him. He closed one eye — iris so dark it was nearly black — against the glare of the rising sun.

He tapped his finger on the window. He touched locations in the city he recognized. Every year that passed, there were less and less. He smiled. The chaos was soothing. The fact he couldn't predict where the city would go put life in his veins. He touched the Marjyal Pits, then the burn scar across the middle of his face. It was a blemish on his sand-coloured skin, but he cared little for appearances.

He ruffled the feathers on his brown coat and turned away. A recently returned expedition had found him a creature they called a 'jump cat.' It sat on a stone slab licking its paw. A dark grey feline, not much larger than the average street cat one could find skulking along the Marjyal alleys. It followed Melifacto's movements with double pupils, two in each eye. Its fur crawled like worms and occasionally it faded for a moment before snapping back to full opacity.

Melifacto's team said the jump cat would flicker around the forest, making it nearly impossible to catch. It cut the throat of a senior trapper before they were able to get it in a cage. All it could do then was hiss and vibrate.

The cat purred as Melifacto stroked it from behind the ear to the tail. Jump cat was too simple of a name, something a farmer would come up with. Melifacto would come up with something better.

There was the sound of footsteps before the door to his lab flew open. The cat recoiled.

"Easy," Melifacto whispered.

The cat settled at his word. The intruder bowed at the door before hurrying past empty cages. Pelady was a sly woman with a wiry frame, but taller than Melifacto when she wasn't slouching. She had short, dark, hair that curled at the tips and in the proper light, her copper skin had a tinge of green to it. She pushed her black feather cloak aside, revealing her leather armour, and bowed.

"Melifacto," she said. When she spoke, her sharp teeth clicked beneath the lips of a too-wide mouth.

"Before you start," Melifacto said. "Can you tell me what's wrong with my laboratory?"

Pelady looked around. "The cages are empty?"

"The cages are empty!" Melifacto laughed. "An unfortunate state to see such a place in. Could you tell me why?"

He hovered his hand over a tray of flux crystals. He plucked a purple one and placed it next to the cat.

"The Sorrow Sea has been wracked with storms lately," Pelady said. "We lost a boat just last week."

Melifacto ran his fingers through his dark hair, striped with white. As the cat faded, the crystal glowed. "Sailing isn't the only way." He touched the crystal and understanding filled him. The cat wasn't teleporting, it made itself appear to be in a different location that it was. An interesting survival technique. "I'm sure there are some animals you haven't found in Adathin yet."

"Yes, perhaps. But—"

"Or take some exodus stones and search Nature's Gra—"

"Master!"

Melifacto stopped. He stroked the cat, feeling for placement of bones and organs. The next words out of Pelady's mouth had better be worth it.

"She's back in the city. The girl."

"Marta?" Melifacto looked at Pelady for the first time. "When? How do you know?"

"I woke up and there was her scent on the wind." She tapped her upturned nose. "It must be fifteen years since I last smelled it."

"Where is she?"

"My nose isn't that good."

"Someday we'll have to do something about that." Melifacto crossed to a corner of the lab where a dusty sheet covered a podium. He yanked it aside, revealing a second purple flux crystal, a little bigger than his index finger, suspended by metal rods and wrapped in runic paper. It pulsed like a breathing creature. "It is her."

"What should we do?"

Melifacto unscrewed the rods until the crystal dropped into his hands. He cradled it like a glass sculpture and handed it to Pelady. "Take this and find her."

"Should I bring her in?" Pelady asked, gazing into the soft throbs of crystal light.

"Yes." Melifacto returned to the cat. "Actually, no. We can do this in a good way. Put her face in your mind. Get her new scent. But let me be the one to approach her."

"Do you not want to come with me then?"

"I wish I could." He picked up a knife, inspecting the edge. "It's the Boar's Banquet today and Bellona will throw a fit if any of the Praetor's miss her little display."

"Of course, master. I'll find her. Don't worry."

Pelady clutched the crystal to her chest and hurried out. Melifacto stared at the closed door long after she left. Something had seemed different about that morning. The sun had risen brighter. The birds sang louder. But that wasn't it. The gods must be afraid — they knew what had come back to him.

The cat rolled onto its side, following the motion of Melifacto's hand. He put the knife against the animal's belly.

There was still work to do.

✷ ✷

Gaul awoke to the sound of metal hitting metal. At first he thought Marta had returned, but no one was at the window. Instead, a guard waited at his door, shouting for Gaul to stand up. Sleeping on hard ground wasn't new for him, but even the firmest grassland was more comfortable than the straw and stone. His body fought against him as he eased to his feet and followed the guard.

Other Untested stumbled out of their cells. A few had to be yanked out, shouting all the way. The guards took them out the door and across the commons to a small mess hall. The couple dozen from the day before blossomed to nearly double. Not everyone wanted to spar. A guard shoved a bowl into Gaul's chest and pushed him into line.

The sun hadn't yet risen and the area was lit by flickering torches. A skinny man with one arm ladled out grey mash into bowls. A wafting of rotten eggs appeared when it flopped out of the spoon and it jiggled when Gaul shook it.

"On the bright side, it won't kill you," a familiar voice said.

Gaul turned to see Tora, already with a bowl of his own. He motioned for Gaul to follow him and headed for a bench not far away. The scars had reappeared on the back of his head and neck.

"I see you didn't try to kill yourself last night, that's good." Tora stretched his left leg out, massaging the thigh muscle.

"The cell didn't give many opportunities," Gaul said.

"People have found ways. Suffocated with straw, or just slam your head against the wall until you're unconscious. Injuries are a good way to keep out of the arena for a day or so."

That would explain the bloodstain on the wall of Gaul's cell. "Everyone's all terrified of this arena business, it's just fighting, isn't it?"

"Most of the time. But this place is about entertainment at any cost. There are torture shows, one-sided battles, anything someone could bet on." He bowed his head, looking at his soggy gruel. "And unfortunately, we're in the middle of the Festival of Vultures. It's much worse right now."

"Festival of Vultures?"

"A celebration of death. Brainchild of the Praetor of Doves. He's the leader of the clergy. They put on much more vicious events to satisfy the bloodlust of the people. You chose a bad time to get captured."

Gaul scoffed. He took a small clump of mash in his mouth. It tasted like the bottom of a boot and had the consistency of moist tar. He chewed until it was somewhat manageable and then swallowed it whole. "I need to get into the arena today."

"Looking to die?"

"Looking to get into the Hall of the Appraised."

"Then you're better off waiting." Tora shoveled some mash into his own mouth, it didn't hit him much better than it hit Gaul. "Barely anyone gets into the Hall during the Festival. I'm surprised two got in yesterday. From what I hear they had to fight some of the Guild of Owls' animal-freaks."

"So you're saying it's possible."

"Yes, but—"

"It's all I need. Have to do something before my luck runs dry." He forced himself through eating more of the disgusting boot slop. It had to be nutritious at least for all its tastelessness.

A woman passed by the bench and leaned toward Tora. "Feyra's here," she said. "Better get a move on before you get pulled into something."

Tora went pale as the woman hurried on. Gaul cocked an eyebrow and asked, "Who's Feyra?"

"Blood of the Praetor of Boars," Tora said, scanning the top of the surrounding walls. "There."

A woman leaned against one of the guard towers. Her chestnut hair wound into an intricate braid with the sides shaved against her skin. Strands of it hung before her eyes, where a jagged scar went across her eyebrow. She was built like a statue, as if formed from clay. Her muscles flexed through her sleeves as she hefted a barbed club onto her shoulder and disappeared into the tower.

Tora abandoned his bowl and jumped to his feet. "Look, my friend. I understand your rush to get to the Hall. But if you wish to pass through the Champion's Walk, today is not your day. If Feyra is here, that means today is the Boar's Banquet."

"What's the Boar's Banquet?"

"Just keep your head down!" Tora shouted over his shoulder.

"Untested!" Feyra shouted, sweeping into the commons. "There will only be one event today. My lady Bellona, Praetor of Boars, offers you a chance to prove your strength to her. No matter the odds. It's time for the Boar's Banquet."

A few of the Untested gasped and cursed. Others looked around in confusion, including Gaul. The woman snapped her fingers and guards stomped across the commons. They grabbed various fighters, hauling the more resistant ones to their feet. One eyed Gaul and reached for him.

"That's not necessary," Gaul said, pushing past the guard and joining those already taken.

Feyra narrowed her eyes. She kept them locked on him as he passed by. For a moment, Gaul thought she was going to grab him. Her gaze was a steel arrow. But like passing ships, they left only their wake.

Gaul was brought along a path that disappeared into the base of the arena. Guards shoved men and woman onto benches lining the tunnel walls. The air was hot, and stank of animals and sweat. Gaul sat himself next to a woman with a black ponytail and a sharp nose who swore when Boar's Banquet was mentioned.

"What's the Boar's Banquet?" Gaul whispered.

The woman looked at Gaul like she was surprised he could even speak. She had bright blue eyes and her pale skin seemed to glow in the dark of the tunnel. She eyed a guard at the far end and leaned closer. "The bad end of life's horse. Thirteen Untested are sent into a maze within the arena. No weapons, no armour. The Guild of Boars' hunters chase us and we have until midday to survive. About two hours."

"And we just need to live to get into the Hall of the Appraised?"

The woman shook her head. "They want honoured fighters in that place. We will be running for our lives, nothing honourable in that."

Gaul ran his hand through his hair, cursing beneath his breath. Tora was right, there was no sense entering the arena. Not that there was much time. If no one had treated the Priest, could he even have survived the night?

Feyra struck the wall with her heavy club, sending a loud thump down the line. It was a wicked weapon reinforced with jagged metal stained with blood.

"On your feet," she ordered, pacing down the line. "It's time for the inspection. For those who don't know, I am Feyra, Blood of the Boars. Believe me when I say that if you speak or step out of line you will be flayed, salted, and given to the Guild of Ashes."

The crowd stayed silent.

"Say yes!"

The crowd shouted yes.

Scowling, Feyra led the fighters through a side door. Further down the tunnel was a large wooden gate. The entrance into the arena itself, if Gaul had to guess. He stretched back, hoping to find some exploit, only to be shoved out onto a wooden platform.

The sun broke across the horizon line, casting its oranges upon Marjyal. The city sprawled from the west sea to the walls. Buildings hung half-crumbled or held up by struts, crammed between a hundred spires. Tendrils of smoked reached into the sky before being blown away by the ocean wind. There were cities that looked better after a war.

People crowded into the square below the door the Untested exited. They cheered when they saw the fighters descend the steps.

"Stop," Feyra said. She lined them up on a lower stage, with stairs on either side into the square. Banners with a flaming horn sigil hung around the area.

A second platform was set up perpendicular to theirs. This one had cover and drinks. Four people stood there, but they were beasts. Three men and one woman covered in muscles and scars, each had a full set of armour and weapons laying on tables next to them.

The Hunters, Gaul thought.

"This is who they're putting in the Banquet?" someone asked.

People in fineries made their way up the stairs and onto the stage. The one who had spoken was a stick man dressed in crimson garb. He played his claw-like fingers along a jewel-laden necklace. His other arm was around a plump woman with a sour look stuck on her face.

"Some of them look like they might die fun," the woman said. "Or at least die loud."

"I prefer if they can fight at least a little bit," the man said. He stopped before Gaul. "What about this one?"

The woman grabbed Gaul's chin and jerked his head around. A choking scent of herbs and some unfamiliar fruit wafted off her in waves. Gaul squeezed his fist. Out of the corner of his eye, a guard tapped his finger against his whip. Gaul relaxed. The woman released his chin with a flick.

"He looks strong," she said. "But have you seen the Hunters? They'll eat him alive. I don't think we should bet this year. Maybe a bounty."

The couple laughed and went on their way. Scores of similar Marjyalian elites, poking and prodding, took their place. The less fortunate had to watch from below. For hours this continued. Gaul thought back to raiding slave towns in Mirral. Unfortunate souls lined up and sold off like cattle. But Marjyal wasn't selling the fighters. They were racehorses. Gaul gritted his teeth and willed his way through the process. The Priest was on the other side.

After the crowd finished their inspections, the guards grabbed each fighter in turn, hauling them off the platform. The Hunters hung back chatting with each other. They weren't prisoners of the arena. Feyra and the other guards shoved the fighters back to sitting down in the smelly, hot tunnel.

Gaul leaned over to the ponytail woman. "They're betting on us?"

"They usually do," she whispered. "Who will survive the longest? Which hunter will kill the most? Things like that. They can put up bounties on the hunters killing us in certain ways."

"They really don't expect us to get out of this, do they?"

The woman rubbed both her palms against her cheeks. "I've never heard of someone surviving the entire Boar's Banquet."

"You seem to know quite a bit about the arena for an Untested." Gaul spotted a guard coming down the tunnel and stopped talking. They passed, eyeing the fighters. "I didn't even hear of Marjyal until waking up here."

"I live in the city," she said. "Spent most of my time hiding in dark corners. But you start owing enough coin to the wrong people and things can get tough. Decided to take my chances in the Pits and maybe in a few years I can be freed."

"Why didn't you leave?"

"I wouldn't dare. Mar grants us freedom. As long as we stay in Marjyal we are spared from the chains that bind the world outside."

Gaul looked up and down the tunnel of dirty and cast down faces. "This is freedom?"

"This is Mar. The Anima of Revels and Hedonism. Patron of Pleasure, as the Guild of Doves says. We are blessed with absolute freedom, and that comes with some sacrifices. I would rather die free than in bondage."

Gaul shook his head. "I'd rather not die at all."

"That would be nice too."

Mar was not an Anima Gaul recognized. The Pantheon of the Divine, of all things, was ordered. Nine Divines with the Anima below them. New gods didn't tend to spring up out of the ground. More than that, why was a city built to an Anima that far south? The Pantheon was mostly a northern religion.

Feyra slammed her club against the wall again. "Time for the Banquet!" Guards with spears stomped in from the commons. A rumble ran through the stone above them. The cheers of the crowd. The gate at the far end rose with stuttering jerks, letting more of the crowd's roar enter the tunnel.

With a smirk, Feyra stepped out the side door. "You have one minute to run," she said, and slammed the door shut.

Half of the fighters sprinted into the light ahead of them, hoping to utilize the head start. Others sunk to the back, shrinking in terror and requiring the guards to motivate them with their spears. No weapons, no armour. Prey waiting to be slaughtered. The fire in Gaul's stomach burned like lava. He pushed it down. He didn't need it. It wasn't him.

"It was nice talking," the ponytail woman said. "Perhaps I will see you in the Great Revel."

"What's your name?" Gaul asked.

"Raea."

"Stick around me, Raea." He started to drop back through the ranks of fighters. "I'm not prey."

Raea stared wide-eyed as Gaul moved closer to the guards with spears. They crossed the threshold, into a screaming arena of sunlight and sand. The gate behind him began to fall. Gaul whipped around, grabbed the shaft of a spear behind the blade, and pulled.

The guard — expecting someone to push back — flew forward. Their head smacked into the falling gate and they released the weapon into Gaul's hands. The metal slammed into the sand before any of the other guards could react.

"Whoa." Raea was the only fighter not to immediately run into the maze, and so she was the only one who saw Gaul's theft.

Gaul faced the maze, spinning his new weapon around his hand. Three paths sat before him. Heavy rumbling and crashes echoed from somewhere deep inside. Raised seats filled to overflowing with bodies shouted to the people down below. Finally, towering over the far side of the arena, an obelisk sat with the sun rising behind it. A bright blue light shone out of its base.

In less than a minute the Hunters would be set upon them, scouring the maze for victims. Gaul turned to Raea and held out the spear in both hands. "Blade or haft?"

"Uh, blade?"

Gaul slammed the spear into his knee. Snapping the shaft — shorter on the side with the spear head — and making essentially a dagger and a short staff. He handed Raea the dagger. "Are you coming with me?" he asked.

She tried a few practice swings. "I'm with you. Do you think we're gonna survive this?"

"Not just survive. You think four kills will get me into the Hall of the Appraised?"

"One kill would get you in."

Gaul smiled and tapped his stick against the ground. The fire in his stomach ached to grow to a full flame and burn out anyone they met. But he had made a promise. Still, the allure crawled along his skin. "Then let's aim to appease."

A red haze grew over the world. That was the most Gaul would give to the fire. He gripped the stick, chose the centre entrance, and entered the maze with Raea on his heel.

* *

Thousands of voices rose from the Pits. Those who had the coin to pay their way into the Festival of Vultures — or had won the seat lottery. Marta loaded the last powder keg onto her cart and looked toward the commotion. She had heard the Boar's Banquet was that day. The stands had to be packed.

"Thanks for the work," the smith said, leaning against his shop's siding. "You gonna be fine with all that?"

Marta looked over the six kegs. "I should be fine. Thanks."

The smith waved Marta off and entered his shop. Marta shook her head and took the cart handles. She worked all morning to get four kegs of powder, joining the two she already had. The smith didn't even blink an eye at that request. It worked out for her, at least. She started towing the cart through the crowded streets.

She had never been to the Pits, but talk of the Banquet always made its way to the gutters. Gaul would have to be pretty unlucky to get picked for it. If he did, then the outlook wasn't good. He would need to survive until midday, then he would be sent right back into the Untested's cells. Marta got the extra powder for the Hall of the Appraised, but she would rather break him out of the cells whether he liked it or not.

Marta was so wrapped up in her thoughts she didn't see a person step in front of her. She ground to a halt, before her face met the stranger's chest. The powder kegs rattled their explosive contents. The person stared at Marta with a cocked eyebrow.

The stranger was tall, easily six feet, and slender. For a moment, her skin appeared green, then it was gone. She looked Marta up and down, her eyes lingering with consideration. Something was off about the woman's mouth, though Marta couldn't figure out what. The woman sniffed the air, smiling as if something delectable reached her nose. Marta was about to apologize, but the woman walked away before she could.

Odd, Marta thought. The city was full of weirdos, though. At least that one wasn't dangerous. She resumed her trek.

As she walked, she kept an eye on the Pits. If Gaul was picked, the cheers needed to continue until midday for there to be a chance he was alive. If he wasn't, then Marta worried for nothing. She had wanted to get to the courtyard while the fighters were out for display to see if Gaul was among them, but the blacksmith's work kept her inside. All she could do was pray to a better god Gaul would be safe.

If he died, she would have a tough choice ahead of her. The journey to the Cradle of the World would be dangerous, and she was the furthest she had ever been. She would walk to the edge of Nature's Grave, willing her body to take the next step. She went in once, and that left her with a lasting scar.

She could go it alone. Through the castle and the wild land, until she found her brother. Or she could turn back. Drown herself in drinks at the Trail's End.

Or Gaul could survive.

Along the edges of the street, shadows darted out of view. Rough-looking people who would duck in and out of buildings, always with their gaze fixed on Marta and her cart. One of them pointed at her. Marta's stomach rolled.

Step by step, the street emptied until it was just Marta. Six thugs stepped in her way, swords resting on their hips. A man with a black curtain of chin-length hair stepped forward, tapping his thumb on his sword hilt still in its scabbard. Marta stopped and lowered the cart handles. She felt the bulges under her coat where her knives hung.

"Is there a problem?" she asked.

"There doesn't have to be," the thug said. "We're gonna take what's on your cart. You can keep your head."

Marta stepped over the cart handles. "That seems simple."

"We're simple people."

He waved to his gang and they started toward the cart. Gawkers waited in the alleys. No one was going to help. No one ever did. Marta gritted her teeth and held her ground.

"I need this stuff," she said. She had four knives and six opponents. It wasn't appealing odds.

The gang stopped. A chuckle ran through the line that faded into the ringing of blades being drawn. All Marta had was the element of surprise, and that was an element that got used up fast.

"Now." The gang leader tapped his sword on his shoulder. "We get to keep your head."

Marta's hand flashed to her hip and forward. A knife thudded into the leader's throat. Another knife. A second thug knocked this one aside. Marta drew her last two and waited. The gang kept their swords at the ready for any further flying blades and closed in.

One of the thugs vanished in a blur. Another thug spun, and his throat collapsed with a vicious jab. The strange woman who stopped Marta knelt on the first thug's chest, pushing his head into the street.

"Get off me!" the thug screamed.

The stranger broke his nose with one punch. The next shattered his jaw. She unleashed wild fury upon him, crushing his skull against the cobblestone. Another thug hurried to save his friend. The stranger flew to her feet and dug her fingers into his throat. Blood poured down her arm. The thug dropped his sword. His chest vibrated, but he would not die.

The surviving gangsters went pale. Their swords shook in their hands. Everything in Marta told her to run. The stranger tensed her fingers until something cracked in the thug's neck. And she moved again. She snaked between blades, tearing flesh and breaking bone.

The final thug dropped his sword and ran. The woman flicked blood off her fingers and caught him by the scruff. The thug screamed and flailed against her vice grip. She kicked his knee hard enough to invert it, then bent him until he looked up at her. She opened her mouth. Marta paled.

The woman's mouth was ringed with a ghastly display of needle teeth. Her lips split too wide for a normal person and a sharp tongue flicked out to taste the air.

The thug screamed. The woman clamped her jaw around his throat, stopping the sound with a crunch. The thug's eyes flicked about, trying to find something in the cloudless sky to focus on. His fingers reached for something to touch. The woman placed one hand on his forehead and the other on his chest. In one brutal motion she thrust the thug to the ground and ripped his throat from his neck. Red viscera scattered into the air and dripped down the woman's chin to stain her tunic. She turned to Marta, the ragged remains of the thug's throat still in her teeth.

Marta raised her knives. She couldn't stop them from shaking. Her knees from waiting to fall out. The woman saved her, but how monstrous of a savior she was.

The woman stretched to her full height. The sun made the blood on her arms and face shine like liquid rubies. She spat the man's throat out. "Are you alright?" she asked.

"I'll live." Marta lowered her knives.

"Are you not from here?"

"I, uhm, don't get to the south much." Marta jerked her head to the right. "I like to stay in the north."

"I see." The woman waved her hands to the corpses at her feet. Blood dripped off her fingers. "These are Flash Killers. You're in their territory. They don't let anyone who doesn't have a Praetor's Sigil get through with their deliveries. You should keep closer to the Pits. The Boars don't like people messing around out there so you'll be safe."

"Thank you." The words came hollow looking at the woman's crimson mask. She sheathed her knives.

"Pelady. My name's Pelady."

"I'm Marta."

Pelady cracked out a horrific smile, chunks of man stuck in her forest of sharp teeth. She bent down and yanked the knife from the leader's throat.

"Stay safe out there, Marta," Pelady said, tossing the knife to Marta's feet. She turned on her heel. "Maybe we'll see each other again."

Marta picked up her knife and flicked the blood off. Her fourth had gone flying off somewhere and she didn't feel like sticking around to find it. When she looked up, Pelady had disappeared, leaving the massacre in her wake.

Marta took hold of the cart and started moving. She took Pelady's advice and turned closer to the Pits. That settled it. Whether or not Gaul made it into the Hall of the Appraised, they were leaving that night. She needed to get out of this crazy town.

She could catch the end of the event. Hopefully Gaul would still be locked in his cell. He seemed like a lucky enough guy. What were the chances he would find himself in the Boar's Banquet?

Something strange happened last night.

I was sleeping in the library. I had moved my quarters from one of the guest rooms into the stacks when my paranoia hit a fever pitch. I feel safer behind the heavy wood doors. But when I opened my eyes last night, I felt a presence.

It was as though someone had sealed me in a coldbox. I couldn't move. I was wrapped up in my blanket, staring at the underside of the second storey balcony. And there were voices.

They started distant. People were screaming. There was a pounding that shook the entire castle. The people were crying out for help. They reached the library and rattled the doors that I had locked. But I was still frozen, unable to move.

The pounding got louder. The screaming got louder.

Then I woke up. Morning had come. I was drenched in sweat.

I need to get out of here.

—From the Journal of Jovin Gutterwake

Chapter Five
Boar's Banquet

The crowd let out a massive cheer — signaling the release of the Hunters. Not ten seconds later, a gut-wrenching scream was heard before getting cut out by another cheer.

"That's someone down," Raea said. "The Hunters work fast. If they don't get you, the maze will."

"Traps?" Gaul asked.

"Traps."

"Better and better." Gaul peeked around the next corner. Another empty hallway.

Gaul and Raea wandered through the maze, choosing turns at random. Every so often the crowd would cheer, someone would scream, or heavy grinding could be heard.

Gaul's red haze threatened to fade. He kept himself barely below the line of Igniting. It was scary how good he felt. His mind kept telling him to Ignite and fall into the battle meditation. But he had made his promise to Anori years earlier. The rage without Ignition should be enough to carry him through.

They turned the corner into an armoured Hunter wielding a short sword and shield. He wore a helmet designed like a weeping face. His arms and legs four tree trunks splattered with specks of blood. In his chest piece was etched with the phrase, *Slaughter the stock.*

"You." He pointed at Gaul and Raea with his sword. "Where did you get those weapons?"

The red haze pulsed like a heartbeat. Gaul growled from the deepest part of his chest and sprinted toward the Hunter. Not expecting the explosive bravado, the Hunter faltered. Gaul snapped his spear haft against the fighter's rising shield.

The Hunter turtled, but Gaul slipped his free hand between the shield and the fighter and knocked it away. He grabbed him by his chest piece and stabbed the broken end of the spear into his throat. The Hunter gurgled out a scream, silenced when Gaul yanked the haft out, and slammed it in again. Then again. And again.

The Hunter went limp and Gaul rammed the haft into his throat one last time, then let the body fall.

The audience became a wall of sound. They cared for blood, no matter where it came from. Gaul left the spear haft in the Hunter's throat, taking instead his short sword. He looked back at Raea, who hadn't moved from the spot he left her.

"Did I go too far?" Gaul asked, taking in heaving breaths.

Raea shook her head. Still, she couldn't look at him. Gaul touched his face. A heavy layer of blood covered his cheeks. He sighed. The red haze began to fade. The look Raea gave him brought back bad memories. He was better than that. He wiped the blood onto his pants.

"Alright, Raea," he said. "Let's get goin—"

"Look out!" Raea skipped backwards and pointed past Gaul.

Gaul spun around. The wall at the other end of the hall had dropped, revealing a stack of clustered barrels pointing toward him. A whirring sound filled the air. Gaul didn't need to understand the contraption to recognize a trap. He grabbed the dead Hunter and took cover.

There was a hollow thump followed by a storm of metal flechettes screaming down the hall. The Hunter's corpse vibrated as the steel tempest flew past. Pain shot through Gaul's right leg and shoulder. He resisted the instinct to jerk away and exit his cover.

The firing wall whirred up and launched another salvo. More flechettes flew past, and more stuck into the right side of his body. His skin was on fire. Red pulsed in his vision, urging him to Ignite. He slapped his forehead. Focus. Sitting in the line of fire would only result in more torment. One more round, then he would have to go.

The wall whirred, fired, tore into his right side, then he took off in a hobbling sprint toward where Raea disappeared. The whirring started up again. The corner was too far away. Gaul dug into whatever reserve of energy he still had remaining to quicken his pace.

Raea appeared from around the corner, grabbing Gaul. A hollow thump. She pulled him around the corner, sending pain screaming up his side. They fell as another wave of flechettes flew by.

"Shit!" Gaul shouted. He grabbed his arm, only to recoil when he touched the flechettes still stuck in.

"Don't move," Raea said, inspecting the flechettes.

Gaul sat against the wall. The arena rumbled and a slab of stone rose up from the ground and cut them off from the firing range.

"I've never seen a machine like that before," Gaul said. "I thought the Imperials were advanced with their siege engines. But this maze is—" Raea yanked a flechette from his arm.

"The entire arena is powered by crystals," she said, pulling more out. "I think four kills was a little ambitious. But you took one down within ten seconds of meeting him — that must have impressed them."

Gaul got started on the flechettes in his leg. "Impressed who?"

"The Praetors." She pointed to a section of seating separated from the rest.

Six figures sat on a balcony separate from the masses, a flaming horn banner fluttering in the breeze beneath them. Some pointed at Gaul and whispered to each other. Clearly, they were the ones in charge of this gruesome performance. There was no room to not impress if they could get Gaul into the Hall of the Appraised. One kill wasn't enough. Gaul pulled out the last flechette and staggered to his feet.

"Are you okay?" Raea asked.

The wounds hurt less without the flechettes moving and tearing the holes. He stoked his fire, careful not to go too far. The pain subsided to a dull pulsing. "I'm sore, not crippled. You still with me, Raea?"

She nodded, slower than she had at the beginning of the maze. Less sure. Gaul ignored it. Hunters weren't the only killers in the maze. He tightened his grip on his new short sword and brushed past Raea.

"Where're we going?" Raea asked.

"Doesn't matter," Gaul said. "They'll find us."

The arena wasn't huge, but the maze's walls sat tight and winding. Gaul and Raea could mostly walk side by side — though occasionally they were forced to walk single file or had the luck of a larger square. It didn't help the maze shifted before their eyes. More than once a hall turned into a dead end or opened into further paths. If it wasn't for the Praetor's podium and the time keeping obelisk, Gaul would have no indication of direction.

Occasionally, figures wearing rags dragged a corpse into holes in the sand. Gaul took chase, but the holes disappeared before he could get close.

"The Guild of Rats," Raea explained. "Sewers and sanitation. But really they just get rid of the bodies. I heard they eat them."

"Seems unlikely," Gaul said. "How many Guilds are there?"

"Six. Doves for clergy, Owls for science, Rats for… you know." Raea stepped around a pool of blood soaking the sand. "Snakes for food, Ants for construction, Boars for military… and entertainment."

"That's not a good combination. What about the Guild of Ashes? Feyra—"

A bloodcurdling scream cut through the air. It was close. Just on the other side of the wall. Gaul and Raea froze, clutching tight onto their weapons.

"I think we're reaching the end of the bodies," Gaul said, creeping around the next corner.

"And we're about halfway through the time limit." Raea pointed at the towering obelisk. More blue lights had appeared, reaching the midpoint of the spire.

The ground rumbled and Gaul threw himself back. The way forward slammed shut, nearly catching his leg. The wall to his right slid open in response. The new hall was tighter than anyone that had come before, with vicious wooden spikes covering either side. They left enough room for two people to walk next to each other.

"Please don't tell me we're going through that," Raea said. The wall behind her rose up as if to say, yes you are.

"Just stay in the middle." Gaul stepped toward the barbed hallways. "And be ready to run if it moves."

The spikes varied from ten to thirty centimetres long, lashed to a crosshatched board built into the mortar of the wall. Dried blood stained the wood red. Gaul and Raea walked single file to avoid being too close.

Ahead of them, a Hunter stepped into view. Her light armour stopped at her midriff and her boots stopped at bare thigh. Scars littered her stomach, arms and legs. A soldier would want to protect their vitals, but she had more style than protection. Didn't seem to bother her. She grinned at Gaul and hefted a trident over one shoulder, holding a net in her other hand.

"Gaul." Raea tapped him on the shoulder and motioned to where they had walked from.

Another Hunter — this one in heavy steel with bloody, thick gauntlets — blocked the passage. He pushed out his chin and slammed his fists together.

"Brother," the woman shouted to her companion. "They appear to have Markus's sword."

"You're right, Sister." Brother pounded his chest. "The whore's will weep tonight without their stallion."

"They would feel better if they could have the sword as a memento, Brother."

"They would indeed, Sister."

Raea placed her back against Gaul's, holding her spear tip at the ready. "What do we do now?" she asked.

"I don't know," he said, never taking his eyes off Sister. "Let them make the first mistake."

Sister hung her net off a hook on her belt and approached the wall. She knocked a brick loose and threw it to the ground, revealing a lever. Somehow, the crowd cheered even louder.

"That's not a mistake." Gaul pointed out the lever to Raea, who gasped in reply. "We need to get out of here."

Sister threw the lever. The spike walls groaned to life.

"Brother or Sister?" Raea asked.

"The one that isn't a wall!" Gaul flared red into his vision. He sprinted into the crimson haze.

Sister laughed, unhooked her net, and held her trident at the ready. Showmanship aside, the Hunter was ready to kill.

Gaul planted and hurled his sword. A moment of panic crossed Sister's face. She flailed with her trident at the flying blade, clattering it against the wall. Her stomach waited bare, the awkward polearm far from its defensive position. Gaul pushed his toes into the hot sand and burst into motion.

Sister was recovering. The walls grinded closer. Metal scraped on stone until it was all Gaul could hear. A long spike caught him by the arm, tearing away his flesh. It cost him a second. But a second was too long. Sister would be ready for him.

A piece of metal flashed past Gaul's ear. It struck Sister's midriff, inches below her armour. Sister stumbled back, gritting her teeth. The tip of a broken spear stuck out from her stomach.

Gaul followed a moment later, crashing his shoulder into Sister's chest. He grabbed the spear shaft and yanked it aside. Blood scattered across the sand. Gaul's nerves vibrated like taut strings. Red shoots invaded his blue eyes, crossing each other into a mesh that overtook him. Filled him. The pain in his body disappeared. Rage pulled the strings in his nerves tighter and tighter. Flames ran through his bones.

Until the strings snapped.

The fury was gone. The arena was gone. Sister was gone. In her place; veins, organs, flesh, and bone. The expanding of lungs and the beating of a heart within a crimson aura. Gaul spun his blade and plunged it into the sack of meat.

The world was cold around him. Peaceful. Quiet. But more crimson auras stained his sight. They filled the empty space with their sound. Thumping hearts. Tensing muscles. Too loud.

A word cut through the distance. "Gaul!" it cried.

The flames receded. The screaming crowd and grinding machinery returned. Gaul was left staring at Sister. The spear tip stuck out of her neck. She sneered before her eyes went blank and she collapsed at his feet.

"Gaul!" Raea screamed again.

She hadn't made it as far as him. She had to step sideways, shuffling between the closing walls. Spikes begun to block her way.

Gaul lunged for the lever. The audience cheered, the wall stopped, and Raea screamed. Gaul's chest tightened.

"Gaul?" Raea's voice squeaked from the passage.

She stood where he had last seen her, gritting her teeth. A few of the longer spikes had pierced her, but only about a centimetre into her chest, arm, and thigh. Somewhere below their feet, gears ground as the walls retracted. Raea clutched her chest wound and stumbled out of the trap.

"Are you okay?" Gaul asked, relief washing over him.

Raea wiped the blood on her hands off onto her pants. "Considering the alternative? I'm fine."

"Sister!" Brother cried as the walls separated. He gave a war cry and charged down the passageway.

Gaul sighed. It was one thing after another. He flipped the lever down. Brother didn't care; he knocked spikes off the wall without breaking his stride.

"Is he going to get through?" Raea asked, stepping back.

"No," Gaul said. Brother was furious, rightfully so. But he let anger get the better of him.

The walls got too close for Brother to ignore them any longer. He planted a hand on each and strained to hold them apart. Mechanics screeched as the walls came to a halt. Brother stepped forward, moving his hands to keep the wall open.

Gaul pulled the spear tip from Sister's body, took aim, and threw. It lodged into Brother's elbow. His arm buckled, and the walls continued to close.

"Come on." Gaul retrieved his sword and handed Raea the trident. "We don't need to see this."

They took their new weapons and left Brother in the ever-shrinking hallway. Not a minute later they heard a muffled crunch and a cheer from the crowd. Three Hunters down, one remained. The whole spectacle made Gaul sick.

"What are you?" Raea asked.

"What do you mean?" Gaul peered around the next corner.

Raea grabbed his arm. She ran her fingers over the spots where the flechettes stuck and the spike tore. The wounds were gone. "How can you mend your flesh like this? Are you a magician? Are you unkillable?"

"No." Gaul pulled his arm away. "Sneak up behind me and put a blade through my neck and I'm sure I'll die like all the rest."

"The Praetors have abilities too. You must be blessed by Mar as they were."

"I'm not blessed by any god."

"We could actually do this." Raea wasn't listening to him anymore. "Mar be praised. You have sent me a reveller with great power.

The ground shook and Gaul leapt aside to avoid yet another trap. Instead the wall dropped. The one behind it did the same, and the one behind that. Every wall in a straight line to what Gaul guessed was the centre of the arena fell into the sand. As the last one disappeared, a figure stood waiting.

"What's going on?" Raea held the trident at the ready.

"We're the last," Gaul said and approached the final Hunter. "The Praetors want a big finish."

Raea kept pace not far behind him. "But that's not fair. We're only supposed to survive the time."

"Since when was any of this fair?" Gaul scowled at the six figures sitting in their private box. The Praetors, far from the cheering masses. They were a unique bunch of men and women. Dressed in cloaks and masks, a uniform where no one looked like the others — yet were unmistakably of the same class.

If they wanted to end with a fight, Gaul could give them that. His body urged him to feed the flames. To Ignite. The excuses flowed through. One more time. You need to survive. You already broke your promise.

His mind raced until he stood in the circular centre of the maze. The final Hunter leaned against the far wall with his hands resting on his sheathed daggers. He wore leather armour with a hood obscuring his downturned face.

"They've never opened the walls before," he said, lifting his head up. He was a sharp-faced man with a permanent sneer. "And there you are with Markus' sword and Sister's trident. Brother must not be faring well either, considering you're still alive. It is a day of new occurrences. Two Untested have taken down three Hunters. Champions of the Boars. Impressive."

"We're about to make it four." Gaul pointed his sword at the Hunter.

"I am Serj Doyn." He bowed with regal flair. "Tyrant of the Sands, Lord of the Pits, The Poet Who Kills, and Champion of the Guild of Boars. And you are?"

"Gaul."

Serj motioned for Gaul to continue. "Just… Gaul? That's it?"

"That's all you need to know."

Serj blinked, then burst into roaring laughter. He slapped his knee and caught his breath. "Simple! Beautiful!" He looked at Raea. "And you?"

"Uh, Raea. And that's all you need to know as well."

Gaul glanced back at her. She shrugged.

"You stand against the Guild of Boars," Serj said, drawing his daggers. He spun one and slid his boots across the sand. "And I stand in judgement of you."

Gaul tightened his grip on his sword. "You ready for one more?" he asked Raea.

"Let's just get this over with." She raised the trident, but her shaking was unmissable.

The crowd screamed for blood. Their cries were joined by the roar of gears. The sand sank and disappeared. Gaul stumbled back until the ground was stable again. Raea dove forward, landing on one of the few platforms that remained.

Serj stood with his head held high and his knees steady atop his own platform. Gaul understood why he was sliding his feet in the sand. The centre of the maze was no longer one solid circular arena, instead it was littered by a dozen platforms. Fingers of flames reached from the burning pit below. Serj took a running leap and bounded from disc to disc.

Gaul waited until Serj jumped towards him, committing to the movement, then thrust his sword. With expert timing, Serj knocked the sword aside and hacked downward with his second dagger. Gaul dodged. The fire below warmed his skin. He placed both feet on the lip and pushed off to the next platform.

It was poor footing, and Serj could get in close with his daggers. He didn't even have to cut Gaul, he just had to force him to take a bad step into the flames.

Serj wasn't stopping for a breath either; he rushed again. Gaul jumped from platform to platform, keeping ahead of the Hunter. Raea kept her trident near her shoulder, owning her area.

Gaul took a hard turn and leapt to join her, kneeling behind her weapon. "Keep the spear up," he said. "He won't come at both of us."

"And how long can we stay like this for?" she asked, keeping the three prongs pointed at Serj.

"About as long as the crowd wants." He glanced up to the Praetors.

A woman dressed in hide armour motioned for a servant and whispered something in their ear. She had an eye patch and her chest piece was mounted with crossed boar tusks. The servant disappeared. Serj smiled and coiled like a snake ready to strike.

The fire around Gaul and Raea's platform flared. Tendrils of flame reached to cook them. Gaul batted at the sparks and jumped for safety, followed by Raea. Serj exploded, barely touching the next platform before landing on the one after.

The clock didn't matter anymore. Someone had to die. Gaul dug his foot into the ground, grinding his bare toes into the scorching sand. He threw himself to the same platform Serj aimed for and swung. Serj blocked with both daggers, leaving his ribs open for Gaul to drive his knee in.

Serj stumbled back, keeping his elbow against his side. "Is this it? You killed three Hunters, didn't you? Come on, Gaul! Show me who you are!"

Red filled Gaul's eyes. He huffed and kicked for Serj's chest. Serj, with a grin and a flair, danced aside. He didn't see Gaul flick his blade back as his foot came down.

A hand clutching a dagger took to the sky. Serj screamed. He dove for another platform, blood spraying from his stump wrist.

His screams turned to laughter. "I did ask for it!"

Gaul steadied his breath. Fire and haze coursed through him. He could stay at the line without going over. Still his gut ached to Ignite.

Serj pulled a small vial filled with silver liquid out of his jacket pocket. He drained it in one gulp. The colour left his face and his gaze grew distant.

"Raea…" Gaul stepped back.

"Kuratah," Raea said. "Mar's Nectar."

Serj charged, sending the last of the sand on his platform sailing. He landed before Gaul and unleashed swipes with surprising speed. It was all Gaul could do to keep Serj's blade from his skin. Occasionally, blood from Serj's stump splattered him or sizzled into the fire.

Serj dropped his elbow into Gaul's temple. Stars blossomed in his vision. He reared back to retaliate, only for Serj to put his foot into his chest. Air ran from his lungs. Gaul went with the motion, pushing off the platform and landing hard on the one behind.

Breath refused to return. Gaul's eyes flickered red, but it stuttered as he urged his lungs to work. Two boots landed next to his head. Serj looked down on him with eerie, disaffected eyes. The blood from his wrist darkened. Thickened. It oozed black from his veins.

Fine, Gaul thought. *I'll show you who I am.* He squeezed the sword in his hand. Heat filled his torso from his stomach to his chest, tightening into a flaming strand. Some dark part of himself screamed in ecstasy. *Again!* it said. *Again!*

Serj raised his dagger, and a trident struck him in his chest. He cocked his head. "What?" he muttered.

Raea followed the trident's arrival, taking it in both hands and pushing Serj down. She yanked it out and stabbed it back in. Serj kept moving as Raea turned his body into a pincushion. Gaul rolled onto his front, red shoots halfway filling his wide eyes. He had to admit; it was somewhat disappointing.

Stabbing and screaming, Raea didn't stop stabbing until Gaul put his hand on her shoulder. Serj wasn't moving anymore. Raea slowed her breath, clutching onto the trident like a blanket. With the back, she pushed Serj's body off the ledge.

The crowd applauded and cheered. The ground rose up as the walls sunk into the sand, until Gaul and Raea were left in a large arena. Serj's corpse smoldered from where it returned to the surface. Gaul looked across the audience — faces filled with fervour — until his gaze landed on the Praetor's box. He moved closer, keeping his sword at the ready.

The Praetor in a flat white cloak and a feathered hat stood up. He had long, fair hair and a trimmed beard, with a scar diagonally bisecting his face. He had pale skin that should be flushed from the heat of the day, but looked cool as a winter evening. He gestured toward Gaul and spoke.

"Very impressive," he said. "Mar has certainly blessed us with some interesting Untested this Festival."

Raea prodded Gaul in the back. "That's the Praetor of Doves. Dianathos."

The Praetor of Doves held himself with an irritating air of superiority and a smug smile. "Anyone who can successfully embarrass my friend, the Praetor of Boars, holds a special place in my heart."

He waved his hand at the woman with the eye patch. She didn't react to the taunt. All her focus was on the man and woman in the centre of the arena. A praetor wrapped in a brown feathered cloak and burn scars on his face leaned in to whisper with Dianathos.

"What are they talking about?" Gaul asked Raea.

"I don't know," she replied. "No one's ever done this before. But if the Praetor of Owls has an idea…"

"There has been a decision," Dianathos spoke again. "It is not only uncommon for Untested to survive the Boar's Banquet, it has never been done. And the fact two of them have survived, and killed four of the Boars' champions, is incredible." He leaned forward, placing one hand on the bannister. "But why have two decent Appraised, when we can have a sole survivor? Kill the other and you will be Appraised."

A scrape on the sand behind Gaul lit the fire in his stomach. He Ignited and the world turned red. He spun, snatching the trident being thrust at him. His sword sunk into a crimson aura. Beneath it, Raea's eyes stared back at him. They widened, welling up with tears. The fire extinguished as Raea's corpse hit the ground.

The world became a hurricane of sound. Gaul acted before he even thought, only wanting to survive the attack. He turned away. His heart quickened.

The Praetor of Boars was on her feet, but she wasn't looking at the arena. She glared at the Praetor of Owls. Another Praetor wearing a rat mask and engulfed in a ragged cloak waved his hand. Two dozen people flooded the arena from holes in the walls, dragging bodies away. The Guild of Rats.

"That was incredible!" Dianathos clapped the Praetor of Owls on the shoulder. "That was an excellent idea, Melifacto."

"This is my banquet!" the Praetor of Boars said. "You had no right to—"

The Praetor of Owls stopped her with a raise of his hand. "Can we discuss this in private, Bellona?"

Bellona kicked her chair back and stomped out of the box. The Praetor of Owls tented his fingers and shrugged at Dianathos.

One of the Rats — all dressed up in soiled rags — grabbed Raea by one leg and began dragging her body away. Her arms left bloody trails and her blank face was raked across the sand.

"Hey!" Gaul stepped toward the Rat. "Have some pity on that body!"

The Rat gave a toothless grin. "The dead get no pity." He disappeared with Raea into the wall.

"What is your name, Untested?" Dianathos asked.

Gaul pushed his fingernails into the palm of his hand. "Gaul."

"Gaul. Just Gaul?" The Praetor rubbed his beard, playing up his contemplation for the audience. "You need to begin collecting your titles. I shall dub you Gaul the Ruthless."

The crowd approved. The Praetor soaked in the cheers like rays of warm sunlight.

"Gaul the Ruthless is yet another display of the truth Mar gives us!" He spread his arms wide. "I have been across the Sorrow Sea and Nature's Grave. I've seen the state of Adathin."

Oh great, Gaul thought. *A speech.*

"Out there, our champion would have been thrown back into chains. But through his force of will, Gaul the Ruthless has shown Mar he deserves freedom." He leaned over the balcony. "You have been Appraised and found worthy. When you return to this sand, you will be something greater!"

Freedom wasn't how Gaul would describe what was happening. He was still caged, no matter how gilded the bars. But the crowd ate the speech up. They hollered until the stands were a wall of sound. Flowers fell at Gaul's feet, creating a multicoloured ring around the arena.

A gate opened and two guards stepped out, but Gaul never took his gaze off Dianathos. Red haze surrounded the Praetor, creating a crimson tunnel directed at his smug smile. Gaul squeezed his blood-coated sword.

"Gaul the Ruthless." One of the guards approached with a spear primed to strike. "You can't take that sword into the Hall."

Half a dozen more guards waited beyond the gate. Just because he was Appraised didn't mean they trusted him. Gaul took deep breaths, quelling his rage. He thought of home. It was so far away, but in his mind, he could make it real. The fire died down, the red haze crept away, and he threw the sword to the sand.

The guards led him away from the roaring crowd into another tunnel much like the entrance. A muffled bell rang, joined by the double doors before him swinging open at the hands of yet more guards. The golden road of Champion's March glittered in the daylight. To his right, the gated window to the commons was packed full of Untested. They cheered as they saw him.

Tora pushed through the crowd. His utterly astonished face changed into an uproarious laugh. Gaul couldn't help but smile too.

Down the road a golden door sparkled in the high sun. Though far from it, it might as well have been paradise. The Priest was close. He'd finally found him. It wasn't easy. It wasn't without loss. That look on Raea's face would never leave

Gaul's mind. But, in the end, it was just another face to add to his morose collection.

I once met a woman who survived the Pits.

The conversation was short, as she didn't want to speak of what she had been through. Not that I wanted to ask. She held herself like no one I had seen before, or would see again. She did what many people deemed impossible. She was a captured slave who went from Untested, to Appraised, to winning her freedom.

I expected her to despise the Pits, but to my surprise, she didn't. She hated Praetors who used the arena for sadistic pleasure. But she saw the Marjyal Pits as a testing hall for strength and glory, and the Hall of Appraised a home of true champions.

It's amazing the beliefs one clings to in order to survive.

—From the journal of Jovin Gutterwake

Chapter Six
Hall of the Appraised

The crowd poured from the stands, hoping to reach Champion's Walk before the new Appraised was ushered away. They buzzed with talk of his victory. How Mar blessed him in return for a revel of death. Gaul the Ruthless was on everyone's lips.

Bellona moved against the masses. They gave her a path to walk, keeping their gaze low and stopping their chatter when she passed. It wasn't with the reverence one would give royalty. They thought it better to stay out of her way. As the waves of people turned to trickles, Bellona stood alone over bloodstained sand. She undid the clasps on her ceremonial armour and dropped it at her side. The image of Gaul, angry in the corpses of his foes remained burned in her vision.

The stands creaked as Feyra crept down the steps, trying not to interrupt Bellona's thoughts.

"What is it, Feyra?" Bellona asked.

Feyra froze. "I just saw you here. Are you alright, my lady?"

An interesting question, Bellona thought. "Who was that man?"

"Gaul?" Feyra stepped to Bellona's side. "I've never seen him in the arena before. Probably a new Untested."

"And already Appraised."

"Do you think he should have been sent back to the commons?"

"No." She walked the lip of the arena. "He deserves his place after what he did to those four. Well, him and that woman. Damn, Melifacto. There was no honour in having them kill each other. He just wanted to play with them."

Bellona descended with Feyra into the tunnels and turned in.

"I'm sorry he killed your Champions," Feyra said.

Bellona scoffed. "Those were never my Champions. They were merely the best psychopaths this Pit can forge."

They exited the tunnel into the arena's centre. It had been a long time since Bellona had been on the sand. She could still hear the roar of the crowd around her. Feel the lives taken and the lives reborn. There was a beauty to it, tainted by the other Praetor's playing their dark games.

"Lady Bellona," Feyra said. "Something has come to mind. When we were recruiting for the Banquet, Gaul practically volunteered. I assumed he was ignorant, or suicidal."

"Did he now?" Bellona paced around dark stains and discarded weapons. She stopped at the sword Gaul had taken from Markus. "Wolves don't stay with sheep."

"Should I retrieve him?"

Could Marjyal forge someone like him? He had to be an outlander, someone from one of the settlements in the east. Perhaps even beyond Nature's Grave. Bellona never feared the lands the Doves preached against. But she never thought much of them either.

"My lady," Feyra said again. "Should I bring you Gaul?"

Bellona snapped from her thoughts. "No. If I act too quickly Melifacto will notice. I'm not sure he doesn't know that I had his pets poisoned in yesterday's fight. No sense giving him a target for his spite."

"Is this man that important to you?"

"I don't know. But did you notice his face? He took no pleasure from killing. He didn't do it because he wanted to, but because the world was thrown against him. He survived in the grinder of existence because he is strong enough." She ran her fingers along the scar peeking out from the eyepatch. "Strength is what kept him alive. See, Feyra? That's what this arena should be. That's why he's Appraised. The best among us. That's what the Pits bring out. That's why he deserves my respect."

Feyra bowed her head. "What about me?"

"The streets were your Pits." Bellona laid her hand on Feyra's cheek. "I found you surrounded by the corpse of the world, just as those in here find themselves. Besides, there's no point. You would kill anyone I could put you up against."

Feyra's face turned red. She stretched her fingers to the sand. The air fractured along the surface. Blood snaked through the grains, pulling itself from the ground to coil around Feyra's hand. "But I would," she said. "I can prove myself. You just have to ask."

"But I won't." Bellona put her hand on Feyra's. Faint red lines glowed along the skin below her sleeves. Bellona pushed her hand down and the blood settled. "If Melifacto saw your ability, he would have you cut apart on a slab by sundown. You're much more useful to me alive."

"Of course, my lady."

Bellona snatched the sword from her feet. "See if you can find anything more about our new Appraised. Subtly, if you can. I should be safe to visit him tomorrow." She paused. "Or maybe later tonight. I could be too paranoid."

Feyra nodded and rushed off, taking care not to run. Bellona took a few swings with the sword. A distant crowd roared.

✳ ✳

The doors of Champion's Walk swung open into a short arcade, packed with Marjyalians hollering to see the new Appraised. Gaul's head rang from all the noise. He backed away, only for a guard to shove him forward again. The crowd closed in, swarming him like flitting flies to touch his chest and arms. The guards forced a path, but mostly succeeded in bouncing Gaul around.

A small figure slipped under the guard's arms. Marta, disguised in the rags of a Marjyalian beggar, pulled down her scarf. Overwhelmed by the sight and sound, Gaul began to speak. "Wha—"

"I love you!" Marta shouted over his words. She slipped something into her mouth then planted a firm kiss on Gaul's lips. With a jab to the gut, she passed the object to him.

A guard grabbed her by the scruff and tossed her back. The masses swallowed her into their waves. Gaul kept his mouth shut as he was guided into the Hall.

He was shoved into the great room that made up the Hall of the Appraised's lounge. "Enjoy the banquet," a guard said, sneering. "Gaul the Ruthless."

It was a large, open space that could be considered elegant when compared to the Untested's home. The centre was a ring with a four-tiered fountain and a number of decorative columns. Alcoves lined the perimeter, some closed with curtains while others showed comfortable lounges with couches and pillows.

The Appraised paid no attention to Gaul's entrance. They gorged themselves on fruits and meat while men and women in the barest amount of clothing walked about. The guard who had taunted him joined others sitting by the exit door.

A woman walked by with a tray. On it rattled vials filled with silver liquid. More of that concoction Serj had consumed. Kuratah, Raea had called it. It must have some recreational purposes as well. A shaking Appraised snatched one vial as it passed by. He took it down in a single gulp and stopped shaking. The man leaned back revealing dark lines on his neck. His blood was turning black as well.

Blood splatters on the floor created a morbid welcome for Gaul. Creeping to the side of the entrance, Gaul leaned against the wall as if to catch his breath. He ran his hand over his face, drawing the object Marta passed to him out of his mouth. A folded piece of paper. Wiping the saliva off, he opened into his palm:

'Fifteen minutes. Western wall.'

It wasn't much time. Gaul's orientation was thrown off, but he figured the western wall was the one with the massive tapestry of soldiers celebrating a victory. With no place to stash the note, Gaul's option was to eat it. He forced it down then inspected the hall.

The blood around him made a trail past the guard station to a door. A carved sign next to it read *Infirmary*. Did a doctor end up helping the Priest after all? He could hope.

Gaul started toward it until he noticed a patch of fresher blood, and a lot of it. It branched away from the main path toward an alcove with the curtain drawn. A passing guard took special care not to walk too close. Gaul approached and peeked inside.

The Priest had not been cared for, that much was clear. He wallowed on a couch more blood than fabric. His clothes were the same bloody armour he had on the day before, and his skin had turned ashen. His chest rose and fell with unsteady rhythm, fingers twitching as his lungs stuttered. Gaul shut the curtains and the Priest stirred.

"You should see a doctor," was all Gaul could think to say. He'd thought long about how he would approach the Priest when he saw him. The broken man was different than the one he demonized in his mind for all those weeks.

The Priest eased his eyes open. "They refuse to see me."

"I hear they do that."

"I am prepared to be a martyr. It's not me I weep for, it's..." His gaze focused and he glanced around the alcove. "Who are you?"

"I'm Gaul. I've been following you for a long time."

"Why would you do that?"

"You took something of mine back in Ulkradia."

The Priest eased himself to sit. "Ulkradia? I apologize, I didn't know. What did we take?"

Gaul pried his gaze away from the thick bloodstain the Priest left on the couch. "A necklace. One with gold and steel links."

"You don't say?" He chuckled, then groaned and clutched his ribs. "I do know the one. You've come far and been through a lot for a simple piece of jewelry."

Heavy footsteps stomped past on the other side of the curtain. Someone shouted for music and a lute filled the air. "It's not a simple piece of jewelry," Gaul said. "I want it back."

The Priest's head bobbed, his gaze growing distant.

"Hey!" Gaul slapped him on the arm. "No dying yet."

With all the speed of a slug, the Priest refocused on Gaul. He was young, younger than Gaul and younger than he had imagined one attempting the mysterious pilgrimage would be. Gaul had seen his face once in passing outside the church in his hometown. The Priest seemed older back then. There was a willpower inside him; it was the only thing keeping him conscious. But it faded with every drop of blood on the floor.

"What's your name?" the Priest asked.

"I already told you."

"Of course. Gaul of Ulkradia. I'm Athas Sorronus of Imperium." He rested his head, sighing. "That necklace must belong to someone important."

"It..." There wasn't any harm in telling a dying man about himself. And it had been many months since he had a person to truly interact with. "It was my wife's, Anori. It's the only thing I have of her. My farm was in debt so I had to give it to the church as a deposit until I got the funds. Two days at the most, but you people came the day after. It was gone when I got back."

Athas laughed, then groaned with pain.

Heat flushed across Gaul's face. "Something funny?"

"Just considering the thin line between coincidence and providence. Your wife must have been very important to you. Coming all the way here for her necklace."

"It reminds me of who I need to be. I need it back."

"I'm sorry, Gaul. They took it when they found me. They took everything. These horrible people. Before they brought us here they forced Matthis, one of my guards, to drink this silver liquid." Athas began to shake, rubbing his wrist. "Something came over him. Then they made some of my other guards swallow the vials whole and start running. Matthis, still in his holy armour, took off after them like a beast. I wonder if any of them survived."

That had to of been the weird soldier Gaul fought. Matthis had been given kuratah, the same elixir Serj took in the arena. What it did to him was disturbing, blackening his blood and thickening his muscles. Gaul had to remind himself there was no way he survived having his helmet caved in.

"Athas," Gaul said. "Do you know where they would've taken the necklace?"

"How would I know that? Ask the guards. They seem to give more leeway to the people in here."

Leaning back, Gaul peeked through the curtain. A guard slapped one of the napping ones on the back of the head. She thumbed toward the exit and took the napping guard's place as he left.

"That may work," Gaul said, turning back to Athas. "Are you going to still be alive when I get back?"

"I'll try my b—"

The tapestry wall blew into the room. A piece of stone took out the fountain, spraying water across the floor. Flaming pieces of cloth fluttered down in a rain of fire. Consorts screamed and Appraised fled from the new entrance. Gaul's fifteen minutes were up.

"Guards! Breach!" the new guard yelled. A knife flew from the smoke and stuck into her chest.

Two more blades shot out of the twisting fog, one taking out another guard while the second cut a man across his arm.

"Gaul!" Marta called from the smoke. "Move now!"

She had terrible timing. He still had no idea where the necklace was. Athas tried to stand, but collapsed back onto the couch.

"What's happening?" he asked.

Gaul took Athas by the arm, supporting him with his shoulder. "An exit just opened up."

He helped Athas hobble across the hall and toward the hole. The many curtains and pillows had gone up in flames. A grey haze filtered throughout the room, strengthening the confusion.

Some of the Appraised cowered in corners, others took advantage of the jailbreak and started fighting back against the guards with stolen weapons and food trays. One man grabbed the lute and smashed it over one of the guard's head.

Marta crouched behind the broken wall. Gaul pulled Athas next to her.

"That was *not* fifteen minutes," Gaul said.

"A Boar came by while I was setting up," Marta said. "I had to act fast. Is that the Priest? He's looked better."

"Marta, meet Athas." Gaul shoved the Priest into her arms. "Get reacquainted."

"Where are you going?"

"I'm not done in there yet." Gaul pulled the scarf off Marta's neck and wrapped it around his nose and mouth.

"Gaul!"

Every piece of flammable material was engulfed in an inferno. The scarf helped him breathe, but the smoke stung his eyes. People were barely more than rushing shadows. There had to be a guard somewhere. A guard with answers.

"Stay back!" A voice cut through the chaos.

A guard with wild eyes plunged his sword through an Appraised's abdomen. Gaul picked up a chuck of stone from the broken fountain and stomped closer. It was far too loud to hear him move. The guard took his sword with both hands, but it wouldn't budge from the Appraised's gut. Gaul brought the stone down on his head. Blood trickled from his skull. He crumpled.

"You're…" the guard groaned.

Gaul leapt on him, pinning his throat to the ground. "Where do you take the jewelry stolen from the fighters?" he shouted, holding the stone above his head. "If someone had a necklace taken from them when they were captured, where would it be? Tell me or I swear I'm scattering your brains across this pretty floor!"

"Storehouse!" the guard croaked out.

Gaul smashed the stone next to his head. "Where is it?"

"West a… a-and then north! Big building in an alley. Has a boar's head drawn on it."

Gaul slammed the stone on the floor again, leaving it there this time. He released the guard's throat and hurried back out to where Marta and Athas waited.

Marta gave him a glare. "Done wasting time?"

"Not yet." Gaul tossed her the scarf. "Northwest to the storehouse."

"A storehouse?" Marta wrapped the scarf around her neck. "We don't have time for this. We need to leave."

"This is the entire reason I came here, do you understand? It doesn't matter what you're going to say, I'm am not leaving Marjyal without that necklace."

"A necklace!?" Marta buried her face in her hands. "This is for a necklace? I am—"

"I am not talking about this anymore. I'll bring you to the Cradle, but you haven't rescued me yet."

Marta huffed. "We can swing north, I guess. I would have preferred to follow the wall." She nodded toward Athas, fighting to stay conscious. "What about him? He looks really bad. Is he coming with us?"

Gaul had gotten what he needed out of Athas. After weeks of lonely wandering on land and sea, he had reached this point. It wasn't what he imagined. And he couldn't bring himself to hate Athas. What a pain. "Yeah. He is," Gaul said, taking Athas by the shoulder.

Marta gritted her teeth but nodded. She helped Gaul lift Athas up. There was enough sense in the young priest's mind to stay on his feet. With some help, that is. Appraised stormed past them. One smashed out a window and climbed into the first building they saw. Someone in the smoky distance barked orders.

"Do you know where this storehouse is?" Marta asked, leading them down slanted streets. "Anything more specific than north-west?"

"A big building in an alley," Gaul said. "Has a boar's head painted on it."

"You know, I actually think I know the one. Saw it a few days ago. The Guild of Boars were guarding it. Can't imagine they're not now."

Great. Those guys again, Gaul thought. "We'll figure it out."

The streets flattened out. Marjyalians stood at their windows with blades, glaring at anyone who came too close. Looking back, columns of smoke rose from the Pits.

"How many explosions did you set off?" Gaul asked.

"A few." Marta shrugged with a smile. "One for confusion. One for distraction. And the Hall of the Appraised has thick walls. With enough chaos I hoped we could sneak out. I don't like how long we are messing around though. Eventually the Guilds are going to regain control."

A shout came from ahead. Boars shoved Marjyalians against walls. They threw people to the ground and kicked until they didn't move. Marta took Gaul by the arm and pulled him and Athas into the ruins of a partially collapsed building. Shadows rushed by the hiding spot. Not all of them were Boar's. Some were rough-looking men and women wearing tunics bearing a flaming horn.

"I see a flaw in your plan," Gaul whispered.

"That storehouse of yours may not be such a bad idea," Marta said. "Could have some weapons for the escape. And for the journey. You can't be wandering around Adathin like that."

The journey to the Cradle of the World. Gaul had forgotten about the deal he made. Marta had kept up her side.

"Let's go," Gaul said. He pulled Athas out from the hole, taking care not to exacerbate his wounds. His skin had turned grey and each breath rattled from his lungs.

"Your friend doesn't look good," Marta said.

"Maybe there's something in the storehouse for him," Gaul said. "Medicine or… I don't know."

"Yeah." Marta chewed on her thumbnail. "Maybe we'll be lucky."

She didn't have to say it. Neither of them had to say it — they were both thinking it. The doctors wouldn't help Athas. They weren't going to find some miraculous potion in the storehouse that could put all the blood back in his body. Athas was on stolen time.

After a few more twists and turns, Marta led them to the mouth of a thin alleyway. They crouched behind a few discarded crates and peered at the building dominating the courtyard at the far end. The storehouse was one storey tall, but every inch of it was covered in vicious wooden spikes. Beneath the porcupine defences was a black boar's head painting. The only entrance visible was defended by two Boars with longswords resting on their shoulders.

"I'm all out of knives," Marta said. "I don't see how we're getting in there. Maybe if there was only one of them."

"I could take them by surprise," Gaul said.

"That alley's at least twenty metres long and you have no cover. They're going to see you coming."

"What if we lure one out?"

Marta poked him in the chest. "How is letting them know we're here going to get us in?"

"Do you have a better idea?" Gaul asked.

"Doesn't mean it's a good one!"

"Wait." Athas forced himself out of Gaul's grasp, holding himself up on shaking hand and knees. Bloody spit trailed from his lips in long strings. "I can distract them. Maybe at least get one to leave so you outnumber the last one."

"As noble as that is," Gaul said. "You can't even stand, much less distract. You start running and you're going to drop after two steps."

"No. I won't," Athas said, reaching into his armour. He pulled out a small vial filled with silver liquid. "Some pitying soul gave this to me. He said I would be alive for a moment before the Gate Beyond took me."

"Is that kuratah?" Marta asked. "It'll help you, but there's no way you'll survive the crash in the state you're in."

"I never planned to survive." He pulled the stopper out. "I was simply waiting for the Divines to show me the way."

"Hold on." Gaul held Athas' arm down.

"It's okay," Athas said. He laid his hand on Gaul's shoulder, caked red with blood. "I left Imperium knowing I may be a martyr. I only have one thing to ask of you. When you find that necklace of yours, there will be a small pendant on it. It appears to be a simple sigil for my order, but it's a vessel for our future. Please, for the sake of all you must bring it to the Cradle of the World."

Marta perked at the mention.

"There is a cataclysm brewing here." Athas squeezed Gaul's shoulder. He coughed red. "Find the Cradle and fill the Chalice. You must finish my pilgrimage." He brought the vial up to his lips. "Coincidence or providence. I haven't decided yet."

He gulped down the silver liquid. A shiver went over his skin. He straightened up more than his injured body should have allowed. Unlike Serj, Athas did not grit his teeth or shake with rage. Instead, the priest held himself proud, with a serene intensity.

Athas grabbed one of the smaller crates. He stalked down the alley. One of the guards shouted and Athas hurled the crate at their feet.

"Come to me, heretics!" he shouted. "I do not fear your wicked god!"

One of the guards hefted his sword into a ready position and approached Athas. Without faltering, Athas took another crate and pitched it into the guard's chest.

The guard swiped at the flying box. It struck his hands and his sword clattered to the ground. Athas rolled forward. Blood stained where his back landed. He grabbed the fallen blade. The guard tried to retreat, but Athas' kuratah fuelled speed was faster. The guard took the blade under his breastplate. The sword slid up and stuck out from his neck.

The second guard pounded on the door. It opened, and two more soldiers charged out. He pointed at Athas, covered in both his own and the dead guard's blood.

"Get him!" the guard shouted.

Athas spun about and dashed off with the Boars at his heel. He dropped blood from oozing wounds all over his body. It created a red trail for the three Boars to follow. He bolted by Gaul and Marta's hiding spot. They tucked themselves against the crates. After chasing the priest for so long, all Gaul could do was watch him run away. It wasn't the confrontation he had built up in his mind.

"He might survive," Marta said.

"Yeah." Gaul hoped Athas found some peace in his god's afterlife.

"We should move." Marta squeezed Gaul's shoulder.

They hurried down the alley, keeping their eyes scanning for any Boars who stayed back. Gaul creaked the storehouse door open. Sparse lanterns lit a mess of overflowing shelves. Armour and weaponry stolen from the unfortunate were cast aside with no care for their worth. A table sat by the door. The Boars had been in the middle of a card game.

"It's clear," Gaul said, stepping inside.

"You better be quick," Marta said, sliding the latch shut on the door. "That priest won't keep them running for long and I don't believe we have another way out."

"I'll be fast."

One of the few bits of organization the storehouse had was a sign over a pile saying *Unsorted*. Gaul pushed his hands into the junk but found nothing that glittered. What were the chances the Boar's kept the necklace? It wasn't pure gold after all.

A terrifying scraping filled the storehouse. Gaul spun about, reaching for an axe that sat atop the unsorted. Marta had taken one of the handles for a crate and dragged it across the floor. Once it was in place blocking the entrance, she let out a huff and flopped onto it.

She noticed Gaul's scowl. "I don't want them barging in here," she said. "We'll move it when we go."

"What's in that chest?" Gaul asked, tossing the axe back into the pile.

"I don't know." Marta rolled off and slid the top aside. "It's a bunch of jars full of something."

She pulled out a small glass jar containing an amber liquid. The cap was thicker than usual and there was a tab with a screw through it on the neck. Something about it was familiar. Not in form, but in function. Gaul froze. His eyes widened.

"You should put that down," Gaul said, stepping back. "I think that's a fluxcracker."

"A what?" Marta turned the jar over.

"An explosive! There's a crystal in the cap."

Marta inhaled. "Oh…" She laid the jar back in the crate and replaced the lid. "A blastjar. I've never actually seen one — before it exploded. I mean."

"Maybe we could not use lithoflux explosives to block the door?"

"There are a bunch of crates and chests," Marta said, pointing. "I just picked the first one."

"Are they all bombs?"

Marta opened her mouth, then without saying anything went to check. "It doesn't look like it," she called back. "Just a bunch of jewelry. Hey, weren't you looking for a necklace?"

Gaul pushed past her. He grabbed the chest and tilted it over, sending valuables scattering across the floor. Some were pilfered from homes. Candlesticks, table settings, statuettes; things that seemed strange to covet or horde. Maybe to show power. Maybe because they could. The rest of the valuables were jewelry. But still no necklace with gold and steel links.

"This necklace of yours must be special," Marta said, leaning over his shoulder. She moved like a cat. "Who does it belong to?"

Gaul kicked over the next chest and kept digging. It had to be here. The Boar's horded things much more expensive than an ugly necklace.

"Who *did* it belong to?" Marta asked.

Gaul slammed a bracelet into the pile, sending gold and silver flying. Marta froze. "What are you doing?" he asked.

"If we're going to travel together, we should know about each other. I, for example, used to be married. Is this necklace for someone similar?" She gestured to the air but got nothing in return. "I'm just trying to learn more about you."

"Don't. If you want to do something, help me look." He threw the top off another chest.

"Fine." She crouched next to the chest. "It should have that eagle vessel thing, right?"

"It's gold and steel."

"That's a strange look. Is it an Ulkradian thing?"

"I wanted it to be all gold." He pulled a necklace out of the pile, holding it up to the light. It was complete. It was the thing one would give someone they loved. "It was going to be all gold."

"You must have loved them very much."

Gaul tossed the necklace aside. Marta was much more talkative when sober. "What is this escape plan?" he asked. "Isn't there still a wall around the city?"

"Ocean to the west, wall to the north and east, and cliffs to the south," Marta said, slipping a silver ring onto her finger. "But we aren't going to the wall. Our best shot is to head into the tunnel."

"The tunnel?

"Yeah! There's an old tunnel near the beach, right in the cliffside. Apparently ancient machines dug a path straight from here to Adathin Castle."

"And no one will stop us?"

"No one goes in there." Marta waved him off. "They say it's full of monsters."

"Monsters? You want us to go into a tunnel full of monsters?"

"I don't think there's actually monsters down there. The Praetor's can't forbid people from doing things, so they lie all the time. No one's allowed to leave the city, and there's guards and gates, but they just trick people into believing it's worse out there. Anyone who is caught leaving is branded a heretic. They're traitors who want to sneak Marjyal's secrets to the wider world and destroy the city."

Raea had been that way, Gaul reminded himself. Even as she was cast to the wolves, she believed a god and her Praetor's cared for her. Marjyal couldn't be bad, because it was worse outside the walls. Anyone who disagreed was a traitor. A simple logic, but twisted all the same.

"That's not freedom," Gaul said.

"But they're told it is. And why would the Guilds lie to them? They love the Guilds. And hate the Guilds sometimes. But they love Mar."

Gaul grabbed a handful of jewelry and was about to throw it away when something caught his eye. Gold and steel. His breath caught in his throat. Link by link, he pulled a necklace free.

"Is that it?" Marta asked.

Though the lantern light was dim, the necklace sparkled in Gaul's eyes. He could see it hanging around Anori's neck. She smiled and laughed every time he apologized it couldn't be all gold. He was going to fix it, link by link. Not anymore. He took it in one hand and dangled the unfamiliar pendant that intruded on his memories.

"That must be the vessel," Marta said. "Vessel for what? Looks empty to me."

It was a glass vial, no bigger than a knuckle. A golden eagle folded its wings over the glass with the necklace knotted around it. Gaul peered into the vial, looking for any minuscule object Athas and his Lightwalkers died for. For a moment, the light reflected strangely through the curved glass. Then it was gone.

What a strange thing, Gaul thought, slipping the necklace through its own loops.

"You're going to throw it away?" Marta asked.

"You don't really believe what Athas was saying about some cataclysm?" Gaul asked. "Priests have been preaching about the end of the world since the start of it."

Marta rolled her eyes. "We're going to the Cradle anyway. It seems rather spiteful to toss it."

Athas dragged Gaul all across the Free Lands, but he didn't know he took Anori's necklace. In some way, he cared for it, using it to hold his strange pendent.

Gaul rubbed his fingers along the links. Athas didn't give it away like it was nothing.

"He did sacrifice himself so we could get here," Marta said.

Gaul let out a growling sigh. He dropped the pendant, letting the chain pull tight around it once again. He flipped the necklace over his head. The vessel bounced against his chest.

The door rattled and banged. It shoved against its latch and the heavy chest but could not move it. "We're out of time," Marta said. "You better get some weapons."

Gaul hurried to the weapons rack, snatching a tunic, pants, and a heavy long coat as he swept by shelves. A man shouted something indecipherable from outside. The pounding resumed harder than before. The building shook under the repeated blows. The Boars were going to take the entire wall down — and probably set off the blastjars, as Marta called them, while they were at it.

That wasn't a bad idea, actually.

"Marta," Gaul said, donning his new clothes. "Find us some string or thread. Something we can attach to the tags in those blastjars."

Marta paused halfway through putting a throwing knife in her coat. "Huh? Why?"

"Because unless you can find another way out, that door's our only exit."

Marta glanced at the rattling door, then around the storehouse. She pocketed a few more knives and disappeared between the shelves. To find some string or a backdoor, Gaul didn't know. All he knew was they were in a bad position. But he got the necklace. Where else did he have to go?

The Boar's hadn't taken his shield or sword. Or one of them had stolen them. Or they were lost in the chaotic waves of the storehouse horde. It all meant the same thing. Gaul took a double sheath and two heavy chopping swords. The shield never fit him anyway.

"I found some string," Marta said, stepping around the corner tossing a spool up and down. She smiled at the sight of Gaul. "Look who got all dressed up for the occasion."

"Give me one end of the string," Gaul said, snapping his coat on. It hung below the tips of his scabbards and its heavy leather was scuffed and stitched. "You take the other end and find us someplace safe. This is going to be… large."

Marta swallowed and nodded. She took the spool and left Gaul with the slack. If there were any reservations to the plan, Marta wasn't bringing them up. Part of Gaul wished she would have. If blastjars were anything close to fluxcrackers, they were in for a brilliant display.

Gaul knelt next to the crate and removed the lid, revealing eight jars with liquid that trembled in time with the door. Below was another row, and another eight blastjars. "Gods," Gaul muttered. They appeared rougher made than the ones the Imperials used. Could be they were weaker. Still, sixteen made the hair on Gaul's arms stand at attention.

"We know you're in there!" a man shouted through the door. "Open up before you get really hurt."

Gaul kept his mind focused on the work. As long as the Boars stayed outside, they could shout all they wanted. He looped the string through the tab on the side of the jar's lid. As long as the screw was in place, it couldn't move. But once it was pulled, the catalyst fluxcrystal would drop in and begin an unstoppable explosive process made to tear people apart with fury and shrapnel.

"Damn it!" the man outside shouted. "Where is that battering ram?"

"It's on its way," another Boar said. "But the south is in a riot. It's hard to get anywhere."

One jail break and the whole city is in chaos, Gaul thought, finishing his knot.

"Looks deadly," Marta said, appearing over his shoulder.

"I sure hope it is." Gaul let out a steady breath and began unscrewing the safety. A few twists and the blastjar was ready to kill.

"Come on. I think I found a good place for us." Marta led Gaul along the path the string left. Far at the back of the storehouse were two shelves stacked with shields and metal armour. A barricade, if one had imagination. "Is this good?"

Gaul put two fingers on a hanging breastplate and pushed. It flexed. He put his full weight against it, but it held. It would have to.

"Wait." Marta glanced over her shoulder. "Did they stop?"

There was no more banging at the door. There was no more shouting. Gaul and Marta looked at each other in confusion at the sudden stillness.

Then a crunch that sent a spike through Gaul's heart. The door had bent against its lock. The crate of blastjars lurched forward, pushed by the door trying to split from the frame.

"Do it now!" Gaul shouted, flipping up the hood of his tunic and taking cover.

Marta took the string in one hand and pulled. The tag went skittering across the floor. Marta dove in next to Gaul.

Nothing happened until the door crumpled again. One more good strike and it was going down.

"Did we do something wrong?" Marta asked.

Gaul shrugged. "They usually have a dela—"

The room filled with sound and fire. Booming echoes became screams and crackling flames. The barricade tipped backwards. Gaul slammed his shoulder against it, for fear they would be crushed. Marta joined at his side. They slid their feet on wood until the barricade settled and they were able to take a breath.

"Did we get them?" Marta asked.

Gaul crept out from behind cover, pulling down his hood and coughing into his hand. Weapons, armour, and jewelry scattered to all corners. Shelves, once bearing the weight of armaments, were reduced to splintered. Fires billowed black smoke that swallowed light like snakes. Gaul put a hand over his mouth and stepped into the haze.

He kicked aside a wooden shield, broken in half and charred. Marta crept in and out of sight. Her scarf protected her mouth from the smoke, but she squinted against the stinging smog. She pulled a knife embedded in a support pillar free and pocketed it.

The smoke thinned as they approached the front of the storehouse. Or at least what used to be the front of the storehouse. It spread down the alley with the sundered remains of the Boars.

"I think we're clear," Gaul said, resting his hands on his pommels.

Marta flipped her hood down, sprinkling dust as she did. "Serves them right."

"Some decorum for the fallen wouldn't be amiss."

"You don't know them like I do." She pulled down her scarf. "Can we please leave now?"

"Yeah." Gaul stepped over the rubble into the alley. They weren't free yet.

I came to Adathin Castle to discover the location of the Cradle of the World. During my research, everything points to the King being exactly what the legends portrayed him as: a misinformed madman with a destructive obsession. The Cradle was in his head.

But there are gaps in the history. I'm finding mentions of events that are ignored in the official calendar. The court historian has omitted selected days from their notes. I had assumed incompetence, but I'm starting to wonder if someone wasn't trying to hide something. The truth always reveals itself in time. And I am incredibly patient.

—From the Journal of Jovin Gutterwake

Chapter Seven
A City Apart

Fire all but consumed the Hall of the Appraised's lounge before the Guilds of Ants and Rats could get their hoses in. An Ant in flame-resistant gear sprayed water over the last vestiges of flame as another pumped at their watercart, sweat dripping off his nose. A tapestry, once a pattern of reds and blacks, crumbled into ash with the slightest breeze through the gaping hole in the wall. It took to the air and swirled about the ruins before coming to a rest on Bellona's cool, umber cheek.

She wiped away the ash and took in the room with a scowl from her one good eye. All the comforts she gave to the Appraised, ruined. Those who accepted the comforts, gone. She had been too soft on them. Next time, chains.

"Praetor!" one of the guards exclaimed. He tried to salute, only to crumple against the wall. His side oozed blood.

"Rest yourself," Bellona said. "Get a doctor to look at your wounds."

"How kind you are to your own, Praetor of Boars," a voice said.

Dianathos, Praetor of Doves, sauntered in from the infirmary. A smug grin plastered across his face, and his robes glistened despite the ash in the air. Next to him was a massive man bathed in grey robes. Dianathos' manservant, Harken, hid any indication of life behind a cloth mask. The fire hadn't touched the infirmary, but Dianathos cared little for flames. He knew preaching to the wounded made him appear sympathetic. Bellona could see the tarnish hiding in his silver and gold.

"Go," Bellona said to the guard, directing him toward the infirmary. She turned to Dianathos. "What are you doing in my Hall? Don't you have a speech to give somewhere?"

"It's not the time for speeches," Dianathos said. "Not yet. Our enemies are still on the move."

Melifacto crept in behind Dianathos. He tapped his fingers along the beak of his owl mask, taking care to be as unobtrusive as possible. Bellona cleared her throat and he stopped.

"And you're visiting the injured?" Bellona asked Dianathos, though her gaze was locked squarely on the Praetor of Owls.

"I'm keeping up morale. And—" He raised his hand. It turned wavy and gaseous. "I was probing for witnesses."

Bellona's chest tightened at the sight of the Ghost Hand. The idea of it reaching into her mind and stealing her thoughts made her blood run cold. Dianathos had agreed to never use it on another Praetor, but as all points in the Accords, it was self-enforced.

"I thought you said no one would dare to assault the Pits?" Melifacto removed his mask and made like he was cleaning it. The smile on his lips might as well of been a kilometer wide.

Dianathos reformed his hand. "It was outsiders. Vile creatures jealous of our way of life. My witness saw a woman with a scar on her face lead the attack. She was working with Gaul the Ruthless and that scrawny fellow from the match yesterday. I gave descriptions to my artists and they're drawing up wanted post." He turned to Harkin. "This is why I tell them we should not be Appraising anyone from outside the city."

Harkin grunted.

"What do you know? I bet the Guild of Ashes was involved. Those heretics have plans to destroy all of us, mark my words. We should have dealt with them when we exiled their leader."

"The Ashes have their uses," Bellona said. She couldn't get her mind off Melifacto. Why would he be here? Usually he slinked off to his manor when any bloodshed occurred.

"What?" Dianathos laughed. "As threats? People respond to hope."

"They respond better to violence." Bellona motioned to the room. The fire crew just finished up. "The ones responsible for breaking my Hall won't be met with hope. They'll be met with a rope, to hang from the trees outside the doors."

"Now, you know I love a hanging." Dianathos threw his robe back and pulled a small doll off his belt. It was a cloth person with a simplistic face stitched with black thread. He held it forth and nodded the head like it was talking. "But is our big Boar mad that someone broke her toys? Or is she mad that someone proved the Boars aren't the strongest folks around?"

"Nothing's been proved!" Bellona shouted at the doll.

Dianathos pulled it away. "It's just a doll, my dear. But it sure is funny how those who find their worth in strength are so easily broken."

Bellona could kill him. She could draw her sword and take off his smug head before Harken could stop her. But that wouldn't be it. The Accords would demand her blood as well, and she couldn't fight against five Guilds. Dianathos put the doll away, hanging it from the tiny noose on his waist.

From the hole in the wall, Feyra came charging in. She huffed and puffed, shoving an Ant out of her way. She hurried toward Bellona, but slowed when she spotted the other Praetors standing by.

"What is it, Feyra?" Bellona asked. Anything to distract her from Dianathos.

"We spotted Gaul and his companions," Feyra said. "The injured man attacked some of our guards at the Pits' storehouse. They chased him down the road where they killed him. I sent some guards back to the storehouse, figuring it might have been a distraction. By the time I got there, it had blown up."

"What had?"

"The storehouse."

Dianathos let out a low whistle. Bellona snapped her gaze to him.

"Everyone's so interested in this Gaul character," Melifacto said, stepping away from his hiding spot against the wall. "Is he dead?"

"We have reports of him and the woman heading westward," Feyra said, bowing her head to Melifacto.

"Why would they go west?" Dianathos paced, running his hand over his beard. "Do they plan on hiding in the city? Stealing a boat from the docks?"

"The tunnel," Bellona said. It was the only option that made sense. These people had a plan, as reckless as it was. "They're going for the tunnel to the castle."

"That's suicide," Dianathos said.

Deliberate movement caught Bellona's eye. Pelady slunk through the front door. The six-foot monster with razer teeth wasn't an easy sight to miss. She crept through the wreckage to Melifacto's side.

"Harken." Dianathos motioned for his servant to lean in. "Spread the word. Two hundred coin to the person who brings us Gaul's head. It would be better for the people to know their terrorizer was dead, rather than letting him disappear in the tunnel."

Pelady whispered something in Melifacto's ear. His eyes widened. "Terribly sorry," he said. "But something has come up. Do let me know when this all resolves itself."

He donned his owl mask again. With Pelady leading the way, he hurried out faster than Bellona had ever seen him move. Feyra scowled at the pair as they disappeared. It seemed Bellona's right hand distrusted the Owl as much as she did. Good girl.

"I too must be on my way," Dianathos said. "The people will need reassurance when this passes. I'll prepare something to say."

"Doing all you can, I see," Bellona said, mockingly.

Dianathos cast her a sly smile, sauntering out of the room with Harken in tow. Bellona waited until they were long out of earshot before letting out an extended groan.

"Are you alright, m'lady?" Feyra asked, stepping toward her.

"I'll live." Bellona walked over the crumbling remains of the Hall of the Appraised. Walls could be replaced. Even Appraised could be replaced. "Did you learn anything more about Gaul?"

"Nothing much," Feyra said. They stepped into the sunbaked city. "He was brought in several days ago. He was gravely injured but a doctor pulled him through. He only woke up yesterday."

They descended stone steps to the city streets. Boars and guards wrangled rioters. People were beaten until they couldn't fight back, then left for someone else to find them. "Let the Guilds fall!" someone shouted, only to be silenced by a large Boar with a club.

"We're taking back control," Feyra said. "Slowly, but it's happening."

"And you haven't had to…" She gestured around Feyra's arm. "Reveal anything?"

"No." Feyra furrowed her brow. "How could you even ask that. I've never broken my word to you. I would never!"

"You've been moody lately. I simply wanted to be sure you haven't slipped. Melifacto's acting strange. He's up to something, I know it. And the more active he is, the more he will leave himself unguarded." Bellona leaned in to Feyra. "We could have a chance to remove him from his position."

"Just say the word, my Lady."

"Not now, Feyra. We have to be smart, which includes no one knowing about your blood powers, so they can be used at the right time. You're the perfect tool for this job, so, yes, I am a little more cautious with you today and will continue to be so. The other Praetor's won't take kindly to the death of one of their own. They certainly didn't last time." She chuckled under her breath. "Despite how well it worked out for me."

"Of course. I understand," Feyra said. Though, Bellona never needed her to understand. She needed her to listen. "Does this mean Gaul's no longer a concern?"

"Why would you say that?" Bellona asked. She leaned against a wall, observing a man push one of her Boars back.

The Boar replied with a skull-crushing strike from his club. The brave man crumpled, yelping like a kicked dog. The Boar didn't stop swinging until the man bubbled foamy blood from his mouth.

"The world still needs strength," she continued. The Boar laughed at how the man twitched on the cobblestone. Bellona curled her lip in disgust. The street had emptied to the point it was her, Feyra, and the cackling Boar. "You have my permission to quiet him."

Feyra twitched her finger. A shard of blood — no thicker than a blade of grass — shot from the pool forming around the man's head and through the Boar's neck. His laugh turned to a choking panic. He clutched his throat, but couldn't stem the tide bringing him to his knees, and collapsed next to his victim.

"We deserve better killers," Bellona said, turning into an alley. "So yes, we are still concerned with Gaul. If only to meet a warrior such as that."

"Then we'll stop him," Feyra said.

"I sincerely hope we don't." Bellona grinned, crazy and wild. "I would be disappointed in him if we did."

The city Gaul saw from the Pits wasn't any less chaotic up close. Marta led him through slanted building skeletons and garbage-filled streets. Men and women rushed in and out of buildings.

A large fellow smashed another man's head against the cobblestone. He stepped toward Gaul, growling. Gaul glared at the thug from under his hood. He pulled his coat aside, letting his swords show. The thug wrinkled his nose and backed away. There was always easier prey. Gaul watched him go, then threw his head back.

"Black Hypogea!" he cursed. "The city went to chaos fast."

"I admit I didn't expect quite so much rioting." Marta grabbed a loose piece of a fence and moved it aside. "It's gotten worse since I was last here. People were looking for an excuse to lash out."

Gaul followed her through the hole and into another road. They turned south, to where the land rose up into a sheer cliff Marjyal swelled against as if to climb. Marta, on the other hand, led Gaul down. Down the steps into the lower city. Under a great bridge that arched across the district, leaving it in constant shadow. They came to a square with nothing but the gnarled remains of a petrified tree, and one massive gate blocking their path.

It was constructed from junk stolen from the surrounding buildings. Part of one of the doors was a well-carved headboard, lashed and nailed to various pieces of wood and metal. The top was lined with downward facing spikes much like the ones in the Pits' commons. They were even facing inside, toward the city.

"This wasn't here before," Marta said, pushing against the double doors. It shook, but didn't open.

"What do you mean it wasn't here?" Gaul asked, flipping down his hood. "It didn't pop up in a day. Didn't you scout the path?"

"Yes! Most of it." Marta pulled her scarf aside and slammed her shoulder against the gate. "I didn't think they would put a gate up! It's just a stupid tunnel!"

"That leads out of the city!"

"Full of monsters!"

Gaul bit his tongue. He eased Marta aside and inspected the blockade. Despite its makeshift appearance, it was solid. A battering ram could crack it, but not much else. Peering through the gap between the door, Gaul could make out the dark ring of a tunnel. So close.

"There's a crossbar on the other side," he said. "If one of us could get there they could open it up."

"Then we can..." Her words trailed off as she took in the surroundings. The gate was built with the right side against where the cliff jutted out and the left into the buildings. Those same buildings were impassable with the amount of ruin scavenging them for the gate had done. Marta traced her finger along the gate then thrust it up and left. "There!"

"You're pointing at the sky," Gaul said.

"No, I'm — look. There was a market over there. They used to use a saferoom to store their goods. I used to steal from that saferoom, so I know it's actually part of the tunnel! We can get in through there."

"This is getting unreasonably more complex." Gaul squinted against the sun. It did appear as though the cliffs receded in that direction. A market could fit in the space. "What if they sealed it like they did here?"

"It's a chance. But what's wrong with a chance? We just have to…" She swung her hand toward the long path back through the winding streets. Her expression dropped. "It's a little bit of a ways. The lower part of Marjyal isn't… hmm."

"Or." Gaul walked toward the ruined building and pushed his back against it. "I boost you up to that window. You get around the gate and let me in."

Marta's gaze shot up. While the first floor had been destroyed, a pair of windows on the second were accessible. "That certainly is faster," she said.

Gaul cupped his hands and braced himself. Marta stepped into his grip and he lifted her up. With a slight hop, she grasped onto the windowsill and rolled in.

"It doesn't look much better up here," she said, poking her head out. "But I think I can find a way out further down. Are you sure about this?"

"I'm never sure about anything," Gaul said. "Be careful, though. I'll be here. I'll…" He glanced around the square. There was the tree, but in general it was an open space with nowhere to hide. "I'll wait."

Voices separated themselves from the general din of the raging city. Gaul narrowed his eyes to the street that curved out of view. Were they getting closer? It sounded like a lot of them. Marta was too focused on the way forward to notice the subtle shift in noise. Gaul couldn't not.

"Then you stay safe!" Marta said, blissfully unaware.

"I will." Gaul backed away from the building. "Just don't take too long."

And Marta was gone.

The voices were getting clearer.

"The tunnel's this way!" one shouted.

"His head is mine!" another bragged.

Gaul tapped a hand on his new swords. He pressed his other against his chest, where Anori's necklace hid below his shirt. "One more time, Anori," he said. "Just one more time."

Fire flared into an inferno in his gut. Red haze filled his vision. The string of his nerves pulled, ready to snap. Ready to Ignite.

Divines have mercy on anyone who entered that square.

Marta shoved a fallen wardrobe aside, sliding through the small gap it left. Years of building and rebuilding had left the home with most of its windows blocked in. But there was light ahead, and so was the way out. Even if it brought her far from Gaul's side.

Gaul was a strong fighter, Marta had to remind herself. He survived the Banquet. Marta could only catch the end, but the end was all that mattered. He lived. The Hunters died. But the speed at which he turned on that woman…

Marta shook her head. That woman tried to kill him. Marta found no fault in killing someone first. Still, she wouldn't let Gaul know about the exodus stone. As long as he didn't know the secret of Nature's Grave, he would need her.

Too wrapped up in her head, Marta didn't notice the bend in the floorboards. They buckled under her feet. She yelped in surprise, tumbling through the collapsed house before being ejected into the market.

"Huh?" a man in a brown cloak exclaimed. The Guild of Owls. He stretched over a stall and his eyes widened. "Hey! There's a woman here!"

Marta scrambled to all fours, tossing an awkward knife at the Owl. It stuck into the awning a metre from his head. Marta's body fought against her, sore from its tumble through the building. She tossed another knife before collapsing and before the Owl could react. He half drew his blade then stopped. The lucky throw stuck into his neck. He stumbled and collapsed chest first onto the stall.

Why were the Owls out in the street? Arcanists didn't quell riots. Marta slapped her hands against the ground and sat back on her heels. She breathed into her sore body.

Her eyes shot open. The Owl had called for someone. She scrambled on hands and knees for a market stall laden with barrels and crates. She crammed herself into a barrel that had fallen over, wrapping up in slick fish. The smell permeated her skin and pulling up her scarf did nothing to stop her from wanting to throw up. She covered her mouth to stifle the gagging and pulled a crate to block the opening.

A thin crack of light was all she had to keep herself from a world of vile odors. There wasn't much to see. The market hadn't been ransacked; it wouldn't have been open on the day of the Boar's Banquet. Between the stalls with empty baskets, Marta saw the cliff and, at its base, the door. Four hardwood planks spread across it, nailed into the wide frame. Sealed, though not well. Things were looking up, if one could ignore the fish.

"The shout came from over here," a voice said.

Marta covered her mouth with both hands.

"And here it was silenced. Observe." The second voice spoke with a slimy cadence that snaked into Marta's ears.

Marta crept toward the crack of light. Two figures in Owl garb stood over the body, still slumped over the stall. Marta stopped herself from cursing. One of them was Pelady. She leaned toward the man's corpse, dragging her fingers through his hair before pulling him up. The knife dropped out of his throat, clattering not far from Marta's hiding place.

The second figure was wrapped in a cloak made of brown owl feathers. He wore a white mask with a longer beak than any of the other Owls. Marta didn't need his face to know who he was. Melifacto, Praetor of Owls.

"But where is the one he was shouting about?" Melifacto asked, removing his mask. He reached into his robes and pulled out a crystal. It pulsed with dull purple light as he swept it about. "She's still in the city. Close. Though I don't know how close. Pelady, you're sure she's the one?"

"She told me her name, Master." Her teeth clicked as she spoke. She dragged one finger along the dead Owl's neck wound. "And her scent was exactly as I remembered."

"And what do you smell now?"

Pelady cocked her head back. "Fish."

Marta smirked. The fish weren't all bad.

Melifacto swept the crystal back and forth. He let it linger, twitched his lip, then continued on. That intense focus, it was as though the crystal was telling him something. A dousing rod for someone. But who?

While Pelady continued to poke the Owl's wound and cover her hands in his blood, Melifacto followed the urging of his crystal out of Marta's view. Pelady plunged two fingers into the Owl's neck, smiling as the blood poured out, soaking the ground below. Marta turned green. She had assumed if she was going to throw up, it was going to be from the fish.

Pelady's gaze followed the trickling of blood, where she caught sight of the knife. The knife close enough to Marta's barrel she could touch it.

No, no, no, Marta thought.

Pelady crouched under the stall. She never let go of the Owl's head as she stretched out for the knife. Marta kept still. Her eyes stayed fixed on the blood dripping off Pelady's fingers. They could rend Marta as they did those thugs. The back of her mind screamed at her to hide, to push down to the bottom of the barrel. But movement could alert the monster. With a final reach, Pelady snatched the knife and stood up. Only then did Marta allow herself to breathe.

"She did like to throw knives," Pelady said. Melifacto reappeared at her side. "It could have been her."

Melifacto nodded. He put the crystal away and threw his arms out to the air. "Marta!" he shouted.

Marta clenched her teeth until they hurt, just to keep from gasping.

"It has been so long, my dear. Years upon year since Jovin stole you so cruelly. I knew you would return, though. You were always destined to return. If you're here, tell me!" His voice echoed off the cliff walls. "Let us finish this."

Another Owl ran in from across the market. "My lord!" he said. "We have reports that Gaul the Ruthless is at the tunnel gate."

"I told you we should have gone straight to the tunnel," Pelady said. "Instead of following that useless crystal."

Melifacto didn't change, and yet the glare he sent Pelady was so cold it put shivers up Marta's spine. Such a darkness seeping out of one man.

"I apologize, Master," Pelady said.

"Perhaps when I fix that nose, I should remove that mouth as well." Melifacto replaced his mask. "Gaul means nothing to me. But if Marta helped him escape, perhaps she will stay by his side. The tunnel is it."

"Master." Pelady held up the Owl's corpse as if it was nothing but a doll. "Do you require his body?"

Melifacto considered. "He's all yours."

A jagged grin cracked Pelady's face. She stuck her bloody fingers in her mouth and followed Melifacto out of the market, dragging her toy behind her.

Marta didn't move. She couldn't move. The Praetor of Owls spoke to Marta like she was an old friend. Marjyal as a youth stayed in her mind with frightening clarity, and he wasn't among those memories. Maybe he had her confused with someone else.

But he knew her name.

And Pelady. She had protected Marta. Was it under Melifacto's orders? He wanted her alive. But why?

Marta shoved the crate aside and crawled out of the barrel. She had to leave. She had to get out. She had to reach Jovin. Her heart pounded against her sternum, trying to tear itself right out of her chest. Hot sickness roiled in her stomach. She stumbled to her feet and sprinted toward the tunnel door. She grabbed a plank and pulled. The nails were long and driven deep. But with a couple tugs it wiggled loose. Adrenaline and weak wood, she figured, before yanking the next plank off.

Once the door was clear she threw it open. The saferoom had been long abandoned of the goods it once stored, now home to thick cobwebs. The second door was easier to open. Only a couple latches she had to slide aside and it was into the tunnel.

She took a moment to catch her breath. Her heart settled into an easy rhythm and her stomach stopped trying to take her down with it. The tunnel was built for carts. To her left, it dipped down into inky blackness. To her right, sunlight burned and the other side of the gate waited.

Fear and confusion told her to go left. Run from Melifacto and Pelady. They would be at the gate soon. Something deep inside her — a part of her she'd never felt before, primal even — was terrified at the idea of Melifacto getting his hands on her.

You can't leave him, she told herself and ran with all her speed for the gate.

She crashed against it, throwing the crossbar aside. "Gaul!" she shouted, pressing her hands into the grime of the gate and shoving it open. "We need to—"

Bodies filled the street. Weapons stuck out of flesh and wood, pinning some corpses to walls and others to the ground. Blood scattered like leaves in fall. And at the centre of the macabre maelstrom, was Gaul.

He faced away from Marta, the branches of the petrified tree reaching twisted fingers toward him. A man was pinned to the tree by a broken halberd. Gaul had his head down, his back rising and falling with heavy breaths. In one hand he clutched a red object. Marta stepped closer, a moth to the flame. Then she realized what that object was. Gaul clutched onto some poor soul's jaw, torn free from the rest of his skull.

"Gaul," Marta said, barely more than a whisper.

His shoulders trembled. He shook his head and turned to her. His distant gaze scanned her up and down, though never truly took her in. He tossed the jaw aside and stomped by.

"You took too long," he said, snatching his swords out of the carcasses he left them in.

Marta hurried to catch up. Her gaze went between him and the massacre he left behind. She helped him shut the gate and put the bar across it. Still neither of them said a word.

What had she gotten herself into?

Gaul stared down the dark tunnel, tapping his hand against his chest. That was where the necklace hung. The necklace that strange man went across the world for. Marta flipped her bag over her shoulder and tossed Gaul a sunstone. He struck it down his arm and it burst into brilliant white.

Should I say something? Marta wondered. *What does someone say after something like that?*

"I hope you brought food," Gaul said.

Marta tossed him a piece of dried meat. *I suppose that works.*

Sunstones in hand, they descended toward Adathin Castle.

They found the Cradle of the World — and it destroyed them.

—From the journal of Jovin Gutterwake

Epilogue

"Today has been a test of faith!" Dianathos shouted from his balcony. Marjyalians packed into the courtyard of his manor and spread out into the streets. They hung off awnings and sat on rooftops to get a better look at the preacher.

"Our enemies have shown their jealousy. While they toil in chains out there, we are bathed in the freedom only Mar can offer us. But it is this very freedom that invites terror."

Four Praetors waited inside Dianathos' sitting room. The setting sun cast orange light through the windows, complimented by the rising of the cool night breeze. Four Praetors, and one was late.

"Now we upkeep the walls, strengthen the guards, and work to keep you safe. They want to bind you. They want to tell you no." Dianathos put his hand to his chest. His words trembled with practiced sorrow. "This is about more than faith. This is about truth. If you're not free, you are the walking dead. The revels are freedom. The revels are life. We revel for freedom. We revel for life!"

The crowd cheered. They banged on roofs and drainage pipes. Dianathos raised his hand and they fell silent. He let the moment hang in the air.

"Do not let the events of today make you afraid. Go. Praise Mar with every raised glass and close friend. We will ensure that you are never chained!"

Dianathos left the balcony with his arms raised in glory. The crowd sang his praises as he shut the doors and let out a contented sigh. Bellona had to admit; Dianathos was full of bluster, but he knew how to use it.

Taking a drink from his bar, Dianathos flopped into s chair. He glanced about. "Where's Melifacto?"

"Late," the Praetor of Snakes said. Yomat was an athletic man dressed in furs, even during the scorching heat. He scratched the snake tattoo that peeked out of the collar of his armour. "He wants to make an entrance, I'm sure."

"He was the one who called the meeting," Ettik complained. He was the Praetor of Rats. A small, gaunt-faced figure swallowed up by the ragged coat he wore. His clothing looked like he had taken a tumble through a weapon's rack. "He thinks he can waste our time like he's better than us."

"Do you have some bodies you need to be dragging off?" Yomat said with a sneer.

"I have an important job, Snake." Ettik pointed a crooked finger. "Why don't you preen your furs a little more?"

"Watch your tongue, Rat. Else I'll take it as a trophy."

Ettik jerked forward, only to be stopped with a look from Bellona. The final Praetor, the Praetor of Ants, Kygan, stayed silent with his arms crossed. He was the youngest among them, ascending to the position two years earlier. He had long brown hair, braided to his upper back.

"How are the repairs going, Kygan?" Bellona asked.

Kygan took a moment before turning to her, moving without urgency or care. Bellona tried to remember if she had ever seen him smile, or frown, or give any form of emotion.

"How should I know?" he said. "I'm stuck in here."

Ettik burst out laughing. The door swung open and Melifacto entered, cutting Ettik off mid-guffaw. He looked at each Praetor in turn from beneath his owl mask.

"They escaped," he said, but they all knew that already. "I saw the aftermath. It was… intriguing." He removed his mask. His eyes looked past the room, as if he could inspect the sky itself. "I don't believe we should let them go."

"Why shouldn't we?" Yomat asked, lounging back in his chair. "That tunnel's a deathtrap."

"Even you?" Melifacto turned to Bellona. "What about making an example of them?"

The emotion on Melifacto's face was a new one for him. Desperation.

"Why are you so concerned about these fugitives?" Bellona asked, resting her head on her knuckles.

Melifacto clenched his jaw. He took careful, calculated steps toward the sitting area. "The woman with Gaul," he started, speaking as if each word was delicate glass. "The one with the scar. Her name is Marta. She is incredibly important."

Bellona leaned forward and spoke to the Praetors, but never gave Melifacto her attention. "And yet I can't see it being worth our trouble chasing these people down across the country."

"What if I make it worth it?" Melifacto asked.

Dianathos chuckled. "What? You're going to take the coin we forge and give it back to us?"

"Not with any material wealth." He raised his gaze upward. "Something greater. Power unimaginable. Marta is the key and only I know how to use her."

Bellona cocked an eyebrow. There was a damned assurance in his words. She had known him to be evasive, but never exaggerative.

"What are you talking about?" Ettik asked.

Melifacto gave a knowing smirk. He ruffled his coat and swept around the room, stopping at an empty seat. He sat, drinking in the bated breath from his audience.

"Tell me," he said. "What do you know of the Cradle of the World?"

ALL GODS FALL: SEASON ONE

PART TWO

CRADLE OF THE WORLD

One day, the King of Adathin gathered his three daughters in the throne room of his castle. His search had failed. His kingdom once spread across the continent but had collapsed to a quarter of its former glory and size. The only thing that had not faded was his obsession. The crawling and corrupting mania that controlled his entire reign. And so, the King laid out a decree to his daughters.

Find the Cradle of the World.

—From the Journal of Jovin Gutterwake

Chapter Eight
Three Days Underground

"Do you know why that tunnel was built?" Kygan asked Bellona.

Bellona leaned against the bridge's parapet. "How about you tell me?"

The pair stood above the tunnel square. Once home to a lonely tree and a seldom used gate, the square had become the headquarters for the search for the fugitives. Bellona was enjoying the view from the bridge stretching over the lower city — from the shops to the Grand Cathedral — when the Praetor of Ants took it upon himself to join her.

"Marjyal was founded by Isildia," Kygan said. "She was the King's youngest daughter. Apparently, also his favourite, because while the city was being built, the King used ancient machines to dig a passage between Adathin Castle and Marjyal."

"Which is—" Bellona gestured toward the tunnel. "That."

Three days earlier, Gaul and Marta had fled into the tunnel. It was also three days earlier Melifacto put forward the reward for the person who caught them. The key to the Cradle of the World and what lay within. The Guilds of Owls, Snakes, and Rats each set up in front of the tunnel gate, hoping to be the one to claim the reward. The Guild of Doves had set off for the overground route. Though, that was only after they spent a day gathering tithes from the city. So far none of them have been successful.

"Indeed." Kygan brushed some dust off the parapet. "Adathin Castle is surrounded on three sides by a deep chasm. At the bottom, the King gave his daughter a church she could use to return to him, if she ever wanted to go home."

"Did she?"

Kygan shrugged. "I know buildings, Bellona. People don't concern me."

People concern me too much, Bellona thought. She leaned toward Kygan. "Do you trust what Melifacto is saying?"

"I trust he believes what he's saying." Kygan checked his pocketwatch, counting off the seconds before snapping it shut and returning it to his waistcoat pocket. He started walking toward the shops with Bellona following. "Maybe he knows where the Cradle of the World is. Maybe he can open it. Maybe he can take the Chalice of Light and use its power. What matters is Melifacto is sure. That makes him dangerous."

"So you do think he's dangerous?"

They passed a group of beggars. The beggars reached out, then stopped when they saw who Kygan and Bellona were. Kygan flicked them several coins without looking.

"He's always been dangerous," Kygan said. "He clearly only cares for his own goals. Marjyal, the citizens, even your Pits are just tools for him."

Bellona looked back at the beggars clutching onto their meager wealth, mouthing 'thank you' at the back of Kygan's head. *People don't concern you, huh?* she thought.

"Then what about this new talk of the Cradle?" she asked.

"I don't believe its new talk." He stopped at the edge of the bridge. The shops were busy, and each had an armed guard outside, ready for someone to try and steal something. "I think it's just new to us. Melifacto has been a Praetor for a long time, hasn't he?"

"Longer than me."

"None of us have been a Praetor for more than ten years. Other than Melifacto." Kygan narrowed his eyes, looking through the crowd. "Isn't that your shipmaster?"

Pushing through the crowd was a familiar face, Ortun, the head of the Boars' naval fleet. He was a stocky man, wearing a long doublet that had seen better days. His pants and boots held the scars of repeated patch jobs and the bandana around his head had a long tail laden with good luck charms. Most striking of all, he wore a metal mouthpiece that covered a horrific jaw injury, strapped on with heavy leather bindings.

"Lady Bellona," he said, muffled by the mouthpiece. "I came as soon as I got word."

"You got word?" Bellona asked.

"A crow. From Melifacto." Ortun crossed his arms, thick from his days hauling rigging. "The message said you wanted me and my boats to help with a search?"

"That cragger," she cursed.

"I apologize, m'lady."

"It's not your fault." She shouldn't have been surprised Melifacto made that play. Other than the Snake's fishing vessels, the Boars had the most boats. "Don't tell me you brought all the ships in?"

"Broken Island Fort is still well equipped." He rubbed his metal jaw. "What's all this about?"

"Melifacto." Bellona turned to Kygan, who was just about to make his silent exit. "Where is he right now?"

"Still in the tunnels, I believe." Kygan cocked his head. "Do you want to confront him?"

"Not yet." The idea fermented in her mind. If she didn't act on it, her moment may pass. "What about the rest of the Praetors?"

"Dianathos has left with his guild to take the overland route. I think he wants to set up somewhere to the south of the Castle. I suppose he doesn't want to tussle with the thing inside. Ettik and Yomat are still fighting about who gets what part of the east. Of course that all relies on them getting out of the underground."

"Excellent." She pointed at Ortun. "Ortun. Feyra is overlooking the reconstruction at the Pits. Retrieve her and meet me at my manor."

Ortun bowed before hurrying toward the arena. Kygan stared at Bellona for a long time, playing with the hem of his jacket.

"What are you planning?" he asked.

"Getting ready to go after the fugitives, of course." She started toward the manors.

"Bellona."

She stopped, but didn't look back.

"Why do you think the King built a tunnel for his daughter?" he asked.

Bellona shrugged. "So she could come home, like you said."

"I don't think he ever imagined Isildia would come back."

Bellona turned around. Kygan rolled a gold coin back and forth along his knuckles, lost in the yellow glimmer. It didn't look like a Marjyalian piece.

"Fine," Bellona said. "Then why did he build it?"

"Hope." Kygan flicked the coin skyward, then snatched it. "Hope can keep buildings standing when they should have fallen long ago."

"I thought people didn't concern you?"

"People don't, but what they do does." He put the coin in his pocket. "Or maybe we're both bad liars."

Bellona narrowed her eye. Every time she thought she had Kygan pegged, he would add another layer to himself. He wasn't on Melifacto's side, but was he on hers?

Kygan sauntered toward the bridge. He waved over his shoulder. "I hope you find whatever you're looking for," he called back as the crowd swallowed him up.

Bellona kept her gaze fixed on the point in space Kygan vanished from. The people swirled about as fish in a stream, and yet none dared to step too close to the Praetor of Boars. Just as Kygan's words circled her head without ever touching. He was as skilled at double-talk as Dianathos, and without all the pomp. But words were a flimsy shield.

The crowd parted for Bellona to pass, wide enough to not even risk the waving hem of her fur-lined coat touching them. Pseudo-inspirational rhetoric aside, Bellona had bigger concerns. Melifacto was in the tunnels. He brought his animals and his arcanists. He put everything into finding Marta.

And that left his manor free for a curious mind.

Marta couldn't help but be pleased with herself. She wanted to journey into Adathin ever since her brother had left, but she kept stopping herself at the edge of Nature's Grave. The one time she had gone farther, her husband came after her. That didn't end well for anyone. But as she sat in the tunnels leading away from Marjyal, warming herself by a fire, she couldn't imagine why she was so resistant to leaving Landus. Of course, having company didn't hurt.

Gaul ducked under a partially collapsed door frame into the room. He tossed a dead sunstone to Marta and stretched back until his bones cracked. "There's light in the distance," he said, ruffling his fingers through his hair. "Could be fire, could be sun. If the sun's up. We've been underground for too long I don't even know what time it is."

"Jovin always knew what time it was," Marta said with a lopsided smile, the scar coming out from the corner of her lip preventing a full one. "Didn't matter where we were. Once we spent four days straight down in Guttertown, where the only light is torches and stolen stones. Smelled terrible. But all the while Jovin would say sunrise and sundown. Sunrise. Sundown. We left and he said it would be dusk. And when we came out of the sewer the first thing I saw was the sun sinking into the sea. It was like magic."

"Not magic," Gaul said, tossing his coat to the floor. "Suppose he could be fluxblooded."

Marta leaned her elbows on her knees. "Flux… blooded?"

"Just a person who can push around a little bit of flux. Minor weaving talent. Something specific, like knowing exactly what time it is."

Marta blinked. "Nothing you just said makes any sense."

"We really are at the end of the world," Gaul muttered. He sat on his coat and poked the dying fire with a stick.

"What about you?" Marta asked

"What about me?"

"Are you fluxblooded?" Marta clasped her hands, rubbing her thumbs against each other. "You certainly are hard to kill. Not everyone can turn an army to a field of parts."

"That was hardly an army."

"It was still a lot and you…" That image burned into her mind. The image of Gaul with the jaw he had torn out of some poor soul's head. Brutal. "You took them all down. You weren't even injured."

Gaul tossed the stick aside. "Some people are just good at killing."

"It's got to be something more than that."

"You don't know what you're talking about."

"I've seen fights. I've been in fights. And you're telling me you killed, what? Twenty? Thirty people? And all you got were some cuts on your coat." She shook her head. "You're not a simple soldier."

"As I said." Gaul rubbed the spot on his chest where the gold and steel necklace hid. "Some people are just good at killing."

Marta clenched her jaw. Gaul was hiding something. He was company, but that didn't mean he was good company. Their relationship was based on a deal. She freed him from the Pits, he would help her get to her brother, then she would give him the secret to getting through Nature's Grave — a fist-sized wooden shard with a rock through the middle. A rare exodus stone she kept in her bag where no one could see it. Especially Gaul. It was the only way she had to control him.

"We should go," Gaul said. "I'm still not sure that Marjyal isn't tracking us."

Marta wrapped her scarf around her neck and stood. "They have no reason to."

"And yet." Gaul grabbed his coat and swept it on, the long tail flicking out with the movement. He stomped on the remains of the fire until it was dull embers then lit a new sunstone across his arm.

It seemed too much to ask that her and Gaul could be friends. But they needed each other. In place of friendship, reliance wasn't terrible. Still, soon Marta would be reunited with her brother and Gaul could return to whatever lonely life he had.

It's difficult to describe the search for the Cradle without describing the nature of it. Saying it's a location isn't wrong, but it doesn't capture the entirety of the matter. According to the legends, the Cradle is a part of Meza that was, somehow, removed.

When the First Gods fell to their corruption and the Divines needed to seal them away, they chose the Cradle of the World because of the innate power the area held. It was the location of the Chalice of Light and where the First Gods first appeared on Meza. The Divines lured the First Gods to the Cradle then, using the might of the Chalice itself, separated the Cradle from our reality. They sealed it behind a door with no knob, only a lock.

—From the Journal of Jovin Gutterwake

Chapter Nine

Rotted Parish

Gaul rested his hands on the pommels of his swords as they walked through the tunnel. It wouldn't have been a bad trip if it wasn't so tedious. Only simple stonework and the ever-present smell of old dust and mildew growing stronger with nothing else to focus on. Each footfall filled the space like a clap of thunder. Marta tapped one of their last sunstones against her thigh, making their shadows dance across the walls. With any luck, the light Gaul spotted earlier would be a way out to the surface. He had enough of that infernal tunnel.

"What was this tunnel used for?" he said, keeping a watchful eye on the side paths and holes in the wall.

"I don't know exactly," Marta said. "Direct route from Marjyal to the castle? I'm sure some people wanted that."

"It's a very long tunnel. That's a whole lot of work."

The light ahead grew. It didn't flicker like fire or possess the pure white of sunstones. It was daylight. A dull brilliance, but a sign the open sky wasn't far off. Marta hastened her steps. Gaul, burdened by pessimism, kept grounded, his eyes scanning the surroundings.

From the darkness came the sound of feet sliding. Metal grazing against rock. Bestial growls. Sounds that barely made it out from being lost in the oppressive shadows. Marta slowed until she was at Gaul's side again.

"Marta," Gaul whispered, keeping his eyes locked on the light.

"I heard," she whispered back.

"They're surrounding us."

"Do you have a plan?"

More footsteps padded around them. Counting was useless. Could be six, could be two dozen.

"Running seems like a good option." Gaul shifted his hands to grip his swords.

"Where?"

"Forward."

"On three." Marta's shoulders rose.

"Just say when."

"One, two—"

They broke into a dead sprint. Creatures leapt from the darkness, forms flashing by in shadows. Marta hurled the sunstone. It struck something with scales and teeth before bouncing away. They barrelled for the light, the only hope of escape.

They burst from the tunnel — only to stumble at the edge of a sheer drop. Rubble crumbled from the ruined steps, disappearing into infinite depths. Gaul cursed. They had gone deeper than he thought. The surface was high above them, letting in the faintest view of the sky. The chasm before them was interspersed with dark waterfalls. Some tumbled down the cliffs in roaring waves, others freefell, but vanished much like the rubble before. Ramshackle bridges and buildings stuck out from the walls, creating a dizzying town hanging over a bottomless pit. Dots of firelight littered the distance like angry eyes. Through the cracks to the sky was the silhouette of towers. Adathin Castle, so close and yet terribly far away.

Which brought them back to the original problem. Gaul drew his swords and turned to their pursuers. Daylight spilled into the tunnel, and their hideous forms were revealed. They were squat, only half the size of Gaul, and covered in scales. Upright lizards, clothed in rags or scraps of leather. They snapped at their prey, but Gaul kept them back with swings of his swords. Some had spears or broken blades, but none yet risked rushing an armed foe. First three, then six, then a dozen creatures kept Gaul and Marta backed against the sudden drop. And they only kept coming.

One with white scales and a broken sword hopped forward and back. Side to side. It screeched something in an unknown language. Drool dripped from its spike-filled maw.

"There's a small ledge to our right," Marta said, keeping herself behind Gaul's blades.

"Does it go up?" Gaul followed the white lizard's movement.

"I only see a path down."

"Black Hypogea," he cursed. "Better than nothing. Lead the way."

The white lizard leapt forward. Gaul caught it with a flick of his sword, slicing its throat open. Black blood cast into the air and its body dropped down the chasm. Marta hurled a knife into another's chest. The pack withdrew, pacing the edge of the light, waiting for their chance to strike. Marta took off down the rickety wooden ledge, Gaul sheathing his sword and chasing after her.

Gaul kept his feet before him, trying not to go too fast as each step shook the ledge and dropped splinters of wood. Lizards skittered out of holes in the cave walls. They clambered across stone and struts, reaching out at Gaul and Marta's feet. One got brave and came in with a two-handed snatch from below. Marta kicked it in the jaw, sending it howling into the darkness.

"There!" Gaul pointed at a bridge that crossed the chasm. At least it put them on the right side, but they would have to cut through a suspended slum to reach it.

Marta leapt from the ledge to a shack roof. The planks snapped like twigs, sending her crashing through. Gaul followed, landing on his feet inside the shack.

"This place is terrible," Marta said, throwing a chunk of rubble off her chest.

A lizard dropped from the hole in the ceiling. Grabbing a broken plank, Gaul struck the lizard then plunged the splintered edge into its chest. Another fell in, only to be hit by Marta with a throwing knife. Gaul pulled Marta out of the shack as it filled with the reptilian flood.

The two ran and leapt across the underground city, always keeping the bridge in sight. More torchlights appeared above and below. The chasm rumbled with warning cries, calling the strange denizens to descend upon the intruders.

An unlucky step from Gaul cracked the boards and dropped his leg through. He pushed himself up, but the splintered wood pressed into his thigh. Marta rushed back, pulling on Gaul's shoulders. It only served to make the shards bite harder.

"Keep going!" Gaul shouted, slamming his fists into the wood. The path cracked around him and he dropped through, landing chest first on the supports before tumbling to a lower section of the city.

Gaul shook the stars from his head and glanced about. He was in some sort of town square. Dirt fell from above, shaken loose from Marta sprinting toward the bridge. Hovels split from the main road, though some left gaps where they had fallen away. In the centre was a statue made of wooden chunks wrapped together with rope and adhesive. Dirty threads created long hair draping over the effigy's shoulder. There wasn't any time to inspect further; lizards were filling the square.

He put his shoulder to a door, turning it to splinters. He knocked aside a table laden with clumps of vile meat and continued out the far window. As he landed the ground shifted, dropping him deeper. Every movement was instinct. The path to the bridge was winding and full of detours. He scrambled up and down ladders, kicking away any lizards who got too close. Occasionally he would spot Marta above him — but he couldn't see a way back to her.

A lizard came bursting out of the building before him, taking down the entire wall in its fury. Gaul twisted on his heel and took a sharp right turn. The passages got tighter. He put his head down, pushing away the burning in his lungs, and focused on one foot in front of the other. The buildings ended and he had to skid to a stop, barely holding himself back from falling into the pit.

The bridge stretched above him. Marta was halfway across, but lizards blocked her path forward and back. She drew two knives and pointed them at either group. There wasn't much room to fight, and the bridge swayed with each step she took to steady herself.

Ropes hung from the platforms above Gaul, suspending cages with dusty skeletons inside. He grabbed one and sliced the cage free. He gave it a few tugs. It shifted before locking in place. There was a clatter and he glanced over his shoulder as three lizards slinked down the path with spears in hand. They snapped when they saw they had been spotted and broke into a run. Gaul wrapped the rope around his arm and threw himself off the ledge — the lizard's dirty claws snatching nothing but air.

Wood cracked as the beam the rope was tied to dropped. Gaul's heart stopped until the beam caught itself. Marta braced for the oncoming lizards, while below Gaul kicked at the support struts. They snapped. The bridge twisted as one side crumbled. Lizards rained down. Marta held onto the bridge as more supports bowed and broke.

"Marta!" Gaul cried. His swing began its return trip.

Marta spotted him. She gritted her teeth and released her grip. The bridge split, dropping the rest of the lizards into the shadows below. Gaul reached out his hand, catching Marta by the forearm before she could join them.

The pair swung back to the lizards Gaul left behind. Growling with exertion, Gaul swung Marta forward. She slammed both feet into the lizard at the front. It stumbled back against the rest of the horde and Gaul and Marta kept moving by. They flew back across the chasm. Gaul released the rope and they landed in a heap on the far ledge.

Marta rolled onto her hands and knees, drawing in deep breaths. "Why did you do that?" she asked.

"I couldn't see any other way to get you out of there," Gaul said, cracking his neck and sitting up. "Sorry it wasn't comfortable."

"You could have died."

"Yeah? You could have too." He hopped to his feet. "Next time I'll find a way to save you that does not involve destroying a bridge. Or I could drop you to Black Hypogea. Your choice."

"That's not what I…" She sat back on her knees and sighed. "Thank you."

Gaul cocked an eyebrow. "You're welcome? I guess."

Lizards screeched, standing at the ruins of the bridge. They tossed spears that made it barely halfway across the chasm. But most were already running off for other crossings.

"They know this place better than us," Gaul said, helping Marta to her feet. "We need to go."

There was no clear way of scaling the cliffs; they could only traverse the unstable town stretching between natural stone pillars. With only light scattered in from the holes above, it felt like the cavern went on forever. The cries of the lizard monsters echoed off the walls, surrounding them in hostile noise. And, with each step, they got further from the sun.

After crossing a suspended bridge that swung unnervingly with each step, they came to an unusual sight. A stone pillar separated from the natural cave walls. The spray from the nearby waterfall fed a thick mat of moss and vines. Gaul pulled it aside and revealed worked stone blocks. He stepped away and followed the pillar upwards with his gaze, until it split into a series of arches attached to the ceiling.

Are these supports for the castle? Gaul wondered. *Did people live here before the lizards?*

"Hey, over here," Marta said. She grabbed two handfuls of the vines and gave it a sharp yank. She jerked her head, indicating for Gaul to follow, then stepped forward and disappeared into the vegetation.

Gaul glanced around to make sure no lizard had snuck up on them, then crept toward where Marta had vanished. There was no indication anything was different about that spot, but when he pushed the vines aside he saw Marta waiting inside a small break in the stonework. It was difficult to see with the little light that got through and as Gaul stepped over the collapsed part of the wall and let the vines drop, it became pitch black.

He didn't risk moving, not wanting to bump into Marta. Cloth rustled and, with a scrape, light filled the space. Marta cursed and pulled the scarf down from around her neck. She wrapped it around the sunstone, turning the bright light into a dim glow — enough they could see where they were.

Not that there was much to see. It was a simple room with mushrooms growing in the corners. There were stairs leading up and down — or there would be if the structure hadn't collapsed in and blocked the passages.

"It's part of Adathin Castle," Marta whispered. "It has to be."

"Doesn't matter." Gaul pulled on a piece of stone, but the rubble blocking the way up wouldn't budge. "We're still stuck down here with those things.

"I think I know what they are."

"The lizards?" Gaul pressed his back against the stone and peered out between the vines.

"Not lizards. Some of the books my brother read talked about the King's daughters and their hunt for the Cradle. His eldest was this woman named Forta. I guess she thought the Cradle was underground, because she tore the land apart trying to find it. She worked her people to death." Marta sat on a broken chunk of the ceiling and rested her head on her hand, gazing into the limited light of her sunstone. "She was not a kind leader. But apparently while digging she found the corpse of an ancient dragon. It must've still had some blood, because she was able to use it to create things that… what was the quote? 'Were not man and were not dragon. Dracolings that could work and dig and never tire.'"

Gaul ran his hands over his hair. "You think these are those creatures? Dracolings?"

"People said the tunnel was built with machinery, but maybe also little dragons? I suppose it doesn't really matter what they are, as long as we can find a way past them and out of here."

"These towers appear to lead into the Castle. We just need to find one that's in better shape."

Gaul crept out of the hiding place. Marta buried the sunstone under the rubble and followed him. They hadn't seen a dracoling in a while, but the sharp yaps and echoing growls never faded. Gaul approached the edge of the platform built out from the tower and scanned the cavern.

Now he had seen one, he was able to spot similar manmade towers that littered the area. Unfortunately, they were all far away and didn't have a clear path to get to. Climbing got more enticing by the second.

Marta appeared at his side, wrapping her scarf back around her neck. She didn't look up like Gaul had — she looked down. "There!"

She pointed to a wooden building that sat at the bottom of one such tower, and at the lowest point of the cavern they could see. Gaul recognized the form. A Pantheon Cathedral. Two bell towers stuck up from the square structure, but the stained glass on all sides had been smashed.

"What's a cathedral doing this far underground?" Gaul wondered. It was an extravagant piece of work considering the surroundings.

"Who knows. But it's connected to that tower. It must be the way up to the castle."

"Seems as logical as anything in this place has been."

There was a clatter of footsteps from around the corner. Gaul and Marta scrambled back into their hiding place. The vines barely fell as a group of dracoling stomped by. They wielded short swords and some even had cobbled together plate armour. Gaul let out a breath of relief as they rushed across the bridge and disappeared once again.

Marta grabbed his arm and pulled him down to her level. "I saw a way." She slid past him and stood at the edge, pointing straight down. She sported a smile that made him worry.

Coming out of hiding, Gaul saw a madman's idea of a slide. Collapsed shacks and crooked paths led right to the cathedral doors — if one could survive the trip.

"That's not ideal," Gaul said.

"Do you have a better idea?"

"Doesn't mean it's a good one."

A shrill cry cut the air. Gaul looked up in time to see a javelin flying toward him. He leaned back, feeling the wind from the jagged tip brush past his neck before it bounced off the wall. A dracoling stood on the bridge, pointing and shouting something that even in another language sounded accusatory.

"Fine," Gaul said. "Let's take the slide."

"Alright." Marta didn't move.

"Come on!"

"Give me a second! It's higher than I thought."

"No more seconds." Another javelin flew by. "Go now!"

Marta leapt off the edge and Gaul followed suit. He hit the slope and started sliding on his side. Arrows and javelins bounced around him. He got his feet beneath him just in time to leap the gap to the next piece.

Marta laughed up a storm, gliding down the ruins like a child down a hill. She moved side to side, avoiding the shots from distant archers. She was so occupied with her fun, she failed to notice the archers that dropped onto a walkway much closer.

Gaul gritted his teeth. He leapt from the ruins to a tilted walkway, then from that to the archer's post. The dracolings couldn't turn fast enough. Gaul twisted through them like a bladed hurricane and came out the other side without losing momentum. He sheathed his swords and jumped back onto the slope.

Marta waited for him at the bottom. He struck the stone floor with both feet and rolled to a somewhat graceful stop.

"What took you so long?" Marta asked with a smile.

"Saving your life." Gaul swept past her and headed toward the church. "Again."

The church was built on a stone outcropping. A broken archway marked where a bridge must once have been. It pointed at the tunnel exit far above them and across the cavern. In simpler times one would have been able to walk from the tunnel.

Gaul pushed against the rotting wood of the church door. He was hit with a wave of sour scent. He snorted, as if he could force the smell away and threw the doors open. A massive beast swelled up before them, sending Gaul and Marta grasping for their weapons. But it didn't move. A decaying form with wings and four legs dangled from the ceiling. Its long neck was held up by chains and bile dripped from its mouth into a dish in the middle of the nave. Lit torches lined the walls, casting the beast's flickering shadow onto the ceiling.

"I think that story of yours is true," Gaul said, shutting the door behind them.

"A dragon." Marta walked forward, mouth agape. "A real dragon. The one that Forta created the dracolings from. It's here!"

"How is it so well preserved?"

"It's an ancient dragon. Its body isn't like anything from our era."

Gaul picked up a cup from next to the bile-collecting dish. The same liquid caked the inside. "They've been drinking the fluid from this creature." He sniffed, recoiling from the sweet scent.

"Why would they do that?"

"Look at this place. The pews are busted, but there's not a speck of dust. It has an upkeep I haven't yet seen in this entire place. It's still a church to them." He pointed at the dragon. "And that's their god."

The designs on the stained-glass windows were long gone, but the dracolings had scratched strange symbols into the stone. Marta spun in a slow circle. All motifs of the Divine had been destroyed and replaced with offerings to a more draconic entity. A steady thudding grew in Gaul's mind.

He could have been on his way home. Instead he's sliding down underground cities to help some women he met drunk in a tavern find her brother. Everything had been falling apart since he lost Anori and he had just floated along like a corpse in a stream.

"This is what the hunt for the Cradle created," Gaul growled. The thudding got louder. "A kingdom destroyed and out of it came the City of Revels and this rotting place. This land is made to corrupt and decay."

"Gaul."

"And you bring me here!" Gaul hurled the cup right past Marta's head. She was so shocked she didn't even move. "You extort me into coming with you deeper and deeper into this cesspool!"

"Gaul! Calm down!"

Her voice was distant. It was her fault he couldn't return home. Instead he would die in a pit in the earth filled with monsters. Red filled his vision. *Thud. Thud. Thud.*

Marta threw her gaze around the room. It landed on the dragon and she narrowed her eyes. She grabbed Gaul by his arm and dragged him to a back corner.

"What are you doing?" he growled.

Marta said nothing. She kicked a door open to a stairwell leading up. Gaul yanked his arm away but she grabbed him again. Heat flooded through his body. Marta grabbed a burning torch off the wall and pulled him through.

As she led him further up the stairs, he fought less. He didn't care as much that she pulled him along by the wrist. The rage quelled and he couldn't remember why he was so mad. The thudding faded away.

They arrived a small guard's station and Gaul softly removed Marta's hand before dropping into one of the dusty chairs.

"What happened?" He clutched his aching head with both hands.

Marta placed the torch into a holder on the wall. She knelt in front of him, laying her hand on his knee. "It's an ancient dragon, I told you. My brother read me old tales about them. Some say certain dragons had an aura that would cause creatures to lose their mind. They could destroy towns simply by existing. Even a corpse… I felt it too, but I don't know why it got you so fast."

"I tried to tell you Marta." He wanted to kill her. He might have… "You've hitched your cart to a broken horse."

Marta ran her hand along her scarf. "Your eyes were red."

Gaul clenched his fists.

"And don't tell me I don't know what I'm talking about." She pushed up onto her feet. "I was looking right at you! Talk to me."

"We're not friends, Marta. I don't owe you anything." He grabbed the torch from the holder. "I'm here to get you to the Cradle. After that's done, we're done. Just know if you do ever see my eyes turn red, you better not be around me."

He stomped past her. Marta kept her eyes affixed to the wall. She let out a low sigh then followed him up the stairs.

Gaul did feel bad for being so harsh. But at least he was honest. He didn't mind a friend. He just knew friends didn't tend to hang around when they knew what he was.

I am tempted to say that I don't believe it was the Cradle, specifically at least, that the King was looking for. For all the legend that surrounds it, it's still just a place. The King wasn't a historian or a preservationist. Or at least it doesn't seem that way from what I've researched and seen.

There's a sitting room in one of the towers. It's close to the King's bedroom, so I imagine he spent a lot of time looking out the windows in that room. There are three walls covered in glass — glass that has miraculously survived the centuries since the King's time.

The only thing is, two of those windows are boarded up. The north and south windows that once overlooked the chasm far below. This way, one would be unable to stare down into the dark depths that always sat just below the throne. The King feared those depths, of the darkness that awaited all people, so he sealed them away from his sight until all he could see was the horizon.

No, he didn't want the Cradle, he wanted the Chalice of Light, and all the power that came with it.

—From the Journal of Jovin Gutterwake

Chapter Ten
Castles

Walking the city as a Praetor was a bizarre experience. When Bellona was young, the Praetors would wear masks when they were acting in any official capacity. It created distance and allowed the citizens to truly embrace freedom, as if the Praetors were forces that watched over them rather than people.

It also, unfortunately, created much unrest. The Praetors were mysterious shells that never seemed to change or grow. When Dianathos became the Praetor of Doves, he convinced the others to remove their masks and give human faces. It worked, and the people were content. Two years later, Bellona ascended to her seat, so she never had to wear a mask.

The Marjyalians didn't give servitude to the Praetors, but they gave respect. They understood the power the Praetors had and none would risk insulting them. And so, when walking the city, Bellona would get the occasional stare and the crowd would give her plenty of room. She never felt like a monarch, but she never blended in.

So, when she had to lurk around the Praetor manors, she did something she never had to do. She wore a mask. Not the mask of Boars, that would be too conspicuous. She wore a wooden beggar's mask, painted with colourful sprays to entice the wealthy to hand over their money — and to cover any scars or disfigurements that might scare them off. No one paid her any mind as she slipped past the gate, across the courtyard, and into the Owl manor.

Melifacto had pulled every spare hand he had, even the cleaning staff was gone. Though, Bellona never once seen a cleaner enter or leave the gate. She walked under the grand staircase. She had spotted Melifacto through the large window on the back of his manor nearly every morning. That was where his lab was located. That was where Bellona could find out what he was up to.

She checked her corners before crossing hallways — but, there was no one to be seen. Those empty corridors swallowed Bellona's footsteps and spat them back as haunting reverberations. She ran her fingers over a console table. They came away clean. Not a speck of dust existed on any surface, nor dirt, nor scuffs. There were no paintings or tapestries. Not even a gaudy statue. Sterile, as though caring hands never touched it. The only indication of life was a well-worn path in the wood floor Bellona followed to the lab.

The sun high in the sky cut a hard line across the floor from the south facing window. The rest was dim. Empty cages lined the walls, stacked two high with straw along the bottom. Strange machines made with runes and crystals sat like monsters in the shadows, with more hiding under heavy cloth. On the slab near the window was the dissected corpse of a small animal. Bellona paid it no mind, hurrying past to a writing desk in the corner.

She checked each drawer. There were stacks of paper and she took a moment to read each one, but they were almost indecipherable. It wasn't just the content, Melifacto wrote in a peculiar shorthand. The best Bellona could tell, he had dozens of experiments and projects going on.

In the centre drawer, she found a book bound with twine. She opened the leather cover and inspected the pages. It was in a different handwriting, and the bizarre shorthand was mostly absent except for notes in the margins. The author wrote on numerous subjects. Lithofluxy, arcanology, long and dense treaties on the 'malleability of the spirit.' Whatever that meant. She placed her mask down and flipped through. It was intense, to say the least. Near the end she found two pages sun-faded to a light beige — the book spent a lot of time open to that section.

The shorthand was back en masse. The pages were overflowing with alchemical recipes, some scratched out, others circled, still others circled then scratched out. They were iterations on the same process, where they changed ingredients and techniques to create something called *elys sang*. Bellona had never heard of such a thing — though alchemy was never her game. It had to be important for Melifacto to spend so much time looking at those pages. One of the sections she could parse from his shorthand laid it out simply. *Elys sang* is the key. *Elys sang* to the Cradle.

If there's a key, Bellona thought, *then there's a lock. The lock must be the Cradle of the World, and Melifacto has been trying to create the key for years. But what role does Marta play?*

Bellona ran her finger down the lists of formulas. Melifacto had tried minerals and herbs mixed with heat and cold. Nothing seemed to of worked, any yet some were circled with a star. As if to indicate 'maybe this one.' Did Melifacto even know what he was looking for? Bellona's finger reached the bottom of the page were the writing shifted. No longer formulas, Melifacto instead had written a single phrase, surrounded by dots from a tapping quill.

All Gods Fall.

What an odd sentence to dote over. She flipped to the next page where a stack of folded, loose papers was stuck into the margin. She spread them out on the desk before her. Dozens of reports labelled from outposts one to seven. Outposts that shouldn't exist. They were organized by date and went back years. Each was a simple list of five-digit numbers, each labelled as nonviable, unconfirmed, or untested. Every three months a new report appeared from each outpost. Bellona plucked the most recent ones from the batch. Six reports all received in the past two weeks. Outpost Four was missing, or hadn't reported in.

Bellona tapped her fingers along the beggar's mask. *Elys sang* was the big one. Melifacto's driving force. Important enough to build seven secret outposts working dawn to dusk on creating it. What she wouldn't give to find one of those outposts. Bellona replaced the book, ensuring each page was in the exact position it was when she found it. The Cradle was more than just a momentary passion for Melifacto. It was his life's work.

Which, of course, meant she had to take it.

Old hinges creaked as Gaul opened the door at the top of the stairs. Marta peered around him. They had arrived on the lowest floor of a dark dungeon, with empty cells to either side. Those same cells reached six floors up until they disappeared out of torchlight. And on the ground, the start of construction to build deeper.

"Adathin was having some criminal trouble it seems," Gaul said. He raised the torch to each cell where skeletons lay curled in the corner. Everyone had one — many had more.

"How could they just leave them here to die?" Marta pulled on the cell doors and they rattled in reply.

"Maybe there was no one left to keep them alive."

They crossed the floor to the stairs. The placement of the stairways alternated sides, so they had to walk past each depressing cell as they ascended.

"You clearly know more of this place than you let on in Landus," Gaul said. "Do you know what happened here?"

Marta sighed and ran her fingers along the bars. "No. All of the writings my brother found stopped at a certain point. Some cataclysmic event silenced all voices at once. A revolt against the king seemed as likely as anything else."

"A rebellion wouldn't have left the people in the dungeon to starve." Gaul kicked a bucket off the level they were on. It struck the floor with a satisfying crack.

The castle above them groaned in reply. Gaul and Marta froze, sharing a glance. In silent agreement, they started walking faster.

"This place feels wrong," Gaul said. Each breath was a sick miasma. Each step was on cemetery dirt. "Let's get through this castle and on our way. Where's the Cradle from here?"

"Uh." Marta scratched the back of her head. "There is one thing…"

"You do know the way to the Cradle, right?"

"It's not that easy."

Gaul grabbed her by the arm and pulled her back. "You told me you know the way."

"I do!" She pulled her arm away and hopped backwards toward the next stairway. "I know how to find the way."

"That's different things, Marta." He took wide steps to keep pace. "You better start explaining. And no more half-truths!"

"My brother never knew where the Cradle was, but he thought the information may be here in the castle's library."

"The King found the Cradle of the World after all?"

"Maybe. But my brother figured this is where all that information would be kept, so if he was going to have any chance of finding it he would have to come here. Either he's here, or he found the location of the Cradle which means we will too."

Gaul shook his head. Hope was a punishing strength to possess. "How long ago did your brother leave?"

Marta stopped at the top floor. "A year. And I know what you're thinking, but it's not true. He's still alive."

"Marta…"

"I can feel it! Every time he came back to Landus from a trip he would stand at the edge of Nature's Grave and say, 'It must be in the Castle.' He's going to be here or at the Cradle. We just need to get to the library. He always finds himself surrounded by books."

"And I'm sure it will be clearly marked," Gaul said sarcastically.

He stepped around Marta and headed for the door he hoped would lead out of the dungeon. Marta had lied to him, but at some level he understood. He crossed two countries to find his wife's necklace, and he wasn't honest the whole way. Marta was doing the same to reunite with her brother.

The door at the top of the dungeon opened into a smaller tower. The exit was bright sunlight that made Gaul squint and cover his eyes. He put the torch in a wall holder as Marta rushed past him.

They stepped out of the tower into Adathin Castle's courtyard. Marta bounded across the pristine white coating on the ground.

"Snow?" Gaul said, taking a handful. "How is there snow here?"

Marta leapt onto a bench, sending powder flying. "We're really here. This is amazing!" She flipped off the bench and landed back first into a snow drift.

Gaul took a staircase up the castle walls and looked over the surrounding landscape. For kilometres in all directions there was not another speck of snow. Just plains that gave way to lush forests and lakes. Somewhere to the north would be Marjyal. Coming from that direction, figures dotted the grass. Gaul strained his eyes, just to make sure they weren't a figment of his imagination.

"Marta!" Gaul called.

Marta burst out of the snow. She shook flakes out of her hair and rushed up the steps.

Gaul pointed at the figures. "Marjyalians?"

"They look like it but… they wouldn't chase us. It wouldn't be worth their time."

Gaul turned back to the courtyard. "You can always trust insane people to act insane. I should leave."

"What?" Marta jogged to catch up. "We're not done yet. We haven't found my brother."

"Clearly the Marjyalians aren't done with me." With the chasm enfolding the castle on three sides, the only way out was the main gate. It would be easy enough for Gaul to find. "You'd be safer if I wasn't with you."

"You don't know that."

"Do you have another reason why Marjyal would be coming out here?"

Marta shrank into herself.

"Exactly." He stepped around a fountain filled with inches of solid ice.

"No," Marta said. "I still need you to watch my back. I still need you to get me to Jovin. That's the deal."

Gaul stomped his foot into the snow and came to a stop. "And you told me you knew where he was. Let's say for a second he is still alive. What if he found where the Cradle is and left? Took all the clues with him too. Then you're stuck here and the trail is dead."

"Then I'll find another way."

"And drag me along with you? Don't get me wrong, I'm thankful you got me out of that city but this is absurd. And if growing up in Marjyal is so bad then you should be able to handle yourself."

"Adathin is dangerous." Marta stepped toward Gaul, unwilling to back down. "That's what my brother said over and over. Adathin is dangerous. And after what I saw you do in Marjyal, I have no doubt you're dangerous too."

She was determined, Gaul could give her that. But he wasn't about to wander with a drunk while Marjyal was after him. She would need to feel comfortable parting ways. He glanced around the courtyard until he spotted two branches lying in the snow beneath a tree. He snatched them free, shaking the snow off and snapping the twigs off the main branch. He tossed one to Marta, who caught it out of the air. "Defend yourself."

"You're kidding me," Marta said.

Gaul stepped in with a slow chop. Marta batted it aside, bored.

"So what?" Marta shook the stick at him. "You give me a ten-minute sword lesson, pat me on the head, and be on your way?"

"Or you can keep throwing knives."

Marta crinkled her nose. "Fine. Let me make this simple in case you've forgotten. You can't get past Nature's Grave. You should know by now it's not your average forest. I know its secret and I know how you can get through it. But you're not getting that until you bring me to the Cradle of the World. You said we weren't friends, then fine. I'm the reason you're not rotting away in the Marjyal Pits or dying in the sand. You may think you don't owe me anything, but you're not getting home without my help."

And that was it. Gaul was Marta's prisoner. Her hired guard with his freedom as the prize. He shouldn't have expected any more. He snapped the branch in half, making Marta jump with the sharp sound, then tossed the pieces away. "Let's find that library, maybe Marjyal will walk on by."

Marta followed him as he continued across the snowy courtyard. His blood pumped hot into his face, but the cold and ice were kind reminders of Ulkradia. Though even they couldn't cover the abhorrent atmosphere surrounding Adathin Castle. They walked past crumbling gazebos and fallen statues — disappearing reminders of their former glory — until they found a door to enter the castle proper.

Snow billowed in when they opened the door. The inside was colder than the out. Their breaths puffed in heavy clouds, creating ice crystals along the scarf wrapped around Marta's face. The initial enthusiasm was gone, now it was only the chill.

"Are you gonna be okay?" Gaul asked.

"What do you care?" Marta's teeth chattered as she spoke.

Fair, Gaul thought, bundling up his own coat and turning down the hall. They walked the empty castle, preserved against the entropy of years. There was frozen elegance to the structure. Guest rooms were ready for people to stay in, iced into a state of constant hospitality. They passed by a garden courtyard with tiny plants poking out through the snow. Everywhere they went Gaul swore he could hear a groaning and dragging. He was sure Marta heard it as well, but neither of them said a thing, hoping it was just the natural sounds of an empty castle.

Marta stopped by a large portrait at an intersection. Gaul stood beside her and looked up at the massive golden framed painting. It showed a grey-haired man surrounded by three young women. Their faces had been torn out.

"The King and his daughters," Marta said.

The King was as regal as a man of his position could be, dressed in flowing robes and with a crown of five spikes. His intense glare followed Gaul's every movement.

Marta pointed at the women. "One of these would be Isildia, the youngest daughter who founded Marjyal. Then there's Forta, the eldest and the creator of those dracoling monsters we found below the castle. I don't know the middle daughter's name. I guess she didn't do anything special."

"What about their mother?"

"She died in childbirth of Isildia." Marta ran her fingers along the canvas. "A doomed family."

"That's poetic of you."

"It's carved in the frame. Someone didn't like them."

The groan came again, followed by a wet dragging sound. Gaul was sure of it this time. He left Marta at the painting and wandered into the next hallway. Doors lined both walls, interspersed with several broken vases. The carpet was stained green and black in long stripes, as though some rotting thing had been dragged through.

Gaul covered his nose against the horrible smell seeping into the hall. It got stronger as he stepped forward. The groan came again and he stopped.

Something reached around the corner. It grabbed onto the wall. Each finger wasn't a finger; it was an arm or a leg. It pulled itself forward as Gaul stumbled back. The thing was made of people, bound and fused together by bone and sinew. It filled the hall with writhing flesh.

At its front, a single corpse stuck out from the rest. He had long grey hair and wore a crown with five spikes. The King of Adathin. He swayed his head like a searching snake, his eyes covered with scarred skin. The monstrosity sat in the juncture between the hallway Gaul stood frozen in and the one it was moving down.

Gaul stepped back as slowly and quietly as he could. He went around the corner and hit something. He spun around to see Marta standing there.

"What are—" she started before Gaul clamped her mouth shut.

The monster groaned.

"We need to go another way," Gaul whispered.

"What are you talking about?" Marta matched his volume. She moved to the corner and peered around. Her face went pale and she backed up. "We need to go another way."

"Great idea." Gaul rolled his eyes. He grabbed her by the arm and pulled her back the way they came.

"Was that the King?" Marta said once they were far enough away.

"His corpse at least." Gaul glanced out a window. The sun sank below the horizon. "We need to find the library before dark. I'm not walking these halls with that thing stalking about."

"That thing was people."

"Not anymore."

They continued to search the castle and thankfully didn't see any more of the monster. The halls were expansive, but they followed a form and were easy to navigate. They sun had just set when they stumbled upon a large two-level hall packed with books. The library, just in time.

Gaul shut the door and wedged a chair against it. It was almost a joke against the scale of the thing he wanted to keep out. Marta had already grabbed some books and started flipping through. The long tables were stacked high with leather bound tomes and candles.

"Look!" Marta held up a book. Someone had scratched a graphite drawing of a tower onto the paper. "It's my brother! We could see this from our home. It was a tower that sunk in the bay. We would try to guess what was in it. He was here."

"Well. He's not here now." Gaul walked toward the other side of the library, only to be stopped by Marta slamming a book against his chest.

"Then he found the Cradle." She pulled him closer. "And so will we."

* *

In the Boar Manor's sitting room, Bellona had finished telling Ortun and Feyra what she had done. Feyra sat at a corner table with her armour. She worked oil into the supple leather until the rag was dry, but she still rubbed. Her thoughts stayed with Bellona.

"All gods fall," Ortun said. He rubbed his metal chin as he paced the room.

"Does that stand out to you?" Bellona reclined on her lounge, tapping her fingers along the beggar's mask resting on her knee. "Melifacto seemed to be considering it quite a bit."

"Yes." Ortun spoke in a clipped, deliberate manner that riled Feyra. He could never simply get his point out. "It's part of a quote from a philosopher. When Dianathos became the Praetor of Doves he pushed to return Marjyal to one god."

"I remember," Bellona said.

"Do you remember when he sent his clerics to gather dissenting texts? Most don't. He did it secretly. He burned books that could cause people to have uncooperative thoughts. The book this quote is from was one of them. The full quote is 'The only truth when it comes to divinity in this world is that it, by its nature, is passing. Though new gods rise, all gods fall.'"

"You have that memorized?" Feyra asked, looking up from her monotonous work.

Ortun glanced over his shoulder. "I read the book."

"And you remember everything you read?"

"Don't you?"

Feyra ground her teeth, until she couldn't stop herself from laughing. Ortun may have smiled, but it was hard to tell with his mask. He tossed Feyra one of her bracers for her to continue pretending to treat the leather. He didn't need to say a word, Feyra knew he was onto her. They'd known each other for too long to not recognize when the other was upset.

"Then what does it mean?" Feyra put down the bracer and rag. "All this talk of keys and gods falling? And what was that? Someone singing?"

"*Elys sang*," Ortun said. "I believe it's another language. An old one. Elysium is God's Land, according to some beliefs. A similar root could indicate a similar etymology."

"Yeah." Feyra rubbed the back of her neck. "That."

Bellona stood up, handing her mask to Ortun. "Melifacto has big plans. He's going to bring down the gods."

"What do you mean?" Feyra asked. "How is that possible?"

"All gods fall." Ortun shut his eyes. "It's the history of the world."

"Well then." Bellona had another one of her crazed smiles across her face. "We'll have to beat him to it. The Cradle of the World is an appetizer, Melifacto wants us to fight over it while he uses the Chalice of Light and goes for the main course. Ortun, start gathering the troops and readying the boats."

Ortun bowed. He passed Feyra, giving her the mask and making fleeting eye contact before leaving the sitting room. Feyra wasn't one to second guess Bellona, but there was too much intrigue for her liking. She needed Bellona to give her an order. But the Praetor stared silently at a half-completed map of Adathin, tapping her thumb against her chin.

"Lady Bellona," Feyra said, pushing herself away from the table and to her feet. "I would like to speak openly."

"Is there a problem?"

Feyra squeezed on the edges of the mask. "I don't like this. I don't like you having to hide in the shadows like some common thief."

"Oh?" Bellona crossed her arms. "What do you think I should do?"

"Show Melifacto you're not afraid of him."

Bellona laughed, so loud that Feyra recoiled. "Do you think I'm afraid of him?"

"I… I don't…"

"Subtlety is not for the cowardly." Bellona placed her hand on Feyra's shoulder. "It's for the clever. I'm not afraid of Melifacto, he's the one afraid. He's the one pounding on doors of gods. He's the one chasing fugitives into tunnels."

Feyra couldn't stop smiling. Bellona's energy crossed the distance between them and filled her. When she spoke, the world stopped to listen. Bellona put her hands on Feyra's face. A jolt of hot lightning shot up Feyra's spine.

"If we can take this from him," Bellona said, her breath caressing Feyra's face. "Then we will have power over him. It doesn't matter if any of this is real, it will crush him if we hold it in our hands."

"Then…" Feyra swallowed. She tried to keep her voice steady. "We take his hope from him."

Bellona blinked. She removed her hands and stepped away. "Yes. Hope."

She spun on her heel. Feyra touched the spot where Bellona had placed her hands, still feeling the residual warmth.

"What do you need me to do, my Lady?" Feyra said with a deep bow.

"Huh?" Bellona looked over the map of Adathin again. "Oh. Be ready to move when Melifacto does. We must stick to him until we can take our chance."

Feyra grabbed her armour and rushed out. Whatever Bellona needed her to do, Feyra would do it. She would drown the world in blood to ensure her lady's dreams came true.

The Daughters had access to all the resources that Adathin had left. The King believed the Cradle was somewhere in the lands he still controlled. There was evidence of monsters from legend and locations that match ones written about in stories. To him, it could be nowhere else. And the daughter who found it would inherit a kingdom, as decrepit as it may be when they were done.

—From the Journal of Jovin Gutterwake

Chapter Eleven
Undead Dole

The days passed quickly. Marta tore through books like she used to when she was young and hiding with her brother. Gaul worked much slower. He told Marta to stay in the library and went out to search the castle. At first she was worried he wouldn't come back. But he still needed her exodus stone to get through Nature's Grave. He was stuck with her.

They ran out of the food Marta brought on the second day. Gaul disappeared for six hours and returned with dried pork.

"These were behind a ward in the larder," he said. "I had to shatter the crystal to turn it off, but look. Hundred-year-old meat that looks freshly made. These Adathinites were ahead of their time."

Marta didn't tell him how nervous she got every time he left. The monster they saw when they first arrived and the figures coming from Marjyal were stuck in her mind. She had nightmares where recruiters in boar masks would break in and drag her back to the city.

"Can you read?" Marta asked Gaul.

Gaul threw another book onto the pile. "I've been doing it for the past three days. Do you think I'm tricking you?"

"You could be shy about it," she said. "There's nothing to be embarrassed about."

"Many soldiers in Ulkradia can't read. None of them are embarrassed, because they know reading won't help them keep a sword out of their gut. I, however, can read. Anori taught me."

"Anori? Who's that?" Marta grabbed a book and tossed it to him. "Mother? Sister? Wife?"

"She was my wife. Though not at the time. I'd known her since we were young. She used to sit under the trees and read books brought in from Imperium. She seemed to enjoy them, so I asked her to teach me."

"That's a lovely story." Marta used her book as a headrest. "My brother taught me to read, and our mother taught him."

"Jovin," Gaul said.

"Yes. Jovin Gutterwake."

Gaul swung his finger at Marta. "Which would make you Marta Gutterwake, right? Where'd you get a name like that?"

"We were born in Guttertown. Nearly everyone there gets called a Gutterwake. We just decided to embrace it. You got a last name? Can't imagine you're going to keep using Gaul the Ruthless."

"It doesn't matter."

Marta smiled and opened her book. "Nice to meet you, Gaul Doesn't Matter."

They continued to research into the night, when they slept on beds made of books. Marta would always wake up early and light a candle to get more research done. On the fourth day they heard a commotion from outside the window. Gaul crept over and swore. Marta joined him. On the bridge to Adathin Castle was a group of people dressed in white robes. One of the figures gestured angrily at another as they were cleaning the contents of a fallen bag. The yelling figure slapped the other one across the face.

"Marjyalians?" Gaul asked.

"Yes, but..." Marta had seen the white robes before, but only among one group. "That's the Guild of Doves."

"The clerics?" Gaul leaned out the window. "Why are they chasing us?"

"I don't know. If anyone would be chasing us, it would be the Boars. I can't imagine a reason why the Doves would come out this far."

"Hmm." Gaul left the window and picked up his swords from the table where he left them. "How about we go ask?"

Gaul stood alone in the entrance hall of Adathin Castle. He had his swords drawn and waved one about his feet, fanning the sprinkling of snow. He hadn't seen the King since the first day they arrived, but the groans and dragging were always on his mind. He was ready to run at the first hint of either of them.

He looked up at Marta waiting on the balcony, ready to give throwing knife support when the Doves attacked. She told him Doves weren't a very aggressive Guild, but dangerous just the same.

The doors opened and snow billowed into the main hall. The Doves entered — and stopped when they saw Gaul. Their robes hid heavy plate armour. They looked like Imperial Lightwalkers. In fact, Gaul was certain some of their armour was just repainted from when they belonged to Athas' guards. That would protect them from Marta's throwing knives. All the same, they were invested now.

"Welcome to Adathin Castle," Gaul said. "What brings you to my humble abode?"

A massive Dove stepped from the back of the group. He was clad in armour rusted with blood and a helm covering his face. The image of Matthis, the twisted Lightwalker, flashed in Gaul's mind. He tightened his grip on his swords.

A fair-haired woman stepped forward. "I recognize you from the Pits," she said. "Gaul the Ruthless. Where's your little friend, Gaul? The one who rescued you."

Gaul kept his gaze from revealing Marta's hiding place. "Why do you ask?"

"Because, my pretty." She drew her sword, followed by a symphony of metal from her half-dozen companions. "We're here to claim the reward."

Gaul narrowed his eyes.

"Melifacto has put a bounty on the girl that freed you. Give her to us and you can join in the wealth."

Gaul paced. He was wrong. Marjyal wasn't after him. The Praetor of Owls wanted Marta.

"She's gone," Gaul said. "Freeing me was part of paying back a debt. We separated as soon as we left Marjyal. You're better to look in the sewers for her."

"You left her for the little dragons?" The woman looked at the massive Dove.

"He's lying, Gret," the massive Dove spoke with an inhumanly deep voice.

Gret pointed her sword at Gaul. "Last chance, Gaul. Else Harken will have to break you."

"I'm not afraid of monsters," Gaul said.

"I'll bring him to Dianathos," Harken said, creaking his gauntlets. "Everyone answers when the Ghost Hand asks questions."

Harken stepped forward, then in a burst of smoke, he grasped Gaul by the throat. He hurled him against the grand staircase. The stairs punched into Gaul's back. In another burst of smoke, Harken was on the stairs as well.

Gaul thrust a sword into Harken's neck. There was no resistance. Harken grabbed Gaul and tossed him yet again. He smashed into a suit of armour on the first stair landing, sending the pieces clattering to the ground. His swords flew to either side.

"Gaul!" Marta shouted. Knives flew at the Doves and they defended themselves with their shields.

They were too heavily armoured for Marta to take them out hurling knives. She would have to jump down, something Gaul prayed she wouldn't do. Marta had a different idea. She grabbed the rope she had set up and slid down to the main floor. A Dove charged her with a sword. She parried the blade away and sunk her knife into his neck.

"Get the girl!" Gret shouted.

Harken turned to Marta and started smoking. Gaul grabbed him by the neck plate. The armour solidified, the smoke twisting until it faded away. Harken couldn't disappear while Gaul had a hand on him, lucky for Marta.

Fire burned in his gut as he yanked Harken back, sending the big thing clattering to the ground. Gaul couldn't fully unleash, not with Marta there. He grabbed the gauntlets from the broken suit of armour and put them on. Harken tried to smoke again, but Gaul put a hand on his chest.

"Your fights with me, will-o'-wisp." Gaul dropped a heavy fist to Harken's chest, crumpling the rusted metal.

Harken pushed Gaul off him and stood. He was more interested in fleeing, but every punch Gaul threw stopped him from smoking.

Out of the corner of his eye, Gaul could see Marta battling with the other Doves. She could put up a fight, but it was all defensive. The Doves were circling. It wouldn't be long before they got her.

Gaul swung at Harken. Harken didn't block, he stepped aside and pushed slightly on Gaul's arm. It wasn't much, but Gaul was off balance just long enough for Harken to turn to smoke.

"He's coming for you, Marta!" Gaul tossed his gauntlets aside and grabbed the closest of his swords.

Marta had just pushed a Dove aside when Harken's smoke got to her. He formed and drove his fist into her chest. Marta flew back, clutching where Harken had struck.

Gaul kicked off the railing and flew down the stairs. He slashed the back of a Dove's calf then across his face as he collapsed. Marta was back on her feet. She was much faster than her opponent. Each of Harken's swings went wide when she twirled out of the way.

Gret and her two remaining Doves stepped in front of Gaul. "Get her out of here," she called to Harken. "We'll deal with him and follow."

"You'll fall before I do," Gaul said.

The Doves readied their spears. Gret held her shield and sword firm. A tunnel of red grew around them. Until a groan came from one of the hallways leaving the entrance, followed by a slow dragging. The monster had impeccable timing.

"What is that?" One of the Doves spun toward the groaning, spear shaking in hand.

"Support." Gaul stepped back onto the stairs.

A hand made of bodies grabbed the balcony supports and the monster dragged itself into the entrance hall. The King stuck out the top, grasping with his own withered hands at air.

"Mar save us," one Dove said under his breath.

The monster oriented on him and pulled itself closer. The Dove screamed and charged with his spear. A malformed hand crushed him, splattering blood across the stonework floor. When it drew back, the Dove's body was being absorbed into the fleshy mass.

Gret grabbed the other Dove and shoved him forward. He too was smashed and absorbed.

"Run! Flee!" Gret dropped her weapons and turned tail.

The monster swung and clipped Gret. She sailed through the air and crashed into the front wall as a bloody mess.

Harken looked up at the creature as it turned toward him. He growled, then exploded into smoke. His armour dropped as an empty shell, leaving Marta to face the King alone.

Gaul charged up the stairs and grabbed one of the gauntlets he had used earlier. The monster pulled itself closer to Marta. He aimed for the ridge of bodies constituting its spine and threw the gauntlet. It bounced off and the monster stopped.

"Over here!" Gaul picked up his other sword. He stood at the top of the grand staircase as the monster dragged itself around.

Marta ran into view. She pointed up. Gaul followed her finger to the crystal chandelier. On the balcony was the winch mechanism. He pointed toward it and Marta took off at a sprint, scaling a cracked pillar.

Gaul sheathed his swords and grabbed the other gauntlet. He hurled it at the King's head. The monster took the hit and swung back. Gaul dove out of the way. Its massive fist cracked the stone wall where he once stood.

"Faster, Marta!" Gaul cried as he rolled under another swipe.

The monster's arms were so long it didn't need to climb the stairs to reach him. With each swing it sprayed putrid fluid across the hall. It never tired. Gaul, on the other hand, was already beginning to feel burning in his lungs. He let the fire grow in his gut to offset the drain. Crimson shoots faded in and out of his eyes.

A mighty downward blow sent Gaul jumping backwards. The stairs cracked. The monster stopped and King's corpse rose its eyeless gaze to Gaul. The air grew cold in his lungs. He tried to move, but his legs refused to respond. A sick grin spread across the King's lips. The monster grabbed both handrails and pulled itself up the stairs.

Steel screamed and the chandelier dropped. It landed on the thickest part of the monster's back, sending repulsive green blood into the air. The King unleashed a wheezy scream.

"Don't stand there like an idiot," Marta yelled, standing next to a broken winch. "Run!"

Gaul took the second set of stairs to the balcony three at a time. Marta waved him into a small room and followed. They charge into a lounge, complete with once impressive furnishings now covered in frost. Gaul headed toward a door on the other wall when Marta screamed.

The monster had stretched itself as much as it could and grabbed onto her bag. It looked almost dainty as its massive finger-like appendages grasped onto the thin leather. Marta held onto the door frame for her life. Gaul slid forth, drawing and slicing the bag's strap in one movement. Marta flew forward, but stayed on her feet.

She turned back to the door. "My bag!"

"It's not worth it!" Gaul grabbed her and threw her toward the second door. "Let's go."

She looked between Gaul and where her bag disappeared. Gritting her teeth, she ran out. The monster howled a pitiful sound, until it became like weeping. Gaul found himself listening for any sign of humanity in those cries. Deep in the wretched echoes, he heard words.

"I'm sorry."

Or maybe he imagined it.

He left the baying of the monster and returned with Marta to the library. Marta slapped life into her face and headed for the books.

"You can't be serious," Gaul said.

"We still need to find where Jovin has gone." She picked up the book she was last reading.

Gaul tore the book from her hands. "You have some questions to answer. Why does Melifacto have a bounty on you?"

"I don't know." She snatched for the book, but Gaul kept it behind his back. "Look, when I was trying to find a way around the tunnel gate, I saw him. He was looking for me. He called me by name."

"Do you know him?"

"No!" She leapt from her chair, chewing her thumbnail as she paced. "I don't think so. He doesn't seem familiar."

"He certainly wants you bad enough." Gaul handed the book back to her. "Any idea what the smoke-man was?"

"A homunculus. The Guild of Doves' ultimate weapon. They're made from dust and don't really have a body. Only the Praetor of Doves can create them. He has a doll that acts as the creature's heart — it can always return to it. That must be where it went."

"That means the Guild of Doves knows we're here." Gaul rubbed the back of his neck. "We need to get out of the castle. If that monster wasn't bad enough, we have more Marjyalians on the way."

"We haven't found where Jovin is yet!"

"I think your brother would rather you be safe than dragged back to Marjyal for who knows what."

Marta poked Gaul in the chest. "Would you rather we wander randomly? We need a direction."

"No." He slapped her hand away. "We have a direction. North."

"But—"

"I have given you my time and you have repeatedly lied to me. The trail is cold and we have a city looking for us. I'm sorry, but we're done."

Marta squared her jaw. Her grip tightened around her book and she stared at the floor. Gaul crossed his arms, unwilling to yield.

"One night," she finally said.

"What?"

"Give me one night. They're not going to get here in that time and that creature hasn't found us yet. I don't even think it could fit through the door."

Gaul looked at the double doors. They were big, but the monster filled entire hallways. He took off his coat and tossed it aside. "One night, Marta." He unclasped his sword belt and slammed it on the table. "One night then we are leaving. And I don't mean this castle. I mean we are leaving this entire accursed kingdom."

Marta said nothing. She watched Gaul as he settled into a chair. The sun would be down soon, so he wanted to get some rest. He was sure Marta wouldn't find anything, but still she wouldn't be sleeping any time soon.

When Gaul awoke, he was met by Marta wielding a candlestick and a smile. The library was bathed in shadow, save for the glow from Marta's light.

"I found it," she said.

"What?" Gaul shielded his eyes from the candlelight.

"Come on."

She grabbed his arm and dragged him out of his seat. Gaul was drowsy enough to allow it, and she led him to an open book. It was set out next to a map of a land Gaul didn't recognize.

"What is that?" Gaul asked.

"It's a map of Adathin Castle and the surrounding lands," Marta said. "Goes all the way to the Sorrow Sea and some ways east. I don't know. I don't know much outside of Marjyal. Oh! It has Marjyal." She pointed to a mark north of the castle.

"Where'd you get it?"

"I found it in, uh, another part of the castle"

"You left the library with that thing moving around?"

"I haven't heard it since I got it with the chandelier. Maybe it's recovering somewhere. Besides…" She sighed and leaned against the table. "I was looking for my bag. No luck."

Gaul tapped on the open book. "Just tell me what you found."

"Alright." She put down the candle and picked up the book. "This is a written account by Sebanna, The King's middle daughter."

"I thought she didn't do anything special."

"I thought so too, and then fourteen years after the King made his decree, she returned. And she brought the Chalice of Light with her."

Gaul wasn't tired any more. "She found the Cradle of the World?"

"Here, listen." Marta began reading from the book. "'I returned triumphant to find my home a shadow of its former self. My younger sister had lost Dothrin to poison and now overlooks a new city with a man who calls himself the Voice of Mar. My older sister is dead. The land she worked on destroyed and the people despising her. I returned home with the prize, not that it meant anything anymore.

"'I had given the Chalice to my father and slept. When I awoke, the castle was empty. I walked the lonesome halls, calling out for anyone to answer me. It had grown cold in the night. I found them in the throne room. The king's court had joined into one. They writhed pathetically on the ground, and at their head was my father. The good King was bound to this creature. He clutched onto the Chalice with all of his might.'"

Gaul held up his hand to stop Marta. "That thing is everyone who served in the King's court? The Chalice of Light made that?"

"Let me continue. 'I removed the Chalice and left him there, praying he would find death soon. It seems clear now mortals are not meant to wield the power that comes from the divine. The search for it has destroyed my family. I will return the Chalice to the Cradle and complete the work on the archive around it. My followers will ensure no one trifles with powers beyond their control again. I, however, will descend to the bottom of Black Hypogea and repent my actions. I'm sorry, Father. I should never have returned.'"

The last syllable echoed through the empty library. Gaul leaned against the table and crossed his arms. He couldn't imagine what Sebanna felt when she returned home. Her sisters were gone, one to Mar and the other to the Gate Beyond. Then her father became that monster.

"That's a sad story," Gaul said. "But it doesn't tell you where to go.

"But it does." She closed the book and turned to the map. "Sebanna's Archive is actually marked on here. Look."

She pointed at a cove on the west coast. It seemed to be several days walk from the Castle. Someone had added the note 'Sebanna's Archive.'

"What's that?" Gaul pointed at a scratching around one of the rivers between the castle and the coast.

"I think that means it's a swamp."

"We're going to have to go through it if we want to get to the inlet."

Marta looked up from the map and gave him a bump with her shoulder. "So you're still in for the journey?"

"I made a deal." He rolled the map up. "We're leaving at first light."

Marta gave a squeal of excitement and hurried to the stack of records she had made a bed out of. Gaul rubbed his eyes and walked back to his own makeshift bed. He reached into his tunic and pulled out Anori's necklace. He tapped the pendent Athas had left on it.

"Find the Cradle," the young priest had said, "and fill the Chalice."

Was he talking about the Chalice of Light? The Cradle is just a place, any place one might want to call holy, but the Chalice was something else. What was Athas doing? What did he want Gaul to do?

Those questions would have to wait. Gaul and Marta would be on the road again come morning.

The youngest daughter, Isildia, was a priestess. She turned to religion to find the Cradle, praying to gods for guidance. Even as her faith began to waiver, she rallied her people to darker arts. She would sacrifice anything to achieve her ends, a trait she inherited from her father. The gods must have hated her cruelty, for they sank her city, Dothrin, in a bog of poison.

After this, she abandoned the search and took up the worship of Mar, Anima of Revels.

—From the Journal of Jovin Gutterwake

Chapter Twelve
Fallow Fen

Gaul and Marta departed the castle across the same bridge the Doves entered. The King's Court left a horrid smelling pool of blood in the entrance hall, but the creature itself was nowhere to be found. Not that they were looking for another encounter. They hurried across the snowy bridge.

On the other side was a hand cart with a flaming horn, Marjyal's symbol, on the side. It had some weapons and supplies, some rations fresher than the salted pork they had taken from the castle. They each took a satchel and filled it with food. Gaul grabbed some sunstones and, of course, Marta replenished her stock of knives.

"With all this food we shouldn't have to hunt for at least the trip to the archive," Gaul said. "Maybe even the way back."

Marta nodded as she snapped into a carrot.

They headed westward, following the river toward the marshland in the distance. The snow disappeared soon after leaving the castle. When Marta looked back, she could still see the faint shimmer in the air and the white caps of the roof.

They walked throughout the days and at night they slept under the stars. The oppressive atmosphere was gone, and they could enjoy the night air. Marta spoke of the history of Adathin, but it never felt like she added anything Gaul didn't know by now. Her conversation partner was hardly engaged. Gaul, already a quiet man, had become more withdrawn since they left the castle. Now, as they sat on the riverbank, listening to the nighttime hum of the Adathin countryside, their distance from each other felt miles apart.

Marta laid her bundled up scarf on the ground as a pillow, but didn't lie down. Gaul had his elbows on his knees and a handful of rocks he flicked into the water. Every plop as the stone disappeared under the slow current punctuated the silence.

"It would be nice if we had some bedrolls or something," Marta said. "In case it gets any colder."

Plop. Another stone struck the water.

Marta sighed. They worked so well together when they were in danger. Getting through the dracolings, escaping the Doves, running from the King's Court. They were a good team — but that was it. Gaul tossed the last of the handful of stones. He reached into his shirt and pulled out the gold and steel necklace. Athas' pendant dangled off it, but Gaul's focus was on the links, running his fingers back and forth across the metal.

"Was that Anori's?" Marta asked.

"Yes." Gaul spoke like Marta wasn't there.

"How'd she die?"

Gaul dropped his head then tucked the necklace away.

Marta hugged her knees to her chest. "I just figure you don't go through all this for someone who is still alive. I'm sorry if it came out rude, or something."

"It's not your concern." He shut his eyes and hung his hands limply off his knees.

The river burbled along, but Gaul didn't say anything else. His breaths got slower, but more rhythmic. For minutes Marta watch in confused interest as Gaul's chest swelled and shrank, the only motion on an otherwise still form.

"Are you sleeping?" Marta finally asked.

Gaul's eye twitched. "I'm meditating."

"Is that how you turn your eyes red?"

"No. Well… no, it's not. I'm clearing my mind. It helps me sleep."

Marta mirrored his position, with her elbows resting on her knees and her hands hanging forward. "I haven't seen you do it before."

"It's been a trying few days. There are things that I would rather keep pushed away. Images and feelings I need to quiet."

"Oh." She shut her eyes. "When I want to forget things I just drink."

"That's not really an option now, is it?"

Marta gave up on the meditation and threw herself onto her makeshift pillow. "That's true. I'm probably distracting you from clearing your mind, huh?"

"Yes."

"Have fun with that." Marta turned to the side, trying to squirm into a comfortable position in the grass. Gaul's breaths became a lullaby as she drifted off to sleep.

* *

Another day and night passed before the land turned from hard ground to soft marsh. The trees became thin and sickly. A light fog rolled off the water and the air grew damp.

Marta stepped onto a partially submerged piece of stone. It looked to be a collapsed fortification. "Was there a city here?" she asked.

"You're the one with the map," Gaul said.

"It only showed a swamp. It also warned not to come here."

Gaul hopped onto the wall with Marta. "Which makes me all the happier we came."

"That same warning could apply to everywhere around here." Marta laughed and leapt to the far shore.

Gaul was about to follow when something caught his eye. "Don't touch the water, Marta," he said.

Marta spun back and followed his gaze. One of the trees had toppled into the water. Its leaves had gone black and the bark peeled off in rotting clumps. Marta stepped back from the shore.

"I know where we are," she said. "This is Isildia's first city."

"First city? Before Marjyal?"

"Dothrin, remember from Sebanna's note? It was supposed to be close to her father's castle but sunk into a poison swamp at some point during her search for the Cradle."

Gaul looked at the collapsed wall he stood on. As he scanned the marshlands, he spotted towers and buildings sticking out of the muck. As Marta explained it, he could see where a city once stood.

"Why do we always find the worst places?" Gaul said, throwing his hands into the air. "Underground city of little dragons, castle with an aberration, and I'm quite looking forward to the monster that lives in a poison goddamn swamp."

"We're in a land of ancient gods!" Marta spread her arms as wide as her smile. "Here there be monsters!"

In the distance, wood cracked followed by a tree falling. Birds cawed and rustled leaves as they flew away.

"Maybe we leave the grandiose speeches for later." Gaul leapt next to Marta. "Keep to the shore."

They continued into the marsh, taking care where they found their footing among the decaying roots and submerged buildings. Gaul made the jump from a stone wall to the base of a tree, catching himself. As he pulled his hand away, sap stretched from his palm to the bark. Clear water pooled around the roots with green algae and tiny ripples from skittering insects. As the water spread into the marsh it became cloudy and polluted once again. Life was coming back, or barely hanging. It would depend on your outlook, Gaul figured.

"Hey!" Marta called from ahead. "I don't want to spend the night here. Let's go."

Gaul wiped his hand clean using the bark and leapt after her.

The day turned into early evening when Gaul spotted a plume of smoke over the trees before them. "We better avoid that," Gaul said, pushing through the brush. "Could be more Marjyalians."

"I wouldn't be surprised anymore. I'd rather not see anyone until my br — Ow!" Marta clutched her hand.

Gaul stopped and turned back. "What happened?" he asked.

"I just scraped my hand." She stretched her left hand open and closed. "It's kinda burning."

Gaul rushed back to her. The skin on the back of her left hand had turned red around a small abrasion.

"Actually." Her skin turned pallid. "It's burning a lot." She screamed, clutching her hand. Her knees buckled and Gaul caught her. "It's crawling up my arm!" She scratched at her shoulder.

"Calm down, Marta!" He looked around, hoping to find an herb or poultice hanging off a tree or something else so miraculous. All he saw was the smoke trail curling into the sky.

"It doesn't feel so bad now." She spoke through deep gasps. "Almost… numb."

Marta's fingertips had gone black and the veins in her arm were a visible crimson. Her hand shook, even as she tried to hold it still. She tried to stand but fell back into Gaul's arms. Gaul swept her legs out and picked her up.

"Where are we going?" Marta asked.

"The smoke." Gaul started walking with Marta in his arms.

"But… Marjyal… the Guilds."

"If it's them, I'll kill them and take any medicine off their corpses."

He stepped over a log into a clearing. The smoke wafted up from the chimney of a small cabin in the middle of the glade. A white fence surrounded the entrance. It was an idyllic sight to be seen in such a dark place.

He took another step and was greeted by the sound of a bowstring being pulled back. Gaul froze. Footsteps squelched on wet grass.

"What are you doing here?" A woman stepped into view. She was clothed in hide and furs with a stone arrow nocked and pointed at Gaul's neck. Her copper hair was tangled up in thick clumps and wrapped with a scarf. A bundle of hares hung off her belt. Her gaze flickered to Marta for half a second.

"She's been poisoned," Gaul said. "Scratched by some plant in the—"

"Deaththistle. The name says it all." The woman stepped back. "But it's none of our concern what fate befalls fools who wander where they don't belong."

Red haze seeped into Gaul's vision. But, he couldn't rightly drop Marta to the wet ground. "Help her," he growled.

"You didn't say please."

"Please."

The woman narrowed her eyes. "You aren't a slave to pride. Interesting. Move to the house and if I see something I don't like, you get an arrow through the back of the head."

Gaul walked toward the cottage. Marta muttered nonsensical sounds under her breath. Her eyes flickered but never opened. When they reached the door, the woman circled back around and opened it. She stepped in backwards.

Candles upon sconces lit the interior, bolstered by a crackling fireplace. Plants hung from the ceiling and the furniture was raw wood bound together. Another woman covered head to toe in wolf's fur was at a stove. The smell of cooking stew filled the air.

"Who have you brought with you, Lenn?" the second woman asked, turning around.

She was older, with grey hair bundled up on her shoulders. A simple linen head wrap covered her forehead and reached down to shield her eyes. Yet, she stepped casually around the furniture that could trip her to meet the visitors.

"They were on the edge of the glade," Lenn said. She never took her eyes off Gaul and Marta, holding her bow down but with an arrow still nocked. "The smaller one was scratched by deaththistle."

"By the Spirits, Lenn-ya. You know how much time matters in this." She waved Gaul over to a bed in the corner. "Come, put her down over here."

"Ba-ya, I was being careful. They—"

"Are injured. We cannot heal the land by forgetting the people. Try to be more accepting."

Gaul laid Marta onto the bed. Ba-ya yanked a yellow herb off the ceiling. Lenn had already grabbed a cup of water and handed it to her. They had done this before. Ba-ya put a sprig of the herb into the water and mixed it together with her finger. She eased open Marta's mouth and poured the solution in. Marta tried to cough it back up, but Ba-ya held her mouth shut. Her breathing steadied.

"Is she going to be okay?" Gaul asked.

Lenn started to speak, but Ba-ya took her by the arm. "The doldranite will keep the Gate at bay for now," Ba-ya said. She knelt next to Marta and took her infected hand in her own. "She's very strong. Something inside her is keeping her alive. What are your names?"

"I'm Gaul, and that's Marta." He leaned next to Ba-ya. "What else does she need?"

"Gathos' Tongue. Have you heard of it?"

"It's a flower." He ran his fingers through his hair. "It grows here?"

"In the places life still finds hold." She rested Marta's hand onto her chest and patted it. "I need at least twelve bulbs. Lenn, go with him."

"Ba-ya," Lenn stepped toward the older woman.

She stopped her with a look. "If you distrust this man so much, consider this a way to keep an eye on him."

Lenn growled. She grabbed her bow, tossed her bundle of hares aside, and pointed for Gaul to go first. Gaul gave Ba-ya a wary glance.

"Do not worry, young dust." Ba-ya returned to her stew, still simmering on the stove. "Lenn-ya will not shoot you unless you provoke her. So, do try not to provoke her."

She cackled as Gaul stepped out the door, followed by Lenn. Lenn jerked her head northward. Deciding to take Ba-ya's advice not to provoke, Gaul followed Lenn's directions and headed into the swamp.

Gaul searched for an hour but only found two Gathos' Tongue. They were small blue flowers with five petals curling out from a dark core. The entire time Lenn would stand back from him, occasionally on a tree root or fallen stonework for better vantage. She always kept one hand stroking the feathers on a nocked arrow.

Gaul pulled aside some brush, but yet again found no blue. Lenn let out a small laugh.

"You clearly have a problem with me," Gaul said, tossing a handful of leaves aside.

Lenn sat on a collapsed tower's parapet. "Was I not subtle enough? Ba-ya may be trusting but I know the terror that comes from these lands. This place used to be a thriving city and now look at it. Poison flowing like a river. And you think I should just trust someone I don't even know. Where are you from, Gaul?"

"Ulkradia."

"Can't say I've heard of it. Is it to the east?"

"North." Gaul stepped onto the tower. "Far north. Past Nature's Grave."

Lenn's eyes flashed wide. "You're an outlander?" She returned her arrow to her quiver and a sly smile spread across her lips. She scanned Gaul up as down as though seeing him for the first time and stuck her hand to her hip. "Very, very interesting. I saw a patch of blue bulbs this way. Come on."

Gaul let out a puff of air and squinted at Lenn. She looked back over her shoulder with a grin. The fact he wasn't from Adathin had certainly turned her opinion of him around.

Lenn led Gaul through the twisting roots and dangling branches of the swamp. Her keen eyes picked out the deep blue of Gathos' Tongue long before Gaul could have a chance. They didn't talk and she still kept an eye on him. Though the eye had a different feeling behind it. They returned to Ba-ya with twelve blue bulbs in hand.

She pushed the bulbs to her nose and inhaled the sweet scent. "This will do fine," she said. "I'll whip a tincture together."

Gaul crouched next to Marta's resting form. Her coat had been hung up, revealing the dark veins tracing up her arms and around her neck. Her chest rose and fell with constant rhythm and her eyes flickered beneath the lids. "How is she?" he asked.

"I told you before, there is something strong inside keeping her alive." Ba-ya motioned for Lenn to hand her a muddler. "You're fighters, both of you."

"I suppose," Gaul said.

"Most who walk with blades are." She put a drop of brown liquid onto the bulbs and crushed them with a pestle. "This'll take some work. How about you go wait outside and take your mind off it?"

"No offense, ma'am." Gaul stood up. "But while I appreciate you helping Marta, we still don't know you."

"At this point, it would be too late if you truly distrusted me. We need to have faith in each other when the world turns dark. I'll take care of your friend, but you need to rest."

Gaul looked to Lenn. She sat by the stove, picking at her nails and smiling.

"Let me know as soon as she wakes up," he said, heading out the front door.

The sun had set, but he was shocked to find the clearing aglow. Tiny lights rose from the ground and filled the air. They cast a warm radiance that made the field look like it was full of small twinkling stars.

"They're called sparkbugs," Lenn said, stepping out of the cottage. She carried two chairs. She left one next to Gaul as she passed by. "They live underground during the day then crawl out when the sun goes down."

"I've never seen anything like them before." Gaul took the chair and set it up within the fence boundaries, next to Lenn's. "But even with them, why would you live in a place like this? The water's poisoned — or is poison."

"For exactly that reason," she said, leaning toward Gaul. "We are here to cure the swamp of its infection. When we arrived, it was entirely toxic. The place you sit right now was the worst of it, a fallow pool of deterioration. But now the sparkbugs have a place to play."

"That's a noble endeavour."

"We were born for it." Lenn twisted around in her chair until she could lean over her arm rest. "So, that woman in there, what's your relationship with her?"

"We're travelling together. It's a long story, but let's just say we're kind of stuck together for now."

"You're a good man to care for her if you're just stuck together." She propped her chin on her hands. "Tell me about Ulkradia."

Gaul told her about the mountains that hid his village from all the went searching for it. He told her about the plains where they would go on summer hunting expeditions. They even discussed the battles Gaul fought in, with other tribes or invaders from the east. Lenn always had more questions, and she always had an elated smile.

"Have you heard of an archive on the coast?" Gaul asked. "It would be on an inlet just west of here."

"There's a building in a cove about a day away," Lenn said. "Can't say I've ever been inside, so I can't tell you if it's an archive or not. Why are you going there?"

"We're looking for someone."

"Who—"

The cottage door swung open and Ba-ya stepped out. "Gaul," she said. "Your friend is awake."

Gaul jumped up from his chair and rushed inside. Marta sat up on the bed, rubbing her face. Relief washed over Gaul.

"Where are we?" she asked, ruffling her hair.

"I followed the smoke to a cottage," Gaul said, sticking his hands into his pockets. "The people inside saved your life."

Marta looked at her left arm. The black had disappeared, and her scrape nothing more than a light-red line. Lenn and Ba-ya stepped up behind Gaul.

"This is Lenn and Ba-ya," Gaul said. "This is their cottage. They—"

"I know who they are." Marta slid to the edge of the bed. "They're druids."

Lenn laughed. "She must be from the area."

Gaul turned to Lenn and Ba-ya. "What is she talking about?"

"Let's see what she has to say," Lenn said, crossing her arms.

"Just stories," Marta said. "Stories of an old blind woman and a young huntress who live in a cottage and kill all who enter their lands."

"We kill them because they attack us." Lenn sat in a chair and leaned on the dinner table. "If they take this land back it will return to poison. So, I stop them."

"The stories say they've been here for centuries."

"Are you immortal?" Gaul asked.

"No, no." Ba-ya laughed. "But we are not human, if that's what you're wondering. Tell me, young dust, do you know of the Fool King of Adathin?"

Gaul nodded.

"His youngest, Isildia, founded two cities. The one that still stands is Marjyal, the city devoted to Mar, Anima of Revels." She tilted her covered head toward Marta. "Your home city, I believe."

Lenn sat forward in her chair.

"How do you know?" Marta asked.

"Marjyalians have an aura they can't ever escape from," Ba-ya said. "But we aren't talking about Marjyal, this is about the home she built first. The city used to stand on this very spot. Dothrin. It was built before the King made his decree. A city of prosperity and faith. But after the search for the Cradle started, Isildia changed. Her inquisition spread across the land and her followers' prayers changed to finding the home of the First Gods. Maybe it was this selfishness that cursed Dothrin to fall, for soon poison came to the land. It sprang from the ground like water and the city began to sink. Isildia's followers abandoned her, and she abandoned her faith. It was then the Voice of Mar found her and turned her to the cult of revels. When they left, our ancestors arrived. The Spirits of the World abandoned this place and so us druids will return them and heal the land."

Lenn nodded. She stood from her chair and rested her hands behind her head. "And that's what we've been doing," she said, making pointed eye contact with Marta. "And dealing with any Marjyalians who are foolish enough to come back."

"We should go, Gaul," Marta said. She stood, and promptly fell back onto the bed.

"You should rest," Ba-ya said. "There is still some poison in your system and besides, it is far too dark out for us to force you into the night. Stay at least until morning."

"It's not a bad idea," Gaul said to Marta. He took off his coat and hung it next to Marta's jacket.

"We'll be in the next room over if you need anything," Ba-ya said.

"Gaul." Lenn stepped forward. "I was thinking we could talk a little more before we go to bed."

"No, no." Ba-ya pushed her toward the door in the back corner. "It is much too late. Everyone needs their sleep."

Lenn gave silent protest but was eventually forced out of the room. Gaul glanced about. There wasn't much furniture to speak of. He took a chair from the table and placed it against the wall.

"What are you doing?" Marta asked.

"I've slept in more uncomfortable positions."

"That's…" Marta slid over on the bed, squeezing herself as hard into the corner as she could. "There's enough space for both of us."

"That's really not necessary."

She slapped the fabric. "Hop on, and don't get handsy."

"Don't make this any weirder than it already is." Still, he removed his swords and flopped next to Marta.

They both stared at the ceiling. The buzzing of insects filled the silence.

"How long has it been since you've slept on a bed?" Marta asked.

"They had beds in the infirmary in Marjyal," Gaul said. "I was unconscious for most of that, though. You?"

"Not since Landus. That was a long time ago." She sighed and tapped her fingers on her stomach. "Hey. Uh, thank you."

"I wasn't going to let you die."

"You need me to get home." Her voice crackled with the words. "I know."

"That's not why…" He turned to look at her, while she stared at the ceiling without ever looking at it. "I'm sorry you think that of me."

"It's the only thing I know of you. That and you had a wife, her name was Anori, and you chased down a priest to get her necklace back."

"I don't know what you expected, Marta. I told you no after you tried to follow me out of that bar in Landus. I never wanted to travel with someone. I'm fine being alone."

"I'm not. I'm tired of being alone. My entire life it was me and my brother. Us against Marjyal. Then in Landus…" She tapped her head against the pillow. "No one wanted me in Landus."

"Didn't you have a husband?"

"He was nice. He liked me and I thought if I was married they would have to accept me. But I don't think I ever loved him." She let out a long breath and closed her eyes. "He was less nice after we were married. One day, I decided I wanted to go after Jovin. My husband followed me into Nature's Grave. I don't remember what happened next, but I lost a week. They found me at the edge of the forest. They never found my husband, and I had this." She dragged her pinky along her lip scar.

"I'm sorry."

She opened her eyes again. "I'm not that broken up. I guess you could say I wouldn't do for him what you're doing for Anori. Still, for a moment it was nice not to be alone. And when I find Jovin..."

When she found Jovin, Gaul would be free. He could go home. That's what he wanted, wasn't it? To go home to an empty house. To people who hated him, or were afraid of him, or both. He knew what it was like to be alone in a crowd.

"I understand," he muttered, barely loud enough for Marta to hear.

She rolled onto her side, pressing her back against the wall, but she didn't say anything. She stared at the side of Gaul's head, waiting.

Gaul continued, "I was never welcome in my home either. You want to know about me? About why my eyes turn red? I'm what my people call a trublüdar."

Marta didn't react. He shouldn't have expected her to.

"It's an ability written into my blood. A few Ulkradians can Ignite. Sends us into a something like a battle rage, serene and furious at the same time. It takes training and patience and a surprising amount of self-control. That's why people like me are taught to read and meditate. But we're still weapons, pointed to destroy enemies and raze villages. Each of us worth ten soldiers or more."

"That's what turns your eyes red?"

"It turns everything red. Faces become nothing. All I can see are hearts beating blood. It makes it easier. People aren't people anymore." He shook his head. "Invaluable in war, but in peace... in peace they sign us into the auxiliary and send us home. They give us the army weaponry like we were one of them but, no, we had no homes. Once our ability manifested we grew up in camps that taught us how to kill, so all they could do was send us back to where they found us. People weren't happy."

"That's horrible," Marta said.

"Anori thought I could be better. She believed in me. She thought I could be more than this fire in my blood. I promised her and myself I would never Ignite. And I failed. She's gone and I'm that monster again."

"That's ratshit, Gaul."

Gaul whipped his gaze to her, tensing his brow in confusion.

"Just because you have this ability doesn't mean you're a bad person. You're not a sword with one purpose, you're a living thing."

"You don't know me."

"Ugh." She twisted and flopped onto her back. "You keep saying that. You've saved me enough times I think I have a good feel for you. I'm sure it's crossed your mind Marjyal can also traverse Nature's Grave. But you didn't turn me over."

"I wouldn't leave you to people like that."

"That's my point. You're not a monster."

"You don't get it," Gaul said. "Anori understood, but she thought I could be better. I guess she was wrong, because I don't feel better. I've Ignited before and I will do it again."

"A lot of people put a lot of bad into your head." Marta spoke with a hard conviction that made Gaul want to believe her. "They want you to feel worthless.

In time, you believe them. It took a lot for me to walk away, but you can do it too. You're not worthless."

Gaul squeezed his fingers into his arm. Marta was nicer to him than he deserved. He wished he could see things from her point of view. But these voices in the back of his head kept screaming at him. Monster. Inhuman. Worthless.

"We should get some sleep," he said.

"Yeah." Marta settled into her side of the bed. "Thank you for telling me."

"Thank you for listening."

They drifted off into a well-deserved slumber.

Marta found herself staring at the wooden ceiling of the druid's cottage. The smell of herbs and flowers tickled her nose with their mashed-up scents. But that wasn't what woke her, or what kept her up. There was a pounding in her head. Dull at first, but it had worked its way from her spine around to the front of her brain. At first she was worried it was the deaththistle coming back, but it wasn't the same burning sensation. It was steady, and while it wasn't painful, it was unnerving all the same.

She looked at Gaul sleeping at her side. Someone like him, Marta would have expected loud snoring. But Gaul was silent when he slept. So much that if it wasn't for the rise and fall of his chest, she would have thought he was dead. Marta sat up, the bed groaning in reply. She had to stretch over Gaul, her foot barely touching the ground before she gave a little hop and stood free. She needed some air.

A cold breeze cut through Marta's shirt and pants as she stepped into the night. The clearing around the cottage was heavy with shadow, Meza's large moon partially hidden behind the clouds. An occasional dot of light flickered by in the distance. Glowing bugs that danced between the trees. Marta took a deep breath. The chill air filled her lungs and the pounding began to fade.

"Marta."

She spun around. No one was there. She waited to hear the voice again. It was soft and airy. It had to of been the wind or mishearing some odd bird. A shiver climbed along Marta's skin. She spun back.

Still nothing.

What's happening? she thought. *Nothing. Nothing's happening. You're close, don't lose it now.*

She sat on the grass, not caring about the cold dirt that froze her backside. The pounding had turned into a repetitive tap. It was like something was knocking on the door to her brain. She couldn't let them in.

It was when the eastern sky turned orange that Marta crept back inside.

The middle daughter, Sebanna, though few know that name, turned to history. She read book after book and eventually faded into obscurity. She seemed to enjoy collecting folktales. Here's one I found about a place called the Teeth of the Sea:

Yoderi, Anima of Storms, was being harassed by an earthen spirit. During the day, Yoderi would work to shape the coastline. She would smooth stone or form cliffs to try to create something beautiful. But during the night, an earthen spirit would tear the coastline apart. It would create ugly cracks and terrible reefs to rip at ship's hulls.

Yoderi could never catch the spirit, for it was clever and fast. And so it continued, undoing Yoderi's work and cackling as the morning came.

Thankfully, Yoderi eventually came up with a plan. Her father Gathos, Lord of the Wilds, assisted her by turning her into the very coastline itself. That night, the spirit arrived. As it landed on the shore, Yoderi struck. With Gathos' power, she turned the landscape sharp with spikes, piercing and slicing the earthen spirit apart. Its cackles faded, becoming the songbirds sing when the sun rises, reminding all beings gods are not to be trifled with.

The veracity of the story is debatable, but the landscape that inspired it is not.

—From the Journal of Jovin Gutterwake

Chapter Thirteen

The Teeth of the Sea

Gaul woke up to find Marta eating breakfast with Lenn and Ba-ya. Hare stew, by the smell of it. He stretched his body out with a series of satisfying cracks.

"Good morning," Lenn said cheerfully.

"I guess I slept deeper than I thought," Gaul said, swinging his feet off the bed. His swords were still right where he left them.

"We decided you needed some well-deserved rest." Ba-ya grabbed a wooden bucket from the corner. "Though, could you help me get some water from the well? My old bones aren't what they used to be."

"I… Yes, I suppose." He pushed his hands into his knees and stood, stumbling as the last of the sleep left him. He shook it out of his head and looked to Marta. "Are you going to be okay?"

"I'm alive," Marta said, her mouth full of stew. She swallowed and swung her spoon in his direction. "Help the lady."

Ba-ya offered the bucket. Gaul took it, but his gaze stayed on Marta. She leaned on one hand and scooped another piece of hare into her mouth. Her own gaze was locked on a long scratch across the table's surface.

"Come on," Ba-ya said, opening the cottage door. "The well's around back."

Gaul swung the bucket by the handle and followed Ba-ya out the door. Birds chirped, fluttering from tree to tree in pairs. The sun shone but the air was still crisp. Dew puffed up with each step Gaul put into the soft earth. Lenn and Ba-ya had truly found a beautiful place. One would be surprised to learn it was in a poisonous swamp.

"You're going to the Cradle," Ba-ya said.

Gaul snapped his gaze to her. "Marta told you?"

"No."

"Lenn told you about the archive?"

"No."

Gaul stopped. Ba-ya walked a few more steps, then stopped as well. She tilted her head back, listening for his reply.

"You're more than you seem to be, aren't you?" Gaul said.

Ba-ya smiled. "So are you. But what incites you to find the Cradle? You surely know how much pain it has caused."

"I made a deal."

"Oh, of course." She turned around and hobbled closer to Gaul. "Or perhaps you were searching for something, and now found yourself with no future and no destination. So, you chose one."

"What do you mean?"

She took the bucket from Gaul and headed toward the well. "Oh, who knows?"

"You certainly know how to say a lot that means absolutely nothing."

Ba-ya tied the bucket to the rope then lowered it into the well. "The meaning will become clear with time. Can I see the pendant?"

Gaul balked at the mention of Athas' pendant. Had it slipped out of his shirt at some point? Did Ba-ya search him in the middle of the night? She had figured out they were headed for the Cradle, why shouldn't she figure out the pendant as well?

He unclasped the necklace and handed it to her. She offered the rope in return.

"I do need your help getting the water," she said.

Gaul hauled up the filled bucket as Ba-ya held the pendent to the sun.

"Tell me about the pendant," Gaul said through puffs of air. "Athas called it a vessel."

"A vessel to contain Light. Not the kind that comes from the sun, no, no. The source of divine power. The Light that came from the Chalice and birthed the First Gods. There is merely a speck in here, but it could be enough to reseal the Cradle."

"Reseal the Cradle?"

"My, my, Gaul." Ba-ya leaned on the well. "They don't know much outside of Adathin do they? The Cradle is where the First Gods are imprisoned."

Gaul pulled the bucket out of the well and plopped it onto the ground, untying the rope. "What are you talking about?"

"When the First Gods were corrupted and overthrown, they were sealed by their children, the Divines, into the Cradle of the World. They used the Chalice of Light to lock the door. But, when Sebanna entered and removed the Chalice, she started an unbreakable chain of events that could end with the First Gods returning. Her Unseen scholars saw fit to form the Pantheon Church to fight against the oncoming darkness. Unfortunately, Adathin is devoid of Light, as it had been since the First Age. So, they make pilgrimage to the Cradle and place a spark into the Chalice to keep the world as it is for a time. Now, it is you who must finish the journey."

"Are… you want me to reseal the Cradle?"

"I'm merely telling you what you can do, young dust." She motioned for him to pick up the bucket. "No one can make you do anything. Invigorate the Light, or don't. But the choices you make — Marta too — will define much of the coming age."

"What will happen if the First Gods return?" Gaul asked as they walked back to the cottage.

"That's not for a little old lady to speculate."

"But, is that… bad? They defeated the Primordials after all. I thought they were supposed to be righteous and powerful, or at least that's what the elders would say."

"Things change over time — even gods."

A bird sang in the distance. They were almost back at the house.

"I don't know what you want me to do," Gaul said.

"Do what you will, young dust." She placed a hand on the fence and stopped. "I am also aware Lenn-ya fancies you."

Gaul stumbled to a stop, sending a cupful of water sloshing to the dirt. "Uh huh. You noticed?"

"I'm blind, not stupid," Ba-ya said with a smile. "And she's infatuated with the fact you're not from Adathin. See, this swamp is our home."

"Is she not allowed to leave?"

"We are druids. As long as the contract is unfulfilled, our life comes from our home. We can leave for short periods of time but if we don't return we will wither and die."

Gaul put the bucket down and leaned against the fence next to Ba-ya. "If the druids have been here since Dothrin fell, how are there only two of you?"

"We are not like mortals, young dust," Ba-ya said, "There are only ever two. Soon — sooner than perhaps I would like — I will return to the earth. And my spirit will create the next druid." She drooped her head. "And Lenn will have to teach them."

"Does that concern you?"

"Lenn will have to grow up quite a lot. And I'm worried I did not teach her well enough."

Gaul scratched the back of his head. He wasn't sure how to ease the mind of a druid. Instead he grabbed the bucket off the ground. "Let's go back inside."

For the first time, Ba-ya looked directly at Gaul. Even with her wraps, he could feel her eyes on him. She stared at him for several seconds. The birds chirped playfully. Then, a small smile grew across her face. She motioned for him to crouch and clasped the necklace back around his neck, patted him on the cheek, and turned to the cottage.

Marta watched Gaul and Ba-ya leave, followed by a minute of tense silence as Lenn spun a spoon on the table.

"So," Marta said. "You don't like that I was born in Marjyal."

Lenn glowered at Marta. She kept spinning the spoon.

"I'm not exactly proud of it. And I got out as soon as I could."

Sighing, Lenn laid the spoon flat. "Marjyalians come into the swamp. Try to take me or Ba-ya. I kill them. They try again. I kill them. They try again. Now I kill every one. Nothing good comes from Marjyal."

"Once again, I don't like it."

"It doesn't matter." She leaned toward Marta. "Marjyal gets in you. Twists you, even if you don't see it. Gaul already told me you're heading toward the building west of here. I know about the others."

"What?" Marta leaned in as well, not letting Lenn think she scared her. "What others?"

"Some Marjyalians came through a few days ago. They skirted along the north, too afraid to step into the swamp. Smart. They set up in the ruins on the western edge."

"What did these Marjyalians look like?"

Lenn cocked her head. "They wore white cloaks. The man leading them had this scar across his face."

"The Guild of Doves. We took out a few of them while we were in Adathin Castle."

"You killed them?" Lenn leaned back.

"A few. Some monster got the rest."

"You met the King's Court?" A grin grew across Lenn's face. "And you lived?"

"I didn't just meet it." Marta lifted her hand, then slammed it onto the table. "I dropped a chandelier on it."

"Incredible." Lenn shook her head. "I went there a few years back and after seeing that monstrosity, I wasn't itching to go that way again."

"Oh, don't get me wrong, I'm not looking to go back. The chandelier only stopped it for a short time. I'm sure it would be very upset to see me again."

They laughed. Lenn rubbed her temple. Marta figured she was probably bothered she shared a laugh with someone from Marjyal. It was a small victory for her, nonetheless.

The door swung open and Ba-ya entered. She weaved between the table and the counter, stepping over a footstool without any warning it was there. *Amazing*, Marta thought. It had to be some kind of magic. Maybe she was fluxblooded, like Gaul had mentioned. Or, it was simply because she was a druid.

Gaul entered second, holding a bucket full of sloshing water. Lenn lit up upon seeing him and helped him get the bucket onto the counter.

"We have a problem, Gaul," Marta said.

Gaul didn't respond. He was lost in thought, staring into the water.

"Gaul!" Marta said louder.

Gaul snapped back to reality. He turned to Marta with a confused look. "Did you say something?"

"Yes," Marta sighed. "I was talking with Lenn and she told me more of the Guild of Doves have set up in a ruin on the west side of the swamp."

"Ah," Ba-ya said, resting back in her chair. "The ruins of Dothrin's castle."

"Great." Gaul leaned on the counter and crossed his arms. "Another castle."

"Not a complete castle, mind you." Ba-ya wagged her finger toward Gaul. "So do try to have some positivity. It was never completed and even before sinking it was simply a shell."

"Still, it's full of Doves and I'd rather avoid them."

"You can't go south," Lenn said. She rested her arm on Gaul's shoulder. "The river that splits the ruins is far too wide to cross without a boat. You aren't likely to find a crossing anywhere close either."

"Okay. Then north?"

Lenn smiled. "That will bring you to the Teeth of the Sea."

"That would be perfect," Ba-ya said. "The river goes underground before that place. It's a landscape of jutting stones and narrow passages. Impossible to see in from the outside. They'll never know you were there."

"I see a problem." Marta stood from her chair and paced. "The homunculus that was in Adathin Castle returned to its heart, which I have to imagine the Praetor of Doves is carrying with him. That means they know we were in the castle, and if they aren't going to go through the swamp they likely will go through the Teeth."

"Are you saying we should take the long way?" Gaul asked.

"Of course not." Marta stepped closer to Gaul, making sure her gaze did not flicker to Lenn. "But considering what their goal is we should be aware."

Gaul nodded. He couldn't know the extent Marta feared being taken back to Marjyal, even if he suspected it. Melifacto's voice calling her name still echoed in her mind in moments of silence. She didn't want to find out why he asked for her.

"We need to get moving." Gaul stepped out from Lenn's arm. "Thank you so much for everything you've done for us."

Ba-ya bowed her head. "Good luck on the rest of your journey."

Gaul and Marta collected their things. Marta forced Gaul to eat before they left, but within half an hour they were stepping outside the cottage.

Lenn and Ba-ya waved from the fence line as Gaul and Marta headed back into the swamp. Lenn had described to them the safest way to the Teeth of the Sea, a path they had cleansed of all poison. Marta looked back as the cottage disappeared behind foliage.

"You know Lenn was into you," Marta said.

"I know." Gaul hopped over a tree root. He didn't look back.

"You didn't feel like…" Marta made various odd noises.

Gaul turned to her with a bewildered look. "No."

"I hope it wasn't on account of me being there."

"No."

"Her mother being there?"

"No."

"On the way back you could—"

"Marta." Gaul stopped. "No."

Marta raised her hands in defeat.

Gaul rolled his eyes and resumed walking. "I'm not getting attached to someone I won't be seeing again," he said.

"You know." Marta jogged to walk beside Gaul. "You're allowed to have moments of happiness. Even small ones."

Gaul sighed then patted Marta on the shoulder. "I'll figure it out eventually."

* *

After a week and a half in the tunnel, Melifacto returned. There was no triumph, no cheers from the crowd when the Owls emerged tired, dirty, and in fewer numbers. Bellona kept her smug satisfaction hidden when she went to meet Melifacto at the tunnel gate.

To her surprise, Kygan was already there. Bellona glided through the crowd of Owls and mercenaries to where Kygan and Melifacto waited. Pelady, Melifacto's pet monster, stood not far away. She was the first to spot Bellona and whispered in Melifacto's ear.

"I hear you're finally joining in on the search," Melifacto said, slinking over. "Kygan has graciously volunteered to take over running the Marjyal guard while you're gone."

"Oh, has he?" She looked past Melifacto to Kygan.

Kygan rolled his eyes and shrugged. "Apparently."

"I need you, Bellona," Melifacto said, his words saccharine. "With your troops and your boats, we could find these fugitives. Then all would know the Cradle was found by the Boars, and it will grant you anything you need."

"Yes, my boats. It was fortunate my shipmaster returned when he did." Bellona held herself back. She could play nice with Melifacto. It would be him groveling soon enough. "How did the journey into the tunnel go?"

"We were beaten back by the lizards that live at the bottom." Melifacto muttered something profane against the scaly monsters. "Dianathos said he was taking the overland route. He left, I assume."

"He left with several companies of Doves nearly a week ago," Kygan said. "Planned on setting up in the ruins near the swamp, I believe. Send out search parties from there."

"Good, good." Melifacto rubbed his hands together. "He's a passionate man. How about you, Bellona? What is your plan going forward?"

"I thought with you returning, we would let you take the lead. Figured you would need help—" She looked at the stream of weary-faced men and woman passing them by. "—bolstering your forces."

Melifacto narrowed his eyes. "That would be splendid. Perhaps we should set out this evening?"

"As you wish."

Melifacto was agreeable, but his body language said something else. Bellona was being helpful, and that put Melifacto on edge. He didn't have a choice though, it was Bellona or nothing.

"I'll have my carriage prepared." Melifacto pulled his feather cloak tighter. "I'll see you at the southern gate."

He waved for Pelady to follow him. Pelady gave Bellona a long, suspicious look as she shadowed her master.

"I'll do my best to keep the city together while you're gone," Kygan said.

"I know you will." Bellona watched Melifacto and Pelady disappear before turning to Kygan. "There's been something weighing on my mind. It's your fault."

Kygan's head twitched. "I apologize if that's the case."

"Why did you tell me that story of the tunnel?" She stepped toe to toe with him. "Why the message about hope?"

"I figured you'd see." He looked left and right, taking in the crowd still surrounding them. "Come on. It's too busy here."

Bellona flipped up her furred collar and followed Kygan out of the square. Kygan took a deliberate path through twisting streets that made Bellona's head spin. Eventually he led her to a small building squeezed under a walkway and between two overwhelming apartments. He brushed the dust of the handle and stepped inside.

It was a church, as small as it was. There was no light coming in through stained glass windows, or large altars to crowd the area. Just a simple set of pews and a raised podium.

"This used to be a place of worship," Kygan said, striking a match and lighting a candle. "It was dedicated to some god that's not Mar, I'm afraid I don't remember which one. Dianathos pulled all the parishioners away. Not by telling them they couldn't pray here, but by making the worship of Mar feel better. He asked, Bolan, my predecessor to squeeze this chapel until the prayers ran all the way to the Doves."

One by one, Kygan lit the candles. Bellona brushed the dust off a pew at the front and took a seat. The church glowed in the yellow, flickering light of a dozen flames. It was then she could see windows did exist, but they were blocked by the walls of the buildings intruding on each side.

Kygan stopped at the podium. "Tell me, do you like the state of Marjyal?"

"What kind of question is that?"

"A real one. An honest one." He clutched the sides of the podium. "A question we avoid. I can tell you what I think. Marjyal is cracked."

"You better get to a point real soon, Ant." Bellona flipped her coat down below her shoulders and leaned on her knees.

Kygan pulled down on his waistcoat. "You're not disagreeing, because you see it. I know your story. You fought in the Pits, right? Tell me about it."

"You're kidding me?" Bellona rubbed her face. Kygan wasn't speaking like any Praetor had before. It intrigued Bellona enough she wanted to see where it went. "I wouldn't say I fought. I survived. The last Praetor of Boars had a thing for torture shows. I was brought in to see how much I could take. I didn't just take, I gave it back. The torturer slipped up, I slipped out. Smashed his head in with my chains, but not until after he took my eye. The cragging crowd cheered."

"Terrible." Kygan shook his head. "And yet years later, you took his place."

"I proved I was strong. And I kept being strong, every day until—"

"You killed the Boar."

"It was a duel." Bellona clutched her hands together before her. "I wanted something. I took it. It's the way of the world, Kygan. Now will you please make some sense?"

Kygan raised in hands in mock surrender. He stepped around the podium and sat next to her. "After you became Praetor, something happened. There were more fair fights in the Pits. The Hall of the Appraised was expanded. Of course, it couldn't change completely, not with the other Praetors having their fingers in the pot."

"Kygan!"

"Sorry. I promise I'm getting somewhere. You changed something. Even to a small amount. Why?"

"Because I found my strength in the arena. It wasn't built to turn punishment into a spectacle. It's a place for people to find their glory in the moments of combat. For people to take their lives back or lose it all. Only the strong survive, the arena just proves it."

Kygan chuckled. "Of course. But you don't believe you could change all of it, do you?"

"Of course not. The Boars aren't even all under my control. I know they take orders from Melifacto, Yomat, and Dianathos. They raid and steal people away to keep the Pits full. But those people can still be champions." *Like Gaul*, she thought.

"But you strive for change, because?"

Bellona groaned. Kygan wouldn't be satisfied unless she came to the conclusion herself. "Hope. You want me to say hope. I'm not a child, you know. You don't have to play all these games."

"It sticks better when people figure it out for themselves." He pushed himself off the pew. "That's what Bolan thought at least."

Bellona certainly would never forget this meandering talk. "Fine. What about it?"

"I can't change a lot, Bellona. I'm a carpenter, building walls as they crumble. But you have an honest shot. You could make things better. Pull Marjyal out of its death spiral. I'm sure you're up to something, and I don't need to know what it is. I just want to know the hope in you is real."

Bellona wasn't sure if she cared about making Marjyal better, or pulling it out of any spiral. She wanted to bring Melifacto down, to put her boot on his throat. But she thought too small. It wasn't just Melifacto, it was all of them. The Praetors who looked down on her because she rose to her station by proving she was better than her predecessor. She could raise the Marjyal Pits to where they belonged. Cast aside that cruel name and turn it into a home of glory and strength. Just as Kygan said, she needed hope.

"Yes." Bellona stood. "I have hope."

With the power Melifacto hid, she could turn Marjyal into a city that would even surprise Kygan. But why stop with just one city?

"Good," Kygan said. "You'll need it. That's the hope that built that tunnel, the one that died in this chapel. With it, you can bring about some real change."

She snapped her coat over her shoulders and turned to leave the church. "I'll just need to find Gaul and Marta before Melifacto does."

The path Lenn told Gaul and Marta to take through the swampland kept them safe from the poison, but it was muddy and slowed their progress. Marta caught Gaul looking back a few times, but said nothing. The ground hardened once again and before long they were looking at a wall of twenty-foot-high stone spikes.

Marta approached one of the many spaces between the spikes and peered into the maze-like structure within. "We're going to get lost if we go in there," she said.

"Ba-ya seems to think we can get through," Gaul replied. He considered the spikes. "But she may have overestimated us. Just keep an eye on the sun. We'll be heading away from it until noon."

Marta adjusted her bag and followed Gaul into the Teeth of the Sea.

It wasn't quite as confusing as it seemed from the outside. Many of the paths converged or were split by a single spike. Occasionally it got too thin to walk through, so they had to hoist themselves higher to where the spikes were thinner. While doing this, Marta could peer through the gaps in the stone and spy the ocean beyond.

"I didn't realize we were so close to the sea," she said.

"That would explain the name." Gaul leapt from the two spikes he held himself between.

"Still." Marta hopped down herself, stumbling on the dismount. She brushed the dirt off her knees. "I always liked the sea. It was the only thing that wasn't touched by Marjyal's evil. Me and my brother used to watch it from the library."

"I was landlocked. Would swim in a lake or the river, but never the ocean."

"I think it's lovely." Marta closed her eyes, letting the slight breeze flowing through the Teeth ruffle her hair. "To stare into something that has no other side. It's freedom."

"Or it's just water."

Marta sighed. As she followed Gaul, the breeze got stronger. The smell of salt became clear in the wind. Then, as they stepped around the next corner, a clear view of the ocean appeared. Marta rushed toward it.

She stood at the cliff overlooking another stretch of land below before giving way to an infinite ocean. The wind was strong enough to push her coat back and billow her short hair. She shut her eyes again and allowed the salt air to envelope her.

"Marta!" Gaul said through his teeth.

"It's fine." She turned around to wave Gaul over.

She froze. Coming down another path was a group. At their head was a figure clothed in white robes, and behind them were a dozen armoured Doves.

Marta was too far from Gaul to join him in hiding. She dropped. She pressed her back against a spike and slid along the cliff as far as she could go. It wouldn't be good enough. The path would lead right past her hiding spot. She tried to hold her breath, but her heart beat faster with each second.

"Hey!" Gaul shouted. "You going somewhere?"

Marta couldn't bear to look. She simply hoped Gaul was smart enough to run.

"Hey! You going somewhere?"

Gaul stood on a piece of stone, staring down at the collection of Doves. They spun at his voice and drew their weapons. The figure in robes turned slower and raised a darkened hood toward him.

"Gaul the Ruthless," he said. His voice was less metallic, but no less recognizable. Harken the homunculus.

"I see you've come crawling back." Gaul drew his swords. "Or are you going to run away again this time?"

"No." Harken pointed with a clawed gauntlet. "This time you are coming with me."

Gaul cracked out a smile. Marta was nearby, but she was out of sight. Hopefully she was smart enough to run when the fight started.

Some Doves encroached on Gaul's perch. Gaul leapt forward. He caught one Dove across the face while the other parried his swipe. Gaul kicked him in the chest, sending him stumbling back.

The other Doves moved in. There were a lot of them, and it looked like they could handle themselves in a fight. He needed to hold them off so Marta could run. But, if he could kill them, even better. *Stay out of view, Marta*, he thought.

The string tightened as Gaul put his thoughts elsewhere. His mind Ignited and the world became bathed with crimson. The Doves became red auras. They pulsed in time with their heartbeats.

A Dove moved toward him. Gaul batted his weapon aside; his arm went with it. He dropped screaming and Gaul advanced.

They were tough, more well trained than the masses in Marjyal. Gaul swung wild, and they parried or dodged. But, when he did land a blow it was hard, vicious, breaking bones and carving muscles. They died gurgling as the others retreated.

Gaul caught one in the ribs. He left his sword inside her and ducked beneath a swing from another one. Catching the next Dove by the throat, Gaul brought him to the ground. He wrenched hard enough to snap his neck with one hand.

A mighty kick to the stomach sent Gaul stumbling back. Harkin had no aura.

"Why are your eyes red?" Harkin asked.

Gaul charged, but the homunculus turned to smoke. He planted a foot, pivoted with the wisps, and swung with his remaining sword as Harkin reformed. Steel sunk into the oddly soft cloth shoulder and Harkin grabbed it. He clawed upwards, scattering blood and sending Gaul stumbling, disarmed.

Heat burned across Gaul's face. Lightning leapt from his wound. He gritted his teeth as the skin knitted together.

"How… bizarre," Harkin said, tossing Gaul's sword aside.

A Dove leapt forward, sword first. Gaul caught the strike with his forearm. The blade stuck into his bone, sending yet more lightning shooting out.

The Dove recoiled, leaving her sword sticking out of his flesh. Another swept in from behind. He planted his sword into Gaul's shoulder. Dull pain, nothing more than a push on his nerves, radiated from the spot. Gaul pulled the first sword out of himself and smashed the pommel into the second Dove's crown, cracking bone like a carrot, then hurled it hilt deep into a third.

Gaul's wounds oozed blood and vibrant energy. Doves attacked in crashing waves, each blow adding more lightning to the air. The pressure was euphoric.

He kicked a Dove's knee. It shattered with a horrifying crack and the Dove collapsed — only for Gaul to drive an uppercut into his throat. Another grabbed his arm; Gaul broke the grip and plunged his thumb into the Dove's eye. The next leapt over her ally. Gaul caught her before she touched the ground and tossed her screaming off the cliff.

A large metal hand shot from the crowd and took him by the throat. Harkin reformed from that point and hoisted Gaul into the air like a small puppy. He punched, breaking his hand on Harkin's arm. Energy crackled as his bones reset.

Gaul struggled, but there was no give from the homunculus. Air refused to enter his lungs. The red faded from his vision, replaced with dimming lit.

"Your red eyes turn blue once again," Harken remarked. "Dianathos would like to meet a being such as yourself."

Harken struck Gaul in the head. Then, darkness.

✳ ✳

Marta couldn't believe what she had just seen. Gaul had torn through a squad of Doves with unbelievable fury. The remaining few were staring at each other wide-eyed, except for the one who clutched where his eye used to be.

Gaul had recovered from every wound inflicted upon him. Lightning leapt from his body to pull him back together. That was how he took down the Marjyalians at the sewer gate without a scratch. However, not even while Ignited was he invincible. Harken dropped Gaul's limp form over his shoulder and motioned for the surviving Doves to follow. They glanced at their fallen comrades but followed Harken without a sound.

Marta waited another ten minutes after they left before stepping out of cover. She stared where Harken disappeared with Gaul, then to a westward path. She was so close to the Cradle, where her brother would be waiting.

"No," she whispered. She couldn't even think that. Gaul had done so much for her. She wasn't going to let him face the Praetor of Doves alone.

Steeling her will, she picked up Gaul's swords and followed Harken.

The eldest daughter, Forta, led the King's armies and had conquered much of the land before her father lost it. She wrote many times about her hatred of her father and how she planned to return the kingdom to glory.

She turned to industry and her people created terrible machines to tear the land asunder. It was her search that covered the most area, from the northern prairies to the Banshee Coast and even to the islands beyond. She seemed most likely to find the Cradle and inherit her father's kingdom. However, she too eventually faded into history along with the Kingdom of Adathin.

—From the Journal of Jovin Gutterwake

Chapter Fourteen
Ruined Dothrin

Marjyal's south gate slammed shut behind the hundred or so soldiers Bellona had gathered together. She had sent Ortun with all the ships in her fleet to dock at every port town down the west coast. Feyra and Bellona waited at the rear on their horses, watching the last of the troops exit the fortifications. With the carts and soldiers, they weren't moving fast.

Across the marching order, Bellona spotted Melifacto and Pelady. They were away from the troops, hiding in the shade.

"What are they doing?" Feyra asked.

"Melifacto said he was going to send word to Dianathos we're on our way," Bellona said, never taking her eye off the pair.

"Then why do they have two crows?"

Two black birds sat on Melifacto's arm as Pelady tied messages to their legs. If one was going to Dianathos, where was the other going? Melifacto ran his hand over each of the crow's heads, then lifted his arm, sending the birds to the sky. One went south, the other east.

"We need to find out where that second bird is going," Bellona said.

"Do you want me to intercept it?" Feyra asked.

"No. Melifacto was missing a report from one of his outposts. Outpost Four. I'm willing to bet that crow is going to collect. Can you track it?"

"You want me to leave you alone with Melifacto?"

Bellona's eye flared. "Are you questioning me again? We will not succeed if every one of my orders is second guessed."

"I don't trust him."

"That's because you're smart." Bellona took a deep breath. "Don't trust him. Trust me."

Feyra squeezed her reins until her knuckles went white. "I won't fail you."

"Then go."

Feyra spurred her horse eastward. Bellona turned back to Melifacto as he stepped into his carriage. Pelady was already on her horse. She shouted, then galloped to the south. Bellona urged Skyborn, her own horse, into motion and trotted next to Melifacto's carriage as it rattled down the road.

"Where's your lieutenant off to?" Melifacto asked.

"She's going to get some troops from Fort Rockhill. They'll put up wanted posts in some of the local towns. We don't want Gaul and Marta slipping our nets."

"I only care about Marta."

Melifacto picked up a wanted post. He had printed enough to coat Marjyal with paper. It offered enough coin even the wealthy would take notice and had depictions of both Gaul and Marta as recited by Dianathos after using his Ghost Hand.

"What about your subordinate?" Bellona asked. "Where is she riding in such a hurry?"

"I sent her ahead to assist Dianathos if he is in need. It's just you, me, and a hundred soldiers."

"Do you think he's in trouble? Are Gaul and Marta too much for the Guild of Doves?"

"Dianathos is, at his core, a showman." Melifacto folded up the post and slid it into his robes. "I doubt he would fare well against those two."

* *

Gaul woke up to hazy vision and his head screaming at him to go back to sleep. He pushed the pain away and focused his gaze. The Teeth of the Sea stretched below him, reaching to the ocean in the distance.

He tried to stand but found himself tied to the chair he sat on. The platform was at the top of some tower, open to air. Judging from the broken stone above, the tower once went much higher.

"Beautiful," a familiar voice said.

Gaul pulled against his bonds to see the man talking. His long, fair hair was in a ponytail and he was dressed in less ceremonial robes. Still white. Still unmistakable. Dianathos, Praetor of Doves, ran his fingers along the dusting of hair on his chin.

"I am not so foolish to believe Mar controls all we see." He paced along the lip of the tower. "Mar is but one of the Anima that dictate our world, but a glorious one at that. For all Mar asks is you be true to yourself. Nothing is forbidden in their eyes. This sight is the doing of a lesser god."

Gaul played with the idea of lunging at Dianathos and knocking them both off the tower. But as he stretched against his bonds, a clawed gauntlet grabbed his shoulder. Harken held him in place.

"Gaul," Dianathos said. "Gaul the Ruthless. I gave you that name, remember? And you have lived up to it." He sauntered closer and grabbed Gaul by the chin. "I can feel the death of every Dove you killed. You will answer for them, but first there is the mystery of where Marta is."

"I'm not talking," Gaul said.

Harken's grip tightened until his fingers cut cruelly into Gaul's shoulder.

"My friend there told me a funny little story." Dianathos sat cross-legged, smiling at Gaul. "A tale of a man whose eyes turn red and fights like a monster. And when he is cut, lightning spills from the wound and heals him. This is a man Melifacto would pay extremely well to have for his experiments. To cut apart and find out how he ticks. But first."

Harken pulled Gaul back, tipping his chair. Dianathos followed, leaping over Gaul's knees and landing with one hand pressing down on his chest. He put his other hand in front of Gaul's face.

"Let's see where that wretch is," Dianathos hissed. His hand turned white and billowed like mist. "Beautiful."

Dianathos plunged his hand into Gaul's head. He felt cold, then hot. Dianathos reached around Gaul's mind, searching and pulling at information. Gaul pushed against the intrusion.

"Tell me where Marta is."

The castle. Gaul could see Marta at the castle, working in the library. He pushed harder against Dianathos. It was no use. Dianathos was the wind twisting through each crack in Gaul's defenses.

So, he stopped pushing. Instead, he cleared his mind. A red haze trickled into Gaul's vision, but there was no rage to Ignite with. Dianathos' grip kept searching, but there was nothing to find.

"Gah!" Dianathos yanked his hand back. It coalesced back into material form. "You are full of surprises, Gaul."

"What happened?" Harken asked.

"He cleared his mind." Dianathos started rubbing his hand and stepped away from Gaul. "It's an amazing amount of self-control coming from a barbarian. Throw him to the Doves, Harken. Let's see how well he can concentrate after some playtime."

He spun around and a ragdoll hanging from a corded noose bounced on his belt. Harken's heart. Gaul pulled against his bonds again, but they were still tight. Harken grabbed the rope around Gaul's chest and lifted him like a child picking up a toy. He carried him to the ledge opposite the Teeth of the Sea and tossed him over.

The chair splintered on impact. The air evacuated Gaul's lungs. He groaned in pain. At least that side didn't go down as far as the other. He was within the destroyed walls of what could have been Dothrin Castle. There was movement at his peripherals. Surrounding him were men and women in white robes. At least a dozen, probably more. They turned at the sound of Gaul crashing to the ground and put down their food. They kept their knives though.

"Do not kill him!" Harken shouted from above. "But ensure he is very uncomfortable."

"Well, well," a man said. He put the tip of his dagger against Gaul's chest. "It sure is going to be unfortunate when you aren't as handsome anymore."

The other Doves laughed, cut short when a throwing knife struck the man in the neck. He sputtered, grasping with weak fingers at the hilt, then collapsed. Everyone looked to where the knife had come from.

Marta stood just outside the ring of destroyed buildings. She sauntered forward. In one hand were Gaul's swords — she leaned those against the closest wall — in her other was a knife tied to a rope. She turned her wrist, making the makeshift weapon hiss through the air. Gaul shoved the dead Dove off him and rolled away.

"Grab her!" Harken shouted.

The Doves charged. Marta spun the knife into a frenzy then slashed it across the chest of an approaching Dove. Without their armour, they were at the mercy of Marta's spinning blade. Marta stepped past a thrusting Dove and swung her knife across their calf, then arced it wide and embedded it into the back of their head.

Marta put her foot against the Dove's back and kicked him down, pulling the knife free. It flew in a high arc before driving into the dirt at a Dove's feet. The Dove chuckled and stepped onto the rope. Marta pulled, but he didn't budge. The Doves spread out, circling her. In a flash of steel, Marta tossed a knife into the throat of the Dove pinning her rope. The man dropped and Marta pulled the rope into a spin.

"Enough!" Harken jumped off the tower. The earth shook at his landing. Dirt and Doves were pushed aside. He rose a finger to Marta. "You have an appointment with Melifacto."

Marta hurled her rope-knife. It dug into Harken's chest to no effect. She yanked it back and started spinning again. Harken stepped forward, then disappeared into smoke. Gaul pushed his fists into the ground and stood. Marta was impressive, but no one can fight air. She couldn't kill him, but Gaul could. He grabbed the dagger from the first Dove to die and scrambled to the stairs.

It was only one floor up, but after falling that same distance he found himself staggering. He caught himself on a stair. *Marta's going to die if you don't do this*, he thought. He pushed the pain away and finished the climb. Dianathos stood at the top, watching the fight below. He clutched a rapier with an intricate basket hilt, his knuckles white from the tension. The Praetor turned to Gaul and gave his blade a flick.

"Malcontents," he said, rage in his eyes. "I have a god on my side. What do you have?"

"Nothing." Fire grew in Gaul's belly. "And that should terrify you."

Dianathos cried out and thrust with his rapier. Gaul parried the strike and punched him in the jaw. The ragdoll on Dianathos' hip bounced with every movement. Gaul didn't need to kill him. He gritted his teeth against the pain in his back and focused, ready to Ignite.

"No, you don't!" Dianathos lunged in.

Gaul raised his dagger to stop him, but Dianathos' hand went straight through, turning again to strange mist. Two of his fingers entered Gaul's forehead before Gaul could jerk away. An icicle shot through his mind and sent him stumbling.

"Harken told me about your eyes turning red." Dianathos spun his rapier, the blade whistling. "This isn't the Pits. I have no interest in fighting a monster."

Gaul caught himself on a wall and pushed his body to Ignite. The cold spike wouldn't go away, muddling his thoughts around a pillar of ice. He turned in time to see a rapier tip being thrust at him. In sheer instinct, he lifted his hand and watched as the tip pierced through his palm. He squeezed his hand shut. The rapier stopped a centimetre from his eye, his own blood dripping onto his cheek. Dianathos dug his boots in. Gaul pushed the sword aside, letting it strike the wall instead of him.

Now he was in a bad situation. One hand was skewered against the wall. He flipped the dagger around in his other and swung back. With the swagger of a king, Dianathos caught his arm and smirked.

"I am a Praetor," he said, his breath hot against Gaul's face. "What could an outlander savage like you hope to achieve against me?"

"Stop talking!" Gaul kicked him in the thigh and tore his arm away. He jammed his dagger on the rapier tip, wedging it between the blade and the crossguard. With a sharp twist — and more than a little blood — he snapped the sword.

Dianathos bounded back. He inspected the broken blade with a curled lip. "I like this sword."

Between the cold sensation clouding his thoughts and the four-inch steel in his palm, Gaul couldn't say he was doing well in the fight. But he couldn't stop. Marta was alone with Harken. The doll had to be destroyed. Pain was nothing. "Don't worry," he said, gritting his teeth. "I'll be breaking you too." He clapped his hand against the wall, sending the rapier tip shooting out, and barreled in.

Steel on steel clashed in the broken tower. Dianathos had perfect form, his feet tracking across the stonework like dance steps. With only a dagger, and his Ignition quelled, Gaul couldn't fight with the full ferocity he was accustomed to. The Praetor had the edge. Gaul moved in with a flurry of blows. Dianathos simply stepped out of the way then parried the final strike with all the joy of swatting a fly. Gaul took the momentum, raised his injured hand, and with a flick of his fingers sent a spray of blood into Dianathos' eye.

"Ah, you bastard!" he cried, trying to wipe the blood away.

A moment was all Gaul needed. He flipped the dagger into a reverse grip and stabbed for the heart. Dianathos flailed, half-blind, and knocked Gaul's attack aside. He missed the heart, but he drove the dagger up to the hilt into Dianathos' shoulder. With a scream that could wake the dead, Dianathos shoved Gaul away — leaving the dagger sticking out of the wound.

"Insolent!" he screamed. "Arrogant! How dare you!?" He grasped the hilt and with agonizing effort pulled the dagger free and tossed it aside. "I'm done tolerating you." He lunged forth. The blood fell from his hand as it turned ethereal and plunged into Gaul's chest.

Blinding pain shot through Gaul's body. He pulled away, but that only put ice through his veins. He dropped to his knees. Dianathos towered over him, curling his ghostly fingers around Gaul's heart.

"I would tear your will to live right out of your chest," he spat. "But it's been too long since I've had a good hanging." He sheathed his rapier and reached into his robes. Sneering and shaking with rage he pulled out a thick rope. The end was already tied into a noose.

Gaul tensed his fist. It was like moving his fingers through mud. That ragdoll — the strange effigy — hung from thin cords. Tantalizingly close. If he didn't do something, he would be like that doll. Hanging from his neck.

"The Guild of Ashes likes to burn," Dianathos said. "My predecessor preferred decapitation. But when you hang someone, they have just enough time to think about all the sins they've committed. They can repent them. They can ask for forgiveness. Then they're gone." Like a practiced executioner, Dianathos gently laid the noose over Gaul's head with one hand. With a sharp tug it tightened up. Then, he pulled. "I wonder what sins you'll regret?"

"I said…" Gaul grabbed Dianathos' arm with both hands. "Stop talking!" He pulled the ghost arm deeper into his chest.

Pain blossomed from his heart. His eyes flared deep red. Lightning coursed along the hole in his palm, closing the skin. For a moment, he was at peace. And close enough to the ragdoll. He grabbed and pulled, snapping the cord.

"Marta!" he cried, and hurled the doll over the edge. She had to hear him. She had to still be fighting.

"No!" Dianathos lunged for the doll, abandoning Gaul to collapse. It slipped past his fingers and down to the ground below. His eyes went wide. "What is this?"

The removal of the hand from Gaul's chest didn't removed the pain. The noose was still around his neck, but he dragged himself forward to see what got Dianathos so shaken.

Carnage. Pure carnage.

The remaining Doves were dead, sliced to ribbons. Blood puddles littered the dirt. In the centre of it all, Marta stood with her rope-knife at her side. In her other hand, held above her head, was the doll. Harken's robes were shredded, revealing more of the blackness underneath. Smoke seeped out from these fabric wounds. It seemed like, beyond all expectations, Marta had been winning. She looked over the doll.

"Stop her!" Dianathos screamed.

Harken moved, but Marta was faster. She tossed the doll into the air and, with a quick wind up, cut it in half. Harken turned to smoke for the last time, blowing past her and into the wind. His cloak fluttered to the bloody earth.

"How is this happening!?" Dianathos cried, slamming his fist into the stone. His gaze crept toward Gaul. "This is your fault. Everything I've done…" He lunged and grabbed the noose. Gaul reached for the coil around his neck, but Dianathos planted a foot on his back and pulled. "I've hung hundreds of heretics from the rafters of their own blaspheming homes! I am the only reason Mar's light still shines in Marjyal! I am a servant of God!"

The light faded. Drawing breath was impossible. It wasn't a bad end, fading away. Maybe it was better.

"You think I care about some dead priests or remaking a homunculus? With the Cradle of the World, Mar's grace will be proven absolute. Every living soul will be my flock! And I will be their shep—"

The rope went slack. Gaul collapsed to his hands and knees. He drew in breath after burning breath. Everything hurt. He tore the noose off his neck and turned back to Dianathos.

A knife tied to a rope stuck in his neck. He sputtered on blood before the knife was yanked back out. He clutched at the wound, blood pouring unheeded through his fingers. Gaul returned to his feet and stared Dianathos dead in the eyes. The smugness was gone, instead there was fear. The white robes turned red. He moved his lips to say something but a gurgling, wheezing breath was all that came.

"Sermon's over," Gaul said, and walked away.

Boots scraped on stone. A thump. A sigh. The Praetor of Doves had fallen.

Gaul descended the steps to where Marta waited. She stood in the middle of a ring of corpses, rope knife laying in a pool of blood. She stared blankly at her feet.

"I didn't actually expect you to come for me," Gaul said, rubbing the spot where Dianathos' ghost hand entered his chest. "But I am glad you did."

Marta turned to him. She stepped closer, stopped, then stepped again. Her movements were considered, but unsure. She got faster, more sure of herself. The knife dragged behind her, leaving a small rut of blood. Instinct told Gaul to run. To be ready to fight. But Marta stopped before him. She lifted a single finger and pressed it against Gaul's chest.

"I'll see you later," she said with an evil grin.

Her eyes rolled into the back of her head. She buckled. Gaul caught her under her arms and kept her from falling. He dragged her to the base of the tower and sat her against the wall. He tapped her cheek, but she gave no response. He put his head against her chest. She was breathing, and her heart beat strong. What could he do now? His swords were still where Marta had left them. He needed those — what if there were more Doves? He hurried over, keeping Marta in sight.

He stepped over the corpse of a Dove who had taken the rope-knife across the neck. There were over twenty, including Harken. Gaul saw her take out two or three, but standing in the mess the enormity of it became clear. The scale of what Marta was capable of.

It wasn't Marta though. That look in her eyes was someone different. It was pointed, focused as an arrow piercing through the back of his skull. But what was it? What was she?

As he came back from getting his sword, she was already coming to. Her head bobbed and her eyes flickered open. "What happened?" she said.

Gaul tried to piece the words together.

"I was fighting Harken," she continued. "The Doves were getting close. He knocked me in the head." Her eyes focused on the field of corpses. "I guess you cleaned up my mess."

Gaul frowned. Something in the back of his mind told him to hide the truth. She killed all the Doves, Dianathos, and fought Harken to annihilation. But it wasn't her. It was that other thing. The Not-Marta.

"It was my mess," Gaul said, helping Marta up. "And it's not like you did nothing. You made… that."

Marta looked at the rope-knife, laying where she dropped it. "I found the rope and they weren't wearing any armour. There was a fighter in the Pits who used a weapon like this. There were so many of them. Then I thought, 'what would Gaul do?' He would swing on a rope to break a bridge. He would throw something at a giant monster. He would go all in. No risk, no reward."

"I don't know if that's an insult or not," Gaul said.

"I don't know either." She looked west. A smile spread across her face and she rushed to a low wall and leapt on top. "We made it, Gaul! There's nothing in the way anymore, just straight in that direction and we're at the Cradle… and Jovin."

"It couldn't just be the Guild of Doves." Gaul vaulted over the low wall Marta stood on. A long bridge crossed the river outside of the ruins ahead of them. Downstream, the water dipped into the underground before the Teeth of the Sea. "If Melifacto really put out a bounty on you then others could be looking."

"All the more reason to keep going." Marta hopped off the wall. "Before they find us."

Marta clapped Gaul on the shoulder and walked out of the ruins. Gaul took a last look at the catastrophe left in Dothrin's never-was castle.

"Gaul!" Marta shouted. "Look at this!"

Gaul sprinted around the corner then stopped in his tracks. Marta stood next to a cart attached to a massive brown horse. She stood on the cart's bench, arms held wide with pride.

"We can get to the Cradle in no time!" she said.

Gaul stared at the horse. He stepped back. "They already cleared the cart of supplies, it'll be another hindrance. Let's just walk."

"We've been walking for days." Marta sat on the bench. "Let someone else do the work for once."

"It's only another day!"

"Get on the cart!"

"I don't want to!"

"Why not?"

"I…" Gaul averted his eyes. "Don't like horses."

Marta leaned forward. "What was that?"

"They upset me, okay?" Gaul crossed his arms. "Their bone structure, their hooves, they're upsetting."

"How about I take the reins?" Marta said. "And you can lay down in the back."

Gaul groaned. He took a wide path around the cart, coming straight into the back. He sat on the edge, took a deep breath, then laid down. Marta snapped the reins and Gaul's entire body seized as the horse pulled the cart into motion.

Gaul's legs dangled off the back, bouncing with the dirt trail they rode along. He stared into the sky and shut his eyes. He put his mind elsewhere until Sebanna's Archive.

The Cradle.
I've found it.
Divines save us all.

—From the Journal of Jovin Gutterwake

Chapter Fifteen

Sebanna's Archive

By evening, Marta spotted a large building on the horizon. It was the only structure other than Dothrin's ruins she had seen all day. It had to be the archive.

"Gaul," Marta said and turned to the back of the cart.

Gaul sprawled across the cart bed, his fingers laced over his undulating chest. Even a night at Lenn and Ba-ya's didn't give him the rest he deserved. Marta reminded herself Gaul had been on the road for much longer than she had. Every ache she felt, every bout of homesickness, it was all amplified in him. She decided to let him sleep.

The sun had set when Marta stopped the cart at the archive's doors. It sat lonely at the cliffside. A gentle salt breeze blew over Marta as she left the cart and patted the horse on the haunches. It whinnied in appreciation. She led it to a patch of grass and let it graze. She walked around to the back of the cart and climbed up. She crouched next to Gaul, still fast asleep. A wicked idea came into her head. Leaning close to Gaul's ear, she neighed.

Gaul flew off the cart like a bird taking to the air. He landed and drew a sword, pointing it at Marta. Marta collapsed against the cart wall with laughter.

"Not funny," Gaul said, putting away his weapon.

"It was kind of funny." Marta hopped off the cart. "But look where we are."

Gaul gazed up at the archive. It was a three-floor manor built out of faded wood, with an archway over the door. Some of the windows were cracked, but overall, they held up well considering the age of the building. Marta snapped a brown leaf off a rotting bush and approached.

She opened the door and stepped into a baroque antechamber. A fading carpet of white and red design was partially rolled up at their feet. Along both walls down the passage were broken mirrors with silver frames. Gaul picked up a chunk of mirror and looked it over.

"Someone didn't like seeing themselves," he said and tossed the shard away.

Marta chuckled and headed to one of the side doors. She peeked through to a sitting room furnished with plush chairs and elegant curtains. The moon had risen and shone through the window, casting sinister shadows into the corners.

"We need a light," Marta said, shutting the door. "Or we're never going to find anything."

"Good thing the Marjyalians were prepared." Gaul dug through his bag and pulled out two sunstones. He struck one to life and tossed it to Marta.

"Do you want to split up?" Marta asked.

Gaul struck the other one. "Shout if you find something."

Marta gave a faux salute then headed for the door at the end of the antechamber. Gaul took the door opposite the sitting room and disappeared.

Marta flitted from room to room, looking for any sign of her brother. The building was more than just an archive. It had living spaces and a kitchen with rotting food. Rodents scurried to hiding places as she leapt into the room. Everywhere she found chairs with lines in the dust where they had been recently pulled out, plates that had food residue on them, and books placed out for someone to read. Jovin had been there.

The first floor was easy to clear, but Jovin was nowhere to be found. She wanted to call out his name, hear his voice in reply, but she stopped herself. There was still danger. Jovin could have left, or something else could have taken his place.

Instead, she gripped the sunstone harder and moved to the second floor.

* *

Gaul crept through the archive. It was ornate, yet with an underlying feeling of utility. Most rooms had tables and comfortable chairs. The kitchen had spread from its humble beginnings into the surrounding areas once laden with research equipment — now shoved into the corners. It hadn't been a scholarly place for a long time. It was simply home.

The archives weren't as well preserved as Adathin Castle, but more recently lived in. He walked through bedrooms, each with one or two beds and empty wardrobes. In the closest one to the stairs, he found the only bed that had been used any time soon. Marta's brother had been there.

He spotted Marta half-jogging through the halls, trying to get through the rooms as fast as possible. There was no point in both of them searching the same floor, so Gaul ascended straight to the third.

Upon reach the third-floor landing, Gaul spotted a body. It was slumped against the wall across from the stairs. It wore robes made from overlapping metal plates and a strange helmet with red glass eyes, though one was broken. Gaul's heart sank, but he noticed a skeletal hand clutching the metal robe's chest. It wasn't a new corpse. It wasn't Jovin.

Gaul took the odd helmet off and tossed it aside so Marta wouldn't be fooled as he was. As he did, he spotted something tucked into the robe's neckline. A parchment.

They've all gone, it read, *Generations of Unseen have passed through Sebanna's Archive, learning all she had and passing it on to those who would hear them. But long before I was born people stopped listening. Adathin has died. Those good and noble that filled this land have all but disappeared. Our proximity to the Cradle of the World, the history of the earth beneath our feet, that is the cause.*

My fellow Unseen are ready to enact Sebanna's solution, devised when the order was first founded. They are going north, past the still moving husk of a city, Marjyal, and creating the forest. A single seed, the only remains of ancient archtrees, will grow a tombstone for Adathin's grave.

I am much too old for the journey. My son begged me to come and join his family, but I declined. My wife went to the sea, and I would like to join her. Until then, I will keep writing. I don't believe even the archtrees can hide Adathin forever and they may return. For those who do, and seek mortality's curse, look to the bookcase at the bottom of the spiral stairs. Remember Sebanna's greatest mistake.

May the Divine's look upon you,

Grandmaster Altriss Formwater.

Gaul folded the note and looked down at the skeleton. Altriss wore armour, but it was unscarred by battle. As far as Gaul could tell, he simply sat down and never got back up.

Gaul hauled Altriss' body onto his shoulder. The metal robes added a great amount of weight, but Gaul carried Altriss down the hall. He found a balcony overlooking the ocean. He rested Altriss onto the wide railing and put his hand on the chest of the robes.

"Go find your wife," he said and pushed Altriss into the sea.

Altriss splashed into the water far below, disappearing among the waves crashing against the stone. Gaul muttered a prayer, something hollow to him but he thought Altriss would respect.

He looked at the note once again. He had seen a bookcase at the bottom of the stairs, it could be the one Altriss wrote about. Gaul headed back to the first floor. He didn't see or hear Marta as he passed the second and considered calling out to her. There was no assurance he was on the right track though. Better not get her hopes up.

Ragged volumes of information on the Kingdom of Adathin filled the shelves from side to side, bound with titles on their spines. "Sebanna's greatest mistake," Gaul muttered, running his fingers along the books.

Halfway down was a simple brown book with the title 'The Chalice of Light.' Gaul pulled, but it wouldn't move. Instead, he pushed. A click came from within the wall and the bookshelf popped backwards. Bracing his shoulder, Gaul forced the secret door open the rest of the way.

He held up his sunstone, shining light into a dark stairwell leading ever downward. Gaul took a deep breath. His nose filled with the smell of mildew and wet wood. A soft splashing could be heard as he entered the secret tunnel.

Gaul went deep into the earth. The unworked stone walls had regular sconces. Each had a torch, but not an ancient one. Someone had been keeping the tunnel alight. Jovin once again, no doubt.

At the bottom of the staircase was a small tunnel which grew into a massive water-filled cavern. Gaul arrived on a thin stone bridge. Ocean water was a few feet below him, sending its spray across the rocky path. At the far end was an opening to the broader sea, and the moonlight silhouetted a rectangular formation at the end of the bridge.

Gaul approached, taking careful steps on the slick stone. He moved past a blanket with a lamp and some writing supplies. Books were placed where the splashing water couldn't reach them, though the salt air had caused the pages to warp.

The light from his sunstone crept along the ground, until it could illuminate the formation. In the middle of an archway of rough obsidian nearly thirty feet high was a slab of intricately carved stone. Words in an unknown language wrapped around pictographs and sharp motifs. A thin line ran from the top to the bottom, an opening for a door.

Gaul stared at the monolith. He repeatedly reminded himself he was awake. There was no way what he was looking at could be real. The Cradle of the World. Or at least the door to it.

At the bottom of the door was a lone figure. He was too far decomposed for Gaul to recognize even if he knew who he was. But Gaul suspected.

"Gaul!" Marta's voice echoed from the entrance. "Gaul are you down here?"

Gaul closed his eyes. The thought of pushing the body into the sea crossed his mind. It wouldn't be right. It was going to be hard. Gaul sighed as he heard footsteps on the stones behind him.

The footsteps slowed. Her breath became laboured. The footsteps started again, faster, toward the body. Each footfall became staggered, first rushing side to side then stumbling. A scream — primal and angry.

Gaul opened his eyes. Marta knelt over her brother's body.

They had found Jovin.

Gaul hadn't spoken to Marta in a day. The morning after they discovered Jovin, Gaul found Marta sitting next to the body. She leaned against the door, forehead resting on her hands. The cavern was cold and the body's smell filled it mercilessly, but she didn't care. As Gaul approached she lifted her head and looked at him with tired eyes. Gaul left her breakfast and returned to the archive.

While Gaul looked over the numerous confusing books in the archive, he spotted Marta leaving the secret door. She clutched onto a small black object. It appeared to be a book, maybe a journal. But with Marta gone, Gaul returned to the door to the Cradle.

Jovin was still right where Gaul had last seen him. It was a few months of decay at least, but Marta recognized him. Could have been the clothes, could have been the journal, or maybe she just knew.

Gaul stepped past Jovin's body and approached the door. He ran his fingers over the cold stone. At the edges, where the carved stone met the obsidian, Gaul noticed a darker patch. Not even black, almost a hole in space. It seemed to seep out from the door. Gaul walked around the back.

It wasn't obsidian. Something had oozed from the door and darkened the glass-like substance that constituted the arch. In the glass it had sheen and texture, but as it spread from the back of the door toward the sea there was nothing. Absolute dark. A hole in existence.

A burning grew on Gaul's chest. He yanked out the necklace. Within the seemingly empty vial was now the smallest speck of a glow. Gaul retreated from the door and the heat disappeared with the glow.

"Gaul?" Marta appeared at the entrance, holding Jovin's book to her chest like her life depended on it. "Could we have a ceremony?"

Gaul hid the necklace back inside his shirt. He glanced at Jovin, then back to Marta.

"Of course," he said.

In Marjyal they burned the dead, Gaul learned. It was the only way to keep the Rats from dragging the corpses of their loved ones into the sewers. He helped Marta gather wood from the surrounding trees and build a pyre. They laid Jovin on top and wrapped him with a sheet. By the time the sun sank into the sea, they were ready.

Marta lit a torch. She gazed at the ocean, looking far over the horizon.

"Do you want to say anything?" Gaul asked.

"No." Marta turned from the sea to face the pyre. "No one would hear it."

She lit the kindling. The fire spread through the wood and wrapped its feverous fingers around Jovin. Smoke curled into the twilight sky until it disappeared into darkness. When the pyre was nothing but raging flames, Marta left with her head down. Gaul stayed. He listened to the popping of dry wood and the cracking of sparks. Loss was never easy, no matter the form it took. The structure crumbled, sending a flood of sparks floating past Gaul, over the cliffside, and drifting into the endless sea.

Gaul puffed out a breath into the cooling night air and stuck his hands in his pockets. When he returned to the archive, Marta was outside. She leaned against the wall, looking at the embers in the distance. Gaul gave her a half-hearted smile then stepped toward the door.

"I can't get you back," Marta mumbled.

Gaul stopped.

"The only way through Nature's Grave is with an exodus stone. Mine was in my bag but I lost it at the Castle. I thought Jovin would have one but he… and I couldn't find it anywhere."

She pushed off the wall and paced the entrance. She swung her hand, covering her eyes or mouth then gesturing for words to come to her. "I can't, Gaul." Her voice cracked. She took three deep breaths. "I can't get you home."

Gaul ran his hands through his hair, forcing himself not to tear it out.

Marta clutched her head in one hand. "I tried to find it in the castle but it was gone! I'm sorry, Gaul. I'm so, so sorry."

Her lower lip trembled. She held Jovin's book to her chest with her other hand. Gaul was about to begin yelling, until he saw the way her fingers trembled. When he brought her breakfast, she looked tired. When she ran out of the archive with the book, she looked focused. Even at Jovin's pyre, she made no indication of sadness.

But now, she was barely holding together. Her entire body quaked. She had been more worried about not getting Gaul home than mourning her brother.

"Only the Praetor's know where the stones are grown," Marta said. "But they have stores of them. We could go back! I could go back!"

"Marta."

"I know the way around. I know where they keep the stones."

"Marta!"

She froze.

Gaul looked her in her wide eyes. "I don't care."

Her gaze fell. Her shoulders shook and her breaths turned shallow. Gaul wrapped an arm around her and she burst into tears. She held around Gaul's waist, pressing her face into his chest, muffling the sound of crying. Gaul squeezed harder.

Marta let everything out. Gaul was upset about the stone, of course, but it wasn't the time. There was a solution to every problem. But at that moment, Marta needed a friend. And in some way, so did he.

* *

The morning was darker than the one before. Storm clouds formed above Marta as she stood on a balcony. She picked a bedroom with a view of the ocean so every morning she could look into the infinite distance.

It was freeing being in a place where she knew no one was around except for her and Gaul. She had done something she had never been able to do before. She had locked the door, to prevent Gaul from accidently walking in, and slept naked. It was amazing. Freeing.

Now she stood completely nude, letting the ocean air touched every inch of skin on her. For the smallest of moments, all worries left her. She was like a child again. Then a wave of self-consciousness came over her and she rushed inside to get clothed. Back in her gear, with her scarf hanging loosely off her shoulders, she went to find Gaul.

The archive was massive. Marta walked the halls, calling out for Gaul with no answer. She arrived at the ground floor and continued down through the secret entrance.

Taking her last step at the bottom of the stairs, Marta stopped. The smell was still in the air, not as strong, but unmistakable. She let out an uneasy breath, then stepped into the cavern. Gaul stood at the strange monolith. Jovin's journal called it the door to the Cradle of the World. Gaul looked down, then began to raise his hand.

"What are you doing?" Marta asked as she stopped next to him.

Gaul cursed out of surprise. He looked Marta up and down, as though confused she even existed. He must have been deep in thought.

"I don't really know," Gaul said. He held out his wife's necklace with Athas' pendant. There was a single point of light within the glass. "Ba-ya said there was some sort of power within this. It was being brought here to reseal the First Gods into the Cradle."

"That must have been what Athas was talking about before he died." Marta stepped closer to the stone.

"Apparently." Gaul rolled the pendant between his fingers.

"So, what are you waiting for?"

"It just seems like this is the last confirmation of what I thought was simple legend and story. A priest travels across the continent to stop old gods from escaping."

Marta craned her neck back to look up the entire carved surface. It was beautiful in a terrifying way.

"I said no to the gods a long time ago," Gaul said. "If this works, it feels like some kind of divine joke. Or maybe I just don't do anything. Let the god's fight their own battle."

"What will happen if the First Gods return?"

"She didn't say. I would assume they would be gods again. Might not be a good outcome for the Divines, but considering the state of Adathin, maybe it's not such a bad thing to have someone new in charge."

Marta tapped against the door. The crack that ran down the middle didn't split the stone; it was only a centimetre deep.

Gaul gave a loud groan and put away the necklace. "How about some breakfast?"

"Sounds good to me," Marta said. "Bring it down."

"Are you sure?"

Marta looked around the cave. The bad memories weren't here. "Yeah. Besides, we still have a decision to make."

Gaul nodded. He took a lingering look at the door then ascended to the archives.

Gaul was getting sick of dried meat. He took some of the fruits and vegetables from the cart they looted off the Doves. The fluxcrystal on the icebox had died ages ago, but it kept the food reasonably cool. With their breakfast in hand, Gaul turned around to find Ba-ya sitting at the table.

"So, you found it," she said.

Gaul stopped. He laid the food onto the counter. "Druid fluxweaving?" he asked.

"In their last days, things can shine like never before." Ba-ya bowed her head. "My end is soon."

"I'm sorry."

"Such is life." She smiled at Gaul. "I could sense your trepidation."

"And Marta thinks *I* use big words."

"You're afraid, young dust. The responsibility to make a choice that could change the world can be crushing."

Gaul sat down next to her. "Athas would have fixed the seal in an instant. I don't have as much faith in the gods. I've seen senseless wars and killing from people who claim to be good. This entire kingdom is a monument to the failing of those who are supposed to look out for us. Gods and kings both lost everything here. Maybe the Divine's time is done."

"You believe since things are bad, they can't get worse?"

"So, releasing the First Gods would be a mistake?" Gaul waited for an answer. Ba-ya shrugged. "I just need to know what to do."

"You say the Divines don't care. It seems to me they are doing the best they can. The Primordials ruled the world when it was at its cruelest. The First Gods usurped them, but the harder they held on, the more darkness was allowed to seep in. When the Divines overthrew their parents, they looked upon reality and decided it cannot be controlled, not without becoming corrupt like those before them. So, they ascended, deciding to help the world, not control it."

Gaul sank into his chair. He had seen men try so hard to keep power they became cruel. Kings who became tyrants. Or who wanted the power of the Chalice so badly his entire kingdom paid for it.

"You remember," she said. "I told you this before. The choices you make — you and Marta — will define the coming age. The impact of what's to come will resonate far into the future, and make it what it will be."

"Why do we have to make this choice?"

"Because you're here."

Gaul stuck his fingers in his hair, leaning on his elbows. "That's not fair."

"Few things are." She rested her hand on his arm. "A druid is supposed to stay neutral in all things, but I'm sure you've seen that substance extruding from the door. It is called Absence. It is what was left behind when the First Gods lost their Light. It will consume the world and revert it to a state we haven't seen since the time of the Primordials. I'm not ashamed to say I'm afraid of this evil. There is darkness in our world, you know this. Marta knows it as well. But as long as a single light remains, no matter how small, you cannot allow it to be snuffed."

Gaul raised his head, a weak smile showing. "Thank you," he said.

"You're a good man. You wouldn't have punished the world for your own anger." Her body turned to green leaves and spread across the kitchen floor. Her words carried on the wind. "You would have made the right choice."

Gaul walked with purpose back to the Door. The pendant grew warmer with every step.

"Where's the food?" Marta said as he arrived.

"We're sealing the Cradle," Gaul said, stomping past her. "We can't let the First Gods return."

"Uh, okay?"

The pendant began to burn as Gaul approached the door. He held it up by the chain. Light spewed forth from the vial, filling the cavern. The void on the glass arch shrank into the edges of the door. In a few seconds, the archway sparkled like diamonds and the vial was dark once again.

"That was fun," Marta said, stepping next to Gaul and crossing her arms. "But I'm still wondering where the food is."

Gaul opened his mouth to speak but was interrupted by a horrible screech. The door trembled. The hole in space tore back into the glass arch. It didn't stop with the door. Absence spread like water across the land bridge. The scream intensified.

"Get back!" Marta pulled on Gaul's arm.

They ran away from the oncoming flood, clutching their ears to protect them from the scream. As fast as it started, the sound stopped. Gaul skipped to a halt, with Marta not far ahead of him.

The bridge had become nothing. A liquid void dripped over the edges into the water where it swayed along with crashing waves.

"Was that supposed to happen?" Marta asked.

"I don't think so," Gaul said. "It cleaned the Absence, but it came back stronger."

"The Absence?"

Gaul pointed to the archway, now looking like obsidian once again. Marta cocked her head, then began tearing through Jovin's journal. Gaul approached the substance. It still spread, just much slower. He held up the vial. The spark had disappeared — he couldn't feel any heat from it either. The Light was gone, but the Absence wasn't giving up. What could they do now?

"I found it!" Marta cried. She rushed to join Gaul, glancing at the Absence, then pulling Gaul closer to the entrance. "'The blackness in the glass arch is not natural. When I first arrived, it was only a centimetre into the glass, now it's three. Some of the books talk about a corruption that needs to be quelled with the power of Light. Apparently Light can't be gathered here, so they must slowly let it grow within a vessel elsewhere.'"

She flipped to the next page and continued.

"'I don't know what to do. The corruption keeps spreading and doesn't appear to want to stop. When I look at it for too long my head starts to hurt. I have never seen something so... enthralling. Maybe one of these Unseen will arrive with some Light, I would love to talk to them. I haven't found any way to open the door and see the source of the corruption. It seems Sebanna kept much of the information on the Cradle to herself. Even these Unseen are still in the dark.'"

"Alright." Gaul scratched his head. "I don't really see how that helps."

"Sebanna would know so much more about this Absence stuff." Marta paled as she took in the reaching void. "I mean, we can't just leave that, right?"

Absence would consume the world, Ba-ya had said. The First Gods would wake up. Gaul stepped up to the edge. "While I was following Athas I learned he was telling everyone the end of the world could be coming from the south. People seemed to believe him, many were fleeing north. Maybe he knew this was going to happen. Or at least suspected."

"The end of the world." Marta followed his gaze. "I don't think we can walk away from this."

"As long as a single light remains, no matter how small, we cannot allow it to be snuffed." Gaul ground his teeth until his jaw hurt.

"I'm done with gods," Marta said. "The last thing I want is more waking up."

"We need to know what Sebanna knew," Gaul said. "But her account back in the castle said she planned to go to Black Hypogea."

Marta kicked a stone into the dark water. "What is Black Hypogea, anyway?"

"It's, uh, a place for evil people." Gaul searched for the right words to explain the concept. "Where the spirits that the Gate Beyond judges as evil go to be punished and cleaned. Where monsters are born. The opposite of Elysium. It's kind of hard to explain something like it."

"Oh..." Marta pulled a large sheet out of her bag. "Because it's on the map."

"It's what?"

Marta,

I'm sorry I left you behind when I left for Adathin. I couldn't bear the thought of bringing you anywhere close to Marjyal again. You were so young when we left. I remember how tired you got once we snuck through the city walls. I had to carry you up to Nature's Grave. I only regret we didn't leave sooner.

I hope to be the one to give you this journal. I hope I can share with you all I've learned. I hope I can explain why I did what I did. How it was all to keep you safe. But if I am just shouting into the void here, then I hope my thoughts can reach you.

I love you, Marta. And I will explain everything one day.

—From the Journal of Jovin Gutterwake

Epilogue

Feyra rode hard, but even her prized stallion couldn't race a bird and win. Arion would tire fast if they kept moving at a gallop, but Feyra wanted to make some distance between her and Melifacto. The crow was nearly a dot on the horizon when Feyra made her move.

She reached into her saddlebag and sliced her thumb on one of the jagged blades on her club. Rubbing the blood over her index finger, she focused on the distant crow. With a quick flick, she launched a blood bolt from her finger, her tattoos flashing. It stuck into the crow's feathers.

Feyra pulled back on the reins, bringing Arion to a gentle trot. The bird was now a beacon to her and she could follow it, no matter where it flew off to. Her blood would be her guide.

Bellona had asked Feyra to trust her. But Feyra had always trusted her. She would do anything for the woman who took her in. Who taught her to be strong. Bellona was the first person to make her not feel alone in the world. Feyra had shown Bellona her power over blood, the markings on her arms, and Bellona said they were glorious, not monstrous. She never asked herself what was wrong with her when Bellona was close by.

Feyra would follow each order her Praetor gave to her. She would kill anyone who got in her way. And maybe, when Bellona's dreams come true, there would be room in her heart for Feyra.

ALL GODS FALL: SEASON ONE

PART THREE

BLACK HYPOGEA

There was an age before the First. In this time, the five unkillable Primordials ruled Meza. Each held uncontested dominion over their section of the ancient world: Earth, Sky, Sea, Dark, and Fire. Every time mortals gained a foothold in those vicious lands, a Primordial would inevitably stomp them out. Meza could never progress.

There was no more dangerous creature for these early humans than Earth King Behemoth. A towering beast who stomped flora and fauna below his feet and whose shadow could freeze the crops. His skin of stone repelled arrows and swords from those foolish enough to challenge him. Good and evil fail to describe something like the Earth King, he simply consumed and destroyed everything he came upon. No more evil than a storm at sea, but no less dangerous to human life.

How many years did our ancestors starve under the weight of the Primordials before the Chalice of Light appeared? And with it, the five gods to face them?

—From the Journal of Jovin Gutterwake

Chapter Sixteen
Sebanna's Rest

Pelady came riding back, telling of the massacre at Dothrin. Of Dianathos face down in a pool of blood and the Doves slaughtered in the ruins. The troops muttered about druids or how Gaul the Ruthless could have slain the Praetor. None of them saw Pelady take Melifacto's ear and tell him how the ruins reeked of Marta's scent.

When they arrived at Dothrin, it was just as Pelady had reported. While Bellona went about setting up camp and dealing with the corpses, Melifacto carried on. "It's too close," he told Pelady. "It's too much of a coincidence."

Pelady drove his carriage across the Fanged River to a building on the seaside cliffs. Sebanna's Archive. It had been years since Melifacto last went there. But someone had intruded in the meantime. Doors were left open, beds were slept in, and the secret passage in the bookcase was revealed to the world. He struck a sunstone and descended the steps, echoing thudding footfalls to the cavern below.

The door to the Cradle of the World was there, as it always had been. But a strange ichor spread from it, barring the path. Where it touched were gaps in space to pure blackness.

"What is that?" Pelady asked. "It doesn't smell. At all."

"It's Absence." Melifacto dug into his robes for a purple erudition crystal. "The lack of all things. It's what replaced Light in the hearts of the First Gods."

He held the crystal close to the substance and his mind blossomed with information. The Absence was spreading. Imperceptibly, but the crystal perceived the tremors in the flux. There was something else too — faint, but unmistakable. Light. Marta had brought Light to the Cradle. She tried to lull the First Gods back into their slumber, but something went wrong. Absence lashed back, consuming the power meant for the Chalice. And if Light couldn't stop it…

"What does this mean?" Pelady asked.

"That the Chalice is emptier than I assumed," Melifacto said. "*Elys sang* is only part of the puzzle now. We'll need Light, and a vessel. Neither of which is easy to come by in Adathin."

"What about Marta? Her scent is fading. She hasn't been here for a while."

"The Praetors will find her." He pulled his cloak against the blustering sea winds. The feathers ruffled like a bird in flight. "But even if we have her, it won't mean anything if these gods reawaken, or if this Absence consumes the country." He spun on his heel. "We'll leave Marta to other beasts. Wherever it is she's going now."

The bartender placed two sloshing beers onto the counter. "Black Hypogea?" he said. "Never heard of it."

"Never?" Gaul said, pushing one beer to Marta. "What about the Abyss? The Stagnant Dark? None of these names catching your ear?"

"They're creepy, but no. What is it?"

"A pit to the centre of the world."

"Oh." The bartender scratched his head. "We don't much mess with that stuff around here. You got ranchers and farmers and traders — people don't go looking for a big ol' hole. Simple folk, you know."

"What about Marjyal?" Marta asked, wiping the froth from her drink off her lip. "Don't you worry about them?"

"Yes, well, you don't live in Adathin without knowing about the City of Revels," the bartender said. "But they're far away. Sebanna's Rest was founded by our last true Queen before she left this world to join the Divines. As long as she looks over us, I'm not concerned with some Boars." He raised an eyebrow, shifting his gaze between the strange pair. "Where are you from that you're asking about Marjyal?"

"South," Marta said. "But we've heard to avoid the city."

"I find people will worry more than warranted," he said. A voice came from the back of the bar, taking his attention. "Ah, sorry. The name's Dorin if you need anything else. Though we have some other lazy ass workers here somewhere." He gave them a shrug and pushed away from the bar.

Marta elbowed Gaul in the side and jerked her head toward a table in an empty corner. She took her drink in both hands and pushed through the busy crowd, disappearing among the simple folk taking in a night of drinking. The Resting Rose was the only bar in town, and people made use of it. A man stumbled in through the front door and a group cheered for him to join them. Gaul let the man stagger past before grabbing his beer and joining Marta.

She slouched in her seat, tapping fingers against her drink. Ripples met in the centre with each hit against the glass. She would tense her brow, only to loosen it a moment later with a puff of breath.

"Something's on your mind," Gaul said, taking the seat next to her.

"It's just…" She clutched the drink. "It's weird a town like this exists down here. After Marjyal, the castle, and the swamp, this seems too normal." She turned at the sound of laughter. "I always figured Marjyal was Adathin, and Adathin was Marjyal."

"You heard Dorin," Gaul said. "Marjyal is far away. Even with horse and cart it would be weeks here and back."

"Then do you think they're still chasing us?"

Gaul slung an arm over the back of his chair and sighed. "Whatever Melifacto is offering for you is enough to die and kill for. They wouldn't give up, but it's a big country. At least according to that map of yours."

"Ugh. That map hasn't been helpful for days. I know I'm no mapmaker — what do you call them?"

"Cartographer."

"I thought they made carts."

"That's a cartwright."

Marta shook her head. "Well, I'm neither of those things, but it seems to me like scale is important on maps. Rather than writing essentially, 'Black Hypogea this way.'"

"If it even exists. We're wandering half-blind toward the afterlife."

"Oh, cheer up." She pushed his shoulder. "We can't both be depressed. Do you think we should have stopped in the swamp on the way back? We could have asked Lenn and Ba-ya for directions."

"No. It was better to stay south and avoid any Guilds. Those druids don't leave the swamp anyway, I don't feel they're best for directions."

"Ba-ya seemed proper mysterious, who knows what's bouncing around beneath that messy hair."

The last time Gaul had seen Ba-ya she was scattering as leaves across the Archive floor, talking about how powerful things became in their final days. If those were her final days, then she had certainly shown some power. But that also meant there was a chance she wouldn't be in the swamp when they returned. Cold as it may seem, Gaul didn't wish to meet another mourner.

"It doesn't matter," he said. "We're here, the swamp's back there. Now drink up so we can make some friends. Someone must know something about Black Hypogea. That, or it doesn't exist."

"Why wouldn't it exist? Sebanna said she was going there, after all."

"Because…" He pinched the bridge of his nose. "It's not really a place on a map. It's a concept for where you go after you die. Or at least where the evil souls go."

"Evil souls?"

"The wicked souls will be judged by the Gate Beyond and cast into the dark pit of Black Hypogea — where even light dares not tread. There they will be one among the monsters and lost, until their soul can be cleansed and returned to the cycle."

"Wow." Marta took a drink from her beer and checked to make sure no one heard them. She leaned toward Gaul. "Did you come up with that?"

"It's from the Book of Divines." He took his own sip and frowned. It was a harsh drink, but would get someone drunk fast. "Despite all that, at its core, Black Hypogea is a prison created by Lord Tyran, the First Knight. He cracked the earth with his blazing sword to keep the Primordial Earth King Behemoth from ever rising again."

"So, giant hole in the ground."

"More or less."

"Why would Sebanna go to a place like that?" Marta asked, chewing on her thumbnail.

"I don't think she went there. I think she went to a place that shares the name, or maybe inspired the legend. When she wrote she was going to Black Hypogea I figured she ended herself." He brought his hand to his waist and tapped his thumb on the pommel of his sword. "It doesn't matter where she went, as long as she kept writing. If we can't find anymore information on what to do about the Cradle then… then I don't know what. That Absence will keep spreading."

The Resting Rose's door slammed open with enough force to rattle the mounted antlers on the wall. An out of breath young man stood in the frame. "Marjyal is coming!" he shouted, eyes wide with terror.

A murmur ran through the crowd. Gaul caught Marta seizing. He placed his hand over hers.

"Don't move," he whispered. "React as everyone else reacts."

A woman with greying hair stepped out from behind the bar. She hobbled to the young man's side, the crowd giving her plenty of room. "Foggus," she said softly. "Catch your breath and sit down. Someone get this boy some water."

She walked with Foggus to a nearby table. The room waited with bated breath. Dorin rushed in with a cup of water and Foggus took it down in one gulp.

"Now tell me what this is all about."

Foggus took a few deep breaths, steadying himself. "I was bringing some hay out for the horses when I saw a bunch of carts and torches on the horizon. Figured it might have been a trade caravan on its way back into town, but they were coming from the northwest. I snuck a little closer and spotted a flaming horn on their cart."

"Why would Marjyal come 'round?" a man leaning on the bar shouted. "We ain't seen them in years."

The shouts of agreement and fear stopped when the old woman raised her hand. "They're probably passing through to their mines. If not, we've dealt with Boars before and so we will again."

"They weren't Boars, Nana Stundel," Foggus said. "Not like any I've seen before."

Nana Stundel nodded, considering what Foggus had just said. She coughed into her hand. "How far out are they?"

"They'll be here any minute."

"Then we shall be here to greet them. If they mean us no harm, we shall treat them as any other outsider who passes through."

The crowd nodded, unquestioning at the command of their apparent leader. But near the edge of the bar, Gaul spotted a skinny man sinking into the corner. His gaze burned into the back of Nana Stundel's head. As the crowd settled in to wait for their new arrivals, the skinny man leaned against the wall and shook his head.

Outside the Resting Rose, a horse cried and carts rattled. Someone shouted, and someone else screamed. Marta picked at the table with a knife, glaring at the open door. A few seconds later, a figure cloaked in rags wandered in, followed by four more dressed the same.

"Rats," Marta hissed. "It's the Guild of Rats."

The Rats paced the room, staring at the crowd awaiting them. No one moved. No one spoke. One of the Rats motioned at the door. A small man in a black coat — shredded to pieces — and a rat mask sauntered in. He had a hunched gait, diminishing his already small frame. In essence he blended in with the rest of the Guild, just another rat in the pack, but Gaul had seen that mask before. In the Praetor's Box at the Pits.

The Praetor of Rats grabbed his nose and pulled the mask aside, handing it off to one of his companions. He was a gaunt-faced man, who smiled a thin-lipped evil grin when he saw Nana Stundel.

"Welcome to Sebanna's Rest," Nana Stundel said. "I am Hertrude Stundel, but people around here simply call me Nana Stundel. How can we help you this night?"

The Praetor turned to the crowd. He paced the line, staring up at the faces with that same smile he gave Nana Stundel. He waved for one of his men and they passed him a rolled-up bundle of paper.

Nana Stundel wriggled in her chair. "Excuse me, sir—"

"Ettik," the Praetor said, unrolling the paper at an infuriatingly slow speed.

"Excuse me, Ettik. Is there something we can do for you?"

"I believe so." He snapped his fingers.

A Rat shoved people aside and grabbed a chair. He gave a toothless sneer to the crowd and skittered back. Gaul nearly leapt out of his seat. It was the Rat from the Pit, the one who dragged Raea's body away. Red grew in Gaul's vision.

Ettik stood on the chair and held up two papers. At the top they proclaimed in bold letters 'WANTED.' One was a drawing of a short-haired man with stern features, 'Gaul the Ruthless.' The second was a woman with chopped off hair and a scar running from the corner of her mouth. That one read 'Marta Gutterwake.'

Marta crept her hand to her cheek, covering her scar. The image of Gaul wasn't anything spectacular, but Marta's distinctive scar was a problem. She kept still, slowing her breaths with each exhale.

"We are looking for a man and a woman!" Ettik shouted. "They will be travelling together. The woman can be known by the scar on her face. If you assist us, you will be rewarded. If you oppose us… don't oppose us." He tossed the wanted posts to his guild and hopped off the chair. "We will be in town for the foreseeable future, so it will be in your best interest not to anger the Guild of Rats."

Ettik disappeared back out the door. Some of his troops followed him, while others approached the bar and demanded drinks. Nana Stundel nodded to the crowd and hobbled to the back of the room. With the urgency of molasses, everyone returned to what they were doing before Ettik barged in. Though the conversations were quieter and the smiles were smaller.

The Rat from the Pit circled the room before heading out as well.

"Stay here," Gaul said to Marta.

"Where are you going?" She kept her hand over her scar.

"I need to deal with something." He strode after the Rat before she could reply.

The flickering oil lanterns from home interiors gave Sebanna's Rest plenty of shadows for Gaul to stalk through. He hopped off the side of the Resting Rose's porch and pressed his back against the next building. A few young townsfolk were checking out the caravan of carts, pointing at the flaming horn emblazoned across the side.

"Get away from there, ya whelps," the Rat said, drawing a short blade from his side. The metal crackled as it left the scabbard and was a greenish-red.

The townsfolk scattered. The Rat tapped his sword against the cart, sending a flaky substance off the blade. The street emptied. Windows closed, leaving only the waning moon to give its light. The Rat pulled himself onto the cart and dug under the tarp. Gaul flipped up his hood and stepped forward, easing his feet into the soft dirt without a sound.

"Where did they put it?" The Rat mumbled.

Gaul grabbed him by the coat and pulled. The Rat let out a strangled yelp and flew off the cart, into the earth.

His eyes widened. "Gau—"

Gaul slammed his hand down around the Rat's mouth. He pushed his head into the mud and swatted away the Rat's hands as they clawed for him. Red filled his vision. He squeezed his fingers into the Rat's cheeks, feeling the musculature and bones under his flesh, and dragged him across the street by the head. Once he got the Rat into the alley, Gaul released his grip and drove a fist into his temple, then again into his chest. Breath shot from the Rat's lungs. He rolled onto his stomach and crawled, drawing mud and air into his mouth. Gaul kept slow pace, his soft shadow casting across the Rat's form and joining with the darkness in the alley.

"W… wa—" the Rat wheezed.

Gaul grabbed the Rat by the scruff and slammed him against the wall. Dirt rained down on them from between the slats of the building. The Rat steadied himself on his knees, only for Gaul to take him by the forehead and smash his head back. More dirt scattered as Gaul repeatedly drove the Rat's skull against the wood, leaving behind a splash of blood and splinters.

Voices came from inside the building, too obscured to make out the words. They wouldn't be alone for long. Gaul grabbed the Rat by his coat — his vision a wavering crimson — and dragged him further from the street. Clouds separated from the moon, showing a slanted shack not far from the building line. An unlit lantern hung from a hook next to the door. Gaul tossed the Rat against the frame.

"Let's… talk…" the Rat said, holding himself.

Gaul lit the lamp and stared into the new flickering flames. He couldn't Ignite. Too much rage filled his veins and his bones. That was fine with him. He wanted to engulf himself in madness, not serenity.

The Rat's hand crept from his ribs to his waist. Gaul grabbed it as his fingers tickled the pommel of his sword. The Rat's joints popped in his grip as Gaul scraped the weapon out of the sheath. The blade was caked with rust and muck. A lining along the edge turned blue in the lantern light. It was ill-kept and yet terribly sharp. Gaul flipped the sword around and pulled the Rat to his feet before shoving him through the shack door. Taking the lantern, he peered inside.

Light danced off wicked metal implements hung on the walls. Farmer's tools. A saw. A hammer. A hook. Gaul placed the rusted sword on the workbench, his eyes lingering on the serrated blades.

"Wait," the Rat croaked out, blood seeping from his toothless mouth. "We don't want you, only the girl. We can share the reward."

"I don't need you to talk anymore," Gaul said.

"Please. I'm nothing. I'm just a Body Dragger. They only brought me along to watch the cart. Have some pity."

"What was it you said?" Gaul rested the lantern on next to the sword. His heart beat steady, but strong. Rage. Red. "Oh right, the dead get no pity."

Gaul slammed the shack door shut.

Marta waited in the Resting Rose, keeping her hand against her cheek to cover her distinctive scar. Surely someone noticed her sitting motionless, not even daring to drink. But with the Rats slinking around the room, flaunting their minimal amount of power over the people, no one paid attention to the lonely woman in the corner.

Gaul was taking too long. Where did he go? Marta couldn't stay in there. She had to get out. But how to do it without revealing her scar? She dragged her fingers along her scarf, lifting it up to her face and wrapping it around her neck. It wasn't subtle. It had to do. She got one wrap around her when she spotted a skinny man in the corner giving her a crooked look. He had been sitting back from the discussion with Nana Stundel earlier. He caught one of the barmaids by the arm and whispered something to her.

Marta threw the scarf around her shoulders a few more times and leapt to her feet — only for the same barmaid to be upon her. A beer flew out of the barmaid's hand, splashing all over Marta.

"Oh!" the barmaid exclaimed. "I am terribly sorry!"

She whipped out a cloth and patted the alcohol stains. Nearby patrons stared. A few chuckled at the scene. The barmaid laid her cloth over Marta's cheek, where the scar was, and smiled at her.

"Come on, let's get you cleaned up," she said.

Marta opened her mouth, but the barmaid hustled her out the backdoor and into the night. The skinny man lounged against the back fence. He stared toward the moon-lit mountains, his hands in his pockets. He was a rakish man with shorn hair and dark skin, almost preternaturally thin. As the bar door shut, he turned and scowled.

"Black stars," he cursed. "What did you do to the poor girl, Miribelle?"

"I got her out." Miribelle crossed her arms in a huff. "That's what you asked."

"Not by giving her a beer bath."

"It worked, didn't it?"

"Excuse me?" Marta said, squeezing the beer out of her hair with Miribelle's cloth. "But what's going on?"

"Where are my manners?" The bartender gave a deep bow. "I am Fortunis of Rest, this is my sister, Miribelle."

"Charmed." Miribelle gave a sarcastic smile with her curtsy. The familial similarities were present now that they stood side by side. Their hair was a similar dark brown, with Miribelle's done in a long braid over her shoulder.

"Why did you help me?" Marta asked, eyeing the strangers cautiously.

"Because it was the right thing to do," Fortunis said.

"Excuse me if I don't take that at face value." Marta tossed the beer-soaked cloth back at Miribelle.

"You don't have to. But you should know if Nana Stundel found you, she would give you to Marjyal without a second thought."

"How can you be so sure?"

"Because she's a monster," Miribelle said. She was suddenly behind Marta. "She sends people to the Boars without the rest of the town knowing. Takes payment for sending out the strong ones."

"The Boars would take them anyways," Marta said, stepping away from Miribelle.

Fortunis crossed his arms. "I'd rather fight."

"You would die."

"And still I'd rather fight."

Marta flashed a smile, but kept it hidden under a facepalm. "This still doesn't explain why you would stick your neck out for me."

"Marjyal wants you." Fortunis beamed. "It's nice just being able to stick it to them."

"Fortunis is a madman," Miribelle said, now leaning against the back of the tavern. She was fast. Too fast. "But he has a heart of gold."

"Go back inside, Miribelle. Don't let them get suspicious."

Miribelle nodded. Then she was gone. Nothing but empty air where she once stood.

"What?" Marta blinked hard. *What just happened?*

"Miribelle's gifted," Fortunis explained, peeking around the corner of the Resting Rose. "She's not supposed to do it in public."

"Fluxblooded," Marta muttered. "That's more impressive than telling time."

"What was that?"

"Nothing. I can't leave yet. I need to find my friend."

"You need to get off the street." He motioned for Marta to follow. "You can stay at our place. I'll keep an eye out for your friend. You were sitting with him, right?"

"Yeah." A dark thought crossed Marta's mind. "How do I know you're not just turning me over for your own gain?"

Fortunis turned back to her. He ran his hand over his hair and considered the question. "I suppose you don't. But there are Rats out in the street. I could call them over right now if I was going to betray you."

"I'd kill you."

"I suppose you would." He put his hands in his pockets. "I don't know what to tell you. There must be some trust. Can you trust me?"

"No. But I can hope."

"If that's all we have..." He stepped past Marta and froze. Lights bounced down the road that curved out of the little hamlet. "Black stars. You have got to be kidding me."

Marta rushed forward, past Fortunis. She leapt over a fence and crossed a pig pen. A massive hog paid her no mind as she took position beside it and peered at the newcomers.

The crystal lamps barely illuminated the convoy. People dressed in furs with bows strung over their shoulders. A painted snake curled along their carts, beneath the flaming horn of Marjyal. Marta swore silently. The Guild of Snakes. Two of Marjyal's guilds had descended upon them.

Fortunis crept next to her, hiding behind the hog. "More Marjyalians? You're a popular one."

"How do you know they're here for me?" Marta kept low, moving with Fortunis back out of the pen.

"Let's not play dumb. Why else would so many of the Guilds come this far?"

Marta didn't answer.

"Fine. Let's get you off the street."

"I need to find Gaul. They're looking for him too."

"I've seen the post. They're not going to figure out it's him unless someone calls him by name." He motioned away from the main street, but Marta walked past him unabated.

"Gaul fought in the Festival of Vultures," Marta said. "And he won. Some of these people could recognize him, and the Praetors definitely will. I'm not going anywhere until I know he's safe."

"You're going to get both of you..."

But Marta wouldn't be stopped. She grabbed the bar's door handle. Fortunis put his hand against the wood and kept it closed. He let out a big sigh.

"Okay. I can see your point," he said. "Wait out here. We'll find him."

"You better." She leaned toward him. Fortunis was at least a head taller than her, yet he still leaned away from her glare. "I'm not going anywhere without him."

Fortunis nodded, shuddering from the intimidation. "Just keep out of sight."

Marta gave the handle a last squeeze then relented. Fortunis entered the Resting Rose with a flash of light and sound. Then the door shut and it was dark again. Marta found a tree not far from the bar and sat against its roots.

Gaul's going to be fine, she thought to herself. She drew her knees to her chest, watching the crack of light haloing the bar door.

Marta lost track of time before the Resting Rose's door swung open and a silhouetted figure in a long coat stepped out. Gaul scanned the area, backed by Fortunis. Marta leapt from her hiding spot and stomped towards them.

"Where did you go?" she asked, thrusting a finger at him.

"I was dealing with something," he said.

"You left me alone with no idea what was going on." She punched him in the shoulder. "What happened to sticking together?"

Fortunis eased the door shut, making sure no one heard them. "Could you two keep your voices down? We're trying to be subtle."

Gaul looked at his feet. "I'm sorry, Marta."

"You're damn right." She punched him again, softer this time. "I'm glad you're okay. The Guild of Snakes just arrived."

"Yeah, I just saw their carts. It doesn't look like either group is happy."

"Go back to your gutters, Rats!" a voice shouted from the street.

Marta jerked her head toward the thin alley.

"We were here first, Snake!" a second voice insisted.

Marta pulled her scarf over her mouth. It still smelled like the remnants of beer, but she ignored it and took off at a jog. Gaul flipped up his hood and followed, crouching against the wall and peering into the street. Fortunis could do nothing but throw his hands into the air and sneak after them.

A Snake stood on the front cart of the convoy, backed by his guild. Rats lined up across from them. Hands were on weapons and tension was thick. The Snake on the cart reached back and grabbed a bow.

"Step back from the cart or I'm taking an ear," he said, nocking an arrow.

The Rats drew their rusted swords. The Snakes pulled out spears and axes. They shouted and gestured, urging someone to make the move. One of the Rats pulled a glass jar from his bandolier. A blastjar. Civilians poked their heads out from between the curtains in their windows.

"Maybe they'll kill each other and save us the trouble," Gaul said, pulling his hood tighter.

"They're posturing," Marta said. "They'll never break the Accords."

Ettik came charging in from the back of the crowd, shoving a Rat aside. "Put down your weapons! Everyone!"

"But, Ettik—"

"Now!"

The Rats followed his orders. The Snakes eased, much slower than the Rats did. Ettik turned to the Snakes, his skeletal fingers playing nervously along the rat mask hanging off his belt.

"What are you Snakes doing here?" he said.

"Have you not heard?" A Snake wearing the heavy white fur of some massive beast pulled himself onto the front cart. He was a confident man with a tattoo of a snake curling out of the collar of his armour and ending on his neck. Another Praetor. "Have you not been cleaning your ears?"

"Yomat," Ettik growled. "I thought you and your hunters were heading to the Gottick Caves?"

"We were. I got a message Dianathos' body was found in the ruins of Dothric Castle."

A murmur ran through the Rats. Ettik silenced them with a hand. "Dianathos is dead? Was it the fugitives?"

"There's no way to know. Did you not get Melifacto's crow? Ah, well. I'm sure it's keeping someone fed." Yomat jumped off the cart. He paced through the crowd of Rats, tapping his finger along their heads. "My spies sent word a couple fitting Gaul and Marta's description were heading this way. The only town for days is Sebanna's Rest."

"You can't come riding into town like it's nothing. There is an order to this." Ettik stepped in Yomat's way, his crooked posture diminishing any intimidation he may have been trying. "We were here first."

"You spent a week in Marjyal scouring the sewers, wasting time. I told you they would be long gone. How many Rats did you lose to the dracolings?"

Ettik gritted his teeth and turned away. "If it wasn't for the Accords," he muttered.

"What was that?" Yomat circled Ettik. He sneered — the Praetor of Rats was a toy to him. "You think if it wasn't for the Accords, you would kill me? If it wasn't for the Accords, I would have ground you into dust when you first hobbled into Marjyal and took your position. And if you're not careful now, I will tear your pitiful guild apart. Damn the Accords."

Yomat snapped his fingers. The convoy lurched into motion, using the horses to separate the crowd of Rats. He clapped Ettik on the back and followed his guild.

"It's a nice town, Ettik," Yomat called over his shoulder. "We'll be sharing it."

The convoy rolled down the main street, Snakes jeering at the Rats as they went past. Ettik clenched his fists, his breath staggering along his chest.

"Tear this town apart!" he shouted. "Don't let those Snakes find the fugitives first!"

Fortunis grabbed Gaul and Marta by the shoulder. "Can we go now?"

"Yeah," Gaul said. Rats kicked into buildings and dragged people into the street. "Let's get out of here."

Tyran, The First Knight, set his sights on the Earth King Behemoth.

He forged himself a greatsword made from Light. He crossed the landscape, following ruins that marked the path to the monster. Tyran was small to Behemoth and the Primordial did not see the new god as a threat. The First Knight lifted his golden blade and cracked Behemoth's stone shell in one blow.

—From the Journal of Jovin Gutterwake

Chapter Seventeen
The Day Ahead

Feyra walked in the clouds. Or, at least that was what it felt like. The eastern salt flats had been flooded by a season of heavy rain. The resulting centimetre of water turned the landscape into a mirror, giving no line between the horizon and the ground. Feyra rode Arion across one of the few strips of land in a hundred kilometres. It led her to the plumes of black smoke in the distance.

She had been chasing Melifacto's crow for nearing a week. Bellona said it could lead to one of his secret outposts, and Feyra didn't want to fail her Praetor. But with time and rain the blood marker faded. When she awoke that morning and set about cleaning up her camp, she found it was gone. But it gave her an area to search. Somewhere in the expanse of water and salt was Melifacto's outpost. She would need someone who knew the area. Fortunately, Marjyal already had a presence in the salt flats. Unfortunately, they weren't easy too work with. Still, Feyra had ways of making people agreeable.

She arrived at her destination to the choking smell of smoke. The ground had been torn away, replaced with the heat and noise of a mine. A kilometre across, the Blasted Land Mines were a scar on an otherwise beautiful landscape. Bridges were suspended across the levels like an overlapping web. At the centre was the castle, Ashkeep, square and stalwart among the columns of black fumes. Everywhere were ash-covered banners displaying a flaming horn.

Feyra rode to the gatehouse, crinkling her nose to the oppressive atmosphere. A man wearing nothing but a simple tunic and breeches met her outside the rundown building. He looked up at the woman on the horse — dressed in leather and furs with the handle of a club sticking out of her saddlebag — in utter shock.

"I am Feyra, Blood of the Praetor of Boars," she said. "I wish to speak to the Praetor of Moles."

"Oh!" The gateman snatched a tabard off his chair and threw it on. It had the sharp face of a mole in front of a pickaxe. "Vickor — er, the Praetor of Moles should be in his keep."

"Then I'll surprise him." Feyra dismounted and handed the reins to the gateman. "Ensure my horse is well taken care of."

"Of course. I'll bring him to the stables right quick after I get you into the mines."

Feyra stopped the gateman and reached into her saddlebag. She drew her jagged club, a length of heavy wood over a metre long reinforced with metal spikes and blades. The gateman flinched as she swung it up and rested it on her shoulder. He kept his head low as he tied Arion to a hitching post and led Feyra into a room at the back of the gatehouse.

The gateman threw a switch and the room descended. Out the windows, the landscape disappeared, replaced by stone walls and black skies. They reached the bottom with a bump and the gatemen hurried to open the door.

"Just follow the bridges and you'll get to the keep," the gateman said. "It's impossible to miss."

Feyra stepped out of the moving room. A second gateman was waiting outside, bleary eyed and yawning. As soon as he saw Feyra, he snapped to attention.

No discipline at all, Feyra thought. She ignored him and exited the lower gatehouse into Blasted Land Mines.

She stepped onto a stone platform built out from the wall. The heat was intense, and she had to remove her coat before she began to cook. She tucked it under her arm and made her way toward the keep. The mine consisted of constructed platforms and natural pillars connected by bridges. These bridges were the veins of the mine, moving miners and crystals anywhere they needed to go.

Feyra glanced over the edge. Miners were plentiful in the upper levels, searching for crystal clusters and working any they did find. The absolute bottom — where the bubbling pools of lava made it inhospitable for people — was where the living armours worked. Moving masses of steel, shaped like hulking humanoids with lamplight eyes. They were animated by ancient runes that filled them with flux, a technology even the arcanists whose job it was to keep them running didn't understand. The knowledge had passed, but the machines still moved.

Ashkeep was built on the largest pillar in the mine, right in the centre. Guard posts that looked like they hadn't held a person in months were placed at the end of each bridge. Feyra circled the keep until she came to the front door, ash dusting the front steps to the wide-open entrance. The dining hall sat before her, complete with two long banquet tables. Stairs led to the balcony above.

"I'm here for the Praetor of Moles!" Feyra shouted. "Come out, Vickor!"

Footsteps echoed through the keep, bouncing off empty walls. A stout man rounded the corner with three guards. He wore a billowing robe of brown and red over light clothing, perfect for someone who presided over a sweltering mine.

"What is the meaning of—" Vickor stopped. "Feyra. I wasn't aware you'd be visiting."

"To be honest, neither was I," Feyra said. "We need to talk."

"Of course. Why don't we go to my study?"

Feyra motioned for Vickor to lead the way. He brought her up a nearby staircase to the second-floor balcony, overlooking the dining hall. His guards were never far behind. At the front of the keep was a nook. Tall windows let grey light through. A desk with maps of the various floors of the mine was in the centre. Vickor sat in his large wooden chair. Feyra stood, club planted tip-down on the ground, and waited for Vickor to speak.

"Alright, Feyra." Vickor placed both elbows on the desk. "What brings you all the way out here?"

"Have you received a crow in the last few days?" Feyra asked.

"No. The only time we hear from Marjyal is when something has gone wrong. An emergency shipment of crystals is needed, or our drivers were attacked by cragwolves. The rest of the time we might as well not exist."

Feyra tapped her fingers against her club, deciding whether or not Vickor was lying. The Mole Guards didn't possess the same fearlessness as their Praetor. They had Feyra surrounded and outnumbered, but that didn't stop them from shaking.

"I know for a fact Melifacto sent a crow this way," Feyra said. "If it didn't come here, where did it go?"

"I don't know. Frankly, I don't care." Vickor pushed his fists into the desk and stood. "If you want to play your political mind games, fine, do it back in Marjyal. We, meanwhile, have actual work to do. I need to keep this mine running, sending my drivers all across the country so you can get your cragging crystals!"

"Hush." Feyra raised one finger. Vickor turned bright red. "All across the country? Where do you send the crystals that isn't Marjyal?"

"I am a cragging Praetor! It is not my job to feed you information like I'm your tutor! If Bellona wants to know something, she can come here her own—" He slammed his desk. "Damn!" Again. "Self!" The mapping tools rattled to the floor.

Feyra flipped her club around and brought a spinning blow into the head of the guard standing behind her. The Mole crumpled, neck broken and face torn. The two remaining guards drew their swords, hands shaking. Feyra turned back to Vickor, pointing at him with her crimson club. Vickor fell back into his chair.

"The only reason that wasn't you was because you're still useful!" she shouted. Blood dripped from the club, staining the maps red. "But I will tear through your pathetic excuse for soldiers until there's only you. Then I will drain you of blood, drip by drip until you answer my questions!"

Vickor stammered over his words. "I… I forgot the question."

"Where are the crystals going that isn't Marjyal?"

"A bunch of places."

"Who ordered this?"

"We've just always done it. They're outposts for the Guild of Owls."

"One last question." Feyra stepped forward until her club was pressed against Vickor's head.

The guards stepped forward, but Vickor held out his hands for them to stop. "Anything I can do to help," he said.

"Where's the closest of these outposts?"

"Not far. An hour to the northeast. We bring a cart out there every few months and pick up the empty one."

"What do you bring them?"

Blood dripped down Vickor's nose from Feyra's club, joining with his sweat. "Any crystal that isn't a catalyst, the teal ones."

Feyra pushed Vickor back until his chair toppled over. The guards sheathed their weapons and ran to help. Feyra tossed her coat onto the desk.

"Take care of that until I get back," she said.

She rested her club on her shoulder and left, stepping over the body of the Mole guard. She could tell already, it was going to be a bloody day.

Gaul woke in an unfamiliar place. He stared up into the pointed ceiling and worked his brain from sleep. He was in Fortunis and Miribelle's cottage, not far from Sebanna's Rest. He and Marta were given a corner and some blankets, the best the siblings could do for their unexpected guests. Gaul sat up with his back cracking and grabbed his swords. Marta laid next to him, her own eye fluttering open to the orange sunlight.

"Good morning," Miribelle said, tightening up her braid. She grabbed two apples and tossed them over. "Just in time for breakfast. Sleep well?"

"Well enough." Gaul took a bite and stood, dangling his sword belt from his fingers. He pointed out the front window, a heavy curtain blocking any prying eyes from looking in. "What's the situation like out there?"

"Bad." Miribelle took a cup of tea and sat at the table. She wore her tavern wear, a heavy skirt and a stained apron. "Once the Snakes figured out the Rats were tearing the town apart, they joined in. People were dragged into the street, houses were destroyed, beatings — this town can't take it for long. On the other side, Nana Stundel and her goons are doing their own search. They're not much gentler. The quicker you leave, probably the better."

"That's not a bad idea," Gaul said.

"But it's not going to stop them." Marta said, flopping into a chair, her scarf hanging off one shoulder. "They'll still be looking for us."

"We'll tell them you left," Miribelle said.

"They won't believe you. Or are you going to tell them you sheltered us for a night?"

"I don't…" Miribelle rubbed her temples. "It's too early for this."

The door swung open and Fortunis entered. "There's been a development," he said, placing a basket of groceries on the counter. "Cassandra found a Rat in the shack behind the general store. He was — in her words — butchered. The Rats think a Snake did it."

Gaul took a loud bite from his apple. Marta cocked her head at him and narrowed her eyes.

"What do you think?" Miribelle said to Fortunis.

He shrugged. "Could have been a Snake. Could have been someone who just got tired of Marjyal in Sebanna's Rest. Sometimes someone has a darkness inside them. I hope it was a Snake though, let them kill each other."

"What if we make sure the Rats believe a Snake did it?" Gaul asked, resting his apple core on the table.

"What are you thinking?" Marta asked.

"Currently the Guilds are focused on the townsfolk. If we can make them focus on each other, we could force a conflict. Weaken them to the point they'll have to leave — or get forced out."

"Absolutely not," Fortunis said. "I'm not turning Sebanna's Rest into a battlefield. Just be on your way and everything will be fine."

"They're here because of us."

Miribelle stood from her chair, pleading to Fortunis. "And we can't tell the Guilds they left or they'll know we helped them."

"But they won't find them," Fortunis said, putting his hand on his sister's shoulder. "If we keep out of the Guild's way, they'll figure out these two aren't here and move on. They have no proof they're in Sebanna's Rest." He turned to Gaul and Marta. "I don't blame you for bringing Marjyal here, it's not your fault. But please leave before any more trouble begins."

"If that's what you want." Gaul slapped his knees and stood. "You don't happen to know about any place called Black Hypogea in the area, do you?"

"No. But if you head north there's a town—"

"What about the bartender?" Marta asked. The room turned to her. "Dorin, wasn't it? We talked with him for a while. He saw me at least."

"Dorin." Miribelle squeezed her eyes shut. "That's a problem. He's a nice guy, but he's not going to keep that a secret."

Fortunis ran his hand down his face. He paced to the window and leaned against the frame. Was he starting to regret helping Gaul and Marta? Turning them over would be the simplest and fastest way to end the occupation, Gaul knew that. That was unless Gaul could give them another option.

"Which brings us back to getting them both out of town," he said, stepping toward Fortunis. "You saw last night, they're ready to explode. Snakes kill a Rat, let's make them think a Rat killed a Snake. Then anything we do to them they'll blame on each other."

"How do we do that?" Miribelle asked.

"We get a Rat's sword." Marta leaned forward, rolling her apple between her palms. "They use these disgusting blades that leave infected cuts. It's unmistakable."

If only I had kept that one I got, Gaul thought. He gestured between Marta and Miribelle, while Fortunis kept his back to them, staring out the window. "At that point they'll be willing to believe anything was because of the others. We twist the knife, burn some of their supplies, make them angry."

"Last thing I saw were the Rats moving into an empty church on the other side of town," Miribelle said. "That thing is a tinderbox at best, even with all the rain. The Snakes have been keeping their carts near townhall."

"The Rats had blastjars," Marta said. "Set it on some of the Snake's carts and they'll be right pissed. Might be enough for someone to break the Accords."

"And turn Sebanna's Rest into a warzone," Fortunis said. He spun away from the window. "Listen to yourselves. Stealing weapons and lighting fires. It's going to get someone hurt."

"Didn't you say you wanted to fight?" Marta asked. "The warzone's already here. You said it yourself, they're dragging people into the street."

"A fight like this comes with sacrifice," Gaul said, standing toe to toe with Fortunis. "Only when you're very lucky does it get to be yours alone."

Fortunis flapped his jaw, looking around the room for any sort of help. Miribelle stepped in, taking her brother's hand in her own.

"Let them fight each other," she said. "If they're weak enough — if she thought she could win — Nana Stundel would get them out of town. Come on! Let's show Marjyal they can't push us around. For Dad. First Marjyal, then Nana."

Fortunis gave a tight smiled and folded his hand over hers. "I still don't like it, but let's do it."

"We have to be fast," Gaul said, crossing his arms. "We can't give them time to think. Rat kills a Snake, Snakes burn down the church, Rats blow up Snake's carts. One right after the other."

"We do this right," Marta said, gesturing with her apple, "and we could have them fighting by sundown. We just need that sword and blastjar."

Miribelle danced away from Fortunis, her skirt bouncing with each jump. "Now that would be a job for someone like me. Easy."

"Miri—" Fortunis started.

Miribelle took one step and vanished. Gaul blinked and looked about. She was gone.

"Yes," Marta said. "I was going to tell you about that."

Fortunis ran to the door and threw it open. "Miribelle! Damn it." He slammed it shut. "She can only go about a dozen metres, but if she doesn't want you to catch her, you're not going to."

"Good, I suppose," Gaul said. He wanted nothing more than to ask about Miribelle's sudden vanishing, but time was better spent forging ahead. "I can get the Snake, that won't be a problem. But Fortunis, do you think you can burn down that church?"

"I've never burned anything down before." Fortunis nervously dug his thumb into the palm of his hand. "I can't imagine it would be that hard, though."

"You can't let them see you."

"I know." Fortunis paced the room, his gaze never meeting with Gaul's.

"What do I need to do?" Marta asked, crossing her legs on her chair. "I can blow up the Rat's stuff. I'll enjoy it too."

"You're staying here," Gaul said.

"What?" Marta toppled over, stomping her feet to catch herself. "Why?"

"Marta, you'll get recognized the second anyone sees you. I at least have the chance to blend in."

Marta ran her fingers along her scar. She let out a groan and lounged back, taking a bite out of her apple. "Fine."

Miribelle appeared in mid-step from the wall. She held up a sword in a sheath wrapped with fraying rope. "Some Rats passed out upstairs in the Rose. Told you it'd be easy." She tossed the sword to Gaul.

"You certainly did," Gaul said, snatching the sword out of the air. With a sharp tug, he drew the putrid blade from its scabbard. It was the same as the one from the night before, complete with the blue-tinged edge. It reeked with the smell of blood and decay. The process of creating such a weapon was sickening to imagine.

"One problem," Miribelle said, putting her elbows on the windowsill. "They weren't carrying around any of those jars."

"They must be keeping them with the rest of their supplies," Gaul said, placing the sword on the table. "That would be the church, then."

Miribelle pushed off the sill. "Consider it done."

"No, you don't," Fortunis said, catching her by the arm. Miribelle pulled, but Fortunis held tight. "You're not going anywhere while I've got you."

"All the more reason for you to let go," Miribelle said, working her fingers under Fortunis'.

"Sneaking around your job is one thing, but it's another to go to the middle of their operation. You're not invisible. If they catch you — if they see what you can do…" He shut his eyes and took a breath. "Let's figure something else out. You can get alcohol. Let's just make a firebomb or something."

"It's not the same thing," Marta said, picking at her nails with a small knife. "I've seen firebombs and blastjars. The Snakes can tell them apart."

"And they could blame the town," Miribelle said.

Gaul tapped his thumb on his bicep. "I can make a blastjar. I saw the alchemists making them dozens of times."

"I've seen shepherds sheer sheep," Fortunis said, holding his sister close. "Doesn't mean I can do it."

Gaul scowled at Fortunis. True, the alchemists had never cared much to teach Gaul anything. But, hauling supplies and cleaning up meant he had seen all the ingredients needed. He was certain he could replicate it — but they didn't need all the details. "I've done it before. I can write up a list of ingredients, but it'll be useless without a catalyst fluxcrystal. Anywhere we can get one of those? It doesn't have to be big."

"Occasionally traders pick up a crystal," Miribelle said, pulling herself from Fortunis' grip. "Nana Stundel throws whatever coin she needs to scoop them up. I think she keeps them in her house. I could get in."

"Wait." Marta took the Rat's sword and pulled it partway from its sheath. She turned her nose up. "Gaul, there's no way you'll have time to both find and kill a Snake *and* make the blastjar. They're going to check this cottage, it's only a matter of time. Someone else has to deal with the Snake."

"I will," Miribelle said, pushing the sword back into the sheath. Marta let her take it and rest it on her shoulder.

"Miribelle!" Fortunis stepped forward.

Miribelle spun around and shoved her finger into Fortunis' chest. He stumbled back. "Stop that! I am not a child and I don't need you shouting my name like I am. I know you killed that Boar who saw my ability, and I'm just as strong as you. You can help Gaul get into Nana Stundel's house; I'm going to do my part. Okay?" She shook her head. "Actually, I don't need you to answer that."

She turned and was gone. Fortunis grasped at the spot she once stood, his jaw slack and eyes vacant.

"I was going to say I could do it," Marta said, sticking out her bottom lip. "But I guess that works too."

Gaul put his hand on Fortunis' shoulder, only for Fortunis to tear it away. "Let's get that crystal," Gaul said. "It's all we can do now."

Either Fortunis agreed, or didn't want to fight anymore. He grabbed a knit cap off a wall hook, nearly knocking the groceries to the floor in his wide motions. Nothing was said as he threw the front door open and stomped out.

"Be careful out there," Marta said, rolling out of her chair, returning to the spot on the floor she designated as her bed.

"And you keep an eye out," Gaul said, putting on his sword belt. Fortunis stood at the gate outside, squeezing onto the wood with both hands. "We're causing a lot of problems for these people. If they turn on us—"

"I know." Marta rolled over. "But I like helping them."

Gaul gave the belt a few tugs to keep it firm. Helping Sebanna's Rest was secondary. If the plan succeeded — if they could cripple two guilds — that would give him and Marta breathing room. Black Hypogea could be the end of the journey, or the start of something new. No way to tell until they were there.

Amid the clashing of these giants, the landscape bent and bowed. Mountains were formed and basins were carved. Even far from them, continents split in fear. Though hard-fought, Tyran did eventually best the Earth King.

—From the Journal of Jovin Gutterwake

Chapter Eighteen

Blood Stains

Nana Stundel's house was a two-floor not far from the tavern. Its back faced the woods, giving Gaul and Fortunis privacy as they opened a window and inspected the room. A piano sat in a corner, the wood polished to immaculate splendour. Several chairs and a lounger gave Nana and her guests plenty of space to rest in and listen to the music.

"Hold up," Fortunis said, taking Gaul by the arm. "I don't like you getting my sister involved in this."

"Your sister involved herself," Gaul said, pressing his back to the cold wood wall. "From what I saw, no one can tell her what to do."

"You saw her jump-step?" Fortunis asked.

Gaul nodded.

"I've never seen anyone else do anything like it," Fortunis said, his expression turning to somber remembrance. "As a kid my mother told her to be careful with it. To keep it hidden. You hear about Marjyal around, how they take people. A few years ago, some Boars came through town. One of them got his sights on Miribelle. He wouldn't take no for an answer and followed her all the way back to the cottage. I caught them outside as he was putting his hands around her throat. I shouted, he let go, and Miribelle jumped."

Each word of the story pulled Fortunis away. Part of Gaul wanted to ask if it was the time for a talk like this, but emotion caught in Fortunis' throat. If that choking serpent wasn't let out, his mind wouldn't be on the job.

"I saw the look on that Boar's face," Fortunis continued. "He was half-drunk, but he slurred out that she was gifted by Mar. I didn't know what that meant but it made me sick. I could see greed in his eyes. I had a spade I had been using earlier that day. And I thought Miribelle had run. So, before he got up, I hit him. He fell, but he was still breathing. I used the edge and I cracked his skull open. I threw up and then I buried him. I didn't think Miribelle saw, but she never did ask what happened. That should have been a sign."

"You protected her," Gaul said.

"And I will continue to protect her." He squeezed his knuckles until they popped. "But now she's off hunting down a man to kill. It's far too dangerous, and it's your fault!" He grabbed Gaul by the coat and pulled him close. Tears hid at the corners of Fortunis' eyes, but his grimace was all anger. "If she gets hurt—"

Gaul pushed on Fortunis' elbow, bending it and pulling him even closer. They were eye-to-eye. Gaul swelled, looming over the man who held him. Fortunis, now realizing he bit off more than he could chew, tried to pull back. But Gaul clutched his forearm, keeping it against his chest.

"Some advice," Gaul said, a low growl coming from behind his words. "If you want to protect someone, you let them fight beside you, not hide them away. Porcelain dolls will always get broken."

Gaul released and Fortunis stumbled back, rubbing his arm. There was a mark from where Gaul had pushed his fingers into the skin. Fortunis stared hard at the abrasion, everything in him working to keep the tears where they belonged.

Now Gaul felt like an asshole. He ran his hand along the back of his neck and moved away from Nana Stundel's house, speaking softly to keep their covert mission covert. "One of the things about being alone is you don't have anyone to protect, so maybe I don't know what you're feeling. I just know the world will hurt people, it's what the world does. Trying to keep Miribelle away from harm is impossible. She knows that too, don't think she doesn't. This is why we fight. To be strong enough to withstand those blows."

"I… think you may be right," Fortunis said, rubbing his eyes with his arms. "I don't know you are, but the way you said it makes me want to believe it." He turned to Gaul, a small smile on his face. "And how can you say you're alone? Aren't you and Marta fugitives together?"

"That's a way to look at it." Gaul didn't know what to make of his time with Marta. It was better than when they left Marjyal, but he still couldn't shake the feeling they were separate ships heading to the same port. "Speaking of her, we should move along before she gets too restless. She knows she's recognizable, but she also doesn't like sitting around."

"Sounds like Miribelle," Fortunis said, shaking off the last of his outburst. "Come on. I've never been inside the house, but I think she has a study upstairs. Might be where she keeps the crystals."

"It's worth a look."

They returned to the window and checked to make sure there weren't any onlookers. Fortunis scanned the alleyways while Gaul hopped over the sill into the parlour. Fragrant flowers greeted him with the smells of nature. Fine curtains hung across the walls in long sweeps to break up the crimson colour and ostentatious paintings. This room was built for entertaining, not for any sense of belonging.

Fortunis threw his leg through the window, sending a creak as he pressed into the floorboards. Gaul grimaced, but sounds like that were unavoidable in an old house.

"Sorry," Fortunis whispered. "We should hurry. Nana spends at lot of time at the Resting Rose in the mornings, but with the Guilds around, who knows what her schedule is."

"Why does she buy all the crystals?" Gaul asked, stepping through the parlour to a hallway. Here a thin staircase circled around to the second floor.

"I don't know for sure," Fortunis said, following Gaul up the stairs. "I don't think anyone does except Nana herself. I always figured she didn't want anyone in town having any semblance of power. Even just a little crystal."

They came to the second landing. A small space with four doors that went off in different directions. The red analogous colours from the floor below gave way to neutrals and fine décor. Fortunis opened the door to his left with a long creak. Past it was a room centrepieced by a large desk and seats for serious discussions.

"We should spread out," Gaul said, opening the next door to a bedroom. "Call out if you find anything."

They scoured the top floor for half an hour. From the knickknack-filled study to the sparse bedroom and the elegant bath. Gaul picked up a gold candlestick that sat on Nana's bedside table. Sebanna's Rest wasn't wealthy by any stretch of the imagination, but her she was burning on gold. Opening the wardrobe and carefully ruffling through clothes gave nothing but lint.

Pulling aside a dour dress, Gaul found clothes that should have been for a much younger lady. Fine dresses and form-fitting blouses. Perhaps from Nana's younger days, and yet they seemed in too good of shape to be reminders of the past.

"Find anything?" Fortunis asked, stepping into the room.

"No luck," Gaul said, replacing the clothes and shutting the wardrobe. "Does Nana Stundel have a daughter? Granddaughter?"

"I don't think so. She doesn't seem like the family type. Though I think she was married once." Fortunis' gaze lingered on the gold candlestick, a scowl crossing his face. "Let's check downstairs."

They returned to the sitting room. Gaul ran his fingers along the wall, feeling for any depression or other irregularity. He peeked beneath paintings and tapestries, but it was as devoid of crystals as the top floor.

"Are you sure they're kept in her house?" Gaul inspected a painting of Sebanna cresting a cliff point. She looked majestic, long dark locks framed by a halo of white light. A far cry from the dour family portrait he saw in Adathin Castle.

"I can't think of where else she would," Fortunis said. "She owns the Resting Rose, but that seems somewhat public if she wants to keep them a secret."

Something clicked down the hall. Gaul froze, half-kneeling next to a couch. Fortunis stood by a cabinet, a bundle of curtain clutched in his hand. There was a long creak as the front door opened.

"Bring him into the sitting room," Nana Stundel said, her voice echoing from the front hall.

Fortunis threw the cabinet doors open and leapt inside. Gaul dropped to his stomach and rolled under the couch, ending up in a small space made by the couch and the corner. Four pairs of feet came thumping into the room, three boots and one low-heeled shoe. One boot-wearer was shoved to his knees, bracketed by the other two. The last one — Nana Stundel, Gaul would imagine — shuffled to the couch and sat down. The wood creaked next to Gaul's head. He kept his breathing slow and quiet. Nana Stundel broke into a coughing fit, shaking the couch.

"Dorin," Nana said, recovering. "You say you saw these people, Gaul and Marta, in the Resting Rose?"

"Y-yes, Nana Stundel," the man said. It was Dorin, the bartender from the Resting Rose. "They were asking for directions to some place called Black Hypogea."

"Interesting," Nana said. "Did you see what happened to them?"

"No. The Rats came in and I couldn't think. I was serving them all night and it wasn't until this morning I saw the post and recognized the scar."

Told you, Marta, Gaul thought.

"I understand." Nana Stundel coughed. One of the men stepped forward. "I'm fine. Now, Dorin, when Riggin here came to me, he said you were planning on telling the Rats about this. Why would you do that?"

Dorin shook. Even on his knees, ready to collapse. "Once they got who they came for, they would leave."

"And why the Rats?"

"Because…" Dorin let out a stuttering breath. He couldn't come up with a reason — or a lie.

Nana Stundel leaned forward, the couch creaking. "Is it because they offered a reward?"

"Yes, Nana Stundel," Dorin said, his voice heavy with shame.

"Do I not pay you enough?"

"It's not that."

"You're greedy." She let out a single, squeaky, laugh. "Nothing wrong with that. Greed can be a fine motivator if you're smart about it. There are many things I want. I would even say I'm greedy. But you, Dorin, are greedy and stupid. If you leave, you won't tell the Rats, will you?"

"No! I won't tell anyone. Just you! I just told you!"

"Then I will take your fate into consideration."

Metal hummed and Dorin gasped in shock. His body seized. Gaul stretched forward, trying to see what happened. Blood trickled to the floor about half a metre from the front of Dorin's body. With a wet slurp, Riggin drew his sword from Dorin's back and let the poor bartender fall. He collapsed to his side and in those last moments, as the blood pulsed from his chest, made eye contact with Gaul. Then he was still.

"Oh, Riggin," Nana said. "I wish you would have done that where it wouldn't have stained my carpet."

"Sorry, Nana Stundel."

"It's quite alright." She stood with another creak from the couch. "But it's now your job to clean it. Take the money the Rats already paid him with and put it in the stockpile."

"Yes, Nana Stundel."

"Come on, Jon." She and the other pair of feet walked out. "Someone in the Rose must have seen where they went."

Nana Stundel and Jon left Riggin in the sitting room. He pulled a pouch from Dorin's belt and moved to the piano. Gaul crawled to the edge of the couch and looked through the space between it and the wall. Riggin lifted the top of the piano and dropped the pouch inside. If that was where Stundel was keeping her money, it could also be where the crystals were.

Riggin shut the lid and returned to the body. He flipped both sides of the rug over Dorin and dragged him out of the room. Gaul waited until the back door shut, then another minute to make sure Riggin wasn't coming back. He stood up and stepped over the couch.

Fortunis exited the closet and pointed at the piano. Gaul nodded and they crept over. One eye stayed on the back window, ready to run if Riggin's form reappeared. Beneath the cover was a platform built above the strings, full of pouches, wine bottles, and other such luxuries. Gaul took a bag that had sharp shapes pressing against the fabric and untied the string. Catalyst crystals, pulsing in steady rhythm, cast their teal light against his face.

"Will any of these work?" Fortunis whispered.

Gaul laid the bag on the piano bench and picked through. Some were too big, or too murky. He found a nice coloured one that could fit in a jar and held it up to the light.

"I'm not really an expert," he said. "This looks fine. I'll take two just to be sure."

He grabbed a similar looking one then placed the bag back where he found it. Fortunis softly shut the piano and they crept to the back window they entered through. Gaul glanced around the curtain. The back was clear. Riggin was still doing his gravedigger duties in the woods. Fortunis pushed on the window and scurried out with Gaul at his back.

"Dorin was annoying at times," Fortunis said, looking toward the forest. "His answer to almost everything was ignoring it. But he was a good man. I can't believe we're relying on Nana Stundel to run the Guilds out of town."

"The enemy of your enemy isn't always your friend," Gaul said, shutting the window. "Sometimes they're just a tool. So let's use them."

Fortunis squared his jaw. "A few more ingredients. Then I'll burn down that church and we can get at least some of the monsters out of Sebanna's Rest." He fixed his collar and stomped away from Nana Stundel's.

Gaul rested his hands on his sword pommels. "Well then. At least you're getting into it." He flipped his coat forward and chased after Fortunis' fleeting form.

* *

After riding northeast, Feyra found herself standing before a bizarre sight. In the middle of the salt flats, with nothing for kilometres in all directions, was a birdhouse. It was a metre tall, made of a dark wood. It stuck out of the shallow water like a lonely lighthouse. Try as she might, Feyra couldn't figure out why it existed.

Out of ideas, she put a finger on top of the birdhouse and pushed down. It sank easily. Below her feet, muffled by the earth and water, a bell rang. She released the structure and it rose up again. There was silence. Then, the metallic grinding of a heavy latch split the air. A dozen metres away, the ground rose up. Under the water, disguised as part of the salt flats, was a hatch. It splashed against the flats and woman climbed out of the hole. She stopped with one hand on the top rung, eyes locked on the intruder who was distinctly not a bird.

They stared at each other in uneasy silence. A gust of wind made waves across the water. The woman lunged for the hatch door. In one smooth motion, Feyra sliced her thumb open across her club and shot a blood bolt. It struck the woman on the arm, splattering her blood across the salt flats. It didn't stop her, and she still scrambled to shut the hatch.

Feyra charged forth, kicking up water in her wake. The woman swung the hatch closed, but not before Feyra wedged her club in and threw it open once again. Water poured from the surface into the depths below. The woman was halfway down the shaft. Feyra flipped her club around then, like a javelin, hurled it straight down. It struck the woman on the head and she rattled between the ladder and the shaft walls all the way to the bottom.

Anyone down there would know she was coming. All the better — Feyra was getting restless. She took the top rung and swung herself down, descending the shaft lit by inset sunstones. She leapt off near the bottom and landed with a splash, one foot to each side of the first guard. Her neck twisted awkwardly, and she leaked blood from her head. But she was dead, and the least of Feyra's concerns.

Ahead of her was a staging area littered with crates that had been lowered down the shaft. A dozen men and women wearing heavy leather aprons had stopped what they were doing. They stared at Feyra, eyes wide and mouths agape. Owl's heads were painted on the walls.

She had found it.

An Owl dropped his crate, spilling fluxcrystals across the floor. He ran to a weapons rack against the wall and started tossing swords to his allies. Feyra untied her wrist cuffs, rolling them down her arm to reveal arcane scribblings inked into her skin. They flowed around her forearms and biceps like leaves dancing on the wind. As she clenched her fist, the very space around these words cracked for an instant and they turned deep crimson.

Feyra stepped forward, letting her hand dangle behind her. Blood pulled away from the first Owl's hair and skin, becoming fractal shapes that followed Feyra's fingers. She lifted her arm, letting the shifting blood bead float just below her outstretched hand. The Owls shared glances, trying to figure out what was going on. The wounds on the Owl weren't large enough to get much blood, but it would do.

A particularly courageous Owl let out a battle cry and charged in, sword at the ready. Feyra flicked her fingers and the bead became a spear, plunging through the

Owl's stomach and out through his spine. His sword clattered to the ground. Feyra yanked her hand back, pulling the spear free and adding blood to her supply. The other Owls watched as their companion collapsed dead, while Feyra floated an orb the size of her fist over her palm.

"Aren't you Feyra?" an Owl asked, the tip of his blade following her movements. "You're a Boar. Why are you here?"

Feyra spun the orb around her index finger, taking slow steps forward. "How many are there of you?"

"What did you say?" the Owl asked.

A second Owl stepped up, shaking her sword. "How are you doing that? How are you moving that blood?"

"I only need one." Feyra swung her arm across her chest, the orb turning into a scythe-like curved blade. Half a dozen more Owls came running in from deeper in the complex, clutching swords, shields, and spears. "The rest of you are witnesses."

The shaking Owl leapt forward. Feyra parried the sword and swung her arm. The crimson moon pierced cleanly through the Owl's chest, drawing yet more blood as it exited out her back. A dozen steel edges reached for Feyra and she pressed against the horde. Blood ebbed and flowed with her movements, crashing and retreating like waves on a rocky shore. She caught a wide sword swing with her bloody wall then threw both arms forward — snapping the blood around the blade and clamping its wielder like the jaws of a wolf.

An Owl swept in from behind, only for Feyra to drive her heel into his stomach, twist around, and drop a heavy guillotine into his shoulder. It broke apart his collarbone and cut to his upper chest. As the Owl screamed, Feyra snapped her fingers. The guillotine burst into spikes that skewered those behind him and ending the Owl's suffering. Feyra drew the blood from their wounds and turned to the few that remained.

"To the workshop!" one shouted, shoving his companions out of the way.

A whip of blood caught him across the back, sending his own scattering into the air. The droplets slowed into vibrating points that hung above the two Owls caught in macabre mystification. Feyra lowered her fingers and the droplets fell to the earth, turning the Owls into pincushions. The rest scrambled over each other into the next room.

Rivers of blood crossed and spiraled, all with Feyra as their nexus. She sauntered forth, a crimson queen in her regality. Yet more Owls arrived in the workshop, clutching weapons and wearing aprons from their recently abandoned work. But they had done nothing to impress her. They were as useless as the ones in Marjyal.

One pushed through the crowd, knocking over jars with crystals and fluids. He hurled a spherical object. Feyra snapped her blood around it, suspending it in the air between her and the group. It was made of some sort of clay, and as the room held its breath in anticipation, a small rune lit up on the side. Feyra gasped, moving the rest of her blood to cover the blastjar.

A dull thump cracked the air, sending blackened blood splattering across the workshop and striking Feyra in the chest with a concussive blast. She stumbled back and grabbed onto the door frame, holding herself up as her body ached with sudden pain. She wiped the blood off her face. Most of it had burned to the point it was unusable. She clenched her fist, drawing back any blood that remained.

They're going to pay for that.

An Owl raised his crossbow and fired. The bolt whistled through the air. Feyra raised a handful of blood, catching the bolt before it could pierce her eye. The crossbowman dug into his pouch for another bolt. He didn't see Feyra snap the first in half and charge forward. Owls retreated to the back of the workshop, leaving the crossbowman alone. He placed the bolt in position and raised his weapon. Feyra was quicker. She vaulted a table and knocked the crossbow away.

The Owl staggered and reached for his sword, fear filling his eyes. Feyra pooled the blood in her palm and slammed it against the man's chest. The blood roiled and ripped through his skin. As Feyra pulled her hand back, she brought with it the Owl's own gore.

The two of the eight remaining Owls gripped their swords hard and rushed forward. They had figured out the best time to fight Feyra was when she was low on blood. Unfortunately for them, they figured it out just too late.

Feyra spun the Owl in her grip around and planted her palm against his back. A long, thin, blade oozed out of his chest. A charging Owl chopped for the man's shoulder, intending to cut through his ally to get to Feyra. The blood parried the strike instead.

Keeping one hand on her puppet's back, Feyra gave ground. The two Owls fought with the intent to overwhelm. Her blood blade zoomed from one foe to the other, but when one was left alone he would attempt to sneak around, meaning Feyra had to move the blade back to him. Her brain ached from exertion. It was getting hard to focus. She needed to end it before she passed out.

Feyra took the Owl by both shoulders and threw him down. The two she fought with were so surprised they jumped back. They kept their eyes on Feyra, trying to figure out what she would do next. They ignored the man she cast aside. A mistake. Feyra swung up two fingers. The dead Owl's back vibrated before two jagged spears leapt from his corpse. They went through the other Owls' chests and heads, leaving them suspended on their feet as their swords clattered from loose fingers.

Feyra's vision went fuzzy. She pulled the blood back into an orb at her side. Three Owls left.

Weren't there four a second ago?

The missing Owl stepped in from a side room clutching onto a long tube with a crossbow grip. Dials and tubes lined the outside, pulsing with red arcane energy. He pointed it at Feyra and pulled the trigger. A flickering light grew inside the mouth.

On instinct alone, Feyra raised a barrier against the shooting flames. She had never seen a device like that before. It cooked through her defenses, dropping clumps of useless blood to the floor. Sweat rolled down Feyra's brow into her eyes. She was nearly out of blood, but the unbearable heat from the flamesprayer was nonstop. She flipped one of the metal tables, sending half-finished experiments flying, and dropped behind it as the shield gave way.

She kept her head low, the Owl locking her down with spurts of fire. The metal of the table grew hot against her back. Without any blood, she had few options. She looked around, hoping to find something that could give her a way out.

The hasty retreat of the Owls and Feyra's wide-sweeping combat had knocked many of the arcanist's devices to the ground. Most were foreign things with piping and ruins. Even if she had them she wouldn't know what they did. But among the detritus were two blastjars. The flamesprayer closed in, nearly reaching around her cover. Feyra grabbed both blastjars and pushed herself against the quickly heating table.

She pulled the blastjar tab and tossed it over her cover. The Owls gasped in shock. Feyra covered her head. There was the sound of the blastjar hitting the ground… then nothing.

"They don't have crystals," the Owl said, laughing.

Feyra stared at the one still in her hand. Without a catalyst, there was nothing to set off the formula, nothing to activate the runes.

"Get a bird for Melifacto," the Owl continued. "We'll take her alive. If not a little crispy."

Feyra scrambled out from cover, facing the Owls that remained. The one with the flamesprayer raised it to his shoulder. Smoke trailed off the lips of the barrel, obscuring his angry eyes.

"I don't know why you came here, Boar," he said. "But you're going to regret it once Melifacto hears about it."

Feyra couldn't let that happen. Melifacto would know it was Bellona behind it. Worse, Bellona would know Feyra failed. The Owl crept forward, keeping the flamesprayer trained on her. Setting her jaw, Feyra raised the blastjar clutched in her grip.

The Owl stopped, then smiled. "We don't keep live explosives around. Good luck using that without a crystal."

The blood in Feyra's veins grew hot. She focused her willpower on the blastjar, squeezing her fingers harder against its ribbed surface. She'd only done this a few times, but a final push, the runes on the blastjar lit up. The Owl's face dropped. She smiled and rolled the jar between his legs.

Feyra dove out of the room and rolled aside as the blastjar exploded, sending fire and shrapnel tearing through the air. The Owl with the flamesprayer flew through the open door. The weapon went sailing away as he cracked his skull against the hard stone. The back of his coat was torn apart, revealing burned flesh and embedded clay. Crackling blue smoke rose from his ruined spine.

Exhaustion wracked Feyra's body. She forced her knees beneath her, then further forced them to let her stand. Using the walls as crutches, she stumbled into the now destroyed workshop.

Desks and arcane tools were shattered. The back half of the lab was a horror show of blood and mangled bodies. Feyra groaned, grabbing her head. Her brain rung a shrill bell and she had trouble focusing her eyes.

Amid the devastation, there was one Owl still moving. He crawled through the remains of the lab, over the bodies of his allies. Feyra let out a scratchy sigh and lurched, step by step, across the room. The Owl grabbed onto the leg of another, pulling himself forward. His arm was a mess of shrapnel. Spit and blood foamed between his teeth.

Feyra caught him before he could get out of the room, stomping on his heel and pinning him in place. She leaned in. "There," she said. "I said I only need one."

The Owl gazed up to her, fear in his eyes and sweat dripping off his nose. Feyra pushed down harder on his heel. The Owl screamed, then passed out from the pain.

The workshop was a scene of devastation, but the outpost was now quiet. They had to be working on something important to fight so diligently. Feyra rolled down her sleeve, covering up the ink along her skin. She smiled. There must be a god guiding Feyra. They had granted her a path to serve Bellona. They had granted her someone to interrogate.

Sitting around in the cottage was driving Marta crazy. She had looked in every cupboard and sat in every chair. She peeked out the windows when she got a chance, but only to make sure neither of the Guilds were sneaking up on her. She was bored — and liked to put up a fight — but she would never leave as long as Marjyal haunted the streets. That old fear still gripped her.

She was lying on the floor, tossing an apple up and down, when Gaul came back. He emptied his pockets of vials, a bottle of alcohol, and an empty jar.

"How'd it go?" Marta asked.

"Better than I expected," Gaul said, taking two teal crystals from his pocket. He inspected then against the sunlight then laid them next to the vials. "Fortunis is going to set fire to the church. Has Miribelle come back yet?"

"No." Marta caught the apple then dropped her arms to the ground. "Figured it would take her a while. Get everything you need?"

"I think so."

Marta pushed herself up from the floor. "You can make this, right?"

"Sure I can." He inspected a vial with dark grey leaves inside. "Or, I should be able to. I'll fill in the gaps with alcohol. It'll look like a shoddily made blastjar — because it will be."

Gaul lit a fire in the hearth. He dumped half a pint of grain draught into a pot with water and hung it over the flame. He sorted out the vials of regents on the table. His fingers hovered over them and his brow furrowed. Marta crossed her arms and waited as Gaul gave intense thought to the reagents before him. It seemed he may have been somewhat over-confident. Finally, he snatched up the two vials with leaves and roots in them and added them to the concoction, turning the ale into a pale grey.

"Gaul," Marta said, sitting on the table and rolling a vial of thick silver powder between her fingers. "Why did you kill that Rat?"

Gaul cocked his head but kept his eyes on the pot. "What are you talking about?"

"You disappeared last night after the Rats arrived. They found a Rat this morning. It could be a coincidence, but…" She placed the vial next to the crystals. "Don't get me wrong, I'm sure they deserved it, I'm just wondering why you did it."

Gaul took the powder and popped the cork. He sprinkled it over the darkening liquid, stirring the pot slowly to make sure it all mixed.

"Gaul," Marta said.

"I was angry," he finally said. "When I was in the Pits I didn't fight alone. There was a woman, Raea was her name. I wouldn't have survived without her. But when it was done, we were told only one of us could get out."

"I saw," Marta said, picking at her nails. "I saw that part at least."

"Then you saw that I killed her."

"I also saw she was going to kill you."

Gaul took a knife from the counter and absentmindedly tapped it against the back of his hand. "I could have done something different. Maybe. Maybe if I hadn't become lost in the red. It doesn't matter now. But that Rat, he just dragged her away like she was nothing. I wanted to hurt him. Thought it may make me feel better."

"Did it?"

"No." He winced, not from pain but from memory. "Pass me a crystal."

Marta took one of the catalyst crystals and tossed it over.

"Why should it of?" Gaul asked, spinning the crystal in his palm. "We could leave, you know."

"Leave?"

"Leave Sebanna's Rest before the Guild's find us. I was worried that Miribelle and Fortunis might turn us in if we became too much of a problem, but they're gone now. We could get out of town before they even know."

Marta bobbed her head. She crossed her legs onto the table. "And would you feel comfortable about that?"

"It's our fault," Gaul said. "But it's not our problem."

"Just a second ago you were all sad about that woman from the Pits." Marta leaned forward. "All that talk about fighting and sacrifice was just so Fortunis wouldn't turn us in? I don't believe that. I think if we leave, this would be another thing for you to regret."

Gaul bounced the crystal in his hand. "I've gotten used to regret."

He had only said what they were both thinking. Marta's plan had always been to run and to hide. Actually, her plan had been to follow Jovin. Now her plan was to run. Gaul held the crystal over the pot and started chipping at it. Powdered crystal flaked into the mixture, multi-coloured sparks jumping as it touched the surface.

"I like having the chance to help," Marta said, sliding off the table and peering over Gaul's shoulder, entranced by the lightshow. "It doesn't come by everyday."

"Yeah," Gaul said quietly. "I do too."

With one big hit on the crystal, a purple flame burst out of the pot. Gaul and Marta recoiled, but rather than giving off heat, the flame sucked it in and left the air cold. It flared for several seconds then subsided.

"Was that supposed to happen?" Marta asked, brushing the frost off her coat.

"I think so." Gaul put the lid on the pot and pushed a layer of ice off his chin. "It's going to sit for a while now."

"I really hope you aren't going to blow us up."

"Me too."

Miribelle appeared in the middle of the room, holding a sloshing bucket of water. She dumped it into the basin and tossed the bucket aside. Grabbing both edges of the basin, she stared into the water.

Marta took a step toward her. "How'd it—"

Miribelle dunked her head into the water. It splashed over onto the counter and then onto the floor. She shook her head, sending more water flying into the air and soaking Marta's pants. Finally, she yanked her head back.

"It's done," she said, pulling her braid out.

Gaul and Marta shared a glance. Miribelle slid a chair out from the table and took a seat, cradling her head in her hands. The silence continued. She looked at Gaul and Marta, at the mess she left by the basin, then back to them.

"It's a stress thing." She pulled at her long hair, squeezing the water out. "Don't tell Fortunis."

They nodded. Marta sat next to Miribelle, with Gaul taking the seat across from them. The young woman had a distant look and would periodically stop running her fingers through her hair — as though something caught her attention — only to start back up a moment later.

"So—" Gaul started.

"It took forever to find a Snake that was alone," Miribelle said. "I followed this one for twenty — thirty minutes. He would just threaten people and laugh when they ran away. This poor guy bumped into him and he slammed his head into the wall until he was unconscious. Figured that was a Snake I wouldn't feel bad about. Eventually he went behind the carpenter's and I snuck up behind him. He heard me, but I was still able to get that sword into his stomach. He grabbed my hand. I covered his mouth so he wouldn't scream and twisted the... He looked so sad. Or scared." A shiver ran across her. "His eyes were blue."

She let out a puff of air and bowed her head. Marta patted her on the shoulder, and she grabbed her hand.

"Could be worse," Gaul said, standing up.

"How's that?" Miribelle mumbled.

"You could have liked it."

She chuckled. She released Marta's hand and lounged in her chair. "They're not going to be happy when they find him."

"Perfect." Gaul turned to the pot and lifted the lid. The mixture let out a strong smell of burnt leather and was taking on a more yellow-ish colour. "Won't be long now."

"I'll take a walk then," Miribelle said, standing. "See what the situation is like out there."

"You might want to…" Marta pointed at her dress.

Miribelle looked down. Her dress was soaked from dunking her head. More than that, a fist-sized bloodstain sat on her waist, once hidden by the table. "Oh," she said. "I'll go change." She took a slow step and vanished.

Gaul brushed off the talk with Miribelle and grabbed the jar from his supplies. He took the knife and began scratching into the glass runes he had drawn on a piece of paper. The squeak of metal on glass and the bubbling of amber liquid filled the silence. Marta reached across the table and lifted up the corner of the paper. Her own emotionless expression stared back at her. Crafted by an artist and pressed over and over into hundreds of wanted posts, Marta's face would be across the country. They're only hope was to keep ahead of the information.

Marta laid her head on the table, closing her eyes to the scratching and boiling. If she could find out why Melifacto wanted her, she could do something about it. She could make it clear he made a mistake. She could finally sleep without nightmares of returning to Marjyalian streets.

Or maybe someday, once the rest of the Praetors fail or fall, Melifacto would come himself. When he was within reach, Marta could end all this. Miribelle showed regret for killing even a Snake or a Rat. Marta didn't have the same softness.

She would like it.

Knowing Behemoth was immortal, Tyran came up with a perfect prison. He cracked the earth with his blazing sword and thrust Behemoth to the edge of the Dark. To the bottom of Black Hypogea.

—From the Journal of Jovin Gutterwake

Chapter Nineteen
To Break

Feyra took a walk through the outpost. It was sprawling, with a few dozen rooms hidden beneath the salt flats. She found more shafts to the surface, where supplies could be lowered down through trap doors. In these rooms were storage, labs, and cells. Though 'cell' was generous. They were metal boxes, either too short to stand up in or too thin to lay down. Plates hung from the doors like name tags, but with five-digit numbers instead of letters. Not prisoners. Test subjects. Now they were all empty.

Feyra grabbed a chair from the mess hall and dragged it back to the destroyed lab. She tied the surviving Owl to the chair and waited. The lab stunk with burned meat and metallic grit. When the Owl awoke, Feyra was waiting, seated on a throne of corpses.

"What are you?" the Owl croaked.

"You're not in the position to ask questions," Feyra said.

The Owl's gaze flickered to Feyra's club, leaning against her leg.

"That's not what you should be worried about." Feyra pointed downward.

Blood leaked from the pile and surrounded the Owl's legs. When Feyra moved her hand, a ripple followed. It circled the Owl's chair like a sea serpent. He turned pale.

"Now." Feyra leaned back, limply swinging her hand back and forth. "What's your name?"

"What?"

Feyra flicked one finger. A blood spike shot into the Owl's calf. He howled and pulled against his bindings.

"What is your name?" Feyra asked again.

"Drayton," the Owl said through gritted teeth.

"Very good, Drayton." The spike retreated and the ripple moved again. "What do you do here?"

"Me? I'm an assistant. I clean up and help with the experiments where I can."

Another spike shot through his thigh. "Maybe that's my fault," Feyra said. "I wasn't clear. What is Melifacto having you all do here? And do be detailed, Drayton."

"Research." Drayton took in a gasp of raspy air. His chest was burned from the blastjar explosion and it seemed to be affecting his breathing. The spike slowly retracted from his body and he continued, "Weapons, mostly. Uses for esoteric fluxcrystals."

"Uses for what?"

"Esoteric fluxcrystals? Most fluxcrystals are bluish-green, you know? Catalyst crystals? But they can mutate into different colours that have different purposes." He winced in pain. "Oh gods, my leg. White ones are sunstones, they're technically esoteric. Or… or at least that's what I heard from the arcanists."

Feyra rubbed her temple. This was too boring to be important. "No. No. No!" A spike pierced through the bottom of Drayton's foot. Feyra leapt forward, leaving her club to clatter about, and grabbed him by the jaw, catching his scream in his throat. "What does any of this have to do with *elys sang*?"

"I don't know!"

"A crow arrived this morning. What was the message?"

Drayton's eyes fluttered. Every bit of his energy was going to finding an answer. His foot twitched against the pulsing blood construct turning in his flesh. "You want to know about the people," he finally said.

Feyra kept his head pushed back but allowed the spike to leave his foot. "Continue."

"It was asking about the subjects." Spit dripped down the sides of his mouth, leaving tinges of red in his stubble. "I don't work with them. We used to keep people, but we haven't had any in months."

"There has to be something else." She released him and stepped back. Strands of her chestnut hair — fallen from her intricate braid — hung in front of her eyes. She absentmindedly swirled her hand, the blood at her feet following the motions. "The gods saved you for a reason. They allowed you to live. You must know something. You must." The blood around Drayton's chair grew into cracking, bladed ribs — as if the space around it was folding in and snapping back. "I simply haven't hurt you enough."

"I don't know anything!" His panicked eyes flicked between the blood arcs reaching for him like wicked fingers. "I'm not lying! I was just brought in to do grunt work, I'm not even from Marjyal!"

Feyra let out a long sigh. There was truth in his fear. The blood began to recede.

"Just please let me go," Drayton said, letting his head loll about on his shoulders. "I won't tell anyone. I don't even know anyone! I was a sailor, I hauled cargo. That's why Melifacto send me here after that bitch Bellona the Boar sunk my ship."

Half a dozen blood spikes shot into his body. He let out a scream that cracked his throat. Feyra twisted her hand, the motion being followed by the spikes cutting into Drayton's torso and legs. Anger filled her, vibrating through her chest. The tattoos on her arms shone through her sleeves. Flux pulsed through them like blood through veins under her skin.

"What did you say?" Feyra asked, her voice husky and dark.

"I di — didn't—" Words could barely eke out between his gritted teeth.

"You didn't say it? You didn't know?" Her eyes grew wild with anger. "You didn't understand that someone like you doesn't deserve to even speak her name!?"

"I'm sorry!" Drayton cried.

"You're not sorry, you're scared. Scared of death and pain." She squeezed her fist, pushing the spikes into Drayton until they protruded from the other side of his legs.

"Please! Stop!" Blood dripped from his lips.

"Louder!"

Blood rose, creating a field of gory pillars. Crimson threads twisted toward Feyra's hands. Reality cracked and folded under the weight of the flux moving through the room.

"Stop!" Drayton begged. "I said I'm sorry!"

"Say it so the gods can hear you!"

The blood from Drayton's body floated toward the ceiling. He had stopped screaming — the air in his lungs no longer sustaining such a thing. "I…" he said, his voice cracking. "I can use the birds. I can get Melifacto! I can learn what you—!"

A spike shot from between Drayton's legs and through his mouth. His fingers twitched, reaching for something to hold onto. The spike rippled then exploded. Thousands of drops of blood flew in all directions, only to stop, frozen in unmoving constellations.

Feyra screamed in rage. The pillars broke from the ground into geometric shapes shaking with her voice. Her mind was back in Marjyal, in the gutters where she once had to hide. Bellona pulled her out. Made her free. Kept her safe. Gave her purpose. No one could be allowed to slight her.

She went quiet. The blood fell.

"Oh, no." She clutched her head. "No, no, no, no." She spun to the Owl and grabbed him by the shoulder. "I'm sorry. I got angry. I need to know about *elys sang*. You have to help me. Tell me anything!"

There wasn't anything the Owl could say without a head. Feyra pounded against his chest. She kicked the chair over and stumbled back. A beat hammered in her skull. She lashed out at the lab with bloody weapons, shattering what wasn't already broken. When it was rubble, Feyra collapsed to her knees.

"Bellona. Please don't be mad. It happened again."

Bellona was on a tear through the Dothrin camp. They had been burning the Dove's bodies, but one important corpse was missing. Bellona knew exactly where it would be. She kicked open the door to one of the few towers that had a roof. Melifacto had turned it into a temporary lab, complete with cold boxes and trays of fluxcrystals. Pelady squatted on a chair, sinking her blade-like teeth into a mystery meat. In the centre of the tower, on a table stolen from the mess hall, was a blood-stained sheet with a human form beneath.

"Can I help you, Bellona?" Pelady said, standing and tossing her meal aside.

Bellona stomped to the table. She flipped the top of the sheet over. It was Dianathos, his torso recently stitched closed. In particular, his right hand was a mess of piping and needles connected to a strange crystal array. On a shelf nearby were five jars filled with, what she had to assume were, his organs.

"Where is Melifacto?" Bellona asked, replacing the sheet.

Pelady slunk next to the operating table. "He's out. Should I take a message for him?"

"Pelady. I know you're proud of being Melifacto's pet monster, but know this, I could slit your throat and turn you into a puppet show for the troops and there's not a damn thing Melifacto could do about it. Instead, how about you stop acting like a queen and show some cragging respect."

Pelady's sharp-toothed smile faded. "He followed the river south. I don't know what he's doing."

"And that's it?" Bellona took Pelady by the chin, forcing eye contact.

Pelady twisted her lips, like she had just eaten something sour. "Yes, Lady Boar."

"Good puppet." She released Pelady with a flick of her wrist and marched out. "Someone bring me my horse!"

A Boar came rushing up, holding the reins of her chestnut mare, Skyborn. Bellona mounted up and cut through the camp before following the river south. As long as Melifacto kept within sight of it, she would find him soon enough, since she doubted he rode there. The Praetor of Owls always preferred to be driven.

Sure enough, only a few minutes later she spotted a trail of broken branches into the forest. She left Skyborn near the water and followed the path. They were still close enough to the poison swamp Bellona couldn't let her guard down. The druids didn't take kindly to Marjyalians who wandered on their own.

She found Melifacto in a clearing, staring into the brush ahead of him. He hummed an unfamiliar tune and held a blanket to his chest.

"Melifacto," Bellona said, approaching.

"Hello, Bellona," Melifacto said. "What brings you out here? Taking in the lovely scenery?"

"I'm wondering what possessed you to chop up Dianathos."

"That's simple. I had an agreement with Dianathos that upon his death, his body was mine. I was curious how his Ghost Hand worked."

Bellona grimaced. She never liked Dianathos, sure, but she had respect for the dead. "And do you know now?"

"I'm beginning to." He stroked the mask on his hip. "There's something about him that allows the manipulation of flux, albeit in a very specific way. It manifests in his right hand, but that's not where it originates. I'll have to continue the biopsy to discover what that is."

"You're detestable." Bellona crossed her arms. She raised her eyebrow at the blanket in Melifacto's arms. "Then we can't burn his body?"

"Absolutely not! I could potentially recreate the Ghost Hand in others, but I will need access to my full lab. Please send the cadaver back to Marjyal at your earliest convenience." The trees in front of them shook, sending leaves fluttering on the breeze. "Now step back. I have some work to do."

Melifacto moved toward the shaking treeline with the blanket over his shoulder and his hands extended. Wood cracked and there was the sound of vegetation being crushed under the feet of something big. Bellona stood her ground but kept her hand ready near her sword.

A tree came crashing down, landing a couple of metres from Melifacto. From the overgrowth, three massive creatures appeared. They looked like canines, but with the size of a warhorse. Their fur was shades of grey and bone spikes jutted from their joints. It was as if their skeletons were too big for their bodies and wanted to break free.

One snapped at the largest as they approached. The big one retaliated with a quick bite to the aggressor's haunch, spilling his blood onto the grass. Melifacto turned his palms face up and the creatures calmed, sitting before him like trained dogs.

"What are those?" Bellona asked.

"I haven't given them a proper name yet," Melifacto said. "But my research team called them devastation hounds. It's fitting for now."

Melifacto reached up and the largest hound lowered its head so he could stroke it. Bellona kept her face emotionless, but her mind was racing. She had known Melifacto had a way with animals, talking to the crows and the livestock as easy as people. But he called on such terrifying creatures and turned them into lapdogs without a word.

The hound sniffed the blanket and after a few minutes, Melifacto stepped back. The beast barked, then took off with its pack back into the woods, knocking full grown trees aside like saplings.

"What did you just do?" Bellona kept her gaze on the bounding forms of the hounds.

"We need to accelerate our search," Melifacto said, bundling the blanket. "There have been some unforeseen complications. The devastation hounds will follow Marta's scent and bring her back. Alive, and hopefully in one piece."

"What about Gaul?"

"If he gets in their way?" Melifacto chuckled. "They'll kill him."

Bellona couldn't let this happen — Melifacto could not get Marta first. She was Bellona's bargaining chip. And Gaul was a survivor, but against those things who knew what could happen. She needed him alive. She needed to look into his eyes and see the soul of strength in person

The blood from the hound was still visible in the grass. Melifacto walked away, humming that same tune, giving Bellona the opportunity to bend down and smear it on her finger. She hid it in her palm and turned to catch up to Melifacto.

"Was there anything else you needed?" Melifacto asked. "Or was this all about Dianathos?"

"I need to send a message to Feyra," Bellona said. "With the Doves routed, I need her to move troops to the south."

"Do you know where she is?"

"No."

Melifacto gave a proud smile. "No problem, my crows can find her, they always do. Just tell me what you need me to say and I'll write up a missive."

"She's not going to listen to you," Bellona said as they arrived back at the river. Skyborn whinnied as Bellona took her place in the saddle. She kept her hand to her side, making sure her bloody finger didn't touch anything. "I'll write the letter, just bring me a bird."

"Are you going to offer me a ride?" Melifacto asked.

"No." Bellona turned north and spurred Skyborn on.

The hounds could not be allowed to find Marta. Even if Feyra could intercept them and follow to Marta's location, it would be too dangerous. There were still questions about *elys sang* and what Melifacto's true plan was. Better to be safe. Better to kill the beasts before they ever had the chance. Marta's time would come. Time was the one thing they had.

Fortunis returned near sundown with good news. It took some time, but he snuck in through the storm cellar and set a fire below the church. It had burned through the floor and into the main room before the Rats standing guard noticed. He had joined the crowd gathering as the Rats tried to put out the fire and save their supplies.

"By the time I left," he said, resting at the kitchen table. "They were already blaming it on the Snakes. Entire place went up like a bonfire too. I don't know how much they lost, but the building is rubble."

"Was it weird burning down a church?" Miribelle asked, braiding her hair once again. She had changed out of her tavern clothes and wore britches with a long coat and blouse.

"I'm sure Sebanna would understand," Fortunis said.

"Then all we need is this," Gaul said, placing the blastjar on the table.

Marta leaned in to inspect the liquid. "Is it supposed to be that dark?"

"That's the alcohol," Gaul said. "It'll work."

Hopefully Fortunis and Miribelle didn't notice the hesitation that Marta did. They put a drop on the other fluxcrystal and it gave them some sparks. A good sign, Marta figured, but sparks weren't going to convince the Guilds to break the Accords.

"I'll do it," Miribelle said, flipping her finished braid over her back.

Fortunis snapped his gaze to her. For a long moment, it seemed he was going to forbid her once again. Until he grinned. "You are the best at getting in and out."

Miribelle smiled back.

"Then it's yours." Gaul slid the blastjar toward her. He held out a second lid with the crystal tied to a string running through a hole in the top. "When you're ready, put this lid on and hold onto the string. Once you let go—" He released the string and the crystal fell to the counter. "—the countdown starts. The runes will keep it from exploding immediately, but you'll only have five seconds to get away." He paused. "Around five seconds."

She put the lid into her coat pocket and picked up the blastjar. "Can't throw this one, huh?" she asked.

"Not with the way I made it."

Miribelle turned to her brother with a smug smile. "Who could do this better than me?"

"Just be careful," Fortunis said. "I think once this goes off the guilds are going to go to war."

"Let's be there to make sure," Gaul said, tightening his sword belt and grabbing his coat.

"There's a ladder that leads up to the roof of the doctors," Fortunis said. "It's not far from where the Snakes are keeping their carts and it's right on the main street. It would be a good vantage point; we can hide behind his sign."

Marta cracked the curtains and looked out the window. Dust was falling over Sebanna's Rest bathing the town in an orange glow. It was the perfect setting for a fight, and she wasn't about to be stuck inside once again. "I'm coming too," she said, putting on her own coat.

Gaul slowed, his arm halfway through his sleeve.

"It's dark," Marta said, wrapping her scarf around her neck. "No one's going to see me."

Gaul narrowed his eyes as if to start arguing, but instead simply shrugged and snapped his coat over his shoulders.

"I'll head over," Miribelle said. "It'll take me a few jump-steps, but I'll meet you on the doctor's roof."

"Wait." Fortunis took Miribelle's hand. "Dad would be proud of you."

Miribelle smiled. She stepped to the door, holding the blastjar to her chest. She gave a small wave, then disappeared. Fortunis stared at the space Miribelle was for a long while before turning back to Gaul and Marta. Marta cocked her head at him.

"Our mother disappeared years ago," Fortunis said. "The rumour was she was taken to Marjyal, sent there because she was the only one who would stand up to Nana Stundel. Our father ran trade routes. He said there was nothing we could do." He clutched his hands together. "Then one day he changed his mind. He tried to get the town to turn on Nana Stundel. He tried to keep it a secret, but someone must have told her because on his last trade caravan he was somehow the only person who died when bandits attacked."

"That's why Miribelle hates her so much." Marta turned to the spot Miribelle disappeared from. The fact she could even live in the same town as the woman who ordered her father's death — if Marta knew who killed her brother they would already be dead.

"I hate her too." Fortunis grabbed the door handle. "I just hide it better than my sister. Maybe for once Nana can be useful and get these guilds out of our town. Then we can take the fight to her."

He left the cottage. Gaul raised his eyebrows in Marta's direction.

"Guess we all have reasons to be angry," Marta said, opening the door.

"I think they should just wait until she dies of old age." Gaul pushed past her, stopping at the threshold to whisper, "Revolutions tend to just get people killed."

"That's rather dire for the man who went so far for his dead wife's necklace. You're more sentimental than you let on."

"That's..." Gaul leaned against the door frame, turning his eyes from Marta. "That's hard to explain."

"Seems simple to me. Sometimes you need to stand up for something. What happened to 'As long as a single light remains?'"

"Those weren't my words."

"So? I believed them when you said them."

"Marta, we can't stop for every sad story." He squared his jaw. "If you want to be a hero for the people, then why don't you save Marjyal, rather than run from it?"

Marta took a sharp breath through her nose. "That's not the same thing."

Gaul scoffed and flipped up his hood, leaving Marta at the door to fume. She pushed her annoyance down and slammed the door shut. Gaul changed the subject to rile her up. He didn't know anything about Marjyal.

Fortunis waited at the fence, looking at the town down the slope. The guts of the church glowed beneath the setting sun, though the fire had died down to embers. Gaul swept past, hiding his face beneath his hood, while Marta leaned next to Fortunis and took in the sight of Rats abandoning the ruins of their storehouse.

"You said Sebanna would understand you burning the church," Marta said. "What do you know about her?"

"She was human before her ascension," Fortunis said, stretching his back out. "She created the line of trees that protect Adathin from the outside. She gave hope to people who had been abandoned in cruelty and indifference and led them here, to where rains come plentiful and the lakes are clean."

Marta bowed her head. All she knew of worship were the revels — where they were told the world was evil but they could hide and celebrate and ignore it. Mar gave them not salvation, but distraction. "She sounds perfect," Marta said.

"She wasn't. She wasn't supposed to be. The stories tell of a Great Mistake. Though we don't know what it was, it was terrible enough to end the reign of her father and necessitate the planting of the northern forest." He pushed himself back from the fence. "But that's why I take her words to heart. A mistake does not define someone. Sebanna doesn't ask for perfect, she asks for a life of kind intent. But she understands those shades of grey. That's why she was allowed to ascend to Elysium."

But did she ascend? Marta wondered. How much of her life was known to the people who saw her as a saint? Marta was born in Adathin, her brother devoted himself to uncovering the truth, and still she had believed the King was hung in a revolt. That was wrong. When they find Black Hypogea, would the truth change once again?

Gaul waved at them from down the path. "We should go."

"Of course," Fortunis said. "Follow me."

He took the lead toward town. There were no shouts or screams. Lit candles hid behind the drawn curtains of the homes they crept by. The lively town Gaul and Marta arrived in only the day before had shrunk into its shell. But more than that, the Rats and Snakes had disappeared. They weren't banging down the doors anymore. All of Sebanna's Rest was holding its breath, basking in the calm before the storm.

Fortunis brought them to a simple wooden building with a large sign that read, simply, 'Doctor.' They climbed the ladder at the back to the roof. From behind the sign they had a perfect few of the main street. Fortunis pointed near the Resting Rose where a crowd had formed under the awning.

"There," he said. "Rats."

There were a few dozen of them, with one or two owning the conversation. They kept their voices hushed, but the violent gesturing and occasional shout made it clear. They were furious.

"I hope Miribelle's doing fine," Marta whispered.

In reply, a ball of smoked plumed up from further down the street. The Rats turned in surprise, drawing their weapons. Shouts rose up from the direction of the smoke. The Rats flooded into the streets, waiting to see what all the commotion was. With a creak of wood, Miribelle appeared next to Fortunis. Soot and dirt were packed into her hair.

"Those Snakes are not happy," she said, brushing the grime off her coat. "But I don't think anyone saw me."

"Now we hope it was enough," Gaul said.

The shouts grew louder. Rats came stumbling out of the Resting Rose, rubbing their eyes and pulling on ragged coats. Windows went dark as candles were snuffed. The sun was nearly set, casting long shadows across the street. These shadows were the first to appear before an army of Snakes rounded the corner. Swords laid bare and bows were nocked with arrows. The Rats who just arrived shook the sleep out of their heads and drew their swords, joining the rest of their guild.

"You disgusting vermin!" one of the Snakes shouted.

"Two-faced leech!" a Rat shouted back.

All possibility of communication was drowned out by nearly a hundred well-armed Marjyalians shouting obscenities and banging weapons together. But even as they stood face to face, no one dared to make the first move.

"They don't want to break the Accords," Marta said.

Gaul frowned. "And I thought Marjyalians hated rules."

Ettik charged down the street, the tatters of his coat fluttering behind him. "What's going on!?" he shouted, shoving Rats out of the way to stand between them and the Snakes.

At the same time Yomat pushed his way through his own guild. "Stand down!" He grabbed a Snake by the lapel and threw him back. "Get to the barracks before you lose meal privilege!"

"They're taking back control," Gaul said. "If we give them time to think they'll figure it out."

Marta drew a throwing knife. "Then let's break the tension."

She braced herself against the sign, exhaled, and threw. The knife sailed through the air in a high arc. It was a long trip from the roof to the street, too long for an effective throw. The knife tumbled on the descent. As Ettik and Yomat were reining in control, the knife's hilt hit a Snake in the temple. It wasn't a hard hit, but it struck the match.

A Snake loosed an arrow. A Rat thrusted forth. The two walls of anger crashed, engulfing Ettik and Yomat as they tried desperately to keep the piece. Blood and screams filled the coming darkness. In a flash that brightened the town, a blastjar exploded, sending chunks of people skyward.

"My god," Miribelle muttered, covering her mouth.

"Rat." The voice came from the inside of Marta's head. It was the same as the one she heard in the swamp, but now it was stronger. It sounded like hers. Like Marta's voice had separated from herself to say words of its own.

Or maybe it was her own thought, just one that became unintentionally louder than the rest. Because there was a single Rat sneaking away from the fight. Ettik, with his ragged coat stained dark red, crawled out from between kicking legs. He scrambled to his feet and watched in horror as the Rats and Snakes tore into each other. A Rat fell at his feet, an arrow sticking out of his eye. Ettik curled his lips in disgust and donned his mask. He slunk into the shadows of a nearby alley.

"Rat." The voice said again, and Marta took off at a run.

"Marta!" Gaul whispered harshly.

But she was already gone. She scant touched the ladder before reaching the ground, dropping into a scampering roll before curving around the doctor's office. She pulled her scarf over her face and burst out into the street at full speed, the ends fluttering behind her. An arrow whipped past her head and she jerked away off reflex. But with clashing swords and raging cries, no one cared about the small woman.

Ettik had his eyes focused on the end of the alley, muttering indistinct curses under his breath. Marta lowered her shoulder and caught him around the waist, sheer momentum bringing them a couple metres forward before Marta slammed him face-first into the dirt. He let out a choking squeak as his mask crumpled into his nose.

Marta flipped him over. Blood seeped out the bottom of the leather that once looked like a rat's face, but now more resembled a snub-nosed cat. She pressed her knee on Ettik's chest and pulled down her scarf.

"You," Ettik said, muffled by the leather pushing against his mouth.

Marta grabbed his mask and pulled it clear, snapping the straps at the buckles. Ettik's nose bent at a strange angle and the blood had coated half his face. "Me," Marta growled, the word repeating in her head.

Ettik drew his knife, flecks of rust spitting out from the small sheath. Marta caught him by the forearm and slammed the knife hilt-deep into the dirt. Keeping the arm down, Marta drove her fist into Ettik's face. She unloaded blow after blow against his skull. Her heart vibrated in her chest, sending its warmth into her stomach.

Ever since Marta could remember, the Rats were always around in the Gutter. The other guilds would abuse them, and in turn the abuse would be put on the poor people with no choice but to live in the lowest streets. Marta unleashed years of pain into Ettik's body, until her arm grew numb with repeated blows.

She reared back for another punch when her arm was caught. Gaul held her elbow. Behind him was Fortunis and Miribelle, barely more than shadows in the rising moon.

"We might want to talk to him," Gaul said. "A living Praetor could shed some light on this whole situation."

Marta yanked her arm away. Her heart still raced, but pain grew in her right fist. She stepped off Ettik, stomping on his arm so he would finally release his knife. Gaul took the Praetor by the throat, pulling him to his feet.

"Let me go!" Ettik cried. "Help me! I'm the Praetor of Rats! Help!"

His voice was lost in the sounds of battle still raging. Gaul dragged Ettik by the scruff.

"What are we doing with this man?" Fortunis asked, repeatedly glancing over his shoulder.

"Bringing him to the cottage," Gaul said, driving his forearm into Ettik's spine. "And then we have a talk."

"Marta," Miribelle said. "Your hand."

Marta raised her fist. Blood dripped from a series of splits across her knuckles. "I'm fine," she said. "It doesn't hurt."

As they approached the cottage, Miribelle jump-stepped away. A second later she opened the door to let them in. Gaul shoved Ettik through, knocking him into the table and sending the vials that once held the blastjar ingredients smashing to the floor.

Fortunis paused and looked back to Sebanna's Rest. The light of fires glowed in the main street, framing buildings in flickering auras. Fortunis' face was wracked with worry. "What do you thinks happening down there?" he asked.

"Nothing you want to see," Marta said, pulling him inside.

"Wait," Ettik groaned, using the table to pull himself back to his feet, holding out a hand to protect himself. "We only want her. The reward is big enough for all of us to share."

"I've heard this before." Gaul slammed Ettik's head against the table. "Must be an old Rat saying."

"Could we not brutalize a man in my kitchen?" Fortunis asked, ensuring the blinds were drawn.

Miribelle approached Marta. "Let me see your hand," she said, holding out some linen wraps.

Marta allowed her to begin wrapping the fabric around her bloody knuckles, but all her focus staying drilling into Ettik as he crawled across the floor. "Why is Melifacto sending you after me?" she demanded. "What does he want with me?"

Gaul grabbed Ettik by the greasy hair and pulled him to his feet, leaning him over the table.

"I don't know!" Ettik said. "But he's offering all sorts of luxuries and—"

"Good liar." Gaul grabbed him by the nose, cracking the cartilage between his fingers. Ettik screamed as he twisted. "But a bad lie. There must be something big for you to risk it all."

"Ah… ah!" Ettik slapped weakly at Gaul's wrist. "The Cradle! He offered the Chalice!"

Gaul let go of his nose. "That's impossible. The Cradle is sealed. It's surrounded by Absence."

"I don't know about any of that. But he said if we helped him, we could use the power of the Chalice. The power that created gods, can you imagine?" His eyes crept to Marta. "But he needs her to open it."

A cold tremor ran through Marta's skin. "He's lying."

"What does that mean?" Gaul asked Ettik. "What can she do?"

"He's lying!" Marta tore her hand away from Miribelle, bloody bandage still dangling untied. "I'm nothing special. I was born in the Gutter and I would have died in the Gutter."

"You'd have to take that up with Melifacto," Ettik said.

Marta's face twitched. All eyes were on her. She just wanted to know why Melifacto was after her — why he knew her name. But to say she was the key to opening the Cradle? It had to be a lie. There had to be something cleaner. Something that made more sense. Miribelle gently took her hand and finished with the bandages.

"Melifacto isn't telling them anything," Marta said. "He useless. Kill him."

"If you say so…" Gaul drew his sword.

"Hold on one second!" Fortunis shouted.

"The Abyss!" Ettik grabbed Gaul's shoulder as he raised his blade. "You're going there, aren't you? To Black Hypogea?"

Gaul stopped. He rested the sword on his shoulder and stared Ettik in the eyes, still gripping hard on his rags.

"I know where it is," Ettik said, a panicked smile creeping across his lips. "I used to work the roads around here. Sometimes all you can do is hide out in the wilderness, getting chased far from any roads. That's where I found it."

"Or." Gaul pointed his sword at Ettik's throat. "You're lying to save your skin."

"I'm the only one who can help you. People in this country have a narrow view when it comes to religion, all ascended queens and gods of parties. But I'm like you. I came from past Nature's Grave, I know the stories, so I know what I've seen. A scar across Adathin as black as pitch, with the Gate Beyond standing guard. Drove my partner at the time insane, but I know where it is."

Gaul kept the sword at his throat but looked back at Marta. Fortunis and Miribelle shrank into the corner, clasping their hands to each other.

"We can't trust him," Marta said.

"Not trust," Gaul said. "But if he knows the way, we can use him."

Marta turned to Ettik. "How long would it take us to get there?"

"Five days," Ettik said, his eyes locked on Gaul's sword.

Marta took a clump of hair in both hands. Maybe Ettik was lying, but maybe he's the only chance they had to reach their destination. "If you're tricking us, Rat, you're not waking up on that sixth day."

Ettik let out a sigh of relief, sweat blowing with his breath. "I believe you."

"Can you get us some rope?" Gaul asked Miribelle, sheathing his sword.

"And you'll let me go once I show you?" Ettik asked.

"You have a better chance there than here," Gaul said, flicking his nose.

Miribelle brought them a rope and they bound Ettik's hands behind his back, leaving a long end that Gaul could hold like a leash.

"We're leaving now?" Ettik wriggled his hands in the bindings. "It's after dark."

"We've already done enough to this town," Gaul said, shoving Ettik toward the door. "All of us. We'll get a few hours and find a place to camp. You'll like it. Maybe we'll even let you lie down."

Marta opened the door for them to exit. The moon was still hidden behind the eastern mountains, but the stars had filled the sky with tens of thousands of pinpoint lights. Sebanna's Rest glowed below them, though the sounds of battle had faded. All they could do was hope it would end the Guild's brief occupation.

"You don't…" Miribelle started, resting her hand on Marta's shoulder. "You don't have to go right now."

"Gaul's right," Marta said. "We've done enough. Good luck with… whatever tomorrow brings."

Fortunis stepped to his sister's side, wrapping an arm around her. "Thank you. It wasn't always easy but thank you all the same. I hope Sebanna blessed your journey."

Marta smiled. *Wouldn't that be a treat?* she thought.

Fortunis and Miribelle stayed at the cottage door, watching Marta rush out to catch up with Gaul. Blood still dripped out of Ettik's nose as Gaul forced him to take the lead past the fence.

"Time to show your use," Gaul said. "Which direction to Black Hypogea."

"East," Ettik said, glaring over his shoulder. "It's in the mountains."

Marta stomped up to Ettik, him twitching as she approached. She tore off a piece of his shirt and wiped the blood from his face. "We're going to be spending some time together," she said, tossing the cloth away. "You're going to tell me everything you know about Melifacto."

"It'll be a quick talk," Ettik said.

"Then make it interesting." She shoved him into motion.

Looking over her shoulder, Fortunis and Miribelle could be seen in the soft glow of their open door. With people like them, Adathin couldn't be entirely cursed. There was that spark of light.

"Come on," Gaul called back.

With their unwilling guide at their head, and a bedlam at their back, Marta and Gaul continued toward Black Hypogea.

The Gate Beyond is an anomaly in almost every sense of the word. It has shown up in many religions, those closely tied to the Pantheon and those that are not. Even secularists seem to refer to the Gate. The only tale I've found explaining where it came from refers to a time near the end of the First Age.

After the Primordials were defeated, the gods set to giving the world structure. It was from this the Divines were born. One such Divine was created out of a desire to bring order to death. A raven was snatched from the sky, plucked free of its feathers, then buried into the earth. From that spot, a skeletal giant was born. The Gate Beyond was a beacon for passed souls. They would spiral in its breast as sparks of light until they were ready to rejoin the cycle as new life.

The most vibrant of souls would be allowed to pass on to Elysium, the future home of the Divines. The dark souls would be cast into Black Hypogea until they could be cleansed and allowed back into the cycle.

—From the Journal of Jovin Gutterwake

Chapter Twenty
The Gate Beyond

Ettik led Gaul and Marta through the forest to the mountains in the east. They travelled during the day, and at night they would tie Ettik to a tree and take turns watching him. As they got further from Sebanna's Rest, Ettik became less restless. Days went by and they stopped tying him up while they walked. Though he was always firmly bound when the night came.

It only took one day to get everything about Melifacto from Ettik. They wove between trees as he laid it out.

"Praetors don't exactly open up to each other," he said. "Melifacto was around before I even got to Marjyal. And he made it very clear that he wanted to open the Cradle of the World and get the Chalice. The person who brings him you? They get to use it. Now, were not stupid. Melifacto is untouchable because we all want the Chalice, but Melifacto can be dealt with one it's in our grasp. One of our grasps."

"But not yours," Gaul said.

"No." Ettik grimaced. "Doesn't appear that way. Though I do think Dianathos may have truly believed Melifacto would share power. He was never the brightest."

"And why does he need me?" Marta asked, pushing a branch out of her way.

"I don't know. He just does. He said you were taken away before."

Gaul looked over his shoulder to see Marta deep in thought. If Melifacto knew her, it had to be before she left Marjyal. But she said she didn't remember him, and she wasn't that young when she left. Gaul wished he could see into her head, figure out what thoughts were whipping through it. Instead he kept quiet and urged Ettik to walk faster.

The forest gave way to foothills, then to mountains. As they got closer to where Ettik said Black Hypogea was, Gaul felt a sickness growing in his stomach. He would look over his shoulder, wondering if the Absence would soon blot out the setting sun and cover the horizon. He pushed the pain away and followed Ettik down the canyon path.

Marta stumbled over loose gravel. Ettik caught her before she could fall.

"Are you okay?" Ettik asked.

She held her stomach and took deep breaths.

"Are you feeling sick?" Gaul asked, touching her shoulder.

"It's been getting worse the closer we get," she said.

"I've been feeling it too."

"I feel fine." Ettik looked his body over, as if expecting to find a festering wound he overlooked. "What does it feel like?"

"Like I'm sick to my stomach." Gaul sat on a large rock. The pain came and went, he needed to wait it out.

"Same," Marta said. "It comes and goes."

Ettik looked at the sun, halfway though its descent. "Maybe we should stop early, we'll get to Black Hypogea tomorrow. I can see a cave just ahead; it'll be a good place to camp out."

Gaul didn't like the idea of stopping when they were so close. But, with him and Marta suffering from some mysterious illness, they would have to rely on Ettik for any protection. He liked that idea less. They headed to the cave.

It was a small depression on the cliff, enough to protect them from the elements but not much else. Gaul and Marta flopped to the ground, leaning against the wall. Ettik looked them over, then out the cave mouth.

"There may be some berries in the crags," he said. "I'll see if I can rustle some up."

"Ettik," Gaul warned, but couldn't move much to back up the threat.

"Relax." He hopped out of the cave. "Where am I going to go? The closest town is Sebanna's Rest and I doubt they'll be welcoming to me. I'll get the berries and be right back."

He glanced in each direction, then picked left and disappeared. Marta groaned and leaned against Gaul.

"I've been thinking," she said. "Me and you spent a lot of time around the door to the Cradle. It was leaking that Absence stuff. Maybe we got some inside us and it doesn't like that we're on the right path."

"Interesting thought," Gaul said.

Marta nodded, the bobbing continuing until her eyes eased shut. She let out a big yawn and in a few moments was fast asleep. Gaul tried to stay awake, wanting to be aware when Ettik returned. He didn't trust him. But he felt so weak. Sleep overcame him.

* *

Feyra had taken every scrap of research she could find in the outpost with her back to Blasted Land Mine. She wasn't an arcanist, though. Most of the words were indecipherable. The mentions of God's Blood, the translation for *elys sang*, were followed by a string of numbers. Some had more information, the same number as before, but with a string of reagents afterward. In the end of each experiment it was the same result, nonviable. In the end of Feyra's reading she still was no closer to the truth.

The gods had given her a chance to further Bellona's goals, but her temper had stolen it away. She wanted another chance, another opportunity to serve Bellona. A week after discovering the outpost, a crow arrived to give her that opportunity.

Feyra, the note said. It was in Bellona's handwriting. *Melifacto has sent three great beasts after Marta and Gaul. They're called devastation hounds, and I have never seen anything like them before. We can't allow these monsters to reach their targets. Killing the hounds is your first priority and must be done on sight. Leave immediately, H.*

At the bottom of the letter was a bloody fingerprint. It was dry, but the meaning was clear. Feyra tore that chunk of the letter off and ate it. A faint pulsing grew to the northwest. It was bestial, the heartbeat of a large being on the move. The tracking wouldn't last forever, but with the speed the creature was moving it should last long enough.

The crow sat on the desk, primping its dark feathers as it waited for a return letter. Feyra took her club in hand, bouncing it lightly in her grasp. Melifacto's connection to animals was strange. He could talk to them, and so who was to say they couldn't talk back? Feyra took the club in both hands and struck the bird, sending it spinning into the lit fireplace. She tossed the rest of the letter in after it.

She grabbed her coat and hurried out of her room. It was a second chance to serve Bellona. There would be no failure this time.

When Gaul woke, Ettik was back. Marta had slipped off his shoulder and was sprawled across the ground, snoring peacefully. Gaul gave her a small kick and she jerked awake.

"It's not even night yet," she said, rubbing the sleep out of her eyes.

"It's morning," Ettik said. He absentmindedly tapped two rocks together as he kept watch.

"What?" Gaul scrambled to his feet. His guts flared with pain, but he stayed upright.

"You ate the berries last night." Ettik tossed the rocks away. "I guess you don't remember. Feeling any better?"

Gaul stretched back. His joints cracked and popped. The pain in his stomach subsided but hadn't fully disappeared. Marta slapped her cheeks and stumbled out of the cave.

"I'm fine," Gaul said, following Marta. "We better be close."

Ettik shrugged and leapt to the front of the group. He led them deeper into the mountain range until the path became nothing more than a gravel-filled trench between steep cliffs. Hawks and other mountainous birds of prey flew overhead, bouncing their shrieks into the landscape below. Hardy, horned animals paced the tops of slopes, far from the stalking predators. The trees thinned until only the strongest pines with mighty roots could remain. That aroma of sap and needles mixed with the hard smell of crushed rocks.

As they began their belaboured hike up the quickly sloping mountain, Marta dropped back, pulling Gaul out of Ettik's earshot. "What do you make of him?" she asked.

Gaul looked ahead where Ettik breathed into his cold hands. "I don't know," Gaul said. "He didn't make an attempt on us."

"He has no weapons," Marta said. "Maybe he didn't want to risk waking us up trying to take ours."

"Maybe." Gaul couldn't shake the feeling Ettik was up to something. He was a coward at his core, but a cruel one. He could have at least tried to run. "Just keep both eyes on him."

Marta nodded and hurried her pace, sending dirt tumbling the way they came.

The day dragged on. Though the sun rose above the layer of low clouds, the cold mountain winds pressed their chilling fingers through their clothes. Marta's scarf was wrapped tightly around her face, but the tails fluttered like a caught flag in a windstorm. Gaul turned his hood up to protect his ears. Ettik had become an ever-shifting mass of flapping rags slowly making its way up.

A heavy thump shattered the calm. Ettik dropped to hands and knees, jerking his head side-to-side.

"What is that?" Marta asked.

"I don't know," Ettik said. He pointed at a flat rock sticking out of the mountainside, making a sort of lean-to. "There! Hurry."

They charged across the slope, sending mini landslides into the misty depths below. Ettik was first to the cover. He pushed himself deep between the rock and the mountain, scattering the bugs that once filled the space. Gaul and Marta slid in after. The tumbling gravel slowed to a stop for a second before another thump rattled the ground. A hand with fingers like tree trunks grabbed onto the stone that protected them and the beast pulled itself into view.

It was over five metres tall with a hunched posture. Its skin was a cracking grey with red-orange fur along its back, distended belly, and lower body. A sizeable underbite stuck out from below a tiny nose and squinting eyes. The legs were small in comparison to the bulging and long arms it used to help it walk. In one hand it clutched the back half of a goat, leaving a trail of putrid gore as it thumped past the hiding spot.

Gaul gritted his teeth, forcing his breaths to stay steady. The monster's smell, one of unwashed sweat and rotting meat, rolled over them. Marta put both hands against her scarf, pushing it into her mouth and nose to stymie the odour.

The monster raised its head, wisps of the fur along its back shifting in the breeze. Atop a jutting stone ridge that ran next to the path was a lone bighorn sheep. The monster reared back, inflating its throat, before unleashing a gob of sickly yellow spit. It struck the sheep — nearly engulfing it — and sent it screaming off the ridge. The monster slammed both calloused fists into the ground and hurled itself through the air, catching the ridge and disappearing after its new prey. All that remained was a splattering of vile spit that dripped off the stone, sizzling as it burned through low ferns and brave blades of grass.

"We're getting close," Ettik said, brushing a centipede off his shoulder.

"What does that mean?" Marta asked. Ettik ignored her and crawled out of cover. She turned to Gaul. "Why would he say that?"

"Black Hypogea is the birthplace of monsters," Gaul said, creeping out. "Or at least that's what the legends say."

"And you don't fear the legends?" Ettik smirked in their direction. "Do you know what you're getting into?"

"That's not your concern, is it?" Gaul loomed over him. "I'm not afraid of stories."

"What about when the stories are real? What do you do then?" A deep roar wiped the smile from Ettik's face. "We shouldn't talk here." He wrapped his coat around him and continued up the path.

Gaul kept pace, ensuring Marta wasn't too far behind. "What're you on about, Rat?"

"My former partner was a lot like you," Ettik said. "He wasn't afraid of the old stories. Until he saw the Gate Beyond himself. All those lights dancing in its chest, drove him mad. 'That's where we'll end up,' he said, before diving headfirst into the dark." He looked over his shoulder. "I wonder if you'll fair much better."

"You can be sure I'd drag you in with me."

Ettik turned back, but for a brief moment Gaul spotted a grin cracking across his face.

"Gaul..." Marta said.

He paid no attention to her. For the rest of the day the trio walked in silence. Their path turned from a slog up a rocky slope into thin ridges that wound through the mountain range. Between the peaks were forested valleys where clouds would cut through trees like water moving around stones in a river. Occasionally, on far mountains, they could see large monsters traversing the landscape. But it was in the misty forests below where Gaul swore he saw the back of a beast, a mountain in its own right, knocking down trees with its lumbering gait.

At least we're not down there, Gaul thought.

The sun set on another long day and they set themselves a small fire at the back of a cave. Marta gnawed on a stick of dried meat, flicking her gaze between Ettik and Gaul. Ettik leaned against the cave wall, his hands tied behind his back and his legs bound at the ankles. Gaul glared at him from across the flames, tapping his fingers along the sheathes of the swords laying on his lap.

Ettik didn't need to say a word to worm his way into Gaul's brain. That dead-eyed look did it all. They were going to Black Hypogea. They were going to the Gate Beyond. Gaul's stomach twisted inside him. Maybe Marta was right and the Absence infected them, but now it was pushing back.

Or maybe it was Ettik's words.

Gaul took his swords and stormed out of the cave. Cold air greeted him, sliding its cooling fingers along the sweat on his neck. He fell against the mountain and listened to baying of beings that haunted that valley below. Feet crunched on loose stones as Marta approached.

"What's going on with you?" she asked.

"It's this sick — or whatever it is," Gaul said, resting his head back. "It'll pass."

"That's not what I mean."

"You can't actually feel for that man."

"That's also not what I mean." Marta squatted at the cliff's edge. "You're acting strange. You talk like you're already defeated. You've never been a ray of sunshine, but the Gaul I'm seeing now would not have survived Nature's Grave or the Pits. Something's changed."

"I haven't changed. I've just been thinking." He pushed away from the wall and joined Marta at the edge, looking into the misty valley. "Ettik's right. I don't know how I will react when I see our destination. A confirmation of legends."

"You've already seen the Cradle."

"I've seen a stone door. Call it what you want. Even 'Chalice of Light' is just a name given to a powerful artifact. If I start tossing one of these swords around, calling it the Sword of Kings, who's to say it's not? It just a name. But the Abyss… the Gate…" He took in a deep breath. "Stained souls are sent into Black Hypogea, that's all the teachers ever said. Trublüdar souls are born to be sent into the dark. I'm walking to the place where my soul will end up when I die."

"After all that, you're just overthinking things. Figures." She pressed her hands into her knees and jumped up, stumbling back and holding her stomach. It seemed the sickness was still in her as well. She shook it off, though. "Have you ever seen a soul?"

"No."

"And neither have your teachers." She clapped his shoulder. "Don't let people assume what's inside you."

Gaul chuckled under his breath. Marta patted him against before returning to the cave. The next day was going to be interesting — one way or the other. Gaul's stomach began to settle. After all that, it was only Ettik's words that were causing him to feel ill.

Though there were tinges of pain stretching through his stomach as he laid down to sleep.

The next morning came with no relief from the ever-present grey of the mountains. Gaul stepped out of the cave, flipping his coat up over his shoulders. Ettik, his breath visible in the early morning chill, joined him.

"Are you ready?" Ettik said with a sneer.

"I'm not the one whose usefulness is about to come to an end," Gaul said. "What do you think comes after that?"

Marta came out from the cave, spinning a throwing knife around her finger. She eyed Ettik as she slid the knife into her coat. "You keep talking about Black Hypogea, but I don't think you ever mentioned your feelings. Your partner went insane, but what? You felt nothing? You're a bad person, Ettik, isn't that where you'll end up? Aren't you scared?"

"Oh, only fools are scared of the future," Ettik said, following the ridge line. "I only worry about surviving the present."

Marta leaned toward Gaul. "Why didn't we think of that?"

"It certainly would have saved us some time," Gaul said, rubbing the sleep out of his eyes.

Their path wound between peaks and through passes. The deeper they got into the range, the less animal sounds greeted them. Only the occasional bird crying from high above. In time, all they had were their footfalls echoing through the stone walls.

Ettik brought them to where the mountains grew close. A crack of dim light split where a landslide narrowed the way. Ettik went first, holding his rags against him and sliding through. Marta followed. Gaul put his hands on either side of the crack and stopped. The pain in his stomach flared. They were getting close.

He slid between the rocks. The tips of his swords knocked against the narrowing passage. The light ahead grew brighter and he could see Marta and Ettik's shadows waiting for him. Taking a deep breath, he shoved himself through.

It was like stepping into a dream world. Gaul stood atop a high ridge that overlooked a massive caldera. Wind blew waves across the amber ocean of low shrubbery and long grass, swaying and dancing below the torso of a humanoid skeleton as large as the mountains that encircled it.

The Gate Beyond.

Its spine began in a crystal-clear lake before reaching nearly a kilometre into the sky. One hand pushed into the ground, as if the Gate was frozen halfway from pulling itself free. On its back were skeletal wings casting long, thin shadows across the caldera. Twin waterfalls fell from its eye sockets, past its bony grin, and into its other hand where it spread between its fingers and ended in the lake. The sheer sight of it took the feeling from Gaul's legs.

"There you have it," Ettik said. "The Gate Beyond."

"Is it... alive or dead?" Marta asked.

"Both." Ettik shrugged. "Neither? Who's to say it has to be just one thing, or anything at all?"

"I don't think we're meant to understand something like it," Gaul said, his eyes locked with the shadowy sockets of the Gate Beyond.

"So I don't even try." Ettik pointed past the Gate. "But that's where you're heading."

A canyon followed the base of the far mountain range. It arced behind the Gate Beyond and to its right. Impressive in size, of course, but after witnessing the winged skeleton, Black Hypogea ended up somewhat underwhelming.

They took a switchback path to the caldera floor. From there it was simply a long walk, and the Gate Beyond looming to meet them. Grass brushed against Gaul's knees and hid small meadowland creatures. A flock of small birds burst from a nearby patch, disappearing against the brilliant blue sky. A family of rabbits burrowed from beneath the hand, each fingerbone rivaling the size of a castle.

With each step, the Gate grew larger until they stood at the lakeside. Gaul and Marta stared up at its distant face, crying tears of flawless water. Ettik stopped a short distance away and waited.

"Wow," Marta said.

"I agree." Gaul's mind had all but stopped. The Cradle was a door. The Chalice was a cup. The Gate Beyond was… something else.

Marta squinted and pointed at the Gate's chest. "What are those?"

Gaul followed her finger. At first, he couldn't figure out what she was pointing at. As he stared longer, he saw a spark fly through the Gate's ribcage. It could have been a fluke, but then there was another spark. Then another. Nearly invisible with the bright sun in the sky, but now Gaul was sure. There were sparks of light moving within the Gate Beyond's chest.

Dozens. Hundreds. Thousands. Millions. More.

"Those are souls," Gaul said, his mouth going dry. "From all over Meza. Kings, paupers, criminals, priests. They all swirl in there in the end."

"Then what?" Marta asked.

"I guess the evil ones go into the Abyss. The pure ones go to Elysium. The rest are sent back into the cycle."

"Oh." Marta kicked a stone into the lake, sending ripples to meet the ones coming from the waterfalls. "And we're just… staring at it."

"Yeah." Gaul pushed the strands of hair away from his face. The Gate stared down at him with an eyeless gaze, taunting him with a wordless voice. His stomach twisted inside him.

"Seems boring," Marta finally said.

He whipped his head to her.

She gave a wide smile. "There's more to life than the ending."

"Are you an idiot?" Ettik said, stomping over. "This is the end of the road, sweetheart. And that dark hole over there is where people like me go. What kind of ending is that?"

"I thought you weren't scared of the future," Marta said.

Ettik's eyes flashed and his face turned red. "I built myself from dirt. I'm the only outsider who ever became a Praetor. I did all this to be thrown into the Abyss?" He pulled on his rags, puffing hot, rage-filled breath. "I'm not scared of the future, I hate it. It's unfair. With the Chalice I could change the ending. Maybe live forever. Maybe crack Elysium and sneak in."

"Too bad," Gaul said, putting a finger against Ettik's forehead. "Guess you'll have to deal with it like the rest of us."

Marta suddenly dropped to one knee, clutching her stomach. Gaul spun to her side. "I'm fine," she said. "That sickness is still hanging around."

"You too?" Gaul asked.

"Seems I'm not the one who should worry about the end," Ettik said, turning on his heel. "Not far now."

Gaul wrapped one arm around Marta's waist and lifted her to her feet. His own stomach rebelled against him. An acidic taste worked up the back of his throat. As much as he supported Marta, she supported him. Ettik became a blurry oblong, and it took everything to follow him. They had to keep moving. It would pass, it always passed.

Everything became enveloped by a mental haze. Every bird, blade of grass, even thoughts mixed and muddled into indistinct noise. Gaul's skin went cold until the breeze felt like needles piercing through him. The waving grasslands made the ground shift and turn, as if it could twist completely around and drop him into the sky.

One foot, then the next. One foot, and he stumbled. Marta caught him by the shoulders. Before them spread a dark expanse. Wide and overwhelming, and yet light dared not pass below its upper lip. Black Hypogea.

Marta collapsed, dropping Gaul with her. He fell to his hands and knees as Marta curled around her gut. Ettik stood proud, with his hands clutched behind his back, his eyes locked with the ravine before him. His jaw trembled with fear as he stared into the infinite depths.

Marta was wrong. It wasn't Absence poisoning them. It had to be Ettik. Somehow it had to be him.

"It's unfortunate it took so long," Ettik said, tearing his gaze away from the pit. "I couldn't risk killing Marta as well. But here we are." He walked the lip toward Gaul, spreading his arms to embrace the freedom. "Think of it this way, I saved your soul the trip."

Gaul urged his legs to carry him. His arms to push Ettik away. Nothing worked. He fell onto his chest. His breath puffed against the dirt and brought gritty particles between his teeth.

Ettik knelt next to him. "I wonder if you were a good person. I wonder if you deserve to be reborn as someone else, or if you'll…" He turned to Black Hypogea. "I wonder if you're afraid now. I'm not. I'll have the Chalice and I'll choose my destiny."

Gaul's eyes flared. He pulled until everything hurt. Ettik just laughed.

Behind Ettik, in the distant blur of Gaul's consciousness, a figure approached. Ettik noticed Gaul's gaze and spun around.

The stranger was dressed in all white, glowing in the high sun. He was a thin man with a delicate gait, long coat brushing the dirt as he walked, turning the hem to brown and black. A wide-brimmed hat blocked his face. As he approached, he lifted his head, revealing a blank mask with slits for his eyes and mouth surrounded by burn marks. Head-to-toe, there wasn't a single piece of his skin that wasn't covered. "What a sight this is!" he said, gesturing forward. From his fingers to just past his wrists, stains turned his white gloves red.

"Who are you?" Ettik shouted.

"Ettik," the stranger said. "Have you forgotten me so quickly."

Ettik's eyes widened. "We exiled you. You shouldn't be here!"

"You exiled me from the City of Revels, true. But we aren't in the city anymore."

"I'm warning you," Ettik said, legs shaking in fear. "Don't come any closer."

"You're warning me?" The stranger cackled. "Have you gotten brave? A poor day to grow a spine."

Ettik's gaze crept to Gaul, then to the swords on his belt. The stranger took his time, swaying playfully with each step. Ettik lunged for Gaul. In a blur, the stranger was upon Ettik. He caught him by the throat and shoved him back. Ettik stumbled to the edge of the pit, windmilling his arms to keep himself from falling in.

"Poor little rat thought he was special because they gave him a title," the stranger said. "Of all the people I wished revenge on, I cared about you the least."

Ettik ran left. The stranger was there. Ettik ran right. The stranger was faster. "Please." He glanced into the pit. "Don't put me in there."

"Your life was your own choice." The stranger grabbed Ettik by either side of his head and squeezed. "This is simply a fitting end."

The stranger forced Ettik screaming to his knees. He put his thumbs over Ettik's eyes and drove them in. Blood poured down Ettik's face and he screamed louder, tearing at the stranger's hands but unable to move them. There was a sickening crack and Ettik went silent. The stranger released his grip and dropped Ettik's corpse into the darkness below.

Gaul's stomach tried to tear itself out of his body. He cried out — the only response he could give with the oncoming paralysis. Marta, meanwhile, was quiet, rolling gently as she clutched her gut. The stranger turned to face them. For what seemed like forever he stood like a statue and watched Gaul and Marta writhe in pain. What was he thinking? Just because he was Ettik's enemy didn't mean he was their ally. He could as easily watch them die.

But he didn't. He pushed Gaul onto his back and pulled a metal flask out of his pocket. Holding Gaul down by the forehead, the stranger forced the bitter fluid down his throat. Gaul tried to cough it up, but the stranger held his mouth closed. Ettik's blood spread across his cheek.

"You'll need to sleep now," the stranger said.

The world became blurry.

"Don't worry. I'll watch over you."

And everything went dark.

* *

Wake up, Marta.

Marta's eyes flew open to a rocky ceiling. She sat up, resting herself on one hand and holding her head with her other. She was in a dark cave — no, not dark, pitch black. A blue-grey light emanated for several metres before coming to stop at a darkness that seemed liquid and heavy. It barely allowed Marta to see the floor and ceiling, and as she turned around, she saw a figure sitting on the edge of the light. He wore a wide-brimmed white hat and a charred mask, with his elbows resting on his knees. Marta yelped and scrambled back. The light retreated with her and the man was swallowed up by darkness.

"Oh, come now," the man in white said, his raspy voice echoing off the cave walls. "If I wanted you dead, I would have let Ettik finish his work."

Marta spun onto one knee, ready to run if the need came up. She ran her hand through her coat. She still had her knives. But the light that followed her didn't give her much indication of where to go. Gaul laid half-covered by darkness, his chest rising and falling in peaceful sleep. He would be a deadweight to carry, so Marta steeled herself and crept forward until the man in white reappeared.

"There we are," the man said. "A modicum of trust for the one who saved your life."

"Who are you?" Marta asked.

"No." The stranger shook his head. "That's not a very interesting question. Who someone is doesn't mean anything about what they are. Why they do the things they do."

"Alright, why did you help us?"

The stranger chuckled and focused on Marta with his charred eye slits. "That is an interesting question."

Gaul coughed and groaned, slowly rising to a sit. Marta shifted until she was next to him, all the time keeping one eye on the stranger.

"What's going on?" Gaul asked, pushing his hair back.

"That is also an interesting question," the stranger said. "You were poisoned by Ettik."

"How's that possible?" Marta asked. She was upset the stranger seemingly passed by her question, but she wasn't going to let him go until he answered her.

"Before he was Ettik the Rat, he was Ettik the Poisoner." The stranger rose to his feet and paced barely inside the light. "Those who spent time with him and raised his ire would inevitably succumb to a terrible sickness, as if the Poisoner's mere presence was enough to infect them. The Praetors of the time made him one of them if only to keep an eye on him. They also had antidotes made against Ettik's particular brand of death. Fortunately for you."

It wasn't the Absence after all. All that time Gaul and Marta spent with Ettik — when he was tied up, when he touched them on the shoulder to hurry them on, when he leaned close enough to feel his breath — it was all poison. He had to of had a way to control it to ensure Marta didn't die. Or maybe an antidote of his own.

"You seem to know an awful lot about the Praetors," Gaul said, rising to meet the stranger. Marta joined him; her fingers ready to draw a blade. "Why did you help us?"

"I was about to answer that before you joined us," the stranger said, a hint of a smile in his voice. He spread his arms wide, throwing out the tails of his coat in a grand flourish. "My friends! We are fortunate. Though I do not know why you run with Marjyal at your back — nor what goals you hope to achieve — the means to our ends have harmonized. I simply wish to see the Praetors of Marjyal slaughtered.

"We're not out here to kill Praetors," Gaul said, stepping forward and sliding his hand to his sword hilt.

The stranger stopped pacing. He cocked his emotionless mask to Marta. "How about you, angry one? Are you against the killing of Praetors?"

"No," Marta said. She knew Gaul wasn't either, but the stranger had a chilling aura. The featureless white porcelain mask, the cackling laugh, and the blood-staining his gloves. Marta knew better than to believe the enemy of an enemy would be her friend. "But that's not what we're trying to do."

"What you mean to do and what happens are very different. You have achieved something I never could. The leaders of Marjyal have presented themselves to risk. They want you. They will come for you, and you will kill them. For that, I will be eternally thankful."

"What're you implying?" Marta asked. "Should we expect you to tag along?"

"Not at all. I was simply in the area when I heard about the Praetor's coming through. I had hoped you would discover Ettik's ruse, but when you didn't, I had to intervene. I won't lie, I was thrilled to kill him myself. You don't know how disappointed I was to learn the Ghost Hand had already been dealt with." He let out a longing sigh. "But there are other Praetors, other places to go. And as I said, the Praetors will come to you, and you will kill them. Don't disappoint me."

"Why do you want the Praetors dead?" Gaul asked. His hand never left his sword.

"Why are they chasing you?" He ran his fingers along the bottom of his mask, as if to rub his chin in mocking contemplation. "We all have our secrets. Why don't we keep some of them for now?"

A drop of light appeared behind the stranger. It fell from somewhere above, illuminating the chasm outside their little cave. The far wall was a mess of caverns and ledges only visible for a moment before the spark disappeared out of view. Something about it felt familiar to Marta. She had only seen them in the light, but it could have been one of the sparks that swirled inside the Gate Beyond's ribcage.

"Was that a soul?" Marta asked.

The stranger tilted his head toward the cave entrance. "That it was. Down here in the Stagnant Dark, the only light that exists is that which your soul provides. Though, while it's inside you only you can see it. That'll be your light on the journey down."

"So, you really are leaving?" Gaul asked.

"You will be fine. Or you will be dead, and I will be heartbroken." He put his hand on his chest and spun his back to them. "Oh, a warning. The Snakes haven't given up on you, and they aren't what they seem. That guild isn't just hunters of food for Marjyal, they're problem solvers of a sort. Assassins. Secret-keepers. Yomat is as much their leader as they are simple trappers. I was hoping to discover the true Praetor of Snakes, but they still elude me. Perhaps they'll reveal themselves for you."

Yomat isn't the real Praetor of Snakes? Marta thought. Who was this man in white that seemed to know so much about Marjyal and harbour such hatred for its rulers? Marta had never seen him before — not that there was much to see with the mask and long coat.

"And as for your first question," he threw back over his shoulder. "You may call me Goodsmile if we should see each other again." He disappeared into the darkness, though his final words still echoed, "Go left if you wish to follow this path to the end."

Gaul and Marta shared a look of confusion and followed after Goodsmile. He was gone, but their limited light showed them the lip of a dark chasm. Above and below was nothing but shadows. It was impossible to tell how far down they already were, as light didn't pass into the Abyss.

Out of that darkness came a falling spark. It didn't show them the sky, but it did reveal a long ledge that would lead them deeper into Black Hypogea. To the left, just as Goodsmile said. Then the spark was gone, and all Marta had was that glow from her body. Gaul had one of his own, one that she couldn't see. They would need to stay close if they didn't want to lose each other.

"Do you think we should trust him?" Gaul asked, looking right.

"He's not working with Melifacto or else I wouldn't be here," Marta said. "But I don't think that means we should trust him. He admitted we're effectively bait."

"Another thing to keep our eye out for." Gaul picked up a rock and tossed it off the cliff. They waited, but it never hit the bottom. "Time to start walking again."

Marta motioned for Gaul to take the lead. With only their souls to light their way, they descended into Black Hypogea.

Before the creation of the Gate Beyond, there was nothing to ensure souls rejoined the cycle. Some would stay on this plane, twisting the world around it and, in turn, being twisted by it. In these early writings, everything would be blamed on a malicious ghost. Storms, droughts, sudden deaths, or even something as simple as a lost cow.

Sometimes a ghost would find its peace and move on. Other times, when the soul was particularly twisted, it may stay and continuously grow in power and rage until they would collapse in on themselves, rejoining the cycle whether they wanted to or not. These souls were a danger to the newfound peace of the First Age, but the First Gods already had a prison. And so it was decided Black Hypogea would hold these souls until they could be cleansed.

(Noted in the margins) Found account implying Gate Beyond existed before First Gods. Need more research before finalizing.

—From the Journal of Jovin Gutterwake

Chapter Twenty-One
Black Hypogea

It was a steady march down and forward. Every few minutes, a spark dropped from high above. They were the only other source of light in Black Hypogea, and as they passed by it gave them a brief view of the depressing canyon system they found themselves in. As this momentary light faded, Gaul swore he saw movement in the distant walls.

The deeper they went, the quieter everything became. Black Hypogea seemed to eat up sound as much as it did light. Not that there was much to say as they walked. There was only one question that hung over them like tantalizing fruit; how would they find any sign of Sebanna in a place that big and that dark?

Gaul figured hours had to of gone by, but he couldn't be sure. It was mind numbing. He was reminded of the days they spent travelling the tunnel from Marjyal to Adathin Castle. In many ways he preferred that. At least in the tunnel he had a sense of surrounding, rather than the inky darkness of the Abyss. That felt like forever ago.

"So then, is Mar real?" Marta asked, as if carrying on a conversation Gaul wasn't a part of.

"I don't know," Gaul said. "I've never heard of them before."

"But the Divines are real?" Marta scratched her head. "And Animas are like little Divines."

"I don't know if Divines are real, Marta. I don't think anyone does for sure, some people just believe it."

"Isn't that why we're doing all of this?" Marta asked, matching her steps with his. "The Divines sealed the First Gods away, and now the Cradle of the World is opening. You said we can't let the First Gods return; doesn't one existing mean the other does?"

Gaul let out a contemplating hum before replying, "When I was very young, my father told me thunder was clouds colliding. As I got older, I was told it was wild flux cracking the air. Consensus now is that it has something to do with lightning leaving space." He paused. "I'm probably not describing it well. The point is thunder still exists even as we understand it better."

"Sound to me like you're making excuses to not commit," Marta said, pursing her lips.

"You're not incorrect."

Marta let out an exasperated sigh and hurried forward. "Uh oh," she said, stopping about a metre ahead.

Gaul joined her and his light revealed what had gotten her so concerned. The path diverged. One through a gap in the wall to the left, while the other continued forward. A spark dropped, but both paths still led into darkness as far as they could see.

"What do we do now?" Marta asked.

"I don't know." Gaul looked between the two choices. There was nothing to signify which way Sebanna went all those years earlier. "What would Sebanna have done?"

"How are we supposed to know that? She wanted to go to the bottom, didn't she? Let's go down."

"I think everything here goes down. It's a massive gulley leading to the bottom. I don't think it matters which way we go."

"Okay." Marta looked left, and right, and back left. "Let's go that way."

"Why?"

"Sebanna wanted punishment. She blamed herself for what happened to Adathin. She wanted to get lost. It's easier to lose yourself when you take more turns."

Gaul bobbed his head. "That's flimsy reasoning."

"Do you have a better idea?"

"Doesn't mean it's a good one." Gaul searched the ground for a rock. "But I did say either way would bring us to the bottom. Left it is." He found one that fit easily in the palm of his hand and begun scratching the cavern wall.

"What are you doing?" Marta asked, leaning over his shoulder.

"I don't know how much of this place we'll have to look through, we need to mark where we've been." He made a large X on the wall and pocketed the rock. It should be easy to see if they looked for it.

Taking the side path did have one rather stark disadvantage, without the periodic sparks the dark space was even darker. The tunnel walls were barely visible on each side. They didn't have to go far before Marta grabbed Gaul by the collar, stopping him.

A clicking sound broke the absolute silence. Gaul focused on the noise. Occasionally there would be a wet squish or a sudden pop like from a bone joint, but the clicking never stopped. It only got louder. Gaul pulled Marta against the cave wall.

A clawed hand landed in the light, followed by a cruel mess of a body following it. The thing moved on all fours but swayed like a human rather than some beast. Bones jutted from red, bleeding flesh while other parts were more skeleton than muscle. Grey-black liquid oozed from open sores on its back and face. It swung its head back and forth, revealing milky eyes and clicking its teeth at the air.

Marta squeezed Gaul's shoulder. The creature wheezed, but continued on despite them, disappearing into the darkness. Gaul reached back and tapped Marta's hand. They crept on. Neither made a sound.

The clicking continued. It became more intense, growing in volume and multiplying until the tunnel was nothing but echoing chatter. A fleshy clump of some meat landed a few feet from them. Gaul cursed silently, then looked up.

The ceiling was covered in those same creatures. They gripped onto each other and stalactites, moving like one large pulsating entity. One stretched its neck out and clicked its teeth in Gaul's direction.

Gaul pushed against Marta's stomach, forcing her to step back. Her eyes were wide with fear, staring at the horrible mass covering the ceiling. They kept a hold on each other and crept back. Gaul worried they were going to bump into the first one who wandered past, but they were able to make their way back to the intersection. Only then did Gaul allow himself to breathe.

Marta threw her head back, drawing in a big gulp of air. Even the stale underground atmosphere was better than the rotting scent excreted by the monsters. "I don't like this place," she said, spitting on the ground.

Something giggled behind them. They drew their weapons and spun to the noise. Sticking out of the wall was a statue of a desiccated man, half covering his face while he screamed in fear or pain. Had they walked past it without noticing?

"I see you have met the forlorn." The bird-like voice seemingly came from somewhere within the statue. "Forlorn, forlorn. Borne from the blood of the beast Behemoth. Buried in the bottom of Black Hypogea. Blocking the path to the cursed Queen of Adathin."

"Sebanna?" Gaul lowered his sword. "Are you talking about Sebanna?"

"Sebanna, Sebanna. Sorrowful and sweet sovereign of scourged Adathin. Sebanna's her name. Sebanna, Sebanna. What's yours?"

Gaul inspected the statue. There weren't any gaps in the stone for a creature to live. The man's torso was fused with the wall and at where they met was half an X scratched into the stone. "We're looking for her," Gaul said. "Or maybe something she left behind?"

Marta pulled on Gaul's arm. "Can I talk to you for a second?" She led him away, so the light only barely illuminated the statue. "I don't like this thing. We should go."

"This thing," Gaul said, pointing at the statue, "could tell us about Sebanna. It could let us know if she left anything behind, or at least where she went when she came through. It's either this or we wander down here blind, with those forlorn around every corner."

"We don't even know what it is."

"My name is Kumuru!" the statue said. "Kumuru! Kumuru! What's yours?"

Gaul give an urging look to Marta, who let out a huff and spun her knife away. Gaul sheathed his swords and approached Kumuru. "My name is Athas."

"Athas!" Kumuru chirped. "Athas adventures into the Abyss. What's your name?"

There was no movement from the statue, but Gaul turned to Marta. "I think it's asking you."

Marta frowned. "Lenn."

"Lenn!" Kumuru said. "Lenn languishes in loathsome locales. Why are Athas and Lenn in the dark? For Sebanna, Sebanna?"

"Yes," Gaul said. "We're following her path. Do you know where she lived? Or where she is buried?"

"Yes, yes. No, no." A scratching came from the statue. "Deep in the depths the second daughter disappeared. To atone for the ruin she wrecked upon the world. Down and down she went. Staying in the Sunken Citadel. Built the Unseen Church in which to now pray for pity."

"Now? Is she still alive?"

"Of course! Of course! Where can you die in the land of the dead?"

Of all the things Gaul imagined finding in Black Hypogea, Sebanna herself wasn't one of them. They could get answers — real answers not gleaned from ancient writings. Marta jumped in front of Gaul.

"Where is she?" she asked. "Where's the Unseen Church?"

"In the deepest parts of the deep. The darkest parts of the dark. Down, down, down, down. All paths converge in the down. The forlorn hunt the quickest way. Do not go! No forlorn. No forlorn. I can show you another since we are friends now, Athas and Lenn. Sebanna needs more friends too!"

"How long will that take us?"

"Days? Days?"

"How many days?"

"Five days! Five days!"

Gaul pinched the bridge of his nose. Marta let out an audible groan.

"Are you hurt?" Kumuru asked.

"I'm fine," Marta said, adjusting her scarf in frustration. "Show us the way, Kumuru."

"Straight then right! Straight then right! Cross the bridge!"

Gaul waited for something else to happen, but as far as he could tell, nothing changed with the statue. "I guess we go straight then right," he said.

They turned from the statue and headed down the canyon ridge. Occasionally, they passed another offshoot into the wall that Gaul would mark with his stone. As he was making his third of such marks, Marta planted herself next to him with crossed arms.

"I'm not crazy for distrusting a statue," she said.

"I never said you were." Gaul finished the X and continued walking.

Marta followed at his side. "Do you think Kumuru's telling the truth? Is Sebanna still alive down here?"

"This is where souls go," Gaul said. "I can't even begin to fathom what the rules are. But I do know that if Kumuru is leading us to get eaten by something like that thing we saw out in the mountains, we need to be ready to fight or run."

"Let's say run." She spun a knife between her fingers. "I'm not going to be doing much pinpricking something of that size. I need to steal myself a sword."

"If a giant monster comes after us—" He used his thumb to push one of his swords out. "—you can borrow one of mine."

Marta rolled her eyes. "What a gentleman."

Gaul laughed and let the sword drop back into his sheath. Before long they arrived at a natural bridge that reached a stony arm into the darkness. A spark dropped, revealing a thin stretch of earth spanning across Black Hypogea. Gaul took a few careful steps out.

"It's holding," he said. "But let's move quick."

Marta nodded, but there was a sluggishness to her movements. She looked out into the expanse with an exhausted dread. Gaul could feel it too. It was draining to have nothing but a few metres of world around him at a time. The week ahead was looking terrible. Gaul gave a smile that said he understood, and they crossed the bridge.

Gaul reached the end of the bridge first. His light brought in the far wall, revealing another statue. Only it wasn't just similar to Kumuru's, it was the exact same — a man protecting his face from some unknown attacker.

"Hello! Hello!" Kumuru chirped.

"How did you get here so fast?" Marta asked.

"Because I am fast! Sebanna says I'm very very fast." Pulsing chitters echoed from the statue. Something Gaul figured was a laugh. "I'm glad you didn't fall off the bridge, Athas and Lenn. Do you want to wait for your friends? Friends or forward? Friends or forward?"

"Friends?" Gaul asked, glancing behind them like someone would be right there. "What friends are you talking about?"

"Wandered in willfully with weapons in hand. Just like you! Just like you! Many with weapons. Sour face. Just like you!"

"I don't have a sour face," Gaul muttered.

"Not you! Lenn!"

Gaul turned around and caught Marta mid-scowl. She shook her head in protest. "Hey!" she exclaimed. "He's much more sour than me."

"We're going to keep moving, Kumuru," Gaul said.

Marta muttered under her breath, "You just caught me on a bad day."

"Left!" Kumuru said. "I'll see you ahead." Once again, nothing changed in the statue. Either Kumuru was gone or waiting to move when out of view.

"It's the Snakes," Marta said, taking off at a brisk walk so that Gaul had to chase after. "Goodsmile was right! After all that, they're right behind us. They've been behind us since we left Sebanna's Rest! We should've… we should've killed them when we had the chance. Instead of sneaking around with blastjars we should have just slit both Praetor's throats."

Marta kept her eyes affixed on the edge of her light. Her hands were deep in her coat pockets and her chin was hidden in the folds of her scarf. It didn't take much to read her.

"Maybe," Gaul said. "If that would make you feel better."

Marta slammed one foot on the ground and came back at Gaul, stopping him in his tracks. "You're allowed to work out your anger on some Rat and I'm supposed to keep calm?"

"That's not what I mean."

"Only you can kill Praetors?"

"That's also not what I mean."

Marta shoved two fingers into his chest. "Then what do you mean?"

Gaul ran his hand through his hair to the back of his neck. He shouldn't have gotten involved. It would have been better to say nothing. Marta didn't even remember she was the one who finally killed Dianathos. "Nothing," he finally said.

"Then just shut up." She stomped away. "Every time we let a Praetor live, it comes back on us."

"Is this about Ettik?" Gaul asked, hurrying to keep up. "I'm sorry. You were right, he was tricking us."

"Of course I was right! Praetors are in charge because they have outmaneuvered every other asshole in Marjyal, you can't underestimate them. And he almost succeeded! It took pure luck that he didn't kill you and take me prisoner."

"What were we supposed to do? We had no idea where Black Hypogea was, and how was I supposed to guess Ettik was fluxblooded? Do all the Praetors have abilities?"

"I don't know! I don't know anything!" She booted a rock off the side of the cliff.

"The only reason we even stayed in Sebanna's Rest was because I was trying to keep Fortunis from turning you in. You're the one who wanted to play hero."

"What do you think we're doing?" Marta stopped and stared Gaul in the eyes. "I don't want to go back to Marjyal — I can't explain how much the thought of it terrifies me — but what does that matter if Absence covers everything? Or if the First Gods make all of us their subjects? Jovin was trying to find a way to stop it, the least I can do is continue his work. That's why I'm here; why are you?"

Gaul clenched his jaw. "Because you told me you would show me the way out."

Marta's eyes went wide. She fluttered her lips for a second, then hurried away. Gaul tapped his palms on his swords. *Good job*, he thought, and followed before Marta could leave his light.

The path curved right into the valley wall, before expanding into a cavern. Marta stopped at the base of a statue nearly twice her height. It wasn't another of Kumuru's, this one was a man in heavy armour with a full-face helm, his head tilted down as if to observe those who stood his base. He held the hilt to a golden greatsword to his chest, with the point down at his feet. Lichen and fungus were spread at the base — offerings to the statue.

"Is this Lord Tyran?" Marta asked.

Gaul stood next to her. "It's how he's depicted. Lord Tyran, the First Knight. The one who cracked Black Hypogea open and defeated Behemoth." He leaned down to inspect the offerings. They were still fresh. *Tyran won't hear you in the Cradle,* he thought.

Marta brushed her finger along the sword. Yellow chips fell from where she touched. "I was hoping it would be real gold."

"Tyran used a greatsword that crashed like lightning." Gaul left the offerings where they were. "Perhaps that's what it was made from as well."

"Oh no!" Kumuru's voice pierced the dark. Gaul and Marta spun to where a statue now stuck out of the wall. "Run! Athas and Lenn must run!"

"Why?" Gaul drew his swords. "What's happening?"

"It's supposed to be asleep! Not awaken for a decade more. Run, run, the baadageist comes!"

Filling the chasm with so many evil souls changed it. Before long, even light didn't dare to pierce the space below. The gods refused to acknowledge it and turned their eyes elsewhere. Monsters began crawling out of the pit. Slithering, flying, crushing beasts that stalked Meza to this day.

If that's what came out, I would hate to see what remained inside.

—From the Journal of Jovin Gutterwake

Chapter Twenty-Two

Run! Run!

The earth shook with the pounding of mighty footfalls. Gaul raised his swords toward the sound. A six-fingered hand — as big as Gaul's torso — grabbed onto the wall. The baadageist ducked under the ceiling before standing to its overwhelming full height in the cavern.

Its skin was like a rocky wall, complete with mossy clumps and fungal growths. Drawn lips pulled back over a mouth overflowing with needle teeth. A whip-like tongue flopped out of its mouth and tasted the air. It turned sunken, beady red eyes upon the pair of them with a vague interest before stomping forward, reaching for Gaul.

Gaul slashed it across the palm and jumped back with Marta. The baadageist inspected its hand, as if surprised its prey would fight back. It reached again with its other hand. Gaul cut that one too, shoving Marta out of the cavern with him.

The baadageist looked at its palms. Strangely, no blood trickled from the wounds. It began to shake and slammed its fists into the ground, letting out a bone-rattling roar. It swung a backhand. Gaul stumbled back, while Marta ducked underneath and rose throwing two knives. They stuck into the baadageist's broad chest. It didn't even flinch.

"Just run!" Gaul shouted, grabbing Marta by the scarf and pulling her in front of him. As he turned to follow, something wet wrapped around his leg and yanked him to the ground.

The baadageist's tongue stretched out of its mouth, slowly drawing Gaul toward its horrible maw. Marta hurled a knife at the tongue. It bounced off the stone but took a sizeable chunk out of the side. Gaul tugged his leg back. The remaining flesh on the tongue tore free — still no blood. Gaul shook the tongue off his leg and scrambled back.

"There's no way that thing can cross the bridge," Marta said, helping Gaul to his feet. "We'll lead it there."

They turned to run — only to come face to face with Yomat and his Snakes. They weren't looking at Gaul and Marta, though. They were gazing much higher, at the baadageist stomping behind them.

Yomat loosed an arrow into the baadageist's face. It grunted in annoyance then reached over Gaul and Marta to the new pest. Yomat dove aside and the baadageist grabbed the Snake standing next to him. The Snake screamed and struggled against the six meaty fingers.

"Loose!" Yomat shouted.

A dozen arrows stuck into the baadageist's hand. It growled and tossed the Snake across the cave. The sound of a human body turning to paste came from the dark. The Snakes spread out, launching arrow after arrow. The baadageist swatted at the missiles as if they were annoying flies. Gaul and Marta retreated from the fight — putting it out of their light range — only to be stopped by Yomat drawing back another arrow.

"Not another step," he said.

"You don't want to be here either," Gaul said.

Marta drew a knife and reared back. She was about to throw when a voice came from the dark.

"Gaul!" Fortunis appeared from the shadows. His hands were bound behind his back and a Snake held him by the shoulders. Next to him was Miribelle, similarly bound. Coming into the light last was Nana Stundel, showing off a cruel grin.

"We found those who helped you." Yomat nodded and the Snakes put knives to Fortunis and Miribelle's throats. "We may not be able to kill you, Marta, but try anything and these two are dead."

Marta breathed through clenched teeth. The knife shook in her hand, but eventually she lowered it and returned it to her coat.

"Take her," Yomat said. Another Snake grabbed Marta by the arm and dragged her away. He started digging in her coat for knives and tossing them off the cliff.

Gaul tapped his swords against his legs. He could kill Yomat easily enough. At that range, slipping past the bow would be simple, but there was no getting to Fortunis or Miribelle in time. As much as he wished he was heartless enough to sacrifice them, he couldn't add that to his heavy conscience.

With a pained grunt, the mangled corpse of a Snake came tumbling out of the dark. They couldn't forget the baadageist. It roared and thumped about just outside of Gaul's light. They needed to move before it finished with the Snakes and moved onto more prey.

Yomat didn't seem to worry. He let down his bow and circled Gaul, taking gentle steps that barely made a sound. The steps a hunter would take to not spook his prey. He stood before Gaul and tossed his head back. "You never did impress me in the Pits," he said. "Impress me now."

He drove his foot into Gaul's stomach, pushing him back. Yomat disappeared and Gaul spun about in time to dodge a Snake being swung by the monster's tongue — now seemingly whole. It tossed the Snake aside and faced the returning prey. Pieces of people were strewn about, with a lone Snake clutching a sword in his shaking grasp.

"I'll give you one minute, Gaul," Yomat shouted. "If you live, you can come with us."

The baadageist leaned toward Gaul. It puffed out hot breath that smelled like rotting meat and mildew. The remaining Snake looked between Gaul and the monster, not sure if he should run — or if he even could. Gaul smiled and rested his swords on his shoulders. For the first time in a long time, there were no bystanders.

Time slowed. Gaul bent his knees. He focused on the fire in his gut. He pulled it out until it was a flaming strand that ran from his head to his feet. Blood dripped from the baadageist's teeth as it opened its mouth, revealing dozens of whip-like tongues. As a drop of blood struck the stone, Gaul snapped the string and the flames Ignited.

He struck the beast across the cheek, digging a deep gouge across his face and knocking a mushroom shelf off its brow. There was still no blood. The baadageist recoiled, showing pain for the first time. Gaul rushed in and cut it just below the knee.

There was a tearing of wind. Gaul felt his skeleton compress as the baadageist slapped him aside. He tumbled across the stone. Lightning skipped off the ground where he struck. He never released his grasp on his swords, and as he turned with the momentum he ended up on both feet and hands. His shoulder cracked into place with a burst of energy and he raised his head. The baadageist was out of his light, but he knew the way.

Gaul exploded into motion. A crimson aura appeared before him. He brought a blade across the aura's throat and carried on before the Snake even hit the ground. An arm reached in from the darkness. Gaul curved to the side, keeping his momentum up. The hand struck where he once was, scattering fungus and moss off the baadageist's skin. With Gaul's next step, the monster's horrid face came into the light.

Lashing tongues were already working their way out of its toothy maw. Gaul hacked at the fleshy mass, sending chunks of tongue flying in all directions — their red glow disappearing as they splatted against the ground.

Gaul crouched low, bounding between the baadageist's legs and cutting at its ankles. The monster reached back with both hands. Gaul swayed aside, like a marionette on loose strings, and came back with a double chop that took off one of his meaty fingers.

The baadageist clutched his finger stub in his other hand, letting out a low groan. Gaul moved toward its exposed leg and began chopping down the tree. He cut through cracked grey skin and thick fungus. Even as he hit bone, there was no blood for the baadageist to bleed.

The baadageist teetered atop its suddenly thinner leg. Gaul stepped back, unafraid of the mass that threatened to crush him. He spun one of his swords and planted his feet. The baadageist crumpled — first to one knee, then to all fours. As its head came forward, Gaul brought a sword up to meet it. He stuck it just underneath the jaw, sinking deep into the baadageist's throat. He gave his other sword a spin and stuck it up in next to it.

A gurgling came from the baadageist's throat. It held itself, shaking, on all fours, pitched like a living tent. Gaul turned his grip about on his blades. Tensing his chest and shoulders, he pulled. They refused to move. The baadageist's neck muscles were like steel. But with a primal roar — like a giant pair of scissors — the swords tore apart the beast's throat. Its heavy skull dropped at Gaul's feet, tongues lolling from its open mouth.

Gaul dropped his swords and took the baadageist by two of its teeth. He planted a foot against the monster's shoulder and pulled. The little skin that remained on the baadageist's nape tore under Gaul's strength, and he hurled the head in the direction where the Snakes should be. With a long exhale, Gaul quenched the flames. There were no more beating hearts demanding his attention.

After retrieving his swords, Gaul staggered out of the cave. He took in deep breaths, trying to force his heart to beat slower. He found Yomat standing next to the baadageist's head. He was tapping his sword against its brow. Marta, Fortunis, and Miribelle were still being held by their Snakes, while Nana Stundel leaned on her cane between them.

"Adequate," Yomat said, sheathing his sword. "Drop your weapons."

Gaul threw his swords down.

"Take them," Yomat said to one of the Snakes.

"What now, Praetor?" Gaul asked, strolling forward.

"You're in no position to ask questions," Yomat said, shaking his finger.

"I'm not asking you." Gaul's eyes weren't on Yomat. They were locked, unblinking, with Nana Stundel. "I'm asking the Praetor of Snakes."

A smile crept across Nana's lips — and then begun to spread further than her mouth should have allowed. "Someone has been tattling," she said, her voice now deeper than before.

She ran her fingers along her cheeks. Flecks of skin flew away at her touch. She continued until just under her ear, where she pushed her fingers into her flesh and pulled. Like a snake shedding, she tore off the disguise of Nana Stundel and became a much younger woman with golden skin and an upturned nose. Her eyes were grey slits and the faintest hint of scales were visible on her neck and wrists.

"I've been hearing so much about you, Gaul the Ruthless," she said, slinking closer. As she walked, she tossed aside her shawl and woolen overcoat. She tore her skirt away to reveal pants and knee-high boots. Piece by piece, the disguise of Nana Stundel fell away. "I am Handai, the Praetor of Snakes. I heard shocking things about your fight in the Pits. Survivor of the Banquet. But not only survivor, you conquered all who stood in your way." She cast her glance to the baadageist's head. "And the trend continues. But I'm curious, who told you about my identity?"

"Why else would an old bag come in here?" Gaul said. "This is important enough to oversee yourself, isn't it?"

"True." Handai had grown with each step, until she was eye-to-eye with Gaul. She put a finger under his chin and push it up slightly. "But who sent you looking for a true Praetor? Only the elite of my Snakes and those I trust know of this. Who betrayed me?"

"I guessed."

Handai chuckled. She ran her finger along Gaul's jaw, caressing his neck with her long nails. "Such confidence. Such courage. Melifacto said we are free to kill you, but I think I would like to keep you around."

Yomat's eyes flared with anger at the words, something Handai didn't see, but Gaul did.

"Most of my companions tend to… break far too quickly." Handai rested her hand on Gaul's cheek. A shiver ran down his spine. "Perhaps you'll do better."

"Tempting offer." Everything in Gaul told him to back up, but his legs were frozen in place. "Afraid I'll have to decline."

Handai pulled Gaul closer to her. "It's not an offer." She opened her mouth, revealing a long, forked tongue that she used to lick up his cheek. Pressing her nails into his skin, she whispered in his ear, "You'll find I'm much better company than Melifacto."

"Excuse me," Yomat said. "We should move on. It's going to be night by the time we reach the surface."

"Of course," Handai said, pulling away from Gaul. She coughed into her hand as she walked. It seemed that wasn't part of the act.

"Was there ever a Nana Stundel?" Miribelle asked as Handai passed by.

Handai paused, inspecting Miribelle. As if deciding she was worth her time, Handai spoke, "Or course. You need to kill someone to wear their skin. If it means anything, she was a right old bitch before I found her." She patted Miribelle on the cheek and kept walking.

"You're in the middle," Yomat said, pushing Gaul into motion. He kept his eyes on him, flicking his bowstring.

The group moved forth. With the limited light it took a while to count, but Gaul figure there were about a dozen Snakes. They split with half at the front and half at the back, with the prisoners in the middle. Yomat walked just in front of them with Handai, occasionally glancing back to glare at Gaul. The Snake who took his swords walked just in front of Yomat. Miribelle was the only one with a Snake keeping a solid grip on them — they must have figured out she couldn't jump-step while being touched.

"Are you alright?" Marta whispered.

Gaul wiped some of Handai's saliva off his cheek. "I have rarely been more unsettled."

"You don't want to go home with that woman."

"I wasn't planning on it, but thanks."

They marched right back the way they came, quickly coming upon the thin bridge. Something that narrow, a quick attack could favour them. If Gaul could knock a few Snakes away, they wouldn't risk killing Marta. But they could just as easily send him into the depths. Same with Fortunis and Miribelle, whose hands were still tied.

"Stop," Yomat said. He pointed at a few of the Snakes. "Take Lady Handai across the bridge first. The prisoner's will be next." He thrust a finger at Miribelle. "And if you're not there when you get to the other side, my Snakes will kill your brother on sight. Now be good."

Miribelle nodded, something barely visible amongst all the shaking. Yomat was smart, he wasn't going to risk his guild on the bridge with them. Gaul would need to keep his eye out for another chance.

Handai and her Snakes went out first. Another coughing fit hit her as she disappeared across the bridge. They waited in silence for a minute or two before Yomat sent the four prisoners out. They were soon surrounded by darkness on all sides.

"I'm sorry," Miribelle whispered. "We tried to convince Nana Stundel to run the Guilds out of town but…"

"We saw how that turned out," Gaul said. "It's fine. You couldn't have known. Why did they bring you along?"

Fortunis sighed. "I told them we helped you. Nana was resistant so I thought maybe it would convince her to help. It was a dumb call."

"We can't worry about that now," Marta said, scanning the darkness ahead. "This bridge is gonna end soon. We need to figure out an escape plan. Fortunately…" She slid a knife out of her sleeve. "They missed one."

"There's always the forlorn," Gaul said.

"That's… an option," Marta said, hiding the knife in her palm.

"Do you have a better plan?"

Marta sighed. "That doesn't mean it's a good one."

"Clarify something for me," Fortunis said, leaning in. "What did you say? Forlorn?"

"Monsters," Marta said. "Look, we're going to be passing a few turns with X's on them. On the third one—"

"Fourth one," Gaul cut in.

"—fourth one we're going to make a break for it."

"Yomat seems prone to anger," Gaul said. "And I know just the nerve to hit. I'll make a distraction. Marta still has her knives so she can cut Fortunis free, and Miribelle, once you get your guard to let go, just run.

"And what's this about monsters?" Fortunis asked.

"Just keep running. No matter what happens, never stop. We'll meet up when it's safe."

Fortunis opened his mouth, only for Miribelle to shush him. They soon arrived at the other side. Handai waited with Snakes holding their bows at the ready. One of them grabbed Miribelle as soon as she stepped onto the ledge. A few minutes later, Yomat and the last of the Snakes joined them. He silently checked to make sure Handai was fine, then waved for the group to keep moving.

The silence was crushing, only the sound of their feet sliding on the earth. Occasionally a spark dropped and gave them some sense of location. The path to the forlorn was close. It seemed much closer on the way down.

As the boredom took over, the Snakes unknowingly spread apart. Since each person could only see their own light, the distance between them would be an advantage for the prisoners. They could use that confusion. Gaul's gaze fell on the Snake who took his swords. He was a target for sure. But first, time to get a reaction.

"Handai," Gaul said, slightly speeding up. "I've been thinking about your offer."

Handai tilted her head but did not look back. "It's adorable you're still thinking of it as an offer. Snakes don't mind a struggling prey."

"Will it keep me out of the Pits?" Gaul asked, keeping one eye on Yomat, who was watching with great interest.

"The Pits are far too public for my tastes." She shrugged playfully. "And as long as you're entertaining, I won't get bored."

"I can be very entertaining," Gaul said, a smile in his voice.

Handai tittered behind her fingers.

Yomat fumed, looking over his shoulder at Gaul. "It's a long road back to Marjyal. Anything can happen."

"Are you worried, Yomat?" Gaul asked. "I can take over navigating if you don't think you can handle it."

"I would rather you be quiet so I can focus on leading us out of here."

"Lady Handai doesn't seem to mind me talking." Gaul grinned. "And she is the Praetor after all."

Yomat dropped back to walk next to Gaul. "You better watch your tone. You're not untouchable, Gaul. Melifacto has said that you mean nothing, and the only one who needs to be returned unspoilt is Marta. So keep talking, I dare you. Lady Handai doesn't have need of your tongue."

"Actually," Gaul said, spotting the half X on the tunnel to his right. "I think she does."

Yomat, face red like he'd spent a week in the sun, opened his mouth to reply. Gaul slammed it closed with a rising elbow, dropping Yomat flat.

Marta flipped around her hidden knife and drove it into the closest Snake's throat. She grabbed Fortunis with one hand and used the bloody knife to cut his bonds. With the initial surprise gone, the Snakes shouted and drew weapons. Gaul caught one in mid-draw, punching him in the throat before pushing him into another one. Yomat staggered to his feet — clutching his jaw — and barely got out of the way before the Snakes tumbled off the cliff.

Fortunis ran by in a blur, catching the attention of the Snake with Gaul's swords. Gaul caught the Snake by the scruff and threw him into the cave wall. He readied a fist to hit him on the return, but the Snake never did. His back was stuck to the stone. Panic overtook him as he struggled to no avail. Dark grey veins snaked out of his collar, running along his cheeks, and into his mouth. There was a crack and his jaw locked open. A voice came from inside.

"Not friends!" It was Kumuru. "Run, friends!"

Gaul wrenched his swords from the Snake's grasp. He gave them up easily, now that he had bigger concerns. The grey veins grew denser along the Snake's skin. His eyes pleaded for help, but his body was locked in that state of perpetual fear.

Miribelle appeared behind Gaul for a moment, her hands still bound behind her, before vanishing again. This was followed shortly by Marta sprinting past.

"Go!" she shouted, slapping Gaul on the back.

Gaul left the Snake to whatever fate Kumuru had for him and followed. He glanced to his left. Yomat met his eyes.

"We need the woman!" Handai shouted. "Forget the rest!"

Yomat drew back his bow as the light left him. Gaul paused, and with a whistle an arrow flew where his head was about to be. He turned sharply into the tunnel to the forlorn. Blurs of arrows flew through his light, disappearing again before breaking against the wall. One such arrow whipped past his head, the wind tickling his ear.

He focused on his feet, driving his toes into the stone. Each step was the only indication he was making any headway, as the walls and ground looked all the same. Soon he caught up with Marta. She let out a breath of relief upon seeing him and begun to slow.

"We're not stopping!" Gaul said, tossing her one of his swords.

Marta caught the blade and looked back. An arrow flew by, taking a lock of her hair with it. She recoiled, cursing under her breath, and ran at full speed.

"You're going to hit her!" Handai said. "Keep your arrows on your string before I choke you with them!"

They found Fortunis cutting through Miribelle's rope. With a twist, it fell free and Miribelle shook the feeling into her arms. Fortunis raised the knife to Marta. "Do you want your—"

"Still running!" Marta said.

Miribelle jump-stepped while Fortunis scrambled into motion. The four of them sprinted forth, keeping each other in their lights. Soon a familiar clicking filled the air. It was more interested this time, frenzied even. The forlorn were waking up.

"What is that?" Fortunis asked, whipping his head around.

Gaul adjusted his grip on his sword. "No matter what happens, don't stop."

A forlorn leapt into view. Its jaw clicked open until its cheeks were nothing but stretched tendons. Miribelle screamed and Fortunis stumbled. Gaul caught it on the brow with the pommel of his sword and knocked it away. He grabbed Fortunis' coat and pushed him forward.

"What did I say?" He sliced the arm off another reaching forlorn.

Marta thrust her sword through a forlorn's chest. She twisted around and with all her might, yanked the sword out, catching another monster on the downswing. She was less graceful than she was with two knives, but she kept the forlorn at a distance and cut deeper. She pushed the first forlorn aside as she ran.

A face of jagged teeth lunged for Gaul's arm. He met it with his boot. The forlorn thrashed on the ground until Gaul stomped on his throat as he stepped over. Gaul and Marta fought on the move, letting Fortunis and Miribelle take the lead. The forlorn were barely more than beast, they simply had to beat away the ones who lunged at them. There was a bloodcurdling scream from the direction they came. As long as they kept moving, the forlorn would be awake and ready for the Snakes.

The horde of forlorn broke as Gaul came to a stumbling stop at the start of a rickety bridge. He caught Marta before she could take her first step. Miribelle was partway across, helping Fortunis out of a broken slat in the bridge. The other side was past the reach of their light, but if it was a precarious as the rest, then too much weight was going to break the entire thing in half.

"You go first," Gaul said, turning to face the forlorn. "I'll Ignite, buy some time, and meet you on the other side."

"No way." Marta planted herself at Gaul's side. "It held the two of them; it'll hold the two of us. Let's just give them time to get across."

"I can't Ignite while you're here. It's too dangerous."

"Then we spread out. I stay out of your light; you stay out of mine."

Gaul grabbed her arm. "I won't be able to tell if it's you."

"Don't worry about me." She tore her arm away. "And don't you dare hold back. I'm not dying because of your problems."

Gaul wanted to argue more, but the forlorn were closing in. He stepped forward, sword resting on his shoulder, until he couldn't see Marta anymore. The forlorn circled him, snapping their teeth and shaking their heads. They would break the bridge of any followed. It wasn't enough to buy time — everyone needed to die. Gaul took a deep breath and Ignited.

The forlorn burned with red light. Gaul rushed forward, catching the first one under the jaw and bisecting his head. He spun with the momentum and slashed the next one as it reached forward. Fingers flew into the air and Gaul returned with a deep gash across its back.

A forlorn caught him in the shoulder with its clawed hands. Heat flared in the wound and lightning leapt forth, knitting the flesh together. Gaul caught the same claw with his healing arm and wrenched it back before slicing it off at the shoulder.

The wounded forlorn retreated, only to be replaced by an ocean of more red auras. Gaul hacked and chopped. A forlorn grabbed him by the foot and yanked it aside. He fell onto his front and rolled over. The forlorn lunged. Gaul stuck his sword out, impaling the beast as it leapt.

Another swipe came from the left. Gaul moved the stuck forlorn in the way. The crazed monster tore at the corpse as Gaul pulled his sword out and rolled back onto his feet.

Pain shot up his leg as a forlorn bit down on his calf. Lighting fought back against the wound, but its powerful jaw was crushing down on his bone. Gaul swung at its neck. It bit down harder. Gaul hacked away until he was finally able to decapitate the creature. He kicked the head off, striking a fleeing forlorn. Lighting poured from the wound like water, healing the mangled limb.

The red auras fled from him like a flood. Gaul's turned in a slow circle, letting the blood drip from his blade. More hearts were beating. They pounded like needles into his brain. He swayed forward until spots of red appeared at the edge of the darkness. He held out his sword and let the weight of the blade carry him forward. More red. More noise. He needed to silence them.

With his next step, a blazing sun grew in the centre of the sea of red. An aura of pure gold that burned against Gaul's brain. Until the screaming red hearts, it was quiet. It shocked him so much, his flame flickered.

The gold faded and there was Marta. She sliced at a forlorn's nape then drove her heel into its jaw. Golden light pulsed along her frame, an in crosshatched patterns across her skin. Gaul shook his head, regaining his sense. They were still in trouble. He flicked the blood off his sword and refocused. The auras returned — forlorn in red, Marta in gold.

Gaul bullied his way through the crimson sea. Marta braced herself, but Gaul slid past, driving his knees into a forlorn and sending them off the cliff. Marta recovered and jumped away, giving Gaul plenty of space.

Gaul struck a forlorn across the back. It wavered on its thin limbs and Gaul struck again. He brought the blade against it until its spine snapped and it crumpled. It stopped moving and the red faded away.

Only the golden aura remained. It outlined every one of Marta's features — along her jaw and nose, pushing through her clothes like they were windows. Gaul was wrong, it wasn't quiet. There was a beat that came with it. It wasn't discordant like the red ones. It was steady and strong. Like a distant drum, echoing across cold mountains.

Gaul quenched his flames and Marta's form returned. She had a severe look in her eyes and held her sword at the ready. As the aura disappeared and Gaul's eyes turned blue, she relaxed.

"See?" she said, tossing the sword to Gaul. "Nothing to worry about."

There was something going on with her. Between her attitude in Dothrin and the strange gold aura — either she didn't know or was hiding it well. Gaul sheathed his swords, but kept his thumbs tapping along their pommels. Staring at Marta wasn't going to get him his answers.

"We need to go," he said, starting over the bridge.

Marta kicked a forlorn's arm out of the way and followed. The wood creaked with each step and they had to hold onto the rope handrails lest they be shook off. Gaul eased his foot onto the next slat. It splintered at his touch and he pulled back. He indicated it to Marta and stepped over. Better to be slow than dead.

"Don't move!" Yomat stepped out of the dark, bow drawn. Blood poured from a split on his brow. The bridge swayed beneath him, but he stood steady like a sailor aboard a ship.

Marta placed herself in front of Gaul. She was smaller than him, but as Gaul turned to the side and slouched, it gave just enough doubt that Yomat wouldn't risk killing her. But with the precarious nature of the bridge, any movement could give Yomat a target. They were at a standstill.

"You will return with me to Handai," Yomat said. "You will get her the Chalice, and it will get that sickness out of her."

"I'm not going anywhere with you," Marta said.

"I may not be able to kill you," Yomat said. "But there are so many ways I can hurt you and keep you alive. Melifacto may be upset, but I've never concerned myself with other people's opinions."

Gaul pushed a sword free with his thumb. "Hold onto something, Marta," he whispered.

"You'll want to stay still," Yomat said, lining up his eye with the arrow. "I would hate to miss."

Marta twisted the bridge rope around her arm. Gaul clutched his sword. He would have to be quick.

"You have until three." Yomat lifted a finger from the grip. "One."

The bridge shook. The three of them froze. From the darkness, the clicking of the forlorn grew. Yomat lifted his bow and spun, loosing into a forlorn creeping across the bridge. It took the arrow through the mouth and collapsed. The weight of it hitting the bridge caused the ropes to fray. More forlorn crawled into view, straining the bridge to its max.

Yomat loosed arrow after arrow, but the forlorn never stopped. Marta slapped Gaul on the arm. "Do it now!" she said.

Gaul drew his sword and in the same motion, sliced through one of the ropes holding the bridge together. Everything turned. Marta dangled by one arm while Gaul had to grab onto a slat to keep from falling. Yomat hooked his bow onto the bridge and pulled himself closer to the rope to hang on. The bridge swung wide, dropping forlorn into the depths.

With the next bounce, the remaining rope began to unfurl. Its strands frayed and split until with a final snap, it collapsed. Gaul and Marta went one way, while Yomat and the forlorn disappeared in the other. They hit the wall with a rattling force. The slat Gaul held snapped. His shoulder struck Marta and sent them both tumbling.

But only for about a metre. Gaul laid on his back, clutching onto his sword and taking heavy breaths. The remains of the bridge settled above him. A few more slats clattered onto the fortunate ledge he and Marta found themselves laying on. Marta broke out into a laugh that filled the cavern.

"Gaul! Marta! Are you down there?" Fortunis shouted from above.

"We're alive," Gaul said, rolling over and stretching back on his knees. Marta rolled her shoulder and staggered to her feet. She waved at Gaul, letting him know she was fine. "For better or worse. Are you alright?"

"Yes. We were off the bridge before it fell."

"The cave keeps going," Miribelle said. "Is there anyway you can get back up?"

"I don't think so," Gaul said. A bridge slat fell at his feet. "Definitely not."

"There's a path over here," Marta said, walking the edge of the light. "It goes down, though."

"Okay." Gaul pushed back his hair. "Fortunis, Miribelle, here's the plan; we're heading to the Unseen Church, it's in a place called the Sunken Citadel. Don't worry about the names. Every road down here eventually leads to it, so if you keep walking we'll meet up. This is supposed to be the fastest way but… I don't know how long it'll take."

There was a long silence before Miribelle spoke, "Fortunis has that worrying look on his face, but we hear you. Be careful."

"You as well."

Marta waited for Gaul to catch up before following the path along the chasm. It went straight for a few metres before taking a hard downward turn.

"Maybe they'll find a way up," Marta said, taking careful steps so she wouldn't slip.

"Still a long walk back to Sebanna's Rest," Gaul said.

Marta shrugged. "It's better than being in here."

There is a legend about a city that almost succeeded in the Age of Primordials. It was in a distant corner of the world, far from any other form of civilization. They built upon a tough land and infertile soil and nearly devoid of water. But they were resilient.

They dug deep until they found an underground spring. They turned the soil and grew hardy crops. In time, a great city grew out of the small settlement. The people could live easy and forget about the world outside their walls.

Only, as it grew, it became more noticeable. Behemoth eventually found it. As if he was furious something would dare thrive in a harsh land, Behemoth shook the earth until it split open. The city fell and its name faded into history.

—From the Journal of Jovin Gutterwake

Chapter Twenty-Three

Sunken World

There was nothing to break the cycle of stone and darkness. Marta had become uncomfortably familiar with not knowing what was around her. What lurked just outside of that few metres of light. She discussed with Gaul the idea of bedding down for the night. Was it even night? Could they be safe? They never reached a definite decision on that, but rather continued to walk in silent agreement that when they were too sore to move, that would be the time to sleep. And that time was coming soon.

However, it didn't come before Marta saw the light. Something ahead was glowing — in a place where nothing glowed.

"There's no way that's the surface, right?" Marta asked Gaul.

"Not unless we're coming out the other side of the world," he said.

It wasn't the other side of the world, but it was a new one. They entered from the top of a massive cavern, illuminated by a blue-white sphere hanging like a sun above the grand city. It stretched out to crowd the space. Stone buildings of an ancient design pushed against the walls like moss climbing a tree. Roads intersected in a drunken spider's web.

"This isn't a citadel," Marta said. "This is a city."

"And that is a church," Gaul said, pointing.

Far on the other side was a large building built higher than the rest of the city. Its architecture was reminiscent of the church that sat far below Adathin Castle — blocky and symmetrical. A Pantheon Church. This one was much bigger. Yellow light flickered out of the ground-floor windows.

"Let's go meet Sebanna," Gaul said, turning down the ridgeline.

Marta took a moment to look over the city. She focused her eyes on an irregular circle that seemed to separate an inner portion from the outer. It could have been a wall — hard to tell from a distance. Maybe the Sunken Citadel at one time was, in fact, a citadel.

They reached the outskirts and headed in. The buildings changed as they walked toward the centre of the city. Along the edge they were more utilitarian, pushing up against the cavern wall to eke as much space as possible. As they moved inward, the architecture became more beautiful and inspired. They were of a different era; built by different hands. The city was still empty, no matter what the buildings looked like.

In the centre of the city they found a large square. Broken stalls rimmed the edge. Once it was a marketplace — now it was a graveyard to what the city used to be. Marta knelt by the fountain filled with water. Logic dictated it should have been dry or at least murky, but it was clean. Marta ran her hand along the surface and inspected the motifs ringing the basin.

"Have you seen anything like this before?" she asked.

The designs showed workers building and harvesting. Marta had only seen tributes to the Anima of Revels, whether they be carved into the base of fountains or built as sculptures in town squares. These people, however, revered their workers over the gods. Either that, or they had no gods to revere.

"We don't get much fountains where I come from," Gaul said. "But it could be from the First Age, maybe even before that. It's a city at the bottom of the world. I don't know everything."

Marta stuck her hands in her pockets and paced the square. The city smelled of earth and wet mold. She looked across the buildings surrounding the square. There was a flash of movement as a window shutter closed.

"There's people here," Marta said.

"What?" Gaul hurried to her side as another shutter slammed closed. "Hello?"

No answer.

"We should hurry to the church," Gaul said. "If there are people here, they seem to want to hide. I say we let them."

"Yeah." Marta glanced over her shoulder as they left the square. Hopefully Fortunis and Miribelle would find their way to the city as well.

Old scorch marks began appearing on the buildings as Gaul and Marta got closer to the church. First it was the occasional black smear, but it wasn't long until entire buildings were turned black. It was as if the stone itself had lit aflame.

Then came the people. Blackened bodies. Some clutched weapons while others were laying half out of doorways. Piles of them leaned against walls — the ones at the bottom crushed as the ones at the top tried to climb away from the flames. Other held themselves in their last moments, now locked in emaciated positions of terror.

Marta covered her mouth against the ash and seared flesh. "I thought people couldn't die down here."

"Seems we don't have all the information," Gaul said.

"How can it still smell?" Marta gagged into her hand. "This can't have been recent."

Gaul said nothing but quickened his pace. Marta spotted a corpse holding a spear in both hands. They were resting against a building, but the flames that had taken him were so intense they fused his flesh to the stonework. What sort of fire could do that?

Marta followed Gaul through barricades that had been cracked in half, giving them passage to the grand stairs. These stairs were covered in similar corpses and broken barricades. They were defending the church, not assaulting it. But as Gaul and Marta climbed the steps, they found less evidence of a fire, until the ground was untouched at the base of the Unseen Church.

Two bell towers rose out of the structure, facing the city below. Tall stained-glass windows ringed the outside. Scenes of gods and saints, or at least that's what Marta figured they were. There were no people dancing around bonfires or sacrifices to Mar. It was as Gaul said, a Pantheon Church.

"This was built long after the city," Gaul said, gazing at the magnificent structure. "These depict the sealing of the Primordials, miracles done by the Divines, and whatever else my tutors nailed into my head. They're all from the Book of the Divine."

"All those people died to protect this place," Marta said. "From what?"

One of the double doors opened. Gaul and Marta stopped as a figure dressed in metal robes stepped out. They wore a helmet with red glass eyes that glowed in the light from the orb. The layers of their robe clinked against each other as they drew a halberd from behind the doors.

"What brings you to this fallen city?" she asked. "You are not dead. This is not your home, nor a place you should wish to be."

"We're looking for Sebanna," Marta said, stepping forward. This had to be an Unseen. "We need to speak with her."

"The Queen is not accepting visitors. She is in counsel with herself as she has been for many years." The Unseen turned back to the door. "Do find your way out."

"Hey!" Marta shouted. "This is important! Absence is growing from the Cradle of the World. The First Gods are waking up."

"We are far from the world here. It does not concern us in the deep."

"We came from your archives! The one you abandoned! Of course this is your concern!"

"My child," another Unseen said, pushing the door open the rest of the way. While he wore the same robes, his head was bare. He had a gentle face with greying hair that was cut short on the sides. "Lady Sebanna wishes to see the visitors. She's been expecting them."

The first Unseen's expression was hidden by her helmet, but she froze in place. "Of course, Master Junter."

She stepped aside and let Gaul and Marta past. Junter beckoned them to follow him into the church. They entered into the nave, lined with wooden pews down each side.

"How did Sebanna know we were coming?" Gaul asked, gazing at the chandelier high above.

"That is not for me to explain," Junter said.

He led them down the aisle. Other Unseen moved slowly through the church. Some wore the metal robes and helmets, while others donned simple cloth. They stopped as they saw Gaul and Marta pass by. One by one, the entire church froze to watch the strangers.

"How many of you are there?" Marta asked.

"A dozen. Less than there were once." He spoke gently, as if he were gazing into the past at that moment. "We discovered down here time has no meaning. We do not age, but that does not mean we do not die."

"We saw that," Gaul said. "Someone attacked you. Was it recent?"

"No. But just as we do not age, the bodies of our fallen do not rot. Even though their souls became… different."

Marta's eyes widened. "The forlorn."

Junter stopped at the back of the altar, near a stairwell leading into the rock wall. "That is also not for me to explain. I simply serve the Queen. Lady Sebanna indicated you would have many questions. She is willing to answer them, though you may not like what she has to say." He motioned to the stairs. "She is waiting for you."

"You're not coming with us?" Gaul asked.

"She wished to speak with you alone." Junter bowed. "It's a great honor to be asked. Please don't leave her waiting."

Marta shared a look with Gaul. He shrugged and stepped down the stairs. Marta followed, wary about what they were getting into. They descended into a simple chapel with unworked rock walls. Across from them was a shrine covered in nothing but dozens of candles dripping wax to the floor. A figure dressed in black robes bowed before it.

"The little creature in the walls told me you were coming," Sebanna said without turning around. "You have been through much to get to me, but I do not believe I can help you. I have discovered when I help, it does nothing but destroy."

"We've been to the door to the Cradle," Gaul said.

Sebanna tilted her head. She calmly rose to her feet and turned to face them. She wasn't as old as Marta thought she would be, but older than she was in the painting they saw in the castle. Her black hair was in a bun, greying ever so slightly. She clasped her hands before her and stepped gently toward them.

"You have been to the site of my greatest success and most terrible mistake." She closed her eyes. "I felt the darkness growing on the door when I left. It was unstoppable."

"The descendants of your Unseen have been keeping it sealed for hundreds of years." Gaul took his wife's necklace out. Athas' pendant still hung off it, but the spark once inside was now gone. "They've been gathering Light and using it to keep it shut."

Sebanna chuckled. "That was what we used to do. I had intended to simply stop in my archive to return the Chalice before journeying here, but my followers had a plan. Light was what sealed the door. My removal of the Chalice was what broke the seal in the first place. We were fighting against the natural decay, but we could never truly fix it. Light could not grow in this land, the presence of the door made sure of that. But the Unseen would travel with specially made vials and harvest Light from elsewhere."

"This time it didn't work," Marta said, stepping forward.

"The Light was always destined to fade." She turned back to the shrine. "There's nothing to do."

"I don't believe that!" Marta put her hand to her chest. "My brother died while he was trying to find a way to keep the door closed. There is Absence pouring out of it. Are you just going to sit here and let whatever's inside come out?"

"I know what's inside. It's nothing. Pure Absence. I walked fields of it held back only by the power of the Chalice. And like a naïve child I didn't even think about what it would mean to remove that sacred artifact. I am here to atone for my sins." She knelt on the pillow, stained with wax. "To punish myself for what I did to the world."

"You're hiding." Marta stomped up next to Sebanna. Gaul followed, slower. "Rather than doing something you're going to stare at a bunch of candles and feel sorry for yourself."

Sebanna bowed her head. "I must pray for forgiveness."

"Who are you praying to? Who even cares? There are people out there who believe in you! They see your failure as a sign of humanity and that redemption is possible. But this isn't redemption!" She threw her arms out to the damp cave, smelling of wax and humidity. "This is depressing. This is… Gaul, what's it called when you don't care?"

"Apathy," Gaul said.

"Apathy!" Marta couldn't believe how much time they wasted. It would have been better if they just found some writings.

"Let's go, Marta." Gaul turned away. "She can't help us. She's just a sad woman in a cave."

Marta shook her head. They would have to find another way.

"Light," Sebanna said weakly. "Light is the only thing that can keep that door closed. Light was the weapon of the First Gods. They were born from it. It was what allowed them to defeat the Primordials. The only Light that may remain in Adathin is clinging to the flesh of those primal lords."

"We tried Light," Gaul said. "The Absence seemed to feed on it."

"This is godly power straight from those who breathed it. A hundred years of gathering will be nothing to a single drop of this pure energy. When we first discovered the door, we learned it was being kept shut by five locks. The Divines used the First Gods' own Light to seal it and keep the Absence back. My arcanists theorized the Light of a First God is different in some way, more powerful or purer. You'll need as much as you can get if you wish to seal the door." She shook her head. "But it will fade. The door will open someday. We will all lose someday."

"I would rather fight a losing battle than lose a battle never fought," Marta said.

"You must have not lost many battles." Sebanna leaned forward and blew out a candle, breathing in the scented smoke. "There are three sources. Three Primordials still within our grasp. Behemoth is close. He dwells in his sunken cage.

If you can pull Light from him, you'll be able to pull it from all of them. He would be an adequate test in that way. Ziz was captured by the Apostles of Wind and her wings have been clipped. South is the Tower of Samadel, where you may ascend to the sky. The King of Rot, Architect of the Dark, is underground, but far from here. The idiot worm was bound and used as the foundation for Lady Sanguine's Cage. Of course, the Firespeaker is lost somewhere beyond the Gates of Flame — I would not bother with him — and Leviathan is dead. Shiller, Father of the Flux, killed the unkillable." She paused. "Though, her bones are said to be laid to rest in Boboros Vale. If you can find such a place — I never could — there may be Light on those remains. Four sources then, if you can find the Vale."

Marta held her head in her hands. It could never be anything easy. Sebanna couldn't just have a key to a lock they could turn. Gaul stood back with his arms crossed, tapping his thumb against his bicep. He stared at the candles expressionless. All Marta wanted was for someone to bring her to her brother.

"That's the only way?" Marta asked. "How long is that going to take? The Absence is spreading now. What if you send the Unseen out and we split up?"

Sebanna raised her robed hand and pointed at the pendant dangling from Gaul's fingers. "That is the only vessel I have seen in ages. Moreover, I do not lead the Unseen anymore. They are their own people, and I will not act as though I can tell them where to go."

"They would disagree."

"They would be fools to look for leadership from failure. If you want to keep the sun rising for a little while longer, then you've heard my offer. Take the Light from the Primordials — all the ones you can reach — and bring it to the Cradle. It's the only answer my once Unseen had ever found. We concerned ourselves more with opening it, less with how to close it again."

"How did you open it?" Gaul asked, finally breaking from his thoughts.

"I can't tell you." She clutched her hands to her chest. "I won't tell you. I ensured every record of our research on opening the Cradle was destroyed. I will not allow that door to be reopened, and so I did the one thing I swore I would never do. I destroyed the knowledge."

"That may not be entirely true." Gaul turned his head to Marta.

"Oh." Marta shut her eyes for a second, centring herself. It was her story after all. "The Praetor of Owls from Marjyal, Melifacto, is scouring the country for a way to open the Cradle. He's looking for me." The words felt like poison as they left her lips. "How's that possible?"

Sebanna didn't say a word for the longest time. She stared at the line of candles, playing one thumb over the other in her clenched hands. "It's not," she finally said. "He's lying."

"I told you," Marta said, punching Gaul in the shoulder.

"Why would he lie about it?" Gaul asked.

"Wealth. Power." Sebanna blew out another candle. "Even a simple promise for something great can sway hearts and minds. This Melifacto doesn't need the fulfil it, he only needs the foolish to keep chasing it."

"That's easy to say when you stand at a distance," Gaul said, running his hand along his jaw. "But if you could figure out how to open the door, then it's possible someone else could as well. Pretending you didn't do what you did has changed nothing but make it harder for us to try to fix it."

"I am not pretending I am without sin!" She slammed her hands into her knees. "I saw everyone I cared for become twisted into a horrific monster with my father sitting atop. He was a good king. He cared for his subjects and wanted nothing more than to ensure his kingdom stayed together. The Chalice turned that against him. Mortal minds cannot comprehend the power contained inside. It will always destroy them. I did my part to seal it away, even if I knew someone would follow my footsteps. At least then it wouldn't be my fault. I did everything I could to slow that inevitability."

"Then why are you still here?" Marta asked.

Sebanna sank into her robes. "Go. Behemoth isn't far. Or stay, it doesn't matter in the end." She blew out the last of her candles, though the cave never dimmed.

Part of Marta regretted choosing such harsh words, but Sebanna was nothing that she hoped she would be. She was a shell of a human being.

"Marta," Gaul said, turning to leave. "Come on."

They headed toward the stairs back up to the church, Gaul putting the necklace back on, when Sebanna called to them, "Did he say your name was Marta?"

"Yes," Marta said, pausing at the foot of the stairs.

"'Of Mar.'" She sighed. "What an unfortunate name."

Marta started climbing. "At least we agree on that."

As they left the cave, the final remains of the candle smoke disappeared. Beneath its odor was another stench, similar to one Marta caught in the city below. Burned flesh. Sebanna struck a match and begun lighting the candles once again, hiding that sick scent beneath the smoke.

Earth King Behemoth.
Defeated by Lord Tyran, The First Knight.
Imprisoned at the bottom of Black Hypogea.

—From the Journal of Jovin Gutterwake

Chapter Twenty-Four
Behemoth

Gaul and Marta returned up the stairs to where Junter greeted them. His expression was solemn and apologetic. The stairs weren't long, and Gaul was sure he had heard everything.

"Don't judge her harshly," Junter said. "She wasn't always this way."

"What happened to her?" Gaul asked. "Is this all because of the Cradle?"

"Not all of it." Junter motioned for Gaul and Marta to step away from the stairs. He led them to an alcove as he explained, "It's true, in her darkest moments, Sebanna sought to entomb herself here in Black Hypogea. But as we travelled, we found others. Lost and lonely people were drawn to us. Sebanna talked to them. She knew how they felt and so she helped them. Some left better than they arrived, while others stayed with us, even though they knew the journey's end."

He sat on a bench in the alcove, the metal on his robes clinking together. Gaul and Marta sat next to him. Junter slouched against the stone wall, showing the weariness expected from one as ancient as him.

"What started as a march of penance, became something different," he said. "Black Hypogea was still our goal, but there was a new passion in Sebanna. I asked her one night why we were still continuing on. 'Because,' she said, 'If I deserve redemption, so do they.' I didn't understand at the time. But when we found this city, I began to. Black Hypogea is not an evil place. The gods decreed it to be where souls could be cleansed, but how can you cleanse evil with evil? Sebanna brought them patience and love and hope. She gave them something the gods never could."

"There's people in the city," Marta said. "Are they souls of the dead?"

"Yes, they are. Souls fall from the Gate Beyond and enter that cold sun you've seen. Now you can imagine me thinking, 'how are we supposed to help a big ball of light?'" He chuckled under his breath. "As it turns out, a soul will eventually create itself a body. Not alive, but flesh and bone like any others. They never remembered who they were in life. They were like children. Though, the more corrupted the soul, the more twisted the flesh. Sebanna had this way of coaxing the gentleness from a soul, and we would give them home and community until they could someday rejoin the cycle."

"This story has an ending," Gaul said, standing from the bench and looking over the Unseen toiling in silence. "One that involves fire."

All traces of a smile left Junter's face. "It wasn't just souls we found down here. We found the Descendent of Tyran."

"Descendent?" Gaul scratched his neck. "Wouldn't that make them a Divine?"

"No. Something different. Tybalt, as he called himself, explained it. He actually was very forthcoming with information, the savage. The Divines were the first children of the fallen gods, but not their last. As the Light faded from the Chalice, the First Gods grew to distrust the Divines. They mixed Light with their own blood and breathed life into creatures with the sole purpose of killing gods. They were failures. Abandoned by their parents, the children hid and were sealed away in the Cradle as well."

"And then Sebanna opened the door!" Marta exclaimed. An Unseen dropped the stack of book they were carrying and glared at her. "Sorry. I got excited. I think this was the first thing I actually understood."

The Unseen grumbled under their breath and collected her books together.

Junter continued, "The Descendants weren't put to sleep like the First Gods were, and so slipped out. When we first met Tybalt, he was helpful and kind. For a long time we worked together to ease the afterlife. But all of it was so he could learn how to open the Cradle and retrieve the Chalice." Junter's hands began to shake. "Sebanna refused — we all refused. That was when he started the fires. I can still hear all those people screaming. The scent of their skin fills this church no matter how much we try to hide it. He ensured they died in such agony and fear that all their souls can create are those mindless beasts that stalk the caves. He marched upon this church, surrounded by fire, but then he stopped."

Junter held his head. His voice wavered as he spoke, overwhelmed with emotion. Marta laid her hand on his back.

"I'm sorry for my outbursts," he said. "I thought Tybalt was going to destroy the church and us with it, but he wanted us to live. He wanted us to look out over the ruins of our work. So, he left. That was when we lost Sebanna for the second time. Now we, the Unseen, keep ourselves busy. We tidy and rearrange, and I watch as forlorn drop from that cold sun and scurry away from the light."

Gaul looked to where the dark steps descended into Sebanna's chapel. That was how someone could be broken. She blamed herself for two acts of ruin, and not without reason.

"Sebanna only ever wanted to do the right thing," Junter said, sniffing the tears away. "That's why we all stay. We still believe in what she said about redemption. Even if she doesn't."

"Master Junter!" It was the same woman who met Gaul and Marta at the door, clanking across the church. "There are two more strangers approaching the church. Another man and woman."

"Fortunis and Miribelle," Marta said, leaping to her feet.

"Open the door," Junter said, standing with a groan. "It seems our guests have further guests."

The Unseen removed her helmet, revealing a woman with a sour expression across her face. She shook her head and returned with the group to the door. She pulled it open to catch Fortunis with his fist raised to knock. His eyes widened and his mouth opened, but it was Miribelle who got the first words out.

"You're alive!" she shouted.

"I was going to say the same," Marta said. "Glad to see your path wasn't much longer than ours."

"This place wasn't hard to see," Fortunis said, shrinking away from the glare of the Unseen guard. "And you said you were heading for the Unseen Church and this seemed… church-like."

"And you would be correct." Junter stepped forward with a bow. "This is the Unseen Church. Home of Queen Sebanna."

Fortunis' eyes widened. Miribelle's open and closed her mouth a few times before getting out the word, "Sebanna?"

"Yes."

The Unseen guard looked between Junter and the slack-jawed expression on Fortunis and Miribelle's faces. "Could someone go in or out? Because I do not like having the door open."

"We're leaving," Gaul said, pushing past the siblings.

"Wait," Miribelle said, breaking from her stupor. Her gaze darted around the church. "Do we have to leave? Why?"

"Miribelle," Fortunis said, taking her hand. "We have to go home."

"To what? What's up there for us? We'll be right back where we started."

"Nana Stundel is gone." He grabbed her shoulders. "We've won."

"She didn't work alone. People supported her. Marjyal was in our town and we didn't even feel them pulling the strings. But here…" She stepped out of his grasp and turned to Junter, her eyes wide as dinner plates. "Sebanna is here? She didn't ascend to Elysium? Could we meet her?"

Gaul made brief eye contact with Marta, still standing just inside the church doors. They both knew Sebanna wouldn't live up to Miribelle's expectations. The lonely woman at an altar was nothing like the paintings and stories of her. But he didn't know how to be the one to tell her. The way Junter averted his eyes told Gaul he knew that as well.

"The Unseen are not what we used to be," Junter said. "We toil in this church, doing Sebanna's will, but all she wills is solitude."

"But…" Miribelle looked about. Unseen had stopped their work but turned away as Miribelle's eyes fell on them. Even the stern guard had hidden her face. Miribelle deflated. "This can't be it."

"What happened to Sebanna's apostles from the stories?" Fortunis wrapped an arm around his sister's shoulder. "The warrior-scholars who protected Sebanna and fought back the darkness."

"What happens to everything?" Junter asked. "Time."

Miribelle clenched her fists. With the flip of her coat, she stomped away from the church doors.

"Miri!" Fortunis shouted, chasing after her.

The Unseen watched them go, passionless expressions on their faces. Junter bowed his head.

"You've been in this pit for too long," Marta said. "You already think you're dead." She followed Miribelle and Fortunis out of the church.

Gaul gazed over the crowd of Unseen. They couldn't even look at each other. The door guard put her helmet back on and shrank away. Junter leaned against the door frame, head down like a scolded child. *What a disappointment*, Gaul thought, turning away from the church.

His footsteps echoed lonely over the still cavern to where Miribelle and Fortunis sat at the grand stairs. Marta crouched at the wall's lip, staring up at the orb they now knew was the collected souls of everyone in Black Hypogea.

"I'm sorry," Gaul said, approaching Miribelle and Fortunis. "I'm sorry they're not who you want them to be."

"Sebanna was supposed to of ascended to Elysium." Miribelle spoke with her arms wrapped around her knees. "But it wasn't true. None of it was true. Dad believed in her and he fought Nana Stundel because of that belief. He died because of that belief."

"Miri," Fortunis said, covering his mouth. His fingers were shaking.

"What about those stories?" Miribelle continued, not noticing her brother's reaction. "He said that because Sebanna refused to give up, she could leave this world for a better one. That's why he never gave up. That's why he fought."

"Miribelle," Gaul said firmly.

Miribelle turned to him and stopped. Fortunis was holding his hand against his mouth, tears running down his cheeks and across his fingers. He bowed his head and took in breaths between his sobs.

"Fortunis," Miribelle said, resting her hand on his knee. "What—"

"Dad didn't die because of his belief in Sebanna," Fortunis said, his voice as unsteady as his hands. "I pleaded with him. I told him Nana was the reason Mom was gone. I called him a coward for not doing anything. I called him…" His voice broke. "He died because of me."

Miribelle wrapped her arms around him, holding his head against hers until his tears soaked her shoulder. "No," she said. "He fought because of us. He stood up for what was right and even if he failed, you know what he would say?" She held him closer. "Who cares if you failed? Other people never tried at all."

Fortunis broke down, clutching onto his sister with everything left in him. They cried against each other. The world didn't matter anymore. Gaul stepped back to give the siblings rooms and bumped into something metal. Junter stood there. He placed his hand on Gaul's shoulder and guided him aside before stepping in with great care.

"Failure is only what you accept it to be," he said, his voice soft as a breeze.

Miribelle glanced over Fortunis.

Junter crept to the edge of the stairs, looking over the charred remains of the city. "I once held that saying close to my heart. Our order was founded upon failure and mistakes. We believed they could not be ignored but needed to be embraced. We've held onto these mistakes for so long we've forgotten that part of the purpose is to grow and move past it."

Gaul looked back at the church. He could visualize Sebanna still in her chapel, kneeling in front of the altar, unaware or uncaring of how much pain she caused her followers. She could only see her own mistakes and held onto them as if they keep her floating. But they only dragged her down. A feeling all too familiar to Gaul.

"You remind me of those people who joined us," Junter said, smiling at Miribelle. Fortunis lifted his head. "You see, it wasn't the Unseen who first said such things. It wasn't even Sebanna. We were all ready to throw ourselves into the dark as punishment for what we did. It was the people we met, the towns we stayed in, the stories we heard. We saw life, in all its messy ways. We couldn't change the things we did, but we could pick ourselves up and start doing good. Some Unseen went to collect Light for the Cradle, but others continued on. The gods had long ago turned their gaze from Black Hypogea, but we could ensure these souls are not forgotten." He furrowed his brow. "Or at least we used to."

"Failure," Fortunis said, wiping the tears away, "is only what you accept it to be, right?"

"Yes," Junter took in a deep breath. "And its never too late to learn how to stand up again. The Unseen have been hidden for too long. We can still comfort these souls, find some purpose again. Even if Sebanna stays in exile, we are still Unseen, but felt everywhere." He turned to the siblings. "You're welcome to stay for as long as you like. I'm sorry we're not what you expected, but maybe we could be again."

Miribelle and Fortunis returned to their feet. They shared a momentary glance — eyes still red — but it seemed like they both had already made up their minds.

"We want to stay," Fortunis said. Miribelle nodded with him. "For at least a little while."

Junter smiled. "Then perhaps there is hope for the Unseen. Our time is not yet over."

"That's something at least," Gaul said

The siblings beamed with pride. Fortunis turned to Gaul and Marta, and the grin faded into a resigned smile. "Did you get what you needed?"

"No," Gaul said. "But we got something."

"Are you moving on then?"

Gaul glanced at Marta. She stood at the edge of the steps, looking over the city. She was furious at Sebanna for giving up but had gotten quiet once Junter started talking. The Unseen's words had touched Gaul, maybe they had touched her as well. "Yes, we are," he said. "We still have things to do."

"Then I suppose this is goodbye," Miribelle said, smiling. "It was… interesting."

"I apologize for getting you involved in all this. It wasn't our intention."

"I was the one who saw Marta and decided to help," Fortunis said. "I involved myself."

"Marta!" Miribelle called, catching Marta's attention. "We heard you're leaving."

"It won't be the first time we've said goodbye," Marta said, leaving the stairs. "And you'll be fine down here?"

"I would like to see what it's like," Miribelle said. "Maybe we'll go back home eventually, but I'm not in any rush."

"And we shall show you the way if that day comes," Junter said. He turned to Gaul and Marta. "Just as we can show you the way after you've finished your work. Follow the cavern wall and you'll find the entrance you seek."

"Thank you," Gaul said.

"Now." Junter raised his arm to the church. "Would you like to see our home?"

Fortunis took Miribelle's hand. They followed Junter to the front door, glancing back briefly before stepping inside. The heavy door thumped shut.

"Sebanna better not disappoint them," Marta said.

"She will." Gaul started in the direction Junter indicated. "But they'll get over it."

Marta hurried to catch up. "We're walking again?"

"We're certainly not flying."

"I meant we're doing this? Collecting Light from Primordials? I was hoping we would get here and find some easy answer. Like we'd just have to say some magic words and it'd fix everything." She chuckled and bowed her head. "It's pretty stupid now. I don't want the world to end. I know it's not perfect, it's not even close, but these First Gods sound… I'm just thinking what it would be like if Mar could walk the streets."

"Let's focus on one thing at a time," Gaul said. "We'll see what happens with Behemoth and then decide what happens after." He looked out over the city, destroyed by the desires of the Descendent of Tyran. "I don't want the world to end either."

The path ringing the cavern dipped down. Ahead of them was a crack in the wall, framed by an archway. Marta had been chewing on her thumbnail and tapping her fingers along the pocket where she kept her brother's journal. The one she read at night by the light of the moon, after she thought Gaul had gone to sleep.

"Gaul," Marta said. "After all this is done, I'm going to get you home."

Gaul laughed. "Is that so?"

"Yes." Marta wasn't laughing. "I brought you into all this and I swear I'm going to see you out."

"You don't…" Gaul stopped at the crack into the wall. It was the same heavy darkness as when they first looked into Black Hypogea from above. "You don't have to worry about me. You shouldn't worry about me, I'm not worth it."

Marta squared herself with him. "That's not your decision."

"I don't know how I'm supposed to make this clear to you. I am angry and I am unstable. People don't care about me. I'm pointed in a direction and told to destroy and that I am good at. I am a broken human, and I was born that way."

"What about your wife?"

Gaul rubbed the back of his neck. "She's gone."

Marta scowled at Gaul, until her expression softened. She stepped into him, pressing her head against his chest and wrapping her arms around him. "I don't know who told you broken things don't deserve love, but I'm sorry."

Gaul looked at the top of her head. Water dripped from stalactites and struck against stone — the only sound that could be heard. His heartbeat slowed and filled his head. Slowly, he returned the hug.

"I never had a friend before," Marta said. "I'm fine with a broken one."

A smile crept across Gaul's face. They held for a moment like that, amid the cool glow of the orb and solitude of the sunken world. "Thank you," Gaul mouthed.

Marta stepped away from the hug and smiled up at him. "And now," she said. "Want to meet a Primordial?"

"Why not?" Gaul tossed her one of his swords. "We're already in the land of the dead?"

Marta gave the sword a spin and took the lead. Down, into the depths to find Behemoth.

Marta bounced Gaul's sword in her hand, making sure he was close behind her. Their lights seemed darker now. Maybe it was just her imagination. What wasn't her imagination, was the occasional rumble from far below.

Marta had not grown up with the legends of the Primordials. Jovin had told her stories, of course, but before leaving Marjyal she believed the only god was a cruel one. From what Gaul had said, and from what Jovin's journal explained, the Primordials were gods before gods. The sword she held seemed small next to the threat, but she kept it ready all the same.

They reached the bottom of the stairs and looked forward into a cavern the size of the city above. A path of worn stone with dirt to either side led them on. The air stunk of something foul. Nothing Marta could discern, but made her nearly gag when she first smelled it. As they approached the edge of a chasm, the rumbling stopped.

"What now?" Marta asked.

"I have no idea." Gaul pulled Athas' pendant out. "I guess we wait?"

The cavern was silent. If it wasn't for that, Marta never would have heard the sliding on the rock behind them. They both spun around, Gaul drawing his sword.

A bloodied figure stumbled into their light. Handai, Praetor of Snakes, clutched a bow with a nocked arrow. Blood poured from a wound on her head and pasted her hair to her face. Her right leg was torn to shreds — barely able to support her weight.

"Marta," she said, panting. "It's time to come home."

"It's done, Handai," Gaul said. "We know you're not going to kill her."

Handai shifted her sights to Gaul. "But I could kill you. And she cares for you. She uses her body to protect you. You're her weakness."

Marta stepped in front of Gaul. She didn't care if Gaul was her weakness. It may make it easier for Marjyal to take her, but Gaul was her friend. She didn't want to lose him.

Handai circled them, with Marta keeping her body in front of Gaul's. She was smaller than him and couldn't cover everything. But would Handai risk it?

"I will not be denied when I have come this close." With great effort, Handai pulled the string back further.

They were standing close to the chasm. If Marta could move fast enough…

"You will come with me," Handai said. She coughed and her aim wavered. "And through you I will receive the Chalice and cure this damned poison in my lungs."

When she coughs, Marta thought. She could attack when she coughed and knock her off the cliff. She bent her knees, ready to spring forth.

Handai steeled herself. "Last cha—"

A hand the size of a building smashed Handai into nothing. Marta and Gaul stumbled back, only for a second hand to slam down behind them. They sprinted away from the cliff as whatever beast owned those hands pulled itself into view.

They spun back and came face to face with the Earth King Behemoth.

He was impossibly large, with Marta being barely the size of one of his sharp teeth. His skin was like stone; grey, lifeless, and weathered from many battles. Two bull-like horns stuck out the side of his head, but one was broken on the side of his face also missing an eye. The rest of his body below his upper chest was hiding in the dark and below the cliff edge.

With a deep, booming voice, Behemoth spoke, "Why is this young dust at the gate to my prison? You smell of dead gods."

Gaul grunted and pulled Athas' pendant away from his chest. The metal on it had grown visibly red hot.

Behemoth bent forward — the crackle of lightning creating a wall and keeping him from reaching them. "What is that? Is that what smells?"

A trail of brilliant white light traced along the injured side of Behemoth's face. Seeing this, Gaul removed the necklace and held it out. The Light tore itself from Behemoth's face and flowed into the vial in Athas' pendant. Behemoth collapsed. Dust flew as he landed on the cliff.

"I see," he said, dirt puffing out with its breaths. "The power of the gods must have waned for you to come to me. Am I the first you have seen? Or have you already torn the Light from my brothers and sisters? The gods are falling and soon the strong will return."

He slunk back into the chasm. A bloodstain was all that remained of where Handai once stood. Gaul held the pendent up to his face. Marta leaned in with him. Within the vial was the tiniest spark.

"Okay," Marta said as Gaul donned the necklace. "One down."

"One down."

Marta turned to leave. There was a whistling before an arrow struck deep into her chest. Her body went numb. Yomat lowered his bow as Marta dropped.

Gaul caught Marta before she hit the ground. The sword clattered as it fell from her grip. He eased her onto her back. The arrow stuck straight up out of her chest. Bubbling blood oozed from the wound. Her eyes flickered in and out of focus, staring into the sky confused.

Gaul spun to Yomat, rage already building. "You are supposed to take her alive!"

"I don't care about Melifacto." Yomat tossed his bow aside. "Handai's dead. She's all I ever cared about. And she died fawning over a worthless brute like you."

Gaul squared himself with his opponent, dangling his sword ever so slightly. He couldn't help Marta while Yomat was there.

"We will all die down here, Gaul." Yomat drew his straight sword, holding the hilt to his chest. "But your life will be mine."

"Then let's stop talking."

Yomat thrust forth. He moved incredibly fast. Gaul knocked his sword aside, twisted his own, and slashed downward. Yomat stepped aside and the attack slid past his chest. He braced himself and unleashed a powerful sidekick into Gaul's gut.

Gaul stumbled back, grabbing his stomach. He tried to Ignite. He felt his rage turn into a string. Crimson grew and shrank in his vision. But then he saw Marta, her fingers twitching at her side, struggling to breathe with the arrow in her chest. He couldn't focus — he could only rage.

Gaul roared. He rushed forth with a flurry of blows. Yomat blocked each one, leaping back as the final slice cut too close. Gaul dipped low and rose with a stab for Yomat's face. Yomat caught the blade with an inch to spare. Blood trickled down the steel, seeping from the cut in Yomat's glove. He pushed the sword aside and retaliated.

They traded blows, neither able to land a solid hit. Their blades chimed in the dark. They collided in the middle, locking up face-to-face. Yomat sneered.

"Why do you think you matter so much?" Yomat said. "What are you doing that's so important? The world is dark and rotten. Anything bright in it will eventually die."

Gaul pushed against Yomat's sword. "Then make your own light."

They broke the clash. Gaul leapt and brought both feet to Yomat's chest. Yomat flew, and both landed hard on their backs. Gaul took a handful of the dirt and returned to his feet.

Yomat unsteadily got his feet under him and reared back. Gaul caught him in the eyes with a toss of the dirt. Yomat shouted. Drawing out all his strength, Gaul cut Yomat's sword arm from his body. The arm landed with a puff of dirt, still clutching the sword.

Crying out in pain, Yomat dropped to his knees. He clutched the stump — once his arm — and glared up at Gaul. "The other guilds will know where you're going," he said through gritted teeth. "I wasn't the only one who heard you talking to that monster. We know you're searching for the other Primordials. My Snakes are on their way to spread the word. Melifacto has access to great amounts of knowledge — he'll find where they are. Call it a contingency for if I did not kill you. Your reckoning is still coming."

Gaul placed his sword on Yomat's shoulder. "We'll kill them too."

"Not my concern anymore." He gazed into the shadows, where he imagined Handai's bloodstain still was. "I was at her side when she became Praetor. I'll be at her side again in death."

Gaul drew his sword back, then removed Yomat's head. The Guild of Snakes was decapitated.

He didn't have time to catch his breath. He dropped his sword and sprinted to Marta, sliding on his knees to her side. Her breathing was shallow, but she was still breathing. Each rise and fall of her chest made more blood leak out of the wound.

"Gaul," Marta said weakly.

"I'm still here." He inspected the wound. The arrow couldn't come out without tearing her insides more.

"Marjyal won't chase you anymore." She shut her eyes and smiled. "You find the Primordials. Save the world. Then you can go home. I told you I would get you home."

"Yeah, *you* would get me home. You need to be there to do it."

She shook her head. Gaul grabbed her by the collar. He needed to get the Unseen. They must have something to help. But they were so far away.

"Open your eyes!" Gaul shouted. Panic set in. Her pulse was so weak.

Marta's eyes flickered open. There was something in her brown eyes. Red shoots that crossed her iris before fading away.

Something came to Gaul. The golden aura he had seen while Ignited. Could it be a sign of untapped potential? He put both hands behind Marta's head and held her up.

"I need you to focus on me," he said.

"Can I just sleep?" The red began to fade from her eyes.

"No!" He shook, perhaps more violently then he should of. "Picture the ocean."

"I love the ocean."

"I know you do." He shifted her body, cradling her in his arms. "Imagine the serenity from the sea. The wind, the crashing of waves, the cawing of sea birds. Clear your mind of all but that. Remember this feeling, you're going to have to recreate it. But first get angry.

"I don't—"

"Think of your brother. Someone killed him, right? They're still out there. Marjyal is still out there, chasing you down. Feel your anger in your stomach like fire. It may even make you feel sick."

Marta had a sharp intake of breath. "I can feel it."

"Pull it tight. Imagine a string from the top of your head to your feet. That fire is that string. Feel it vibrate, feel it want to burst. But it's tough, it's unbreakable. The only way to snap it is to all at once lose your rage and replace it with serenity, like you had when you thought of the ocean."

"I can't."

"Yes you can! Your body wants to! It wants to live! Let it! Pull that string tight until the fire is gone and with one strike of the match, Ignite!"

Marta's eyes shot open. Red shoots invaded her iris, crossing over each other rapidly until even her pupil was swallowed up by the crimson swell. Sparks leapt from her wound. Gaul grabbed the arrow shaft and pulled. Marta screamed, bloodcurdling and angry. Lightning filled the cavern, the arrow tearing flesh as it was removed. This energy reached threads across the wound, pulling the skin tight until it was whole once again, nothing to show what was once there other than the blood staining her light-brown skin.

Marta passed out. Her chest rose and fell with calm breaths. Gaul held her close.

The cave was silent.

I've been watching that strange black substance ooze out of the Cradle for weeks now. The growth is exponential. What was only a few millimetres of movement being now centimetres. The feeling of dread has increased as well. Whether that's an effect of the substance, or just my own anxiety is yet to be seen. I'm a historian, not an arcanist, after all. Not anymore, at least.

However, there are supplies in the Archive. I could do some tests on the substance. It could be natural. Some unknown form of flux. It's been a long time since I've done work like that, but you don't forget it.

I don't know if I can, though. Morally. I wasn't a good arcanist. I did things that I would rather stay buried in the past.

But maybe this is important.

Maybe.

—From the Journal of Jovin Gutterwake

Epilogue

So, they're going to find the Primordials, Feyra thought. *I wonder where they are?*

She stretched her arms toward the sky, loosening the tightness in her shoulders. She had been sitting on the Snakes' cart for hours. The pulses in her mind indicating the devastation hound's location had been getting weaker as her tracking faded, but they were close. It should be any minute. Fortunately, she ran into the Snakes just as they sent off their crow to Melifacto. They were shocked to see her but explained the situation.

Their corpses laid a few metres from the cart, leaking blood into the earth.

With the massive cliff faces to either side, the devastation hounds would have to go through the path Feyra waited on. She knew where they were going to be, making setting up a trap trivial. Her thoughts drifted to Gaul and Marta. She learned from the Snakes they were in a canyon deep in the mountain range. With Handai dead and Ettik missing, they weren't likely to stay in the area.

Birds flitted away as a rumbling came from the forest. Heavy footfalls beat against the ground. Feyra stood and looked into the treeline. Three massive beasts of fur, muscle, and bone rocketed out, knocking down trees in their way. Feyra pointed at the clearing between her and the hounds. The leading hound saw her, but didn't stop. It snapped its teeth. Feyra waited.

Closer, she thought. *Come closer.*

One of them stomped on a Snake's corpse. Feyra raised her finger to the sky.

The blood in the dirt burst up like spears. The devastation hounds were each skewered by a dozen spikes. The leader didn't die instantly. It pulled against the blood, its black eyes focused on Feyra, but soon it too passed away. Feyra lowered the spikes and hopped off the cart.

She knew where the hounds would be. It was easy. But, she didn't know where Gaul and Marta would be, and she wasn't much of a tracker without using blood.

Perhaps Bellona knows of the Primordials, she thought, going to retrieve her horse from where she tied him up. *Melifacto surely does. Until then, I'll wait at the mines.*

Feyra mounted Arion. She looked over the devastation hounds, killed so easily by a simple trap. They had no hope. No escape. Once she knew where Gaul and Marta were going, there would be no escape for them either.

ALL GODS FALL: SEASON ONE

PART FOUR

TOWER OF SAMADEL

When Sebanna disappeared and Isildia began the prayers in Dothric, King Adathin's eldest daughter took a more aggressive approach to discovering the Cradle of the World. Forta went east, to the lands beneath the Tower of Samadel. Here she reopened the mine that Samadel once used to get crystal and ore out of the earth.

She built a manor at the base of the tower, but rarely stayed there, too consumed with her industrial hunt for the Cradle. Her followers tore the land apart until fire oozed at their feet. They harnessed this fire and built marvellous machines of moving armour to dig where people could not reach.

—From the Journal of Jovin Gutterwake

Chapter Twenty-Five

Blasted Lands

Bellona woke up to the sounds of footsteps and shouts. She put on her fur coat and exited her tent to find the Dothrin camp half-packed up. A couple Boars waited outside, looking around in confusion. One of them spotted Bellona and gave her a look that said, *what's happening?*

Bellona was itching to find out.

She found Melifacto supervising his workers as they carried out the pieces of his makeshift lab. "It seems like we're leaving," she said.

"Marta is going to find the Primordials," Melifacto said, staring into empty space. "I know where they are, and so I know where she's going to be. We'll move to intercept."

"You know this is all fantasy, right? Immortal beasts from before history, locked away somewhere in Adathin. It's nonsense."

"You don't believe in the Primordials?"

Bellona breathed deeply and put her hands behind her back. "I believe in the allegory."

Melifacto turned to her. "Good will overcome evil?"

"Strength rules."

Melifacto grinned. He followed his workers bringing the last of his supplies to a cart.

"Have you ever seen a Primordial?" Bellona asked, joining him on the walk through the ruins.

"I thought you don't believe in them."

"You do."

"A long time ago. You don't have to believe in them, Bellona. They're still very real."

Melifacto wasn't one to lie about something like the Primordials. He wanted to catch Marta, just as Bellona wanted to catch Gaul. Perhaps there was something to the legend; something that was embellished throughout the years. The workers hefted a box onto a cart. Jars of samples of rattled. Melifacto looked to the horizon.

"Feyra is to the east, right?" Melifacto asked.

"Yes," Bellona said. She hoped Feyra had stopped the devastation hounds. What would be better was if she discovered the secret to Melifacto's outpost. Feyra couldn't contact Bellona, not without Melifacto noticing, and with them leaving Dothrin Feyra wouldn't know where they were.

"I need you to send her a message with one of my crows," Melifacto said. "Since she will only listen to you. Tell her what we learned about the fugitive's destination. If they're leaving from Black Hypogea, then I have to assume the Tower of Samadel would be their first stop."

"There's a Primordial in the Tower of Samadel?"

"That's not all there is." Melifacto gritted his teeth, like his memory was hurting him. He turned away from the cart. Pelady waited by his carriage. "Marta has embarked on a very dangerous journey. We must retrieve her as soon as possible. Instruct Feyra that once she has Marta, she will meet me at Barrowfield in two weeks time."

"I don't like you hiding things from me."

"There are so few of us Praetor's left. It's only you, me, and Kygan. If I'm hiding something from you, it's to protect you." He grabbed onto the carriage's handrail, then stopped. "I wouldn't want anything to happen to any of us, I'm sure you don't either. After all, I'm the only one who knows how to enter the Cradle of the World."

"That makes you useful." Bellona crossed her arms.

"Don't worry. You're useful too." He pulled himself into the carriage then leaned out the window. "I have something I need to deal with to the south, but could you take your ships and meet me at, say, Dancer's Inlet? Do you know where that is?"

"If it's on a map, I'll find it." She sauntered closer to the carriage. "Are you getting rid of me?"

"Of course not. Time is simply against us. I left you some crows, one will find Feyra, the other your shipmaster. Keep yourself safe."

He waved as Pelady pulled the carriage away, followed by the rest of the Owls and even some Boars. Bellona finally unclenched her jaw. Melifacto was right, he was still useful. But if Bellona could discover how to open the Cradle, she would have power over him. Marta certainly had something to do with it, but what? Hopefully Feyra would discover something at the outpost.

She turned toward the camp where her Boars were waiting.

"What do we do?" one of them asked.

"Pack up," Bellona said. "We're going to the sea."

The sun burned hot on the mountain side. Gaul poked the fire as two rabbits hung on the spit above. He hid in a cave high above the Gate Beyond so the scorching sun would not cook him like the rabbits. Juices dripped from the meat into the flames. It was a nice step from the dried jerky they ate for weeks after their raid in Castle Adathin.

Marta was outside the cave. She had the sword she stole from Yomat, the former false Praetor of Snakes, in one hand and was practicing. Step, lunge, back, slice.

"Watch your feet," Gaul said.

She did a big horizontal cut. "I'm not tripping."

"That's cause you're fighting air. A real opponent could catch your front foot. You have more range than with a knife, use it."

Marta put the sword away. She grabbed the collar of her shirt and fanned herself with it. The giant skeleton that was the Gate Beyond seemed to watch them from the valley. Marta crossed her arms and looked at the chasm of Black Hypogea.

"When are you going to teach me to berserk like you?" she asked.

"It's not berserking," Gaul said.

"Then what is it?" She joined him in the cave.

"It's... just not berserking. There are berserkers." He took the spit from the fire and snapped it half between the rabbits. "Just eat. We'll practice after."

They ate in silence. Gaul looked beyond Marta to the birds that circled the Gate Beyond. They had barely made it out of Black Hypogea. If Marta hadn't discovered her trublüdar nature, she would be dead. He touched the spot on his chest where Athas' pendant was hidden. How many more Primordials would they need to seal the Cradle?

"You know," Marta said, mouth full of rabbit. "I already did the red eye thing once, why is it so hard to do it again? I'm doing what you said with the string and the fire and the ocean, but it's not working."

"You were dying," Gaul said. "It was half instinct."

"Thanks for the faith." She pointed at Gaul with her skewer. "Upset that you're not the only special one?"

"I've never met a trublüdar outside of Ulkradia. I thought it was trait purely of my people."

"Then how do you explain this?"

Gaul thought about it. "Everything seems to lead back to this land in someway. I can't trace my ancestors, but maybe they came from here."

Marta leaned back. "I wish I knew I had this when I was younger. No one would have messed with me or Jovin if I could heal myself with lightning. I wouldn't have..." She touched her mouth scar.

"It needs to be triggered." He poked the fire with a stick. "If your family line has a history of trublüdars, you'll be forced to go through the makkenblüd. A trial in the wilderness to force you to trigger your nature. After that, it can be taught and cultivated."

"That's what happened to you?"

Gaul lowered his head. "No. I was playing with some kids on a frozen lake and the ice broke. Me and another boy fell through. I smashed my way back out of the water and I was able to survive until I could get someplace warm. The other boy didn't. A week later I was packed up and shipped off to the capital where they trained me to be a killer of men. I never had to endure the makkenblüd. But, if I ever have a child, they will."

"That's terrible."

Gaul shrugged. "That's life. Ulkradia's in the far north. It's a big country, but most of it is uninhabited. We have mountain wolves and stone wyverns. Wandering trolls that will attack without warning. Cold winters and thaws that flood the land. Even without nature biting at us, we're right up against Imperium and Mirral. Imperium especially is known for their conquering spirit."

Marta slid closer, enthralled by the story. "Why didn't they try to conquer Ulkradia?"

"Oh, they did. I heard the story when I was in the capital. One day, an Imperium general rode with a contingent into Ulkradia. There's not much on the edges so the first person he ran into was a farmer. This general said to the farmer, 'We are here from the glorious Imperium. This land will become part of our whole. Tell your king that we come as benefactors, or conquerors.'

"This farmer took a long look at the general and the warriors he brought with him. He stared the general dead in the eye and said, 'Welcome to Ulkradia. We are a separate people, but fight as one. If you come here demanding submission, you will not find it.'

"The general was incensed. He clearly thought the Ulkradian were simple people and would give up easily. 'Do you truly think you can stand against the might of Imperium?' he asked. 'Our army is greater than you can imagine.'

"The farmer stood his ground. 'Here's what I imagine: your army has men. Those men have swords. I have a sword; my wife and son have swords. But swords break, and when yours do, what then? When our swords break; we will fight with tools. When those shatter; we fight with bone and flesh. You may conquer a land, but never our people. We will salt the earth and burn the forests. Poison the wells and slaughter the livestock. When all Ulkradians lay dead, with five of your warriors around each one, you can ask yourself if you were a benefactor or a conqueror.'"

Marta's eyes widened. "That's incredible."

"Embellished for effect, I'm sure," Gaul said. "But it certainly is a good story. Imperium and Ulkradia were at war for some time in the past. The hostilities remained until Mirral attacked Imperium. They asked Ulkradia for help and the Winter Council said yes."

"You fought in that war, right?" Marta asked.

"Plenty of people did. Trublüdars were used as a battering rams against the Mirralians. You sneak one in and they could take out an entire unit or more. I never fought with another trublüdar, we were always told we would just tear each other apart."

"But, the aura. You said you saw a gold light around me."

"Yeah." Gaul had it hammered into his head to never Ignite when another trublüdar was around, or else they would tear each other apart. Did they know about the golden aura? If trublüdars could recognize each other, the makkenblüd would be useless. An army of trublüdars would be frightening indeed. The Winter Council had reason to fear it.

Trublüdars had been mistreated for as long as Ulkradia knew they existed. They began as berserkers, but when a few learned to truly tap into their power, things changed. They were called monsters and hunted down by warriors specially trained to combat their violent, explosive style and near-invulnerability. Others were captured and kept in cages to be unleashed upon other tribes.

Even as times changed and trublüdars were given certain rights, the stigma never completely faded. Perhaps, the Winter Council was afraid of what unified trublüdars would do. The trust still wasn't there.

"Gaul," Marta said, snapping her fingers in front of Gaul's face. "You have haven't eaten yet."

Gaul looked at his untouched rabbit. He began eating. Marta tossed the remains of her meal aside and hopped to her feet. She drew her sword and started practicing again.

Gaul finished his food as Marta trained with her straight sword. She was picking it up fast. Gaul left the cave and drew a weapon.

"Ready for an opponent?" he asked, flicking his sword.

"No berserking," Marta said with a smile.

Gaul groaned and raised his sword.

* *

They left Black Hypogea far behind. The only direction they had was Sebanna saying the Tower of Samadel was south. And so south they went. The mountain range fell away to a flooded salt flat. A centimetre of water spread in all directions and off to the horizon. They took a night there on the edge, knowing that once they started the crossing there would be no camping on the watery plain.

When the sun rose in the morning, they began their crossing.

"Ever heard of this tower?" Marta asked, watching the clear water became murky with each step.

"I was going to ask you the same question," Gaul said.

"You're the one who knows all this Cradle stuff."

"I don't recognize the name." He drew his sword and ran it through the water, cutting a line through the smoky dirt. "But names change. Ziz was told to be sealed in the Windscar Manse. Not entirely sure what that's supposed to be."

"And who or what is Ziz?"

Gaul flicked the water into the air. It sparkled in the sunlight as it fell. "The Sky Queen. A massive bird that ruled the air until Dimiya and her Apostles of Wind clipped her wings."

"A big bird." Marta chewed her thumbnail. "Let's get there, get the Light, and get out. There's still more Primordials to find."

Marta didn't know what her own hurry was. After they resealed the Cradle and Gaul returned home, where would she go? Jovin was gone. She could go back to

Landus. Since all the people left, she didn't feel as many eyes on her. Maybe she could go with Gaul. Ulkradia sounded nice.

"I was thinking," she said.

"Do you see that?" Gaul pointed forward.

The shallow lake made a perfect mirror for the sky. That made it easy to see the black smoke that was pluming upwards and down. A massive fire was burning, as if an entire town was set aflame.

Gaul hurried, though the source had to still be an hour or more away. Marta figured she'd ask her question another time.

They discussed lightly what the fire could be. Gaul hoped for a place they could sleep. They still couldn't see the edge of the flooded salt flats, and that would require they keep walking, even through the night. The fact it was on fire was a surprisingly small afterthought.

As they got closer, the water got shallower until it disappeared entirely. The smell of smoke grew stronger. They stopped at the edge of a hole that dipped down into a fiery landscape. The smoke that billowed into the sky was the combination of dozens of molten pools. As far as they could see, fire and ash covered the land. The Blasted Lands.

"What happened here?" Marta asked. "Some disaster?"

"It's a mine," Gaul said. "But I've never seen one like this before."

There was a whistle and they dropped prone. In the network of bridges that spider-webbed below them, figures moved. They held pickaxes and shovels and another hollered at them.

"Miners," Gaul said. "This place is still being worked."

Marta stretched forward to see more. "What do you think they're mining? And who's doing it?"

"I don't really care." He crawled away from the lip. "This place is massive. We're going to have to go through it if we don't want to walk through the night."

They crept along the edge of the mine until they found a ladder down. Gaul took the lead, descending into the scorched land. They stayed along the upper catwalks. The heat was incredible, Marta couldn't believe working much lower. She peered over the edge and saw something bizarre far below.

Walking among the pools of lava was a metal creature. It was a massive humanoid, hunched over like its own weight was pulling it down. Light poured from its lamp-like eyes as it swept them back and forth, looking for something. It reached the wall and began digging with powerful hands. It was as if armour had been given life to move on its own.

She prodded Gaul, but he was already looking at it. The creature reached into the hole it made and pulled out a teal crystal. It let out a whistle like the one they heard earlier. Two more metal monsters lumbered from elsewhere in the mine and began digging with the first one.

"It's a crystal mine," Gaul said. "Those things must be able to survive the heat and dig where humans can't."

"Yeah," Marta said. "But what are they?"

Gaul continued moving. "Something I don't want to see close up."

The three moving armours slowly carved into the wall. Marta tore her gaze away and followed Gaul.

The pillars of smoke made it tough to see far, as if the bridges were a maze among twisting stone walls. As they moved into an open-air shack on a stone platform, their worst fears were realized. A keep stood in the middle of the mine, high above the workers below. Banners were hung with a flaming horn design.

Marjyal was the one working the mine.

Forta travelled further than either of her sisters. She reached the edges of the ever-shrinking kingdom of Adathin, believing that prayer and research would be nothing in the face of her blunt exploration. Everywhere she went, she brought a contingent of moving armour with her, and later, dracolings. The people sent letters to their King, asking him to call Forta back so she would stop ravaging the land. The King, of course, cared only for the Cradle.

Though Forta sailed the sea and dug deep into the ground, she always returned to her manor and the Blasted Land Mines. It was where she learned the secret of moving armour. It was where she found the corpse of an ancient dragon. It was where, after an illness got hold of her, she passed away surrounded by loyal dracolings, empty suits of armour, and a land on fire.

—From the Journal of Jovin Gutterwake

Chapter Twenty-Six

The Bloody One

"This is where Marjyal gets their crystal from," Marta said. "This is what keeps the machines in the Pits running."

"We need to move faster." Gaul turned away from the keep and cursed, "Black Hypogea."

A group of miners were coming down the bridge toward the platform they were on. Marta turned to backtrack, but another group of people were further down that path. Gaul turned to her. She cocked her head toward the keep. Gaul groaned, but they sprinted toward it.

Empty guard stations sat on either side of the bridge leading to the keep. Gaul dove into the station and Marta vaulted after him. They pressed themselves against the low wall and waited. The miners went past first, talking about work and some card game that night. The next group was different.

"They may decide to go around," one voice said. A woman. "So, put some guards along the outside of the mine."

"Are these two really worth all this effort?" A male voice asked. "We can't work all the slaves with guards off in the far reaches."

They were talking about Gaul and Marta. The Snakes got the word out fast. Marta had hoped they would get at least one Primordial before Marjyal caught up.

"They are worth every bit," the woman said.

The man scoffed. "Then what if I keep them for myself? Why should the Boars get the respect from their capture?"

Shit, Marta thought. The Guild of Boars was there. Or at least one of them was. She wanted to peek over the lip, but the voices were so close they were bound to spot her if she moved.

"Do you believe that the best decision?" the woman asked, amused.

"I believe," the man started. "I believe that the Guild of Moles gets no respect in Marjyal despite us doing all the work."

Gaul gave a quizzical look and mouthed, "Guild of Moles?"

Marta shrugged. She had never heard of them before. She wondered if they were a new addition, much the like Guild of Ashes. But, the crystals had been used in Marjyal since she first lived there. They must oversee the mining operation, with no power in the city itself.

"Settle yourself, Praetor," the woman said. "It's the Guild of Boars that have been speaking for you in the city. Bellona has been very kind to you, don't throw all the good will back at her."

The Praetor of Moles grumbled something unintelligible. "Let's take this conversation inside. This heat is unbearable."

Their footsteps faded away. Marta popped her head over the lip. A tall woman dressed in leather armour with a spiked club resting on her shoulder must have been the Boar they were hearing. There were three shorter men, but only one wearing a royal coat. It was sprinkled in ash, but still clearly elegant. He was a pudgy little man and Marta guessed he was the Praetor of Moles.

Gaul clapped her on the shoulder and pointed in the opposite direction. "Let's get out of here."

"Can't we shut down this mine or something?" Marta asked. "We can cut off the supply of crystal to the Marjyal Pits."

Gaul snorted. "And how do you suspect we'll do that?"

"Kill the Praetor of Moles."

"That won't stop production."

Marta crept toward the exit of the guard station. "It's something."

Gaul grabbed her. "We need to keep moving to that tower."

"You don't understand." She pulled her arm out of his grasp. "The Pit is a symbol of the Praetors power to every good person in Marjyal. A sign that the people who just want destruction and pain are more powerful than them."

"Even if you can shut down the mine, it won't stop the Pit," Gaul explained. "People have been killing each other since before we started using crystals."

Marta pushed her fist into the ground. She wanted to do anything to help the good people in Marjyal survive against the bad. Finding the Primordials was important as well. The Tower couldn't be far.

"Okay," she finally said.

Gaul gave her a soft look. He peeked over the low wall, then stood and hurried around the other side of the keep. Before he could look back, Marta sprinted in the other direction. The Tower wasn't far, but the Praetor was right here. She paused at the corner to make sure the coast was clear, then followed the group to the front of the keep.

She hid at the next corner. The Praetor and the Boar stepped into the keep while the others guarded the entrance. Marta scanned for a way into the building. A few feet above her was a window, cracked open. She stepped back, then kicked off a perpendicular wall and grabbed into the windowsill. The sword and sheath were still new and bounced strangely at her hip as she pulled herself up. She opened the window the rest of the way and entered.

She was in a nice sitting room, a few books and half-used candles were at the table where someone spent their time. The room was open to the main hall. A balcony looked over the floor below. She crept to the railing and observed the

Praetor and the Boar cross to an iron throne. The Boar sat in the throne, to the Praetor's obvious displeasure.

The Boar grinned cruelly at the Praetor and hung her leg over one armrest. She had a scar that ran across her brow. Marta wasn't sure if she'd seen her around, but she must have been someone important in the Boars.

"Feyra," the Praetor stepped forward.

Feyra slammed her heavy club, reinforced by jagged metal, against the ground. "I apologize. Were you saying something, Vickor?"

"Feyra," Vickor said again with a grimace. "We will not be pushed around by you or your Praetor."

Feyra smiled. "Not pushing. Suggesting. You're far from Marjyal. Far from the protection of the Accords. These two have already killed three Praetors. I simply don't want you to be scared."

"I am still a Praetor," Vickor said. "And I will not be spoken to in such a way. If Melifacto wants these fugitives so badly, I'm sure he's willing to pay a hefty sum. Go back to Bellona. Tell that cow, Vickor won't bow to her."

Feyra's eyes flared with anger. Vickor turned his back to stalk out. That was his last mistake. Feyra rose from the throne, club held in both hands, and brought it across the side of Vickor's head. His neck broke with a horrifying snap. Blood flew from the mangled half of his face and he fell to the stone floor.

Feyra didn't stop. She pounded her massive club against Vickor's skull. Marta had to cover her mouth to keep herself from screaming — or vomiting.

"Never! Slur! Lady! Bellona!" With each word, she drove the club into Vickor. His head collapsed until Feyra was hitting nothing more than a viscous pulp. Blood flew with each hit until Feyra was coated in his gore.

The two Mole guards rushed in — far too late. They drew their swords. Feyra stretched her back and glanced sideways at the Moles. She looked like madwoman, covered in blood with strings of her dark hair pasted to her face. She stepped toward the Moles, dragging her club behind her and leaving a red trail from Vickor's corpse.

"You can die," Feyra said, "Or you can guard the edge of the mine."

The Moles stumbled back. They took in the sight of their massacred Praetor, and the crazed woman slowly moving toward them.

"Yes, Lady Feyra," one of the Moles said. They spun to the exit.

"Wait." Feyra pointed at one Mole. "Draw me a bath."

The two Moles shared a look, then the one who wasn't pointed at rushed out the door. The other one looked at Feyra, smiling sweetly at him beneath the blood, then hustled to follow her orders.

"I'm sorry, my Lady." She was talking to herself. "I lost my temper again. He would not listen. But, I will find Marta and the world will be yours."

She let out a terrifying cackle that bounced off the lonely stone walls. Humming a dissonant tune, she followed where the second Mole went to draw her a bath. The bloodstained club dragged behind her as she disappeared.

Marta finally let out the gasp of air she was holding in. The guilds were brutal to each other. Feyra killed Vickor without a second thought. He was dead, though, that's what Marta wanted. Gaul was right, the mine wouldn't stop without him. Now Feyra was in charge. But, she would be unarmed in the bath. Marta could kill her and leave the mine without a head. Surely that would at least slow them down.

At the very least it would get another Marjyalian off her trail.

Marta crept along the second-floor balcony. She found a staircase to the main hall. Feyra was easy to follow, her club had left a blood trail down the hall. Marta grabbed a knife from the table and followed the blood to a closed wooden door. She heard the same dissonant humming from inside. Feyra was inside. Marta pushed very slightly against the door, but it was locked. She peeked through the keyhole.

All she could see was the lip of a copper bath with a bare leg hanging out. The Mole had not left. Maybe Feyra thought an assassin could be close and kept the guard near? Strange — but Feyra seemed like a strange woman.

Marta left the door and entered the next room over. It was a bedroom, with a nice down bed and blue curtains. A window was across from the door. Marta could shimmy from that window to the next one over, where Feyra was bathing. Bash through the window and take out the guard and the Boar before they knew what was happening.

She creaked the window open, letting in a flurry of ash. She peered out. The back of the keep hung over a sheer drop into the mines below. Smoke billowed from the dizzying height.

Nothing to shimmy on, Marta thought, putting her knife in her coat, But there is a banner. She lifted one leg over the windowsill and grabbed the edge of the banner. She pulled it into a rope and gave it a few test tugs. It held firm. With a deep breath, she brought her other leg out the window. The banner supported her full weight, holding her over the lethal drop.

Pressing her feet against the keep wall, she swung back and forth. She reached out and grabbed the railing with one hand. She dug her fingers into the stone. With the banner to steady herself, she pulled closer to the railing until she could sit on it and ease herself silently onto the balcony.

She crept to the double glass doors and looked in. Feyra was lounging in a copper bath against one wall. She rolled her neck and had her eyes closed. As she lifted a hand, letting water drip off her fingers. It was red as blood. A much deeper colour than it should be if Feyra had just cleaned herself of Vickor's.

Marta knew what had happened to the Mole. In the corner, partially hidden by the bath, he laid limply against the wall. She could only see half his face, but his throat was slit. Feyra happily hummed and ran the Mole's blood — mixed with the water — over her skin.

Feyra was a standout of viciousness, even among the Marjyalians. Marta would be glad to put her down. She drew the knife slowly, not daring to make a sound. She pushed against the door and it swung apart from its partner. She was slow, methodical. There was nearly enough space for her to get through—

Creak.

Marta froze. Feyra continued splashing in her bloodbath. Marta pushed again and the door was silent this time. She was almost in. Feyra took a deep breath and dunked her head, disappearing entirely under the red water. Marta squeezed her knife and took a step inside.

The bathwater exploded to the ceiling. Marta stumbled back, but the blood arced toward her, wrapping around her throat and throwing her across the room. She slid across the floor and hit the wall, coming to a stop next to the Mole's corpse. From the bath, Feyra rose like a spectre, soaked in blood.

"Incredible," Feyra said, drawing a line from the corner of her mouth with her finger — imitating Marta's scar. "That was simple."

Marta stumbled to her feet. What had just happened? Was she attacked by the bathwater? Feyra stepped out of the bath. Her muscular arms were covered in tattooed words in some other language. They spread long around her strong shoulders and across her clavicle. As she turned to grab a robe, Marta could see the tattoo continued along her shoulder blades and spine, down her just above her tailbone.

Feyra spun on the robe, staining the white fabric crimson. Her club was in the corner furthest from her. Marta drew her sword and slid toward the club, keeping Feyra from her gruesome weapon. Feyra cocked her head, then raised her hand to the bath.

The tattoos peeking out from beneath her robe turned blue and the blood rose from the bath, leaving behind crystal clear water. It floated through the air and encircled Feyra. The Mole's body vibrated as the last of the blood was pulled from his neck wound and joined the spiraling mass.

Marta took a fighting stance, though nothing could tell her how to fight something like this. Feyra moved the blood around her body, then sharpened it into a spear hovering just over her shoulder. Her hand twitched. The spear flew forth. Marta dodged to the side and it cracked the stone where she once stood.

The spear retreated to Feyra's side. She couldn't kill Marta, but she could maim her and drag her to Melifacto. Marta tried to call up the same feeling she had when she nearly died in Black Hypogea. *Think of the sea, think of rage.* Red grew into her vision, but it couldn't take hold. She needed to Ignite. She couldn't go back to Marjyal. Where was Gaul? Why did she leave him?

Feyra smiled. "I can hear your heartbeat, little one. Why don't we finish this before you hurt yourself?"

Marta dove for the front door. The blood slammed against it, holding it shut. *Be unexpected*, Marta thought. She dug her toes into the floor and charged straight at Feyra. The blood formed into a shield, but Marta ignored her. She sheathed her sword and leapt at the balcony doors, the left one was still open from when she snuck in. Her shoulder hit the other door that remained closed and shattered the glass as she exited onto the balcony.

Marta stumbled to a stop, nearly barrelling over the railing to the mine below. She glanced briefly back into the bathroom. Feyra stepped on the broken glass, cutting her feet — though she didn't seem to care. Marta pushed herself off the railing and headed toward the side with the banner. She jumped to the railing, then forward again and grabbed the banner.

She bundled the fabric into her hands and began climbing. Feyra stepped out of the bathroom, she wasn't in any hurry. She spotted Marta and pointed. The blood construct flowed into the air and shot toward her.

Marta pushed away from the wall and the blood spear stuck into the stone. She swung back, put both feet on the spear and — before Feyra could pull it away — leapt even higher up the banner.

"Fall!" Feyra cried. "I will catch you!"

The blood spear fluxed and turned into a scythe-like blade that tore through the wall. Feyra was aiming to cut the banner instead of Marta. There was a balcony diagonally from the one Feyra was waiting on. Marta swung her body away, then toward the balcony. The blood blade cut through the banner just as Marta leapt off. She grabbed the railing and the banner fluttered into the smoke.

Her fingers slipped. She tried to readjust, but the ash that coated the stone gave her little grip. She shut her eyes, then she stopped. Easing her eyes open, she saw blood wrapping around her wrists. It pulled her over railing and onto the balcony. The blood retreated from her wrists and became a blade once again. Marta drew her sword.

"Let's not do this, Marta," Feyra called from below. "If you fall…"

Marta knocked the blade away. It flew back, then shot forward once again. She stepped around it, battling the flying sword. It flowed strangely, making it hard to keep up with the movement. As Marta stepped toward the balcony door, the blade moved more sluggishly. Feyra couldn't see where they were fighting.

Marta took her sword in both hands and smashed the blood blade. It broke into a crimson rain. Marta kicked the balcony door open and rushed into the office. She dropped her sword into its scabbard as she moved through the keep. She needed to get out. She couldn't handle Feyra on her own.

She was back on the second floor. She arrived on the balcony over the throne, across from the one she came in on. She kicked off the railing and landed on the banquet table with a roll. The mutilated corpse of Vickor flashed in the corner of her vision, but she kept herself oriented on the doors before her.

There was a bang from behind her. She turned to see Feyra stomping into the main hall. She pulled the blood from Vickor and joined it with the pool she was already using. The liquid congealed into a whip. She spun her arm and flicked the blood whip toward Marta.

Marta slid feet first, knocking table settings aside. The blood whip snapped over her head. Marta got her feet beneath her and leapt high into the air. She landed hard on the edge of the table, tipping the massive structure up and sending the rest of the utensils, plates, and cups flying. Marta stumbled forward, regaining her footing on the floor.

The table flipped up, but couldn't make it all the way over. It slammed back onto its legs. A Mole guard stepped through the front doors to investigate the commotion. Marta bullied him aside, knocking him off the door.

She turned left to where she had split from Gaul. Glancing back to see how far away Feyra was, she saw the Mole pick himself up. He raised his crossbow and squeezed the trigger. A red spike shot through his throat. The bolt went wide and Feyra stepped into view. She pulled the blood out of the Mole's body, turning to Marta just as she disappeared around the corner.

Marta barrelled past the two guard stations she and Gaul had been hiding in. Gaul was still nowhere to be seen. She crossed a bridge, the only one Gaul could have taken considering the direction he was going. The wood bounced with each step.

On the other side, she found him. Gaul pulled one of his swords from the chest of a Mole — with two more already on the ground. He wiped the blood off the sword and spotted Marta rushing up.

"There you are," he said, sheathing his sword. "What in the world were you thinking?"

Marta grabbed him by the coat. "No time. Keep running."

Walking across the bridge behind them, Feyra spiralled three corpses worth of blood around her head. Marta pushed Gaul, trying to get him to run. He stared at Feyra with something between amazement and confusion.

"She's fluxblooded," Marta said. "We can't fight her." Gaul wouldn't move, no matter how much she pulled at him.

Gaul shook his head. "No. She's a fluxweaver."

Feyra reared back to strike, but stopped. "What did you say?"

"Gaul!" Marta punched him in the stomach, pushing him back. "Move, now!"

"Sorry." He spun on his heel and rushed away from Feyra with Marta at his side.

"Stop!" Feyra shouted.

Arrows made of blood flew past them. Trails flowed from their back, touched other arrows, and bound together to create trap lines. They spun at Marta and Gaul, trying to wrap around them. Feyra wanted them both alive.

Ahead of them was a hoisting system to haul small amounts crystals and other ore to the top of the mine. The rope looped through the bucket and the counterweight. Marta formulated a plan and — judging by the look he gave her — Gaul came up with the same one.

Gaul rushed ahead as Marta spun to Feyra. She planted her feet and tossed the knife she stole at the oncoming Boar. Feyra pulled back her blood and formed a shield to protect herself. Gaul had one arm with the counterweight rope wrapped around it. He reached out for Marta with his other. She grabbed his arm and with her free hand, sliced the rope.

The rope shot them up. Marta held tight to Gaul's hand as the rock wall flew past. The whining of a pulley grew into a scream until they burst into a flat landscape. Gaul released the rope and they landed in a less-than-graceful heap at the upper lip of the mine. Brushing the dirt off themselves, they looked back down.

Feyra, robe covered in blood and ash, glared up at them. She dropped the blood she was using and turned to the keep in a huff.

"She's not going to give up," Gaul said. "I thought she was mean in the Pits."

"It's not all bad." Marta pointed away from the mine. "Look."

Without the smoke covering the horizon they could see further. A tower rose from the ground and disappeared into the clouds high above. It fit the description of the Tower of Samadel. Unfortunately, it was still very far away, but its sheer size made it seem closer.

At its peak should be Ziz, the second Primordial to harvest Light from. They needed to move fast — Feyra would be on their tail.

Feyra watched Gaul and Marta sail up and disappear from the mines. She was surrounded by heat, but her skin felt cold.

What did he say? Feyra thought. *Fluxweaver? Was that the word?*

Feyra had never heard that word before. Gaul had said it as soon as he saw her blood ability. She looked at the tattoos that glowed on her arms. They burned slightly as she held onto the blood orb. Bellona had always told Feyra not to question her ability. She had said it was the will of a god, though Feyra knew it was simply the will of her mother. The mother who pinned her down when she was a child a cruelly carved those words into her skin.

She made Feyra into something else. Something different than the Praetors and their abilities. They couldn't activate runes with a touch, after all. She had followed Bellona's orders to keep it hidden and tried to accept it for what it was. But if Gaul had answers. Any answers at all…

Bellona comes first, Feyra thought, dropping the blood orb with a splash. *I can't be selfish.*

Feyra returned to the keep as a group of Moles came stumbling out. They stopped when they saw Feyra and made space for her to pass them. Feyra looked up at the Marjyal banner hanging in the main hall, then spun around and pointed at the closest Mole.

"Get me a detachment to go after the fugitives," she ordered.

"That, uh." The Mole shook. "That might be difficult. We don't normally leave the mines, we're guards. We aren't prepared for an expedition."

Feyra glared at him.

"But we can make it work," the Mole said. "We'll just have to stock the horses. And a cart."

"Go." Feyra leaned on the banquet table.

"Do you want the message?"

"What?"

The Mole was handed a piece of paper and offered it to Feyra with a shaking hand. "We got sent this before Vickor…"

Feyra took the paper and unfolded it. *We have learned that the fugitives are visiting the Primordials*, it read in Bellona's writing. Feyra already knew that of course. The Snakes told her. *Their first stop will most likely be the Tower of Samadel. Melifacto will be waiting for you in Barrowfield in two weeks. Make sure he doesn't know Gaul is still alive.*

"We're going south," Feyra crumpled up the letter. "You have until morning to prepare."

"South?" The Mole looked at his allies. "We don't go south. We've lost a dozen or more caravans that have gone that way. We take a large loop west rather than go south."

"What did you lose these caravans to?"

"We don't know."

"Maybe you'll be lucky enough to find out." She leaned in. "We leave at dawn."

The Moles scattered. Feyra sat on the lip of the table. Bellona wanted Gaul, and of course Feyra would retrieve him for her. But maybe, just maybe, he could answer some questions first.

The Tower of Samadel — also known as the Tower of Gods or the Gifted Tower. In the First Age, Tyran looked up to the sky and saw Dimiya. He was enraptured by the way she could dance on the wind and fell in love the instant he saw her. He wanted to give her a gift, a monument and a place Earth and Sky could be together.

Tyran called on the spirits of nature to grow a tree that would stretch past the clouds. Then, he carved out the most beautiful pieces of the earth and sent them skyward. He asked spirits of fire and earth to forge great chains to bind the chunks of land to the tree. When it was complete, he met Dimiya upon the highest point and said it, along with him, was hers.

Dimiya loved the tower. Goddess of innovation that she was, she went to building machinations to speed Tyran's ascent so that they would not have to wait long to be together.

Unfortunate that such a lovely gift would have its name tarnished by a man like Samadel.

—From the Journal of Jovin Gutterwake

Chapter Twenty-Seven
Palace of Dust

The sun gave little respite to the weary travellers as they marched south. Marta's legs burned with exertion and her muscles trembled with each step. It had been hours since they left the mines, but still the flooded salt flats continued. Every few minutes she would look back and wonder if that blood-wielding woman was chasing them at that very moment. If they slowed down, would she catch up?

Gaul never looked back. He kept his eyes on the great tower, cutting the sky like a vertical horizon. To see it from so far away, it had to be kilometres tall. Climbing that thing was going to be a pain.

As the western sky turned to shades of red and yellow, the water around their feet receded. They walked until the ground turned into ruddy rock and sand. There was finally some definition to the landscape as they came to a series of canyons containing tall rock spires. A long slice out of the earth blocked the way forward.

"We need to stop," Gaul said, coming to the edge of a sheer fall.

"What about Marjyal? If we stop—"

"If we don't stop, it's going to be worse." He pointed at the dark spike jutting into the clouds. "And we don't know what's in that tower. What if we need to fight? I'm sensing a trend with these places, so we shouldn't go in there unprepared."

Between Marjyal at their back and the Primordials on their horizon, every choice was going to come with a consequence. Marta grimaced. There were times where she wished she had stayed in Landus. But then what? Gaul would have stayed in the Pits, she would never had known of her brother's fate, and the Absence would keep spreading from the door with no one to stop it.

"Besides," Gaul said. "They would have to get their people together and with that Praetor dead there's going to be some disarray. I imagine they won't leave until the morning. They know where we're going to be after all. Come on, let's find a place to sleep." He turned down a narrow path toward the canyon floor.

Marta took a final look back. Still nothing. The desert was already getting colder without the sun to heat it. She pulled her scarf out of her pocket and squeezed it tight as she followed Gaul.

The canyon floor was a few dozen metres down at its highest and kept descending the further they walked. A fairly shallow canyon, though after Black Hypogea Marta's scale of depth was way off. Any hole she saw the top of might as well of been a stumbling block. Wind funnelled through the twisting passage, blowing around the patches of long yellow grass and low-lying shrub life. There had to be a cave somewhere. A place they could light a fire where no one would see. They trekked on. And still it got colder.

The pass became tighter as the worry that they would not find a way back up set in. Neither said a word, both being strong for the other. Marta adjusted the sword on her hip and scrambled to the top of a boulder.

"I don't see a cave," she said, her breath visible in the chilly air. "But maybe we could use that."

Gaul circled the boulder and followed her gaze. Part of the canyon wall had crumbled, leaving a ramp up to a winding path. The remains of the sunlight turned the top half into a blazing white landscape. "That'll do." He tapped his foot on a ring of small rocks near the base of Marta's perch. "We're not the first ones to come this way. It's not a bad place to camp."

Marta hopped down, crushing a small fern under her feet. It took half an hour for them to collect enough wood to start a fire. Some trees had taken the long drop to the canyon floor and splintered their wood into easy to use chunks.

The flames gave them a modicum of heat in the small alcove between the boulder and the wall. The flickering lights cast dancing shadows on the canyon around them. When the sun finally set, it became the only indication they weren't lost in some dark void. Again.

"I'm sorry," Marta said, her soft words sliding into the long silence.

Gaul tossed her a large rolled-up leaf. "For what?"

"The mine. Running off like that." She unfurled a chunk of rabbit meat from the leaf. They were running low on food again, and it was difficult to hunt the large game that lived around the canyons with swords. "I thought I could do something. Destroy their source of crystals and maybe make some difference."

Gaul took out his own meal and bit off a chunk. He stared into the fire and chewed slowly.

"I didn't want to abandon you," Marta continued. "But an opportunity like that doesn't come up everyday. You're the one who asked why I don't try to help Marjyal rather than run from it? And sure, maybe looking back I didn't have a chance. The Praetor's dead now and the mine's going to continue. It just seemed worth it."

Still, Gaul ate quietly.

Marta's face grew hot. "I couldn't shake this feeling — maybe not a feeling, but these words. Jovin said to do nothing makes you as bad as them. He always had these quotes from books that he would repeat to me like they meant something. Inspirational words that are stupid when you hear them. And they made me act stupid in return. I'm not going to run off—"

"Marta." Gaul squeezed the bridge of his nose. "I don't... I don't care."

Marta's mouth was stuck halfway between one word to the next. A bird fluttered from the brush into the sky. The fire crackled in reply.

"What do you mean?" was all Marta could think to ask.

"If you want to go and save Marjyal, that's your prerogative. I won't stop you. I can't stop you."

"Don't use big words like it makes you smart." She tensed her jaw. Gaul had been on a bridge in the mine when she found him. He wasn't waiting for her. "You were going to leave."

Gaul rolled his head back. "Yes. I was. But what are we doing? That monster at the bottom of the world? There are four more just like it. One of them is dead, another is locked behind a fire gate, and one is in a place called the Dark. The chance of anyone succeeding is… bad. But I can do it alone."

"I said I was going to get you home."

"Yes. You did. You should get yourself home." He leaned forward. The campfire illuminated a sorrow-filled face. "You said you know where to get exodus stones from. Get through Nature's Grave, back to Landus, and even beyond that. That was where you were safe before."

Where Jovin left her. Even as he promised to bring her with him, he had been lying. To keep her safe, it would seem. "Do you think they would stop hunting you just because I left? Do these seem like that sort of people?"

"They won't stop. I don't care. But I'm used to being alone."

"You need me to get back. I know where the stones are." She stared Gaul down, but he quickly averted his gaze. He took another bite of his food. "Gaul, you are planning on going home after all this?"

"Ba-ya said I was lost and didn't know what to do." He took a deep breath that puffed up his chest. "I do now. Without purpose, what's the point? To do nothing makes you as bad as them, right?" He cast her a joking grin.

Even through the momentary bravado and jollity, cracks were apparent. Marta could see them as clear as day. "I'm not leaving. You don't get to be alone just because it's what you think you deserve."

The smile faded. "You already almost died once."

"What's the chance of that happening again?"

Gaul finished his food and flopped back onto the boulder. He wrapped his coat around himself and disappeared into the cloth. That was the end of that conversation. Marta wrapped her scarf tighter and picked at her meal.

"Thank you," Gaul said. His voice was nearly lost in the whistling breeze outside their little hovel.

Marta smiled and began to eat.

* *

The morning came with birdsong and an elk wandering by Gaul and Marta's camp. It snorted in their direction as if their very presence was an insult. But it went on its way so the pair could climb out of the canyon.

Through the rest of the morning they could only walk and watch as the huge tower grew larger and larger. The Tower of Samadel was a ragged, ancient-looking wooden structure. It had stone outcroppings and other additions, but at its core it seemed to be — strangely — a tree. It rose out of a manor house that was clearly built after the time the tower was formed. Despite all the time they had stared at the monstrosity, the cloud cover had never parted to show them the top.

"Do you think they're on the move?" Marta asked.

Gaul tore his gaze from the sky. Marta was walking backwards, focusing on the direction of the Blasted Lands. "Probably," Gaul said. "We should work fast. Last time I saw Feyra was the Pits. She's somehow gotten less friendly."

"You said she was a fluxweaver?" Marta spun into a forward march.

"She has to be to use flux to do anything like that."

"Does that mean she can do other things?"

"The weavers I've met can." Gaul scratched his chin. "Though I've never seen tattoos like those before. And did you see how confused she got when I called her a fluxweaver? I could be wrong. She could be something different."

They entered a courtyard of dead trees and hedges. An extravagant fountain sat in the middle, though now it was crumbled. Its basin was cracked open as if from some heavy impact. But it wasn't overgrown. The grass was all dead like the trees.

A shadow flew past one of the windows. Gaul slowed. Did he just see that? Was it a curtain? An animal? His hair stood on end. Something was wrong.

"But fluxweavers are still human?" Marta asked, blissfully unaware.

"What?" Gaul kept his eyes out for anymore movement. His fingers shook. "I don't know, that's just what the Imperials called them. Hold on." He put his hand on her arm. "I just need a second."

"For what?"

One of the two heavy wood entrance doors was ajar. It was sturdy. Too sturdy for any simple breeze to move. Yet as Gaul watched, it creaked open.

Gaul yanked Marta behind the fountain as there was a snap. A projectile whistled through the space they once filled.

"What was that?" Marta kept her head below the lip of the basin.

"A crossbow," Gaul said.

"Could Marjyal have beaten us here? Is that possible?"

"I don't think so." He crawled on his belly around the fountain. He wanted desperately to take a look, but he didn't know how good of a shot the crossbowman was.

"Then what do we do?"

"Hey!" a woman shouted. It came from the manor. "What are you doing here?"

Gaul made eye contact with Marta. She shrugged and motioned for him. "We're travellers," Gaul called back. "We're just looking for a place to hole up."

"This far south?" The woman let out a quick laugh. "That's unlikely."

"It's true," Marta said. "We're from Sebanna's Rest. We saw a tower and got interested. We're out of food. We've been on the road for a long time."

There wasn't a reply. Gaul kept scanning the parts of the manor he could see. If the woman wanted to kill them, she certainly had many vantage points to do it from.

"Alright then," the woman finally said. "Come on out slowly."

"Are you going to shoot us?" Gaul asked.

"If you don't come out slowly."

It didn't give them many options. The fountain was the only cover worth a damn. A run might be worth the risk. Hopefully they simply spooked the occupant and they weren't looking to make any bodies.

Gaul put his hands over the basin lip, then rose to his feet. Marta moved with him. No quick movements. They stepped from behind the fountain to meet whatever fate was in store for them.

The woman was tall. She had a stern expression and wore a vest and trousers. Everything about her was sharp. From her pointed nose, to her polished boots, to the nocked crossbow bolt at the ready. She stood in the entrance to the manor. A long distance to run, but far too short at the speed of a bolt.

"You have weapons," she said. "Put them near that pot." She motioned with the crossbow to a stone planter with a dead fern. "One at a time."

Gaul went first. He kept his hands over his shoulders until he got to the wall. All the while, the woman kept her weapon pointed at him. He removed his sword belt and dropped it at his feet.

"Now come here," the woman said. "Slowly or you're getting a bolt through the heart."

Gaul approached. The tower loomed over him. Its shadow was beginning to extend again as the noon sun moved on. The woman descended the steps to meet him. Gaul stopped. With one hand, the woman gave him a quick pat down. She was thorough. She had a process. It wasn't the first time she had done this.

"Alright." She put both hands on the crossbow again. "Go back with your friend. Send her over."

There was a bright side to all the fuss. No one would go through all that trouble just to kill them. Gaul got back to Marta's side and whispered to her out the side of his mouth. "Don't play with her, just drop your sword."

Marta curled her upper lip. But when her turn came she unbuckled her belt and tossed the sword nonetheless. After the pat down Marta was back at Gaul's side.

"Don't move." The woman crept down the steps once again. She scooped the swords in her arms then hurried into the manor.

Minutes went by without the woman returning. Gaul and Marta were stuck in the middle of the garden, wondering what just happened.

"Is she—" Marta started, only to be interrupted by the woman reappearing at the door. Only now she was unarmed.

"Sorry about that," the woman said, now cordial as though she didn't just steal from them. "You can never be too careful out here. You know. My name is Veidecke. You said you're out of food? Come in. I have some stew for lunch."

Marta squeezed her eyes shut as if she could wake up from a dream. "What is going on?"

"She's not the strangest person we've met," Gaul said.

"Come on!" Veidecke insisted. "I won't bite."

"Maybe." Marta pulled her scarf to her face. "But she's very close."

They followed Veidecke into the manor and were struck by an underlying sweet smell. It wasn't a good sweet though, it was sickly and if it was any stronger it would be choking. As they moved it came and went in waves.

There was a path from the front of the manor straight through to the centre courtyard where the tower sat. The manor ringed around the tower like a castle wall. The footprint of the two structures was acres in size. Only one person living there was so much stranger than no one.

Veidecke took a hard right and led Gaul and Marta away from the front entrance and the sight of the tower. The manor ring was nothing more than a series of rooms. Drawing room, study, music room, kitchen, and finally, a dining hall.

It was a sight of forgotten opulence. A crystal light hung from the ceiling, though the actual light came from the windows and half-melted candles. Broken chairs were piled in the corner. A few holes had been knocked into the walls, letting streams of dusty light in. Sitting on the table was a pot of stew.

"I was planning on saving this for dinner," Veidecke explained. "It's yours if you want it. I never mind sharing."

"Thank you." Though Gaul wasn't sure how thankful he was. "Where did you take our stuff?"

"I locked it away." Veidecke ladled out some vegetables and meat onto a plate. "People are much kinder when not surrounded by tools of death." She put the plate down with a wooden spoon. "I only have one."

Gaul and Marta sat down on the few intact chairs. Marta poked the stew a few times with the spoon. It seemed fine. It even seemed tasty. She gave it a tentative try. A smile spread across her lips and she dove in with gusto.

"You really are hungry," Veidecke said, sitting across from them.

"We've been on the road for a long time," Gaul said. "But you live here all by yourself?"

"I do. It's quiet and I like that."

"It must be lonely."

"I have plenty of work to do."

A half-eaten plate of stew slid across the table, stopping in front of Gaul. Marta offered him the spoon. "It is very good." The corners of her mouth were stained brown until she cleaned them with a flick of her tongue.

Gaul took the spoon and laid it on the plate. "What work do you do?"

"One of a private nature." Even when being welcoming, Veidecke kept a proper demeanour. She had yet to smile. "What about you? You're travelling from Sebanna's Rest?"

"The town's been going through some issues," Marta said. "We thought it might be nice to get away. The tower seemed as good a place as any to stop."

"The Tower of Samadel as most call it." Veidecke turned in her chair to gaze at the stone wall — all that was visible of the tower from the dining hall. "Interesting thing."

Gaul chewed through the pieces of the stew. It was delectable. "Is there any way inside?"

"Not as far as I know. You'd need to climb a hundred metres at least to reach the first window."

A series of chimes rang out. They started further in the manor, then rushed their way through the other rooms until a tiny bell — nearly invisible in the corner — vibrated. The sound continued back through the rooms Gaul and Marta had already seen. A series of bells with strings through eyelets.

Veidecke narrowed her eyes and straightened her spine. Marta's gaze flicked between her and the bell. "What was that?" Marta asked.

"An alarm. Of sorts." For the first time, Veidecke smiled. "I've had a rodent problem in the cellar for a while now. That's all. I must go deal with it. Enjoy your meal. Make yourself at home. I'll be back soon."

She stood and smoothed out her pants. She walked out, but with the urgency of someone who wanted to run. Gaul and Marta glanced about the room. Silence resumed.

"What do we do now?" Marta asked.

"We have to get in that tower." Gaul hurried to the window and peered into the courtyard. It was filled with the same dead plants as the front one. The place must have been vibrant and full of life long ago. Now it was like the rest of Adathin, a pale shade of former glory.

Marta joined him. "She said there was no way inside."

"There has to be a way. Though, I wouldn't mind getting my swords back first."

"How long do you think until Marjyal gets here? I can't imagine that woman protecting us."

"It depends." He leaned against the windowsill. "If Feyra's alone she can move fast. But a larger group would have trouble crossing that canyon. They would have to go around, especially if they have carts. Could be a few days, could be a few hours."

"Then what do we do?"

Gaul gazed in the direction Veidecke disappeared. "We play nice. And we hope we have time."

I believe I've discovered what the substance seeping out of the Cradle is. The most common term I've heard for it is Absence, though I've seen it described as Nothing, darkore, and void shard.

It's a peculiar element that, despite its unnerving appearance, is quite natural. It's reactive to flux and has the notable quality of being a liquid that hardens into a metal at high temperatures. It's incredible rare, to the point that in all my travels I have never seen it in person. It's one of those rumours you here around markets and parlours; they would say a queen in a far-off land had jewellery made of the blackest black. Of course, rumours are hard to substantiate.

—From the Journal of Jovin Gutterwake

Chapter Twenty-Eight

Storms

Returning to Marjyal felt like stepping into a jail cell, but it was the closest place that Bellona could embark with her Boars. It had only been a few weeks since they left, but the atmosphere of the city was different. Ortun, her shipmaster, met her on the docks.

"Welcome back, M'lady," he said, bowing. "I'm glad to see you're alright. There have been rumblings that some Praetors have been killed."

"Has there?" Bellona gazed around the docks. Citizens were hiding in the shadows.

"Anyone who rumbled too loud was found face down on the beach. Don't concern yourself with that." Ortun adjusted his metal mask. "But is there a truth to these rumours?"

"We should talk in private." There were too many prying ears on the docks.

"Of course. Welcome aboard."

He led her up the gangplank onto the *Steel Jaw*, the flagship of Marjyal's navy and Ortun's personal vessel. They entered the captain's quarters where he drew the blinds and locked the door.

"Dianathos is dead." Bellona poured herself a drink from the bar. "I saw his body myself. We received word that the Praetor of Snakes has fallen. Ettik has gone missing, which means he's dead as well or ran off. Either way, it's the same outcome." She downed the port in one swig.

"All this chasing that Marta girl." Ortun sat in his chair and swung his feet onto his desk with a bang.

"They're chasing the Chalice of Light. Marta is just a tool."

"Bellona, I've known you for fifteen years now. So, I mean this with all due respect and as your friend. What are you doing?"

Bellona furrowed her brow. "What do you mean?"

"Why play along with Melifacto's chase? You're giving him what he wants and he won't share power once he has it."

"I know." She sat against the bar and put the empty, cool, glass to her temple. "Cragging Kygan got into my head with all this talk of hope and making Marjyal better."

"You want to make Marjyal better?"

"I want to make the world better. The Chalice of Light is strength and that strength can be used to lead. I can strip away a world of weakness and replace it with one built of steel and blood."

Ortun pushed him out of his chair and paced the room. "What about Gaul?"

"What about him?"

"You're obsessed with him. Ever since he killed those monsters you called your champions."

"They were the best that Marjyal could forge. Until Gaul."

"Then tell me, Bellona." Ortun stopped and faced her. "Is he going to be your new champion? Or your replacement?"

Bellona lowered her gaze. "Someone needs to lead."

"Why not Feyra? Why not you?"

"Feyra is too emotional. Too easily compromised. And I… I can be surpassed."

Ortun tapped his mask pensively. "So you want him to kill you?"

Bellona snapped her gaze to Ortun. She slammed the glass down and turned for the door. "Prepare to set sail," she said, unlocking the exit and stalking onto the deck.

Ortun followed her out and shouted, "Prepare to sail!"

The boatswain repeated his call and the sailors went to work on the rigging. Bellona looked off the side of the ship toward the dock. Boars had set up on the boats and Marjyalians watched them go. In the back of the crowd, Bellona spotted Kygan. He was flicking his weird coin up and catching it. Bellona grimaced, squeezing the railing until her fingers hurt.

He had put a bug in her brain that was driving her mad. Hope was nonsense without the power to act, but with power would hope become viable again? She wanted to pull her hair out. The sail's rose and the ship lurched into motion. Kygan disappeared into the crowd. Maybe after Bellona dealt with Melifacto, she would kill Kygan as well.

Half an hour went by and Veidecke hadn't returned. Did she leave Gaul and Marta to wander the manor at their freedom? It felt strange after their crossbow introduction. But as time passed by with no sight or sound of the woman, the pair got restless and began to wander.

The manor was only one floor, much of it collapsed from time. Still, it didn't seem as ancient as the tower it encircled. Some of the architecture and the decorations that survived were even familiar. Oddly so. Reminiscent of Castle Adathin. And much like the Castle, there were no bodies. It was abandoned, not ransacked. Only that wavering sickly smell followed their passage through the rooms.

They circled around into a study and library. The stacks were packed thick toward the back. A simple row of chairs and tables was the only place one could sit and read. An afterthought, it seemed, to the crumbling immensity of the texts.

On the inside wall, lit by dusty light from vaulted windows, was a portrait of an austere woman. Years had all but faded it away, but her regal armour and a gaze that looked over imaginary horizons remained. Laying on a pillow at her side was a five-pointed crown.

"A daughter of Adathin," Marta said. "Must be Forta."

"I wonder if she ever found a way up the tower," Gaul said, turning to continue on his way.

Marta gave the portrait a few more seconds. There were places around Forta's eyes and cheeks that were evocative of her sister, Sebanna's. But Forta was harder. Carved from stone and ice. Gaul was nearly out the study door when Marta snapped back and hurried to catch up.

The stone wall of the tower dominated the interior windows as they passed. It continued to be a solid structure. There were no visible doors or easily accessible windows. Veidecke seemed to of been telling the truth, and there was no way into the Tower of Samadel.

If that was the case, where was Veidecke? They finished their circuit and ended up back in the entrance hall. No sign of their host. No sign of their weapons. No sign of any way to get to any cellar.

"Tell me I'm not the only one who has a bad feeling about this," Marta said.

"You're not." Gaul stepped out the door into the centre courtyard. Amber grass crunched under his boots. He craned his neck back to watch the tower disappear into the white landscape of the sky. Vertigo filled his head and he stumbled back.

"Are you okay?" Marta asked, putting her hand on his back.

"Yeah. But you know, once you look high enough, I think it's a tree. Trees have roots. Maybe the way in is below us?"

"In the mysterious cellar." She glanced at the door to make sure no one had snuck up on them, then leaned in. "There's another option. What if we move on? There are other Primordials. Even if we climb that tower, Marjyal's going to be waiting when we come back down."

"I thought about that too. But there's nowhere else to go. Boboros Vale, Sanguine's Cage, we have no idea where those are. And if Marjyal does, we can expect to find them everywhere we go. At least we're here first."

Marta ground her teeth, then relaxed. He had a point, unfortunately. "Forta spent her life looking for everything to do with the Cradle. That study 'round the other side wasn't in bad shape, could be some information there."

"More books." Gaul groaned.

"You're supposed to be the well-read one." She re-entered the manor and froze. "What's that?" She furrowed her brow at the open front door.

Sand was being whipped up into a frenzy by growing winds. The horizon disappeared behind a ruddy cloud. Particles were already trickling through the open windows.

Gaul rushed forward and slammed the door. "Shut the windows."

They hurried from room to room, closing whatever shutters were still intact. The sandstorm hit and the manor screamed in reply to the buffeting squalls. The manor — once silent as the dead — now a cacophony of rushing wind and creaking wood. Sand was making its way through the cracks and piling up against the walls.

When they reached the kitchen, the storm was at full force. Sharp sand flew in one window and out the other. Marta covered her face with her scarf and went for the closest of the four windows.

The wind fought back against her attempts. She closed her eyes to keep the sand from blinding her. The window slammed shut. Marta nearly crashed headfirst into the shutter. It was as if the wind reversed direction.

Easing her eyes open, she saw a scrap of fold paper stuck between the two shutter doors. She tossed down the latch and snatched the paper before it flew away.

How did that happen? Did the paper come from outside? None of that should have been possible. Gaul was across the kitchen, dealing with his own windows. He certainly didn't throw the paper or help her.

Marta backed away from the rattling window to inspect the paper. She unfolded it to find a drawing of a man. He had a kind smile and long hair. Soft features. Whoever had drawn him spent loving time on his eyes and a slight crook in his nose. It was too precise to not be a real person. But who?

Gaul finished forcing the last of the shutters closed when Veidecke sauntered in. "A sandstorm," she said. "Infuriating. At least you were here to batten down the hatches. Very good."

"Is this place going to hold up?" Marta asked. She jumped as the manor groaned an answer.

"Maybe," Veidecke said. "The sandstorms normally last for a few hours. It seems you'll be staying for at least a little while. There's plenty of rooms. Take your pick. I have more work to do."

"You don't mind us staying?" Gaul asked.

"It's not my home. I don't care. I'm a squatter here as much as you are."

"And yet only you're allowed to know where the weapons are."

"Think of it this way." She flicked a stray hair out of her face. "If I wanted to kill you, I could have killed you with my crossbow or any time while I've had you in this unfamiliar space. I have not. I have proven my lack of a desire for violence. Yours is still unknown. Meaning the weapons are safest with me. Logical." She gave a curt bow and spun on her heel.

"Hold on," Marta said, holding out the paper. "Is this yours?"

Veidecke cast a disinterested gaze over her shoulder. Her eyes widened. "Where did you get that?"

"It was blowing around in the wind. Who is it?"

Veidecke's fingers twitched, as if she barely stopped herself from snatching it out of Marta's hands. "It's my husband. It was my husband. He…" She set her jaw. "I have to go. Work." She rushed out of the kitchen.

"Odd," Gaul remarked.

"Grief can make people do odd things." Marta folded the paper gently and pocketed it.

Gaul traced her body up and down. "Are you alright? It's been a while since—"

"As you said." Marta smiled. "It's been a while. Now, books?"

"Yeah. Let's go read." The manor groaned like a sleeping bear. "Before this place falls apart."

They circled the manor to the study in the rear. It might as well have been night, the way the sandstorm blocked the sun. And in the places where the walls had crumbled there was nothing to stop the sand from filling the hallway. Still, closing the windows was a nice effort.

They entered the study to find one of the windows they had shut blown open against the raging wind. Gaul shielded his eyes and rushed to close it again. He reached for the latch, only to find a loose nail where it once was.

"Shit," he said, letting the shutters slam open. Sand billowed around the room, filling shelves and seats. "Okay. I saw some boards and nails in a cabinet while we were looking around. I'll grab them, just stay on the other half of the room, maybe."

Marta pulled her scarf over her face. "I'll manage."

Gaul left and Marta began pulling books off the shelves. They were documents of a time long forgotten. Personal accounts from kingdoms that stood and fell even before Adathin. They had stories and poetry. Who was the last person to read those books before Marta? Jovin could have spent a lifetime pouring over the stories. It felt wrong that Marta had to tear through them so fast to find a map.

The sandstorm grew in ferocity. Marta snapped a sunstone down her arm and travelled deeper into the stacks. The room was medium-sized, but the shelves were unbearably tight, turning it into a massive labyrinth. Some were knocked over or had their books pulled onto the floor.

"This is going to take forever," Marta muttered, leaning against a collapsed shelf.

"Excuse me." Veidecke stood at the entrance to the aisle. She ran her fingers along the shelf, leaving an unbroken line in the dust.

Marta pushed her back against the crooked bookcase. She was trapped with Veidecke getting closer. The light from the sunstone cast heavy shadows across her face. Marta swallowed.

"I want to apologize," Veidecke said. "I believe I was curt earlier. I've been alone for so long. Contact is unfamiliar. I never even asked your name."

"I guess not. I'm Marta, and Gaul is off grabbing some boards. He'll be right back." She made a move to leave, but Veidecke didn't notice. Or didn't care.

"Do you still have it? May I?"

Marta handed the paper over. Veidecke unfolded it with great care. A sad smile crossed her face.

"I made this drawing of Antigonus when I worried I would forget what he looked like. I threw it away in a moment I feared that I should. He was a light in the dark. Then sickness took him and never let go. He was the only one I had. It tends to make me emotional. I apologize."

"You don't need to." Marta pulled down her scarf. "My brother died recently. He raised me and was my only family, the only one I remember, at least. He was the only one I had too."

"Then you understand." Veidecke put the paper away. "What would you do to be with him again?" She sauntered forward, looming over Marta. "I followed his spirit to a massive skeleton in the mountains. Despite my efforts I couldn't pull him from the monster's ribs. He passed through the Gate Beyond."

Marta shrank away, but couldn't tear her eyes from Veidecke's. The woman eschewed personal space. Her body heat washed over Marta, and yet she felt cold to the bone.

"Life is too beautiful to be cut short. I find no trespass in tearing back our loved ones from uncaring gods." She brushed her hand against Marta's cheek. "Humanity deserves better than such loss."

"You want to raise the dead?"

"I want to return the living. Necromancy merely creates an artificial soul to animate a corpse. It's the puppeteering of a body. But to truly bring back the spirit requires something more. Tell me, Marta." She lifted Marta's chin. "Do you want your brother back?"

Marta's heart pounded against her sternum. It was crazy, but something in her wanted to believe Veidecke. To see Jovin again. So while the claustrophobia made her shake, her mouth said, "Yes."

A smile crept over Veidecke's face. She flicked her finger off Marta's chin. Across the study came a thumping sound.

"What is that?" Veidecke wondered.

"Probably Gaul fixing the window." Marta pushed past Veidecke, knocking a few books off the shelves.

Gaul finished hammering the third board into place when Marta arrived. Veidecke stayed at her heel.

"It should hold," Gaul said. He looked over the room stained earth yellow by the sand. "Though the damage may have already been done."

"May I have that hammer?" Veidecke asked, planting herself before Marta.

Gaul played his thumb along the hammer's handle. Veidecke gestured again for him to hand it over. For a moment, it seemed like Gaul was going to refuse. Until he flipped it over and slapped the handle into her hand.

"Thank you," Veidecke said. "I suppose there are all kinds of things around this place. Something to keep in mind." She scowled at them. "What are you doing in the study?"

"We were..." Marta scratched her scalp. "Have you ever heard of Boboros Vale?"

"No." She pointed into the stacks. "There are maps in the back corner. I never had use for them. But I must return to my work. Pick whatever room you'd like if you're staying. Mine's already locked." She tapped the hammer against her palm and scurried into the depths of the creaking manor.

"What work do you think it is that keeps her so busy?" Gaul asked.

"Necromancy," Marta said.

Gaul whipped his head in her direction. "What's that?"

"She wants to bring her husband back from the dead." Marta walked toward where Veidecke indicated. "She seems confident too."

Gaul followed. "That doesn't sound good."

"What if she can do it? If she can bring back her husband, she could bring back Jovin. How can that be bad?"

"I don't know."

"What about Anori? If you could have your wife back, wouldn't you take it?"

"Marta. Anori's..." He rubbed his eyes. "Look, you can't just play with the line between life and death. Something like that has to have a cost."

"Maybe I'm willing to pay it."

"Don't say that until you know what it is."

They came to a map table, complete with a rack of diamond shaped holes overflowing with rolls of parchment. Dozens — if not a hundred — maps crumpled, torn, or simply thrown about by years of disuse.

"You know," Gaul said, picking a map from the pile. "Considering how long this place has been abandoned, it could be worse."

"That's it. Keep positive." Marta unrolled a map on the table. Unmarked. Unlabeled. She groaned. "This is going to take a while."

It seems foolish of me — who has devoted so many hours to filling these journals with my knowledge — to not mention the one legend about Absence that follows it wherever it goes. When Light fades, Absence takes its place.

I am still hesitant to claim Light as fact. I've always imagined it was a form of, or exaggeration of, flux. Those who can properly weave flux seem to do similar things to those that had been done by gods using Light. Albeit on a smaller scale. There was no evidence that Light had to be its own phenomena, though a good arcanist is always open to new ideas.

Now as I sit by this door, watching Absence ooze out of it, I begin to wonder. The Cradle is supposed to be full of Light. If Absence takes its place, then what remains behind the door?

—From the Journal of Jovin Gutterwake

Chapter Twenty-Nine
Flesh Foundry

The sun set, but the storm raged on. The rattling shutters and roaring wind faded into white noise as Gaul and Marta poured over maps. Despite the din, there was serenity in the study. The glow of the sunstones was warm, easy to read by. As maps went through their fingers, time gave way to peace.

"I hate this," Marta said.

"It's never as simple as opening a book and finding the answer." Gaul put a map into a pile he had designated as 'maybe Adathin.' Forta was quite the collector of cartography.

"That's not what I mean." Marta leapt to her feet and stretched out. "Feyra's out there. Melifacto's doing something I can't comprehend. Absence is pouring out of the Cradle. But look at us now and you wouldn't even know."

"Would you rather we be constantly running from little dragons and women who can wield blood?"

"Maybe not but…" She turned her chair to face Gaul and sat with her knees to her chest. "It would be more like the stories Jovin would read to me."

"What sort of stories?" Gaul asked, setting a map aside.

"Knights. Adventurers. Romantic heroes pitted against evil." Her face glowed. "Stories where good overcomes and battles are epic."

"And they don't spend hours pouring over badly labelled maps?"

Marta laughed. "I never read that. Didn't you read a lot of books as a fancy berserker?"

"Histories, philosophies, texts that were supposed to focus our minds, not put our heads in the clouds." He tapped the map on his knee. "It wasn't fun. And we had our own adventures, though I imagine they were significantly gorier than the ones in your stories."

"I think sometimes Jovin gave me the kid version. I don't think he ever stopped seeing me as a kid." The glow left her face. She sank into her knees.

Gaul tensed his fingers around the map. All Veidecke's talk of resurrection could do was give Marta easily shattered hope. It was easy to forget how little time Marta had to grieve Jovin before they packed up and crossed the country.

Gaul unfurled his map. "Marta," he said, sitting up. "I think this could work."

Marta brought her head out of her knees and slid closer. Gaul laid out the map and slammed his finger down.

"If this land bridge here is Nature's Grave." He slid his finger around the map. "And this coastal city is Marjyal. The castle down here and this inlet is where Sebanna's Archive is. Mountains, salt flat, and the tower." He swept his hand over the landscape. "This is Adathin."

"And where's Boboros Vale?" Marta asked.

Gaul pushed his fist into the desk. "I don't know. What good is a map that's not marked?"

"Maybe people back then knew the landscape. And look." Marta ran her finger along the southern edge where two words were written. "Banshee Coast. They labelled that."

"You're not wrong." Gaul flopped back, running his fingers through his hair. They had been avoiding the obvious decision for too long. "We have to focus on finding a way into the tower. Feyra be damned. I'd rather be up there than down here when she arrives."

"If you're right and the entrance is underground, we need to find that cellar before—" Her gaze went past him. She leapt back. "Gaul!"

Gaul turned with her. Standing toward the front of the study was a woman in a flowing gown. Gaul jumped to his feet, sending his chair clattering to the ground. The woman observed them without care. Strange lavender hair sat braided over one shoulder. Her skin was dark, offsetting brilliant, icy, blue eyes that glowed in the sunstone light.

She smiled, then stepped out of view behind one of the shelves. Gaul charged forward. The woman was gone, leaving the study empty again.

"Who was that?" Marta asked, holding a sunstone like a brick ready to be hurled.

A cascading chime of plucked strings filled the air. It came from a few rooms away where a dim candlelight flickered. Gaul crept closer with Marta at his back. With each step, the light grew and the sound of the storm was replaced by the plinking of a harp.

The music room had changed. The walls returned to a clean white and the red and gold patterned curtains hung in front of a beautiful — if foggy — day. The sickly-sweet smell disappeared, replaced by a soft fragrance of flowers. An indistinct murmur of polite conversation as if heard through water filled the air, but the only person was the lavender-haired lady at the golden harp.

"I wonder," she said, her voice a cool breeze upon ethereal shores. "Do the insects skittering on roots comprehend the tree? The curse of mortality has always been to only see a part of the larger picture. Such as a little necklace that contains something that has not touched this tower in millennia."

Gaul brought his hand to his chest, where the Light vessel hung. Marta opened her mouth, but the woman continued.

"Don't concern yourself with who I am. Wonder instead about the host who makes promises of miracles. The legacy she bears. She already lies to you. She has climbed the tower. She has seen the horrors humanity inflicted upon a once great world, and she felt nothing. A tower that was a gift from a King of Earth to his Queen of Sky. Until the Conqueror Above took it for himself and turned the land as foul as he was. The Necromancer at his side."

She shifted to a lower octave. The fog from outside started to seep in through a crack in the window.

"By the time the Adherents of Tyran stormed the tower, it was already a writhing graveyard. You can still hear the screams of the people who once called this place home. A symbol of love, now a tombstone carved from the avarice of humanity."

She pulled on a string until it snapped. The discordant note faded with the ghostly chatter until they were left with only their breathing. Gaul and Marta were frozen in place, stuck attempting to comprehend what they were seeing. The woman looked them over, lingering her gaze at Gaul's chest, as if she could see the necklace under his clothes.

"You can be done," she said. "Leave the Light upon this harp and you can go. Be free from this unfair burden put upon you. Grieve who you must grieve, and be in peace."

Was it as simple as that? Gaul wondered. But the temptation never took hold. He already made his decision, and the way that Marta rolled her eyes told him that she did too.

The woman shook her head. "You are mortal after all." She drew a silk scarf from her gown. "Then see what people like you are capable of."

She released the scarf and it flew upon an absent gust, catching onto one of the wall sconces. When Gaul and Marta looked back, the woman was gone. The walls had become stained and damaged once again. The roaring of the wind, pushing sand into the music room, returned in force. Marta had to hold up the sunstone so they could see. In the far corner was the broken remains of a harp.

"I am beginning to dislike this place," Marta said.

Gaul turned to the sconce the scarf indicated, now too vanished with the lavender-haired woman. It looked like all the other brass sconces, long missing the candles that once filled them. But as Gaul grabbed it, there was a shift in its base. He twisted it and the wall next to him popped open, spilling light into the room.

The woman's voice came again, "We shall meet again upon the tower." The reverb was swallowed up by the storm outside.

Marta tossed the sunstone away and leaned past Gaul to see the secret passage. Lanterns hung upon the walls of the worked stone staircase that spiraled down into a cellar.

"I wonder if we'll find rats," Marta said with a wry smile.

Gaul ignored the joke, stepping in to lead the way down.

With every step deeper, the sweet smell came back stronger. After a few spirals the tunnel came to an iron door, with a thin beam of light on its open edge.

"Wait," Gaul said, holding Marta back. He shut his eyes to focus on the sounds. Silence.

"Where's Veidecke?" Marta asked, pulling up her scarf against the smell.

"I don't know, but let's be careful." Gaul put his shoulder against the door and pushed. Its old hinges creaked, but nothing reacted to the noise. He got it open just enough to squeeze through, letting Marta come in after him.

Two dozen stone slabs were spread out in a grid. On most were corpses — some new, some preserved to an extent. Their mouths were sewn shut, and in place of eyes were polished black stones. Gaul lifted the sleeve of one. The skin beneath was stitched together and while one side of the stitch was an ashy brown, the other side was stark white.

There was an order to it. It wasn't a funeral rite. Someone had been working on the bodies to create… something.

"What has Veidecke been doing?" Marta wondered. She lifted up leather bindings attached to the head and toe of each slab. "You don't have to tie corpses down."

Gaul ran his fingers over indents on the stone. They ran in lines from the corpses and across the floor. They seemed to be either leading or coming from a man-sized bell in the corner, next to an open wooden gate.

"It goes deeper," Gaul said. "Let's find our way into the tower. Leave Veidecke to… whatever this is."

"Hello?" said a shaking voice. It was coming from the far room. It wasn't Veidecke. Metal clanged. "Is someone out there?"

Marta jerked her head toward the room, and they crept closer. The room was a pen lined with cages. In the far corner was a bloody smear below some sort of chute from the manor above. Next to the smear was the only occupied cage, where a woman dressed in white and blue robes rattled the cell door. A cut on her head left her covered in dried blood — though likely it wasn't all hers. Her robe was torn and burnt to reveal trousers beneath.

"Thank the First," she said, breathy and tired. "You must get me out of here before she and that thing returns."

Marta stepped forward. "What thing?"

"The corpse prospector." The woman spoke with an unfamiliar accent — one that was bouncy and bright. "A monster made of stitched together men. He's working with that woman doing unholy things with the bodies that they drag down here."

Gaul inspected the lock. It was heavy, not easily broken.

"Who are you?" Marta asked. "How'd you end up here?"

"I'm Penelopa of Bahrstor. I'm a cleric. I came across the eastern ocean with a group on a very important mission. That's why you must unlock this cage. I've spent the last three days watching that woman bring people into the other room and they never return. She prefers men. I don't know what she'll do with me."

"You're in luck, Penelopa." Marta knocked against the cell bars. "I'm Marta and this strapping fellow is Gaul."

Gaul stepped back from the cage. "I don't suppose you know where the key is. We're not breaking that lock."

"The woman has a keyring," Penelopa said. "I don't know where she keeps it."

"On me." Veidecke stood at the pen door, a large bone saw in one hand. "At all times."

Gaul spun on his heel, ready to fight. But Veidecke wasn't alone. From around the corner came a monstrous creature.

He was nine feet with pallid skin and built like a rampart wall. Stitches — much like the ones that covered the corpses — lined his body. His face was covered by a steel mask that bowed his head from the weight. A broken chain hung from the back of the mask, draping over his shoulder. A motionless body hung over one brawny shoulder. A corpse prospector, if Gaul had to guess.

"I'm not angry," Veidecke said. "On the contrary, the next experiment is about to begin." She turned to the prospector. "Prepare the body."

"Forge," the creature said, thumping off with the man over his shoulder.

"You can't do this!" Penelopa cried. "I must climb the tower! Let me go!"

"Hush." Veidecke motioned for Gaul and Marta. "Come. Let me show you my work."

Gaul glanced briefly at Penelopa. She was collapsed against the cage wall, clanging her head against the bars. Gaul felt the same way.

"Let's play along," Marta said. "She's bound to slip up."

All Gaul could do was hope Marta was right. They returned to the room with the slabs to find the corpse prospector had bound the man to one. Veidecke came from another door — next to the one they first entered from — wheeling out a contraption of crystals and piping as well as a small chemistry set. The corpse prospector stepped aside so she could plug pipes into the man's body. He groaned as she stuck a needle between his ribs.

"He's still alive," Marta said.

"Yes." Veidecke laid a pad on his chest. A teal catalyst crystal sat in a clawed holder in the centre of it. "Necromancy is a flawed art. It's not the returning of life. It's the imitation of it. But I came to this tower because Samadel didn't work alone. Tales tell of the Necromancer who showed him the secrets of unlife. Unfortunately, his writings are unfinished. I'd had to fill in the gaps myself. Trial and error."

Gaul's gaze drifted over the corpses that filled the room. Each corpse was multiple bodies, making the count impossible. How many had fallen to Veidecke's work?

A flame ignited under a glass, making the clear liquid boil into a glowing green. Veidecke watched the change intently and spoke as if she had done this a hundred times. "I had to begin at the beginning. Obvious. Animating corpses is easy. I found my assistant here"—she indicated the prospector—"on one of the upper floors. He lives to forge corpses into the undead."

She turned off the flame and dropped a light blue crystal into the concoction. It puffed vapour as droplets formed on the glass. Veidecke snatched it out of its setting and splashed it onto the slab. The green liquid spread through the indents with a mind of its own, filling everything with verdant light.

"But returning a true soul is much more difficult," Veidecke explained. "Once a body is dead, it wants to stay that way. The Necromancer theorized returning a soul to a corpse is impossible. But to swap a living soul with a dead one could work."

"You're going to kill him!" Gaul stepped forward.

The corpse prospector dropped a meaty hand on Gaul's shoulder, pinning him in place.

"I'm going to save Antigonus," Veidecke said, pulling out a vial of blood. "With my blood to call him back. And if it works, Marta. I can bring back Jovin as well. We won't have to be alone."

Marta's fingers twitched at her side. Her gaze danced around the room, finding nothing to gain purchase on. Veidecke sprinkled her blood into the green fluid, causing it to flicker for a moment. She flipped a switch on her contraption, filling the room with an electric hum. The man on the slab seized. His eyes flew open and though he tried to scream, his body wasn't his anymore.

"Stop this, Veidecke!" Marta screamed.

Gaul slipped through the prospector's fingers. He could destroy the machine. Knock Veidecke out. Anything.

Veidecke waved her hand. "Assistant."

The corpse prospector bounded into action. He grabbed Gaul in one hand and Marta in the other, slamming them both against the wall and pinning them there. Gaul punched the meaty slab that held him by the chest, but it gave him nothing. Stitches unfurled and split. More natural-sized arms snaked out of the prospector's wounds and grabbed for Gaul. One pushed his head against the stonework, giving him only the barest view of Veidecke's procedure.

Electricity shot from the contraption, filling the air with snapping and whining. Green light wrapped long fingers around the man, piercing into his flesh. Finally, a scream left his lips. Gaul had never heard anything like it. It was as though the man's lungs were being pulled from his chest.

The machine let out one final thump, and the light disappeared. Veidecke whipped her head around. "No, no, no! Not again. What's wrong? Not enough power? Was the body too weak? Damn it!" She slammed her fist into the man's corpse, his face twisted into an expression of utter fear.

"Forge," the corpse prospector said.

"Shut up!" Veidecke's eyes were wild. Many strands of hair hung in front of her face. "I need more bodies. I'm close. We'll start with Gaul."

Marta cried with exertion, tearing her arm free from one of the prospector's limbs. She grabbed the lantern hanging next to her and slammed it against the corpse prospector's back. Flames burst along his rotten skin. He dropped Gaul and Marta, patting at the fire devoid of all urgency.

Gaul hit the ground running. He barrelled his shoulder into Veidecke's stomach, lifting her off her feet and bringing both of them to the ground.

"Assistant!" Veidecke cried.

The flaming prospector yanked Gaul off his master, sending him sailing across the room. Marta raced over to make sure he hadn't cracked his skull open.

"Ring the bell!" Veidecke struggled to her feet, clutching her ribs.

The prospector lumbered across the room, uncaring to the flames that continued to cook his skin and snap his stitches. He took the mallet from next to the massive bell and struck. The bell rang dull, but with a booming pulse that shook their bones.

He struck again. The corpses on the slabs stirred.

He struck again. The corpses on the slabs groaned.

He struck a final time. The corpses rose.

"I'm sorry, Marta," Veidecke said. "But maybe I can bring you back too." She dashed for the iron door.

Marta took chase, only to be stopped by a risen lunging for her. Gaul grabbed her wrist and dragged her back from the growing horde. Veidecke disappeared with the slamming of the door and the turning of the latch.

Risen lumbered toward Gaul and Marta. Slow, but unstopping. One reached out, only for the stitching on his arm to give way and fall to the ground. The arm laid motionless, but the risen stepped by without a care. The corpse prospector stood at their back, a burning juggernaut. The risen pushed their way forward, forcing Gaul and Marta back into the pens where Penelopa was pressing against the bars of her cage.

"What's going on?" Her eye's widened. "They're back."

The pen was a dead end. The risen pushed their way through the door and the smoke from the corpse prospector was already choking the air. Even if Gaul Ignited, going against a horde of undead unarmed was a losing battle. Maybe if Marta could do it too. Still unlikely. At least they could go down fighting.

Marta snapped her finger's in Gaul's face. "Hey! Look!" She pointed at the chute for dropping. It was at least eight feet off the ground, but it was a way out.

"Alright," Gaul said. "Let's go."

"What about me?" Penelopa rattled her cage door. "You can't leave me here!"

"Don't worry." Gaul knelt by the cage and jingled a keyring. The results of a well-timed pilfering after tackling Veidecke. "We're all getting out of here. Hope you can climb."

Penelopa's face lit up. "Like my life depends on it."

Gaul swung the cage door open and Penelopa scrambled to freedom. She rushed to the corner where Marta was bracing herself for a lift.

"Step into my hands," Marta said. "And be ready to push against the walls."

Penelopa nodded. She glanced back at the encroaching risen. Her gaze fell upon a long-haired man, shambling with his jaw busted open.

"Oh, Harrod," she said, more sad than scared.

"Penelopa! Now!" Gaul kicked a risen back, sending the whole group tumbling — only to be stepped on by the ones behind.

Penelopa tore herself away from the grizzly sight. She planted to her foot in Marta's palms and leapt into the chute. Metal rattled and shook as she shimmied her way up.

"Now you," Gaul said, pushing Marta aside.

"Wh—"

"I'm taller! Go!"

Marta huffed, but took the leap into the chute. She pushed her boots into either side of the slide, holding herself on small indents in the metal and reached down. "Now jump!"

The corpse prospector — seeing its quarry escape — picked up speed. Risen were flung aside by his imposing gait. Gaul braced against the wall.

"Gaul!" Marta cried. "Now!"

The prospector lunged with a grasping strike. Gaul unfurled, landing on the prospector's hand then leaping again. The chute rattled as Gaul stopped face to face with Marta.

"That was unnecessary," Marta said.

"We're not done yet." Gaul looked past his feet to where the corpse prospector peered up the chute. Yellow eyes flickered in the slits on his mask.

Tiny Marta clambered up the tube. Gaul had to push himself against the walls, with less room to work in, and slide himself best he could. Metal groaned like a weary animal as the prospector shoved his arm into the chute. Gaul kicked at the fingers, lifting himself higher. Stitches split and the smaller arms continued the prospectors reach.

Gaul couldn't look down anymore. He focused on the climb. Hand then foot. Arm then knee. He shoved himself up the chute until the air broke and he came tumbling out of a hatch to join Marta and Penelopa on the floor of a small room.

The three of them laid there, breathing in stale air. Far below were walking corpses slamming uselessly against stone walls.

"Hey," Marta said. "Look at that."

Gaul flopped his head to the side. Propped up in the corner were their weapons, as well as one taken from similarly unfortunate adventurers.

"Oh!" Marta turned over and picked up a throwing knife from a pile. "I've been looking for these."

Gaul rolled onto his feet, though part of him wanted to stay on the floor. He snatched his swords and half-fell onto the door handle.

The door swung out from where it blended into the wall. They were back in the entrance hall. The sandstorm had died down, letting the moonlight sneak through the shutters.

"How many more secrets do you think Veidecke knows about this place?" Gaul asked.

Marta went to her knees and crouched over Penelopa. "Are you okay?"

"For a moment, I believed I would never be out of that cage," Penelopa said, sitting up. "The First still watch over me it seems."

"The First?" Marta asked.

"The First Gods. They watch over us from their place in the Cradle of the World."

"Oh." Marta locked eyes with Gaul.

Something clattered from elsewhere in the manor. Gaul flicked his swords, letting the sheaths drop to the ground. "We're not done yet," he said, stomping toward the noise.

Marta scrambled for her gear and chased after him. Penelopa moved slower, but still followed.

Gaul took wide steps through the manor halls. Red flickered in the corners of his vision. He blurred past rooms.

"Calm down," Marta said, tightening her sheath around her waist.

"Don't I look calm?" He glanced at her. Shoots of red went in and out of his irises. "That woman killed how many people for her selfish wants?"

"She was trying to get her husband back."

"So? You can grieve without becoming a monster. She didn't want him back for him, she wanted him back for herself. As I said. Selfish."

They entered the living quarters as Veidecke came stumbling out of her room, two bulging bags thrown over her shoulders. She turned to see Gaul stomping toward her, both blades bare, and threw her hands forward.

"Wait!" she exclaimed, her bags dropping with heavy thumps.

Gaul spun his swords. "Let me think about it."

"You want to climb the tower, right?"

Gaul slowed. Marta and Penelopa joined him at his side. Veidecke's gaze flicked between the three of them. Her stern demeanour was long gone, replaced with panic.

"There's another way up," Veidecke said. "In an outbuilding in the back gardens you can lift up the floor. It's how I let the corpse prospector out. It'll bring you around the foundry to a lift up the tower. That's all you wanted."

"What? And let you continue your work?" Gaul asked.

"I'm just trying to get my husband back." She reached out to Marta with sad eyes. "You understand. You understand the pain of this grief."

Penelopa pushed past Marta. "My people came here injured and in need of help! You locked us in that basement and killed them! Damn your grief!"

"Everyone is in this world for themselves," Veidecke said. "I am not evil for knowing this."

"You're not going to hurt anyone else." Gaul stepped forward.

"Just…" Veidecke pulled a piece of paper out of her pocket and bowed her head. "This are the Necromancer's notes, with my additions. Maybe someone can find a way to bypass the sacrifice. Maybe my work can help people."

Gaul glanced over his shoulder at Marta. She had been quiet in the confrontation. Maybe there was a part of her that still felt for Veidecke. If not for the actions, but for the motives. Marta reached for the paper.

A smile crossed Veidecke's downturned face.

"Marta!" Gaul pulled her back.

Veidecke revealed her other hand, clutching a small catalyst crystal. She flicked it into the centre of the paper. Runes popped along the surface. Reality seemed to fold around the rapidly shifting page. With a crack, the distortions became an ice wall that swelled with force to shatter the wooden ones around.

"Damn it!" Gaul exclaimed, hammering his sword pommel against the icy barrier. Snow chipped off, but no progress could be made. It was too hard.

A shadow moved on the other side. Veidecke's laughed echoed before she vanished.

"We can circle the building," Gaul said. "She can't of gone far."

"She's gone," Marta said, putting her hand on his chest to hold him in place.

"Marta, like it or not, she's evil."

"Marta's right," Penelopa said. "But justice will always catch up to those deserving of it. And I still have my duty." She spun about, her ragged robes flaring. "Thank you for your assistance. But you should be on your way. I must find that outbuilding she spoke of."

"We're going for the tower too, Penelopa," Marta said.

Penelopa stopped. She bowed her head. "You should think better of that. The Gifted Tower isn't for the faint of heart."

"The Gifted Tower?"

"I refuse to call it by Samadel's name. He does not own it. He never did." She took a deep breath. "Please don't follow me. I have a very important mission."

"So do we," Gaul said. "You're not getting rid of us."

Penelopa glanced over her shoulder, taking in Gaul and Marta for the first time. She opened her mouth, but closed it without saying anything. It didn't matter the argument, Gaul and Marta didn't have anywhere else to go. Penelopa walked away — not quite fleeing, not minding if she left them behind.

"She doesn't seem grateful that we freed her," Marta said. "Now suddenly we're unwelcome."

"You heard her," Gaul said. "She's on a 'very important mission.'"

Marta followed Penelopa with Gaul. "So are we. I doubt she's on a mission to save the world."

"Who knows?" Gaul rested his swords on his shoulders. "Maybe she is."

Not much is known about Samadel before he arrived in what would someday be called Adathin. He came across the sea to the east with a small contingent of soldiers. As he moved across the land, his charismatic nature got him many supporters. He was a man who had a simple, but grand, wish. He wanted to build the greatest empire the world had ever seen.

He found the Gifted Tower and built himself a throne in the highest room. He had windows so he could see in all directions — see the lands he was intending to conquer. After he claimed his tower, he started to work on claiming the nearby kingdoms. At its peak, his kingdom stretched far past the peninsula that Adathin would someday rule.

Samadel was not an idiot brute. He found a mine where he could gather crystals and rare ores. He would bring royals up his tower and make alliances to grow his land. Samadel was an innovator, and I have found writings that talk about him making moving armours to guard his doors.

These armours became his sole protection after his mind failed and the Necromancer found him.

—From the Journal of Jovin Gutterwake

Chapter Thirty
Tower of Samadel

The trapdoor in the outbuilding was easy to find, knowing it was there. Pulling the barn doors aside let the moonlight cast off the floor, revealing gaps in the floorboards that were too clean to be natural. Gaul and Penelopa slid their hands between the wood and lifted the floor to a ramp below.

"I can see some light," Marta said, crouching at the top of the ramp. "This is supposed to bring us around that room with the bell, and the slabs, and the risen dead, right?"

"That's what the woman said." Penelopa stepped to Marta's side.

"Then let's be quick," Gaul said. "But careful. Find that lift and get into the tower."

Penelopa took off at a rushed walk. Marta uncoiled from her crouch, springing after her. None of them wanted the other there, but wasn't easy to leave someone behind. It was better to be close than be abandoned. Gaul shut the trap door behind them, sending sand tumbling with the thump.

The shadowy tunnel brought them to a large room dimly lit by crystal lanterns that hung from the stone ceiling. They were on the upper floor that was ringed with a wooden railing. Marta stepped to the edge of the balcony, overlooking a work floor crowded with large iron machinery. Long cold forges lined the walls. Dust sat where flames and sweat once did. Whatever was built there was large and intricate. Was it Forta's? Or Samadel's?

"What do you think they made here?" Marta wondered out loud. She touched the railing only for it to topple over and clatter below.

"We're done touching things," Gaul said, pulling Marta away before she could make any more noise.

Penelopa was already on the move. She paid no attention to the strange technology below — her gaze was locked on the other side of the foundry. There was a staircase up to a room where four chains hooked onto the floor and stretched up and out of view.

"Penelopa," Marta said, practically jogging to keep up with the cleric's wide steps. "What is your very important mission?"

"It's personal," Penelopa said.

"It has to be, since you came right back down here after all you've been through." Gaul used his long legs to be the first up the steps into the lift.

Penelopa scowled at his speed. She brushed by him toward a lever sticking out of the wall.

"You also didn't seem upset by the risen," Marta said. "I've never seen something like them before."

Penelopa grabbed the level and stopped. "Last chance. You don't know what's up there."

"Do you?" Gaul asked.

There was a pause so heavy it could have flattened the tower. Penelopa tapped her fingers along the lever. She hadn't taken any time to wipe the blood off her, leaving a scowl accenting crimson mask. "Let's see if whatever's powering this thing is still working," she said, and flipped the lever.

Metal rattled as the heavy chain links went taut. Crystals appeared on the walls, dotting lights up into the darkness above. With a tremor, the lift rose. Marta breathed a sigh of relief. With their luck, she wouldn't have been surprised if the lift had been broken.

"Penelopa," Gaul said, stepping in with his hand to his chest. "We can help you. Marta and I are trying to get to Ziz. She's supposed to be imprisoned at the top of this tower."

"The Primordial?" Penelopa asked. "Legend says she was sealed away in the Windscar Manse, upon the Floating Records. Pieces of Meza that were chained to the tower."

"See?" Marta crossed her arms and grinned. "You're already helping us. Let us help you."

"I have to do this alone. I..." Penelopa clasped her hands together. She rubbed her fingers along the red that stained her ivory skin. "I am descended from heroes. The Adherents of Tyran. They were the ones who stormed the Gifted Tower to stop Samadel and the Necromancer's vile deeds. Twenty knights entered this place and did not lose a single one." She grew bolder with each word. "But though the Necromancer was gone, he left a death curse with Samadel. These Adherents, who saved the land from a madman's undead plague, were infected with a malignant destiny. Them and everyone who share their blood are cursed to die and rise again as revenants dedicated to the destruction of their loved ones."

It seemed so strange, Marta thought it must have been a lie. But Penelopa's impassioned words cut right to the heart. A generational undead curse. It wouldn't be the weirdest thing she'd seen lately.

"You're right," Penelopa said, turning to Marta. "I was not shocked by the appearance of the risen. It wasn't the first time I've seen the dead walk again. My father, my cousins, my family would all die, only to rise and have to be killed again."

"You found a way to break the curse," Gaul said, coming out of his stupor. "That's why you're here. It's the only reason why you would do all this."

Penelopa nodded and dug through her torn robes. Out from a well-hidden pocket, she drew a dagger with a silver hilt. She pulled it from its sheath. The blade was a void in space. Blacker than black. The antithesis of reality. Absence. Marta's blood ran cold.

"An Oblivion Dagger," she said. "Forged from Nothing. Plunging this into the corpse's heart would shatter him from existence, taking his curse with him. It is the last hope of my line." She sheathed the dagger. "I am the last hope of my line. We aren't quite the Adherents of old. They left with twenty and returned with twenty. We left with twenty and now it's me, the twenty-first. The one who wasn't supposed to be here."

Her shoulders shook. She put the dagger back into her robes, hiding her face to disguise the tremble in her lip. Gaul turned away, while Marta lowered her gaze. Better to pretend they never saw that break.

"We were nearly here when we were attacked by a masked man in white." She squeezed her fist until all signs of sorrow were replaced with anger. "I could have killed him. I know I could have but Harrod…" Her eyes widened. She had said too much. "I'm reaching the top of this tower, no matter what."

"I believe you will," Gaul said.

Goodsmile, Marta thought. *What other freak in a mask could it be?*

The lift came to a stop at a double door. "This can't be the top of the tower," Penelopa said, throwing the doors open.

The doors thumped against the walls and brilliant light filled the room before them. Crystal chandeliers hung in rows from the ceiling, leaving no shadows across the elegant entrance hall. The floor was scuffed marble around a four-tiered fountain. There was a beauty to the room, soured by the presence of spiked barricades and rusted weapons.

"This is it," Penelopa said. "This is where the Adherents attacked."

Marta picked up a sword. "Where are the bodies, though?"

Gaul cleared his throat. He pointed down, back to the flesh foundry.

"Oh." Marta tapped the blade on the fountain and it snapped in two. "Hey, more knives!" She scooped a few old daggers to refill her coat before joining Gaul and Penelopa in pushing through the breaks in the barricade.

"We still have a lot of the tower ahead of us," Gaul said. "We might have to think about taking the night."

"It's not safe in the tower," Penelopa said, stalking toward the grand staircase.

"Not that it is anywhere," Gaul said.

Marta took a wide circle around the hall. There had to be a quicker way up. It was a tower of gods after all; they didn't take stairs. She came to a curtain that covered part of the wall next to the stairs and yanked it aside. Behind it was a small room with a moveable grate.

"Hey, wait," Marta called. "I think I found another lift. Not to ruin your stride or anything."

Penelopa stopped with one foot on the stairs. She let out a sigh then spun on her heel. Gaul, however, had his head cocked, his ear pointed toward the ceiling.

"Gaul." Marta stepped toward him. "There's no horses in the lift."

"Do you hear that?" Gaul asked, holding up a finger.

Something thumped against the floor above them. Heavy footfalls that moved in circles, joined by the clanging of metal. As the trio listened, the noise paused, then resumed heading toward where the stairs joined with the floor above.

"There's someone up there," Marta said. "Some person wearing armour I think."

"There's no people in this place," Penelopa said.

"That's even more of a reason to take the lift." Gaul tapped his palms on his sword hilts. "I don't want to fight anything we don't have to."

Penelopa pulled the grate open. "We could stay to see what it is. Might give us an idea of what situation we're walking into."

Now she wants to be part of the team, Marta thought.

Gaul looked back at the stairs. The metal footsteps were coming clearer. "I don't know if seeing it would help us — oof!"

Penelopa buried her shoulder into Gaul's stomach. He stumbled back, more out of shock than the impact. Penelopa skipped backwards into the lift. The grate slammed shut before Marta could even react.

"What are you doing?" Gaul shouted. He grabbed the grate, but Penelopa twisted the latch. All he could do was rattle the steel.

"I'm sorry." Penelopa rested two swords on her shoulders.

Gaul's eyes widened. His hands flew to his now empty sheaths.

"Please leave," Penelopa said. "You have no idea what you're getting yourself into. Primordials are not to be trifled with. This tower is not to be trifled with. Leave before you get yourself hurt. Go home."

"Penelopa!" Marta kicked the grate. "We can't leave!"

Penelopa shut her eyes. "Only you can." She lifted the lever and rose out of sight.

"Shit!" Gaul tapped his thumbs on the empty holes in his sheaths. "Why did she have to take both?"

"And there it is." The lavender-haired woman sat upon the fountain lip, running her fingers over crystal clear water that trickled from the top. "Even when trying to do the right thing, mortals are selfish. Yet we're supposed to believe gods left the world to them."

Marta rubbed her eyes. Everywhere they went were more people talking down to them. If that woman even was a person. As Penelopa said, there were no people in the tower.

"You're correct," the lavender-haired woman said. "There is no life in this tower. Though it was once full of such beauties."

Did I say that out loud? Marta wondered. *How can she know what I'm—*

"The human mind is not so impenetrable." The woman flickered out of existence and reappeared in a lounging chair. She softly swirled a glass of red wine. "And no, Gaul, I'm not a devil nor a spirit. I am the Descendant of Dimiya. This tower is my inheritance, and that Light you carry around your neck is my birthright. I'll give you one last chance to put it where it belongs."

"With you?" Marta asked. "You want to return the First Gods?"

"There is so much more Light can do than close a little door. And to our parents, my brothers and sister and I are failures. That's why we are Descendants, rather than children. Why would I wish for them to return?"

"Then why do you want the Light?"

"Because I can do so much more with it. I can seal the Cradle, getting Light from the Primordials is nothing for me. I even know where Boboros Vale is." With another flicker, the Descendant was on them. She was taller than before, and the room darker. "Give me the vessel and I can save this world."

"It won't happen," Gaul said. "We made a promise to see this through, no matter how difficult."

"A *promise*? To a sad mortal in a cave? This is all her fault, you know. Her and her mortal greed has brought ruin upon everything. Don't let your pride do the same."

It took everything in Marta not to back down. The Descendant loomed over them like the tower did the landscape. Each word was a spike driving into her chest. Still, she took a deep breath and set her stance.

"The vessel's going to stay exactly where it is," Marta said.

The Descendant inhaled like she was about to start yelling again, until her lips began to quake. She looked aside, but Marta swore she saw tears welling up in her eyes.

"So be it," she said. "Then I will take it from your corpses."

The Descendent vanished. In her place was a six-and-a-half-foot tall figure in rusted armour. Wicked spikes jutted from its joints and the person inside had to be emaciated to fit within its tiny frame. It gazed over them with dead eyes hidden behind its thin visor.

"Give me your sword," Gaul said, never taking his eyes off the strange foe.

"It's not my fault yours got snatched." She drew her blade and pointed it at the armour.

The armour approached with jerking, staccato movements. It stumbled for a moment then caught itself.

"You're going to leave me defenseless?" Gaul asked.

Marta kicked him an old dagger on the ground.

"Sure." He picked it up. "Though I always figured you were better with—"

"Move!" Marta shouted.

The armour exploded with motion. It stomped in a bizarre, dead-armed gait until it was upon them and whirled about. Gaul and Marta split up. The armour crashed into the lift grate, bending the steel under its body before bouncing off like a drunkard.

Gaul ducked under a wild swing. He rose spinning, sticking his dagger into the armour's eye slit. The armour recoiled. The dagger remained in its eye as fell to all fours, digging chunks out of the marble as it turned its crazed assault upon Marta.

Like a wild animal, the armour scuttled across the floor. It wanted to move faster than its body could possibly take it. And so it tumbled and rolled, leaving gouges in its wake. Marta rushed to meet it. She planted a foot on it's back and flipped to Gaul's side.

"How does a human fight like that?" Marta asked, as the armour crashed through a barricade, sending wood scattering across the room.

"I'm not sure it is human," Gaul said.

The armour flailed to its feet, sending a chunk of wood flying and taking the top off the fountain. It rushed forward.

"There's always someway to kill it!" Marta thrust forward, plunging her sword into the armour's leather midsection. The blade went clean through. Bloodless. The soldier twisted and the sword was torn out of her grip.

Gaul pulled Marta back before the armour could take her head off. He slammed his fist down upon the dagger still in its eye. There was a metallic *ting* as the facemask popped off. Beneath was a mass of spinning gears and springs. Within the mechanical skull was the dull teal glow of a catalyst crystal.

"And that's the way to kill it," Gaul said.

The armour flailed forward. Gaul and Marta dove aside. "Behind all those gears," Marta said. "How do we get to it?"

"Break it till it slows."

"I love how easy you make everything sound." Marta spun out two daggers and rolled under a swing. "Might want to do that thing you do."

Gaul rushed in after her. His eyes turned red and he drove his fist into the armour's chest plate. Bones cracked as metal crumpled. Blue light pulsed under Gaul's skin. He unloaded a flurry against the steel wall.

There was no getting used to seeing Gaul Ignited. It wasn't the perpetual healing or the red eyes. It was the strange calm while he unleashed violence. How while his bones shattered, he never blinked. He said he wasn't invincible, but that seemed hard to believe. It put shivers down Marta's spine. But still she wished she could do it too.

Gaul grabbed the armour's neck and reached for the crystal. His fingers slipped between the gears, jagged teeth slicing his skin and releasing lightning. The armour threw itself back. Marble cracked beneath it. It skittered away using its elbow spikes until it could roll onto its feet.

"Did it do that on purpose?" Marta asked. "It knows to protect the crystal. Guess there's some intelligence in it."

"Just break it," Gaul growled.

The armour threw itself toward Marta. She ducked aside and plunged her dagger into the soft leather in the back of the armour's leg. The dagger vibrated and there was a grinding sound. It dropped to one knee, in time for Gaul to drive a kick into its crumpled chest.

The armour folded with the blow and wrapped its arms around Gaul's leg. Marta stumbled back, barely avoiding Gaul being swung about and tossed like a ragdoll.

"Let's just run!" Marta called. "This thing is slow!"

Gaul staggered to his feet. His eyes were locked with the armour, red still dominating his irises. The armour hobbled in a circle. Its leg vibrated and seized but couldn't bend.

"Come back to me, Gaul." Marta dodged a wild swing. "This isn't worth it."

With a huff, Gaul's eyes returned to normal. "You raise an infuriating point." He burst into motion, sliding under the armour's arm and snatching the sword from its midsection.

"Can I have my sword back?" Marta asked, turning with Gaul for the stairs.

"Not my fault yours got snatched," Gaul said with a smile.

A bell rang. They froze. The armour had its arms spread apart as if to embrace them. The bell had rung from within its chest.

"Don't let it ring four times!" Marta charged forth, two daggers bare.

Second ring. Gaul stayed on Marta's heel. The armour clutched its hands over its head to slam them, allowing Marta to plunge both daggers into its armpits. Its arms vibrated and dropped to its side. Third ring.

"Don't move!" Gaul cried.

Marta obeyed. Gaul thrust the sword over her head. The thin blade slipped between the gears. With a twist, the crystal popped from its setting. The armour crashed to its knees.

"That was close," Marta puffed.

Fourth ring. Marta's heart dropped. Groans and footsteps echoed from the stairs.

"And now we climb faster," Gaul said.

Marta pulled her knives from the armour. The way the tower rumbled above her, she would need every single one.

Marta and Gaul flew through floors. There was no time to absorb their surroundings. The end of one staircase was the search for another. Between that were halls of risen. The walking dead, while armed with nothing but flesh and bone, overwhelmed in number and were impossible to kill. Even decapitated and dismembered, each part moved with the same bloodlust as the whole.

All Marta could do was put her head down and follow Gaul's waving coat.

Time slipped away and still the tower continued. It had to be long past midnight. "How much further can this go on?" Marta asked.

A risen lunged out of a nearby room. Gaul removed its arm at the elbow. "All the way up," he said.

Marta stuck her dagger into the risen's eye and shoved it back. It reached out, scratching her just above the eyebrow. Marta slammed the door in its face.

"How are there so many of these things?" She touched her eyebrow. No blood. She was slowing.

"Haven't you noticed?" Even Gaul was talking through deep breaths. "This is the living quarters. There are beds. And kitchens."

"People lived here."

"People died here."

A tower full of people turned into risen. Floors of corpses who once called it home. The actions of Samadel and his Necromancer? Maybe he felt safer surrounded by the dead. Someone like Samadel deserved to have his tower stormed.

"Hey Gaul," Marta said. "That dagger Penelopa had. Was that thing made of Absence?"

"Seemed like it," Gaul said.

"It's not just coming from the Cradle. Are we… are we fighting against the natural order?"

"Getting eaten by a wolf is the natural order." Gaul slammed his cross-guard into a risen's cheek and pulled it to the floor. "I see no problem fighting against it."

"Yeah. I guess." Marta leapt over the corpse. "It was strange to see it like that."

"As a weapon? It must be rare. Considering how precious she was with it." He glowered. "And she took my swords rather than use it."

They climbed the next set of stairs. Gaul pulled the double doors at the top shut and slammed the crossbar down. Marta twirled, with her arms spread to the bookshelves that lined the walls.

"Hey!" she exclaimed. "Books!" Her laugh turned to a sigh. "It's always books. That's what Marjyal is missing. They hate books."

"Doesn't surprise me," Gaul said, catching his breath.

"Do you wanna sleep here? I'm exhausted. I can't even think of another staircase."

"It's been a long day, but I'd rather put more distance between us and—" He pointed at the door. "—that."

Marta swayed on her feet. She could do one more floor. Gaul stepped past, patting her on the shoulder. Like she'd let him show her up.

"Marta." The voice came and went like a breeze. It was Jovin. But it wasn't. It only sounded like him. The Descendant had played with their senses before. She couldn't trick Marta.

"Don't fall behind," Gaul said, waiting in the next antechamber. "Even without the risen, this place isn't safe."

A gate slammed down between them. Marta froze. Gaul dropped his sword and grabbed the bars with both hands. He gritted his teeth. Even with all this strength, the gate wouldn't budge.

"Hang on." He glanced around the room. "I'll find something to get you out."

"Your persistence is disappointing," the Descendant said, her voice coming from all directions. "And you care for each other. That is the one human trait I find admirable. I take no pleasure in exploiting it. But to save this world…"

The bookshelves rattled. Marta spun around. Something behind the shelves was trying to get out. The door they came through similarly shook on its crossbar. Marta clenched her fists. There was no way out.

"Gaul," the Descendant continued. "Give me the vessel, or you must watch your friend die."

"Don't do it!" Marta cried.

Gaul grabbed the sword and poked the hilt through the bars. "Take it. You can get out of this, but you'll have to Ignite."

"I can do that." Even Marta didn't believe those words. She did it once out of instinct and fear of death. But to call it on cue? She took the sword. She certainly felt the fear.

"This usually takes years. So forgive me if it's a little rushed."

The shelves bowed and flexed, sending books to the ground. The groans of the risen filled the room.

"Let's just get to it." Marta grabbed the gate.

"You need to start with anger. For most, that's the easy part. I feel it won't be any different with you. But that'll only bring you so far. Rage is only the kindling. Now feel that fire in your stomach turn into an inferno."

Marta squeezed the gate until her hand went numb. So many things in her life made her angry. That anger had boiled beneath the surface for years. She felt it grow in her stomach into an unbearable heat that infected her bones. Hands burst through the shelves, and that heat flickered.

"Focus!" Gaul slammed his fist, rattling the gate. "It'll reach a point where you feel like you can't take it anymore. Now, remember the string. Make the fire real and pull it tight. Feel it want to burn out of control but you can't let it. You have to snap that string by losing all your rage at once. Use an image that bring you calm, like the sea. You bring it in like striking a match, or cutting the string, whatever imagery works for you to suddenly clear your mind and feel nothing. Rage and serenity in balance."

Over and over she tensed and released, but nothing was happening. "Is it this hard when you do it?"

"You do it enough, it's harder not too. But you're going to have to consciously think about it. Maybe... uh, try the opposite. Start from that peaceful image, then pull the string tight, then clear your mind. The important thing is control of your emotions. You have to feel two things at once and nothing else."

"Does that work?"

"I've never taught this before! I only have my own technique."

Another shelf splintered. Marta jumped. How was she supposed to clear her mind with those things so close behind?

"You need to focus," Gaul said. "Even if you can get the emotional element, if you can't clear your mind you'll never Ignite the flames. Then you will die."

"Thanks for the pep talk."

"Last time you did this you had an arrow through your chest! Now be terrified or pissed off or whatever it takes as long as you survive!"

Marta bashed her head against the gate. She could do it. She had the anger. She could taste sea air on her tongue. Why couldn't she take the last step? Shoots of red entered her eyes, but they soon faded. A bookshelf crashed behind her, risen pouring out into the room.

"Come on!" Gaul cried.

"Fine," a woman's voice said. It wasn't the Descendant. It wasn't anyone Marta had heard before. Yet it came from the centre of her mind. "I'll do it myself. Again."

Everything went dark.

The necromancer came from the north with nothing but a bag of reagents on his back. He promised Samadel an immortal army — one that would never falter or run from battle. The Conqueror Above was greedy and furious at the losses he had sustained as of late. He set the necromancer to work.

There are indications that before this moment, Samadel's kingdom was prosperous. The poor lived in his tower, well-fed and well-guarded. They made great contributions to art and technology. All this changed when the necromancer began his vile work.

Necromancy poisons the land. The world itself rejects its presence — but the results were staggering. Samadel's kingdom doubled in size. His corpse prospectors would scour the battlefield for candidates for reanimation. And below his tower was a locked room that no one but the necromancer was allowed to enter.

When the Adherents of Tyran stormed the tower, they found it choked with the walking dead. As the frontlines of war stretched further away, Samadel needed more guards to protect him at home. So it came to be that the poor who once lived there roamed the halls as something else.

The necromancer, however, was nowhere to be seen.

—From the Journal of Jovin Gutterwake

Chapter Thirty-One
Different You

Gaul watched as Marta's gaze went distant, then refocused. It was sharper than before. A smile crept over her lips.

"She can't do it," Marta said, resting the sword on her shoulder. "Her mind's a mess. You don't even want to know what's going on up here."

It's her, Gaul thought. *The Marta from Dothrin. But she's not Marta.*

"But I was listening." Marta — or whoever she was — shut her eyes. When she opened them, they were a deep crimson.

The remaining shelves tumbled, scattering books across the floor. Risen stumbled out from alcoves hidden behind the shelves. They struggled over the broken wood and books.

Marta gave Gaul a wink, then pushed off the gate. With both hands, she slammed the sword down on the first risen's crown. Its rotten body split in two. The halves fell to either side and Marta charged through the middle.

Some of the risen held onto rusted or broken swords. They gave wide, uncontrolled swings. Marta didn't even try to dodge. She took a cut on the upper chest. Lightning poured out of the wound and she cackled wildly as her skin knitted.

She caught the next blow with her arm and took off the top of the risen's head. She had lost the grace and balance she normally fought with. Instead she was a beast — reckless and violent. She fought like Gaul.

The risen wasn't slowed by losing the top half of its skull. It swung its rusted weapon in Marta's direction, now blind. Marta skewered it through the stomach and charged forward with it as a shield, bashing other risen aside.

Gaul couldn't stand around watching whoever was controlling Marta destroy her body. There was a limit to the healing Igniting granted. The longer one used it, the stronger they became, but Marta was still fresh. He needed to get through the gate.

The path to the floor above was blocked by a collapsed ceiling. Odds and ends had been shoved into the corner. Some chains and small tools for working leather and wood — nothing that could take down a gate of that weight. Pulling aside a large cloth revealed a small, but sturdy, anvil. Gaul stepped back. There was a window opposite the gate — a black sky beyond. A plan came together.

He rushed to the anvil. Igniting for some extra strength, Gaul lifted it with great effort. He gritted his teeth and hobbled the anvil to the window lip. Marta let out a scream that turned into a crazed laugh. At least she was still fighting. Gaul snatched a length of chain from the pile, tying one end to the anvil and the other to the gate. The chain seemed strong. Strong enough. Maybe.

A risen slammed into the gate — missing half of their right arm and their entire left. Marta stood in the middle of the room, one leg on a collapsed table. Lightning poured out of the numerous wounds on her body. She let out a holler, then reengaged the risen. She was doing well, considering.

Gaul put his back against the gate. He let out two breaths and charged the anvil. It held against it shoulder before scraping free. It dropped out of the tower into the darkness outside. The chain snapped tight. The gate groaned. Metal exploded out of the stone arch as the entire gate was torn free. Gaul stepped aside. The gate shot past him and slammed against the window. There was creaking, followed by the entire wall vanishing into the night.

Unexpected, Gaul thought. He shrugged and rushed to find Marta.

The risen were in pieces. Marta tossed an arm onto the writhing pile of remains. She grabbed a lantern from the wall and frowned. "Crystals?" she growled. "Where's fire when you need it?" Her gaze flicked to Gaul. Red still dominated her wild eyes, but when she looked at him they flickered gold and ivory. A wound on her cheek closed with a spark. "Don't suppose you have any flames on you, golden man?"

Gaul tensed his jaw. He grabbed an oil lantern from the pile in the antechamber and tossed it to Marta. She lit the wick and with a cackling cry, smashed it into the risen pile.

"Who are you?" Gaul asked.

"Is this how it always feels?" Marta shook her hands and bounced on her toes. "It's exhilarating. Why would you ever stop?"

"Who—" He snapped a wood beam under his foot. "—are you?"

"It's me." She curled her fingers and grinned like a lunatic. "It's Marta."

"No. It's not."

"Close enough." Her eyes turned brown and her knees faltered.

Gaul snatched her arm before she could fall into the bonfire. He hoisted her over his shoulder and laid her gently upon the collapsed table. Her eyes fluttered open. The real Marta was back.

"I really am useless," she said, propping herself higher on the table. "You saved me once again."

Gaul rested his head on his heads. In Dothrin, not telling her what she did seemed like the right choice. Sometimes he convinced himself nothing happened. But he talked with that other Marta. She deserved to know.

"I didn't do this," Gaul said, glancing back at the raging flames. "You did."

"I did it?" Her face lit up. "I berserked?"

Gaul rubbed his forehead. "That's not it."

"I know it's not called that, but—"

"No. It's..." He flopped back, resting against the other half of the table. "Remember in the Dothric ruins? The homunculus and the praetor?"

"I got knocked out and you cleaned up the mess."

"That's not quite what happened." Gaul coughed from the smell of burning bodies. He could still turn back. "You weren't knocked out by Harken. I don't fully know what happened, but in the end, it was just you and him. You had this weird look in your eyes. It was like you were a different person. You said something to me."

Marta was looking at her feet, her face emotionless. Gaul couldn't imagine what she was thinking. "What did I say?" she asked.

"See you later."

Marta snorted. "Ominous."

"And that's what just happened again. That other you took control. She was able to Ignite and... this."

Marta tapped her foot on a book. She pushed herself to standing and approached the fire. It had blackened the stone, but remained concentrated on the pile of corpses. Marta stared into the flames.

Gaul followed her with his gaze. "Marta."

"Why didn't you tell me?" she asked.

"I'm telling you now."

"Why didn't you tell me the first time?" Marta kicked a chunk of wood into the flames. "Why would you keep it from me?"

Gaul rested his head back and stared out of the room, to where the wall of the tower collapsed. "Because at the time I figured you'd be gone when we got to the Cradle."

"So, it wasn't your concern," Marta said.

"Yeah."

"And now it is."

"...Yeah."

The wind whistled through the room. It billowed Marta's shorn hair, grown slightly from when he saw her peering in through his cell window in Marjyal. She stomped her heel, then turned away from the fire.

"Let's keep climbing," she said.

Gaul hopped to his feet. "Marta."

"You can't climb with your mouth." She stepped into the antechamber and looked at the collapsed staircase. "Perfect."

Gaul stepped past Marta and looked out the hole in the tower. With the light from Meza's large moon and the breaking cloud cover, they could see the landscape stretching out below them. The bark that covered the outside of the tower was home to giant mushrooms and knots the size of a horse. Scalable, with a bit of effort.

"I have good news and bad news," Gaul said.

Marta joined Gaul at the window. The colour drained from her face. "Hold on a second."

"Do you have a better idea?" Gaul asked.

Marta grimaced. "That doesn't mean this is a good one."

Gaul leapt onto a mushroom cap. It bounced slightly under his feet, but felt sturdy. He turned to see Marta scowling in his direction.

Gaul crossed his arms. "I rode in that horse-drawn carriage because of you."

"A horse-drawn carriage and falling from an ancient tower are not the same thing!" Marta stomped her feet, sending more rubble tumbling to the earth far below.

"Are you afraid of heights?"

"I can climb buildings and trees. This is neither!"

"Technically it's both."

Marta gave him a flat look.

"Fine." Gaul waved her off. "You can head to the base. With the risen. And Feyra. And Marjyal."

There was a thump and Gaul turned to see Marta stumbling. She stared at him wide-eyed.

"I knew you'd be fine," he said.

He grabbed onto a knot and pulled himself up to the next mushroom. Marta readied herself then followed. They climbed from mushroom to mushroom. Occasionally they had to scale the tree itself. The bark was rough, though, giving them plenty of handholds.

They eventually arrived at a mushroom with nothing much around it. The next one was over Gaul's head and out of his reach. Marta pulled herself up next to him and flopped onto her back.

"This is the worst thing ever," she said, gasping for breath.

Gaul stretched his back and looked over the landscape. The clouds had parted, giving him a clear view west. The dry earth eventually gave way to grasslands, lit by the setting sun. Far in that direction was the Cradle and the Absence that was seeping out from the door.

"We need to get inside before we lose all the light," Gaul said. He steadied himself best he could on the spongey ground and interlaced his fingers into a cup. "Come here."

Marta growled and rolled over. She eased herself up and staggered to him. She placed her foot in his hands and he lifted her up to the next mushroom. She scrambled out of view, then poked her head over the edge.

"There's a window up here," she said. "Think you can reach my hand if you jump?"

Gaul rolled his shoulder. "Think you can lift me if I do?"

Marta stuck out her tongue.

"Up and up you little ants go," the Descendant's voice came along the wind like the flitting of wings. "Strong together, but apart you are still nothing but insects."

A scream came from high above them. It was something between the cry of a bird and the shout of a person. Growing dots swept across the tower and dove for them.

Marta fell to her stomach and thrust her hand out. "Gaul! Come on!"

The figures were falling too fast. They unfurled broad wings and turned toward Gaul. They were humanoid, with up to four wings — some fully grown and other stunted, dirty masses of twitching feathers. They reached out with gnarled wooden spears and talon-like fingers wrapped in soiled bandages. Marta wouldn't be able to drag him up before they were upon them. It would get them both killed.

Gaul pulled the necklace with Athas' pendant off his neck. He bundled it into one hand then leapt up to Marta's outstretched arm. He pushed the necklace into her hand.

Marta looked at the necklace, then at Gaul. "What are you doing?"

"Keep climbing." Gaul turned to the incoming birdpeople. "You must get the Light from the Primordial. I'll meet you after."

"Not if you fall to your death! At least take the sword."

"Get inside now!" He snapped his head to her. Gold formed long her skin and consumed her. "Keep the sword."

Marta scowled beneath the golden aura. She moved out of sight. As long as one of them made it back to the Cradle.

Gaul turned back to the birdpeople in time to see a spear being thrust at him. He batted the spear aside and elbowed the birdperson holding it. They were emaciated things, barely more than skin and bone. The feathers that poked out of their inflamed skin were a dirty white. Whether they were birds made human or humans cursed with avian features, it wasn't a pleasant arrangement.

The next birdperson caught Gaul by the waist. Gaul grabbed him back and slammed him into the tree. Two more crashed into him, then three more after that. A mound of scrambling and crying bodies engulfed him.

Two grabbed him by each arm and pulled him out of the pile and skyward. Gaul kicked and twisted against the birdpeople. He flipped up one leg and pushed it against the birdperson holding his right arm, breaking his grip.

Gaul's stomach flew into his throat as he dropped. The remaining birdperson struggled to keep him in the air. The ground below was a distant and foggy painting. The birdperson Gaul kicked recovered and grabbed his arm again. Two more birdpeople swooped in and grabbed his legs. A wing struck him in the back of the head and stars blossomed in his vision.

They held him tight and rose fast. Gaul struggled, but it was no use. Structures, dark against the glow of the moon, grew in the clouds above him. His mind grew fuzzy from the strike and the speed they were ascending. The air was thinning. They passed a great chain coming from the tower to one of the structures. Then, darkness overcame him.

With all this talk of Samadel, I have noticed something. There is a lack of writings on Dimiya. She makes appearances in other stories, but the Gifted Tower was hers. Yet, I hardly see them mentioned together.

I worry that Samadel, in his pride and greed, erased her history. He wanted the tower to be his alone. He wanted his glory to overshadow even a god. But I have travelled far from Adathin and the name Samadel is never mentioned. Despite his efforts, Dimiya has outlived him. Can't say I'm upset about that.

—From the Journal of Jovin Gutterwake

Chapter Thirty-Two

Corpse on a High Throne

Marta kept her back on the wall, peeking through the window she just jumped through. The bird-creatures had focused entirely on Gaul. They had grabbed him and were dragging him into the sky.

She squeezed her fist around the steel and gold necklace. She was useless to him now. The monsters carried him out of view through the next layer of clouds. They weren't dropping him. The Descendant was playing with them, but that meant there was still a chance she could find him if she got to the top of the tower. She put on the necklace and charged up the stairs.

She arrived at the next floor and found a gap where the rising room would pass by. Penelopa was nowhere to be seen. Marta drew her sword and crept slowly through the hallway. She glanced through the open doors of the rooms she passed.

They had all the dressings of rooms for a group of people to live in. There were bunks and washing areas. But, the doors had heavy bolts and were reinforced with steel. They locked from the outside. These wards were built as a prison.

Marta passed a room that was stained with long dried blood. The tower gave her the creeps. If only she still had Gaul watching her back.

At the bottom of the next staircase was a collapsed moving armour. One leg was removed and its chest plate was open with most of its mechanics pouring out. It didn't seem recent, judging by the layer of dust on it. The bell in its chest was crushed, so it wouldn't be summoning any risen. Marta lifted its helm and pulled the crystal out. Just in case.

The gears were etched with strange symbols. Marta pulled one out. Springs exploded into her face and she blocked them with her arm. The symbols were somewhat familiar, though she couldn't tell from where. Maybe in one of the books Jovin had read.

"I recognize those."

Marta spun in a full circle. There was no one there. The voice wasn't the same as she heard earlier, it wasn't the Descendant.

"You're right."

Marta pointed the sword down the hall. Where was the voice coming from?

"Oh, you know."

Marta did know. The voice was coming from inside her head. Marta stumbled back, dropping her sword and clutching her skull.

"I'm so disappointed you couldn't hear me before," the voice said. It sounded like hers, but it wasn't. The same as the one she first heard in the swamp. "I have been trying to talk to you for so long."

"Who… what are you?" Marta asked.

"That's rude. I'm human, just like you. In fact, more like you than you realize."

"No. No." Marta snatched her fallen sword and started up the stairs. "I'm going to ignore you."

"Don't be a child. Don't bury your head in the sand. I'm not going away anytime soon. You and I are together in this, and I would appreciate if you were more careful with this body."

Marta passed pieces of risen spread across the stairs. An arm reached for her, but it couldn't do much from the ground. Must have been remains from the Adherents of Tyran's attack, still moving after all these years.

"Marta." The voice was more distant in her mind. "I will be coming back. Keep a hold on that necklace. I will require it when your body becomes mine."

Marta froze. She waited to hear the voice speak again, but there was nothing. She needed to focus. Gaul must be at the top of the tower and — if not — she still needed to get the Light from Ziz. She tightened her grip on the sword and kept ascending. She was so tired. She would have to find a place to sleep soon.

Gaul awoke on sand. He rolled onto his knees and sat back. A crystal blue ocean spread out before him into the orange sky. Sunrise.

He looked around the beach he had found himself on. The water sparkled brilliantly and lapped against the shore. The Tower of Samadel stuck up like a spike beyond it. The top of the tower. Dozens of islands floated around that central point, chained to the tower by great metal links. Gaul pushed himself slowly to his feet.

"Gaul." It was the Descendant voice. Only, it didn't come from everywhere.

She sat upon an elegant wooden chair. The sand around her was littered with half-buried armour and weapons. They poked out of the sand like a mountain range. Behind her were the corpses of malformed giants. The Descendant crossed her legs like a royal and smiled gently.

"Those who know me called me Dynah," she said. "The Apostles of Wind were gracious enough to bring you to me. I thought, perhaps, you may be more receptive alone."

Gaul put his hands in his pockets. "For someone who can apparently see my thoughts, you make some wild assumptions."

"I can not see your thoughts, I can merely skim them." She ran her fingers through strands of her hair, letting the wind play with them. "Much like a sailor reads the breeze on the sea. My mother held domain over the Apostles of Wind and some believed she could read their minds and act as one. A flock of birds that took down a roc."

"I'm not giving you the vessel."

Her gaze fixed upon Gaul, turning cold with realization. "You don't have it. But you do have the ear of the one who does. Look around." She gestured to the abandoned battlefield. "I thought a warrior like you would appreciate this place. During the First Age, Hunter Gran the Unbent led his soldiers into battle against overwhelming odds. He fought demons let loose from the Fire to save a town from destruction. They died, but not without slaying every demon that threatened the townsfolks. To respect their sacrifices, Tyran cast the battle site into the sky and chained it to the Gifted Tower. Dimiya asked Time to miss this place, so their weapons may never rust and their memories may never fade."

Gaul shrugged. "And yet, I've never heard of it."

"That is because the Divines sealed the First Gods away." The Descendant leaned forward. "All their deeds were buried in the twisting halls of time."

"But you don't want the First Gods to return? You're lying."

"I'm not." Dynah chuckled. "Our parents deemed me and my siblings failures. We were designed to kill gods, but came imperfect. No, I don't want them free. I want to save the people that they once saved. The mortals that the Divines left behind."

She reached forward, eyes wide, her mouth cracking into a wicked smile. The beautiful façade was giving away to someone more desperate.

"If you give me the vessel," she said. "There is no limit to what we can do. All your desires become possible. A new world will grow at our feet and you could help usher it in. Stand at the top of it."

Gaul groaned. "I have no interest in ruling the world. And less interest in letting you do it."

Dynah's smiled faded into a blank expression. She sat back in her chair, looking down her nose at Gaul. "I could rule better than the Divines."

"You just want revenge."

"I want to help you!" She slammed her fist onto the chair arm. "Is it arrogance that won't let you see that?" She calmed herself, smoothing out her dress. "If I can't appeal to your goodness, then perhaps your greed. You can't think of single thing you would like to do with unlimited power? What do you want most?"

Gaul held himself firm, but the smile on Dynah's face told him she got what she needed. She bowed her head. Her lavender hair darkened until it became raven black. Her dress fluttered and changed from a sophisticated gown into a simple dress. The Descendant looked at Gaul with familiar brown eyes. Anori. Gaul's wife sat upon the chair.

"Death isn't so large a divide here." The Descendant spoke in her voice, torn from Gaul's mind. "I can make anything possible."

Gaul's mouth twitched. She shut his eyes to get her smiling face away. "You should look deeper."

The Descendant's eyes narrowed and her smile dropped. "Oh, I see it now. You really are pathetic."

"Yeah." Gaul grabbed a polearm from the sand and rested it on his shoulder. "But I'm not without purpose for the moment." He walked toward her. "Here's the deal, I need to go find Marta. Either you do something more than just making smoke, or I keep walking."

Dynah squeezed her chair arms, still in Anori's form. She did nothing as Gaul sauntered past.

"I thought so." Gaul draped both arms over his new weapon.

He glanced back. The Descendant was gone. In her place was the shattered remains of a chair. It wouldn't be the last he would see of her, though. Gaul needed to find Marta.

* *

Marta had the worst sleep she remembered in a long time. Her sword was unsheathed at her side and she sat against the wall. She wanted to keep climbing, but as the night wore on and the floors seemed infinite, she knew she needed rest.

She found a few more gaps in the wall to an empty shaft. More of the rising rooms. She lost count of how much further she climbed after that. Cracking her back, Marta continued up the tower.

A dozen or so more spirals and Marta arrived at a different kind of floor. Rather than a tight hallway, this was a massive hall. Two lines of intricately carved columns directed Marta to a grand staircase. Chunks of risen and a few moving armours lead to the foot of the stairs. Laying among the remains of battle was a figure dressed in white and blue, pierced by half a dozen spears.

Marta sheathed her sword and rushed to the stairs. "Penelopa!"

The young woman opened her eyes. "Marta? Why did you come?"

Marta slowed to a stop. The spears stuck out of Penelopa's torso and arms, adding fresh blood to her stained robes. She still held onto Gaul's swords, even as she lay dying.

"I was so close," Penelopa said. "The throne room is just up these stairs. But… I can't move. I was so close."

Tears mixed with the blood coming from her mouth. She coughed and tried to catch her breath. Blood poured from the wounds on her chest. Marta bowed her head.

"Could you imagine?" Penelopa shut her eyes and smiled. "How proud everyone would have been when I returned? The unwanted daughter ended the curse. But this figures."

Marta furrowed her brow. She knelt by her side. "Give me the dagger."

"An Oblivion Dagger," Penelopa said, half opening her eyes. "Plunge it into the heart of the corpse on the high throne and the curse will be lifted."

"Then give it to me." Marta offered her hand. "I'll do it for you."

Penelopa released one of Gaul's swords. As if she was using every ounce of energy left in her body, she reached into her robes and drew the silver-handled dagger. She shakily lifted it. Marta caught her hand, keeping it steady. She took the dagger.

"Please leave," Penelopa said. "I don't want to hurt you when I come back."

She breathed a final sigh and released the other sword.

Marta stood. Penelopa had fought hard to get where she fell, and she took every risen and machine with her. Marta pulled the void blade from its sheath. The haunting hole in space still gave her shivers, but she tapped it closed and tucked it into her jacket. She would finish Penelopa's mission.

Marta recovered Gaul's swords before continuing up the stairs. They split at the top and curved back to the next floor. She arrived at the throne room. Penelopa really was so close. The columns from below continued into this top room. Windows ringed her with views of large chains that went past, all could be seen from the throne ahead.

Upon the throne sat a decaying corpse, swathed in a red and gold flag that spread across the floor. As she approached, Marta was surprised to see that Samadel still had skin. It was greenish grey and pulled tightly across his skeleton. His eyes were gone, only sunken pits where they used to be. Marta placed Gaul's swords on the ground with a small clatter — every sound might have well of been cannon fire — and drew the dagger.

A wild wind whipped through the throne room. It was strong enough to nearly knock Marta off her feet. The flag fluttered as the wind moved across it and formed into the visage of a young lady. It was the Descendant. She curled around the throne, still half-smoke, and draped her arms over Samadel's shoulders. She leaned forward and whispered into his ear.

Samadel's corpse stirred.

Marta drew her sword and took a ready stance. She held the Oblivion Dagger forward with her straight blade as Samadel pushed himself off his throne. The flag fell away, revealing a glorious armour that had not tarnished with time and a great sword that looked ready to crush bone. He took his sword in both hands and stepped toward Marta. With each stride, he gained speed. The misty woman perched atop the throne grinned.

Marta waited until Samadel had fully lifted his sword, then dodged aside. The sword cracked the marble where she just stood. Samadel pivoted the blade, pushing the flat edge toward Marta. She took it on the shoulder. Her boots slipped across the smooth stone floor. She dropped, rolling under the sword and popping up to face her foe.

He stumbled slightly, thrown off balance by the sudden disappearance of Marta's resistance on his sword. He stared down at Marta through void eyes. His heavy armour protected his chest, giving no access for Marta to stab his heart. She would need to figure out something.

Samadel shifted closer to Marta, forcing her back. He swung a wide cut. Marta recoiled. Her back touched the railing. She glanced down at Penelopa spread across the stairs below.

Samadel spun into a heavy overhanded swing. Marta placed one foot on the railing balusters and threw herself to the side. The railing exploded into splinters. She scrambled across the floor and clumsily thrust her sword into Samadel's exposed armpit. Samadel spun, but Marta kept her hand on her sword and moved with him. She kept in his blindspot, where his great sword couldn't touch her.

Marta ducked as Samadel swung his elbow at her. She stabbed the break in his armour with the dagger, but couldn't get deep enough to reach his heart with the short blade. Samadel lifted his great sword over his back and flicked it toward Marta. She had to release her sword and dive away.

The sword remained stuck in his armpit, but it seemed to do nothing but annoy him. He rested his great sword against the railing and reached for Marta's blade. His armour was too broad for him to grab it, though.

Marta stumbled to her feet. She was getting tired. The Oblivion Dagger was heavy in her hand. She needed to Ignite or else she would lose this fight. What was it that Gaul had said? There was a string and rage and something about an image.

She imagined the sea, the same one she saw through the destroyed wall of the library her and Jovin grew up in. The infinite expanse. She didn't care about the smell or the sound, only the possibilities it promised to her.

Leaving the sword under his arm, Samadel took up his weapon again. He dragged it along the floor as he approached Marta. Marta let the anger rise within her. A hot sensation grew in her belly, just like when she tried lower in the tower. She was almost there.

Samadel leapt forward, swinging his great sword one-handed. Marta dodged and the fire dimmed. Samadel lost some mobility with his one arm propped up, but none of his ferocity. He bowed and staggered, whipping his blade back and forth. Marta had no time to clear her mind, she had to focus on dodging.

No. She was fighting a losing battle. She had to Ignite. A distant voice screamed at her.

She stopped dodging. Samadel spun and dropped his sword down onto her shoulder. A hot pain spread across the wound as the blade cut in. Her bones cracked under the weight. Marta pushed the sensation aside until only the flame in her stomach remained. She pulled it from foot to head into a fiery string that vibrated with the pain in her mangled shoulder.

"Fine," the voice in her head said.

Crimson filled her vision.

The red didn't encircle Samadel like Gaul said it would. Maybe because Samadel wasn't fully alive. Lightning shot out of Marta's shoulder. She pushed back against the blade, drawing more energy out of the wound and into the air. It felt like her entire body was bathed in a glorious warmth.

She pulled herself away from the sword, tearing more of her shoulder out. It didn't stop her. She burst forth, ripping her sword out of Samadel's armpit.

The Oblivion Dagger hummed in her hand. It wanted to find its way into Samadel's heart.

Samadel took his sword in both hands. He swung hard. Marta lifted her sword. The great sword pushed into her shoulder, despite her blocking. She ran down the length of the blade, sending blood and lightning flying.

Marta drove the Dagger over the top of Samadel's armour, plunging it into his tight flesh. He didn't falter. Marta kicked him back. They both prepared to charge once again. The Oblivion Dagger's silver grip stuck out from under Samadel's chin. It wasn't deep enough.

Marta flipped her sword around, grabbing it by the blade. It bit cruelly into her palm. She rushed toward Samadel, ignoring his oncoming swing. She slammed the hilt of her sword into the hilt of the dagger, driving it even deeper. Samadel's great sword struck her side, cutting her flesh and breaking her ribs.

Samadel released his sword and collapsed to his knees. Marta pushed his sword out of her body, clutching where the lightning was already pouring out. A dull ebbing pain surrounded the wound and it closed slower than it had before. There was an upper limit to the healing it seemed.

Light poured out of Samadel's mouth and eyes. He tore at his chestplate, trying to remove it. His skin tore away to muscle, then bone, then dust. Empty armour scattered across the floor and dust flitted in the slight breeze. The Dagger was nowhere to be seen.

Once her wounds had healed, Marta let the fire extinguish. A voice inside her head chuckled and faded away. She sheathed her sword and turned to the throne. The Descendant sat upon it, scowling at Marta.

"You killed my knight," she said.

Marta picked up Gaul's swords. "I'll kill you too if you stick around."

"You and that Ulkradian are a pain in my neck."

"So, he's still alive." Marta breathed a sigh of relief. She knew Gaul wouldn't die so easily.

"For now." The woman grew transparent. Her hair stretched and billowed. "He's lying to you, you know?"

Marta narrowed her eyes.

"Of course not," the woman continued. "In the end, you're just humans. I know you have the Light Vessel, Marta Gutterwake. I abhor violence but… I'm done playing. The Apostles of Wind will kill you and take the Light Vessel from your corpse."

The woman turned into wind. She gusted up the stairs behind the throne and slammed the doors open into another rising floor.

Marta looked back at the remains of Samadel.

Look what you did, Penelopa. She hoped the cleric could find her peace.

Marta rested Gaul's swords on her shoulders and ascended the last steps she hoped she would ever have to take. She entered the rising floor and before she could look for a lever, it started to move. Above her, sunlight blazed in from the open ceiling. She had to cover her eyes to shield them as the floor reached the top with a bump.

She moved her hand and looked upon the floating islands chained to the Tower. A rogue cloud cut through the landscape. Through the billowing cotton was the shape of a manor house with a tall cylindrical building behind it. Hopefully it was the Windscar Manse. With a deep breath and a straight spine, Marta stepped forward.

* *

Gaul pulled his bardiche out of the back of an Apostle. They were even more vile creatures when dead.

The Apostles of legend were followers of Dimiya. When she assaulted Sky, the Apostles of Wind were outfitted with suits that allowed them to ride upon gusts and squalls. It was with their help that Dimiya could defeat the Sky Queen, Ziz.

If these were the Apostles of Wind Gaul had heard about in legend, then something terrible must have happened. Gaul lifted their wings and found leather fused with skin. The flying suits they used had become one with their bodies. Even thousands of years later they stood guard.

Gaul stepped over the three Apostles he had just killed. They didn't fight like humans. They were more like hawks, diving and swooping with spears. Thanks to his polearm, Gaul was able to drag them from the sky.

The floating islands were connected by suspension bridges. They bounced with each step as Gaul crossed. He made sure no Apostles were close before he started, lest they knock him off.

The next island was covered in coarse sand. Each piece of land was plucked from a different part of Meza. This one seemed to be from a desert. There was an oasis full of palm trees and a crystal-clear spring. It was inviting and Gaul wished he could relax by the waterside. But, Marta was somewhere and he needed to find her.

He walked past the oasis and looked to the horizon. On a distant island was a grand structure. Clouds drifted past. Gaul leaned on his polearm. That building had to be Windscar Manse. It was where Ziz would be imprisoned.

Hopefully Marta remembered when he mentioned it. If so, she would head to it as well. He could meet up with her there.

The screams of Apostles echoed from the sky. Two more dove toward Gaul, spears at the ready. Gaul would need to deal with them before he could go to the Windscar Manse.

Hold on, Marta. Gaul readied his weapon.

Finally, some tales of Dimiya.

Dimiya was the second-born of the First Gods. Unlike the others, she was not a solitary soul. She fostered community everywhere she went and in time gave rise to the Apostles of Wind. Tyran led his knights, but Dimiya was truly one with her windriders.

They built suits made of feathers and imbued with ancient magick. With these, they could do battle with Ziz of the Sky.

Ziz — unaccustomed with fighting such small, well-organized creatures — couldn't keep up with the Apostles. They kept close to her body, where her talons couldn't tear them and her beak couldn't snap them. With her Apostles help, Dimiya sliced the wings off Ziz and brought her crashing to the ground.

They built a cage around her, then a home around that. The Apostles made an oath to guard Ziz with their lives. They would not allow the chance that the bird could take to the skies again.

Windscar Manse became a holy site for the Apostles of Wind, even long after Dimiya and the other First Gods were imprisoned.

—From the Journal of Jovin Gutterwake

Chapter Thirty-Three
Floating Record

The *Steel Jaw* bobbed easily along the ocean waves, joined by four other smaller ships: *Far Shore*, *Isildia*, *Spree*, and *Floating Record*. Bellona stood on the bow, watching the shoreline pass them by on the way south. They were a week from Dancer's Inlet, and even then, they would have to wait for Melifacto. They weren't in a hurry.

"When was the last time you were on the sea?" Ortun asked, joining her at the railing.

"Years ago," Bellona said. "Life is stationary as a Praetor. I went to oversee the staffing of Broken Island Fort after the pirates got brazen."

"It's funny you bring that up. I told you pirate attacks have been down, right?"

Bellona nodded.

"Then what do we think—" He pointed away from the shore. "—that is?"

Six ships broke the horizon. They were heading for Marjyal's fleet.

"That would be why Melifacto sent me this way," Bellona said, resting her hand on her sword.

"You knew this was going to happen?" Ortun narrowed his eyes. "And you didn't tell me?"

"I suspected it was going to happen. You would have told me to stay on shore."

"Of course I would have!" Ortun ran his fingers through his hair. One of the sailors had stopped to stare at the interaction. Ortun shouted at him, "Don't just stand there. Battle positions!"

The *Steel Jaw* exploded into a flurry of movement as the sailors prepared for a fight. As the call was passed along, the other ships began their preparations as well. Ortun spun back to Bellona and leaned in.

"You're playing with lives that aren't your own," he said in a harsh whisper.

"This is why I didn't tell you." She brushed past him. "Just get me onto one of their ships."

Ortun scowled at her before sprinting across the ship to take the wheel. He barked orders at his crew. The fleet moved into their positions to attack. They had dealt with pirates before, but they were outnumbered. Bellona slid her coat off and tossed it over a barrel. She stretched her arms out with a series of cracks. Ortun looked at her with disgust. Bellona deserved it, she figured. She grabbed onto the rigging and started climbing the mast.

One of the pirate ships took an early turn and fired all cannons. It was too soon, and the shots missed. The rest of the ships stayed on course. They weren't all amateurs. The *Isildia* unfurled all its sails and headed for the pirate that had fired. Bellona wrapped a rope around her arm and braced herself on the main boom. There wouldn't be another miss.

The *Far Shore* was the fastest, it got within range first. It took a reckless turn and opened fire with its starboard cannons, tearing apart the bow of its target. Another pirate tried to ram it, but the *Far Shore* kept cresting until it could fire on the port side and bombard its first target again.

The thunder of powder and crunching of wood turned the sea into chaos. Smoke filled the air. A pirate ship turned to fire upon the *Steel Jaw*. Ortun moved in reply. The boom she was waiting on was turning to meet the boom of the pirate ship. Bellona coiled her knees, ready to explode.

"Fire!" Ortun cried.

Both ships unleashed. Cannonballs turned wood into splinters. Sailors screamed as the ship around them disappeared. Bellona charged forth. She reached the end of the boom and threw herself forward, landing on the enemy mast. She grabbed a rope and drew her sword, cutting the counterweight and falling to the deck. *Thud!* She landed on both feet.

Every pirate turned to her and drew their weapons. Bellona spread her feet apart and rested her blade on her forearm. The pirates crept closer. Bellona exhaled then shut her eye. She moved with the tossing of the ship until it was like she was standing on firm ground. Amid the roar of cannons, there was the creak of wood. She lashed out, slicing a pirate across the chest. The footsteps of a ship crew stumbled back. Bellona smiled.

For each sound the pirates made, she replied with an attack. She blocked, parried, and killed without opening her one good eye. There was a click as a flintlock pistol was armed. Bellona spun her sword around and sliced off the pirate's hand. She caught the pistol in midair, laid her finger over the pirate's finger, and fired at another one. She tossed the pistol aside and reengaged with her sword.

The pirates had stopped moving. Bellona clicked her tongue and listened for the sound to bounce back. There was someone close. She thrust her blade through the pirate's throat. She clicked again. One of the pirates moved back, but she caught them at the knee. Another click and she killed the pirate with a cut.

She moved across the deck, killing any pirate who stepped too close. She ascended the steps without stumbling, having memorized them from her spot on the mast. When she couldn't tell where an enemy was, she would click her tongue until she found them. It was easier for her to fight with her eye closed, rather than deal with the disadvantage of only having one.

She reached the stern and stopped. There were no more footsteps or cannon fire. There was only the crackling of flames and splintering of wood. Bellona opened her eye to a world on fire. The pirates had been destroyed. Their ships were on fire and floated broken in the waves. Her fleet had their own damages to deal with. The smoke and flames were so fierce that she couldn't see the horizon line.

She wiped her sword clean on one of the pirates, sheathed it, then went to find their captain's quarters. A cannon ball had blown the doors open and punched a hole through the back wall. Paper and glass littered the floor and desk. Bellona pushed it aside with her foot. Hidden under some maps was a paper cleaner than the rest.

It was an offer of payment from Melifacto. In return, the pirates would kill Bellona.

Someone kicked aside a piece of timber and Bellona turned to see Ortun entering the captain's quarters.

"How went the battle?" Bellona asked.

"All ships are damaged," Ortun said coldly. "The *Spree* has a broken mast. We lost the *Floating Record* and half its crew."

"Look at this." Bellona held up the message.

Ortun took it and read it silently. "Melifacto wants you dead. Guess you were right."

"Yes." Bellona took the message back. "Let's keep this between us."

"Why? He broke the Accords, no one would care if you killed him."

"Because he's still useful." She walked to the edge of the boat and dropped the message overboard. "I need to discover how to enter the Cradle of the World. Then we can kill him."

Ortun watched the message float on the wind, then become swallowed up by the waves. "We'll need to fix the boats."

"Then do it." Bellona looked toward the smoky sun. "Melifacto made his move. We'll have to do the same."

Marta peered over the edge of the tower. Her stomach leapt into her throat and she stumbled back. She wanted to find Gaul, of course, but she needed a moment to work up the courage to cross one of the flimsy-looking rope bridges to the floating islands. She wondered if the islands would float away if the chains were gone, or if they would just crash to the earth.

On a distant island was the Windscar Manse. It looked like the mansions the Praetors lived in, in the northern part of Marjyal. The more courageous of the urchins would try to raid the riches from their halls. Few of them came back.

Gaul was still alive, the Descendant woman admitted as much. He would go for the Windscar Manse, and so that was where Marta would meet him.

Marta jumped on her toes, feeling the blood fill her arms and legs. She grabbed Gaul's swords and stepped off the large balcony onto the suspension bridge. It bounced and swayed under her weight. It was firmer than the mushrooms, but still made her sick. She hurried across.

The next island was ring of trees around a lush glen. Flowers of red, blue, purple, and white grew petal to petal. Marta couldn't step forward without risking crushing them. She slid her feet gently through the stems. In all her life, she had never seen a place so beautiful.

Butterflies fluttered around Marta's knees. She moved slowly across the field and into the opposite treeline. She passed through the small forest and across the next bridge.

The island ahead was a similar forested area to the one she just left, but with a small pond close to the edge. She stepped onto the lush grass and looked into the pond. A violet fish leapt into the air and cast a rainbow from its scales. Marta smiled, entranced by the beauty of the islands.

A scream shook Marta's bones. It was the same scream as she heard before the Apostles first attacked. She widened her stance and spun toward the bridge she arrived on. Three bird-creatures climbed from below the island. They held atrocious spears in one hand and dragged themselves over the edge with gnarled, bloody fingers.

They attacked low, their hunched posture forcing their attacks to aim up. Marta coiled and jump over the first thrust. She slashed the Apostle across the face and ran toward the next bridge. Gaul's weapons were heavy and ill-weighted, suited for hacking people apart.

An Apostle blocked her path. He rushed her, spear first. Marta knocked it aside and lifted the other sword at him. The Apostle skewered himself on the sword, knocking both of them to the ground.

Marta kicked the body aside. The other two Apostles weren't far behind. She hurled both of Gaul's swords into the ground and drew her own. *How does he fight with such tip-heavy blades?*

She parried the first spear and drew a knife, plunging it into the Apostle's eye. Leaving the knife, she dropped her stance and flipped the Apostle over her shoulder. The next scrambled across the earth, tearing up clumps of dirt and grass.

Marta drew a knife and tossed it just in front of the Apostle, causing the creature to leap high into the air. Marta placed herself below the Apostle and thrust her sword through her heart. The Apostle howled then went limp, dragging Marta's sword to the ground. Marta placed her foot on the Apostle's shoulder and yanked her sword clear.

More screams. Half a dozen winged beasts spiralled in the sky. The Descendant knew Marta had the vessel. She wasn't going to stop sending Apostles of Wind until it was hers.

Marta held her sword in both hands. The flames rose in her guts, stretching into a string the ran through her nerves. The red crept into her vison. But, that last step was eluding her. She had done it before, not even that long ago. Why couldn't she do it again?

She pushed her body until her stomach ached. She was in just as much danger now, but she couldn't get that last spark. What was so different?

She shook her head. She couldn't Ignite. *Fine. I survived long enough without it.*

He drew some knives and readied herself. With her sword in one hand, knife in the other, and a final blade held in her teeth — Marta waited for the Apostles to strike.

From the island above, a figure appeared, falling toward the Apostles. He clutched onto a polearm and screamed with rage.

Gaul.

"Insane bastard," Marta muttered through the knife in her teeth.

He plunged his weapon into the back of an Apostle and rode him down. As they fell, he grabbed another Apostle's wing. The three tumbled into the pond and disappeared below the surface. The water turned red.

Marta couldn't worry about Gaul at that moment. Four more Apostles rushed to meet her. She lowered her head and charged. The Apostle were moving fast, too fast for them to correct their path. It was the same thing that allowed Gaul to pull them from the sky.

Marta knocked the Apostle's weapons aside, slipping between the gaps in their pattern. She took the last Apostle face to face. Her attack sheered his head clean off.

The other Apostles skipped across the ground. They bounced back and forth, keeping their distance. They were unwilling to make the mistakes the others had.

Water exploded out of the lake. Gaul pulled himself onto the shore, coughing a lungful of water onto the grass. A violet fish jumped off his shoulder, shining out its rainbow before disappearing. Gaul staggered to his feet and looked between the Apostles and Marta.

"Marta!" he shouted. "I need a weapon!"

Priorities, I suppose. Marta pointed where his swords were sticking out of the ground.

Gaul cracked his neck and headed for his weapons. An Apostle leapt forward and stabbed Gaul in the shoulder. Gaul's eyes turned red and lightning shot from his wound. He grabbed the Apostle by the throat and continued walking with the spear still in him.

He kept the Apostle between him and the others, lifted high with one arm. Gaul walked with the Apostle all the way to his swords. He pulled one from the ground, gave it a shake, then buried it into the Apostle's stomach.

The remaining Apostles screamed. One threw caution to the wind and charged forth. Gaul dropped the one in his grip and tore the spear out of his shoulder. In one smooth motion, he pulled his other sword out of the ground and hurled it into the approaching monster.

Gaul followed his throw. He mounted the Apostle and hacked away. Blood and feathers flew into the air. The Apostle reached for him and Gaul chopped his arm off. Even after the Apostle was dead, Gaul kept cutting.

The two Apostles howled and chirped, but neither dared approached. Gaul glowered at them, his two blades bloody with the remains of their companion.

"Get out of here!" he screamed. "Go, or I'll pluck your feathers!"

The Apostles nearly trampled each other trying to flee from Gaul. He wiped the blades off onto the dead Apostle's feathers — the few spaces where they weren't already bloodstained.

"Effective," Marta said. She kept herself from looking directly at the mess Gaul made. Sometimes she forgot how much of a barbarian he could be. "I suppose."

Gaul rolled his shoulders and his eyes turned back to blue. "It's good to see you didn't die."

"Was that ever a concern?" Marta said with a smile.

"It crossed my mind." Gaul looked over his swords. "Thanks for getting my swords back. Where's the cleric?"

Marta lowered her gaze. In her mind, she could see Penelopa on the steps. Bloody, with spears sticking out of her.

"Oh," Gaul said. He slid his swords back into their scabbards. "She seemed like a tough woman."

"She was." Marta put away her knives and her sword. "Took out most of the risen and moving armours on the upper floors."

"Bahrstor clerics are something else, it seems. Did she finish her mission?"

"Yeah." Marta walked toward to Windscar Manse. "She died completing it."

Gaul joined her. "Good for her."

"She's a hero."

"I suppose I should be more upset that she took my swords and made us climb the tower." He rubbed the back of his neck. "But I can't help but feel bad for the poor girl. She came so far and lost so much."

They left the island and crossed the last bridge to Windscar Manse. No more Apostles dared to attack them.

"Goodsmile attacked her," Marta said. "He killed her brothers and her crew."

"Could be another masked man clad in white?" Gaul didn't even sound like he believed it when he said it. "Not likely."

"He saved us and attacked them? I thought he said he wanted the Praetors of Marjyal dead."

"Clearly Goodsmile has more plans than he let on." Gaul shook his head. "Next time I see that guy…"

Marta hoped they never saw his creepy mask again. She didn't mind him wanting the Praetors dead, but what else was he planning?

They arrived at the front steps of the building and stopped. There was no glass in the windows or doors on the entrances. The entire manse was open to the air. The wind that blew through whistled a melodic tune.

"I hope that Dynah has decided to give up," Gaul said.

Marta cocked her head. "Who?"

"The Descendant who's been messing with us this entire time." Gaul crossed his arms, tapping on his bicep. "She says she wants to save humans, but I don't think I believe her. I was a good thing I gave you the vessel."

"Which reminds me," Marta said. She reached into her shirt and removed the chain from her neck, offering it back to Gaul. He took it gently, running his fingers over the steel and gold chain. Marta never saw him treat anything with such care.

Gaul clasped it around his neck and tucked it out of view. "Let's go meet Ziz."

Sky Queen Ziz
Defeated by Dimiya and her Apostles of Wind
Imprisoned in the Windscar Manse

—From the Journal of Jovin Gutterwake

Chapter Thirty-Four
Ziz

Marta lead the way into the front hall. A chandelier had collapsed onto the marble, scattering glass in all directions. There were tables where the Apostles had once sat to eat their meals — back when they were human.

A passageway straight ahead led them past bunk rooms. Others were places for solitary prayer. Did they pray for Dimiya to return? How long after she left did they become those things?

The paintings on the walls were faded with time. Some showed men and woman in wingsuits riding upon the wind. Other were landscapes of various floating islands. One was placed in a spot of pride, at the intersection of two hallways.

A dark-haired man and a light-haired woman embraced. He wore white armour, while she had a feather-like cloak. Marta was about to ask who Gaul thought they were, when he spoke.

"Tyran and Dimiya." He pointed at a lower part of the painting, near the horizon. "There's the Tower of Samadel."

"The Gifted Tower," Marta corrected.

Gaul smiled. "I do like that name better."

They continued past the painting, toward the cylindrical building at the back of the manse. The light was coming in strong ahead of them — there must be plenty of windows in the structure. Marta shielded her eyes and stepped into the room.

Marta's jaw dropped. The steel bars of a cage stretched dozens of storeys to the roof. On the other side was a truly gigantic roc.

Ziz of the Sky.

She had beautiful, red plumage and was large enough that her wingspan could blot out the sun. Except, that is, for the fact she had no wings to speak of. Instead, there were long healed over stumps where her wings should be. She made no noise, but watched them with a wary eye.

"Beautiful, isn't she?" The Descendant's voice wasn't coming from all directions anymore. This time it was frail and coming from the veiled bed at the foot of the cage. Through the light cast from the large windows that ringed the base of the cylinder, they could see a figure moving. "The Sky Queen Ziz, torn from her place above."

Marta and Gaul drew their weapons. They approached carefully.

"My mother tore her wings off." The Descendant gave a wet cough. "But can you imagine how Ziz must have flown in her day? Glorious and graceful. Still, Dimiya had to strike her down so that the world could flourish. The strength to destroy — that's what the First Gods had. The Divines did not share this strength. Instead they ran away and left the world in the hands of mortals like you."

Gaul motioned for Marta to go to the left side of the bed. He took the right.

"Do you know what I found when I returned to this tower? See, after my siblings and I escaped from the Cradle, I wanted to return here. I always loved it. Early humans flocked to it. My mother allowed them to live there. They filled the floors with laughter and music. Dimiya built machines to tend to their needs. It was paradise.

"But that man called Samadel twisted it. He turned it into a prison with him seated at the top. He and that necromancer turned a beautiful place into a wretched hive. I read about it, I saw the results, I felt the pain the coursed through this land. But even for Samadel's pride and sound, he never dared to open the door behind his throne."

The Descendant coughed so hard, Marta thought a lung was going to drop out. She reached for the veil. The Descendant didn't run.

"That is the nature of humanity. To lash out and destroy. But, at your core, you're cowards. That is who the Divines left this world to. The illusion of strength."

Marta yanked the veil aside. She recoiled at the sight, gritting her teeth.

The Descendant lounged on a lush bed, propped up by pillows. She was shriveled and meek. She had few wisps of white hair, rather than the lavender locks of her illusory self. Long bony fingers played along the remains of a dress.

"How can you accept this world?" The Descendant said through thin lips pulled tight around her teeth. "One that had become so twisted. So filled with hate and violence. Samadel, the King of Adathin, they weren't extraordinary evils. They were… inevitable."

"Let's put this thing out of its misery," Marta said, lifting her sword.

"Marta." The Descendant rolled her head, looking at Marta with bloodshot eyes. "Surely you can see a better world. Light has such amazing properties when used by someone like me or my family. Nothing is out of my grasp, not even death. I could return your brother to you."

Marta's eyes widened. Jovin could be alive again.

"You can?" Marta asked.

"Of course." A smile cracked across her bleeding teeth. "I simply need the Light, and you."

"Marta," Gaul said, circling the bed. "You can't—"

"Can't what?" Marta snapped. "She said she wants to help us, didn't she? Why do we have to do this if she's willing to. Besides, Jovin…"

"You can't believe her." Gaul reached for her. "I know how you feel."

Marta slapped his hand away. "Do you!? You have a home. I have nothing without Jovin. Don't make me give up the chance to see him again."

Gaul rested his hands on his sheathed swords. Marta legs trembled and she squeezed the hilt of her sword until her hand hurt. She wanted to see Jovin again more than anything.

"We are in the rare opportunity to decide the fate of the world," Gaul spoke softly, afraid to break the moment. "It's not an envious position. I can't say if we'll like what we've done when it's over. But she doesn't want to save us. She hates us. Remember Tyran's Descendant? Who burned Sebanna's people and home to the ground?" He pointed at the Descendant of Dimiya. "She is no different. I can feel it seeping out of her. Whatever she wants, it's fueled by hate."

Marta shook her head. "And you're not?"

"It's not hate. It's…" He lowered his head. "I don't believe in gods, or kings, or conquerors who live in tall towers. I believe in people. People like Fortunis and Miribelle. I didn't want to help them; you were the one who convinced me to stay. You reminded me of that belief. So, I'm reminding you. Dynah wants to be a new god. We don't need any more of those."

Marta averted her eyes. For a second, it seemed like his words were reaching her. "I could kill you," she said, taking her sword in both hands. "I could kill you and take the Light."

"Can you?" Gaul asked. "I thought you made a promise. Remember?"

Marta scrunched her nose to keep the tears back. Of course she remembered.

"You told me you would bring me back home." Gaul stomped his foot. "So kill me and break it if you're feeling so tough!"

"Shut up!"

"I'm right here!"

"I want my brother back!"

"Then prove it! Or do you need that voice in your head to do that too!?"

Her mind went blank. She thrust her sword forth. The blade went through his shoulder and out his back. The Descendant chuckled.

"Gaul…" Marta withdrew, horrified at what she had done.

The sword stuck out of Gaul. He took the grip in hand and staggered, but stayed on his feet. "Why are you so upset? You're the one that did it."

"But I…" She started to hyperventilate. She was sure he would block or step aside. "I was—"

"You were angry." Gaul grabbed the sword. His eyes flashed red and lightning sparked from the wound as he pulled it out. "I'm sorry I didn't tell you about what happened in Dothrin. I'm not used to having someone around, but I'm glad you are. But sometimes we have to look outside ourselves, as hard as that is for the two of us it seems. We have a world out there. We can't destroy it in the name of those we lost. They deserve better."

Marta squeezed her eyes shut. Her face felt hot. Jovin always believed in a better world — even in the middle of Marjyal. She couldn't rightfully bring him back into anything less than paradise.

Gaul flipped the sword around and offered it to her. "And don't ever say you have nothing. You have me."

Marta snatched the sword from him and turned her back. She wasn't crying. She wasn't a child. She held the hilt to her chest, tensing her body so it wouldn't tremble. Gaul, bless him, kept his distance.

"Beautiful," the Descendant said. "Lovely sentiment."

Marta wiped the moisture from her cheeks and turned. The Descendant had pulled herself to the edge of her bed. With great effort, she stood on stick-thin legs.

"But you don't understand what humanity needs." She walked each step as if through heavy snow, clutching her oversized dress close. "Humanity can only be saved through pain. It must be culled. Returned to zero."

She hobbled past Gaul, then Marta. She made no violent act toward them.

"Though, part of me hopes for your success. I never liked violence. I too lack the strength to destroy that my mother had. I'm glad I didn't have to kill so many people; not for the evil ones who should be cast into flame, but for the radiant souls who love." She paused and glanced back, before resuming her shuffling. "I suppose you'll be looking for Leviathan's bones after this. My brother, the Descendant of Shiller, will be there. He isn't malformed in body as the rest of us are. No, his body was perfectly crafted by the Father of the Arcane. Too bad his mind can't say the same." She stepped onto the ledge of the low window. "I have one request for you, if you'll grant me such a thing. Don't let the other Descendants gain the power of Light. The one who leads them is not as kind as me." She met Gaul's gaze and let out a rattling breath, releasing the exhaustion of centuries. "Tell the truth of Anori, Gaul." She spread her arms wide, letting her dress billow out like bird wings. "I tire of this world. I'll see you in the next one."

She fell and Gaul and Marta rushed forward. Dynah's oversized dress fluttered in the wind as the cloud cover enveloped her. Then she was gone. There was only the wind in her wake.

"What did she say about Anori?" Marta asked.

"I don't know." He turned away from the edge with a shrug. "One last mind game, I guess."

He pulled the pendant out of his vest and he spun the necklace around his hand as he walked, until it dangled just below his grip. Ziz had not looked away from them during the entire exchange. Gaul stopped at the edge of her cage and gazed at the Primordial bird.

"Two out of five," Marta said, joining him. "I hope the rest are easier."

Gaul sighed. "From the sound of it, there's another Descendant with Leviathan. Plus Marjyal's still on our tail."

"She seemed worried about the other Descendants. Why do you think that?"

"I have a sinking feeling we're going to find out someday soon."

"You're a downer."

"You stabbed me."

"How long am I going to be hearing about that?"

Gaul raised the pendant. "Longer than you'd like."

Light grew along the scar left on Ziz's shoulders. She cried out in pain as the Light tore itself from her body. It collected in the vial and faded from sight. Ziz squawked one last time then fell into a deep slumber.

The spark in the pendant had grown marginally. It wasn't much, but it showed progress. A few more and they could seal the Cradle again. Gaul replaced the necklace and turned to the exit.

Marta hopped to keep up with him. Surely he was still furious that she hurt him. She was sure he would dodge. She couldn't believe she acted so irrationally. She thought she was over her brother — that she got all the emotions out at Sebanna's Archives. Grief was a creeping spectre. She would never truly stop grieving Jovin, just as she would never forget him.

Gaul clicked his tongue and rubbed his eyes. "Aww, Black Hypogea. I forgot."

"Forgot what?" Marta asked.

"We haven't seen Feyra since the Blasted Lands," he said. "I bet she's waiting at the bottom of the Tower."

Marta tapped her sword. "We conquered the Gifted Tower. What's a little group of Marjyalians to us?"

Gaul cocked an eyebrow. "Look who's feeling confident. You got one stab on me, don't let it go to your head." He smiled. "But yeah, let's not keep them waiting."

They stepped out of Windscar Manse and looked to the horizon. The sky was looking brighter these days.

In the dark, in the deep, I dream, I sleep.
In the shattered, that which creeps, I shudder, I breathe.
Where a bright world ends, my world begins.
Where your gaze won't drift, my birth will shift.
I am not the beast at your door.
I am not the crack in the floor.
I am not the shadow.
I am not the dark.
I am not the fading spark.
I am you, as you me.
I am the wicked chains, from which you will never be free.
In the dark, in the deep, I dream, but I no longer sleep.

I think of this poem a lot these days.

—From the Journal of Jovin Gutterwake

Epilogue

Feyra craned her head back, but still couldn't see the top of the tower. She thought she saw someone fall a few hours earlier, but decided it had to be a bird diving before taking flight again. Finding a way into the tower had proven to be more difficult than she had assumed. One of the Moles had the idea that if Gaul and Marta went up the tower, they would have to come back down. So, they set up camp and called for reinforcements.

"Now look at all of you!" someone exclaimed.

Feyra turned from the tower. A man dressed in white walked through the camp like others would walk through a park. His long coat swept in the wind and he motioned around with red-stained gloves. As he approached Feyra, he tipped up his wide-brimmed cap and revealed a featureless porcelain mask. Around the eye and mouth slits were black marks.

"Who are you?" Feyra asked, resting her club on her shoulder.

"That's a very boring question." He shook his finger at her. "I'll tell you my name is Goodsmile, but you need to ask me a better question."

Feyra narrowed her eyes. "Why are you here? Are you working for someone?"

"Do I look like a worker? Are these a working man's hands?" He offered his hands and turned them over.

Feyra could recognize blood when she saw it. Was Goodsmile a friend of Gaul and Marta? That seemed unlikely. He could have been one of Melifacto's monsters, but that didn't seem right either. Whatever he was, his presence put Feyra on edge.

"You should leave," Feyra said.

"That sure ruined the mood. Unfortunately, I can't have you here when my friends return." Goodsmile adjusted his hat and paced in a circle. "Instead, I will count to three."

"Why?"

"To give you a chance to run away. One."

The Moles drew their swords. Feyra took her club in both hands. One crazy man would be easy to kill.

"Two."

The air around Goodsmile turned hazy. Sweat beads formed on Feyra's brow from the heat. Goodsmile cocked his head and flecks of fire grew from the blackness in his eye slits. The camp paused in anticipation. The weight of the world folded down upon Feyra. Something was terribly wrong.

"Three."

ALL GODS FALL: SEASON ONE

PART FIVE

BOBOROS VALE

Shiller. The Lonely God. The Father of the Arcane. He makes an appearance in plenty of legends from the Age of Gods. He tends to play the part of a wise, if unwilling, mentor or a convenient way to wrap up a problem. It always goes the same way, Shiller comes in to solve a situation then quickly leaves aboard his ship, the Weeping Sonnet, and sails into storms so others couldn't follow him.

I must admit, if I was alive in that age I would be chasing Shiller down as well. He did so much for the world when it comes to our knowledge of flux. He trained the first fluxweavers, gave the world lithofluxy, and, of course, he was the only god to kill that which was thought to be immortal.

—From the Journal of Jovin Gutterwake

Chapter Thirty-Five

Fort Nowhere

In the mid-afternoon, a few kilometres from the Tower of Samadel, a body fell from the clouds. A loose-fitting, stained dress fluttered like the wings of a broken bird, until she came to a sudden stop in a cloud of unforgiving dust. Her bones shattered, but there was no blood in her to bleed.

A masked man dressed in white arrived shortly after it happened and crouched over her body. With blood-stained gloves, he pushed her onto her back. The barest thin-lipped smile was a taunt against the wreckage her body has become. The man placed one hand over her eye and drew a knife from inside his coat.

"You'll have a greater purpose."

He plunged the knife into her chest and began carving her apart.

* *

Descending the tower was vastly simpler than climbing it. Gaul and Marta took the rising rooms back to the underground workshop and out the auxiliary building exit. There, they sealed the hatch with a couple heavy crates that littered the outbuilding.

By that point they were dead on their feet and Gaul knew they weren't necessarily safe, not with Feyra and the Marjyalians following them. They could be there already, waiting at the bottom of the tower for Gaul and Marta to return. Gaul was in no state for that, and Marta had been distant since their encounter in the Windscar Manse. With the sun setting on another long day, they pushed themselves into the far corner of the outbuilding and slept — Gaul on the ground and Marta curled on top of a crate.

The night was dreamless, and Gaul found himself fading in and out of half-consciousness. He thought, in one of his first moments of flickering awareness, that he heard distant screams. But as he drifted off and back there was nothing else to distract him. When the sun crept through the slits in the outbuilding walls, Marta hopped off her perch as Gaul pulled the coat from his knees.

"Did you get any sleep?" he asked.

"Was someone screaming?" Marta scowled toward the barn doors.

"I might've." He pushed his arms through the coat sleeves, groaning as the soreness gripped his shoulders. "I thought I was dreaming."

"Maybe it was the Marjyalians?"

"They were screaming?"

Marta jogged to the door and looked back. She jerked her head a few times.

"You want to look into it?" Gaul asked, moving closer at a slower pace.

"Kind of. Yeah."

Gaul let out a long sigh then affixed his sword belt around his waist. "I suppose it's flat land in all directions. I don't see us sneaking away from them. Might as well get some information."

Marta pulled the barndoor open and they hurried along the overgrown stone path to the manor's side door. The frame above had collapsed, pinning the door shut. Gaul gave it a few test pushes. No good.

"Maybe we break a window?" Marta whispered.

"I don't want the Marjyalians hearing us." Gaul pointed down the wall, toward the front of the manor. "Let's go around. Slowly."

Marta tapped her thumb against the sword's pommel. She nodded and let Gaul take the lead as they crept toward the front of the manor. The smell of smoke filled their nostrils as they got closer, mixed with burning meat and loud pops and crackles. Gaul had seen villages burned to the ground, and the intensity of the smell brought those memories back in vivid flashes. He peered around the corner — though he already knew what would be there.

The Marjyalian camp had been devastated. Enough tents to house a couple dozen soldiers were burned to the ground. The remains of horses, sliced apart like on a butcher's slab, laid strewn about. Marjyalian soldiers were pined to the earth by their own weapons. In the centre of the massacre was a pile of burning corpses with a figure dressed in white sitting beside it, tending to the flames.

"Son of a—" Gaul stomped out from behind cover, fuming with rage.

Goodsmile looked up as Gaul bore down upon him. Blood was splattered across his strange mask.

"Oh good," he said. "You found your way down the tower. These reprobates were waiting for you with bated breath. I decided to take it from them. The blood woman ran away though. Coward."

Gaul drew his swords, pointing one forward. He didn't stop moving. "You psychopathic freak."

"This is the thanks I get?" Goodsmile cocked his head, letting the sun reflect off his porcelain mask. The blackened areas around his eyes and mouth seemed bigger than they were last time. "I saved your lives twice now, but you still treat me as your enemy."

Gaul stopped with his sword tip a centimetre from Goodsmile's mask. The edges of his vision flickered red until all he could see was that blank expression. "Did you attack and kill some travelling clerics in this area not long ago? Wearing blue and white."

"They dared to call themselves Adherents of Tyran." He tossed his poking stick into the fire and stood up. "I needed to see if they deserved to hold the name of a god such at that. They did not."

Red grew into Gaul's vision. He gripped harder on the swords' hilts. But, he pushed the anger down. If Goodsmile could destroy the entire troop of Marjyalians without injury than he was much stronger than he seemed. Marta held herself firmly next to Gaul, but had not drawn her own sword.

"This is the thanks I get?" Goodsmile cocked his head, letting the sun reflect off his porcelain mask. The blackened areas around his eyes and mouth seemed bigger than they were last time. "I saved your lives twice now, but you still treat me as your enemy."

"We don't know what you are," Marta said.

"I am like you. We are ships in the night sailing on the same wind. You don't think I am curious about you? Curious about what drives two strange bedfellows to travel to such bizarre and dangerous locales. I overheard you're trying to find the living corpses of the Primordials. You don't think that interests me? I simply figured us keeping our secrets would make our relationship simpler."

Marta stepped forward. "We are not helping you."

"The Praetors are not our concern," Gaul said. "If you want them dead, do it yourself."

Goodsmile cackled. "They may not be your concern, but they are definitely concerned with you. Four Praetors have fallen and with Melifacto's bounty on you, there is no one caring to manage the guilds. Marjyal is falling to ruin."

"You want to see Marjyal destroyed," Marta said.

"No." Goodsmile lowered his hat. "I want to see it razed and born anew from the flames. Marjyal must be sacrificed to the fire. I tried once to bring them a great conflagration, but I was rebuked and betrayed and my flames became ash."

Marta's eyes widened. "You're the Praetor of Ashes."

Goodsmile snapped his gaze to her. "I was never a Praetor. I was a speaker of fire and glorious infernos. The Praetors…" His head began to shake. He took a few unsteady, raspy breaths. "I do get carried away. Perhaps I revealed too much. I don't suppose you'd be willing to tell me what your journey is about, then?"

Gaul narrowed his eyes.

"I see." Goodsmile turned to the macabre bonfire. "All the same. The Praetor's are after you. The last of them will reveal themselves in time. And you still need my help."

"No." Gaul sheathed his swords. "We don't."

"With Black Hypogea and the Gifted Tower behind you, where does that leave you to go?" He counted out the locations on his fingers. "Sanguine's Cage is far away in the Dark. The Fire has been sealed since the time of the First Gods. Reasonably, you must be headed for Boboros Vale. But do you know where it is?"

Gaul ignored him. Marta walked past, keeping her gaze low. With a final glare to Goodsmile, Gaul followed her westward. True, they had yet to find Boboros

Vale on any map, but there was a large green area on the west coast. If there would be a valley of any note, hopefully it was there.

"You're going the wrong way," Goodsmile called after them. "There's a secret to Boboros Vale, something lost through time."

Gaul slowed to a stop. Goodsmile wanted them to keep going, why would he lie? Marta noticed Gaul's pause and stopped as well.

"You wouldn't want to wander Adathin aimlessly." Goodsmile wiped the blood off his mask. "The truth is Boboros Vale stems from a misunderstanding — these things happen over hundreds of years. It's quite funny actually. What you call Boboros Vale had a different name for the ancients. The Boboros Whale.

"The only surviving child of Leviathan, Boboros is a creature of incredible size. After Leviathan was killed by Shiller, Boboros Whale was found by his students and colonized. They built a city on his back, dedicated to the study of magic. Now he carries a piece of his mother in the Estuary Academy."

Goodsmile had clarified what the Descendant of Dimiya had said. Boboros Vale was where Leviathan's remains were. Those remains should have the Light Gaul and Marta were searching for. Slim chances seemed to be all they had these days.

"Head south," Goodsmile continued. "Down to the Banshee Coast. If you follow it west, you'll find a small fishing village. Look around. You'll get your vale."

The sharp breeze blew through the plain, scattering ash around. Goodsmile let out a deep yawn then dropped into a sit. Gaul wasn't pleased with his smugness, or the way he treated them openly like tools. He was a madman, no doubt about it. They needed to keep their distance.

"Let's go, Gaul," Marta said, pulling on his arm.

"No 'thank you'?" Goodsmile asked.

Gaul growled and followed Marta. Goodsmile's cackle echoed after them as they headed south.

* *

"Bad luck?" Feyra asked. She stood outside Melifacto's carriage, talking to him through the window. "You think it was bad luck that Goodsmile attacked us. I barely escaped with my life."

"And that's the good luck," Melifacto said. "Everything balances out."

Feyra clutched her fist, holding back the urge to knock Melifacto out. They were surrounded by Owls and Boars. Pelady squatted on the carriage bench, eyeing Feyra. A punch swung at Melifacto would be her last. She took a deep breath and said, "It wasn't a random attack. I recognized him. I should have when he first talked but… he's the Praetor of Ashes. I'm sure of it."

Melifacto sat forward. "So you are. Why would the Praetor of Ashes attack you?"

"He's working with Gaul and Marta."

"I think she's making it up," Pelady said. "Covering for how she failed in grabbing Marta."

"Why don't you say that again with a broken jaw?" Feyra said.

Melifacto leaned out the window. "Be nice, Pelady."

Pelady gave a sharp-toothed grin and slunk back onto her bench. Melifacto gazed down the road to the sign for Barrowfield. He ruffled his coat then settled back into his seat.

"You're early, nevertheless," he said. "Let's get into town. I'm sick of sleeping in a tent."

Pelady snapped the reins and the convoy started on its way toward town. Feyra kept Arion still, waiting for Melifacto and his army to rumble on. Having only Melifacto to greet her was an unwelcome shock. She couldn't wait for them to reunite with Bellona, and her knees trembled with anticipation to see her Praetor once again.

A few days after leaving the Tower, Gaul spotted the ruins of an old fort. An old stone fortification, most likely much older than Samadel's manor. Nature had nearly reclaimed it. Moss grew thick along the walls and trees broke through the collapsed roof. It was a good place to spend the night.

Marta paced the second-floor balcony, occasionally kicking aside a small piece of rubble. The shelter gave them a brief reprieve from camping exposed. Occasionally Marta thought back to the time they stayed in Sebanna's Archive. It was a palace compared to where she grew up, even when abandoned to the ravages of time.

Gaul slept peacefully below, propped up against the wall with his swords at his side. Marta left her coat and weapons next to him. The cool air felt good on her bare arms. It was a beautiful night. It was too bad she wasn't alone.

"You're angry," the voice said.

"I thought you were gone." Marta spoke without words, thinking to the voice instead.

"I will never be gone." The voice crawled along Marta's mind like an insect. "I've been here forever. You just haven't been listening."

"I'm going insane."

The voice sighed. "Yes, and terribly slowly, might I add."

Marta leaned against the railing. The full moon reflected in the river they'd been following. She'd been seeing a lot of the moon lately, looming over her like a giant white eye. Sleep had gotten difficult as night seemed to be when the voice was at its strongest.

She clapped the dirt off her hands and focused. She needed to get this right.

"You can't do it," the voice said, bored.

"I did it before."

"You were dying. Survival instinct."

"When I fought Samadel."

Somehow, the voice rolled its eyes. "That was me, you idiot. You were going to get us killed so I let you use some of my experience since I was too weak to take control again. I didn't wake up until you were running your friend through. Dramatic, don't you think?"

"I missed Jovin," Marta said.

"'Missed?'" The voice broke into laughter. "Don't talk about it like it's a thing of the past. I'm in your head and you whine about it at least once a day. You know, if Gaul didn't have the abilities he does, you would have killed him too. Then you would have been alone again."

Marta clenched her teeth until her jaw began to ache. She brought up images of the sea in her mind, feeling the calming wave that Gaul said was necessary before she could get the fire in her gut going. It wasn't easy with a voice taunting her from inside her head.

"You haven't told him about me," the voice said.

"I'll get around to it." Marta rolled her eyes. "Will you let me focus?"

"Are you scared?"

She rubbed her head. "What kind of question is that?"

"He can play nice it seems. But we've seen his true face — when the blood in him boils. How he tears and rends. That woman in the Pit? Who fought beside him before he killed her so heartlessly? It's easier for him to keep you around, but if you become more trouble than you're worth — if he learns that you have a voice whispering in your head — do you think he will trust you? Or will the doubts grow?"

"Gaul is my friend. We're in this together."

"You coerced him to come with you." The voice felt cold in her mind, an iciness that poured down her spine. "You said you would bring him home after he brought you where you needed to go. You already failed on that. Better keep working on unlocking your inner trublüdar, Marta. It's the only use you have to him."

Marta squeezed her fists until her nails pierced the skin. Red crept into her vision, but it wouldn't fill. She was angry, but it wasn't what she needed. The voice was prodding her on. Gaul wasn't so cruel. They were friends. He was her friend.

"Marta."

Marta spun around. Gaul ascended the steps to the balcony, cracking his neck and rubbing the sleep out of his eyes. He flipped the hood on his jacket up. The wind had grown since Marta started training, but she was too ingrained with her debate with the voice to notice.

"You should think about sleeping one of these nights," he said. He hung his sword belt over the railing and looked out at the landscape. "You're no good to me dead on your feet."

"I've been training."

"Training what?"

Marta tapped her forehead. "Trying to empty the mind. Igniting or berserking or whatever you want to call it."

"Are you having that much trouble with it?" Gaul asked.

"The name?"

"No, Igniting."

"Oh." Marta leaned against the railing and flopped her head back, looking at the moon hanging high above. "I've been trying to follow what you said in the tower. All that talk of the sea and the string and fire."

"The sea was just my suggestion to get you to calm down. Since you talked about it so fondly." He sighed. "It was a rushed lesson anyway. Not the ideal environment. There's more to it."

"Then teach me!" Marta punched Gaul's arm.

"I'm not a very good instructor."

"Yeah well, you're the only person I know of that can do it." She pushed off the railing. "I need to learn how. What do you do?"

"I've been doing it for so long, I barely think about it," he explained. "It's almost a reflex. I have to try harder not to stoke the flames."

"That's not going to help me. The… other me was able to do it. Why?"

"I don't know." Gaul casted his gaze her way. "Anymore developments about that?"

"…No," Marta said. The voice in her head crowed with glee.

Gaul looked her over, probing for any break in her wall. She would tell him, eventually. For now, it was her problem.

"Outside my town was a mountain path," Gaul said, turning his gaze back to the landscape. The trees were nearly diagonal from the windstorm. "It was narrow. Snaked through an area most people wouldn't even look twice at. But, at the other side was a view of Lake Kordan that was unbeatable. I imagined myself walking up the path, thinking of all the trees, the birds, the part where rocks had fallen into the valley below. I can bring it up perfectly in my mind, and as I walked it I let the fire consume me.

"When I reach the end, there's a wooden door. Weathered and beaten like the one to my childhood home. I would open it and then it all would go red and like the snapping of a string, I was gone. That's what I used to do. But during the Mirral Conflict, I just knew what the feeling I had to get to was. I could simply stoke the fire and be there. I haven't walked that path in a long time."

Gaul looked miles beyond the plains. To some far-off place Marta had only heard stories of. Gaul had years to perfect his technique. Marta hoped she didn't take as long.

"You said there has to be anger." Marta stepped closer to him, but still kept her distance. "Your tactic sounds incredibly peaceful."

"I was taken from my home and everything I knew. Put into a cold room, fed brown slop, and told over and over that I'm a monster who if I'm lucky, may prove myself as something more." Gaul shook his head. "Anger wasn't a problem."

A herd of hooved and horned beasts rumbled by in the distance — an ellipsis to Gaul's point. He talked of home with such distain and admiration that Marta couldn't figure out which one he truly felt. She hated Marjyal, but when she thought of the library she hid in with Jovin, it didn't seem so bad. Home was complicated for both of them.

Gaul pushed his hood down and yawned. "I was serious about the sleep. I'm sure it's still a long walk to the Banshee Coast." He grabbed his sword belt and lumbered toward the balcony stairs. "Tomorrow, we can start really trying to…" He stopped. "Berserk?"

Marta smiled. "Igniting works fine. You're right, it didn't feel like berserking."

"I told you." He waved back at her then disappeared down the steps. "Get yourself some sleep."

"Now wasn't that sweet?" the voice said.

Marta smacked her head. It only served to hurt herself.

"You didn't tell him about me."

"Shut up," Marta mumbled.

"You should ask him that question you've been thinking. I want to know the answer too."

Marta crossed her arms and stood her ground. The wind whipped her hair and strands stuck to her mouth scar. She kept her composure. The voice made no sound. With a groan, she hurried to the stairs.

"Gaul," she called as she thumped down to the ground floor. "Could I ask you a question?"

Gaul laid his swords near the embers of the fire. "I don't think anything could stop you."

"Why, uh…" She tried to stitch the words together. "Why didn't you Ignite when you were in the Pits?"

Gaul stopped halfway through taking off his jacket. He stood motionless for a moment, then tossed it aside.

"Well," he started. "See, my wife…"

Marta nodded.

Gaul crossed his arm. He seemed to want to tell Marta, but wasn't sure how to do it.

"You don't have to answer," Marta said. "I just thought it would have been useful when those Hunters were trying to get you."

"Yeah." He stared intently at the ground. "I was very good at fighting, Marta. And after the Mirral Conflict, we weren't at war. Trublüdars aren't useful on defense. They said we were part of the auxiliary then sent us home.

"Everyone in my town knew what I was. I couldn't miss the fact everyone wanted to avoid me. But not Anori. She said she recognized me, I don't know how, we were eight when we last saw each other. We got married a year later. Her family wasn't happy, but they were traditionalist so once we were married there wasn't much they could do. Still, I promised to be the person that she deserved. I was never going to fall back into my nature again, even if I had to die."

A cold chill swept over Marta. Gaul had gone through incredible trials to get his wife's necklace back. She assumed he was simply obsessed with her memory. Now she wondered if he was hoping for death along the way.

"Clearly that changed," Gaul continued with a laugh. He sat on the ground and touched the necklace, running his fingers over the gold and steel links. "If I could prove to her that I wasn't the monster they said I was…"

"Gaul." Marta crouched next to him. "I know I didn't know her. But, don't you think Anori loved you because of who you are? Not despite who you are?"

Gaul took a deep breath. "I can hope, I suppose."

Marta kicked her legs out and flopped down next to him. She had no reason to fear him. The voice was grasping at air.

"I'm getting home, Marta," Gaul said, closing his eyes. "Nothing's going to stand in my way."

The voice laughed her to sleep.

During the time of the First Gods it wasn't uncommon for people to(...)

It feels weird to me to spend all this time writing about the past, when the future is so uncertain. I can't do anything but watch that darkness take over more of the Cradle's door frame. History is important to me. Seeing where we come from should help us create a better today, but what can we do when the past itself is coming to haunt us?

Isildia, Sebanna, Forta, the King, Samadel, even the First Gods paint a history of tyrants and pain. Outside of Adathin, these people are relegated to legend or forgotten entirely. Yet here I sit, within touching distance of the Cradle of the World. It's true, but how much of it? The past is a mystery that even if I had a thousand more years I could never unravel.

And yet, I keep digging.

—From the Journal of Jovin Gutterwake

Chapter Thirty-Six

Banshee Coast

Marta ran ahead as soon as the ocean came into view. Gaul never understood her fascination with it, even after she explained. It was just a lot of water to him. Different people connect to different things, he figured. Though he couldn't think of what would make him react as Marta did to the sea.

"It's a house!" Marta called back.

Gaul hurried to join her. They had seen something sticking out of the ocean, but couldn't figure out what it was. Gaul worried it was another tower — he'd had enough of those.

Gaul stumbled down a sand dune and gazed at the ocean. It wasn't a tower, it was a tree. Thin and twig-like, it curved out of the water about half a kilometer from the shore. Perched precariously at the top was a cottage. The tree bent horribly and looked ready to drop the cottage into the sea at any moment.

"Who do you think lives up there?" Marta asked, catching her breath.

"The state that place is in?" Gaul said. "I'd say a corpse."

Marta nodded toward the beach. "There's a boat. Looks in good shape. Someone must be using it."

A rowboat laid on the sand, pulled away from the tide, complete with oars and devoid of rot or decay. It was certainly recently used — the sand hadn't yet filled in where it was dragged onto land.

"We should leave before whoever it is comes back." Gaul turned west, toward where Goodsmile said the fishing village should be. "Or whatever it is."

"You're not curious at all?" Marta asked.

Gaul couldn't deny the cottage in the tree piqued his interest. "We have important work to do. Stopping old gods, don't you remember?"

"I remember." She kicked at the sand. "I just thought—" She raised her head and her expression dropped. "Gaul!"

Gaul spun around. The sand dune had grown to massive proportions, breaching like a wave over him.

He braced himself. "Get back, Marta!"

The sand wave crashed. He Ignited to keep himself standing, but it was no use. The sand swept him away. He twirled along, becoming lost in the storm. The ground met him violently and he was left buried up to his neck

He spat out a mouthful of sand, mixed with blood and lightning for good measure. He extinguished and glanced around, trying to find Marta.

The sand a few metres from him exploded and Marta pulled herself free. She drew her sword and spun around.

"Who did that?" she shouted. "Show yourself!"

"Marta." Gaul struggled against the crushing sand. "A little help."

"There's someone out there." Marta drew a knife with her other hand.

A man approached from where the sand first attacked them. He moved slowly, but purposely. The long skeleton of some bizarre sea creature hung off his back like a cloak and dragged along the sand. Fine grains flowed around him on invisible wind and in his grip was a large, dripping sack.

"It's been a long time since anyone came this way," the man said. "I'm glad you could make it."

"We'll keep moving." Marta turned her sword and set her feet as firm as she could in the loose sand. "There doesn't have to be blood."

"There always is." The man swept his hand in the direction of the rowboat. "Would you mind terribly joining me in my home?"

"I think we're going to politely refuse."

The sand contracted around Gaul. He cried out in pain, pushing back against the incredible force. Marta clutched harder on her weapon and bared her teeth.

"You both will come with me," the man said. "Else I will crush your companion and sand the flesh from your bones."

"Fine!" Marta lowered her sword. "Just let him go."

"Put your sword away."

Marta bounced her knife in her hand, judging if she could throw it before the man killed Gaul. The sand continued to crush him, pushing the air out of his lungs. Marta's shoulders dropped. She put away her weapons and stood down.

The sand released and Gaul inhaled. The ground rumbled, lifting Gaul up until he was free.

"Let us take the boat," the man said, turning away.

Gaul rubbed his ribs. The stranger was powerful, he would need to wait for his moment to strike. The stranger lifted his hand and the sand moved again. It jumped up at Gaul and Marta's throats, wrapping around them like collars. It bound their hands and pulled them toward the boat. The moment to strike was becoming more distant.

"Woman," the man said, tossing his bag into the boat with a wet thump. "You will row."

The sand around Marta's wrists broke.

"I can easily strangle the life out of him," the man warned, pointing at Gaul. He sat at the bow, facing back.

Marta took the oars and Gaul sat at the stern. They looked at each other — neither of them had a clue what to do. So, Marta started rowing.

"My name is Bara-ban, in case you were curious," the man said. His movements were sluggish and he had trouble keeping himself sitting upright.

"I wasn't," Gaul said. "Where are you bringing us?"

"To my home." He gazed behind him, up at the craning house on top of the tree.

"I've seen a home like that before," Marta said. "I mean, not in a tree, but in a swamp. Are you a druid?"

The cottage had a familiar quality to it. It wasn't exact, but the longer Gaul stared at it, the more it reminded him of Ba-ya and Lenn's home in the swamp.

"What truly is a druid?" Bara-ban stroked the bag at his side. The smell from it was horrifying and rotten. "A being to purify corrupted land? But what if the land does not wish to be purified? What use is a druid then? Nothing but the cruel reminder of a vacuous promise."

He curled inward, breathing heavily. An eerie whining came from his throat.

"The short-sighted ones on the Boboros Whale poisoned the sea," he spat. "Unnatural concoctions that still echo today even as we work to silence them! If the world wants to be corrupt than it shall stay corrupt!" He leaned back. Black fluid stained his lips. "The deepest parts of the ocean will rise."

The druids were purifiers of tainted lands, yet something, something from Boboros Whale, was so evil it could infect even them. If Bara-ban was ever like Ba-ya and Lenn, he wasn't anymore.

Marta rowed the boat to the base of the tree. There was a small dock, with rickety planks spiralling up the tree to the cabin far above. They bumped to a stop and Bara-ban stumbled off the boat. Black bile dripped endlessly from his mouth. His movement seemed slower, more drawn out. He kept the stained bag close to his chest and tied the boat off with one hand. It was awkward, but he was unwilling to drop the strange sack.

"Off the boat," he said, never looking directly at his prisoners. "Climb the stairs. If you try anything, I will snap your necks."

The sand-collars tightened for a moment to prove he wasn't lying. Shards split from the restraints and flew through the air before binding Marta's hands once again. Bara-ban waited for them to disembark and start ascending the uneven stairs. He took up the rear, using the tree to keep his balance.

Gaul wondered if he could take Bara-ban down in his weaken state. But, the druid controlled the sand-collar with a simple thought. While Gaul's hands were bound, there wasn't much for him to do — even if Bara-ban had trouble climbing the stairs.

As the tree began to arc, the stairs turned into scaffolds until they reached the cabin. Fishbones were placed around the doorway, creating a maw-like entrance. Bara-ban pushed Gaul on the back.

"Enter," he said.

The fading daylight barely kept the room lit, but Bara-ban got to lighting some candles. It was a rustic design, reminiscent of Ba-ya and Lenn's cottage in the swamp, but drawn more from the ocean. The furniture was made from bone and driftwood. Clumps of seaweed hung from hooks or in piles in the corner.

Everywhere they looked was a black corruption. It dripped from the counter to the floor and oozed as thick stalactites from the roof. It was raw and lumpy, unlike the darkness from the Cradle which was smooth. It turned Gaul's stomach just looking at it.

Bara-ban shoved them inside. "Sit. Please. There is much to discuss. But first, we must eat."

He thumped across the crooked floor. The sand pulled Gaul and Marta to the chairs and pushed them down. Nothing Bara-ban said was truly a request.

The druid opened a pot and stirred whatever was inside with a ladle. "Dinner is cold, but still good. I left in a rush. I thought I heard it but… it was nothing."

What is he talking about? Gaul rubbed the sand around his wrists on the table leg. It carved away at the wood, but stayed firm around him.

"I'm pleased that someone has been willing to travel this far south." Bara-ban scooped a black sludge out of the pot. "I can't remember the last human I saw. I wonder, is that line of cragtrees still across the northern edge? I've never seen it myself but heard wonderfully strange things."

He piled three plates with the substance and dropped two in front of Gaul and Marta. Bones and what could be confused with meat chunks poked out. The smell was absolutely horrifying. Wet mold mixed with decaying plants.

Marta curled her lips in disgust. "What are you doing?"

"Eating." Bara-ban sat at the head of the table, next to his dripping bag. He took a spoon and shovelled in an overflowing mouthful of grim mash. He paused, then raised his head and stared at his captives. "Are you not hungry?"

Gaul picked up a spoon with his bound hands and poked at the food. Despite how it jiggled, it was oddly resistant to his prodding. "We're not." He dropped the spoon.

Bara-ban shrugged and continued his meal. Gaul and Marta sat in that oozing room as their host noisily slurped down the gruel. Once he was finished, he tossed his plate into a grimy wash basin. Then he grabbed Gaul and Marta's untouched food and dumped it out the window.

"Now we can talk," he said, placing their dishes next to his in the basin.

"Either kill us or let us go," Marta said. "We have nothing to say to you."

Bara-ban returned to his seat. He clutched the bag to his chest. "But we barely know each other."

Gaul scoffed. "You attacked us on the beach and abducted us. We know enough."

"You can't assume you know someone based on one encounter." He stroked the bag. "I am difficult. I know this. I have seen the deepest parts of the ocean, where light is forbidden and the sky is a myth. It has affected me in ways I can't describe. It has taken from me, everything."

He let out the same eerie whine as he did on the boat. More black fluid eked out of the corners of his mouth as he spoke.

"I will not kill you or let you go. You have a greater purpose. Cori-ban, who never returned, needs you. Once the Gillyboith is defeated, all that is lost will be found."

"Where is the other druid?" Marta asked, softly, as if speaking too loudly would wake the darkness in Bara-ban. "There are always two. Where's the other one?"

"Cori-ban, who never returned. She'll come back."

Bara-ban curled tighter around the wet bag, and Gaul had a sinking feeling about what was inside. Marta cast him an uneasy look. She must have had the same thought.

"It's time to sleep." Bara-ban waved his hand and the sand manacles dragged Gaul and Marta out of their seats. They pulled them across the room and pinned them to the wall, sitting. "We have to be up early tomorrow. It's a long walk."

Gaul struggled against the manacles. He still had his swords, but the sand didn't have any give. The fact Bara-ban didn't take their weapons felt like he was taunting them. Gaul's movements bent the wall and dropped a large piece of the black corruption on him and Marta. Marta scowled at him and shook the grime off her head.

Bara-ban doused the candles, slowly bathing the room in moonlight. He stopped at the door to another room, presumably his bedroom, and looked at Gaul and Marta. In the dim glow, it appeared as though the slime that coated the walls and ceiling was reaching for him. Without a word, he disappeared into his quarters.

"Nothing is easy, is it?" Marta asked. A rhetorical question, of course.

"Boboros Vale — or Boboros Whale, whatever people want to call it — must have had something truly evil happen to it," Gaul said. "I was hoping that since Leviathan is a corpse we may avoid another encounter like in Black Hypogea or the Tower. I suppose even a dead Primordial's still a Primordial."

"You're blaming Leviathan for this?"

"Something corrupted that druid." Gaul gazed at the empty frame that led into Bara-ban's dark quarters. "A piece of Leviathan is there. I don't know for sure, I'm just taking a guess."

Marta sighed, rolling her neck inside the sand collar that held her head up. "Doesn't matter anyway, does it? We need to get there and we're stuck here. Do you have a plan?"

"We wait. Bara-ban's slipping, he'll make a mistake and we'll take advantage."

"Will that be before or after he kills us?"

"Aren't you supposed to be the optimist?" Gaul cast her a half-hearted smile.

She didn't respond. She settled into her bonds and shut her eyes. It hadn't gone unnoticed to Gaul that Marta had gotten more dire with each day that passed. Neither of them expected to be in this position a couple months ago. Gaul was going to be on his way home with his wife's necklace. Marta was going to be with her brother.

Instead, Gaul drifted off to sleep in a rotten cottage on a tree.

Digging for what? For truth? Truth doesn't matter. I believed the King was overthrown in a rebellion, but that's not true. Sebanna's account contradicts that. Yet for my entire life, that was the truth. If my research is lost through circumstance or time, will it matter what I discovered?

—From the Journal of Jovin Gutterwake

Chapter Thirty-Seven
The Hanging Village, Galianos

Bara-ban woke them up with the sunrise. He offered them more of the black gruel, but Gaul and Marta refused again. They were hungry, but weren't ready to stoop to consuming whatever that was. Bara-ban ate alone and in silence, then led his captives back down to the boat. Before long, Marta was rowing them to the shore.

"Head that way," Bara-ban said, pointing east. "We'll make landing then walk the rest of the way."

"Where are we going?" Gaul asked.

"To find the Gillyboith." He held onto his bag. This time he clutched it like a child waiting to open a present. "It was screaming last night. I could barely sleep. It knows you came. With you as the lure, I can finally get it out into the open and kill it for good. Then Cori-ban…"

He trailed off, staring into the middle distance with a goofy smile on his face.

"I didn't hear anything," Marta said.

"Then you're deaf. It screamed out for blood so loud I swore it was in my room."

Gaul shrugged at Marta. He hadn't heard anything either. As far as he knew, the night had passed without interruption.

They stopped the boat near a cliff face. A brilliant white wall stretched a hundred metres above them. The stone was worn down to a smooth finish, though the weathering of time was present. Gaul would assume that a waterfall should be there, but not a drop trickled into the sea.

"There's a path up not far from here," Bara-ban said, pulling the boat onto the beach. He reaffixed Marta's hands with the sand manacles. "Stay close to me. You know what will happen if you run."

Gaul and Marta gave no response, but the collars tightened ever so slightly to put a punctuation on Bara-ban's point. He waved for them to follow. His fish skeleton cloak dragged on the ground as he brought them toward the cliffs.

"I'm not deaf," Marta whispered to Gaul. "I didn't hear anything last night. Did you?"

"Not at all." Gaul kept an eye on Bara-ban. "Have you ever heard of a Gillyboith?"

"I was hoping you had."

The path Bara-ban had mentioned was little more than a goat trail that wound up the cliff face like some blind serpent. A few times, Gaul or Marta nearly slipped, only to be dragged to firmer ground by Bara-ban's manacles. It wasn't an easy trek, and took them over an hour to reach the top.

Coming over the cliff lip, they were greeted by the sparkling blue waters of a large lake. Bara-ban stepped forward to take in the soft breeze that crested the surface, creating small ripples that lapped against the stony shore.

Far on the other side of the lake was a stone structure. It was long and tall, a few kilometres wide and taking up much of the northern side of the lake shore. They were a good distance away, but something was on its side, above the water. It disrupted what would have been smooth stone with a speckle of something unknown.

"That's where we're going," Bara-ban said, pointing at the monstrosity. "That's where we'll find the Gillyboith."

They were getting too close to where Bara-ban wanted to use them as bait. Still, he had not slipped up. Gaul wondered if he could draw his sword and kill Bara-ban before the druid could crush his throat. Bara-ban didn't seem concerned that his prisoners might try to kill him, and that confidence gave Gaul pause. Confidence, or was Bara-ban truly insane?

They circled around the lake toward where the land began to rise to meet the top of the structure. The things on the side of it came into focus, they were houses. Wooden buildings, large and small built vertically up and down the height of the structure. Gaul was briefly reminded of the dracoling city beneath Castle Adathin, but these were much better made. Rather than ramshackle tenements ready to fall at any second, these looked sturdy with walkways that gave a sense of safety.

Also as they reached the top, they could see what was on the other side of the structure. It was a lazy river, a kilometre or more wide. The current occasionally slapped against the stone and splashed onto their feet. That was when Gaul realized what they were standing on.

It was a massive dam, bigger than any Gaul had seen or dreamt off. Its stonework was closer to a castle and its size spoke to an unbelievable undertaking. They walked through the remains of an ancient market with clear paths that led off the side of the dam onto the hanging city below.

"This town was called Galianos," Bara-ban said. He ran his fingers along a stall he passed, only for it to collapse at his touch. "The people who lived here didn't build this dam. They found it and believed that it was created by the gods to create the bountiful lake below and push the river toward the Galianos Falls to the east. I think it's ridiculous to assume the gods would care about the flow of a river. In the end, water always overcomes."

Marta's jaw hung open as she took in the sights. Gaul couldn't find any marks of a fight or conflict. The town wasn't ransacked, it was simply abandoned. Everyone packed up and moved on, leaving the skeleton of a town behind.

Bara-ban continued, "This is where the Gillyboith screams. It likes the emptiness of homes that used to be full of life. It knows I'm looking for it. However, it does not know you. I'm sure its hunger will overwhelm its intelligence in time."

He swept his hand forward. The restraints took hold of Gaul and Marta and moved them into a courtyard. They were close to the middle of the dam, near a dock that reached into the river. Planters created paths for the citizens to walk, but now they were overflowing with greenery. Gaul and Marta were brought through the untended walkways, crunching vines and crawlers beneath their feet.

In the centre of the courtyard was a tall fountain. It was expertly carved, with a torrent of fish leaping toward a rune-covered ball, most likely the sun. With a sharp tug, Gaul was affixed to the lip of the basin, forced onto his knees. The stagnant water was topped off with a thick layer of green. Marta was pulled next to him, in the same position.

"If we don't find our moment soon," Gaul said. "We're going to have to contend with this Gillyboith."

"I'm not so sure about that," Marta said. She glanced back to where Bara-ban was inspecting the courtyard, trying to find a place to hide among the overgrowth. She continued softer, "I don't think the Gillyboith is real."

"What do you mean?"

Bara-ban walked further away from the fountain. There was a statue of some figure lifting cupped hands above him, asking for help or raising something. Bara-ban positioned himself behind it.

"I used to have Jovin read me some old folk tales when I went to sleep," Marta explained. "Creepy stories from a book we found in the library. One of them was about the Snatching Crawler. It was from the coastal towns to the south. The fish in the area were the largest anyone had ever seen, but they tended to follow these moving pockets of arcane energy. The fishing villages would pop up then move with the migrations of these magic-eating fish.

"This left dozens of villages on the shore temporarily abandoned until the fish would migrate back. The story goes that the Snatching Crawler lives in the sea and is drawn to abandoned homes. Something about the lingering presence of the people who once lived there. If it finds you alone, it will drag you into the ocean. It was a terrifying story."

"And you think the Gillyboith is the Snatching Crawler?" Gaul asked.

"Seems likely. It's supposed to have a distinct cry, described as a scream. Bara-ban keeps saying he hears it, but I haven't heard anything. Trust me, I did not sleep well last night. I would have heard if something was screaming."

Gaul shrugged. "Doesn't mean it can't be real."

"The book was up front that it was created by parents to keep their children from going back to their old villages." Marta stretched in her bindings and glanced at the river dock. "It's just a feeling I have. I think Bara-ban's fighting a ghost."

Gaul rested his head on his hands. He had assumed that Bara-ban's state was due to the corruption. But maybe he had his timeline wrong. The way Bara-ban talked about the other druid, Cori-ban, and the fact he clutched onto that grotesque bag. It was possible he went mad from grief and that lead to him abandoning his cleansing duties, allowing the corruption.

Minutes turned into hours and nothing came for Gaul or Marta. Occasionally Bara-ban would poke his head out from his hiding place. When the sun completed its rising and began its descent, Bara-ban left his spot in a huff.

"Why!?" he shouted. "Why won't it come for you?"

Gaul cast Marta a knowing look. Bara-ban was coming apart. If he was going to make a mistake, it would be soon. Bara-ban picked up a stone that had broken off one of the planters and hurled it over Gaul's head. It bounced off the fountain and hit the water, splashing Gaul. His manacles were spotted with points of wetness.

"Is there something wrong with you?" Bara-ban stomped his feet, shaking with panicked rage. "Something that makes it not want to eat you?"

The spots where the water splashed on Gaul's sand manacles had been washed away. It wasn't weakened enough for him to break free, but it gave him an idea. There was a tug on his neck and he was pulled away from the fountain. Marta shouted, but her collar shifted up into a muzzle.

Bara-ban grabbed Gaul by the coat and inspected him. "There is definitely something about you. Rage and blood. Purpose too."

"Or maybe." Gaul pushed back, putting his face in Bara-ban's. "Your monster isn't real at all."

Bara-ban's eye twitched. He shoved Gaul to the ground, against a planter. "Are you calling Cori-ban a liar? Have you no respect?"

He clutched on his bag and turned away. He mumbled something unintelligible, occasionally twitching. Gaul crept away. He needed to get more water from the fountain to free himself, then he could kill Bara-ban.

A sharp yank on his collar and his escape grew further. Marta was also released from the fountain and pulled to his side. Bara-ban fumed, more of that strange black bile coated his lips and staining the front of his tunic.

"I know," he muttered, barely loud enough to hear. "I'll drain your blood. It'll come. It'll come when the blood's in the water."

Gaul and Marta were pulled through the courtyard toward the dock. It was closer to water, closer to an opportunity to release them from their bonds, but certainly Bara-ban was aware of the weakness in his sand constructs. He would kill them without putting them in the water. What Bara-ban didn't know was that Gaul knew the weakness as well.

They left the courtyard and swept past a line of vendor stalls. They were only a metre from the water when Bara-ban stopped and drew a bone knife. The sand collars lifted Gaul and Marta until they could barely stand on their toes to keep themselves from being hung.

Bara-ban paced around them, tapping the knife against his forehead. The fluid from inside his body increased. He spat a mouthful onto the ground and wiped it out from under his nose, but that only resulted in it staining his hand.

"Wait," Gaul choked out. "Do you hear that? Something's screaming."

Bara-ban froze. He craned his neck, as if he could make the sound fall into his head. His eyes flickered, wild and frantic.

"There it is again." The pressure on Gaul's neck failed as Bara-ban's attention slipped. He could stand on his heels.

Marta mumbled something through her muzzle. It sounded like agreement, but was hard to tell.

"Where?" Bara-ban shouted. "Where is it!? I can't hear it."

Bara-ban's control over the collar's dropped, and so did Gaul and Marta. Marta took in hard puffs through her nose and clutched at her throat. Gaul knew they didn't have much time. He swung his arms over Marta's head, grabbing her by the waist. With a flare of Ignition, he dragged her off the dock and into the water with him.

Bara-ban shouted. A sand noose tightened around Gaul's neck before the water washed the collar away. Marta looked at her wrists in surprise, but resisted the urge to take in a breath of air. Gaul kept his arms around Marta's waist; they couldn't breach the surface, not yet.

Through the distortion of the river waves above them, Gaul could barely make out Bara-ban standing on the dock. Gaul wasn't sure how much air Marta had taken in before going under, but she wasn't panicking. Still, they couldn't stay under forever. Marta tapped him on the hand and pointed at the dam wall beneath Bara-ban's feet. Taking great care not to disrupt the water and give away their position, they swam to the dock.

Bara-ban didn't give an indication that he saw the pair's movements. He looked over them, perhaps expecting his captives to swim away. The dam wall was irregular and offered plenty of hand and foot holds.

Marta held up three fingers. Gaul grabbed onto a rope used for tying up boats floating just below the surface. His lungs were beginning to burn. Marta held up three fingers, then two, then one.

They exploded into the air. Gaul grabbed Bara-ban's left leg, Marta his right, and they pulled. Bara-ban thudded off the dock and went spiralling into the swirling water. Gaul rolled onto the shore with Marta on his heel.

Bara-ban didn't surface, though a steady stream of bubbles rose and popped. Marta put a hand on her sword and took in coughing breaths of air.

"Is he coming back up?" she wondered out loud.

"I don't know." Gaul readied himself for anything. "But I'm not turning my back on him."

The dam shook with a heavy thump. Marta drew her sword. A black spiral grew within the depths of the river, where Bara-ban had fell, and spread until it choked out all the blue. Another thump and the stone dam cracked. Fractal fissures crawled between Gaul's legs and toward the courtyard. The river water crested the top of the dam.

"It's flooding," Marta said, backing away.

"Worse," Gaul said. "It's breaking."

I wasn't born in Marjyal. I went there due to the legends — curiosity was always my weakness. It was a city of contradictions, one where the people accepted blindness and ignorance and called it freedom. At the time, I authored essays about the world outside the walls. I expected them to be quite controversial, but instead they were ignored by the masses and fawned over by the elite. Of course, it was easy for me to simply take my own history and sell it for attention from the wealthy who would pay just to hear scandalous tales of the savage past. As if the savagery around them wasn't enough.

—From the Journal of Jovin Gutterwake

Chapter Thirty-Eight

Walls Fall

The water bulged upwards into a shadowy dome that poured around Gaul and Marta's feet. In the centre of it all was a pulsating pit of darker than dark.

Gaul pulled on Marta, urging her to run. "We need to go, Marta!"

Marta sheathed her sword and spun away from the oncoming river. Gaul led the way, traversing through the courtyard by vaulting and hurdling planters and railings. The water kept up with them, closely matched with the cracks that formed with each subsequent thump.

"He's trying to take the dam down!" Gaul cried. The water was up to his ankles and each step splashed more up to his waist.

"Then we should be running that way!" Marta pointed right, along the length of the dam.

"If you think you can run a kilometre before this thing breaks, go ahead!" He shoved a stall apart as they entered the residential area. The front of the dam was within sight. "I'm getting to the bottom of that city on the side."

"Oh great. Then we can be *under* the flood!"

"Do you have a better plan, Marta!?"

"That doesn't mean it's a good one!"

The water filled the streets to their shins, forcing them to kick their feet through the torrents as they ran. Behind them, the dome had moved onto the shore. It trembled, then shot out a rushing wave that swept along the street, breaking slats off the windows and snapping awnings.

Marta mantled a crate then bounded along detritus, just above the water. It was faster than slogging through the current, and she quickly passed Gaul.

"Faster!" Marta shouted. She made it to the corner of the street, right on the edge of the dam, and spun around the corner.

Gaul splashed after her, but the wave was closing in. With each step, the water level rose and each step after was more difficult. Marta reached out her hand, urging him to fight harder. Gaul reached back — then he was overcome.

The world became a mess of dark blue and white. He struck the ground, then just as quickly had it disappear. The lake stretched out before him, inviting him to fall into its embrace. First, though, was the hanging village of Galianos. Gaul snapped out a grab at one of the wooden walkway supports. The rope that held it snapped and the pole bent back, breaking more supports as it arched and swung Gaul back into the city, albeit several levels lower.

Torrents of water continued to pour off the top of the dam, raining over Galianos with no end. A few cracks appeared in the dam wall, allowing more to seep through. Bara-ban wasn't going to stop until the dam was entirely wiped out. He was a wild animal, lashing out with loud fury. It was unfocused, but still dangerous.

"Marta!" Gaul shouted. "Where are you!?"

Even if Marta heard him, there was no way she could respond over the sound of water rushing over the dam and pounding against the hanging village. A shack above Gaul cracked then broke away from the wall. He stumbled back as it slammed into the walkway. The anchoring yanked out of the dam and the structure crumbled upon itself.

Galianos was falling. Between the ever-increasing waterfall and the rupturing dam, the village couldn't hold its own weight. Gaul carefully descended a ramp, only for it to shudder and drop him off the side. He landed a level down, cracking the supports and turning it into a slope that kept him falling.

Getting his feet beneath him, Gaul landed awkwardly and stumbled into the door of a house. He took a moment to catch his breath. The break didn't last long, as the walkway he had broken with his back had turned into a water channel. The dam wall cracked, unleashing a flood that aimed to crush Gaul.

Gaul braced himself against the door and turned the knob. The water struck him and tossed the door open. He carried on with the momentum and swung behind the door, allowing the water to rush through the empty home and toward the back room. It grabbed a chair and a stool as it flowed through, moving it all to the back. Supports snapped and cracked as the house tilted from the weight.

Gaul pushed the door against the water, but it was no use. The pressure wouldn't let him close the door or leave. Another crack. Gaul abandoned the door and moved to the window. There was another house, almost twelve metres away. Gaul groaned, but hopped onto the sill.

The lake was far below, a potentially deadly drop. Gaul grabbed both sides of the window frame, let out a puff of air, then leapt. He grasped the bottom of the next house's windowsill and banged his chest off the siding. He looked back as the first house snapped free and dropped into the lake.

A supporting rope from that house flopped within jumping distance of Gaul and dangled a few levels down. Gaul swung himself over and continued downward. Occasionally, he glanced up, hoping to spot Marta among the structure and flood. Perhaps she had stayed on top of the dam and decided to attempt the kilometre run to the edge, but considering how much of the top was currently pouring water, it didn't seem a much safer route.

He was still a good distance from the lake when the water stopped. Gaul looked up, but between the walkways, houses, and struts, it was impossible to tell what was going on. If Bara-ban had decided to leave, that would be great for Gaul and Marta. Something told Gaul that wasn't the case.

As if to answer the question Gaul wasn't asking, the dam exploded.

The centre of the hanging village was gone in an instant, replaced by a raging waterfall. The village bent forward, pulling its anchorings out of the wall and dropping chunks away. Gaul braced himself between two struts. There was no escape now, all he could do was ready himself for the impact. He shut his eyes, held his breath, and submerged.

The rapids pulled him forward, knocking him along the remains of Galianos. A chunk of the dam splashed down next to him. He kicked off the stone and breached the surface. He took in a gasp of air then was pulled under once again.

He swirled chaotically until he lost all sense of direction. All he knew was he was being pulled inexorably toward the white cliffs above the sea. Gaul kicked against the stream, but it did little to stop his momentum.

On his next stroke, he felt the lakebed. He spun around and pushed both feet downward. They sunk into the mud, but didn't stop him. He dug in harder, knocking stones and sand aside as he was pushed along. He breached the surface and breathed deeply. The edge of the cliff was coming on fast.

"Come on!" he shouted.

Finally, something solid beneath his feet stopped him a couple metres from the edge. The water still beat against his back, curling up around his neck and occasionally into his mouth. He looked back at the remains of the dam.

Half a kilometre of the dam was gone. The entire hanging city had fallen into the lake, with only a few of the wider sections rising out of the surface. Kilolitres of water were pouring from the river into the lake and raising the level until it overflowed onto the beach and sea below.

Amid the roiling waters, a dark-haired head swept toward Gaul. It was Marta, trying her best to keep herself above water. They made a moment of eye contact before she disappeared again. Gaul spread his arms out to each side and braced. There was a pull on his left arm and he pulled back. Marta reappeared and he took her arm with both of his.

"Don't let go!" Marta shouted.

The stones under Gaul's feet shifted a few centimetres. He tried to shout back, but a burst of water choked out his words. All he could do was hold onto Marta and strain against the pressure.

"Gaul!" Marta looked past him, eyes wide.

Gaul craned his neck around. Moving across the lake was a mass of water intermixed with black corruption. It splayed out into an impressive wingspan and at its centre was Bara-ban. The corruption focused on him, reaching across his skin like infecting veins. He oriented on Gaul and Marta with frightening intensity.

Gaul made eye contact with Marta. They needed to stop Bara-ban, they both knew that, but both of Gaul's hands were occupied holding Marta and she was in no position to attack. Marta nodded. Gaul gritted his teeth.

"Just make sure you get him," Marta said. "I'll meet you at the bottom."

Gaul grinned, then let her go. She disappeared over the edge. Gaul carefully turned around, making sure he didn't slip off the stones he knew were solid.

Bara-ban had disappeared. There were only the breaking waves that charged to consume Gaul. Pushing against the rushing rapids, Gaul drew a sword. He held it high, tip toward the wall of water. Igniting, the world dimmed into grey and a glowing red figure could be seen within the torrents.

Gaul bellowed with a final burst of exertion. He plunged his blade centre mass on the figure and was swept into the sea.

Marta pulled herself onto the shore, hacking up water. She brushed a clump of seaweed off her shoulder and flopped down onto the sand. Her body ached. With great effort, she got onto her hands and knees and crawled until she could get to her feet.

The lake had completely overtaken the cliffside, turning it into a wide waterfall. Pieces of the hanging village rained into the sea. Marta scanned the ocean, looking for any sign of Gaul. It wouldn't have been a fight between him and Bara-ban, not with the footing Gaul had. He would have had one good strike. Hopefully he made the best of it.

A few metres from the shore, Gaul broke the surface. He drew in some air then moved forward, walking out of the water exhausted. He had one sword bare that he held in the loosest of grasps. Marta ran to meet him.

"Did you get him?" Marta asked.

Gaul stopped, considered her first, then his sword. "I stabbed him, that's for sure. Whether or not it killed him is different."

He sheathed his sword then brushed past Marta. He reached the edge of the water, spun around, then dropped back first onto the sand. Marta sat next to him and looking into the ocean.

"No more water," Marta said, pushing her hair back.

Gaul laughed. "I thought you loved the sea."

"I like the sea. No more water."

There was a sharp, wet cough from down the beach. Gaul bolted upright. Further from the cliffs, Bara-ban laid washed up on the beach. Seaweed wrapped around his limbs and a dark red stain trickled from his body toward the sea.

Gaul growled and rolled onto his feet. He drew his sword and stomped toward Bara-ban.

"I'm gonna put him out of our misery," he said, spinning the blade.

Marta kept pace. After all Bara-ban did to them, she didn't feel bad for ending him. They approached his body and Marta leaned in to see if he was breathing. A wound in his chest bubbled blood along his torso. At his side, the bag he always carried was torn open and empty. Whatever was once inside it was gone. Gaul raised his sword. Bara-ban jerked to life, coughing up a lungful of bloody water.

"Cori!" he cried. "I never faltered. I never faltered in my duties."

Gaul stopped. Something was different about Bara-ban, something ethereal and untouchable. Still, Marta kept her distance, ready to react.

"If anyone tells you I did they're liars!" More blood bubbled out of his mouth. "I never stopped. I cleaned it. Even when you said it was a lost cause. Even when you told me about the deepest parts of the ocean. Even when you never came back." Tears welled up in his eyes. "They're liars. I did my duty."

Marta lowered her gaze. Cori-ban was the first victim of the corruption. Even as it began to take Bara-ban, something inside him told him he was doing the right thing. Marta couldn't forgive him, but she couldn't bring herself to hate him anymore either.

Gaul lowered his sword to his side and knelt next to the pitiful druid. For the first time, Bara-ban noticed someone with him.

"I never stopped doing my duty," Bara-ban said.

"I know." Gaul placed his hand on Bara-ban's chest. "Tell them that."

Bara-ban smiled. A long, drawn out breath, then he was silent. Bara-ban had passed.

"That was nice of you," Marta said, putting her hands in her pockets.

"I see no problem in a kind lie for the dead." Gaul sheathed his sword. "It's what I would want in the end."

The blood at Bara-ban's feet darkened. Marta pulled Gaul back. A shadow oozed from Bara-ban and entered the sea. It shot along the waves, moving westward at an incredible pace.

"Boboros Vale," Gaul said, straightening his spine.

"That's what's corrupting the ocean." Marta stepped forward, the ocean breeze blowing her wet hair back. "We could finish what the druids started."

"More water."

Marta squared her jaw. "More water."

They headed west, continuing their journey to Boboros Vale.

When Dianathos became the Praetor of Doves, it quickly became apparent to me that he was a fanatic. In secret, he had people find any piece of writing that promoted independent thought and had it burned. He couldn't outlaw them, of course, he could only dissuade the authors. Usually violently. I couldn't risk it, not with someone to care for. So, I stopped writing and watched my work turn into ash.

—From the Journal of Jovin Gutterwake

Chapter Thirty-Nine

Descendants

As the Marjyalians celebrated, consuming every drop of liquor in Barrowfield, Melifacto snuck out the back door. Pelady walked with him to the town limits, lit only by the stars and moon.

"Are you sure you want to go alone?" Pelady asked.

"I will be fine." Melifacto put his owl mask on. "Keep an eye on Feyra. Make sure she stays put."

"Of course, master." Pelady slunk back toward the tavern.

Melifacto walked past the horses and into the night. After a short time, he came to a farmer's field. The harvest hadn't been kind, but there were large haystacks littered about. Standing next to one was the man Melifacto had came to see. A man dressed in all white, with a wide-brimmed hat and a porcelain mask.

"I hear you're going by Goodsmile these days," Melifacto said. "What happened to wanting to be known by actions, rather than a name?"

Goodsmile made no motion. He stared up at the large full moon that looked over the pair like a judging eye.

"At least say something." Melifacto took a careful step forward.

"I'm intrigued that you would contact me," Goodsmile said. "After you threw me out of your city of straw, I thought you wanted nothing to do with me."

"You were burning people alive."

"I admit that can be upsetting to those who are more prudish." Goodsmile turned to face Melifacto. "Is this why you contacted me? To remind me when you stole my purpose?"

"No." Melifacto removed his mask. "Things have changed. Absence is spreading from the Cradle."

"Oh, no," Goodsmile said with mock concern.

"This affects us all. It's a clear indication that the First Gods are awakening and that they do not possess a drop of the Light they once held. Their power will come from Absence. Absence is destruction. We will not survive."

"We'll survive." Goodsmile craned his neck out. "It'll just be a different world."

"This is serious."

"Do I not look like someone taking this seriously?"

Melifacto regretted contacting Goodsmile. He had hoped he would put aside their past for a common goal. Clearly that was too much to ask. Goodsmile paced the field, swaying like a drunkard. Behind his charred mask, he kept his gaze on Melifacto.

"We have a chance," Melifacto said, holding his ground. "They can still be stopped. But to do that, we need to open the Cradle."

"So this is about the Key?" Goodsmile asked.

"Yes. But to get it, I need someone." He clenched his fists and his gloves creaked. "Someone that I hear you've been helping. A fugitive named Marta. She travels with a man named Gaul."

Goodsmile stopped. "Oh, yes. We have a mutually beneficial arrangement."

"If you bring her to me, I will ensure that the Chalice of—"

"They're collecting Light, you know."

Melifacto clenched his jaw. "What?"

"They're collecting—" He wiggled his fingers in the air. "—Light. That's why they're visiting the Primordials, it's pretty obvious when you think about it. I imagine some remnants of power from when they were defeated by the First Gods has clung to them."

"That could be possible..."

"It's more than possible." Goodsmile opened his coat and brought out a folded-up sheet. "I checked."

He laid the bundle on the ground and unfolded it slowly. Even with the full moon, it was difficult to make out what was inside. Something small, not much larger than a fist. Melifacto first thought it might be a waterskin, but when he saw the stains on the sheet, it was clear it was something different.

"Lungs," Melifacto said.

"Full of Light." Goodsmile hovered his fingers just over them. "It's the only part of a person that I could find that holds it, even here where none is supposed to exist. But only in very small amounts. These lungs are different. They're bursting."

"What makes them different?"

"These lungs are from a Descendant." He put his palm against his chest. "Lungs like mine." He pointed at Melifacto. "Lungs like yours."

Melifacto narrowed his eyes. His knees trembled. Goodsmile, as he now wanted to be called, spoke with an icy coldness. Melifacto suddenly wished he had brought Pelady. "Who's are they?"

"Dynah."

Melifacto swallowed. "Did you kill her?"

"No. I just found her. I imagine her tumble from the tower was thanks to your fugitives. Don't pretend that you're broken up about it."

Melifacto wasn't, but he couldn't help but feel a pang of loss from the death of such a unique creature. There were only five Descendants after all.

"Our dear sister wanted nothing more than to sit in her tower, alone with her illusions." Goodsmile folded up the lungs gently. "You always hated her because she never wanted to follow you, but you're so alike. You all are. Running away from who you should be. How long have you been talking about overthrowing the Divines? Ascending to a godhood you think was stolen from you? We are imperfect, I've accepted that."

"We should have been rulers." Melifacto's spine tingled. "They never even gave us a chance."

Goodsmile tucked the lungs away and stood tall. "So the plan is to take the Chalice and put our parents to sleep again, but instead it will be you that has the power. You build yourself a throne from the corpses of the Divines and rule as God-King Melifacto? Exciting, but misdirected. You'll always be the flawed child of a god."

"And what makes you so much better than me?"

"I see the truth."

Goodsmile thrust his arms toward Melifacto and the ground burst into flames. A dozen winding rivers of fire twisted through the field, igniting the haystacks. One line cut close to Melifacto and he stumbled back in fear.

"I see the fire in the world." Flickering light danced off Goodsmile's mask. His voice was filled with fervour. "The First Gods will return to set us right. And each soul cast to the flames will prove my allegiance. Powerful souls that will fill the world with a new light. Only then can I be redeemed."

Melifacto shielded his face from the roaring flames. Goodsmile had gone mad. "Would you kill me too? We're brothers!"

"Yes." Goodsmile lowered his head. "But not now. Only once you have watched everything you have worked for turn to ash will I feed your soul to the fire. Marjyal and its people will be the tinder upon which you burn. With an offering such as that, Lord Tyran, my father, won't be able to ignore me any longer."

Goodsmile turned on his heel and walked away, the flames bending away from his path. Melifacto stepped forward, only for a wall of fire to leap up in his way.

"This is foolish!" Melifacto shouted. "You're praying to gods no one believes in."

"They don't have to believe. They just have to burn."

The flames whipped into a frenzy, then Goodsmile was gone. Melifacto retreated from the burning field. He looked back when he was a safe distance away, watching the smoke curl in front of the moon. The meeting had gone worse than he could ever have imagined.

It's humorous to me that Dianathos, who was so afraid of the past, didn't know of the library on the edge of the bay. Most people didn't care about what was left after the collapse except for the people with nowhere else to go. Thankfully, Dianathos was one of those who didn't care.

I found that since I could no longer write, I had more time to read. I carved my way into the back of the library, absorbing every bit of information I could get my hands on. Battle reports, legends from the Age of Gods, even crop yields. But it was never enough. I could see the holes. It was one side of a story, one piece of a puzzle that was our shared history. That was when I decided I needed to leave Marjyal.

—From the Journal of Jovin Gutterwake

Chapter Forty

Fishing Hamlet: Four

They passed Bara-ban's cottage. The tree seemed to bend even more, ready to collapse into the sea. Maybe it felt the death of its occupant. Marta took a moment to take in the sight. Her feelings for Bara-ban were complex, but she believed the druid was once a good person, much like Ba-ya and Lenn.

"Come on, Marta," Gaul said.

Marta jogged to catch up. The fishing village Goodsmile mentioned should be ahead, though there was no telling how far away it was. It could be a few days, or even weeks. There was even the chance that Goodsmile had lied, though that seemed unnecessarily cruel of him.

They spent that night away from the beach, up on the grassy ridge that overlooked it. After seeing the corruption crawl into the sea, neither of them were interested in sleeping anywhere close to it. Marta sat close to the fire with her brother's journal on her knees.

"Any luck?" Gaul asked, trying to dry his coat.

Marta touched the curled pages of the journal. "Most of it is ruined. The ink's too stained to read. I should have read it faster. I was afraid when I finished it, that I would lose my only connection to Jovin. But I lost it anyway." A forlorn smile crept across her face. "Jovin has many journals actually. That's what he was always doing, always writing. Accounts were what mattered, if people didn't write about what happened, in a hundred years no one would know."

"How much older was he?"

"Twentyish years."

"That's quite the difference."

Marta closed the journal. "We had different fathers. Our mother died in childbirth, so it was just us. Now it's just me." She ran her fingers along the damp cover, then tossed it into the fire.

Gaul sat up straight.

"My brother isn't in a book. Jovin always told me the most important thing is to move on. That's what the world does. It moves on. From the Primordials, to the First Gods, to the Divines. From ruler to ruler. Still, they hang around in our minds and our hearts. Jovin is dead, but he's not gone. Not as long as I don't want him to be."

"I'm sorry." Gaul leaned forward on his knees. "I know that means next to nothing."

"No." Marta watched the leather bindings curl and break. "Thank you for being here. So I don't have to be alone. I know I haven't been the easiest to travel with. The exodus stone, Marjyal chasing us to find me, stabbing you in the Tower."

"Don't forget the entire reason why we're here."

"Hey! It's not my fault that First Gods are waking up."

Gaul chuckled, then stopped.

"What is it?" Marta asked.

"Just thinking about something Athas said in Marjyal." Gaul stared into the flames. "He wondered about the line between coincidence and providence."

"What's providence?"

"Holy will. Kind of like destiny."

"You think this is some god's will?" Marta motioned to the landscape around them.

"Either that or coincidence."

"Which one would you prefer?"

Gaul leaned back and puffed out some air. "I honestly have no idea."

Marta fell back onto the grass. "There's a third option."

"What's that?" Gaul kicked some dirt onto the fire, quelling it.

"Bad luck." Marta shut her eyes and drifted off to sleep.

The next day, just as evening crept in, Marta saw a group of about a dozen buildings of various size on the ocean's edge.

The salty sea air had not been kind to the wood and many of the structures were in shambles. The shore had shrunk in the intervening years and the half of the hamlet closer to the sea was covered in a thin layer of water. Gaul stepped onto the fallen planks of a shack, only for it to snap again under his weight.

Marta felt something under her feet. Looking down, she spotted a piece of a wooden board beneath the water and sand. There were designs along the visible edge and she pulled it free. Wiping away the wet sand, it read *Fishing Hamlet: Four.*

"Looks like we found it," Marta said. "These people weren't creative with the names. Guess that's what happens when you move with the fish."

"You think these are the people from that story you told me?" Gaul asked.

"The people were real, even if the Snatching Crawler wasn't." She tossed the sign away and stepped into the village. "What was it that Goodsmile said we had to do?"

"He didn't say anything." Gaul pushed on one of the smaller houses' doors. It swung open without resistance. "All he said was if we came here, we would find our vale."

Marta groaned. She had been hoping for a clear indication when they arrived. A large sign with an arrow. "It's a whale, right? Let's check the dock."

"It's a whale with a city on its back. If it was here, I'm sure we would see it."

"Then maybe we need to call it."

Gaul stopped peering through a dirty window. "You're probably right. That's going to make it more difficult. How do you call a whale?"

Marta couldn't answer that. She left Gaul investigating the village and headed toward the ocean. The shoreline had a long dock that split into a 'T' at the end. There were a number of boats tied to it, though most of them had torn sails or broken masts. One in particular had mostly sunk, with only the tip of its stern above the surface.

At the end of the dock, where it split, was a hut with a large window and a counter. Marta approached, the wood creaking with each step. She couldn't hear Gaul at all, the only sound other than the dock was the whooshing of the ocean breeze. The hut didn't fit. It was too well put together compared to the state of the village. It also was made of different wood.

A shape was inside the shadows of the hut. But as Marta got closer, she saw it wasn't alive. It was a barnacle-covered skeleton held upright against the wall with a fishing net. Marta relaxed. On the counter, stabbed with a dagger, was a piece of parchment. Written in what could only have been blood was a simple message.

I crave black shells.

A hint from Goodsmile? Marta wondered. It didn't seem like the message was a permanent piece of the hut. It would have easily been blown away. Did he put it there before meeting Gaul and Marta at the Tower of Samadel? Or did he beat them to the coast? Either way, Goodsmile got around fast for someone she never saw riding a horse.

She looked around the hut for a black shell, but the dock was clean. She would have to scour the beach if she wanted to get one. There was no way she was doing that alone. She went to find Gaul.

The abandoned buildings were a depressing sight but — at this point in the journey — not a surprising one. Marta checked inside a couple. There was furniture and the occasional critter making waves through the shallow water, but no sign of Gaul. In the middle of the hamlet was a sloped roofed building with a steeple. It seemed like the kind of place Gaul would find himself, so Marta entered.

She was right. Gaul was at the back of the building, standing at a podium in front of a driftwood altar. He was reading a weathered book by the light that poured in through the hole in the ceiling. The water hadn't invaded this space yet, though the floor still felt soft as Marta approached Gaul.

"Listen to this," Gaul said without looking up. He began reading. "'The Fisher's Blessings: I am thankful for the sea and its bounty. I am thankful for the wind and its inspiration. I am thankful for the shore and its safety. I am thankful for Hyloh, Lord of Flux, and his proof that even a god may err. For all these things I am thankful, and for all these things I will share with others.'"

"That's a nice message." Marta took a seat in a pew. "Realizing what you have and deciding to share it with others."

Gaul ran his fingers through his hair. "It's weird."

"Why?"

"I've never heard of Hyloh."

"Okay." Marta cocked her head. "So?"

"It's the Pantheon." Gaul drummed his fingers on the thick text. "There are many Anima, but the Lords and Ladies are set in the scripture. Nine of them, children of the First Gods. But there is no Hyloh, Lord of Flux."

"Who's the Lord of Flux?"

"There isn't one. The priests aren't accepting of flux for just that reason. You have Lords and Ladies of Life, Death, Wilds, Creation, Sun, Moon, Chance, Redemption and whatever the Gate Beyond is, but flux never had a place. There are a few fundamentalist sects that don't even want to use crystals."

Marta leaned back in the pew. All this talk about gods confused her. The only god she had ever known was Mar. "What's the difference between an Anima and these Lords and Ladies?"

"Fundamentally, not too much." He closed the book. "Lords and Ladies are the children of the First Gods, while Anima are figures who ascended to godhood through their actions. It gives people a wide breadth to choose from when they want to pray, I supposed that's a good thing."

Gaul stared for a long time at the leather cover of the book. He had plenty of information on the Divine Pantheon, but it every time he talked about it he got sullen and distant. Marta was interested, but she never felt comfortable talking about it for too long of a time.

"So," Marta said, standing with purpose. "These people prayed to a fake god?"

"It doesn't sound like prayer. It sounds like they wanted to learn from him. There are no calls for help in this book or asking for anything. There are no prayers at all. This doesn't feel like a church, it feels like a school." He put his hands in his pockets and left the podium, walking down the centre aisle. "'Even a god may err.'"

He walked past Marta, wrapped in his mental cloud. Marta glanced at the empty altar behind the podium. Maybe she was wrong, it wasn't an altar, it was just a counter. The door creaked as Gaul exited, so Marta spun around and chased him out.

"I found a note from Goodsmile," she said, catching up to him as he descended the stoop. "I think it's a hint to find Boboros Vale."

Gaul rubbed his temple. "What is going on with that man?"

"I have no idea. But there's a hut at the end of the dock with a note asking for black shells."

Gaul looked down at his feet. He kicked at the water, turning it cloudy with sand. "We're going to have to go looking for that aren't we?"

It took them over an hour before they found a black shell, and the sun had become a slit along the horizon. They had to leave the hamlet and search the drier beach, but eventually they found a shell the size of Gaul's fist that was a shiny black. It had a pointed spiral that felt like it was absorbing all light, a disturbing relation to the Absence they left behind. Marta had never been made nervous by a shell before.

They took it to the dock hut and placed it in front of the skeleton.

"What now?" Gaul asked.

Marta shrugged. She wondered if she was wrong about Goodsmile leaving the note. It could have been a random letter left behind by anybody. Maybe there was a collector who was interested in finding black shells. Marta reached for the shell, to put it in the skeleton's hand, when a deep-toned bell rang behind them.

They turned back to the hamlet, but the bell didn't come again.

"I don't suppose that church-school place had a bell, did it?" Marta asked.

"No," Gaul said. "It did not."

They turned back to the hut and the shell was gone. They checked around to see if it had fallen off or if Marta had knocked it when she was reaching for it, but it was nowhere to be seen. The skeleton had not moved.

Another bell. This time it sounded like it was right behind them. They spun around. One of the boats was alit with a blue torch on its bow. Its rigging was whole and prepared to set sail. Gaul cast Marta an intrigued look. She took a deep breath, and they stepped onto the boat.

"Do you know how to use this?" Marta asked, poking at the rigging.

"Kind of," Gaul said.

Gaul touched the sail and it unfurled. The boat jerked into motion, sending Gaul and Marta tumbling. It made a hard right to get around the edge of the dock, then took off with shocking speed into the dark sea.

"That's convenient," Marta remarked, pulling herself to her feet.

Gaul mumbled in agreement. He went to the bow of the ship and looked to an invisible horizon. The stars were clear, but the moon was waning and the path ahead was nothing but water. He wiped the ocean spray off his face and stepped back.

"I hope we're going to Boboros Vale," he said.

"After all that?" Marta put her hand on his shoulder. "I can't imagine we'd be going anywhere else."

"I knew about Black Hypogea, I'd even heard legends about the Tower." He shook his head. "But this place is completely foreign to me. The stories talk about how Leviathan was the only Primordial to be killed, when Shiller discovered a way to defeat an immortal. That's all I know."

"Finally we're both in the dark," Marta said.

Gaul laughed. "We've always been in the dark.

The boat slowed to a stop. Marta glanced where they came from, but the shore was out of her sight. There was nothing in any direction other than more dark water. She turned in a slow circle, trying to figure out what they were supposed to do, when she spotted a flashing pinpoint of light in the distance.

"Gaul," she said, pointing at the object.

It was moving toward them at a fair pace. It would sweep across the ocean, disappear for a moment, then take its arc again. A lighthouse in the middle of the sea. As it approached it grew taller and, in time, more towers appeared around it. They lifted out of the water, yet were perfectly dry. Buildings grew out of the sea until the horizon was filled with a city skyline.

It was larger than Marjyal. Though the city seemed tight, the architecture was firm and ordered. The buildings were exquisitely crafted wood with tile roofs. The central structure was a clocktower mixed with a lighthouse that overlooked the city below with its glowing eye. All across the city were lights that bathed the ocean in a soft radiance. Barely visible below the surface was the shadow of a massive beast coming to a rest.

Their boat glided silently toward a pier on the edge of the city.

Boboros Vale had arrived.

I should have done it immediately, but I wasn't used to running away from things. Besides, I wasn't the one who needed convincing. The people of Marjyal were told over and over that the world outside the walls was terrible. That we were being kept safe. She believed that with all her heart, and I, for the first time, didn't want to leave someone behind. I should have pushed her to go, even if she hated me.

Maybe if I had, Ellie would still be alive.

—From the Journal of Jovin Gutterwake

Chapter Forty-One
Boboros Vale

The boat docked itself by a hut much like the one that was in the hamlet. This one didn't have a skeleton in it, though, it was completely empty. In fact, despite the city looking alive from a distance, it became immediately clear that something was wrong in Boboros Vale.

There were clumps of the corruption they had seen in Bara-ban's house. Some of it crept up the walls while some dripped onto the street. Gaul stepped off the boat and looked around the pier. It must have once been a bustling area. Streamers stretched between the stalls, their once vibrant colours of red, orange, and blue faded into tints of grey.

"I'm tired of ghost towns," Marta said, hopping up next to Gaul. "Remember Sebanna's Rest?"

"You mean the town ruled over by the Praetor of Snakes in disguise?" Gaul grinned. "Yeah, I remember that one."

Marta kicked a clump of corruption at Gaul's feet. He skipped out of the way and headed down the pier.

"Let's head in," he said. "Maybe there's someone here keeping the lights on."

The streets were narrow, made for walking rather than horses or carriages. Occasionally they would spot a discarded hand cart with rotten food. It didn't bode well for finding someone alive.

When Gaul had heard of a city on the back of a whale, he didn't know what to expect. From where they stood, one would be hard-pressed to imagine there was something living beneath them. The streets were stone and the buildings much like anyone would see on a mainland city. They were more beautiful to be sure. Under the black slime were structures designed by intellectuals and artists.

They headed inward. Goodsmile said the remains of Leviathan were kept inside a place called the Estuary Academy. Without any signs to lead them, they could only guess where it could be.

"Let's look at that clocktower," Marta suggested, pointing between the apartments above them. The light atop the central tower kept spinning. "At least we can get a view of the city. Could even be where the Academy is."

"I imagine if you had a piece of a Primordial, you may put it in a place of importance." Gaul took the next left that should bring them toward the tower.

Boboros Vale was set up like a radial, with streets acting as spokes and the clocktower at its centre. They walked down a main thoroughfare. They passed by cafes and restaurants. Each one had all its candles lit, though their wax was intact like they had never been used. Gaul thought it had to be flux. Boboros Vale was dedicated to the study of it, he shouldn't be surprised if things were a tad strange there.

At the base of the clocktower was a mansion. The front courtyard had a statue of a sea serpent pierced by a spike and reeling back in pain.

"'Leviathan,'" Gaul read from the plaque at its base. He brushed some errant plants off the lower half. "'Smote by Shiller. A spell to kill the unkillable.'"

"'The Estuary Academy,'" Marta finished. "This is it."

They looked up at the academy. It wasn't particularly impressive. Compared to the architecture they saw on their walk, it was utilitarian and simple. A rectangular, two-storey block with a ring of apartments around the lower quarter of the clocktower. It wasn't the same beauty they came to expect from Boboros Vale.

What it was, though, was completely devoid of corruption. The black slime trickled off the buildings on the edge of the circle, but not a drop dared to move any closer. It bunched up at the base of those buildings creating pulsating mounds.

In one of the windows on the second floor, a shadow moved. Gaul had to stop to make sure he wasn't imagining it. It moved again, definitely in a humanoid shape.

"There's someone in there," Gaul said.

Marta tried to follow his gaze. "I don't see anything. Where are they?"

The figure disappeared. Gaul hurried to the front doors.

"Slow down," Marta said, jogging to catch up. "We don't know if they're friend or foe."

"I don't want to meet them." Gaul pressed his back against the door frame. "I don't want them to see us if they're looking out the window. Let's get inside, find the remains of Leviathan, then get out of here."

"I like that idea." Marta leaned away from the wall, trying to sneak a glance at the figure Gaul saw.

Gaul took the handle and turned carefully. The door opened soundlessly. He motioned for Marta to go first, then swept in behind her and shut the door.

They were met by a room full of equipment. Glass vials and larger containers with strange liquid were being piped and mixed with other concoctions. Drawings of runes on paper and others carved into stones were strewn about. Crystals of purple, teal, red, amber, and a collection of other colours were suspended in liquids, held by clamps, or simply left on counters.

"Have you ever seen anything like this before?" Marta asked quietly, walking past a table with a yellow crystal floating in blue gelatin. The crystal pulsed slightly and she leapt back.

"No," Gaul said. "But it looks dangerous. Don't touch anything. And keep your voice down."

A creak of metal shot a shiver up Gaul's spine. Footsteps descended the spiral staircase in the back corner of the laboratory. Gaul pointed at Marta and then at the table she was standing next to. Marta scrambled underneath, pushing herself against the back panel. Gaul hid behind a shelf of beakers as the figure reached the first level.

Gaul kept his breathing slow and steady, suppressing it until it was barely audible. The figure moved around the lab. Their steps were awkward and uneven. Gaul waited until there was a scrape of shoes as the figure stopped, then took a risk and peeked around the shelf.

A slight-framed man with greasy black hair stood in the lab. He was hunched over and shakily ran his fingers along the desk — directly above where Marta hid. His gaze stayed locked on the suspended yellow crystal. Gaul mentally cursed. Every time Marta moved, the crystal pulsed slightly.

"Hello?" The stranger called out. His voice was soft, so much so that hearing it raised felt wrong. "Is there anyone there?"

It wouldn't be long before the man discovered Marta, crouching a few centimetres from his feet. Gaul needed to take control of the situation.

"Yes," Gaul said, stepping into view.

The man spun around. His eyes widened but didn't appear scared. He smiled awkwardly through his thick hair strands.

"Oh, hello. I was wondering why Boboros surfaced." The man bowed slightly. "It's a pleasure to make your acquaintance. My name is Shinn. And you are?"

Gaul paused. He considered lying, but there was more to be gained by testing the waters. "Gaul."

Shinn didn't react to the name. "Ah well, pleasure to meet you, Gaul." He shuffled forward a couple steps. "I assume you're here for Melifacto."

Gaul took a deep breath. He flexed his fingers, widened his stance, and ran his hand along his sheath.

"Yes, we are." Marta slid out from under the desk. She hopped to her feet just as Shinn turned around. "We're with Melifacto."

"That's excellent!" Shinn clapped with excitement. "I'm so glad you were able to make it."

Gaul stopped his hand next to his sword and cast Marta a disapproving look, who rolled her eyes in return.

"And what's your name?" Shinn asked Marta. "If I don't ask now, I'm sure I'll forget. Isolation is terrible for manners."

"I'm Marta."

Shinn's eyes widened. "Marta. Marta you've… gotten older. I suppose I must have been here for a long time."

Marta stepped back. "You know me?"

"Yes! No. Maybe? I met you. One of the times I visited Marjyal. You were young, maybe three or four. I can sense it is you, though."

"You must have known my brother too, right?"

"Who?" Shinn asked, cocking his head.

"Jovin."

"Jovin!" Shinn took Marta by both shoulders. "Yes, Jovin! Dear sweet man. Too sweet, I think, for his own good. How is Jovin?"

Marta opened her mouth but didn't speak. The moment lasted only a second but hung in the air like an arrow fired straight up. Gaul waited to see where it landed.

"He's fine." Marta took a deep breath. "Haven't seen him for a while, but last I heard he was doing okay."

She must not want to tell someone she doesn't remember about her brother, Gaul figured. Shinn seemed harmless enough, but they've been fooled before.

"How do you know my brother?" Marta asked.

"I worked with Jovin." Shinn began tidying the lab, though most of it only amounted to moving supplies into a different mess. "Jovin is a genius, though I don't need to tell you that. But even as a young man he had a talent for ingesting and utilizing. I taught him fluxweaving theory and he taught me history."

"But you also work with Melifacto?" Gaul stepped forward.'

"Of course. We all work with Melifacto."

Marta's gaze flickered around the room. "Jovin and Melifacto—"

"My manners!" Shinn spun to face Marta. "I forgot! Let me show you around. You have just arrived and it is the host's duty to give a tour. Come, come!"

Shinn walked toward a door left of the one they came in through, the tail of his dirty robe dragging across the floor as he moved. Marta pushed her hair back and looked at Gaul. They knew Melifacto had some sort of connection to Marta, so presumably he had to of known Jovin as well. But the fact they worked together? Shinn could have been lying, or was misinformed. Or maybe there was more to Jovin than even Marta knew.

Whatever the explanation, Marta's expression was clear. She had no idea what was going on.

"This way," Shinn called from the door that led deeper into the academy.

Gaul squeezed Marta's shoulder. "We need to stay on our guard," he whispered. "We still don't know we can trust him."

"I'm okay," Marta said. She rolled her neck and adjusted her sword. "Let's go."

Shinn led them out of the lab and into a dusty and worn in hallway. The walls were lined with doors that led into smaller labs or classrooms that couldn't have been used for centuries. The only signs of life were the thick trails in the dust that were left behind by Shinn's robe.

"I set up my lab in the entrance hall for the purpose of efficiency," Shinn explained as he led them around a corner into another hallway. "Not polite for guests, I must say, but I don't usually get them. These classrooms go unused. I do enjoy walking up and down these halls to clear my mind. I think about what it must have been like to be here while the students and scholars were at work delving into the secrets of flux."

Along the walls — between the classroom doors and the below the paintings of men and women — were empty stone troughs. Just below the rim was a white line of salt residue. The stone was wet from where water had only recently stopped flowing. Gaul stooped to inspect the detail carved into the front of the trough. More sea serpents.

"I see you've noticed the channels," Shinn said. "The scholars were infatuated with the power of water and so built paths in the walls and floors so that water could run through the building alongside the supports. When Boboros dives, more is allowed through the top of the clocktower and the perfect cycle begins anew."

"Why water?" Gaul asked.

"Flux." Shinn's gaze unfocused. "An ocean of power."

Gaul had seen a similar look on Marta's face when she talked about the sea. Marta must've recognized this too, as she quickly turned away as they continued through the hall.

They eventually left the hallways and classrooms and entered a library. Shelves littered with tomes stretched into the second and third storey. Rolling ladders were placed in the aisles so that curious readers could climb the heights to grab books from above. Walkways crosshatched the space above them. The back section of the academy was taken up by this great library.

"If I'm not in my quarters or the lab, this is where I spend my time," Shinn said, lifting his hands to the lit chandelier in the middle of the room. "The scholars took meticulous notes on every experiment and theory and I have dedicated myself to read them all."

Gaul gazed around, his jaw slack. This place surpassed the libraries in Ulkradia and shamed the archive in Castle Adathin. Much like the city outside, what should be claustrophobic and chaotic was instead ordered by intelligent hands. Gaul turned until he saw the door.

It was in the centre of the wall, the one that should lead toward the centre of the academy. The water trenches began to either side of it and up the wall were deep carvings in the stone. They were twisting and flowing paths that split and converged again. The water would pour through and eventually exit into the trenches to move onto the rest of the ground floor.

The door itself was made of a white wood — though stained slightly due to the age. A thick metal bar was placed across the middle, keeping it shut with a padlock. If it wasn't for the incredible features that surrounded it, the door would be wholly unremarkable.

"What is that?" Gaul asked, pointing.

Shinn looked at the door in silence for a few seconds. "It's the door into the clocktower. The designs are impressive, I know, but it's really quite boring."

Gaul pulled at his shirt. The pendant warmed his chest. Leviathan's bones were near.

"Your rooms!" Shinn grabbed his hair. "A host should have rooms ready for his guests. I didn't realize you'd be here so soon. Uh, uh, please stay here. I will prepare your lodgings."

He hurried away, knocking over a pile of books stacked on one of the tables. He looked between the fallen books and the stairs. After changing his mind three times, he left the books on the floor and flew up the stairs.

Marta scooped up one — the one that used to be on the top of the stack — and looked it over. She chuckled and turned its cover toward Gaul.

"*The Customs of Gentlemen*," he read. "That explains it."

Marta tossed the book back onto the pile.

"Leviathan is here," Gaul said, keeping an eye on the spiral stairs.

"Where?" Marta glanced around the room.

Gaul thumbed toward the white door. Marta stepped around him and approached it. She looked over the padlock and gave it a sharp tug. Nothing happened. She pulled on the crossbar but it wouldn't budge.

"Are you sure?" she asked.

As Gaul moved toward the door, the pendant grew warmer. "Definitely. The vessel is reacting to something in there."

"Then let's break in."

"With what?" Gaul opened his coat. "We're going to need a hammer to destroy that lock."

"We can chop the door down." She drew her sword and raised it over her head.

Gaul caught her arm. "That's going to take forever, if we can do it at all. Shinn would get here before we can do any real damage."

"I'm not afraid of some wannabe gentleman." She yanked her arm away.

"Who knows what he's capable of. He's allies with Melifacto, remember?"

"Well." She slammed her sword into its sheath. "So was Jovin."

That's what this was about. Gaul hung his arms off the back of his neck. Marta stomped away from the door then slapped both hands onto a table.

"Why was Jovin working with Melifacto?" Marta asked to no one. "*When* was Jovin working with Melifacto? Is that why he's so obsessed with me? What does any of this mean?"

Gaul leaned on the table next to her. "I don't know."

"Why should you?" she murmured. "You didn't know him. Maybe I didn't know him either."

Gaul took Marta by the shoulder and pulled her close. She sighed — a deep sorrowful sound that took all the air from her lungs.

"I just want to leave this place," she said. "I don't want to hear what Shinn knows. I don't care about the answers. Melifacto, him, Jovin." She thumped her head against Gaul's shoulder. "None of it matters."

"Alright." Gaul pinched the bridge of his nose. "I don't believe any of that."

Marta laughed and pushed herself away from him. She rubbed her eyes, even though they were dry.

"I've finished preparing the room!" Shinn shouted from the second storey.

"Let's play along." Gaul put his hands into his coat pockets. "Until we can find something to break the lock with."

"Or a key," Marta added.

"Wouldn't that be a treat?"

Shinn took them past the second floor, up into the dormitories. It ringed around the clocktower for another three floors, and Shinn put them on the topmost.

"I am staying in the headmaster's quarters," Shinn explained, stopping outside one of many identical doors. "It's just around the corner and very easy to find if you simply look for the sign. The one that says headmaster's quarters. You could have figured that out on your own, I suppose."

He opened the door to a stately room, lit by a dozen candles. There was a pair of four-poster beds on opposite walls, with the window between them. The curtains on the beds, as well as the window furnishings, were a subdued blue and cast the room in a somber glow.

"Actually." Gaul pointed a few doors down. "Would you mind if we stayed in a room closer to the corner?"

Shinn stumbled over his words. "That room isn't prepared. There's no sheets or… ambiance."

"We can do all that ourselves, it's fine." He turned to Marta. "That room will be better, right?"

Gaul didn't care about which room they stayed in, but he still didn't trust Shinn. He could have done something to the room. It was better for Gaul to decide where they slept.

Evidently, Marta agreed. "Gaul is very particular about where he sleeps. Thank you for preparing the room, though. You're a very good host."

"Thank you very much!" Shinn clasped his hands, excitedly bowing over and over. "All the rooms are unlocked. You can pick any one that suits your fancy. Are you hungry at all? Would you like any—"

"We're fine, Shinn," Gaul said. "We'll handle ourselves from here. Thank you."

Shinn must've not been used to compliments. Every positive word made him giddy like a child. He gave a couple more bows, then scampered down the hallway. He stopped at the corner and turned back.

"One last thing," he called. "Boboros will be submerging soon. While it's quite a sight to see, I must warn you not to leave the academy while we are underwater. We can tour the city tomorrow, but for now keep to these walls. There are things that only come out when the sky is hidden."

With that warning said, Shinn turned the corner. The academy settled with a creak, as if the building was in agreement with what Shinn had said.

Marta turned to Gaul. "You really think he's up to something?"

"He could be harmless." Gaul opened the door he pointed at. It was similar to the first, but the candles were unlit and the beds were bare. "He works for Melifacto, but it doesn't seem he's kept informed. Living on a whale certainly keeps you separate from the affairs of the world."

"Something he said bothers me." She opened wardrobes until she found one with bedding in it. She tossed a set at Gaul.

Gaul caught the blankets. "Just one thing?"

"Just one thing right now." She flopped onto one of the beds, holding the bedding to her chest. "'I'm so glad you were able to make it.' Like he was expecting us."

"Or he was expecting someone."

Gaul opened a drawer and found a box of matches. He lit a candle and, in reply, the rest of the candles ignited. Gaul looked around the room in confusion. *Flux*, he thought, and snapped his wrist, extinguishing the match.

"That's more of a reason to get into that room quickly." Gaul sat on his bed, rubbing his cheeks. "I'll try to find a hammer or something while we're looking around the city tomorrow."

"You don't want to go out while Boboros is submerged, huh?" Marta asked.

"Shinn could be just trying to keep us inside, but I don't see the point in testing that. Besides, I am very tired."

There was a cry from the great whale. Gaul approached the window that looked across the twinkling lights of Boboros Vale to the sea. Water rose until it was higher than that buildings on the wharf, but not a drop touched the city streets. The ocean was kept back by some force that domed the city.

Boboros dove fast and soon they were completely submerged, and still diving. The world outside the Vale became black.

First, the smallest dot of blue glow appeared in the dark. Then another. Then an orange one. Soon the view was filled with phosphorescent sea creatures of all shapes and sizes. They mixed with the reflected light from the city until the sky was a moving portrait of a starry night.

Gaul couldn't help but smile at the wonder of it all. Marta had practically pressed her face against the glass.

"All the same," Gaul said. "We should sleep in shifts to keep watch. I can take first if you want."

Marta tore her gaze away from the brilliant sight. "Yeah. Just wake me up when you're getting tired."

She glanced briefly out the window, then tossed her blankets on the bed and leapt on top. Her coat thumped to the ground on one side of the bed and her sword on the other. She was asleep within a few seconds, a slight snore sneaking out.

Gaul pulled a chair from the corner and placed it at the large window, looking out. He took off his sword belt and laid it across his lap.

Before him, the ocean swirled a performance of dancing lights and dark waves.

I lost the will to leave for a long time. I stopped reading. I just sat by the sea and stared out into the infinite distance. At times, I imagined myself falling into the waves and allowing it to take me. It had been a long time since I felt loss like that. I didn't even think it possible anymore, that I had hardened my soul with my travesties.

Imagine my surprise when a Praetor found me. A Praetor who asked me if I truly believed what I had once wrote about.

—From the Journal of Jovin Gutterwake

Chapter Forty-Two
Sanguinary Glow

"Marta." Gaul's voice came softly at first. "Marta."

Marta opened her eyes, forcing them to fight against the desire to remain asleep. She reminded herself where she was, in a tower on the back of a whale, and sat up.

Gaul leaned on the frame of the room's large window. His swords laid across a chair that faced the same direction. The iridescent glow from the city outside cast shifting colours across his concerned face.

"Is it time for me to take watch?" Marta asked, kicking her feet off the bed and hopping to them.

"Yes, but—" He jerked his head toward the window. "Look at this."

Marta peered outside. There was still the display of sea life outside the protective dome, but Gaul was motioning lower. There, at the entrance to a thin path between the buildings, was a figure.

"Is that a person?" Marta asked, straining her eyes to make out any features. They had their back to the academy and swayed like they were standing on the deck of a boat on gentle waves

"It looks like it, but they're not alone."

In other roads were more figures like the first. They moved between the buildings, disappearing and reappearing as they walked the streets. They were too distant and the light wasn't quite right to figure out if there were many people or only a few walking back and forth.

"They don't feel right," Marta said. Her skin went cold just looking at the wandering figures.

"I agree. That first one has been standing there like that for at least two chimes of the clocktower."

One of them appeared in the upper room of a building. In the stronger candlelight, it was clear they were terribly pale, if not tinted blue. The figure stopped at the window and turned, seeming to look directly into Marta's eyes. There was something familiar about him. But before Marta could consider it further, the light disappeared and the figure was lost in the darkness.

"They have to be why Shinn warned us not to go outside," Marta suggested, pushing the experience aside.

"Perhaps." Gaul tapped a finger on the window frame. "It only adds more questions, though."

What happened here? Marta wondered. The Primordials were not only kept in places of significance, but places of sorrow as well. Did one demand the other? Or was Adathin truly as cursed as she once heard?

"I need to get some sleep," Gaul said, moving his swords next to his bed. "I'm not sure how the sunrise or morning works here. It could just be we'll be hearing from Shinn at our door. I imagine a few more hours before that happens though."

Marta nodded and settled down into the chair Gaul had used. The room grew quiet until it was just Marta alone with her thoughts.

Are you there? Marta thought.

It had been days since the voice spoke to her. It still stayed silent. It was too much to hope that the voice had given up. It had to be gathering power. It was getting ready to grab her body again. If Gaul knew how much she was struggling with it, would he decide she was too dangerous? Would she be standing in the way of him getting home?

No, Marta told herself. The voice was getting to her. It was whispering clear lies so she would distrust Gaul. They were in this together. They had each risked their life to save the other time and time again.

But it was hard when the words were put directly into her brain. At least things were quiet tonight.

* *

The ocean waves foamed around Feyra's boots. She stared across Dancer's Inlet to the wider sea, the rising sun to her back. They arrived late the night before and Feyra's heart dropped when she saw that Bellona wasn't waiting with her ships. Melifacto had shrugged it off and set up camp, but Feyra waited motionless at the shore, keeping her eyes out for any ship to come sailing in.

"She should have been here first," Melifacto said, coming down the slope from the camp. "I don't know what could keep her."

Feyra squeezed her hands until her nails dug into her palms.

"We can't wait forever," Melifacto said.

"We'll wait longer," Feyra said.

Melifacto shook his head. He returned to the camp, leaving Feyra alone at the shore. She opened her hand and let the blood from where her fingernails cut her drip into the sea. It disappeared into the waves. A warm wind blew the last few drops onto her coat. She looked up and spotted four ships turning into the inlet.

"Melifacto!" Feyra called. "She's here."

The ships stopped away from shore and sent out rowboats. Bellona was on the first one that arrived. She leapt into the water, splashed to the shore, and came face to face with Melifacto. After a moment of tension, she smiled.

"We got held up," she said. "Some pirates attacked and we had to patch up the ships."

"I'm glad to see you're alright," Melifacto said. "The sea is quite dangerous."

"Nothing my guild can't handle. Though, we still expected to be waiting for you."

Melifacto shifted uncomfortably. "My business didn't take as long as I had hoped. But, that only means we need to reach our destination all that much faster."

"And where are we going?"

"We will head into the Southern Sea and go to Boboros Whale."

Bellona cocked her head. "A whale?"

"You may know it as Boboros Vale," Melifacto said, walking past Bellona to look at the ships in the bay. "One of the quirks of the passage of time. It's a city built on the back of a great whale."

"A city on a whale." Bellona shrugged. "Of course. If Primordials are real, why can't a city on a whale exist?" She glanced over her shoulder at Melifacto's convoy. "What exactly do you plan to do with the horses and carts?"

"Uh, some of my people will bring them to Banshee Coast." He dismissed the question with a flick of his wrist. "Time is precious, Bellona. We must reach Boboros soon."

Feyra caught Bellona grinning. It was strange that Melifacto wouldn't consider what to do with his horses. Feyra figured that though he was intelligent when it came to lab work, his lack of real world experience had ended up in him forgetting about that fact.

Bellona motioned to a rowboat. "They can take you aboard the *Spree*. We'll follow you to your whale — unless you have more *business* to take care of."

Melifacto straightened his spine and walked pridefully toward the rowboat. Bellona watched him go with a sinister sneer. Feyra opened her mouth to speak, but was cut off by Bellona pointing at her without looking.

"Feyra," she said. "Let's talk on the ship."

Feyra shut her mouth and nodded. They embarked on their own rowboat to the *Steel Jaw*. The whole way, Bellona was silent. She watched the waves break against the boat's sides. Feyra wanted to tell Bellona how good it was to see her again, but she doubted Bellona cared. She wanted results, and Feyra had little to show. In silence they crossed the water and boarded the *Steel Jaw* where Ortun waited for them.

"Welcome back," he said. "That was quick. Do we have a heading?"

"Not in as many words," Bellona said. She headed for the captain's cabin. "Seems that he wants to bring us to some city on the back of a whale. It's to the south, that's the best I can say."

Ortun took a moment to smile — difficult to see under his mask — and nod to Feyra before they both followed Bellona into the cabin. Bellona looked out the stern windows, a hard but indecipherable expression on her face. Ortun lounged back on a sofa while Feyra waited for Bellona to speak.

"Did you find out anything?" Bellona asked. "I think Melifacto's working toward his endgame. Marta will be in his hands soon and we still don't know how she relates to the Cradle. All this talk of Primordials and overthrowing gods is exhausting, so please tell me you have some information I can use."

"I followed the crow to the outpost near Blasted Land Mines," Feyra said. "Melifacto's been using the mines to send crystals to these outposts all across Adathin. This one was working with esoteric crystal."

"Is that it?" Ortun asked.

"This isn't useful information." Bellona turned and slammed her palms onto the desk. "These outposts are related to *elys sang*. He's trying to figure out the formula. Is there anything useful you got from all this trouble?"

Feyra thought back. She strained for any bit of information from the research notes she read a dozen times. It was complex, with numbers and long words she didn't know.

"There were numbers," Feyra said. "They were all crossed out one by one."

Bellona crossed her arms. "And?"

Why did that seem important to Feyra? "And…" She had walked through the outpost, checking every nook and cranny. "Some of those numbers were on cages. Cages for people."

Ortun leaned forward. "*Elys sang* means god's blood. God's blood is a person? Or it comes from a person?"

"A person with god's blood," Bellona said. "Marta?"

Feyra shrugged ever so slightly.

Bellona shook her head and turned away. "I should have sent someone smarter."

Feyra's stomach turned. She dropped her shoulders, looking like she could crumple at any moment. Ortun looked at her, his eyes soft. It seemed like he wanted to say something to her, but they both knew Bellona didn't care.

"If Marta has god's blood," Ortun said, turning from Feyra. "Then getting her before Melifacto seems more important than ever. Maybe we should forget about Gaul."

"No." Bellona put her fingers on the window glass. She drew a line along the horizon. "He's still important."

"Is this about what Kygan said?" Ortun asked.

"Kygan wants to save Marjyal. He's thinking very, very small. With the Chalice, Melifacto intends to steal the right to rule from the Divines." Bellona turned her hand into a fist and pushed it against the glass until the frame creaked. "And if the gods don't want to use their strength, then maybe they should lose it. But not to the scheming of a coward. They should be challenged and beaten so that the strongest can lead and the weak can be culled. Not out of cruelty, but out of righteousness." She stopped pushing. "Someone needs to take the reins of this unkind world." Then, quieter, so that Feyra could barely hear, "Hope is a terrible curse."

"I saw Gaul," Feyra said. "He saw my abilities and he called me something. He said I was a fluxweaver. Do you know what that is?"

"This again?" Bellona pinched the bridge of her nose. "Why do you insist on questioning your power? You are strong, that's all you need to know."

"But if I could just talk to him—"

"Enough, Feyra," Bellona said firmly. "We don't have the time for this distraction. Maybe if you were more focused on your task, rather than yourself, you could have discovered something more useful."

Feyra lowered her head. Bellona swept past her out the door, slamming it with a wall-rattling bang. Feyra stared at her feet, motionless. At that moment, she was a child again, keeping her head low to avoid drawing attention from the gangs. Ortun ran his fingers along his metal jaw as he approached.

"I failed her," Feyra said.

"You did your best," Ortun said.

"Then my best isn't good enough." She balled her hands and squeezed until it hurt. "I'm too dumb and impulsive. I killed the only witness and couldn't understand what they were writing. I'm useless."

"It's not fair of her to ask everything from you."

"But I would give it to her." She looked Ortun dead in the eyes. "And it doesn't feel wrong."

Ortun ran his fingers over his hair. He paced around his desk then leaned on it with both hands. "I'm worried," he said. "I'm worried that someday she's going to say something that means nothing to her, but will destroy you. Something that, even with all your strength and skill, you will not survive through."

Feyra couldn't tell Ortun he was wrong. She feared Bellona as much as she loved her. She wanted to serve Bellona to the best of her ability, but her thoughts always went back to what Gaul had said — with such assuredness too. She needed to know what she was, and why she never felt like everyone else.

"Ortun," she said softly, walking around the desk. "You're from across the Sorrow Sea, right?"

Ortun cocked his head at the sudden change in topic. "That's right."

"Have you ever heard of a fluxweaver before?"

"I've lived here longer than I lived there. And my world was small. When I left, it was on a boat going south, then a storm, then Marjyal. I can't say I've ever heard of a fluxweaver before you mentioned it. You're not the only one with powers, though."

"It's not the same. It's not just one thing, it's control. I can feel it in the air around me."

"Feel what?"

"Magic, maybe?" She stopped at the window and stared out at the sea. "Who else can activate runes without a crystal? I'm something different, and maybe Gaul knows what it is. Maybe if I know, I won't feel so empty."

Ortun gazed at her sorrowfully. He tapped his fingers along the maps on the desk. The ships outside were starting to turn toward the mouth of the inlet. *Spree* was taking the lead.

Ortun stepped toward the cabin door, then stopped. "When you find Gaul, don't bring him to Bellona. At least not immediately. Ask him what you need to know. Once Bellona gets her hands on him, I don't know what the outcome will be. But you deserve something too."

He exited the cabin to the deck. A warm ocean breeze blew through the open door and wrapped around Feyra. The blood in her veins vibrated with anticipation. It was off to Boboros, and to the truth.

I expected to see one of the essays I had written for the Marjyalian elite. Instead, he gave me something much older. Something I had written before even coming to Marjyal. In it I wrote about the succession of gods. He told me that it put into words thoughts he had for a long time. But what interested him wasn't history, it was when I wrote about the possibility of true resurrection.

That was when I met Melifacto. That was when I should have walked away.

—From the Journal of Jovin Gutterwake

Chapter Forty-Three

Flicker Well

Marta worried she had drifted off a few times through the night. Occasionally she would catch her eyes being closed without remembering when she closed them. That was only because the night was uneventful. The figures disappeared not long after she took over the watch and the only thing she could do was observe the fish moving in the distance.

Eventually there was a cry from the whale, much like the one before they submerged, and they began to rise again. The city became brighter until they broke the surface and radiant light poured in. Marta blinked against the sudden brilliance.

Gaul stirred when the sun hit his bed. Throwing aside the covers, he sat up with a deep yawn. He looked around the room in bored disinterest.

"You know," he said. "I wish something did happen just so I don't feel like we're going through all this concern for nothing."

"Shinn hasn't come by at all," Marta remarked, throwing on her coat. "Maybe we should take the opportunity to look around."

The Academy was empty. Shinn was nowhere to be seen, though the door to the headmaster's quarters was open. There didn't seem to be a concern for privacy or security. Except for the heavy padlock on the door in the library, every room was open to them.

They passed through common rooms and sleeping accommodations for larger groups of students. Lecture halls stood silent and, though they were covered in a layer of dust, didn't seem to be hundreds of years old like the Estuary Academy should be.

When they reached the mess hall they found a breakfast laid out for them. Fresh fruit, biscuits, and of course, water to drink. After the customary concern for a trap, they decided to risk it and indulge.

Marta never had such delicious fruit. When she saw the rotten carts on the streets, she figured they would be in for more meals of waterlogged rations and hunted meat. This was more than she could hope for. She greedily consumed four apples and three biscuits.

She had just gotten into the oranges when Shinn came shuffling in.

"Oh good, you found the breakfast," he said, brushing his hair out of his face, only to have it fall right back in. "I'm sorry it couldn't be warm. I had some last-minute research to do and I wanted to make sure you had something to eat when you woke."

"This is just fine, Shinn," Gaul said, holding up his glass of water.

"So." Marta spoke with her mouth crammed full of gushing orange slices. "What are you researching anyway? What does Melifacto want from you?"

"The same thing he always wants, Marta," Shinn said, smiling sweetly. "Power."

"Is that why you're doing all those experiments with crystals?" Gaul asked.

"Hmm?" For a moment Shinn didn't seem to understand what Gaul was talking about. Then the light came on in his head. "Oh no. I mean, yes, at one time. But that's just a hobby now. My research is hard to explain." He craned his head back. "But perhaps easy to show. Yeah. I can show you it. Come with me!"

He excitedly waved for them to follow him. Marta snatched two more apples out of the basket before they left the mess hall and the academy.

The true beauty of Boboros Vale could be seen in the daylight. It was still lousy with black corruption, but the buildings underneath shone with pink and cream colour facades. Shinn took them down an avenue lined with awnings of vibrant primary colours.

"How is this place in such good shape?" Gaul asked. "It's been around since the First Gods."

"I always supposed it was the protective dome." Shinn pointed up, toward the invisible wall that kept the water out when they dove. "Or perhaps the fact it spends much of its time under the ocean surface. I can't say I understand that perfectly, though I have dedicated some of my hours to figuring it out. You are right though; this city hasn't decayed at all since I've been here."

"How long have you been here for?" Marta asked.

Shinn bobbed his head side to side as they walked. "I'd say about two hundred years."

Marta nearly choked on her apple. "How is that possible?"

"Oh. I suppose you forgot." Shinn stopped and looked back at them. "I'm the Descendant of Shiller. Time has little meaning for me and my kin."

Shinn spun around and kept walking, as if he had simply told Gaul and Marta the time. They, however, were stuck to the spot. Marta worked the mouthful of apple around until it was mush and spat it out.

"The Descendant in the tower did say he was here," she said.

"That's true." Gaul leaned in and whispered, "Let's not tell him about her."

"Agreed."

They jogged to catch up with Shinn, who just turned down a narrow alley between two shops. He assured them it was not much further and brought them up some stone steps to an apartment block.

You should really ask him.

Marta cursed. The voice was back. Gaul gave her a momentary glance, but quickly let it go.

I know you're dying to. The voice was changing. It sounded less like Marta's own. *You're so curious but for some reason are holding yourself back. Are you afraid of what he'll say?*

I just don't care, Marta thought.

Oh, Marta. I've been in your mind for a long time now. I know you. These questions are screaming at you. Don't you want to know why your brother was spending time with a Descendant and a Praetor? How they both know you? Why Melifacto is overturning the country to find you?

How about you? Marta kept an eye on Gaul, but he wasn't concerned with her. He had no idea. *Do you know the answers to these questions?*

Yes.

But you won't tell me.

Where's the fun in that? Until I can take total control, I'm mostly just a voice in your head. I need to find my entertainment somewhere.

I'm not going to ask him.

The voice laughed. *Yes, you are. And when you finally know the truth, we can have a real talk.*

There was an emptiness in her mind. The voice was gone, but it left a bigger hole every time it disappeared.

The truth was an alluring prospect. The truth about Melifacto, Shinn, and Jovin. The truth about her. But in the face of the cataclysm, what did truth matter? They needed to get the Light from Leviathan, and they couldn't risk raising Shinn's suspicions.

Maybe she could admit she had forgotten it, she was very young after all. But Shinn thought that Melifacto sent them. How could she reconcile that she had forgotten with her working alongside Melifacto? She didn't get a chance to figure out the answer to that problem as Shinn shot his hand out to stop the group.

"Wait," he said. "Let them pass."

Coming out of the building in front of them were semi-translucent shapes. Three of them that shuddered with each step like the very fabric of their being was struggling to stay together. Despite the fluctuating membrane, their form was clear.

They were people.

Three people. Two men and one woman. They passed close by without paying attention to the onlookers. They were dressed well, and the woman was wearing a brilliant gown that was both extravagant and wide. They walked to about the middle of the street, then sunk into the stone and disappeared.

"What the pox was that?" Gaul kept one hand firmly on his sword hilt.

"Was that what we saw out the window last night?" Marta asked.

"Those are the wretched inhabitants of Boboros Vale," Shinn said. He gazed upon the spot where the figures disappeared. "They've been left behind by the world and their holy Lord."

"Hyloh?" Gaul asked.

Shinn gave a quizzical look. "Is that name still being passed around?"

"I read it in a book. An old book on the shore. However, the Lord of Flux is not a Divine I'm aware of."

"He abandoned his Divine status when he abandoned his people." Shinn wrung his hands together and continued down the road. "What do you know of how Boboros Vale was founded?"

"Not much," Gaul said, following Shinn with his hands in his pockets. "Shiller built it to study flux."

Marta considered the path the fluctuating figures took for a moment. She peered into the building that they appeared from. It was an extravagantly decorated lobby, complete with a concierge desk and crystal chandelier. Slimy corruption flowed from the ceiling in a long strand until it pooled at the base of the lobby stairs. However, unlike the other buildings along the road, the candles were unlit.

Glass clanked and a bottle rolled out of the shadows behind the desk. It clicked along the tiles until it came to a stop in the middle of the rectangle of light cast from the door. Marta held onto the door frame and leaned inside. The lobby pushed back against her, telling her to leave.

There was a creaking of bones, then more movement from the shadows.

A slender arm reached for the bottle.

Marta leapt back. Her hand twitched to draw her sword, but fear held her tight.

The arm was a painfully drab grey. Its skin was pulled tight and looked too smooth for a person. It grabbed the bottle and pulled it across the floor with a long scrape. Then it disappeared.

She was running before she knew it. She had seen many things and didn't feel as though she was easily scared, but something about that arm shook her to the core. It was unnatural — pure in its defiance of reality. Whatever it was connected to, Marta couldn't even conjure an image. It had to be humanoid, surely.

Marta caught up to Gaul and Shinn as Shinn was telling a story.

"Before Boboros, Shiller had a boat," he began, talking as if the buildings were the ones listening. "The Weeping Sonnet. Shiller liked his privacy, but after he killed Leviathan, he found his boat beset by eager students who wished to study with him the ways of fluxweaving. To combat this, he formed a child from water, flux, and Light. This was Hyloh, Lord of Flux. His true child."

Shinn bowed his head. His steps slowed for a second, but he pushed his woe aside and kept moving.

"Hyloh was the one who found Boboros and built this city on his back. Hyloh didn't stay, though. He left after giving a simple missive to the scholars. 'Surpass me.' So, the people of Boboros began unravelling the mysteries of flux and spreading what they discovered out into the world. They wanted power, but most of all, they wanted immortality. The Gods and Divines never died, so if they were to surpass them, they would have to live forever as well."

They reached a square with a fountain, plastered with corruption. It was heavier here than other places. Despite the size and location, none of the surrounding buildings faced the square. There were no windows to see into it either. There was only the large road that came in one side and left the other.

"I saw something," Marta whispered to Gaul. "In one of those building's back there. It was a creature."

"What kind of creature?" Gaul asked. Shinn was lost in his story and didn't notice them conversing quietly.

"I don't know." Marta shivered. "But it didn't feel natural."

Gaul looked in the direction they had came from, scanning the entrances to the buildings. "Keep an eye out for it."

Marta nodded. She rested her hand on her sword pommel. If that creature showed itself again, she wouldn't be paralyzed.

Shinn reached the fountain. He touched the water trickling off the flower-like projections. It was a multi-tiered structure twice their height. Water shot out the top and made its way down a spiraling path, with occasional outcropping pools for the water to collect in and rain down from.

"The scholars of the Estuary Academy were geniuses." Shinn wiped black slime away and sat on the lip of the basin. "Even among the researchers on Boboros, they were something special. They wanted to find a way to create artificial Light, the only way they could imagine surpassing the Gods. What they developed came to be known as Drowned Water."

"I'm sensing that's not the end of the story," Gaul said.

Marta walked around the fountain, inspecting the motif's carved into the side. There were fish swimming around and toward a carving of the sun, similar in style to the fountain in Galianos. Maybe they were descendants of the people from Boboros Vale?

Shinn continued, "Drowned Water was imperfect. It could give them eternal life, but it took from them what that life meant. Over many years it turned them into those half-formed spectres that you saw earlier. Then it coated the city with this solid miasma." He flicked a chunk of corruption away. "When Hyloh returned and saw what they had become, he turned Boboros to the sea and left his people to fade."

Around the other side of the fountain, Marta found a section where the lip dipped into a concave arc. It was barely a centimetre over the surface of the water at its lowest point. Below the impression was a platform. Marta figured it was a place for someone to kneel or sit, but couldn't imagine why. Possibly they cleaned their clothes in the fountain, but then why would there be only one spot?

"The book that mentioned Hyloh also mentioned that he was proof that gods could err," Gaul said. "What does that mean? What was his error?"

Shinn took a long moment before he spoke. "He left his people behind. He was afraid and he let it impact his judgement. He abandoned the possibility of Drowned Water being perfected and destroyed the technique to create it."

"That's why you're here? To rediscover how to create Drowned Water? How are you supposed to do that when the information has been lost?"

"That's what I want to show you." He stood up and waved to Marta. "Come on, Marta! It's not far now."

Marta put the strange structure aside. She glanced back at the building she saw the long-armed creature in. There was no further movement. It seemed the creature was content to stay inside. Maybe it was harmless.

Just outside the square was a cooper's shop. Finely crafted barrels sat in puddles of corruption. Shinn led Gaul and Marta through the storefront and into the workshop at the back. He held out his hand again, stopping them at the door.

"This is what I wanted to show you," he said. He pointed at the centre of the workshop.

The barndoors at the back of the shop were open to the sun, and if it wasn't for that, they wouldn't have been able to see what Shinn referred to. In the centre of the room sat a sparkle of refracted light. As Marta stepped inside — following Shinn's instructions to keep her distance — she saw the floor in that spot bend.

"This is a flicker well."

As Marta circled the phenomenon she could see the room bend and bulge within, as if she was looking into the waves of a reflecting pool. At the base, the geometry folded in on itself in impossible ways.

"Water carries impressions with it, wherever it goes." Shinn stood across from Marta, resulting in his body splintering in her vision through the Well. "The pipes that move water throughout the city in meaningful patterns has left these localized memories. Flicker wells act as beacons for where the memories can be accessed."

"What do you mean 'memories'?" Marta asked.

"Of the people who used to live here." Shinn gazed into the well, lost within its insane confines. "When Boboros submerges and the water level in the pipes rises, the flicker wells become memories that I can enter and observe. It's through them I can do my research."

Marta spotted Gaul creeping along the wall behind Shinn. He snatched a strong hammer off the board above the workbench and hid it in his coat. He nodded to Marta. Hopefully it was a way through the padlock in the Academy.

"That's why I must work alone," Shinn continued. "The water can still take memories from people and too many in the city can make finding the right one difficult. I have a few of my own memories floating around and I would hate to waste my time in one of them. I've already seen them, after all."

He reached into his robes and pulled out parchment stained with ink.

"I've already seen this one," he said, unfolding it. "A cooper making a barrel and fighting with his son. Nothing interesting at all. I have a few more locations of flicker wells that I am planning on researching when Boboros dives next. There's some places in section four that are possible locations of flicker wells I want to investigate before the dive, though."

He ran his fingers over the parchment and muttered under his breath as he circled the flicker well toward the barn door. He kept his head down — wrapped up in his thoughts as he exited the barrel makers.

"Shinn," Gaul called out. "Where are you going?"

Shinn jumped. He had forgotten he was among company. "Oh, I'm going to find more flicker wells. Do you know the way back to the Academy?"

"Centre of the city." Gaul thumbed at the storefront. "We found it once."

"Of course. Of course. You're free to wander the city if you'd really like. I'll keep Boboros from diving before I'm sure you're back in the Academy. While we're on the surface, the spectres are harmless. But once we dive, they gain a modicum of form."

"They're dangerous?" Marta asked.

Shinn nodded. "They'll try to steal the heat from your body to warm themselves, though it's never enough. I don't have any body heat, so I'll be safe. You won't be as lucky."

"What about the long-armed creature?"

"Ah… you saw the Headmaster." Shinn folded up his parchment and slid it back into his robes. "I try not to think about him too much, doing so makes my head tremble terribly. He tried to undue what Drowned Water had done to his people and his city. Whatever he came up with turned him into that monster. You'll be safe as long as you stay where the candles are lit and you're not outside when Boboros dives. I'll see you back at the Academy."

He waved goodbye and walked down the alley. Marta scratched the back of her neck. Knowing the truth about the creature didn't make it less frightening, but it set her mind at ease about it coming to get them at that very moment. She eyed the lit candle that sat on the nearby workbench.

"Let's get through that padlock," Gaul said, turning away from the barndoor. "I want to leave this damn whale."

Marta couldn't agree more.

True resurrection differs greatly from necromancy, as the latter never brings the soul back, it only creates a false one to animate a corpse. In fact, necromancy is better used to prolong one's life rather than bring it back. This is done by a ritual that will exploit the malleability of the spirit to effectively switch a soul between two bodies. Doing this into a younger body gives one a modicum of immortality with enough subjects to use.

What Melifacto wanted was to bring back someone long dead. When asked, I saw no harm in telling him it was technically possible, though the process was beyond me. Souls were locked inside the chest of the Gate Beyond and somehow we would have to entreat the correct soul to leave those confines and take over a body not its own. A logical expansion on the concept of necromantic immortality, I told him.

Perhaps I should have lied.

—From the Journal of Jovin Gutterwake

Chapter Forty-Four
Ghosts

Gaul couldn't help but walk quickly back to the Academy. Marta kept pace, but seemed lost in her own world. She saw the creature Shinn called the Headmaster and it seemed to have had some sort of effect on her. That wasn't surprising, the city felt wrong since the second they stepped off the boat.

"Do you think this Drowned Water is really as powerful as Shinn says?" Marta asked as they arrived in the Academy. "If it's actually artificial Light, then we may not have to bother with getting to all these Primordials."

"Maybe." Gaul hurried through Shinn's laboratory. "But he's still trying to figure it out. Who knows when he'll have a breakthrough?"

"True. I was hoping for a shortcut is all."

Gaul stopped at the door to the hallways. He let out a tired sigh. "I agree. That certainly would be wonderful." He drew the hammer from his coat. "But this is all we have right now."

Marta nodded, determined. She took the lead on the path to the library.

The door and the padlock didn't look any less secure. The dark iron, if anything, looked stronger than the night before. The cooper's hammer looked flimsy in comparison, but Gaul knew it was a workman's tool. It would hold.

He lined the hammer up with the top of the padlock, intending to snap the locking mechanism. He raised the hammer over his head.

"Shinn!"

Gaul froze.

The voice called again. "Shinn! Where are you?"

He looked back at Marta. She clutched her face, shaking terribly.

"I recognize that voice," she said, speaking through her palm. "From Marjyal. It's Melifacto. Quickly, break the lock!"

"He's going to hear us." Gaul put the hammer back in his coat. "There could be no other way out of that room."

Marta walked backwards, keeping her eyes on the entrance to the library. "What do you suggest?"

"We hide and wait for our moment."

Gaul grabbed Marta's arm and hauled her off into the stacks.

Melifacto stepped into the library. It was as disorganized as ever. Shinn was nowhere to be found, but that wasn't a surprise. He was most likely scouring the city for more memories. He would return to the Estuary Academy soon. He always did.

Droom, a massive man with pale grey skin and black stripes, entered behind Melifacto. "The Owls are searching the Academy."

"There's no hurry." Melifacto shook in his feather robe. "This place is freezing, Droom. Find me a room with a fireplace for tonight."

Droom bowed and departed. He was soon replaced by more soldiers. Ones with feathers and scales and fangs. They kept diligent eyes on all corners of the room.

Melifacto sauntered toward the clocktower door. The padlock had a fine layer of dust. No one had been into the clocktower in some time. That was good, it meant they had beaten Marta and Gaul to Boboros Whale.

Bellona entered the library with an impressed look on her face. She gazed up at the stacks above them while Feyra stayed on her heels.

"A city on a whale," Bellona said. "That's one in your favour, Melifacto. But I don't see your Primordial."

"Leviathan? She couldn't fit on Boboros, she barely fit in the ocean," Melifacto said. "But, you know Leviathan is dead. She's just parts now."

Shinn pushed his way through the soldiers and into the library. When he saw Melifacto, his eyes widened. "Melifacto!" he exclaimed. "I didn't hear your bell. You brought so many people. I don't have rooms prepared for them all. This many people should not be on Boboros. The flicker wells—"

"Calm yourself, Shinn." Melifacto placed his hand on his shoulder. "I hope you spend as much time on research as you do worrying. Have you made any progress?"

"No. No, not as much. There's many memories to sort through and not all of them are helpful."

Melifacto wrapped his arm around Shinn and led him away. Bellona narrowed her eyes and craned her neck, but didn't move to follow.

"We need Drowned Water," Melifacto whispered. "Now more than ever. The Cradle of the World is opening. It's leaking Absence at an alarming rate. If the First Gods awaken fueled by Absence rather than Light, even we won't survive the world they create. If Drowned Water is truly as powerful as the legends say, it's our only hope to cut through the Absence and retrieve the Chalice."

Shinn gave a shaky nod. "I'll increase my efforts."

"Thank you, brother. We're fighting against a foe we've never had to battle before. Time."

Melifacto squeezed Shinn's shoulder then turned away.

"Your people arrived," Shinn said. "I gave them a room on the same floor as mine."

Melifacto froze. He slowly faced Shinn. "My people?"

"Gaul and Marta. They arrived late last night."

One of Melifacto's fingers twitched, the only reaction he allowed himself to have. "Ah, I see." He stomped toward the soldiers. "Pelady!"

Pelady slunk into the room.

"Do you smell something?"

Pelady stretched her spine straight and sniffed the air. She cracked out a jagged smile. "She's here."

"Where? Close by?"

"Very. She's in this room."

Melifacto snapped his fingers to his soldiers. "Spread out. Find her."

The soldiers drew their weapons and started searching the library. Pelady swept her head back and forth, like a cross between a snake and a dog, and crept forward. Shinn had shrunken into himself, clutching his hands to his chest.

"Is everything fine?" he asked.

"Of course," Melifacto said. "I just don't want these two to get lost."

A Marjyalian soldier screamed, then was silenced by a wet thump. There were more shouts and the clashing of metal.

"Are there any other exits to the library?" Melifacto asked.

"Uh, no." Shinn shifted away from the sound of battle. "It's just these doors. But, there is a—" Glass shattered. "—window."

Bellona and Feyra ran out of the library. Melifacto ruffled his cloak and entered the stacks, finding his soldiers standing around a broken window. A couple laid dead in pools of blood. Pelady glowered out the window.

"Chase them down," Melifacto said. "Kill Gaul and bring Marta to me! I am done running across the country for these people. Go!"

The soldiers scattered. Pelady leapt out the window, over the broken glass, and took chase. Shinn walked up to Melifacto, his gaze lingering on the bodies left behind. He shook incessantly. Melifacto hadn't been that close to Marta since Marjyal. He couldn't let her slip away again.

"Submerge Boboros," he said.

"But there are people out there," Shinn insisted. "If we dive, the ghosts will come for them. It's too dangerous."

"Those two are unfortunately tenacious, I'm sure they'll find a way to survive." His fingers twitched. "But I will not allow Marta to leave this whale. Until we have her, we will block off all exits. No boat is going to sail away with my prize! Now dive!"

Shinn shrunk away. He slipped on the blood but kept his footing. With a whimper, he made his way back toward the front of the library.

"Shinn," Melifacto called after him. "You are a very good host."

* *

Marta took wild turns, hoping that if she got lost, so would her pursuers. Gaul kept glancing behind him, but the streets were empty. They eventually came to a stop in a café. They crouched behind a counter lined with a dozen lit candles.

"That woman had feathers," Gaul said through panting breaths.

"It's the Guild of Owls," Marta said.

"Are they all part-birds?"

"Most are part-animal. One of them has my scent. Her name's Pelady, you can't miss her. She's skinny, tall, and has a mouth that's spiky like a bramble patch."

Gaul groaned. "I hate this country."

Marta peered over the counter. A group of soldiers rushed by and Marta ducked down. "What do we do now?" she whispered.

"We get to a dock, get a boat, and get out of here."

"What about Leviathan?"

"Right." Gaul touched his necklace. "You're the one Marjyal is after, so you should still get to a boat. I can return to the Academy and get the Light. We'll meet back up on shore."

"They're after me, which means they won't kill me." She poked Gaul in the chest. "But they'll kill you without a second thought. We're sticking together."

"We don't know what Marjyal wants with you. I would rather we don't find out."

"I'm staying with you."

Boboros sang. Through the café windows, they could see the water level rise over the city.

"I guess we're staying together," Gaul said.

The water reached the top of the clocktower and the phosphorescent fish appeared. A stiff wind blew out the candles, casting the café into deep shadows. A wailing cry echoed through the city.

"I don't think we should stay here," Marta said, stepping around the counter. "If Pelady gets close, she's going to track me down."

"Then we keep moving," Gaul said. "We'll circle around the city then head back to the Academy. We still need that Light."

A bloodcurdling scream split the air. Marta drew her sword and spun around. The scream had bounced off the walls and it was impossible to tell where it came from. Boboros Whale became terribly silent.

"Marjyal isn't our only concern," Gaul said. He let go of his sword hilt. "Remember what Shinn said about the ghosts?"

There was a clattering from behind the counter and they stumbled back. An ethereal young woman stepped through the wall, her skin wavering like ocean waves. Her hair was wet and plastered to her face. A sprinkling of frost dusted her brow and lips. She stopped, then opened her eyes. They were a stark white that pierced into Marta's soul. The ghost let out a sigh and ice encrusted the counter. She stepped forward, through the wood and ice like it was water and reached for them.

Gaul swept forward, drawing and slicing the ghost across the throat. Her head craned back, neck cut open. Rather than blood, water poured over the front of her dress. She crumpled, but before she hit the ground, she began to slow as time dilated around her. In a flash, she was back to standing behind the counter. She opened her eyes again. Two more ghosts stepped through the wall next to her.

"We need to go," Gaul said, stepping back. "We're not going to win a fight with these things."

Marta kept her sword tip pointed toward the ghosts. They walked through the counter and reached for Gaul. Marta grabbed him by the coat and yanked him toward the exit. A long, slender arm cut off their path. It grabbed onto the cobblestone street and pulled itself into view. Marta's stomach fell to her feet.

The Headmaster dragged himself across the ground a massive creature, horribly emaciated. His arms and legs were so long that he moved on all fours, grabbing the floor and walls like a spider. A torn school uniform hung off his thin muscles. He looked over Gaul and Marta with a featureless face — no eyes, nose, or mouth, just cruel scar tissue. He grabbed either side of the café entrance and pulled himself inside. The temperature dropped. The Headmaster wheezed and ice crystals grew along his face and arms. He yanked his head back and the heat from the room was drawn into him. Gaul and Marta leapt aside as a line on the ground they once stood became rimmed with ice.

Gaul grabbed a chair and tossed it through a window, sending glass flying. "Go!" he shouted.

Marta jumped through first. Gaul tossed another chair at the Headmaster and followed. They sprinted down the street. Ghosts stepped through walls, reaching with bony fingers. Fortunately, they were slow and simple to dodge. They were plentiful, however. A dozen blocked off the street ahead.

Gaul cut right, down an alleyway. Marta sliced a ghost across the chest, splattering the ground with water, and followed. Her elbows bounced off the tight walls and she had to jump over a pile of black corruption.

"We can't run forever," Gaul said, looking over his shoulder.

"The only place they don't seem to go is the Academy." Marta dodged a chunk of corruption that dropped from above. "But I bet that's exactly what Melifacto is expecting."

"Then we'll have to find someplace else." He turned to see where he was going. A pale hand reached through the wall.

"Gaul!"

Gaul looked down, but it was too late. The hand grabbed his arm, sending frost up his sleeve. Gaul yanked his arm away, but two more hands shot out of the opposite wall and grabbed either side of his head. He screamed as the heat pulled away from his body. His skin went pale and his lips turned blue. Marta drew her sword and sliced upward, removing the ghost's hands at the forearm. Gaul collapsed to his knees, clutching his chest and shivering.

"Come on, Gaul." Marta pulled him to his feet.

He tried to talk, but his teeth chattered through his words.

"What happened to 'I grew up on a mountain?'"

"Colder."

Marta wrapped an arm around him. His skin was nearly ice. With her help, Gaul limped out of the alley and into the street. The ghosts floated out of the walls and wavered through each other like reflections in a stream. They may be slow, but they never stopped coming.

"You'll moved faster without me," Gaul said, keeping his eye out for oncoming ghosts.

"I'm not leaving you behind," Marta said.

"It's an observation."

"Make a better one."

Gaul pointed at the upcoming intersection. One of the buildings had candles lit in its window. A hanging sign labelled it as *Roi Garuud Hotel.*

"Why?" Marta asked. "Because it has a light?"

"Look."

The ghosts flooding the street took a wide path around the hotel. Where the light cast on the cobblestone, they would not touch.

Marta squared her jaw. "What do you think that means?"

"Shinn said we're safe where the candles are lit."

Thump. The Headmaster dropped off a house and landed behind them. Marta bunched Gaul's coat in her fist and pulled him faster. The Headmaster crawled steadily along the ground, grabbing lampposts and sewer grates to propel himself. The ghosts flanked him on both sides, closing in like the collapsing waves.

With a final explosive lunge, Marta threw Gaul into the hotel and stumbled in after. He rolled to his knees while Marta drew her sword and spun back to the entrance.

The Headmaster stood at the door, at the limits of the flickering candlelight. He wheezed and clicked his long nails on the street. The ghosts stood around him, also unwilling to enter the glow. One of them sighed and wandered off. The rest soon followed until only the Headmaster remained. He let out a creaky wheeze then backed away. Marta relaxed and sheathed her sword.

They were safe, whatever that meant.

It had been a long time since I had any support in my work. Melifacto was hiding things from me, I was sure, but I didn't care. I felt young again. I was reaching my hands into the fabric of reality and feeling it move. It must be how fluxweavers feel. I hadn't felt anything like it since Samadel.

So I experimented with ways to bring the dead back. Marjyal had plenty of subjects, people who could be lost without anyone caring. I worked closely with a man called Shinn and together we reached further than I ever could alone. Soon I became comfortable enough to call myself an arcanist once again.

—From the Journal of Jovin Gutterwake

Chapter Forty-Five
Roi Garuud Hotel

Gaul crawled to a wooden column and rested against it with his eyes closed. His skin was a corpse-like blue and he shivered terribly. Ice crystals had formed on his cheeks and temple. Marta crouched next to him and gently took his hand.

"Can't you Ignite and heal this?" Marta asked.

Gaul opened his eyes. They flickered red, but it couldn't take hold. "It's not working. Too cold. Even falling through the ice wasn't as cold as this. I can't fight — and this place is like a beacon for every Marjyalian in the city."

"If we get in trouble…" Marta rubbed the back of her neck. She had been thinking of this for a long time, ever since they dealt with the Apostles in the Tower. "I can't Ignite. But *she* can."

Gaul narrowed his eyes. "No."

"It's not ideal, but—"

"I need to be able to trust you, Marta." He let out a ragged breath. "I can't trust *her*. I need to know who's in charge of your body."

"I am." This was what Marta was afraid of, seeding doubt in Gaul's mind. Somewhere in her head, the voice smiled.

"Let's move somewhere else." Gaul pushed off the pillar and returned to his feet with great effort. "I don't want someone looking in and seeing us."

Marta supported him as they went deeper into the Roi Garuud Hotel. There were plenty of candles, thankfully, but the lobby floor was barren of most other luxuries. A short distance from the entrance was a ballroom, the floor scuffed by years of dancing and celebrating with a broken chandelier dangling awkwardly by two chains. Marta brought Gaul to the corner, far away from the precarious fixture.

"We can't stay here," Gaul said, collapsing against the wall and sliding to a sitting position. "Someone's going to find us."

"It's dangerous out there," Marta said. "If we're lucky the ghosts will get them."

"Doesn't it bother you that the candles are lit here? Every candle I saw blew out."

"Who would light them?"

The floor near the door creaked. "I did." Shinn stepped into the ballroom.

Marta put herself in front of Gaul. She shot her hand to her sword, but Shinn never seemed like much of a threat. He shrank back.

"What are you doing here?" Marta asked.

"I don't want to hurt you," Shinn said, showing his empty hands.

"You're not the one with the sword."

Shinn shook his head. "That's not what I meant for that to mean. I don't want you to get hurt. I came to help. And I found you." He glanced past Marta to Gaul. "Too late, it seems. The ghosts got to you."

Marta looked back at Gaul, his breaths coming out in broken fragments. "Can you help him?"

"He'll survive. But he needs to be kept warm."

"We need to leave," Gaul said through gritted teeth. "I'll be fine."

"All a ghost would have to do is touch you to kill you," Shinn said. "Please, take some time to recover."

"I don't like this." Gaul rested his head against the wall.

"You don't have to," Marta said. "Let's build a fire."

Shinn helped Marta pull benches, chairs, and curtains into a pile close to Gaul. Marta was about to grab a candle when Shinn put his hands over the kindling.

"*The stars fell,*" he said. The tinder flexed as reality bent around it. It snapped back and fire burst into life. Gaul closed his eyes and bathed in the heat.

Marta's jaw hung open. "What was that?"

"Flux." Shinn tossed a chair leg into the fire. "Stories are how we weave it. I enjoy the tale of when the stars fell to Meza and created the first flame."

Marta thought back to Feyra, who had swirled blood with a terrifying silence. But on her arms were strange designs. Maybe even words. "Could someone do this with words written on their skin?"

"Potentially. A story doesn't have to be told for every spell, they allow the weaver to better control the flux. I was not born with an attunement for flux, so I must use the stories. It's a difficult art, though I've never heard of one using the written word." He took Gaul's arm and inspected his skin. "How are you feeling?"

"Better," Gaul said. "But I still can't feel my fingers. It's hard to breathe."

"We need to get him some blankets," Shinn said to Marta. "The rooms are mostly empty, but there may be some in the closets. We can check the floors."

Marta looked at Gaul.

"Honestly," Gaul said. "I wouldn't mind some blankets."

Marta crouched and whispered, "Should we trust him?"

"I'm the one they want dead, remember? I already feel stronger."

Marta looked at Shinn waiting by the ballroom door, slouched over and wringing his hands. He pushed his long hair out of his face, looking into the empty air as he usually did.

"I'll be back soon," she told Gaul.

He nodded, and she joined Shinn leaving the room.

"Thank you for helping us," Marta said, following Shinn to the hotel's main staircase.

"I like you more than I like Melifacto."

Marta grinned as they climbed the stairs. "What about Jovin?"

"Jovin is a good man. He deserves better than this."

"Yeah…" Marta looked at her feet. "He did."

They reached the second floor, a series of hallways with rooms and a central common area. The stairs continued up from there. The Roi Garuud Hotel was choked with corruption, much more concentrated than the city outside.

"After we help Gaul," Marta said. "I want to ask you some questions."

"I would like to answer them." Shinn smiled, then reached his hands toward to corrupted hallways. "*Grydas cleansed the hearth to feed the many.*"

Reality curled and the corruption pulsed. It snapped back and the corruption turned into white powder that faded from view.

"There's a spell for clearing this stuff?" Marta asked.

"The stories are just ways to weave flux." Shinn shook the feeling into his fingers, the air around him bending with each shake. "It's personal and can be used for almost anything if you can connect to it."

"I don't understand at all."

"Flux is complex. Shiller spent all his time trying to unravel the mystery of how words can affect it. I don't know if he ever fully understood." Shinn turned toward the stairs. "I'll look for blankets upstairs. Be careful, though. All these people on Boboros are causing more and more flicker wells. I can't predict where the memories will be."

Marta nodded then headed into the now clean hallway. The rooms had been stripped, either by the people of the whale or Shinn. She checked some of the cabinets, but, other than the occasional moth, there was nothing inside. She wasn't going to give up and let Gaul freeze. Slamming a cabinet closed, she continued deeper into the second floor.

As she rounded a corner at the far end of the hotel, something wet hit her face. She recoiled and touched her cheek. It was water. The hallway ahead of her was filled with tiny floating orbs of water. She tapped one and it split apart before stopping again. They began to rise until they become long streaks. Rain — inverted rain. She looked up and found the ceiling was gone, replaced by a cloudy grey sky. When she looked forward again, the hotel too was gone.

She stood in a forest with trees unlike any she had seen before. Instead of leaves, they had needles. She walked forward like she was in a dream. The rain turned into snow that floated from the ground into the oppressive sky. The snow crunched under Marta's feet as she continued forth, though she didn't know where she was going anymore.

In a clearing ahead, laid a monster. A green-grey skinned creature, at least twice the height of a person and broad like a draft horse. Its head laid separate from its body, with its stringy black hair stuck to its face with blood. The body was covered in deep wounds. Fingers and toes were missing and pieces of its limbs were scattered about. A massacre that put a curl in Marta's stomach. A man with long hair and two bloody hatchets hunched over like a wild animal next to the corpse.

Gaul.

He was rougher looking than Marta was used to. His hair went past his chin and what was normally stubble was instead a bushy beard. He wore grey furs, stained red by the blood of the creature he just slew. His eyes blazed red from the Ignition and he breathed heavily, visible in the chilly air. His muscles relaxed and the red in his eyes faded back into blue.

A woman stumbled out of the tree line. She had raven hair bound in braids and wore similar furs to Gaul. Gaul whipped around, red shoots filling his eyes, but stopped when he saw who it was. The woman looked at Gaul, then the monster. She stepped back, her hand resting against her chest, before turning in a burst of water and running away. Gaul dropped one hatchet and reached for her.

A sudden wave of water rushed through the forest. Marta braced herself, but the current split before her, washing away the trees to either side.

"No one will love you," a woman's voice said. "No one will love you except for me."

The water brought with it metal poles and wooden supports. They embedded themselves into the ground, creating square skeletons until a town was built around her. The last pieces were metal bars that crossed over each other until it became a cage. People appeared around her — as if they were always there.

They were dirty and huddled against each over for warmth. A blanket laid over the cage that blocked most of the view from outside. It was only the flaps at the front that allowed Marta to see that the square filled with bodies.

Gaul, now in leather armour and with his long hair tied back, reached for the cage lock. Another man in similar armour pulled him away.

"Hey!" the man said, his voice warbling like it was underwater. "Stay away from them."

"I'm just letting them out," Gaul said, a similar effect on his voice.

"Your job is to kill people." The man shoved Gaul. "Stick with that."

There was a heart stopping snap, as if the world itself broke in two. The town blew apart and the snowy copse returned. Gaul watched the woman disappear.

"Anori!" he called.

He stepped forward and the world tilted. Marta tumbled through the forest, over roots and snow mounds.

Voices screamed at her amid flashes of combat.

"You're a fighter."

"You're a killer."

"You were born to make war and that's all you will ever be."

"Monsters have their place."

The dirt turned into cobblestone and she rolled to a stop at the rear of a crowd. She was back on Boboros, but she wasn't in the Roi Garuud Hotel. Her body ached. She got her knees and hands beneath her and stood.

She recognized the square she was in. It was the one with the fountain and no windows facing it. Or, it was at least something like it. People filled the space, dressed like the ghosts that had been hunting her and Gaul. The atmosphere was too somber to be a celebration. Marta put her hand on a man's shoulder and the man disappeared. She walked forward, the people in her way vanishing to create a path for her.

At the front of the crowd, she saw the fountain. Water shot out of the top, sparkling far too much in the sunlight before running down the flower outcroppings. At the bottom, near the dip in the basin lip, were four people in elegant robes. Kneeling on the dais in front of the fountain was a young girl.

Something about the sight made Marta's heart clench. The sound of rushing water filled her ears.

Gaul puffed warm air into his hands, trying to get the feeling back into his fingers. He held them out to the fire Shinn created. Death was wrapping its arms around his chest, and only his breaths drove it back. Getting grabbed by the ghost was the worst feeling he had ever experienced. It was more than cold, it was like his life was being torn away from him.

He looked up at the chandelier. Of the four chains that held it aloft, only two still remained. Many of the crystals had already broken off of their settings, leaving dangling strings in their place. Still, Gaul would have expected it to be in much worse shape considering the centuries Boboros had been abandoned.

In the distance, Marta shouted, "I'm going!"

"Marta?" Gaul called. He forced himself to stand. "What's happening?"

The chandelier chains snapped. The chandelier plummeted and struck the ballroom floor — only to plunge through it like diving into a lake. The floor broke into waves that became water. It rose up to Gaul's waist and extinguished the bonfire. The water crawled up the walls until the ballroom was filled on all sides. Despite the pressure, Gaul stayed planted to the floor. Treetops rose out of the depths and fog crept along the surface. The walls fell to reveal a foggy woodland. The water drained away.

There was no reason why Gaul would recognize the forest he was in, and yet the atmosphere that hung over him was unmistakable. He was in Nature's Grave.

"Come back!" shouted a man.

Two figures crossed between two trees. Gaul whipped around, but they were gone.

"I'm going to join Jovin." Marta's voice echoed without a source. "I'm sorry, Tristen."

"He doesn't want you," Tristen said. "That's why he left!"

"You can't know that!"

Gaul rubbed his face. He thought he had fallen into his own memory of the time he spent in Nature's Grave, when he fought against Matthis. But the memory wasn't his. He tried to step forward, but the trees tore past him, ripping the earth apart and reforming the forest. Marta appeared from around a tree. She had her long hair again, pulled back into a sloppy bun. The scar that normally ran out from her mouth was missing.

A skinny man grabbed Marta's arm, stopping her in her tracks. "Stop, Marta!" Tristen ordered.

"I can't stay here anymore." Marta pulled her arm, but couldn't get out of Tristen's grasp. "Jovin's been gone for months."

"If he wanted you, he would have brought you. He would have told you he was leaving."

Marta bowed her head. She breathed deeply. "I'm going."

Tristen's face contorted into rage. "Everyone told me marrying you was a mistake. If he didn't bring you when he went cavorting around the countryside, why would he bring you when he went into this godforsaken forest?"

"Let go of me."

"You're coming home." Tristen drew a knife. "Now."

Marta sneered back with no fear. "You're not my home."

Tristen backhanded her hard enough to send her crashing to the dirt. Gaul jerked forward, but the forest moved with him and he gained no ground. Marta laughed, a strange unnerving laugh that put chills down Gaul's spine. Tristen balked as Marta returned to her feet, swaying and flexing like she was fitting into new skin. Gaul knew — it wasn't Marta anymore.

"It's good to breathe the air," the other Marta said. "Do you know how long I've been watching from inside that prison? Screaming for one of you idiots to hear me?"

"Marta?" Tristen asked, trembling.

Other Marta looked at Tristen with a crazy grin. "Marta's taking a nap, you mongrel."

She grabbed the knife and drove her palm into Tristen's sternum. Tristen stumbled back, releasing the knife into Marta's grasp.

"Listen to me, insect." Other Marta ran the flat edge of the knife along her neck. "This body is mine. Not yours. Not Marta's. You can't tell it what to do." She brought the knife up to her lips. "But I can do anything I like."

She sliced her cheek open with one vicious cut. Tristen yelped and stepped back, but the other Marta grabbed him by the shirt and pulled him close. She cocked her head to show him the blood pouring down her cheek.

"What's wrong, sweetheart?" she said. "Don't you like the look? It's been so long, even pain is a welcome feeling."

Tristen leaned away. "What are you doing, Marta?"

"Marta—" She stuck the bloody knife into Tristen's mouth. "—is not my name."

She yanked the knife to the side. Tristen screamed awkwardly with part of his cheek dangling. The other Marta cackled.

"Look, lover," she said. "We match."

She flipped the knife around, reared back, then slammed it into Tristan's eye. Everything exploded into water. It swept Gaul off his feet into raging rapids. He fought against the current, but it was too strong and he slammed against a stone wall. The wall became a floor and the water morphed into the shape of a crowd. Everything still felt distant and hazy, Gaul wasn't out of the memories yet.

The crowd looked like the ghosts, now alive — or as close as one would get in a memory. The square was much like the one Gaul and Marta had passed through earlier with Shinn, if not the same one. Gaul pushed his weary body to stand. Four people in robes lined with purple and gold waited at the fountain. A young girl, no more than twelve, knelt on the platform next to them.

Marta, this one with her scar, stepped out from the crowd. She made eye contact with Gaul. She was in clearer focus than the rest of the world. She looked at Gaul only briefly before turning her attention to the event before them.

One of the leaders raised their hands to the sky. He spoke indistinct words. Gaul strained his ears, but he couldn't make out the meaning. Another one put her hand on the young girl's head. The girl had her wrists bound with silk rope. Her eyes were shut. She seemed at peace. The speaker stopped talking, then the person pushed the girls head under the water.

Gaul felt a bubbling in his lungs and he dropped to his knees. Water poured out of his mouth. As it hit the ground, tendrils of yellow energy coursed along the stonework. Marta too doubled over, heaving out mouthfuls of sparking liquid. The young girl who was once so calm thrashed against her bindings. Gaul tried to breathe, but the water was too forceful. The crowd averted their eyes. The girl let out a bubbling scream, but the woman in the robe kept her down.

Gaul's throat and lungs burned. He fell to all fours. The ground turned to liquid under one of his hands and knees. The world pivoted around him as he spun through the ground. He was back in the ballroom of the Roi Garuud Hotel, the bonfire burning like nothing had happened. He took in thankful breaths, now dry once again. Under the hanging chandelier was a spot where the geometry of the room collapsed in on itself. A flicker well.

Being in a memory was like being in a dream. Gaul had been unable to react to most of the stimuli. But it hurt. Gaul wondered if it could even kill. But what he saw hurt more than the pain. The memory was vague, but the meaning cut into his brain with vicious precision.

He knew the truth.

He needed to find Marta.

This is where Marta comes in.

—From the Journal of Jovin Gutterwake

Chapter Forty-Six

Monsters

Gaul's body still felt drained from the ghost's touch, but he pushed it aside and rushed out of the ballroom. Marta sat on the stairs, cradling her head.

"You saw it too?" she asked.

Gaul nodded. "Where's Shinn?"

They found him on the third floor clearing a room. He had a bundle of blankets in his arms and was grabbing another out of a closet. He saw Gaul and Marta and jumped out of fright.

"Gaul," he said, laughing off the reaction. "Are you feeling better?"

Gaul rested his hands on his swords. "We know what Drowned Water is."

Shinn's expression changed. It wasn't what Gaul thought it would be — fear, confusion, or interest. Instead, Shinn seemed sad.

"You already know," Marta said. "Don't you? You know that they killed people to make it."

Shinn sat on the creaky bed, laying the bundle of blankets next to him. "I found the correct memory in this hotel decades ago. This is where they kept the people before they… I didn't think it could be true. I kept searching, hoping that what I saw was wrong or there was more to the story. But everything I learned just revealed something darker." He spread his arms wide. "Boboros is the formula for Drowned Water. The water that runs through the pipes is filled with an impression of the minuscule innate Light that every person carries with them." He flopped his arms down. "But it was just an impression."

"Until they drowned someone in it," Gaul said.

Shinn clutched his head, grabbing handfuls of hair. He rocked back and forth. "The water in their lungs could be removed. That's Drowned Water. A power to rival Light, but only by sacrificing human life. The younger the incubator, the stronger the Drowned Water."

"They used it to extend their lives," Marta said. "And in the end they became ghosts."

"Death can never grant life." The momentary confidence that Shinn had shown disappeared. He looked like the frenzied madman he was when Gaul first saw him.

"I can fix it though. There must be a work around for the incubator. I can still make Drowned Water. I can still do it. I have to do it. Melifacto doesn't have my qualms. He'll drown cities for power. I won't give up on it. I can fix Hyloh's error."

"Hyloh's error was sparking human greed," Gaul said. "Stopping this madness was the last good thing he did before disappearing. That's why he destroyed all evidence of it."

"We can rival the gods."

"Not this way." Gaul turned toward the door. "Let's go, Marta."

"Wait a second." Marta sat next to Shinn. "What did Jovin have to do with this?"

"Jovin isn't involved with Drowned Water," Shinn said.

"I mean." She jumped to her feet and paced. "I think I'm forgetting things, Shinn. I don't remember Melifacto. I don't remember Jovin working with him. What were they working on?"

"I don't know if I'm supposed to say."

Gaul stepped forward. "Shinn."

Shinn wrung his hands. He looked into Marta's eyes. "We were working on you."

Marta froze. Gaul opened his mouth, but couldn't think of anything to say. The question seemed obvious, but no one asked it.

Shinn put his palms into his knees, pushed himself to standing, and said, "When Isildia died, Melifacto lost his Key into the Cradle."

"Wait," Gaul said. "Isildia died over centuries ago, didn't she? How could Melifacto be there?"

"Melifacto is the Descendant of Melakin."

"What?" Gaul and Marta said in unison.

"You really don't know. This can be complicated to explain. I should start from the beginning, when Melifacto and Isildia created the cult of Mar. Melifacto used her to try to discover how Sebanna opened the Cradle the first time. He offered her eternal life, but Drowned Water was out of our grasp. And she died."

Marta's hands shook. She walked from one wall to the other, bouncing around like a fish in a pond. "But what does this have to do with me?" she asked.

"Melifacto couldn't let Isildia be. She was his only way into the Cradle. She knew the secret to *elys sang*. But he met Jovin, so young but intelligent beyond his years. They went to the Gate Beyond and pulled Isildia's soul out before it could pass on. But they needed a body."

"She's in my head." Marta jaw hung open, awestruck and disgusted. "It's Isildia."

Shinn ran his fingers along the blankets he collected. "It took a long time to find a viable child. And when we did, we used the last of the Drowned Water we had found here to put Isildia in, well, you, Marta."

"How could Jovin do this to me?"

"Jovin was the driving force. He was obsessed with true resurrection."

"I'm his sister!"

Shinn did a double-take. His gaze flickered between Marta and Gaul, who waited near the door.

"Why are you so confused?" Marta stepped toward him. "You're the one who helped them put that woman in me."

"But…" Shinn searched for the words. "Jovin's sister died before I ever met him. We found you in an orphanage."

Marta went blank. She put her hand against the wall to keep herself from falling. With her free hand, she clutched her head and started to collapse. Gaul rushed up and grabbed her by the shoulders. He glared at Shinn.

"What are you talking about?" Gaul asked.

"I… I suppose Jovin could have told people she was his sister," Shinn stammered. "I'm sorry. Did I do something wrong?"

"Shut up!" Marta shouted.

"Marta," Gaul said.

She pulled out of Gaul's grasp. "Not you. Her. She's laughing."

"What are you talking about?" A realization washed over Gaul. "Is Isildia talking to you?"

Marta nodded meekly.

"For how long?"

"Ever since the Tower."

"Why didn't you tell me?"

Marta leaned against the wall. She shaded her eyes with her hand. "Because I didn't know how you would react. I've put you through so much. And I just want to get you home."

"Not this again. You're not the reason I'm here. If not for you, I would be rotting in a cell in Marjyal."

"I can't control her, Gaul."

"You're not supposed to," Shinn said. He backed himself into a corner and it was hard to tell who was more afraid, Marta or him. "Isildia will grow in power until she takes total control. Marta will cease to be."

"I want to go." Marta turned away. For a moment, Gaul saw that her face had gone flush before she bolted out the door. "Let's leave."

"Marta!" Gaul went to follow.

"Gaul." Shinn stopped him and leaned in. "Someday Isildia will take over. It's inevitable."

"I'm not losing hope. We still have a lot to do. I know there's a piece of Leviathan in the clocktower, so stay away from the Academy if you don't want to be involved."

Shinn took that in. From his pocket, he pulled out a large iron key and said, "This is for the clocktower. If you need to escape, there's also a way into the sewers from inside the room. I hope you can quiet Leviathan. I'm tired of hearing her screaming."

Gaul took the key.

"I'm sorry if I upset Marta," he continued. "Perhaps there are things we are better not knowing."

"Perhaps." Gaul pocketed the key and followed Marta.

Marta stood in the lobby, looking out the front window into the dark city streets. The ghosts had disappeared, possibly to find better prey, but she wasn't paying attention to that. She wasn't looking at anything in particular, just chewing on her thumbnail and staring into the empty space in the middle of the street.

I used to do that, Isildia said.

Do what? Marta thought in reply.

Chew my thumb when I was upset.

Marta looked at her thumbnail, then tucked it under her arm.

Isildia laughed. *Is it so bad that I'm going to take over your body? In a way, you get to give birth to a queen.* She paused. *You know, my mother died in childbirth too. Funny how these things repeat.*

You're not taking over.

I am. It's inevitable. Very few people get the chance to be a part of something amazing, but you get to be right at the centre of it.

Marta gritted her teeth. *What are you planning?*

I still have to keep some secrets. She faded to a whisper that crawled along Marta's brain. *But you could help me. We're in this together after all. Now that Gaul knows the truth, how long until he deals with you?*

That's not going to happen.

So you say, but you saw the memory. How he killed that troll, how his wife ran away from him, how those soldiers wouldn't let him near the prisoners.

He's been treated badly. Marta shook her head. *That doesn't make him a bad person.*

Or he's been treated badly because he is a bad person. You don't know him, Marta. As much as you think you do. He chased a Priest across countries to get his dead wife's necklace back. That's obsession. That's desperation, and there's no telling what a desperate man could do. Remember what Dynah said. He's hiding something about Anori. He killed her. That's what monsters do. I've lived a longer life than you, I know what true monsters are. I've faced them. I've seen people change like a coin flip and become your worst enemy. Gaul will betray you, unless you act first. Get the Light Vessel and get out.

The floor creaked and in the half-reflection on the window she could see Gaul. Her skin went cold, but she gave no reaction.

"Marta," Gaul said. "Are you okay?"

"I don't want to talk about it," Marta replied. "I don't want to talk about any of it. I want to get the Light and leave."

"There were a lot of revelations just now."

"Yeah. And let's leave them at that. Jovin was lying to me. The stories in his notebook about growing up with his sister, that wasn't me. I was an experiment he kept his eye on."

Gaul stepped around Marta. "He brought you out of Marjyal still, didn't he? Melifacto wasn't planning for that. Maybe to him, you were his family."

Look at how he stands, Isildia said. *Hands on his swords like he's ready to kill.*

That's how he always stands, Marta thought.

Yeah. Around you.

"I guess we'll never know." Marta lowered her head and swept around Gaul toward the open front door. "Let's go before someone finds us. Are you feeling better?"

"Marta, you—"

"Shut up." She stepped toward the door. "That one was for you."

She stalked into the city, uncaring if Gaul followed or not. He did.

They kept to the wide roadways to give themselves plenty of time for if a ghost came through a wall. Boboros stood quiet. Marta nearly relaxed — when they turned a corner and found two dozen Marjyalians barring their path.

Marta and Gaul froze. The Marjyalians turned towards them, as if in slow motion. A group of Boars and Owls, all ready for a fight. At their front stood a seven-foot man wielding a war hammer. The skin on his face and bare arms was covered with black stripes. His slit cat eyes gleaming in the light of the luminescent fish and he smiled with sharp carnivore teeth.

"Marta," Droom said. "You're coming with us."

Marta drew her sword. "You can try."

Isildia spoke, *Hey, that guy is really big. You should run. Or let me fight.*

You don't want to go back to Marjyal? Marta asked.

Of course not! I died to get away from it.

"We shouldn't fight these people," Gaul whispered. "I'm still not fully recovered from the ghost's attack. I've been trying but… I can't Ignite."

The Marjyalians approached carefully and slowly. They still needed Marta alive — to mean they needed Isildia alive. Marta looked back the way they came. There was a sideroad not far back they could take to get around the group. But as she scanned the road, she spotted a trio of ghosts stepping through a building.

"Gaul," Marta said, poking him with her elbow.

Gaul glanced back. "Damn."

"It's only three."

"Yeah, but after one saw us, the rest came."

They were quickly becoming surrounded. Droom motioned for his soldiers to circle the pair. Marta glanced around for another option. A wooden staircase rose up between two of the nearby buildings to an elevated walkway. Marjyal had similar architecture, Marta remembered. The workers started building up to use the most of their space, it could be a way around. Marta got Gaul's attention and jerked her head toward the stairs.

Droom saw where she was looking. "Don't run," he growled.

"Run!" Marta shouted, stowing her sword and turning on her heel.

Gaul kept pace as they raced up the steps. Droom shouted for his soldiers to follow. At the top of the stairs, they turned down a walkway. Much like the streets below, building entrances lined the walls next to them, only tighter here. Marta kept alert for a ghost reaching through as they took turn after turn, always moving toward the clocktower in the distance, its beacon light spinning around at its tip.

Look ahead, you idiot! Isildia screamed.

Marta was so focused on the walls, she didn't notice the Marjyalians stepping in their way, weapons at the ready.

Gaul grabbed Marta's arm, stopping her. "Go back!"

They turned, but Droom's group cut them off. They were stuck on a narrow walkway with no escape.

Gaul drew his swords. "We have to fight."

Marta faced the second group, back to back. She drew her sword and a knife, but her knees shook like twigs in a windstorm.

Let me fight, Isildia said. *I can Ignite. You need me.*

I don't need you, Marta thought.

If you're taken then it's Melifacto using me again. I can get us out of here.

Marta pushed Isildia's voice aside. She readied herself. Her opponents crept forward. She dug her boots into the wood and charged to meet them.

She tossed her knife at the closest one, an Owl. The soldier dodged to the side, but the knife stuck in his arm. Small quills grew out of the area around the wound. He pulled the knife out with his teeth and sneered. Marta drew another knife and jumped into the fray.

The soldiers were skilled fighters, but they were careful not to kill her. That didn't mean they couldn't injure her gravely. They took swipes at her legs and arms. She parried a strike with her knife then lunged forward with her sword. The soldier cross-stepped out of the way, a smug grin across his face. It was different from street brawls with gangsters in Marjyal or a group of Doves. These people knew how to survive a fight.

So Marta changed her tactics. She went in hard. She tossed her knife, but it was batted away. With her sword in both hands she swung wide and aggressive. The soldiers went on the defensive, afraid to kill her.

Marta kept up the assault on the soldiers, even as her lungs began to burn and her arms ached. She struck swords and shields. She moved erratically so the soldiers wouldn't risk a strike.

With a flick of her arm, she got behind one of the soldier's shields and wrenched it aside. She spun, then cut the sword down on the soldier's neck — where their armour didn't protect. He dropped and the Owl with the quills took advantage. He cracked Marta on the temple with the hilt of his sword. She stumbled back, dazed. The Owl grabbed her arm, piercing through her coat with quills that grew from his hand. She pulled her arm out of his grasp, but the quills remained stuck in her flesh. The Owl jumped and drove both his feet into Marta's chest, sending her tumbling through a window into a nearby house.

Marta landed back first on a thin rug that didn't do much to soften her fall. The glass cut her face and hands. She touched the quills the Owl left behind, but they were barbed and stuck firmly into her forearm.

Now can I fight? Isildia asked.

"Go away," Marta muttered, convincing her body to stand.

Isildia sighed. *If not for me. How about for him? He's still injured from that ghost.*

From outside the broken window, Marta heard Gaul let out a cry of pain. He was a better fighter than her, but he was also injured and the Marjyalians didn't care about killing him. If Marta gave her mind over to Isildia, would she be able to come back?

Time's wasting, Marta, Isildia said.

The Owl knocked the glass off the windowsill and threw a leg over.

"Fine," Marta said. "But this isn't permanent."

Isildia chuckled. *Maybe not this time.*

Marta blacked out.

Gaul was in bad shape. He took down two opponents, but Droom still stood and the rest had barely broken a sweat. Gaul hoped he had healed more from having his heat drained by the ghost, but once he started fighting he found his feet dragging and his grip loose. In fact, he already lost one sword — stuck into the wood planks a few metres ahead of him. The other he clutched in a shaking hand as he knelt, taking deep breaths.

Marta's boot stomped next to him. Fresh blood dripped off the tip of her sword. Behind her, a field of corpses, battered and shredded apart. One of them hung halfway out a broken window. More Marjyalians rushed in, but slowed when they saw the state of their allies.

"Marta?" Gaul wiped the blood from his mouth.

She looked down at him with crimson eyes. "One more guess."

Gaul stood. His grip tightened. "Isildia."

"I like you saying my name." She glanced back at the soldiers approached from the back. "I'm here to help."

"I don't need help from you."

"Gods, you sound just like her. Doesn't matter. I'm not letting Melifacto get his hands on me and she isn't going anywhere without you." She raised her sword. "You're both useless. Can you Ignite or not?"

"I've been trying."

"Try harder."

"It doesn't work like that."

Isildia rolled her eyes. "Oh please, save the excuses for your lover girl. I just learned about this a few weeks ago and I can do it. Aren't you some kind of champion?" She dragged her sword along her cheek, sending out sparks. "Or are you just a sick puppy?"

Gaul turned to face her. Red haze crept into his vision, lined with flecks of gold. Isildia was an intruder in Marta's body, and she talked to him like he was some trainee. He reached the point where the haze became a tunnel. Flames stretched from his toes to his crown, burning through the cold that infiltrated his flesh. The world hung still for a moment, and the string snapped.

Gold surrounded Isildia as she grinned. "There he is."

Gaul shouted in rage and charged Droom's group. He kicked his sword stuck in the walkway. It splintered the wood and whistled through the air, embedding hilt deep into a soldier's chest. Gaul followed, grabbing and yanking it free before the soldier hit the ground.

The rest reformed their line, but Gaul moved with unparalleled ferocity. He bashed weapons aside to get at their wielders. The walls were narrow, so he jumped and bounced off them for more forceful strikes. A soldier caught him across the chin. Lightning burst from his skin and he responded by removing the soldier's head.

Gaul stepped forward to continue attacking, but Isildia knocked him aside and he had to catch himself on the wall. Isildia engaged the enemy first. She had none of the grace and coordination Marta usually fought with. She swung her sword like a club and seemed to willfully take hits in return.

"Hey!" Gaul shouted. "You're not immortal!"

Isildia ran someone through. "It sure feels like it!"

Gaul charged forth. He cracked a soldier in the head with a jumping knee and rolled over him to join Isildia. As he rose, he stabbed a soldier in the stomach. Isildia decapitated the same soldier — Gaul ducking to keep his own head.

Droom stomped in. He swung his hammer over his head and down on Gaul. Gaul caught it with his forearm. The bone cracked, then reformed. He swung at Droom's stomach, but he didn't have the force to cut through the heavy leather. Droom kicked him back, then reached for Isildia.

Isildia wasn't paying attention. Gaul lunged forth, catching Isildia by the collar and pulling her away from Droom.

"What are you doing?" Isildia demanded.

"These people want you!" Gaul said, pushing her away from the fight. He swiped at Droom to give them distance. "You can't go diving into the middle of them."

"Don't tell me what to do!"

A scream cut the air. The crowd parted to reveal a ghost grabbing one of the soldiers. The soldier's skin turned first blue, then black, before he collapsed dead. More ghost arms reached out of the walls, grabbing at any flesh within range. The soldier's fought back, but one by one they were grabbed. Only Droom with his quick reflexes and thick armour could stay away.

Isildia bolted in the other direction, but halted. The Headmaster crawled along the walkway, pawing at the corpses Isildia left behind. His aura wasn't red or gold, but an inky darkness. Near Absence. He pulled the last of the heat from the bodies, then turned his eyeless gaze to her. She gulped.

Ghosts poured out the surrounding buildings, providing them no escape. The Marjyalians fought behind them, and the Headmaster crept in from the front. Gaul looked up. The roof of the buildings stretched ten, twelve feet above them.

"Isildia!" Gaul shouted. He sheathed his sword and cupped his hands in front of him. "Up."

Isildia looked at him, then at the lip of the roof. She nodded and ran. She put her foot in his hands and Gaul tossed her. With a grunt of exertion, Isildia grabbed the roof and scrambled up.

Droom broke from the ghosts charged in like a bull. He swung with his hammer and Gaul dodged back. The steel head struck the wall hard enough to splinter the wood and get his hammer stuck. Cold tingled up Gaul's spine and he glanced back. The Headmaster braced himself against the walls. Ice formed along his arms and face as he stretched forward.

"Hey!" Isildia offered her hand.

Droom yanked his hammer out of the wall, sending chunks of wood scattering about. Gaul took a large one and slammed it against Droom's leg. There was a cracking sound, from both the wood and the joint, and he dropped to one knee. Gaul put his foot against his back and springboarded for Isildia's hand.

The Headmaster jerked his head back. Gaul clasped with Isildia and put both feet against the wall. She pulled and Gaul kicked away. Ice shot across the walkway as the heat drained. Gaul sailed to the opposite roof, catching his footing on the shingles before looking below.

Droom had been frozen solid, his arm outstretched, reaching for Gaul. The rest of the soldiers were similar ice statues. The ghosts touched the slick surface, searching for any trace of heat.

"Look at that," Isildia said. "I saved your life. Just like Marta."

"Marta isn't so insufferable about it." Gaul said.

A long pale hand grabbed onto each of their roofs and the Headmaster pulled himself into view. Isildia drew her sword and sliced off the Headmaster's fingers. He fell, slowed down, then flickered back a few feet. His fingers were back. Gaul leapt over the gap to Isildia's side and pointed at the clocktower.

"Start running," he said.

Together they jumped from rooftop to rooftop. Gaul glanced back and saw the Headmaster keeping pace, still cloaked in his black aura. They reached a gap too wide, and Isildia dropped back onto the walkway. Gaul stopped to check where the Headmaster was, only to see a long arm descending upon him. Gaul took a diving roll to the side as the Headmaster's hand cracked the roof where he once stood.. It seemed the Headmaster could truly move when he wanted to.

Gaul drew his swords. The Headmaster crawled forth, supporting himself on his arms. A knife flashed through the air and stuck into one of his scrawny arms, piercing clean through the other side. Water dripped from the wound. He considered the knife with great care. Another flew just over his head. Isildia stood below, a third knife ready to throw. The Headmaster leaned on the lip of the roof and wheezed at her.

Gaul stomped the roof, then rushed forward and cut one of the Headmaster's hands off. Without the support, the Headmaster started to tumble. Isildia ran out of the way, but the Headmaster's fall slowed, preparing to reset his injury. Gaul couldn't allow that.

With a battle roar, Gaul leapt off the roof and planted both feet into the Headmaster's chest. Standing on the Headmaster, ten feet above the ground, Gaul started chopping. He cut deep and vicious gashes into the Headmaster's face and chest, sending slow motion water spurting into the air. The Headmaster flexed his arms in slow motion, reaching for him. Too slow. Gaul obliterated the Headmaster's upper body with inhuman brutality.

The Headmaster let out a wheeze — something like a cry — and disappeared. Gaul fell to the walkway, landing hard on both feet. He looked up at the roof, but nothing came.

"I wish that Marta could have seen that!" Isildia exclaimed. "A true showing of the violence of a monster."

Gaul glared sidelong at Isildia. He blinked twice and the golden aura faded. "Bring Marta back," he said.

"Why? Why would you want *her* help? I can Ignite. And unlike her, I'm not afraid of what you really are — in all the bloody glory that comes with it. In fact, I embrace it. I'm a dead woman in someone else's body. We're both monsters, Gaul."

"This isn't a conversation."

"Is that the deal?" Isildia stepped closer to Gaul. "You and Marta are off to save the world and keep it in stasis for another century? Is that what you are, Gaul? A hero? Your wife didn't seem to think so when she ran off." A wicked smile cracked across her face. "How did dear Anori die anyway? I'm just asking because someone with your abilities, your temperament, it seems likely—"

Gaul grabbed Isildia by the collar and pulled her close. "Shut up!"

Isildia yelped and push Gaul away. Only, it wasn't Isildia anymore. Marta fell onto her bottom. She clutched her chest, taking deep breaths. Her entire body shook and her eyes were wide like dinner plates. Gaul's heart fell to the soles of his feet.

"Marta," he said softly, reaching for her.

Marta waved him off. "I'm fine. I'm fine. Just a little surprised."

"I'm sorry."

"It's okay." Marta stood. "I guess Isildia did her job. We're not far from the clocktower now, huh? Good."

Marta's knees still shook. Gaul squeezed his fists until his knuckles popped. He had seen that look on dozens of people before her, people he cared about. People who left.

Monsters have their place, Gaul thought.

Marta turned down the walkway and Gaul followed. He kept his head low, his mind racing with thoughts about Marta, Anori, and him. Had he reverted back to the man he was years ago? Or had he never truly changed at all? These thoughts plagued him and stuck in his head like an arrow.

So wrapped up in his torturous thoughts, he didn't notice someone rushing him. The woman tackled him in the ribs. Feyra. Together they hit the walkway railing and broke through, tumbling toward the street far below.

After we retrieved the soul from the Gate Beyond and contained it in a vessel, something of my own design in fact, we needed to find a suitable host. Soul exchanging was simple when they were both alive, but a dead soul wasn't conscious. It required more finesse. Perhaps if we had access to their original body it would work, but without that we were forced to look for bodies that were similar to Isildia's. Adults proved useless, as they were too foreign for the soul to take root, resulting in the death of the potential host. Children worked better, and infants even better than that. Though, they too eventually rejected the soul. We were running out of Drowned Water to fuel the ritual as well. Things were looking bleak.

I was wondering if it was impossible without Divine power, when we found her. A dark-haired baby with bronze skin that could cry like nobody's business. The spitting likeness of Ellie. That was the second time I should have walked away.

But I didn't. Melifacto insisted we call her Isildia, but I never liked it. I called her Marta. I told Melifacto it was to honour Mar, calling the girl "of Mar." In reality, I just knew he wouldn't accept anything else and I couldn't bear calling her the name of the woman who would someday take her away.

—From the Journal of Jovin Gutterwake

Chapter Forty-Seven
Chasing Memories

Feyra had been having a bad day. Once Gaul and Marta ran from the Academy, Bellona ordered her to take chase. Feyra ran, but it was easy to get lost in the twisting confines of the city on a whale. For an hour she hunted the streets, looking for any trace of the fugitives, but all she found were frozen corpses of soldiers.

She had done well avoiding the ghosts. It seemed larger groups of people attracted them, while Feyra walking alone wasn't much of a treat. Still, she kept her club ready to smash.

She was on an elevated walkway when she met her first ghost face to face. It stepped through the door of a house next to her and stopped. It inspected Feyra for a second, then reached forward. Feyra cracked it hard on the head. She reached out for the splattering blood, only to have it drop to the ground without fail. It wasn't blood, it was water.

The ghost flickered then disappeared. Feyra stepped back, ready for anything. Out of the same door, the same ghost walked out, inspected Feyra, then reached forward. Feyra hit him again, breaking his neck. Another flicker, then the ghost walked out of the same door. Feyra cursed, then ran.

They're unkillable, Feyra thought. *What am I supposed to do now?*

Ahead of her, she spotted Gaul. He walked slowly behind Marta, lost in his own thoughts. This was her chance. She remembered Ortun's words to ask Gaul her questions before bringing him to Bellona. Gaul knew what she was. She couldn't give up this chance. She lowered her shoulder and barrelled into him before he noticed.

They struck the railing and with a sharp *crack*, the railing shattered and they fell. They bounced off a canopy and Gaul slipped from her hands before they crashed to the hard stone street. Feyra's club clattered away.

Feyra pushed herself to kneeling, clutching the shoulder that hit the ground first. Gaul staggered to his feet, unsteady as he was, a couple metres away.

"Gaul!" Marta shouted from above.

"Go!" Gaul shouted back. "I'll catch up."

"You're going to tell me what I am," Feyra said, pointing at Gaul. "You're going to talk, then I'm bringing you to Bellona."

"I have no idea who that is, but I am not going anywhere with you."

Feyra took a wide stance. "You're not going to beat me."

"I don't have to."

Gaul turned on his heel and ran. Feyra took chase. They both barrelled full tilt through Boboros' streets. Gaul took a sharp turn into an alley. Feyra followed, but the alley became a street, filled to the brim with people. Feyra stumbled to a stop, the bright light from the sudden sunshine blinding her.

It was a parade, though there weren't any spectators, just marchers. They cheered joyously and threw handfuls of coloured dust into the air. A woman coloured red, purple, and green touched Feyra's arm and vanished. Each person Feyra touched similarly disappeared into thin air. Craning her neck to look over the crown, she spotted a trail of people vanishing. Feyra didn't have a moment to consider the strangeness Boboros inflicted on her, she wouldn't lose Gaul.

Feyra sprinted through the crowd without hesitation, the partiers disappearing around her. She saw flashes of Gaul through the masses. Another few metres and she broke from the crowd. She had lost distance from Gaul, but neither of them slowed.

The sun dipped to the horizon, moving faster than it should. Fluffy white clouds filled the sky. The ground beneath Feyra's feet tilted until she was running downhill. It kept spinning and she was sliding. A massive snowy spike poked through the cloud cover. As the clouds parted, an upside-down mountain descended from the sky.

Ahead of her, Gaul lifted off the street, falling upward. When Feyra reached the same point, gravity shifted for her as well. The mountain expanded until it filled her vision. Gaul struck a snow drift on the mountainside; Feyra followed soon after. They rolled down the slope. Feyra grabbed cold handfuls, trying to right herself, but there was no control in the snow.

She reached the bottom of the slope and slid onto a frozen lake, stopping halfway across. With great care not to slip, she got her feet beneath her and stood. Gaul has stopped running and stared into the distance.

Children played on the ice. One of them rushed out and a second followed. The ice cracked, and both the children fell in. Gaul looked to Feyra, then at lake below. He leapt straight up, then slammed both feet into the ice. It shattered on impact and Gaul fell through.

Feyra tried to run, but her feet flew out from beneath her and she landed on her chest. She glanced briefly at the children. Only one had resurfaced, breaking through the ice with bare fists. Feyra scrambled for the hole Gaul made and dove through feet first.

She dropped through a metre of frigid water before falling into a war-torn grassland. Fires and bodies littered the landscape. Grass torn up by hooves and boots. An arrow whipped past her head and struck a man, knocking him off his horse. Feyra's gaze followed the unmanned horse as it ran into the smoke where

Gaul hurried across the battlefield. Brushing off the exertion and pain, Feyra took chase again.

The battle raged around her. She didn't recognize the flags of the armies. All the screams and voices came muffled and distant. A man with orange eyes drew strange symbols in the air then thrust his hands forward and said something Feyra couldn't hear. Reality pulsed around his palms, then fire ignited from them and launched across the battlefield, blowing apart a unit of soldiers.

Is that a fluxweaver? Feyra wondered.

Another explosion ignited next to her. She staggered, but didn't stop running. When the smoke cleared, a door frame and part of a wall appeared where there should've been ruin. Another explosion lit off just ahead of her, and a wall with a window was in her way. She vaulted through and another explosion brought with it a dining room complete with stove and wash basin.

Each explosion painted part of a city that Feyra had to dodge around. People unrelated to the war started to walk by. A street had nearly been built around her when a wave of water washed over the battlefield. Strangely, it didn't knock Feyra off her feet and she could keep running after Gaul as the water receded and the city gained form.

She was in Marjyal. More than that, she was in the neighbourhood she grew up in. There was the store she stole from. The balcony she slept under. The school she never went to.

She passed the spot where she would beg and saw a young girl. A teenage girl with bronze skin and a bleeding cut on her brow. Around her were six gangsters who tried to steal her food. An undulating blob of blood floated around the girl's head and red words pulsed along her tiny arms. Stepping over the corpses, Bellona, approached young Feyra and knelt next to her. Though her words were muffled, Feyra knew them by heart.

"You're special, aren't you?" Bellona had said.

Feyra tore her gaze away, her face flushed with heat. She focused on Gaul, still ahead of her. It was some kind of trickery from the whale. She couldn't get distracted. Pushing her toes into the ground, she closed the distance, his coat fluttering with touching distance. She stretched her arm, only for the world to fall out from beneath them.

They tumbled through empty space, pure darkness, before brilliant light greeted them and they landed face first onto a beach. Feyra spat out grains of sand and prepared to grab Gaul. A deep, resonant roar trembled the earth, stopping Feyra dead. She looked toward the sound.

A massive beast cut across the horizon. Even so far away, it was large enough to make Feyra afraid. Could it be a Primordial? Behemoth? He lumbered on two feet, with a thick shell and two horns. A light burst out from near his feet and Behemoth stumbled back. One of his horns fell to the ground.

From above, a roc swooped down, casting its shadow over Feyra. Winged specks, people in flying suits, attacked Ziz from all angles. The battle swooped amongst grey trees that reached impossibly high into the sky.

"What is this?" Feyra asked, mouth agape.

"A memory." Gaul was similarly stunned.

"Whose memory is this?"

Gaul turned to the sea. "Leviathan's."

The water ballooned behind them until a beast as large as an island breached the waves. A sea serpent. Leviathan. Her pearlescent, draconic head large enough to eclipse the sun. Behind her, arching sections of her spiny body rose and fell out of the ocean a hundred times. To say Leviathan was big would be an understatement. She was world-ending.

A small figure dressed in ragged robes — a grain of sand in comparison to Leviathan — walked across the water to meet the Primordial. Ice formed beneath their feet to give them a path. Leviathan could breathe and the windstorm would dash the stranger across the waves. But there was no fear in their walk.

The robed figure spread their arms apart and shouted something indistinct. The water around them rippled unnaturally, then lifted into the air. Pillars of ocean waves grew like weeds to the sky. The space around the figure pulsed and shook, as if reality was tearing itself apart to get away from them.

Leviathan lunged. The figure clenched their fists. The world fell away and Feyra found herself in a back storeroom of some shop. Bright light shone through the windows, but she appeared to be back on Boboros. The whale had surfaced.

Gaul stood across the room from her. He looked around in confusion before his gaze fell on Feyra. Not giving him a chance to run again, Feyra charged.

"Wait!" Gaul shouted.

At the last moment, Feyra noticed that the geometry of the ground between her and Gaul was wrong, folding upon itself in impossible ways. She passed over the spot, blinked, then she was flat against the wall. Her head spun and her body ached. She tried to stand but fell over. She tried to move her right leg, but her left hand flexed. She tried to wiggle her right index finger, but she shook her head. Nothing worked right.

"I tried to warn you," Gaul said. He ran out of the room.

Feyra screamed in frustration. She failed again.

Marta waited for Gaul in the Estuary Academy library. The building seemed empty, but she didn't want to risk it. So she hid in a stack of books and watched the door to the clocktower. Since Boboros surfaced, Marta was sure people would be returning. The fact they didn't have a guard at the door already was a sign of how desperate Melifacto was. He wanted everyone searching for her.

You should have gotten the Vessel, Isildia said.

Be quiet, Marta replied.

Have you thought about what I said?

I never do.

It was a few more minutes until Gaul entered the library.

Marta stumbled out of her hiding spot. "You made it!"

Gaul took deep breaths. "It wasn't easy. We need to be quick. Shinn gave me a key and told me that there's a way through the sewers inside the clocktower. I think that's the best way out."

There was a shout from the other side of the Academy, echoing through the empty halls. The Marjyalians had returned. Gaul took the necklace with the Light Vessel off.

"Here, take it and get ready to get the Light," Gaul said. He pulled out the key. "I'll get the door."

They rushed to the padlock. It popped open with Gaul's key and he pulled on the door, straining against the years of stillness. Inside was a dark room, with only some light coming in from the clock glass high above.

Marta entered first. "The vessel is getting hot," she said. "Where is this piece of Leviathan?"

Something flew over Marta's head. It was the key. The door slammed shut. Marta spun around and Gaul wasn't there. She sprinted for the door, but Gaul closed the padlock.

"What are you doing?" Marta shouted.

"I'm sorry," Gaul said. "This is where I leave you."

"What are you talking about? Stop this!"

"I really enjoyed travelling with you. It made me think I could be something I never was. Anori did too."

Marta kicked the door. "Your wife was wrong! They're all wrong! You don't have to be a monster! That's not who you are!"

"My wife." There was a thunk as Gaul put his head against the door. "My wife isn't dead, Marta. She left. I couldn't be what she needed me to be. I could only be the soldier, the killer." He laughed at himself. "That's how pathetic I am. I chased a memory of her across a country because some part of me thought I could be the person she needed me to be again. Because I believed somehow that a stupid necklace could bring her back. Bring me back. But I can't go back to being that person, because I never was. And I fooled myself and Anori into believing it was real for six wonderful years."

"Gaul!"

"A delusion sent me chasing that necklace. A delusion made me think I could have a friend like you. I always wanted to save people, but I can only kill them. I was only ever allowed to feel anger, never sadness, or excitement, or remorse. I'm supposed to be alone, Marta. Everyone leaves and the ones who don't get hurt. And I can't hurt you. The world has done so much to you already."

Marta punched the door until her knuckles bled. "Don't pretend you're doing this for me! You selfish, stupid, cragger! Open the door!"

"You should be afraid of me, Marta."

"You idiot!" She put a heavy kick into the door but it didn't budge. She collapsed against it. Tears ran hot down her face. "I'm supposed to bring you home."

"I was never going to go home when I left it. I only forgot that when I was with you. But this is what I deserve."

Marta collapsed. The dark room taunted her with its silence and stillness, amplifying her sobs.

Get up, Isildia said.

Marta hugged her knees, feeling the warmth of the Light Vessel in her hand.

Come on, Isildia continued. *He made this choice himself. He told you he would hurt you. I've been saying the same thing. At least you're not dead. You have me, you don't need that monster.*

You call someone a monster long enough and they start to believe it, Marta thought. *I'm sorry for what the world has done to you, Gaul.*

Marta stood. Gaul wasn't the monster. The monster was the doubt that took her friend away.

Gaul had his eyes shut, pressing his forehead against the door. He could hear Marta on the other side, soft sobs breaking his heart. Marta was strong, she would recover. The world had put so much onto her. But Gaul had brought it all on himself.

She doesn't deserve any of this, Gaul thought. *I wish I could take the journey on myself, but—* A group of soldiers entered the library. *I can still protect her one last time.*

Gaul pushed himself off the door. He wiped the tears from his eyes and drew his swords. A dozen soldiers stopped before him, weapons at the ready.

"I'm losing my life today," Gaul said. "Who wants to take it?"

Gaul Ignited. The soldiers weren't soldiers anymore, they were pulsating beacons of red light. Gaul exploded into action.

He caught the first soldier with two swords through the chest, lifting him and carrying him half a dozen metres before tossing him aside. Gaul didn't even try to avoid any attacks. Spraying blood and healing lightning wrapped around him.

A soldier ran him through the stomach. Gaul stabbed her and kicked her back, leaving his sword in her chest. He took the sword she lost and slashed another soldier across the face. Gaul skewered a man's shoulder with his new sword then tossed the old one so it stuck on the top of a recovering soldier's head.

Gaul wrenched down on his stuck sword, snapping it just above the hilt. He grabbed the soldier's hair and thrust the broken blade into his neck. Someone cut across Gaul's back. Gaul spun around and caught the second blow. He slid his hand down the blade, sending lightning dancing along the steel, then pushed the sword back. The cross guard stuck into the soldier's eye and he fell, clutching his face.

The soldier's kept pouring out of the hallway. Gaul fought with no inhibitions, just pure primal fury. He stole weapons, used them, then discarded them at a rapid pace. His coat turned to bloody shreds with his movements.

With a two-handed strike, Gaul chopped a man's leg clean off. As the man open his mouth to scream, Gaul caught his jaw.

"Die!" Gaul shouted, then ripped the jaw away from the man's skull.

Gaul tossed the jaw away and turned to find another foe. The sea of red parted and a golden light entered the library. Gaul narrowed his eyes. The auras faded slightly. Within the golden light was a man wielding a cutlass. He had a metal mask that covered his face from the nose down. When he saw Gaul, he raised an eyebrow.

"Interesting," Ortun said. "That would explain why you're so hard to kill."

Gaul charged. He scooped up a sword as he moved. Ortun adjusted his stance to face Gaul head on. Gaul thrust his sword through Ortun's shoulder, sending lightning up in reply. Ortun plunged his cutlass into Gaul's collarbone. Gaul pulled his sword back, then swiped for Ortun's neck. Ortun took the hit on the forearm, then pushed the cutlass deeper.

Gaul wrenched himself back, tearing the cutlass from his shoulder. There was no pain, only a growing pulse that went from his heart to his hands. Ortun didn't relent. They battled like mountain goats, clashing over and over. Steel rang and blood flew. Lightning filled the air around them until it looked like they were in an electrical storm.

Gaul knocked Ortun's blade aside then grabbed his hair. He drove his knee into Ortun's nose, exploding it into a display of blood and sparks. He reared back to remove that man's head — but his arm wouldn't move. The blood they had been spraying out floated like frozen abstract sculptures, with some of it wrapped around Gaul's arm, holding it in place.

Feyra made her way through the crowd, staring hard at Gaul. She held her open hand in front of her, then closed it. The blood encased Gaul, sealing him in a liquid coffin. He kicked and pushed, but it was no use.

Ortun returned to his feet and said, "Knock him out."

The blood squeezed around Gaul until he could feel the air being pushed out of him. He had been hoping to die. No such luck.

Sea Queen Leviathan.
Killed by Shiller, Father of the Arcane.
Portion of remains place in the Estuary Academy.

—From the Journal of Jovin Gutterwake

Chapter Forty-Eight
Leviathan

You have to move at some point, Isildia said. *Unless you want me to take over and do it for you.*

I didn't know Gaul was dealing with all this. Marta was numb. *I could have helped him.*

He was weak and a whiner. What more do you want?

"Don't say that!" Marta shouted. "He's strong. Just… a little broken."

Do you think he frets over you the way you fret over him? Isildia sighed. *That strong man is out there sacrificing himself for you. Don't let him die in vain.*

"He's not going to die." Marta rubbed her hands together. "He'll get out of it. He always does. Then I'll see him again. Eventually…"

Whatever gets you moving…

Marta strode forth with confidence. The piece of Leviathan was somewhere inside the clocktower, she would just have to figure out where. The Vessel grew hot. A candle lit at her feet, then another a metre away. All throughout the clocktower, pinpoints of light appeared. Stretching up the middle of the clocktower was one massive, cracked tooth.

Whoa, Isildia said. *Was that from Leviathan? Shiller killed something that big? That's bigger than Behemoth!*

Marta lifted the Vessel above her head. A string of Light grew along the broken section of the tooth. It peeled off and floated into the Light Vessel, joining the Light of Behemoth and Ziz. The Vessel cooled and Marta took it in her hand. Three out of five Primordials, but Marta had assumed Gaul would be with her all the way. He was her guide. Now where would she go?

I know where to go, Isildia said. *But first, find that sewer entrance Gaul mentioned. It won't be long until Melifacto beats down that door.*

Marta looked around. In the dim candlelight, she spotted a trapdoor close to the staircase that lead up the tower. She slid the latch aside and threw it open. It was a ladder down into a dark abyss. The Vessel in her hand began to glow and light the path. But even with the help, it was still a foreboding descent into the unknown.

"I don't like leaving Gaul behind," Marta said.

He left you behind. Isildia pushed on Marta from inside her head. *Keep moving.*

Marta looked one last time at the door Gaul sealed. She couldn't help him if he didn't want to be helped. She could only hope she would see him again soon. As the door began to shake, Marta disappeared into the belly of the whale.

Melifacto charged into the Library with a head full of steam and Pelady on his heel. Gaul was bound with steel links and gagged with a cloth. Ortun and Feyra kept watch over him while others had bashed down the door and entered the clocktower. Melifacto yanked Gaul's gag away.

"Tell me where she is!" he ordered.

"You know as much as me, bird-man," Gaul said, disinterested.

"She went into the sewers," Ortun explained. "They're searching right now, but she has a head start."

Melifacto grabbed Gaul by the bonds. "You know something. Where was she going to meet up with you? What was the plan?"

"Let me think about it for a bit." Gaul pursed his lips. "Nope. Can't come up with a reasonable lie."

Melifacto's eyes flared. He spun to Pelady. "Kill him."

Pelady grinned and stepped forward. Feyra blocked her way. The two women stared each other down, neither backing up an inch.

Ortun stepped in. "Hold on. Marta cares about him. She must. We can use Gaul to lure Marta back, but only if he's alive."

A lure was exactly what Melifacto needed. No more chasing after Marta, she would come to him. Pelady watched Melifacto, waiting for the order.

"Where's Bellona?" Melifacto asked.

"Out on the ships, making sure no boats leave Boboros," Ortun said. "Like you asked."

"Good. Good." Melifacto ruffled his cloak. "Bring Gaul out. Tie him to the front of a ship between here and the shore. Make sure if Marta leaves she will see him out there. Then we'll see if she cares for this man."

Pelady's face fell. Ortun and Feyra yanked Gaul to his feet and pushed him to walk.

"I would prefer to be killed," Gaul shouted over his shoulder as he was hurried out of the room. "But what do I know? I'm just the prisoner."

And he was gone. Melifacto felt like tearing his hair out. Everything had come to this moment and it was all falling apart. With the Absence spreading and Goodsmile going rogue, time was an enemy Melifacto couldn't defeat. His next chance to find Marta would be in the Dark. He trembled at the thought of going there.

Shinn was sitting silently in the corner, curled up so that Melifacto nearly forgot he was there.

"None of this would be happening if you didn't surface Boboros," Melifacto said.

"It was dangerous." Shinn grabbed his head. "The ghosts and the flicker wells and the screaming. Boboros was in pain."

"You'll be glad to know you won't have to deal with it anymore."

Shinn cocked his head.

"We have to go visit our sister." Melifacto motioned for Pelady to follow him. "Down in the Dark."

"Oh no." Shinn covered his eyes.

Melifacto didn't blame him. There was no one quite like the Descendant of Sanguine. But there wasn't a choice. Melifacto walked out of the Academy and into the fading sunlight.

All gods fall.

—From the Journal of Jovin Gutterwake

Epilogue

Pelady found Melifacto waiting on the docks. She slid into a kneeling bow at his feet.

"Where are all the ships?" Melifacto asked. "Have they gone to the other side of the whale?"

Pelady loved giving Melifacto bad news. How it hurt him and made him angry. How he would panic and tell Pelady to kill something. Melifacto had robbed Pelady of tasting Gaul's blood, but this would make up for it.

"They left, master," Pelady said. "After they took Gaul, they left in different directions."

"What!?" Melifacto's face turned red. Pelady smiled internally. "What ship was he on?"

"I do not know. Bellona is aboard *Spree*, Feyra is aboard *Isildia*, and Ortun is aboard *Steel Jaw*. There is also *Far Shore*. They're trying to hide which one Gaul is on.

"It won't work." Melifacto took a deep breath and reached his hands toward the ocean waves. "I'm tired of playing with these people like they're equals to me."

Pelady felt a tug on the animal part of her brain. It told her to leap into the water and swim after the ships. Her human side held her back.

Melifacto scowled at the horizon and said, "These people will learn there are worse things in the sea. And they will send their tiny ships into the depths."

Deep below the surface, gargantuan creatures stirred.

A Sneak Peek of:

ALL GODS FALL: SEASON TWO
PART ONE

ELYSIUM BRUMAL

Chapter One
Bitter Youth

Cold wind sent up snow squalls, ones that battered Tyr's face with small needles. He pulled his mask over his nose and bundled the furs tighter around him. If he had bothered to consider the weather, he would have brought his goggles rather than squint against the prevailing forces. Too late for that now, he made a long trek out to the coastline and wasn't going to turn back and make his friends wait. Svend was eighteen that day, the last of the group to become such. On Tyr's birthday they went to the Gulfyn Crags to see the frozen corpse of Sowwinter, one of the Old Gods. On Arne's it was north to the caves, where one could hear the crystal's sing. So it became a ritual, on their eighteenth birthday they would travel to see one of the wonders of Skarnland and share a drink of apple icewine.

"Come on, Tyr!" Arne called, balancing on the top of a boulder. "Where's all that endurance you've been bragging about?"

Tyr shrugged — the best comeback he could manage. Arne was the biggest of the trio, a boy who started growing young and had yet to stop. He steadied himself with one hand then dropped off the stone, landing ankle deep with his heavy boots. He slapped Tyr's shoulder as he caught up and gave a goofy grin.

"Stop looking so grey," he said. "It's like you were bitten by a dog."

"Of all the places he could've picked, why the ships?" Tyr asked, stepping around him and continuing walking. "There's nothing interesting about them."

"You know Svend, he always wants to do his own thing."

"These are supposed to feel like adventures." He pointed down the coastline. "We're barely fifteen minutes from where the whaler's launch."

Arne threw his arm over Tyr's shoulders. "Just think of how excited he was. That kid barely gets out without us."

Tyr looked ahead where Svend waited at the lip of a promontory looming over the ocean below. He held his arms slightly out, taking in the wind and letting it flare the furs he wore. He did seem calmer than Tyr normally saw him, all bundled up with tension as he cooked blubber at the factory.

"I'll keep my mouth shut," Tyr said.

"Better than nothing!" Arne shoved him playfully and jogged to Svend's side.

Tyr joined them slower. Despite his agreement, the ships did little to excite him. It wasn't even the first time he went to see them; only a few weeks earlier Thordin, his father, and him harvested some wood to repair their shed. It had been a couple months since the wreckage of large sailing ships littered their shores with hull, cargo, and corpses. From atop the promontory, the shards of wood looked like crumbs left on a table from the sea's meal, with the centrepiece a mostly intact galleon nestled against the slope where the storm placed it that day.

"It's so big!" Svend said, pulling his snow goggles down around his neck. He was thin-faced and gangly like a tree. "It's gotta be bigger than the ships from Arkling."

"Not bigger, just taller." Arne shuffled down the serpentine trail, the safest way to descend to the shore.

"Taller would mean they're bigger," Tyr muttered.

Arne and Svend carried on without hearing him. Tyr sighed and followed.

"Where do you think it came from?" Svend asked.

"Somewhere across the sea," Arne said. "It's certainly not Skarnland make. There must've been a couple of them too, judging from the amount of wreckage."

"You think they got caught in that storm and crashed?"

"No, the sea monsters got them," Tyr said. "They found some teeth stuck in the bow the size of goats."

Svend jumped off the path, stumbling as his feet impacted the shore's loose rock. "Sea monsters?" he asked, brushing the dirt off his gloves.

"Oh, yes, the water's full of them." Arne landed next to him and loomed big. "Serpents and tentacled beasts larger than any whale. They come up from the ocean floor, hiding just out of sight, and when they're right underneath the ship they wrap it up and drag it into the depths."

Svend swallowed. "Oh…"

"You have to be out pretty far before anything like them appear." Tyr swatted Arne's hat off his head as he passed.

Arne snatched it off the ground. "I was just trying to scare him."

The boys made their way down the shore to where the ship perched on its smashed hull, keel completely destroyed, and turned around with its bow facing the sea it once came from. One mast remained, though it laid snapped twice over, leaning past the port side with its top resting in the snow. Arne climbed atop the column and carefully made his way up to the deck.

"You go first," Tyr said to Svend.

He nodded and followed Arne on his hands and knees, practically hugging the mast as he made his way up. By the time Tyr joined them, Arne was already at the front, one foot proudly upon the bowsprit and a skein in his hand.

"Not a bad place," he said, braid blowing in the breeze. He grinned at Tyr. "Don't you think?"

"It's great," he replied flatly.

Svend rushed about the wreck. There wasn't much to see anymore, not since the townsfolk picked it clean. The day after it made shore, the people from Lyrne came by looking for survivors, only to find nothing but waterlogged bodies. They buried them in Skarnland rites with stone markers, not knowing what the sailors would have wanted, and took the cargo they could carry. Tyr watched them all the while, Thordin working himself into the night to ensure the dead had their proper resting, lest they return as wights. Or at least that's what local superstition believed, Tyr figured it was just the right thing to do.

Through the decks they searched for anything of note, finding broken beds and tools too worn to be of use. Svend reacted to each find like he discovered gold. With child-like glee he held up a broken sword hilt and pretended to duel a support pillar, despite the less than an inch of blade that remained. Once they journeyed through the ship from bow to stern, they took places on the top deck and passed around the cider, listening to the waves lap against the rocks.

"Who's Isildia?" Svend asked, passing the skein.

"Never heard of her, why?" Arne poured the wine down his throat and wiped away the bit that snuck out the corner of his lips.

"It's written on the back of the ship."

"Probably the captain's lady." He tossed the skein to Tyr and flopped back in a puff of snow. "Men're always naming things after women they've bedded."

"I don't think that's how they name boats." Tyr brushed the snow off the railing and took a seat, kicking his heels against the balusters. "It's just a name, Svend. Maybe it meant something to these people once, now it's just another wreck."

"I was just trying to think of what to name my boat." He rested his head against his hand. "Maybe I'll name it Lise."

"There's an idea," Arne said. "Name a boat you don't have after a girl you never talked to."

"Why do you want a boat anyway?" Tyr offered the skein but Svend waved it off.

"Because I want to go places. I want to see other things. Maybe I don't need a boat, but I need to be on a boat. A boat like this." He slapped the deck around him.

"I imagine one with less holes."

He tossed a handful of snow at Tyr. "Don't either of you get restless thinking about the future?"

"I know my future." Arne leapt to his feet and grabbed the skein. "I'm gonna marry Anette, have lots of kids, and let them work while I fish." He took a swig. "Perfect, right?"

"And never leave the village?"

"My father leaves the village all the time with his wares, he doesn't seem any happier." He dipped with the skein as if he was dancing. "At least here I have glorious Anette."

Svend turned to Tyr. "What about you? What's your future?"

"I haven't thought about it that much." He nodded at Arne, pretending to kiss the Anette-skein. "Guess I'll do the same as him."

"You'll marry Anette?" Arne pitched the skein at Tyr's chest. "Good luck."

"That's not what I mean. As I said, I don't think about it that much. All I know is I don't want to end up buried in unmarked graves because my boat sank."

Svend huffed and stood, walking across the deck to lean on the other railing. Tyr and Arne shared a glance and shrugged.

"Svend," Tyr said, coming down from his perch.

"Come look at this." He waved for the others to join him, eyes locked down the beach.

Tyr and Arne met at the railing, following Svend's gaze. A flock of bird congregated near where the promontory jutted out to meet the sea. They hopped across a large motionless form covered in seaweed.

"Is that a whale?" Svend asked.

"I think it is. Let's see." Arne hopped the railing and grabbed onto netting that hung down the side.

The boys abandoned the boat and rushed across the rocks, racing each other to see what it was that laid at the edge of the waves. The birds took to the sky as Arne arrived, followed by Svend with Tyr lazily taking up the rear. It was a whale, though a small one. Fourteen feet long with a dark blue exoskeleton of many plates covering from its mouth to the tip of its tail and barnacles collected on its jaw.

"Must've beached itself a while ago," Arne said, kicking some of its plating. "It's already dead." His face lit up and he clapped Svend's shoulder. "I have an idea! We may get you out of the boiling room yet."

"But…" Svend couldn't get the thought out before Arne sprinted back for the boat. "…I like the boiling room."

"Just humour him," Tyr said.

They waited for a few minutes before Arne returned holding a metal wedge. "Don't worry, I'm a great teacher; I got the new guy stripping whales in no time. They'll think you're a prodigy once I'm done with you."

"Alright…" Svend gave him some room.

"The older the whale, the more plates they have. This one is pretty young so you should have no trouble getting through." He pressed the wedge between the scale-like pieces. "Usually you need a hammer to get these things off, but I couldn't find one so, uh…"

He readied himself then gave the back of a wedge a hard kick. It shot in a centimetre, but the plating held on.

"See? Easy." He gave it a few more kicks. "A little bit, of brute force, and it pops off."

Despite his confidence, the wedge hadn't moved at all. He took a moment to catch his breath, steadied himself, then planted a solid boot against the wedge. There was a sharp crack and he went knee deep into the whale's side. He screamed and fell back, needing Tyr and Svend to catch him. They hooked his arms and dragged his leg free, releasing a black sludge from the hole that splattered across the rocks.

"What is that?" Svend covered his nose as the wave of nausea-inducing smell came next.

"It must've rotted on the inside," Arne said, trying to shake the muck off his paint leg.

Tyr crept closer. "It doesn't look like rot."

The substance kept sloughing out, a putrid thing of monochrome colouration where the blackness was mixed with sombre grey and even specks of white. Tyr had seen animals when they started to decompose, but nothing ever looked so disgusting or unnatural. Especially not in the cold seaside.

"I need to get this off my leg," Arne said, stomping toward the water.

"Are you sure it's not rot?" Svend asked, staying a good distance away. "It could've been out here for a while."

Tyr picked up a stick and poked the substance. It didn't give easily, fighting back against the stick even after it broke the surface. When he let go, it stayed pointing straight up.

"Hey!" Arne called. "Get over here now!"

Tyr and Svend sprinted over. Arne pointed past the outcropping, to where the rest of the shoreline was visible. Tyr's jaw dropped.

Dozens of whales of all sizes littered the beach. Some of their plating collapsed in as they decayed, revealing the same monochrome sludge that burst from the first one. None of the boys could think of a thing to say. Tyr was right, there was nothing natural about it. Something had come to Skarnland.

The Author

Kevin Weir is an AMPIA Award winning writer of science fiction, fantasy, and comedy. A multidisciplinary storyteller, he has written short films, webseries, stageplays, as well as short stories, featured in Canadian and international publications. His novel *Endless Hunger* was published by EDGE Science Fiction and Fantasy and he has independently published a series of novellas called *All Gods Fall.* He lives in Alberta where he hosts podcasts, works in film, plays Dungeon and Dragons, and lives with two-to-four dogs and a naked cat.

YOU MAY ALSO LIKE

In the near future city of New Montreal, where wireless technology connects everything, Kraft finds himself disconnected due to his ability to see the aura of supernatural creatures hiding as humans. He has accepted that no one will believe him, and so prefers to waste his life away in solitude. No such luck, though, as he is given a job to illicitly clean a mega-corporation's computer system — only to find something has infected the network. Something with a mind of its own.

In a world of high technology and secret magic, Kraft bridges the gap with his unnatural sight and array of inventive gadgetry. Faeries, cults, and corporate espionage collide in a story that has been described as "a riveting, genre-bending adventure", "A fast-paced book full of twists and turns that readers will devour", and "a rocket-fueled tale."

Available now from EDGE Science Fiction and Fantasy Publishing.

CPSIA information can be obtained
at www.ICGtesting.com
Printed in the USA
JSHW081723090723
44301JS00001B/1

9 781777 327415